Alex pushed his way between two of the men, reached the pair in the center, and grabbed that one he'd originally thought was a slender youth by the arm to wheel her around.

She was definitely a woman; large wide eyes blinked up at him in surprise above a straight little nose and full, luscious lips. Merewen Stewart had instinctively brought her wooden sword up to hit at him, but paused abruptly when she saw his face. Recognition flashed briefly through her green eyes, followed quickly by irritation as she jerked her arm free and snapped, "Are ye daft? Ye nearly got yerself skewered. This sword may be wood, but it can still do damage."

Alex ignored her tirade and grabbed her arm again, holding her in place as he snatched the helmet off her head. His eyes widened as a mass of glorious chestnut hair suddenly tumbled out to surround her heart-shaped face. It fell in waves, reaching nearly to her waist, and felt as soft as silk against the back of his hand, where he held her arm. It seemed obvious the girl had got her looks from her mother rather than her father . . . and he was grateful for it.

By Lynsay Sands

TAMING THE HIGHLAND BRIDE
DEVIL OF THE HIGHLANDS

THE RENEGADE HUNTER
THE IMMORTAL HUNTER
THE ROGUE HUNTER

VAMPIRE, INTERRUPTED
VAMPIRES ARE FOREVER
THE ACCIDENTAL VAMPIRE
BITE ME IF YOU CAN
A BITE TO REMEMBER
A QUICK BITE

Coming Soon
THE HELLION AND THE HIGHLANDER

LYNSAY SANDS

TAMING THE HIGHLAND BRIDE

AVON

An Imprint of HarperCollinsPublishers

AVON BOOKS
An Imprint of HarperCollins*Publishers*
10 East 53rd Street
New York, New York 10022-5299

Copyright © 2010 by Lynsay Sands
Excerpt from *The Hellion and the Highlander* copyright © 2010 by
Lynsay Sands
ISBN 978-0-06-134478-7
www.avonromance.com

First Avon Books paperback printing: February 2010

Avon Trademark Reg. U.S. Pat. Off. and in Other Countries, Marca Registrada, Hecho en U.S.A.
HarperCollins® is a registered trademark of HarperCollins Publishers.

Printed in the U.S.A.

10 9 8 7 6 5 4 3 2 1

For Gran

Prologue

Merewen Stewart stabbed the needle into the cloth and tugged it out the other side with an irritated jerk. She was in a foul mood and, as usual, the fault for that lay with her father and two brothers. Unfortunately, the Stewart men liked their drink. Equally unfortunately, while they were lambs when sober and only stupid and clumsy on ale, they were downright mean on whiskey. So, of course, whiskey was their drink of preference, which meant Merry often found herself standing between them and the rest of the clan. Her first lesson on taking over as chatelaine at Stewart Castle had been to arm herself with something heavy when they got like that. Fortunately, her doing so was often enough to keep them in line. However, their whiskey-sharpened tongues could be cutting, and the very threat of violence that shimmered in the air on those occasions was frightening to deal with.

Merry had spent the last six years doing all she could to keep them from drinking the whiskey the Stewart clan made and sold. She'd taken to locking it away in the pantry, keeping the only key to that lock on her person at all times. But they just rode out to the inn in the village, or to Colan Gow's to partake of his whiskey. She then was left to deal with whatever chaos they created when they returned intoxicated. That had been the pattern since her mother's death six years ago . . . Until last week. Last week they'd returned from a visit with Colan Gow so drunk she'd been amazed that they hadn't broken their fool necks on the ride home. She was even more amazed when they still wanted more drink.

Merry had refused them the key to the pantry and suggested they find their beds. She'd then ordered the servants to make themselves scarce and retired herself, hoping that would be the end of it. It hadn't. The three men decided to take battle-axes to the pantry door. The racket had brought her from her bed to find they'd hacked their way through the thick wooden door and were inside, breaking open the casks of whiskey. When she'd tried to stop them, her brother Brodie had pushed her away and raised his axe threateningly as he told her not to interfere.

There'd been nothing else for her to do but to leave them to it. What had followed was nearly a week of them bingeing on their treasure while Merry and the servants had done their best to stay out of harm's way. The trio had drunk until they passed out, and then woke to immediately begin drinking again.

On the third day, Brodie had cuffed one of the kitchen boys who had been foolish enough to return before she gave the all-clear and then had not moved quickly enough for her brother's liking. Fortunately, Merry had been close enough she'd managed to intervene after only the first blow, and while the lad had suffered a bloody nose, he'd also learned a valuable lesson. She doubted he'd ever return to the keep before he was sure it was safe to do so.

On the fourth night Gawain had nearly set the stables ablaze when he'd dropped a torch in the stack of hay in his own horse's stall. However, the stable master had managed to get Gawain and his mount out uninjured and even put out the fire before it spread beyond the one stall.

But it was her father, Eachann, who had committed the sin that upset her most. On the fifth and final day of their drinking, in a maudlin moment of whiskey-fueled grief, he'd taken her mother's portrait from its place above the fireplace to whisper weepy words of longing to it. Then he tripped over his own feet and destroyed the painting when he fell on top of one of the fireside chairs. The chair back had torn through the portrait's face and upper body as surely as a sword. Sent into a sudden fury, her father had then smashed the chair and thrown it into the great hall fireplace. The picture, ruined in his opinion, had followed.

Merry had tried to prevent it, but had been struck to the floor for her efforts. By the time she'd managed to regain her feet, the painting was on top of the chair on the fire, burning merrily away. She'd dropped back to kneel in the rushes and simply wept at the loss of this one and only portrayal that existed of her dearly departed mother, Maighread Stewart.

Once Merry's tears had dried, her grief had been replaced by fury, not just at her father but at both her brothers as well. They ruined everything. There was little left at Stewart that was not mended after one of them had broken it . . . including her heart.

That last incident had moved her father to swear off drink again, and the binge had finally ended three days ago. But the men had spent the time since then doing nothing but moan and whine about their aching heads and nauseous stomachs. Merry had little sympathy, and had simply gone about running the castle as usual, directing the servants and soldiers and overseeing the men at practice in the bailey while her father and brothers recuperated. She also had the pantry door repaired and a new lock placed on it.

For all the good that would do, she thought bitterly. Merry had no doubt once her father and brothers had done what they considered was enough penance, they'd return to the drink like long-lost lovers. They always did.

"Here they come."

Merry glanced up from her mending at her maid, Una's, words, her mouth compressing as she saw the three men crossing the great hall toward them.

"Shall I—"

"You'd best go to the kitchens for a bit, Una,"

Merry interrupted as she noted her brothers were swaggering somewhat. They only did that when they'd been drinking.

"I'm staying," Una said firmly. "You—"

"Go," Merry said firmly.

Una hesitated, but then clucked her tongue with exasperation and stood to head for the kitchens, muttering, "Fine. But I'm watching from the door, and if that devil Brodie tries to threaten ye again like he did with the axe, I'm grabbing the heaviest pan Cook has and coming out here to put him in his place."

Merry shook her head, an affectionate smile briefly claiming her lips as she watched the curvaceous and freckled strawberry blond go. They had grown up together and were more friends than maid and mistress. That friendship had been a real source of strength for Merry these last years, and was the reason she'd sent Una away. Una was very protective of her and could sometimes overstep herself in an effort to protect Merry. All that did was raise her brothers' ire and make the situation worse.

"Merry."

She turned reluctantly to her father and brothers, noting that while her father's expression was diffident, Brodie and Gawain both wore eager expressions that warned the trio was up to no good. She glared at the three of them until they began to fidget before finally snapping, "What is it?"

Her father glanced to the younger men behind him and then took a deep breath and stammered, "I— Ye see— Well—"

Merewen's mouth tightened. The man couldn't

even get out whatever lie he and her brothers had concocted to get into the whiskey. He kept pausing and licking his lips, his expression getting more desperate until she wanted to slap him soundly. Merry was heartily sick of dealing with the trio.

"I— Ye see—" her father said nervously, trying again. He then paused once more.

No doubt his brain was still pickled from their latest drinking binge. If it was not permanently so now, Merry thought with disgust, and set down her sewing to get angrily to her feet. "Let me guess. I heard the shout that a rider approached. 'Tis our neighbor Colan, isna it? And, no doubt, ye're thinkin' his arrival a grand excuse to open another cask o' whiskey."

"Aye," her father breathed, and then straightened abruptly when her brother Brodie elbowed him in the back. "I mean, nay. I mean, aye, Colan has come, but 'tis no' his arrival worthy of breakin' the seal on another cask o' whiskey, 'tis the grand news he brings."

"And what news is this?" Merry asked dryly, not expecting much in the way of news at all. Colan's arrival with a tale of how he'd caught a hare while hunting a week earlier was enough to rouse the Stewart men to celebration.

"Yer betrothed is returned from Tunis," Gawain blurted before their father could continue his stammering.

Merry was so startled by this news she dropped to sit on the bench again. Her eyes widened as her dazed mind tried to accept what was truly news of some magnitude. In fact, it was a dream come true.

A very old dream. In the years just before and just after her mother's death, Merry had spent a good deal of time imagining what her future husband would look like and what sort of man he'd be. In her imagination, he'd been handsome and fine, and he'd ridden into Stewart, swept her up on his horse, and carried her away to a better life. But that had been years ago. As summer after summer had passed bringing excuse after excuse for why he couldn't collect her that year, those dreams had faded and died, and she'd begun to think he would never come, that she was destined to be an old maid, chasing her father and brothers around until she or they died.

Recalling those excuses now, Merry narrowed her eyes on the trio before her and said, " 'Tisn't true."

"Aye, it is," Brodie and Gawain said as one and rushed around their father to sit on either side of her, their expressions eager and full of glee.

"He got word of his father's death and returned to take up the reins," Brodie said happily. "And now he needs to produce an heir."

"So he's ready to settle down and marry now," Gawain added.

"Is that not flattering," Merry muttered.

"Aye," Brodie said, apparently missing the sarcasm in her voice. "So we're to travel to England at once fer ye to marry him. We celebrate tonight and leave first thing on the morrow."

Merry snapped out of her surprise to glare at them again. "Oh. Aye, nay doubt ye'd like that. Hustle me off to England to marry the blackguard now he's deigned to return. Surely that's something to celebrate. Ye'll be free o' me."

Her brothers exchanged a glance before Brodie quickly assured her, "Oh, nay, Merry, we're no' happy about it. Why, without ye here, who will nag us out o' our beds on a morning?"

"Aye, and who will keep us from drinkin' to our hearts' content?" Gawain asked.

"And who will mither us to train at battle and go on the hunt and so on?" their father, Eachann, asked.

Merry turned hard eyes from one man to another. Despite their claims of not wanting her gone, their eager smiles suggested otherwise. Well, it was no more than what she wanted herself. She would love a life where she did not have to chase after these three and try to keep them from killing themselves or someone else. However, they were out of luck. "Aye, well, I'm sure ye'll no' have to face those worries any time soon. Me betrothed has taken his sweet time returning from the Crusades, and nay doubt he'll take his sweet time coming to claim me, too. And until he does, ye're stuck with me," she announced grimly and picked up her mending again.

A pregnant silence surrounded her. Merry was sure they were exchanging panicked glances, but didn't trouble herself to look up and see. She knew they would not stop there when they were so tantalizingly close to having their deepest wish of being rid of her fulfilled.

"Aye, but Merry," Eachann Stewart said finally, " 'tis no' that *we* want ye to travel to England to be wed, but—"

" 'Tis his wish," Gawain said abruptly.

Merry raised her head slowly to scour each man with suspicion. "His wish?"

"Aye. Well, as ye say, he's been away a long time. Three years," Brodie pointed out. "And I gather d'Aumesbery knew not about his father's death and that his absence left his stepmother in charge. Ye ken a female can't run a keep like a man, there is much to set to rights at d'Aumesbery."

Merry's mouth flattened out so much she was sure her lips were no longer even visible. Women couldn't run a keep? Her sainted mother, Maighread, had run Stewart until her death, and then Merry had taken over at sixteen. She'd had to; she'd promised on her mother's deathbed to look out for her father and brothers and run Stewart. The promise had been to do so until either her father died and her eldest brother, Kade—the only sober male in her family—took over as laird, or she married and moved away.

Merry had done her best to keep that promise. However, while she had run Stewart and done her best to keep her father and brothers away from whiskey, she couldn't keep them from the ale. Fortunately, they were more amiable drunks on ale, but the three men were still often too drunk or too hung over to manage making any sensible decision. And even when they weren't, they were pretty much useless, just wandering around whining about how they had a thirst for whiskey and complaining about her keeping it from them. The three were weak, silly creatures who were nothing but a trial to her. But they were her family.

"Aye, d'Aumesbery canna take time away just

now," Gawain assured her. "But he wishes to marry ye as soon as possible and sent word asking us to travel there fer the wedding."

"It seems a grand idea," her father put in. "After all, it means he has to supply the wedding feast and it saves us a load o' bother, doesna it?"

"Aye," Gawain said quickly. " 'Twill save *you* all the trouble of arrangin' a feast and preparin' fer guests and so on."

"So, we'll leave first thing on the morrow. Aye?" Brodie said hopefully.

It seemed to Merry that the three men were almost holding their breath in anticipation of her answer. She could feel their eagerness for her agreement, and that alone almost made her say no. But were she to do so and force her betrothed to come collect her as was proper, she would only be spiting herself. Truly, running herd on a bunch of drunken louts was not fun, and while she would worry about them all, she had no more desire to stay than they apparently had for her to do so. Marriage, hopefully to a responsible, nondrinking man who actually kept his promises instead of forgetting them the moment they were spoken—as her father and brothers were wont to do—would be heaven to her mind. Still, Merry didn't put them out of their misery at once. They had made her life a living hell these last six years and, shameful as it was to admit, she was enjoying their suffering now. So instead of answering, she returned her attention to her mending, fed the needle through the material, and slowly drew it out.

"Merry?" Brodie prompted impatiently.

"I am thinking," she snapped, not looking up from her efforts.

"But Merry, he's sent fer ye," Gawain said.

"Aye," her father muttered. "And ye're well past marrying age."

"Well past." Brodie agreed. "Diya no' think we should—"

"I canna think with the three of ye nattering at me," Merry insisted firmly and kept her head bent to her sewing as she tried to decide how long to leave them hanging before agreeing. The longer she kept them waiting, the longer she could keep them away from the whiskey and, she hoped, the less drunk they could get this night. On the other hand, she had to pack and prepare for the journey. The thought made her sigh. Her life had often seemed an effort to balance on a needle point. It appeared her last night in this, her old life, would be no different. Merry just hoped her new life held more joy for her.

ou should have the blacksmith see to that."

Alexander d'Aumesbery stopped rubbing his jaw and shrugged. "I have no time for it now."

Gerhard Abernathy clucked with impatience. "That tooth has been bothering you since we left Tunis. You should have had it tended the moment we landed back in England, not let it drag on paining you."

Alex smiled affectionately at the older man. Gerhard had always been one of his father's most trusted and faithful soldiers. It was why his father had insisted that the warrior accompany Alex when the prince asked Alex to travel with him to Tunis to join the Crusades. Gerhard obliged, joining him willingly, though Alex often wondered if he'd regretted it since. None of them had expected to remain away so long. Indeed, after just one year, Prince Edward had returned to take the throne on his father's death. But he'd asked Alex to remain in his place and so he—and his men—had stayed behind to carry on the losing battle. It had meant two more years of heat and sand and blood.

During that time, Gerhard had been his friend, his counsel, and at times his nursemaid, mothering him when he was injured or struck down by fever, watching his back in battle, and offering his wisdom when it came to important decisions.

Alex honestly didn't think he'd have survived without him, and he wished his father were still alive so that he could thank him for making him take Gerhard along. Young and arrogant at the time, he'd seen Gerhard—a mere ten years older than he—as old. He'd thought the man would slow him down and be a bother. He couldn't have been more wrong. Gerhard had saved his life more than once, and had become a friend.

"I have had too much to do to bother with it," Alex said now. "I shall tend to it when we get back from Donnachaidh."

"You should tend to it ere visiting your sister and that Devil she married," Gerhard insisted.

"I already sent word to Donnachaidh accepting my new brother-in-law's invitation. I didn't realize then how much work was needed here," Alex said, and scowled as he glanced around the great hall.

The large room was nearly empty, an oddity considering the size of the castle and the number of people it held. The great hall had always been a busy, noisy area when he was growing up, and had remained so even after his mother's death and his father's marriage to Edda. Now, however, it was empty and silent as a tomb.

"I suppose you'll be collecting your betrothed on the way back?" Gerhard commented.

"Aye," Alex muttered, peering down into his ale. It was not a chore he was looking forward to. The marriage contract had been arranged and signed when he was still a boy. He probably should have married the girl before heading to Tunis, but had managed to put it off at the time. He'd expected his father to make a fuss about it, but the man had said the same thing he'd always said when Alex had found an excuse to avoid the marriage. "Plenty of time for that later, son." Having thought about that and the fact that his father had never even taken him to meet his betrothed while growing up, Alex suspected his father had come to regret making the match and would have canceled the contract if he could. However, there had been a penalty clause in the contract for such an action that was so exorbitant it would have beggared them. And still would, Alex thought unhappily.

"Well?" Gerhard asked. "Are you collecting her or not?"

"Aye," he said finally. "The Stewarts are not far from Donnachaidh, so I guess I shall have to collect her on the return journey."

"You do not sound eager," Gerhard pointed out

with amusement, and teased, "Do I sense a little reluctance to claim your betrothed?"

"They call her the Stewart Shrew," Alex pointed
out dryly. "The name does not suggest a sweet, biddable bride and helpmate."

"Aye, and the last thing you need around here are
more problems," Gerhard said sympathetically, and
then shook his head. "These last three years I have
pined for home, but now we're here, I find myself
thinking almost longingly of the dry heat and
bloody battle we left behind in Tunis."

"Edda has that effect on a person," Alex said
grimly, glancing around to be sure his stepmother
was not within hearing distance. He didn't care for
the woman, but wouldn't deliberately insult her.

"She's not so bad," Gerhard said, making Alex's
eyebrows fly up with surprise. Shrugging, the man
said, "She and your father were not well-matched.
He loved your mother dearly and could not see past
his grief to the young bride he had when the king
forced their marriage. As for Edda, she was miserable being stuck up here in Northern England with
a neglectful husband after being feted and pam-
pered at court. I suspect she was overwhelmed by
all the responsibility that landed on her shoulders
when your father died and the running of the castle
fell to her. No doubt that was the reason behind
her harsh treatment of the servants while we were
away."

"Hmm," Alex muttered. It was exactly what Edda
had said in her own defense when he'd returned
home to find half the servants fled and the other
half preparing to do so. It was not the homecoming

he'd hoped for. He'd returned to learn his father was dead, his sister married off to the Devil of Donnachaidh, and the castle half empty. He'd spent the week since arriving home trying to get things in order and convincing the servants to return, promising to provide them with better living conditions and to keep Edda under control.

Alex could have simply ordered them to return. They had sworn fealty to his family, after all, but his father had taught him that an unhappy worker made a poor worker and that he should respect even the lowliest servant. So he'd made no threats, but instead offered promises he intended to keep. Fortunately, he'd managed to get all but a couple he hadn't yet found to take up their positions again. He had even returned order to d'Aumesbery, at least as much as he thought was necessary before he could take the time out to go see his sister and be sure she was all right. He had worried about Evelinde ever since arriving at d'Aumesbery to learn she'd been married off to the Devil of Donnachaidh, and frankly, her well-being was more important to him at the moment.

Alex couldn't believe that Edda had allowed her to be married off to the bastard. The man hadn't been born with the name the Devil of Donnachaidh, he'd earned it. He was reputed to be completely merciless in battle, and a stern laird to his people. He'd also gone through one wife already who had fallen off a cliff to her death under what could only be called suspicious circumstances. The rumors claimed the Laird of Donnachaidh had been seen riding away from the scene around the time of her death. This was the man Edda had allowed Evelinde to be married to.

The thought made him again glance around for his stepmother. Alex didn't know what to think where the woman was concerned. Edda had never been a very warm, kind person. She'd always seemed to resent her life here, but now that he was back, she appeared to be making an effort. He could almost like the woman she'd been since his return. The fact that she'd let Evelinde be married to the Devil of Donnachaidh, however, plus the wary way the servants all watched her, troubled him. He wondered just how bad she'd been while he was away, and how much of her new attitude he could trust.

Alex would know more once he'd spoken to his sister. It was another reason he was eager to make the journey. He would have left at once, had he not needed to get the servants back and decide which of his men to leave in charge while he made the trip. In the normal course of events, Gerhard—as his first—should have been the one left in charge. The man would make a great castellan, he was sure, but Alex found himself reluctant to leave him behind. He depended on his wise counsel and suspected he would need it for this visit, in his dealings with both the Devil of Donnachaidh and his own betrothed.

Alex didn't expect either meeting to go well. He knew he could be a bit hotheaded at times, and loved his sister enough that, did he find Evelinde miserable or abused by her husband, he knew he would be tempted to skewer the man on the spot. Such rash action was likely to see him cut down by one of the laird's men seeking retribution. Gerhard was extremely levelheaded, weighing the pros and cons of everything, and had managed to temper Alex's rashness in the past with wise words. Alex was counting on that when he met up with his sister's husband.

And then there was his betrothed. The Stewart Shrew. Merewen Stewart had been called that since she was sixteen or younger. It was part of the reason he had never been overly eager to claim her. The title didn't suggest a sweet, biddable bride, and he suspected she would be difficult to deal with. Gerhard might have some suggestions there that could come in useful, too.

Nay, he wouldn't leave the man behind to act as castellan, which meant he'd had to train someone else for the task ere he could leave. He'd chosen John, a steady, dependable sort with a level head, and after a week of training him, now felt comfortable leaving him in charge. Last night Alex had announced that they would ride out for Donnachaidh today, and he had no intention of allowing anything to interfere with that plan, not even a nagging toothache.

One of the maids arrived at the table with a tray of cheese and bread for Alex and Gerhard to break their fast. Feeling his stomach rumble, he thanked the girl and began to look over the offering.

"Good morning, gentlemen."

Alex glanced up to see Edda crossing the hall toward the table. She was smiling cheerfully as she'd never done when he was younger, but a smile seemed ever-present on her face since his return. It actually made her more attractive than he'd ever thought she could be. With oddly thinning long brown hair and several teeth missing, Edda would never be pretty, but she was positively ugly when she wore the pinched expression he'd known her to wear before he'd left on the Crusades.

"I see you are just breaking your fast. Good. Then I am not as late rising as I thought. I . . ." She paused and blinked in surprise as she peered more closely at Alex. "Why Alex, your face is swollen. Did you suffer an injury?"

Alex felt his eyebrows rise on his forehead and lifted a hand to rub his face, frowning as he realized that his face was indeed a bit swollen.

" 'Tis a bad tooth," Gerhard explained. "I told him he should see it tended ere we leave, but he's being stubborn."

"Oh, you must not be stubborn about it, Alex. 'Tis obviously infected," Edda said firmly.

" 'Tis fine," Alex assured her quietly, and then disproved the claim by biting into a hunk of cheese and wincing as pain shot through his jaw.

"Oh, aye, 'tis fine," Gerhard said dryly.

Edda glanced to the maid who had brought the food. "Girl, go fetch the blacksmith to your lord."

"There is no need—" Alex began, but she overrode him.

"Aye there is. You are not leaving d'Aumesbery without having it seen to. Better men than you have been felled by infection when they didn't tend a bad tooth."

Alex grimaced, but didn't protest further. Truly, the tooth *was* paining him this morning, and infection anywhere on the body was a dangerous thing. Grimacing at the very idea of what was to come,

Alex turned his attention to breaking his fast, placing the food in his mouth on the good side and trying to chew it there. Unfortunately, that didn't seem to help much. While it didn't cause the sharp pain that biting down on the other side had, his jaw was now throbbing, and moving it about was just exacerbating that ache.

Sighing, he gave up on the food.

"There's the blacksmith." That announcement from Gerhard brought Alex's attention to the door. His eyebrows lifted when he saw the fellow entering the keep.

"*That's* the blacksmith?" he asked with surprise. "What happened to Old Baldric?"

"I hear Baldric went to his reward while we were away," Gerhard said quietly. "This is his replacement, Grefin."

Alex scowled at both the news and the man himself. While Old Baldric had been a large, beefy man, this one was shorter and lean-looking, without the bulk that suggested the strength needed to pull a tooth. Alex knew from experience that pulling teeth took a lot of strength. He'd had to help pull the tooth of one of his men while in Tunis. Teeth could be a devil to pull out. He suspected he was in for a bit of a trying time.

"I was told you had a tooth bothering you, my lord?"

Alexander glanced at Grefin as the new blacksmith paused beside him. He briefly considered not having it pulled at all, but the ache was a steady, pulsing throb now. Besides, the gum was swollen with infection. It needed pulling.

He nodded his head and turned his chair so that he was sideways to the table and faced the blacksmith. Grefin promptly stepped closer and ordered, "Open up and let me take a look then."

Alexander opened his mouth.

"Which one is it?" he asked, squinting into his mouth.

Alexander used one finger to point to it, keeping as much of his hand out of the way as he could so the man could see.

"Aye," Grefin murmured, and as soon as Alex removed his finger, reached in with his own to give the tooth a prod.

Alex managed not to groan at the agony that shot through him at the touch, and squeezed his eyes closed as the man did more prodding.

"How's it look?" Gerhard asked, standing and moving to the man's side to try to see into Alex's mouth for himself.

" 'Tis in there pretty good," he muttered grimly. "Not loose at all. 'Twill be a bugger to get out."

Alexander felt the man's fingers slip from his mouth, but kept his eyes closed as pain continued to shoot through him in slowly decreasing waves.

"I'll need a pitcher of whiskey," the blacksmith announced.

That announcement brought his eyes open as one of the maids hurried off toward the kitchens.

"What for?" Gerhard asked with surprise before Alex could.

"For him," Grefin said dryly, jerking a thumb in Alex's direction. " 'Twill numb the pain a bit at least."

Alex shook his head at once. "I do not want it. We are leaving for Donnachaidh as soon as you're done, and I shall need my wits about me for the journey north. Just pull the tooth."

Grefin laughed. "Oh, aye, you want it, my lord. And I'll not touch that tooth until you've drunk a full pitcher of whiskey. The trip will just have to be delayed."

"I do not want whiskey," he insisted. Alex had never been much of a drinker. He didn't care for the taste, and it did nothing for him but make him stupid. Alex didn't like to be stupid. Even more, he disliked the aftereffects overindulging caused.

"Alex—" Gerhard started, but while he was small, Grefin was apparently as surly as his predecessor and needed no one to argue for him.

He caught Alex by the face and jerked his face toward him, fingers digging into his cheek on the good side, and thumb pressing into the swollen side. When Alex hissed at the pain stabbing though him, Grefin nodded his satisfaction and snapped, "The last man who wouldn't drink ere I pulled a tooth, damned near throttled me to death while I tried to get it out."

Alexander noted a couple of men nodding farther along the table. Apparently, the incident had not gone unwitnessed. He would have asked about it, but the maid, Lia, was rushing back with the requested pitcher of whiskey. He scowled as the girl handed it to Grefin. "Still, I—"

"You'll drink the damned whiskey," the blacksmith interrupted. "Every last drop, and then the men are going to hold you down, else you can pull out your own damned tooth. And that's that!" He emphasized the words by shoving the pitcher of whiskey at him.

Alex ground his teeth with irritation, half tempted to try to pull his own tooth, but the teeth grinding had been a mistake and the pain it sent knifing through him again made him decide otherwise. It looked as if the trip was going to be delayed, he acknowledged with a curse and grabbed the pitcher and began to gulp down the liquid. No drink-induced headache could possibly be as bad as the agony he was now suffering.

"God's whiskers," Grefin breathed with admiration when Alex slammed the empty pitcher down on the table moments later.

"Get on with it," Alex growled. He then leaned back in the chair and grasped the wooden armrests firmly as he popped his mouth open. The whiskey wasn't affecting him yet—he'd drunk it too quickly for it yet to be in his system—but Alex didn't care. He wanted the tooth out and the pain gone.

"Why did we nay finish the journey last night?" Brodie asked in complaining tones. "We were practically on d'Aumesbery's doorstep and could have slept indoors rather than get up at dawn to finish the last mile's journey."

"Because yer sister wished to make herself presentable to meet her husband. Now stop yer whining. The journey is nearly over."

Brodie's grumbling complaint and their father's answer were picked up by the wind and carried back to Merry where she rode several feet behind.

She glanced toward the trio, but none of them was paying her any heed. They'd been riding a good distance in front of her since leaving Stewart several days ago. An attempt to avoid her temper, Merry supposed. She hadn't been at all pleased with her father and brothers the morning they'd left Stewart. While they'd stuck to ale the night before leaving and not tried to force her to give up the key to the pantry again, they'd also "celebrated" until well past the witching hour. Having seen this one too many times, Merry hadn't had the least sympathy with the three of them. She'd roused them from their beds at the crack of dawn and nagged them through breaking their fast and mounting their horses to lead the party out of Stewart bailey.

The three men had been avoiding her ever since, not even daring to complain about their pounding heads the first day of their travels. They'd recovered by the second day of the journey, and had then insisted on picking up the speed, forcing the entire party to travel at a pace that had made her worry for the wagon carrying her belongings. Merry had been sure the cart would rattle itself to pieces at any moment, but it hadn't. The wagon had held together, and they'd arrived in the woods surrounding d'Aumesbery late last evening. The men had wanted to continue on to the castle right then, but Merry had refused. It was late, and she'd suspected the drawbridge would be up and the gate closed. She did not want to rouse the night watch and cause a fuss to get in.

Besides, they'd been traveling for days, getting up at dawn, riding until well into the night and then

stopping just long enough to sleep before mounting up again to continue on. Merry hadn't wished to
ride into d'Aumesbery without first taking the time
to bathe away some of the dust and dirt of the trail
and don a fresh gown.

Now they were nearing the end of the journey. By
her guess, they would arrive just as everyone finished breaking their fast. The thought made a nervous quiver flutter through Merry's belly, and she
found herself biting one corner of her lower lip. She
was surprisingly anxious about the coming meeting. Excited, too, though. Merry had spent the last
several days distracting herself from the discomfort
and boredom of their journey by thinking of the
future. In her mind she'd painted a happy picture.
This marriage was finally bringing an end to her
promise to her mother and freeing her to look to
the future, and she'd done so with both hope and
relief. In her imaginings Alexander d'Aumesbery
was a good, honorable man and a proper husband
. . . nothing at all like her own father and brothers.
She would live in England, with, she hoped, an intelligent, sober man to husband. Someone she could
depend on rather than having to be the dependable
one. Merry was full of hope.

"Still, Merry could have done it in more comfort
at d'Aumesbery. There we all would have had a
warm bath and a comfortable bed at least," Gawain
pointed out with obvious irritation. "Besides, 'tis not
as if d'Aumesbery can refuse to have her, can he?" A
moment passed, and then he added worriedly, "He
canna, can he?"

"What?" Eachann Stewart sounded startled by

the suggestion, and she could hear the uncertainty in his voice as he said, "Nay. Of course not. Why wid ye even ask a question like that?"

"Well, he *has* dragged his feet about coming to get her," Brodie pointed out reluctantly.

"Nay," Eachann Stewart denied quickly. "He was on crusade at the request of his English prince."

"But the prince returned two years ago and d'Aumesbery didna," Brodie pointed out.

"Aye," Gawain said with alarm. "What if he heard that our Merry was a harpy and a shrew and was trying to avoid wedding her?"

"Well, he can't," their father said firmly. "We'll follow him to the ends of the world if need be. He's marrying the lass and that's that. Now hush, I'll not have Merry hear ye calling her harpy and shrew and taking out her temper on us."

Aware that the men were peering back at her anxiously, Merry kept her face expressionless and continued to stare into the woods they were traveling through. She was too weary to put them in their places as she normally would. Besides, it wasn't the first time she'd heard herself referred to as a harpy or the Stewart Shrew. The names had lost their ability to hurt her feelings long ago, but they did make her wonder now. *Had* her betrothed heard she was a harpy and shrew and set out to try and avoid marrying her?

The idea was a troubling one that preoccupied her for several minutes. In none of her imaginings about her future had her betrothed wished to avoid their marriage.

"There it is."

Merry raised her head and drew her mount to a halt behind the men as they suddenly cleared the woods and a castle loomed before them. D'Aumesbery was a large, imposing fortress, perched on a hill and overlooking the land surrounding it. It was much bigger than Stewart, which didn't bother her except to make her wonder how her father had managed to arrange such an advantageous marriage. He'd always claimed it had come about through friendship with the late Lord d'Aumesbery, claiming the two men had met at court while young and started a friendship that had lasted a decade. D'Aumesbery's son, Alexander, had been born five years before her, but the moment Merewen had been born, the two men had sealed their friendship with the marriage contract.

Merry suspected the friendship had not lasted long after that. At least she didn't ever recall visiting between the families. She suspected her father's drinking might have had something to do with it. Her mother had once said that while her father had been a hard drinker when younger, he had not grown really bad until his own father's death when Merry was two. It seemed his grief combined with the new responsibility as laird had pushed him that final step to prefer the happy, fuzzy state of drunkenness to the sober reality of his life.

"Here we are, Merry." Her father turned to beam a smile on her. One that was reflected on her brothers' faces as well, she noted as he added, "Ye'll meet yer betrothed now, and soon ye'll be a married lady with a passel of bairns to chase about."

Aye, rather than three grown drunks, Merry

thought, but didn't speak the words aloud. Why bother? Very soon she would be free of that chore. She'd have a husband of her own, one who, she hoped, would be nothing like her father and brothers.

With that hope firmly in mind, Merry urged her mare past the men and up the hill. It was late enough in the morning that the drawbridge was down and the gate open. Still, they were hailed as they approached, and Merry stopped and left it to her father to answer the hail and explain their presence. She then followed his mount into the bailey and straight to the steps of the keep, knowing the news of their arrival would reach it before they did.

Merry was dismounting when she heard the keep doors open. Once on the ground, she saw that a seasoned soldier was rushing down the stairs toward them. It was not her betrothed. He was only five years older than she, and this man looked to be fifteen or twenty years older at least. Wondering who he was, Merry moved to stand beside her father as the man reached them.

"Lord Stewart," the man greeted, holding out his hand as he stepped off the stairs. "'Tis a pleasure to meet you. I am Gerhard, Lord d'Aumesbery's . . . man."

Merry's eyebrows rose slightly at his hesitation. It appeared to her that he hadn't been sure what to call himself, or what his station was. Odd, she thought as she watched the two men shake hands. Then the Englishman was turning to her, beaming brightly.

"And you must be Lady Merewen. A pleasure, my lady. Welcome to d'Aumesbery."

"Thank you," she murmured, and then waited

patiently as her father introduced her brothers. Gerhard greeted both men politely and then shifted his attention to the rest of their party, who had dismounted and now stood about uncertainly.

"I shall have your horses and wagon attended to directly. In the meantime, perhaps we should go in."

Her father nodded, and took Merry's arm to lead her to the stairs, asking, "Where's d'Aumesbery? He should ha'e been here to greet us. He isna away, is he?"

"Nay, nay," Gerhard assured them as he followed them up the stairs, Brodie and Gawain trailing behind. "In fact, you are most fortunate in that way. Had you arrived on the morrow, we would have already left for Donnachaidh."

"Donnachaidh?" Merry asked with surprise, halting to turn to the man. Donnachaidh was the Duncan stronghold, and less than a half day's journey from Stewart.

"Aye. Alexander's sister, Evelinde, recently married the Devil of Donnachaidh, and he wishes to check on her," Gerhard said as her father urged her forward once more. "Actually, we were supposed to leave this morn, but Alex is . . . er . . . indisposed."

Merry felt trepidation slide through her at his choice of word. "Indisposed" was the term she used when referring to her father and brothers when they were nursing a sore head after a night—or several days—of drinking. And what did he mean they were supposed to leave that morn? The man had sent for her. Surely he hadn't then planned to leave ere she arrived?

"All's well that ends well, eh?" her father said

with a bluff laugh before she could ask any of her
questions. He tugged on her arm once more, drawing her up the last few steps to the keep doors.

"Aye, of course," Gerhard agreed quickly. "But I
should explain—"

"No need, Lord d'Aumesbery can explain,"
Eachann interrupted, pulling the door open and
urging Merry inside. He hustled her several steps
forward, but then paused and they both stood
blinking in an effort to make their eyes adjust to
the sudden dearth of light. As with most castles, the
great hall was much darker than it was out in the
sunlight, and the sudden shift left them both briefly
blinded. That being the case, Merry actually heard
the occupants of the hall before she saw them. Rau-
cous shouts and cheers assaulted her ears and drew
her blinking gaze to a crowd of men gathered in a
small, tight bunch.

"Is he among that group?" Eachann Stewart
asked, glancing about for the man who had greeted
them.

Gerhard nodded as he hurried to catch them up.
"Aye, but—"

It was all her father needed to hear. Waving the
man to silence, he again hurried Merry forward,
this time steering her toward the group by the trestle tables.

Gerhard rushed after them. "But I should tell you
that he is suf— Bollocks!"

Merry glanced over her shoulder to see that the
man had tripped over something in the rushes. He
stopped to pick up whatever it was, and then her
attention was drawn forward again when her father

suddenly drew her to a halt. They'd reached the
edge of the group, and her father was now tapping
the nearest man on the shoulder. The fellow, as large
as a small building, turned a glare on them for interrupting whatever was going on, but quickly killed
the glare when her father announced in a bluff voice,
"I am Laird Stewart and this is me daughter, Merry,
soon to be yer lady. Where is her betrothed, Alexander d'Aumesbery?"

The fellow's eyes widened, slid to her, and crin-
kled slightly as he smiled, but he didn't answer her
father's question. Instead he turned to nudge the
man next to him. Once he'd gained his attention, he
whispered something in the fellow's ear, and that
fellow peered around with surprise before nudging
someone else. Within a moment every face in the
crowd had turned to look at her. No one, however,
was stepping forward and announcing that he was
her betrothed.

Merry was just growing uncomfortable under
their stares when Gerhard caught up.

"Really, Lord Stewart, I should explain—" he tried
again, but paused as a sudden roar of fury sounded
from the center of the group of men before them. It
was followed by shuffling and shifting as the men
whirled back to whatever had held their attention
earlier. Merry stood on her tiptoes, trying to see what
was happening, but couldn't see a thing. Then Gerhard shifted past her and pushed his way through
the crowd, Merry quickly following in his wake.
When he paused, she stood up on tiptoes again to
peer over his shoulder and this time was able to see
what was happening. Two men were rolling about

on the floor, a slender, smaller man attempting to defend himself as a larger man appeared to be trying to throttle him to death. The sight had apparently startled Gerhard to a halt, but only briefly; he was already moving forward, barking at the others, "I told you to hold him down, dammit!"

The rebuke had several men moving forward to help as Gerhard struggled to drag the one man off the other. It took a bit of effort, but eventually they were able to separate the two. Merry suspected it was only because the larger man had grown weary of the struggle, or perhaps he'd got over whatever it was that had made him attack the smaller fellow in the first place. It appeared to her that the larger man simply stopped fighting and allowed the others to pull him upright and away. The smaller man immediately scrambled out of reach and, shaking his head, Gerhard quickly stepped forward. He brushed down the larger man and straightened his clothes, saying, "Your betrothed is here."

Merry sucked in a breath as she realized that the man presently swaying in the grasp of the men still holding him upright was her betrothed. She was not the only one shocked. Alexander d'Aumesbery appeared absolutely appalled by them and gasped, "The Stewart Shrew? What the devil is she doing here?"

The men surrounding them all turned wide and even apologetic eyes her way, and Merry felt herself flush with embarrassment, but lifted her chin as Gerhard hissed, "She's right here, Alex, right in front of you."

He then urged his lord toward her, and Merry's

eyes narrowed as she noted how unsteady her betrothed was on his feet. Gerhard was having to help
him stay upright with the grasp he had on his upper
arm.

"My lord, your betrothed, Lady Merewen Stewart," Gerhard introduced, drawing the other man to
a halt before her. Or at least he tried to; while Gerhard's hold on his lord's arm should have stopped
him, Alexander d'Aumesbery's feet were slower to
get the message, so that he nearly walked right into
Merry before the hold on his arm made him swing
in a clumsy half circle. Gerhard immediately caught
the man by both arms and turned him to stand
before her like a naughty little boy. He then repeated
grimly, "Lady Merewen Stewart."

Seeming oblivious of Gerhard's pained expression, Alex peered blearily at Merry, and then blew
whiskey fumes all over her, saying, "Damn me.
You're pretty. You don't look like a shrew."

There was a collective gasp of dismay from those
around them, and Eachann Stewart actually drew
himself up as if to say something, but Merry placed
a hand on his arm and merely said in dry tones,
"Thank you."

Really, what else could she say? The man was obviously beyond drunk and wouldn't remember any
reprimand anyway.

"You're welcome." He beamed at her and then in
the next moment grimaced and turned to tell Gerhard, "I don't feel so good."

The last word had barely slipped from his lips
before he suddenly fell forward and flat on his face
on the floor.

For a moment, the room was silent and still as everyone stared down at the unconscious man. But Merry's thoughts were not silent. Her mind was wailing in loss and fury as every last dream she'd had on the way here died a sudden, horrible death. She had gone from the pot into the fire, leaving one home of drunks to live in another, but this was worse. This drunk had rights to her bed and body. And he'd been in a drunken rage, throttling another man just moments ago, so appeared to be a mean drunk.

Merry closed her eyes, depression and misery settling over her. She would never get away from drunkards and fools. She allowed herself a moment of self-pity, then she straightened her shoulders and forced her eyes open again. Finding everyone now peering not at the man on the floor but at her, Merry controlled her expression and raised her head.

"Well," she said grimly. "Diya no think ye'd best carry yer laird's worthless hide up to his bed?"

Glances were exchanged, and then there was a sudden rush as every single man present began to shuffle forward. There were too many for the task. In the end only four were needed, each taking an arm or leg to cart him toward the stairs. The others followed, however, even the man whom her betrothed had been throttling when she'd first arrived.

Merry watched them go and then started to glance toward her father, but her gaze caught on a woman she hadn't noted earlier. Standing on the other side of where the men had been, the brunette appeared a good fifteen years older than she. She was also taller, with a thick frame and small eyes presently narrowed thoughtfully as she looked after the men carrying Alexander away. Merry peered at her curiously, wondering who she was. Then the woman glanced toward her, offered an anxious smile, and rushed forward.

"Good morn, Merewen. I am Edda, Alexander's stepmother. Welcome to d'Aumesbery."

"Thank you," Merry murmured as her hands were clasped in the woman's larger, strong hands. "Pray, call me Merry."

"Thank you, dear." Edda smiled, but it was a crooked smile, tinged with worry, and she rushed on. "I am ever so sorry you saw that. Did Gerhard explain matters to you?"

"Aye," Merry said dryly. "He explained when he greeted us that my betrothed was indisposed."

"Oh, good." She looked relieved. "I feared you might get the entirely wrong impression. But truly, while Alexander has been away these three years, I am quite positive he has not become a drinker and normally does not down a full pitcher of whiskey first thing in the morn. These are somewhat unusual circumstances." She smiled wryly and then urged Merewen toward the table. "Come, sit yourselves down. Have you broken your fast yet this morn?"

"Nay," Merry's father answered as they settled themselves at the trestle table. "We reached yer woods late last night and camped out there until this morning, but Merry was up early and through with her ablutions by the time the rest o' us woke so we rode straight here."

Edda nodded and then glanced to a maid who was hovering several feet away. "Lia, fetch some mead for Lady Merewen and . . ." She paused and glanced to Eachann Stewart. "For you gentlemen?"

"Mead fer them, too," Merry said firmly.

"Merry," Eachann protested, "we've been traveling for days without a drop o' whiskey, surely we—"

"—shall manage without it so long as ye're here," she said grimly and then leaned forward to hiss in a voice she hoped Edda could not hear, "I'll no ha'e the three o' ye embarrassing me while ye're here. There'll be no whiskey fer ye."

He scowled but didn't protest further, and Merry turned to Edda and offered a relieved smile. "They are fine with mead, too."

"Mead then for the men as well, Lia, and something for them to eat." The moment the girl rushed away, Edda turned back and offered a smile. "I hope your journey here was a pleasant one."

Merry grimaced. "Riding from dusk until well past dawn fer days on end is rarely pleasant, but we were fortunate and didna run into bandits or trouble o' that sort."

"From dusk until dawn?" Edda asked with surprise.

"Aye, well, meself and me sons are all here, are we no'?" her father said defensively. "We left one o' the men in charge o' Stewart while we're away, but 'tis no' the same as me being there."

Merry snorted at this, earning a glare from her father before he continued, "We wanted to get the gel here, see her wed, and then get back to Stewart."

"Oh, aye, of course," Edda murmured sympathetically. "I suppose you must get back as quickly as

you can. 'Tis a reflection of your caring for Merry
that you would all come to see her wed and leave
someone else in charge."

Merry managed not to snort as her father and
brothers all puffed up under the compliment. 'Twas
not caring but eagerness to be rid of her, she was
sure, but didn't say so.

"Aye, just so," her father said staunchly, and then
added, "That being the case, mayhap ye can send fer
yer priest and—"

"Father," Merry snapped.

"What?" he asked defensively. "Yer betrothed
wishes to get to Donnachaidh and we need to return
to Stewart. There is no reason to delay."

"Except fer the wee matter of the groom bein' unconscious," she pointed out dryly.

"Aye, that does put a bit of a wrinkle in things,"
Edda said with a twinkle in her eye. "But I am sure
he shall be recovered by the sup, or by tomorrow
morn at the latest. There is no reason the wedding
cannot take place first thing on the morrow, and
then everyone may set out on their journeys."

Her father and brothers agreed quickly, but Merry
remained silent. She was no longer eager to be married, but there was really no reason to delay. The
contract was binding and she would have to marry
him eventually. Realizing that Edda was peering at
her in question, apparently looking for her agreement, Merry sighed and nodded.

"Good!" Edda said brightly. "Then after you have
eaten, I shall hunt down Father Gibbon while you
talk to Cook."

"Me?" Merry asked with surprise.

"Aye, well, you will be the lady here by the morrow and in charge of everyone. You may as well begin now. Besides, 'tis your wedding, dear, and while it may be a bit rushed, you should really be the one to chose the menu for the wedding feast and so on."

Merry smiled uncertainly, but again nodded. Put that way, there really seemed little reason for her not to be the one to talk to Cook. She just hoped Cook agreed and would take orders from her despite the fact that she hadn't yet married his lord and officially become his lady.

chapter

Two

Pain was a great monster inside Alexander's skull, slamming a mace around with sharp blows. It made him shut his eyes more tightly and groan as he instinctively fought returning to consciousness and fully experiencing the pain attacking him.

"You can squeeze your eyes closed all you like, but 'twill not stop the pain."

Alex's eyes popped open at those raspy words, and he scowled at the gnarled old woman who stood beside the bed mixing something in a wooden mug. However, the moment he recognized Bet, his mother's old nursemaid, he forced the scowl from his face and squeezed his eyes closed once more. "I feel like hell."

"A pitcher of whiskey on an empty stomach first thing in the morn will do that to you." The woman didn't sound terribly sympathetic. "And you gave yourself a nice goose egg on your forehead when you fell on your face, too. I'm sure that's not helping. Here, sit up and get this into you. It'll help ease the pain."

"Fell on my face?" Alex growled, eyes popping open. His gaze landed on the wooden mug she was holding out and, after the briefest hesitation, he sat up to take it.

"Aye," she assured him. "Right at the feet of your betrothed, too. Made a fine first impression I'm sure. Drink it," she added, sounding a bit impatient when he started to lower the mug full of vile-smelling liquid, his mouth opening on another question.

Alex briefly considered reminding the woman of her place and that he was her lord, but knew from experience that neither reminder would impress her. It was hard to impress someone with your power and position when she'd changed your nappies as a babe. Grimacing, he didn't even bother attempting to argue with the stubborn old woman, but quickly downed the drink. It tasted as bad as it smelled, of course. He wasn't surprised. Bet's medicinals had always been the most god-awful tasting brews, but they also usually worked damned well. He would have been grateful for her vile concoctions and less-than-tender mercies more than a time or two in Tunis.

Managing to down the entire contents in two healthy swallows, Alex grimaced at the taste as he handed the mug back and then growled, "What was that about my betrothed being here?"

"She and her kin arrived just as Grefin was making his attempt to yank out your bad tooth," Bet announced, and there was no mistaking the amusement on her wrinkled face.

Alex ignored it for now, instead scowling as the fuzzy memory of the morning's misery slid through his mind. Just poking at the tooth had caused agony, but the blacksmith's clamping his pincers on it and trying to yank it from his jaw had been hell. The pain of it had been so shockingly fierce that Alex hadn't, at first, even been able to find the breath to roar his agony. But then something had distracted the men holding him, and he'd managed to break free and grab Grefin by the throat to bring his torture to an end. The blacksmith had dropped his pincers and tried to back away, and the moment he wasn't fiddling with his tooth, Alex had got his breath back and roared his fury as he'd followed the man, stumbling to his feet before the two of them had tumbled to the floor.

He could only think it was a good thing he'd roared because that had caught his men's attention and recalled them to their duty. It was probably the only thing that had saved Grefin a good thrashing. Alex also decided it had been a good thing Grefin had insisted on their waiting half an hour for the whiskey he'd downed to take effect before making the attempt. If there was a worse pain than that he'd suffered while numbed by whiskey, Alex had no desire to experience it. Honestly, he'd taken sword wounds in Tunis that had hurt less.

The thought made him search around inside his mouth for the tooth in question. Relief slid through him when he felt a hole where the tooth had once been.

"He got the tooth out once you were in your bed," Bet announced. "Grefin said it was much easier to yank out when you weren't fighting him. It only took him a moment once you were unconscious."

Alex grimaced at the claim and shook his head. Those vague memories of Grefin's struggling to remove his tooth down in the great hall and then his attacking him were the last things he recalled. He had no recollection at all of Merewen Stewart's arrival. "Why is my betrothed here?"

"To marry you, why else?" Bet said with a shrug as she began to put away her pouch of medicinals.

Alex scowled at the woman. "She should have waited for me to go to her, not—"

"You were dragging your feet over the business, were you not?" Bet asked dryly. "It seems she grew weary of the waiting and came to see the deed done."

Alex pursed his lips with displeasure. He wasn't ready to marry. He'd planned to take the time to get matters in order here and then visit his sister. After that, perhaps on the way home, he might have stopped to claim the wench. Or not. There was no rush. Apparently, she didn't see it that way.

"Although," Bet continued when he remained silent, "from what I've seen and heard, I suspect it was really her kin who are eager to be rid of the chit."

"Well, I am not surprised," Alex muttered, feeling

worry rise up in him as he thought of the things he'd heard about his future wife. Noting the raised eyebrows Bet had turned his way, he explained, "She's called the Stewart Shrew."

Bet nodded and commented dryly, "So you said when you saw her."

"*What?*" he asked sharply.

"When she arrived and you first saw her, I'm told your greeting was to say she didn't look much like a shrew or some such thing," Bet explained, her eyes now twinkling with silent mirth.

"I didn't!" Alex said with shock, and felt a frisson of horror slide down the back of his neck when the old woman nodded. While he'd spent much of the last three years surrounded by men, he'd retained enough of his training to know greeting his intended bride that way was beyond rude. It was hardly likely to encourage good relations with the woman.

"Aye, you did," Bet said, and added dryly, "Not the most welcoming greeting you could have offered your future wife."

"Dear God," he breathed in dismay, and then asked, "What did she do?"

Bet chuckled openly as she answered, "I was not there. I heard all of this from one of the maids, but I gather while she looked unimpressed, all she said was thank you . . . and then you fell flat on your face and she had your men pick you up and cart you up here to bed. That's when Grefin finished pulling out your tooth," she added. "After that, the men left you to sleep off the whiskey."

Alex sank back in the bed, his mind whirling with

dismay, but then sat up abruptly and asked, "What time is it?"

"Nearing the dinner hour," Bet answered, putting away the last of her things and moving toward the door. "I thought you might be stirring by now and need a tonic to help your head. Besides, it seemed best to wake you before the girl completely takes over the castle."

"What?" He tossed aside the linens that had been covering him. Much to Alex's relief, he was fully clothed and, despite his aching head, could give chase to the old woman as she tried to slip out of his room on that cryptic comment.

"Get back here, Bet," he growled, rushing forward to catch the door as she tried to pull it closed behind her. Taking the woman by the arm, he tugged her back into the room, careful to be gentle with her frail old bones. He wasn't at all surprised when she came willingly. Knowing her, she was probably enjoying the whole thing. Bet had always had a bit of the devil in her and had enjoyed a good stirring up. "Explain what you meant by that. How is she taking over my castle?"

"Well, once she'd ordered the men to take your 'worthless hide' up to your room—"

"Worthless?" Alex snapped with affront.

"Aye. That's apparently what she said," Bet informed him with a grin that displayed several gaps where teeth had once resided. "And once the men had carted you out, Edda appeared and the two women put their heads together for a bit."

Alex stiffened at this news. He was sure that couldn't be a good thing.

"And then your little Merry rushed around taking matters in hand and running d'Aumesbery as if she were already lady here."

Alex took note of the name Merry rather than Merewen, but merely asked shortly, "What has she been doing?"

Bet shrugged mildly. "Doing what a lady does. She's spoken with Cook and several of the other servants. She's started arrangements for a feast to follow the wedding tomorrow and—"

"Tomorrow?" he growled, horror coursing through him. This was all happening too fast.

"Aye. And now she's down overseeing the men at their training."

Alex stiffened and began irritably, "She has no business—"

"Go tell it to *her*, boy," Bet interrupted dryly, tugging her arm free to turn to the door. "I've too much to do to be standing about here while you bellow at me over what your betrothed is getting up to."

Alex glared after the old woman as she slid out of the room again, but she paused once in the hall and glanced back to add, "You might be wanting to change your clothes and clean up a bit ere you go looking for her. You fair reek of whiskey, and I doubt that will impress her any. From what I have heard, she's had enough of that with her father and brothers."

Alex glanced down at his tunic and then lifted the material to give himself a sniff as the door closed behind the old nursemaid. His nose immediately wrinkled with distaste. It did reek of whiskey, and it was a bitter, stale smell, too.

Grimacing, he immediately tore off the tunic and tossed it across the foot of his bed. Alex then moved to the basin of water on the small table by the window to give himself a quick wash before searching out a fresh tunic from one of the two chests that held his belongings. Once satisfied that he was presentable, he then left his room and rushed below stairs.

Alex had intended to head straight out to the bailey to find his betrothed, but found himself halting on the bottom step to stare at the men presently seated at his trestle table. There were nearly a dozen of them, and every one wore a plaid and looked in need of a good washing. Obviously, these were his betrothed's brothers and father as well as the soldiers they'd brought with them on the journey. It looked to him as if, on arriving that morning, they'd settled themselves at his table and not moved since except to raise their drinks to their mouths. They were obviously drunk and loud and boisterous with it. He wasn't pleased, but wasn't terribly surprised, either. Gossip tended to travel on the wind, often carried by traveling performers as well as salesmen selling spices and other foreign goods. From what he'd heard over the years, Eachann Stewart and his two sons had a reputation for being overfond of their drink . . . and apparently his own, and anyone else's they could get their hands on. His father, James, had not been much for drink himself, and Alex suspected Lord Stewart's tendency toward drunkenness was part of the reason the friendship had ended, and possibly why his father had not been pushing him to marry Merewen Stewart.

Thoughts of his betrothed reminded Alex of the

task he'd set himself and he turned toward the door, but had hardly taken a step before he was spotted and hailed. "Oy! Lad, come sit yerself fer a minute and visit with yer new kin."

Heaving out a breath at how near he'd been to escaping unnoticed, Alex turned back and reluctantly moved to the table, thinking he'd just explain he was off to find Merry and excuse himself. However, before he could say anything at all, before he'd even quite reached them, the oldest man in the group— Eachann Stewart, he supposed—announced, "'Tis glad I am I'm gettin' a chance to speak to ye ere our Merry does."

"Oh? Why is that?" Alex asked cautiously as he paused. Eachann Stewart appeared to have seen nearly six decades. He was more paunch than shoulders, a rat's nest of wiry grey hair springing out of an oddly large head over a face that was flushed from drink and made up of small squinting eyes, thin lips, and a slightly bulbous nose. He was also obviously well into his cups. His speech was slurred, and he was swaying like a sapling in a stiff breeze in the larger of the only two chairs at the table. They were the lord's and lady's chairs. Everyone else used the benches that ran around the tables. The man he thought was Eachann Stewart presently sat in the chair Alexander had occupied since returning from Tunis. A younger version of the man sat in the smaller chair.

"Well, lad," Eachann Stewart said, drawing his gaze back to his face. "Ye see, when we heard ye were returned, we decided to save ye a trip north and bring our Merry to ye, but we kenned she'd no agree. She'd expect ye to collect her all good and proper, ye see. So we fibbed a little to our lass."

Alex let his eyebrows rise in question.

"We told her ye were the one to send fer her," he explained, and then added slyly, "We knew ye would o' course. After all, 'tis well past time the two o' ye were married, and ye wouldn't be wantin' anyone thinking ye were trying to avoid the duty."

Alex managed not to wince at the accusation in the man's voice.

" 'Tis understandable if ye were delayin' as long as ye could," he went on in a friendly manner. "I ken from yer greeting on our arrival that ye've heard Merry's called the Stewart Shrew, and that name's no' likely to make ye eager to claim her, but she isna as bad as all that."

Alex was still. He'd heard she was called that, but had never thought to hear her own father bring up the name.

" 'Tis our fault she's called that," Eachann added almost regretfully.

"Aye," the younger man in the second chair said. He was very similar in looks to his father, but with carrot-colored hair. He also sounded amused rather than regretful as he added, "We gave her the name."

"My son Brodie," Eachann introduced, glaring at his boy, and then he turned to the man on his other side, one who could have been the first's twin, and introduced him as well. "And this is Gawain."

Both younger men nodded, and Alex nodded a bit stiffly back. The brothers were in at least as bad a state as their father. All three were swaying back and forth in their seats almost in time. It made Alex feel like he was on a ship in rough waters.

"Aye, we did give her the name," Eachann admitted. "I fear our Merry tends to worry and fret over us. She doesna understand about a man and his drink. Got that from her mother," he confided. "My Maighread was always disapproving when we had a little whiskey. But that's the only complaint I have with the girl. She's a good chit, generally good-natured, and always willing to lend a hand and take care of things," he assured him, and added, "Why, right now she's down overseeing the men at practice fer ye because ye were too . . . er . . . indisposed to manage the task yerself."

The old man grinned. "To be in such a state ye must ha'e been at the end o' a long celebration. We like to do that oursel'es and understand, but Merry might be a bit testy about it. Ne'er fear, though, she may get angry, but she'll still tend to anything that needs tending and stand in fer ye where she has to."

Alex's brow puckered at these words. It seemed obvious they had no idea he'd only drunk the whiskey that morning to have a tooth pulled, but believed he'd actually just been drinking for drink's sake that early. He found the idea, and their easy and cheerful acceptance of such behavior, absolutely deplorable. Alex had met men over the years too fond of their drink. He'd even had a man or two under him take to the problem. The minute he suspected someone of it, he dealt with it by first trying to get the man to stop, and then by releasing the man from his vow to serve under him. He had no desire to have a drunk under his command. Dependence on drink made a soldier sloppy and undependable and like to get himself or someone else killed.

"I'm getting a crick in me neck staring up at ye," the Stewart complained, and then turned to give the son seated in the chair next to his own a push. "Get out o' the chair, lad, and let our host sit with us."

"There is no need for that," Alex said quietly, having no desire to join the men. "I was just going out to oversee my men at practice."

"But, lad, like I told ye, Merry'll tend to it. She's a fair hand with the men."

Alex stiffened. " 'Tis my place to—"

"There's no need," Eachann interrupted. "Her mother raised her well, Merry's a fine helpmate. She'll tend everything do ye wish it. She does everything at Stewart."

"And what do you do?" he asked curiously.

"Whatever we wish," Gawain said with a laugh.

"Aye. 'Tis a grand life ye're headed for," Brodie informed him, and then snickered as if that were a joke. It brought a glare from his father.

"'*Tis* a grand life ye're headed for," Eachann insisted quietly when Brodie fell solemn. "My Merry's a hard worker. She'll step in and tend whatever needs tending."

"Which would be grand if she did so without glaring at us like we've done something wrong," Brodie put in, appearing irritated at the compliment to his missing sister.

"Aye," Gawain agreed, and warned, "she has a glare that'll singe the hair off yer arse."

"And then there's her fish face," Brodie muttered, gaining an elbow in the ribs from his father. Unsteady as he was, it nearly sent the younger man tumbling to the rushes before he caught at the table to save himself.

"Fish face?" Alex asked with bewilderment.

"Aye," Gawain answered as his brother struggled to sit up straight. "She narrows her eyes and purses her lips like this and looks just like a fish when she's disapproving or—" His words came to an end on a yelp as his father now slammed his other elbow into him. While Brodie had managed to save himself, Gawain couldn't and landed in the rushes. He burst out laughing as if his state of inebriation were a grand joke rather than the sad showing it was, and then his laughter faded and his eyes closed and he began to snore.

"Don't trouble yerself about him," Laird Stewart slurred with unconcern. "We've been celebrating yer upcoming nuptials since arriving and he's in his cups. He'll be fine and fit for the ceremony tomorrow though, I'm sure."

Alex shifted his gaze to the older man as he continued.

"As for Merry, aye, she glares and makes strange faces, but that's the worst o' it, and that's damned good by anyone's standards, especially when ye get the benefit o' her tending to everything fer ye in return. She'll be a good wife to ye."

Alex's gaze moved from Eachann to Brodie and back. Brodie was scowling with resentment, obviously not pleased at the compliments to his sister. As for Eachann, he was looking a tad sad and regretful, and Alex suspected the man was realizing what he was losing. Who was going to run Stewart when these men returned and slipped completely into their cups? He knew from what little gossip he'd heard over the years that the burden had fallen to Merry since her mother's death, and suspected her father, at least, knew what they were losing. It made him wonder why the old man had lied to get her there and not done everything he could to delay losing her to this marriage instead. Alex wanted to think it was because the man had some sense of decency left in him and wished to see her happy and married despite the burden losing her would be, but he suspected the truth was he'd merely bowed to the wishes and demands of his sons, who were obviously happy at the prospect of being rid of her.

Aye, Alex thought, glares and strange faces were little enough in response to the trouble life with these three men must have been. He couldn't imagine what Merry's life must have been like these last six years. After only minutes in their company he was irritated as hell.

Muttering, "Excuse me," he turned away and headed for the door, neither pausing nor glancing around when the Stewart called out to him again.

Alex wanted to get to the practice field and speak to his betrothed. He had no doubt that Merry must now loathe drinking after her experiences with these men, and was very aware that she'd arrived here to find him three sheets to the wind. He doubted it had made a good impression and could only hope someone had explained matters to her so she wasn't now fearing she'd gone from one home full of drunks to another.

He would just find her and thank her for tending

to matters while he was indisposed after his tooth pulling. Her response would tell him if someone had indeed explained things. If not, he'd explain himself, and then perhaps take the opportunity to get to know her better. While Alex had found her father and brothers rather annoying with their drunken slurs and the way they spoke of Merry, it was something of a relief to have spoken to them. For he now did understand how she had come to be called the Stewart Shrew and was positive it didn't reflect poorly on her so much as on them.

Much as he'd like to deny it, her reputation had rather put him off marrying the girl. Alex had been more than happy to postpone the duty as long as possible. Now, if he wasn't eager, at least his stomach didn't roil at the mere thought of it.

The practice field was a hive of activity when he reached it. Pausing on the edge, Alex peered over the people filling it, some practicing at swords, some with lances, some maces. All of them were men dressed in mail and braies, however. Alex had no idea what his betrothed looked like, so had counted on her being the sole female there for him to find her, but there wasn't a woman anywhere to be seen. For all he knew, he might have passed her in the bailey, although he hadn't noted anyone he didn't recognize on his walk down here, but—preoccupied with his thoughts as he'd been—he hadn't really paid attention.

Muttering a mild curse under his breath, Alex started to turn back the way he'd come but stopped when he heard someone shout, "Keep yer shield up or ye're going to be skewered!"

It was a woman's voice with a very definite Scottish accent, and he once again scanned the area in search of a gown. He was frowning with bewilderment over the fact that there wasn't one when she spoke again.

"Good, good! Ye're a fine fighter, Albert, just remember to keep yer shield up else all that fine skill will go to waste when ye're run through. William, 'tis yer turn."

Alex followed the voice to a small group of men at one end of the field. He scoured the gathering with his eyes, but still saw no dress to tell him which was his lady. There were six large men standing in a loose circle around another large man, battling at wooden swords with a much smaller, slender youth in braies, mail, and helmet.

"Damn me, William, stop hesitating. I noted ye tend to do that while ye were fighting with Henry earlier, 'tis why I brought ye here. Now thrust, man, ye'll no' hurt me, and were we in true battle ye'd already be dead."

Alex's eyes went round, horror coursing through him as he realized the little fellow in braies was his betrothed. The crazy woman wasn't just overseeing the training—which would have been bad enough— she was actually participating in it.

"God's teeth!" he bellowed, and rushed forward. Alex pushed his way between two of the men, reached the pair in the center, and grabbed the one he'd originally thought was a slender youth by the arm to wheel her around.

She was definitely a woman; large wide eyes blinked up at him in surprise above a straight little nose and full, luscious lips. Merewen Stewart had instinctively brought her wooden sword up to hit at him, but paused abruptly when she saw his face. Recognition flashed briefly through her green eyes; it was followed quickly by irritation and she jerked her arm free and snapped, "Are ye daft? Ye nearly got yerself skewered. This sword may be wood, but it can still do damage."

Alex ignored her tirade and grabbed her arm again, holding her in place as he snatched the helmet off her head. His eyes widened as a mass of glorious chestnut hair suddenly tumbled out to surround her heart-shaped face. It fell in waves, reaching nearly to her waist, and felt as soft as silk against the back of his hand where he held her arm. It seemed obvious the girl had got her looks from her mother rather than her father . . . and he was grateful for it.

"What are ye gawping at?" Merewen Stewart asked, but while her words were irritated, the way she was flushing and avoiding his eyes suggested discomfort and even embarrassment. "Unhand me and let me get back to work."

"'Tis *my* work," Alex said with a scowl, and turned to drag her, protesting, off the field.

"What are ye doing?" she squawked, sounding alarmed rather than angry.

"Madame, you are in braies," Alex said through his teeth as he noted several of his men pausing in their training to watch them.

Merry's response was a cluck of impatience. "Aye. I can hardly fight properly in a gown, can I? One fall and the skirt flies up and 'tis a free show for all. 'Tis one thing for a Scottish man to be flashing his bum at every turn, 'tis quite another for me to be flashing my—"

Alex stopped abruptly and turned on her with dismay, and she swallowed whatever she'd been about to say and merely scowled at him instead. He took a breath, trying to erase the image her words had brought to mind, and then said, "That is— I— You—"

Before he could quite figure out what he was trying to say, she heaved an impatient breath. "I see ye've the same problem with speech me own da has after drinking too much. Nay doubt yer thoughts are muddled like his, too. Ye'd best take yerself back to the keep and out of harm's way while I see to the men."

Alex briefly closed his eyes and prayed for patience, then opened them again and said as calmly as he could, "Madame, the practice field is no place for a woman. 'Tis my job to oversee the men."

"Well ye were in no condition to oversee them, were ye?" she said pointedly. "So I tended it fer ye. And stop shouting, I am standing right here."

"I was not shouting," he said through gritted teeth.

"Aye, ye were," she assured him, but now spoke in solemn tones as if to a child. She also patted his arm as if soothing a child. "Take yerself on back to the castle and leave me to tend to the men until ye're no' so scattered."

"I am *not* scattered," he denied quickly, and then added, "And the men do not need tending."

"Aye they do," Merry assured him. "Albert there has a habit o' letting his shield drop while he's fight-

ing. It's like to see him killed despite his being a fine
swordsman. And William is too timid, he constantly
hesitates ere swinging at his foe. 'Twill see him dead
in his first battle. And then there's Tom. He seems to
be skilled, but needs to build more muscle or have a
smaller sword made for him. The one he has is too
heavy for him to wield for any length of time."

Alex stared. Everything she'd said was true. They
were problems he'd noticed and had intended to
work on . . . when he had the time. Unfortunately,
he'd been in such a rush to get things in order here
before heading to Donnachaidh that he decided to
tend it when he returned from Scotland.

"Am I wrong?" she challenged.

"Nay," he assured her. "I had recognized those
issues. And I will tend to them as soon as I return
from Donnachaidh."

Merry nodded slowly and then said, "And what if
the castle is attacked while ye're gone? What if those
men die because ye were lax in yer duties and didna
take the time to train them properly ere hieing off to
see yer sister?"

Alex stiffened at the accusation, but merely
snapped, "The chances of an attack are minimal at
best."

"But no' impossible," she said firmly. "And 'tis yer
place as laird to see yer men well-trained and able to
defend themselves and yer castle."

Alex's mouth tightened. As much as he liked to
think he was a good and responsible lord, it did
seem a bit selfish that he was going to delay correct-
ing those flaws in his soldiers in favor of checking
on his sister. It would take only a day or two to tend

the matter. He was considering this when he noted she was a bit flushed and sweaty from her efforts on his behalf that day while he'd been sleeping off the whiskey. It made his mouth tighten further.

"I shall attend the men ere we leave for Donnachaidh," he assured her quietly. "But *I* shall tend it, not you. You shall stick to matters in the castle itself from now on. And this moment, you will go in, wash up and change, and then sit at the trestle table with your father and brothers until the sup."

"My father and brothers are still at the table?" she asked, eyes narrowing.

"Aye."

"They're no' drinking, are they?"

"Aye, and my best whiskey from what I could tell," Alex said dryly.

Much to his amazement, Merry spat out a curse he'd never expected to come from a woman though he'd heard it often enough on the tongues of his soldiers, and then she whirled and hurried away toward the keep.

Sudden concern claiming him, Alex was about to follow when Gerhard appeared at his side and commented, "I did try to steer her away from the practice field, but she's a determined little thing."

Alex grunted, but before he could respond, the man added, "I tried to explain about your tooth and the whiskey this morning when they arrived, but her father wouldn't let me and kept interrupting."

"He probably thought you would say something that would give away that I had not sent for her," Alex said dryly.

"She thinks you sent for her?" Gerhard asked with surprise.

Alex nodded. "I gather her father and brothers thought my sending for her more likely to get her to come, and they seem eager to be free of her disapproval of their drinking. It sounds to me as if they do a lot of it, leaving Merry to run Stewart these last years."

Gerhard nodded, not appearing surprised. "She seems to be very able at it. While I did try to steer her away from overseeing practice, she was good at it, picking out problems and flaws in the fighters and insisting on training them herself. She is surprisingly skilled."

"Aye, so I noticed," Alex murmured, his eyes narrowing on his betrothed. Her steps became stiffer and more militant with every step toward the keep, and he suspected the Stewart men were about to get more than the usual glare and fish face. It suddenly seemed a good idea for him to be there. Glancing at Gerhard, he said, "Tell the men 'tis enough practice for today. 'Tis nearly time for the sup anyway."

He waited just long enough to see Gerhard nod and then hurried after his betrothed. Fast as she was moving, and though she had a head start, Alex had longer legs and had reduced the distance between them by the time Merry reached the keep.

He was just starting up the steps when she reached the keep doors, still he was close enough to hear the shrieks coming from inside the moment the door opened.

Alarm coursing through him, Alex charged up

the stairs even as Merry cursed and rushed inside.
The door closed behind her with a loud thud that
silenced the screams from inside before he reached
it. Those screams reached him again, however, the
moment Alex opened the door himself. He took in
what was happening at a glance. The rest of the Scots
were quiet and wary-looking as they noted Merry's
arrival, but Gawain was still unconscious on the
floor beside the trestle table, and Laird Eachann
himself appeared to have passed out slumped forward on the table. Brodie, however, was still conscious and was presently trying to hold one of the
struggling d'Aumesbery maids in his lap and kiss
her. He wasn't succeeding very well. The girl was
struggling in earnest to be free of his clutches, but
those struggles ceased and her mouth made an O of
surprise when Merry reached them and promptly
smashed her shield down over her brother's head
with a bong that made even Alex wince.

Brodie apparently had a thick skull. He merely
shook his head and stood up, dumping the maid to
the floor so that he could swing around and confront his attacker.

Alex put on even more speed, rushing forward to
be at hand to defend Merry if necessary, but the lass
didn't need defending. When her brother turned
unsteadily and swayed before her, face furious
and mouth opening, no doubt to berate her, Merry
slammed the shield over his head again.

"What diya think ye're doing, ye great gowk?"
she snapped as her brother reached up to rub his
head. "The lass isna willing. Leave her be."

"I was just havin' a little fun," Brodie growled,

swaying like a giant oak whose base had all but been hacked away by men with axes.

"Well *she* wasna having fun," Merry barked, and hit him again for good measure.

The third time was the charm. Where the first two had hardly seemed to do more than get his attention, the third blow finally felled the man, sending him first to his knees, where he blinked briefly with confusion before slumping forward on his face in the rushes.

Alex slowed, his eyes shifting to Merewen Stewart. The expression that crossed her face as she peered down at her brother was a combination of shame, fury, and disgust, and then she turned on the maid.

"I told ye all no' to let them drink aught but ale."

"Aye, my lady, but they are guests and were demanding whiskey and—"

Merry silenced her by grabbing her arm to give her a small shake. "I care naught what they were demanding. Listen to me in future. They're no' to have a drop o' whiskey here. Understand?"

"Aye, my lady. I'm sorry, my lady," the girl said quickly.

Merry patted the girl's arm and then turned to sweep a glance over the three unconscious Stewart men before turning to the soldiers still seated at the table. "Well? What are ye waitin' fer? Gather yer laird and me brothers and take their worthless hides above stairs. They can sleep this off in their rooms."

The soldiers moved at once, getting to their feet to follow her orders. Alex watched them with interest.

He had assumed that they were as drunk as their laird and his sons, but now realized he'd thought wrong. Not one of them appeared the least unsteady on his feet as they began to drag the three Stewart men away. It seemed while they'd kept them company, not a one had drunk as deeply as the men they served. He also couldn't help but notice the respectful deference the men showed Merry. It was only now, seeing the glances and nods they cast her way, that he realized that respect had been missing from their expressions as they'd sat with her father and brothers earlier. They hadn't been openly disrespectful then, but he could now see the difference in their attitudes to each.

Once the men had disappeared above stairs with their burdens, Alex turned his gaze back to Merry. He was just in time to see her head and shoulders droop as if under a terrible weight. He realized then that she had no idea he'd followed her inside. Alex was positive Merry wouldn't allow herself to be seen as anything but strong and capable in the normal course of events and usually hid any feelings of defeat or weariness her family's antics caused. He was glad to see it, however. It allowed him to see a vulnerability he suspected he otherwise wouldn't have been privy to.

It was a very brief vulnerability. Barely a heartbeat had passed before Merry released a heavy sigh, straightened her shoulders, and moved off toward the stairs. Alex found his eyes sliding down over her lithe shape as she went, traveling over the bulky mail jerkin she wore to her behind in the braies. He'd never before seen a woman wear braies. It was

really quite . . . Alex licked his lips as he watched the
cheeks of her bottom move with each step and then
realized what he was doing, gave his head a shake,
and forced himself to turn away as she reached the
stairs and began to ascend them. Moving to the
table then, he sat down and considered the situation
at hand.

It seemed he was getting married on the morrow
. . . to a woman who presently thought him a
drunken lout like her father and brothers. He could
simply sit her down and explain things and tell her
that he wasn't a drinking man, but having dealt
with drunks himself, he knew they were prone to
lying to hide their affliction and doubted she would
believe him if he simply told her. The best way, he
supposed, was to show her by his actions. After a
week or so of their living together, she would see
that he didn't drink and wasn't like her father and
brothers.

chapter

Three

Her husband was a drunk, Merry acknowledged unhappily as she watched him out of
the corner of her eye.

It was dinnertime on the day after she and her
kin had arrived at d'Aumesbery. Her wedding feast,
but that wasn't the only reason this meal differed
from the one the night before. That had been a quiet
affair. Her father and brothers had been sleeping off
their drink in their rooms, and Merry had been so
embarrassed about them that she'd found it difficult
to relax or respond much to Alex's efforts to engage
her in conversation at the table. She'd been relieved
when the meal had come to an end and she could

excuse herself, claiming weariness from her journey to make her way up to her room. Not that she'd slept. Mostly she'd found her mind whirling with worries about her looming marriage and the wedding night that would follow, so that it was quite late when she'd finally drifted off to sleep.

It had been late when her maid, Una, had woken her. The woman wasn't pleased to have to move to England and had been quiet since they'd left Stewart. She'd continued that way this morning, saying little to distract Merry from her worries about the coming bedding as she'd helped her bathe, dress, and fix her hair. The great hall had been empty when Merry had made her way below, but Edda had soon joined her and kept her company as she broke her fast. From her she'd learned that Alex was out passing the morning training the men and would come in to bathe and prepare for the wedding at the nooning hour.

The rest of the day had passed in something of a nervous blur for her; the nooning meal, the wait for the priest and Alex to be ready, the ceremony itself . . . The only thing that Merry really recalled about the wedding was the moment when Alex had pressed his lips to hers to seal the marriage. She'd gone stiff in his hold, but every sense in her had been on the alert and she'd been aware of the fresh, male scent of him wafting into her nose, the feel of his warm, gentle hands on either side of her face, the pressure of his lips brushing softly across hers, and even his taste when she'd licked her lips nervously afterward.

Now, she watched her husband slur out his

answer to a question her father had asked and felt
her heart sink. It was disappointing when the meal
had started with such promise. At first, Alex had
refused the drinks flowing so freely around the
table and she'd felt relieved that, this night at least,
he would refrain from drinking, and she'd hoped
the bedding would be, if not easy, at least less of an
ordeal than she'd feared since arriving to find her
betrothed was as much of a drunken lout as her
father and brothers. But halfway through the meal
her father had stood to make a toast and had insisted
that Alex must have a drink to toast it with, else he'd
be insulting the Stewarts. Alex had reluctantly allowed some whiskey to be poured into the empty
mug he'd been drinking mead from ere that, but had
stopped them after only a couple of drops had been
poured in. However, he'd obviously topped it up
since then. The man was unmistakably in his cups.
Aside from slurring, he was also unsteady in his
seat, and twice she'd seen him reach for something
on the table and miss it.

Merry feared it didn't bode well for the night
ahead. She couldn't be sure, of course. Her mother
had died when she was just sixteen, and the matter
of the marriage bed had never come up between
them. Still, she suspected what was to come was
not going to be made easier by her husband's being
drunk.

A tap on her shoulder distracted Merry from this
worry and she glanced back to see Edda. The woman
wore a smile that was a little crooked and uncertain.
There was a gaggle of maids gathered behind her,
however, who were all grinning widely.

" 'Tis time for the bedding," Edda announced, not sounding sure whether Merry would welcome the announcement or not.

The answer was decidedly "not," but despite wishing she could scream, *Nay*, Merry forced a smile to her own lips and got to her feet. Her brothers immediately began cheering, laughing, and making lewd comments, and she felt a blush claim her cheeks. There was nothing she could do about that, but Merry did her best to ignore them otherwise and—resisting the urge to box their ears— mustered all the dignity she possessed and forced her head up and shoulders straight as she allowed herself to be led away.

With so many to help, Merry found herself stripped and bathed in no time. She was perfumed and oiled until she felt like a boar being prepared for the spit before she was allowed to climb into bed. Most of the women left the room then, taking the bath with them, but Una and Edda remained behind. As Una quickly cleaned up the room and put away her clothes, Edda settled herself on the edge of the bed next to Merry and took her hands in her own.

"Merry dear, I know we do not know each other well yet, but I went to my wedding bed not knowing what to expect and I really think it just made things harder and more scary than it needed to be. I know your mother passed away some time ago and so may not have had the chance to talk to you about your wedding night." She paused then and bit her lip briefly before asking, "Do you know what to expect?"

Merry briefly considered lying. Part of her duties as lady at Stewart had been to help their healer tend to the ill and injured. She'd seen boys naked and even a wounded man or two. She'd also helped with more births than she could recall. She did know the physical differences between a man and a woman. She even had some idea of what actually took place but wouldn't mind knowing exactly what to expect. "Nay."

Edda nodded. "Well then . . ." She paused and bit her lip again and then grimaced and said with a light laugh, "I can see why my mother did not explain, but simply said, 'He will know what to do, just obey your husband and do as he says.'"

Merry smiled, but it was a tense smile, and she said, "If 'tis making ye uncomfortable, ye need no' explain."

"Nay. 'Tis all right." Edda patted her hand. " 'Twill be easier on you do you know."

Merry nodded solemnly and waited . . . and waited.

"Well," Edda said finally. "You see, men are built differently than we women. The man has a . . ." She paused again and chewed on her lip briefly before brightening and saying, "Have you ever been in the kitchens at Stewart while your cook was preparing a chicken?"

Merry blinked at the question, not at all sure what a chicken had to do with this, but said, "Aye."

"Well, think of the neck when the cook has plucked and cut it off to throw it in soup. A man has one of those between his legs."

"A chicken neck?" Merry asked blankly. She

would never have described the few male parts she'd seen as a chicken neck.

"Sort of," Edda said with dissatisfaction. "'Tis straighter. At least 'tis when they are excited. And it does not have the bony ridges and it may be a tad bigger than a chicken neck."

"Oh," Merry said faintly.

Edda nodded solemnly. "'Tis most odd-looking. It sticks out from their body like a misplaced nose, but you must not laugh when you first see it," she cautioned, and nodded to emphasize the point. "They become very offended. For some reason they are very proud of their chicken neck."

"Ah," Merry choked out, trying desperately not to laugh. It would be incredibly rude when the woman was trying so earnestly to help her. Fortunately, Edda seemed to think the amusement she was trying to smother was about men's pride in their parts.

"Aye. Silly, I know, but they truly do strut around with it waving about like a war banner as if 'tis the most wonderful thing in the world. 'Tis really quite sad." She shook her head with mild exasperation and then continued, "And we women have a— Well, 'tis sort of like a sheath for their chicken neck. In fact, they use it as such, wielding their chicken neck like a sword and sheathing it in the woman."

Merry pursed her lips to control her expression. War banner? Sheath? Sword? She couldn't help but notice Edda seemed to use a lot of battle imagery. She waited for the woman to continue, but after a moment noted that her expression was quite satisfied, as if she were done.

"Is that it?" she asked with surprise. "He will just

walk in here and sheath his chicken neck and 'tis over?"

"Oh, well, no," Edda admitted. Much to Merry's surprise the woman was now blushing and avoiding looking at her. "He will no doubt kiss you a time or two, and then squeeze your breasts once or twice, and then if his chicken neck is excited enough and stiff, thrust it in your sheath."

"Humph," Merry muttered, slightly disgruntled. It didn't sound all that impressive or frightening to her.

"I suppose I should mention that it will hurt if 'tis your first time, and I am sure it is," she added quickly.

"Aye," Merry assured her solemnly, knowing the woman had merely misspoken in her discomfort and was not trying to insult her.

Edda nodded. "It shall hurt a lot as he breaks through your maiden's veil. That's a bit of skin inside your sheath," she added, gesturing toward Merry's lap before continuing. "And there shall be blood, and in the morning we will come for the bloodied sheet and it will be hung from the stair rail for all to see the proof of your innocence," she finished in a rush.

Merry was worrying about the hurt-a-lot bit when the door suddenly burst open and a group of men began to crowd into the room, carrying Alexander d'Aumesbery before them. It seemed either the men had grown weary of waiting, or the women had informed the men that she was ready and in bed when they'd gone below. She wasn't too pleased about that. Merry would have liked to ask more about this pain and blood. That didn't sound at all appetizing, but then none of it had. Kiss, kiss, squeeze, squeeze, and in it went? It hardly sounded the most exciting business in the world, and it made her wonder why the maids were so willing to let the soldiers and her brothers have at them at Stewart.

Merry's thoughts scattered when her husband was set on his feet, and he promptly fell on his face. This brought laughter from the men, but made her grind her teeth and glare.

"Oh dear, I hope he is not so sotted he cannot manage the matter," Edda muttered.

Merry didn't comment, but she hoped so, too. Not because she would be embarrassed not to have her sheet hung in the hall, but because she didn't wish to go through the next day worrying about the night ahead as she'd done today. That concern in her mind, she watched the men lift her new husband up off the floor and hold him upright to undress him.

She watched his clothing slip away, noting a little distractedly that he really had a fine physique. It was easy to believe the man had been at battle these last three years. He had none of the bloating and flab her father and brothers had from their main pastime of drinking. His shoulders were wide and muscular, his waist trim, his . . . Merry's thoughts died. That definitely didn't look like a chicken neck to her, she decided as she stared at the erection jutting out from between her husband's legs.

It seemed to her the kiss, kiss, squeeze, squeeze would not be needed to excite her husband. He was already sporting an erection that was large, full, hard, and angry-looking. She wasn't the only one to notice. The men had taken note and were grinning

widely and making ribald jokes, and Edda suddenly
relaxed beside her and patted her shoulder as she
breathed out, "All will be well. The whiskey has not
affected his ability to consummate."

Merry suddenly wasn't sure that was a good
thing. Honestly, it looked more like a small log than
a chicken neck, and the idea of being stabbed with
it was not exactly inspiring either pleasure or relaxation in her right then.

She stopped worrying about that for the moment,
however, when she realized the men were done un-
dressing him and were now carrying her husband
forward to place him in the bed beside her. Merry
steeled herself against what was coming, but still
felt her face flush and her teeth grind together as the
linen was lifted and she was briefly revealed to all
before her husband was in bed beside her and the
linens allowed to fall back over her as well as him.
And then it was over and the men and women were
moving out of the room, leaving them alone.

Merry watched them go, managing an uncertain smile when Edda glanced back encouragingly
before walking out. Her brother Brodie was the last
to leave the room. Merry released a breath of relief
when he went out pulling the door closed behind
him, but then just as quickly frowned when the door
slid back open a crack, and she realized he hadn't
pulled it to.

She wasn't the only one to notice. Her husband
muttered a soft, slightly slurred curse before he
tossed the linen aside and rose to close it. He staggered a bit as he walked to the door, but made it
there fine. It was on the way back that he ran into

problems. Merry was so distracted staring at the part bobbing about between his legs that she, too, was taken completely by surprise when he stumbled over the clothing the men had left strewn on the floor. Eyes widening, she sat up just as he crashed into the upper end of the straw-stuffed mattress. At least his lower body did. His upper body was bent forward as he struggled to get back his balance and he was at an angle so that his head slammed into upper post of the bed.

Alex didn't cry out in pain, but a low moan slid from his mouth and then he collapsed, his chest and arms on the bed and his legs hanging off.

Merry stared at him, wide-eyed, waiting for him to lift his head and speak, but nothing happened. He just lay there. After a moment, she cleared her throat and said tentatively, "My lord?"

When that got no response, she reached out to poke at his arm.

Still nothing.

Merry tossed the linens aside and shifted to her hands and knees to see his face, which was turned in the opposite direction. She had to lean far forward to get a look at it. The man's eyes were closed, his face slack. Worried, she gave his arm a shake. "Husband?"

When there was no response and his eyelids didn't even flicker, Merry sat back on her haunches, unsure what to do. The silly man had knocked himself out. She stared at him for a moment, but was starting to feel uncomfortable about sitting there nude and got out of bed to quickly draw on her chemise. She then walked around the bed to get a better look at him. He was definitely unconscious. At least she hoped he was. It was hard to tell if he was breathing, crumpled up on the top corner of the bed as he was.

Blowing a breath out, she moved forward and began to struggle to turn him over so that he was lying properly on the bed. It was harder than she expected. The man was large and heavy, at least six feet of solid muscle. It took quite a bit of effort and a lot of huffing and puffing to get him turned on his back. Merry then promptly stepped back as she found his erection pointing accusingly at her.

She scowled at the limb, amazed that while he appeared dead to the world, it was still hard and ready to go. Forcing her eyes away from the angry-looking thing, she glanced to his chest, a little sigh slipping from her lips when she saw that it was still rising and falling. He was alive, he'd just knocked himself senseless.

Despite having seen it happen and knowing the clothes lying about the floor were at fault and that even she might have tripped over them had their positions been reversed, Merry couldn't help but think he might have managed to save himself had he not been quite so inebriated.

Grimacing, Merry shifted her gaze to his face. When awake, Alexander d'Aumesbery was attractive, with long, blond hair and strong but pleasant features often fixed in a stern expression. But asleep, that sternness was absent, and she could see that he was much more than just attractive. He was actually handsome, and if he spent less time frowning, scowling, and looking pained . . .

Merry shrugged the thought aside. It mattered little if he was handsome. She would be more pleased to have an ugly but kind and *sober* husband. Unfortunately, that wasn't what she had. Feeling depression and gloom slip over her, she left him as he was, walked around the bed to her side, and crawled back in. Merry then simply sat and stared at him. It seemed all her worry about the wedding night had been for naught. And she *had* worried and fretted over it today as she'd waited to be married and then picked at the food during her wedding feast. She'd tried not to think about it, but it had been constantly at the back of her mind. It had been wasted fretting, and now she could fret about it all over again on the morrow. In the meantime, there was little to do but go to sleep.

Shaking her head with exasperation, Merry shifted to lie down in the bed and pulled the linen over herself. She then turned on her side to face her husband, staring at his unconscious form as she tried to relax enough to drift into slumber. However, it didn't take her long to realize that she wasn't likely to sleep anytime soon. Now she was worrying about the morning and the embarrassment of explaining that they had not consummated their marriage.

Clucking with exasperation, she sat up and glared at her husband with resentment. She was wide awake and fretting while he lay there naked and—

Merry scowled, thinking she should probably cover the man, but didn't do so right away. She would have been ashamed to admit it, but the idea did cross her mind that it wouldn't be a tragedy did he catch a chill and possibly die from it, leaving her a widow. Of course, Merry wasn't at all sure she would be a widow since they had not yet consummated the wedding, as the lack of blood on the linen would prove.

That thought made her mouth turn down unhappily. It would be just her luck did the man never wake up from this blow to the head, but die in his sleep on their wedding night without finishing the job and making her his wife. No doubt she'd then find herself married off to another drunk either in Scotland or somewhere else, and possibly an old man with no teeth and bad breath who would make her skin crawl. Clucking with disgust, she peered at her husband again, this time her attention moving to his erection. The thing was still hard and full, looking as if it was ready to burst open at any moment like an overripe plum when squeezed. She sat there glaring at the overblown chicken neck until she was assaulted by the mad thought that there was no reason she could not consummate the wedding herself.

The idea had barely flittered through her mind before Merry was shaking her head. Nay. She couldn't possibly. Why, that was just—

Why not? another part of her mind asked. She was used to taking matters in hand herself, and this was no different. She would simply . . . Well, Merry supposed, she could sit on it, break her maiden's veil herself with his chicken neck, and 'twould be done. There would be no more fretting about what was to come, no more worry about handing over the linen in the morning . . .

The more Merry thought about it, the smarter the idea seemed to her. She had overseen the men when

Alex had not been up to doing it himself, why not
tend to this as well?

It seemed perfectly reasonable to her.

Never one to stall when something needed doing,
Merry promptly crawled back off the bed and moved
around to her husband's side. It seemed obvious
to her that for her to mount his chicken neck, she
needed to get his feet on the bed. At least it looked
to her as if it would be easier to do so were he flat
on the bed rather than hanging off it. Pausing before
his feet, she bent and caught him by the ankles and
began the long, hard struggle to get him turned so
that she could get his legs on the bed along with the
rest of him. It was no easy task. The man weighed
a ton, and it was something of a delicate operation since every time she dragged his legs toward
the bed, his upper body seemed to want to move
closer to the edge, threatening to tumble off. But by
repeatedly moving his legs to the side a bit, and then
setting them down to move to his chest to push his
upper body farther onto the bed, she managed the
task.

Once she had him safely on the bed, Merry paused
to contemplate him and the logistics of what she intended to do. It didn't take much thought to realize
he was too close to the edge of the bed to allow her
to straddle him, so Merry shoved him away from
the edge and farther toward the center of the bed.
By the time she'd accomplished that, however, she
was a bit weary and dropped to sit on the side of
the bed by his hip while she recovered. Her eyes
immediately focused on his erection. Merry stared
at it, marveling that it still hadn't deflated or what-

ever it should do. It seemed odd to her that a man could be completely unconscious but remain erect. She would have expected it to go back to its resting, chicken neck–like state. But then she was new to all this. Perhaps it was supposed to stay hard until it was used. If so, she could only think that was a good thing since she intended to use it.

She reached out tentatively to poke it, watching curiously as it swayed away and then back. When it stopped, she bit her lip and hesitated. It had seemed hard when she'd poked it, and she was curious to know what it felt like. There seemed little harm in giving it a feel. He was her husband, after all, and she intended to do much more than touch it.

Still, Merry hesitated, her gaze sliding to his face to be sure he was still unconscious before she reached out and brushed her fingers tentatively down the shaft. It was solid, but the skin felt velvety soft under her fingertips. Fascinated, Merry ran her fingers over it again and then took it curiously in hand and closed her fingers around it, measuring its girth and length and moving it about to see just how far it would bend to one side and then the other.

A sudden groan from Alex made her still, her fingers unintentionally tightening on the erection. In the next moment, the chicken neck jerked in her hand, and she glanced to it with surprise as it suddenly began to spit some sort of liquid out of the top. Merry released it at once and stood up. The first thought to flash through her mind was that she'd broken it, but she wasn't sure if she'd broken it or if that was supposed to happen. However, she was pretty sure she'd just ruined any possibility of con-

summating the wedding since it was finally beginning to deflate before her eyes.

Cursing, Merry turned away and paced to the
foot of the bed and then back, her mind working.
Edda had said that he would probably kiss her,
squeeze her breasts, and then, *when excited*, thrust
his chicken neck into her. She supposed that hard
state had been his being excited. Perhaps she could
excite him again.

That thought gave her hope and she moved back
to the bed to peer at his now sadly shriveled chicken
neck, but Merry really had no idea how to go about
"exciting" a man. She'd seen maids on their knees
in dark corners at Stewart Castle, doing things to
the men there that seemed to make them groan and
moan as Alex had done before exploding, but wasn't
sure exactly what it was they did. She supposed it
was something that felt good and tried to think of
things that felt good to her. Her maid brushing her
hair before the fire was nice, though that was more
a relaxing sensation than an exciting one. Rubbing
her feet when they were sore was also nice, but again
relaxing.

Obviously she was approaching the problem
from the wrong direction, Merry decided, and
asked herself what excited her father and brothers.
The only thing that came to mind was whiskey, but
she hardly thought pouring a mug of whiskey over
the man's parts was going to get them working.

Merry poked at his chicken neck again and then
glared at it with irritation. Truly, she hadn't a clue
what to do here, yet she needed to somehow get

it excited and stiff and then mount it to break her maiden's veil to produce the blood.

Or, Merry thought suddenly, she could just cut herself to get the blood, spread it on the bed linen, and pretend he'd done the deed. That thought lifted her spirits at once. It would ensure she didn't have to marry again did the man have the good grace to drop dead on her tonight, and might save her having to worry about his wishing to trouble her in their bed for a while. She had no idea how frequently men liked to bed their wives, but her father never seemed to bother the maids and village women back home much. Of course, he was older, but even Brodie and Gawain did not seem to trouble the women much. Mayhap once a month was her guess, but then she did tend to send the servants away when the three men were drinking, and they did do that often.

That didn't really matter to her anyway, Merry decided. She was more concerned with securing her place as lady here so she couldn't be married off to some other drunken lout should the man die tonight, or stumble down the stairs and break his neck in the morning. Did she cut herself, rub a bit of blood on the bed linen, and give it to them to hang above the stairs on the morrow, then her place as Lady d'Aumesbery would be secure whether the man survived the night or not.

Satisfied with the idea, Merry slid back out of bed and moved to her chest to retrieve her *sgian-dubh* from where Una had put it away earlier. She carried it back to the bed with her, tugged the linens to the bottom of the bed so that they were out of the

way, and climbed in next to her husband. She then
settled cross-legged and hesitated as she considered
where she should cut herself. Her first choice was
her hand, but that would be easily seen, and someone might notice and wonder about it.

She peered over her body considering likely spots.
Somewhere that was covered by her gown was her
best bet. Her eyes settled on her legs, and she peered
at them solemnly for a moment and then pressed
the knife to her left inner thigh and hesitated again.
Merry wasn't a coward, but truly, deliberately hurting herself wasn't an attractive idea. It had to be
done, however.

Sucking in a deep breath, she held it and then
quickly drew her knife across her skin, gasping
in pain as the knife sliced a shallow wound in the
tender skin. Blood immediately beaded to the surface of the cut, and Merry caught it up on her fingers
and brushed it over the bottom linen of the bed. She
did it a few more times before the shallow wound
clotted and the blood stopped coming.

Merry peered at the bed linen then, considering
the small dark smudges on the clean cloth. It didn't
look like much, and she grimaced at the timidity
that had made her hold back and cut herself so shal-
lowly. Still, it might be enough. The problem was,
she wasn't sure. How much blood did breaching the
maiden veil cause? Edda hadn't described that, and
Merry hadn't thought to ask. She shifted impatiently
on the bed, worried that too little blood might give
her away.

Her gaze then slid to his chicken neck, and she
bit her lip at its clean state. Surely if he'd breached

the maiden's veil and made her bleed there would be blood on him as well. There was blood on a knife when it was used to stab someone.

Merry clucked with irritation at this reasoning. There seemed little else for it but that she would have to cut herself again. It seemed to her that it would be better to have too much blood than too little, and she definitely thought she should put some on him. Tightening her hand around her *sgian-dubh* again, she pressed it to her right inner thigh this time, closed her eyes, and quickly, sharply sliced herself again. This time, she didn't merely gasp at the pain, but had to bite her tongue to keep from crying out, and the blood didn't trickle forth to bead on the wound but began to gush out. She'd definitely cut deeper this time, more deeply than she'd intended.

Ah well, at least she'd probably have enough now, Merry told herself, and shifted so that she was in the center of the bed. Her hip rubbed up against Alex, and it reminded her to rub some on his shaft, but once that was done, she ignored him and concentrated on using her fingers to spread the blood about as it ran down her inner thigh and onto the bottom linen. She continued to do so until the blood finally stopped running. Truly, the wound bled an awfully long time, and Merry was growing concerned by the time it stopped. She even considered wrapping the wound, but feared moving about to find something to bind it with might start it bleeding again so merely lay back in bed, pulled the upper linen over herself, and tried to go to sleep.

Unfortunately, while she wanted to sleep, she didn't seem to be able to relax enough to do so.

Merry tried everything she could think of to relax herself enough to manage it, but nothing seemed to work, and eventually she gave it up and simply lay their thinking about her life, past and present, and the bleak future that appeared to lie before her.

It was near dawn before she finally felt sleep overtaking her, and Merry greeted it with a small relieved breath and the hope that the morrow would be a better day.

Alex again woke to a pounding head. He moaned, squeezed his eyes tightly closed, and rolled onto his side to try to bury his head beneath the pillow. He was so groggy that it took a moment for him to realize that what he was trying to bury himself under wasn't a pillow. Eyes blinking open with confusion, he then had to push the linens and furs away so that he could see that he had his hand clasped over one of his new bride's rather generous breasts. The realization brought him immediately awake and—once awake—he recognized that the pounding wasn't only in his head. It was coming from somewhere behind him as well.

Rolling onto his back, Alex peered toward the door as his brain slowly puzzled together that there was someone knocking at it. He scowled at the door and then swung his eyes back to his bride to see that the racket hadn't even made her stir. The woman was pale, shadows under her eyes and dead to the world. It didn't look to him like she was likely to wake up for anything anytime soon.

The pounding at the door became a little louder and more insistent, drawing his attention once more. Alex stared at it with disinterest for a minute, but when his brain finally pieced together that the pounding would not stop until he answered the door, he rolled out of bed and stumbled over to open it.

"There ye are!" Laird Stewart said cheerfully, and far too loudly, the moment the door was open. "We were beginning to think the two o' ye had slipped out while we werena looking."

Alex had a terrible urge to punch the man, but it seemed like a lot of effort so he merely growled, "What do you want?"

"The bed linens, lad," Eachann said, as if it should be the most obvious answer in the world.

Alex was just scowling over that and trying to sort out why they would want his bed linens when Edda drew his attention to the fact that the man wasn't alone by saying gently, "For proof the marriage was consummated."

Alex blinked, absently noting that the priest and Merry's brothers were there as well, but most of his brain was processing the bit about proof of consummation. The bed linens. Proof. Blood from the breaching of her maiden's veil, his mind put together, and he whirled to peer at the bed. Merry had burrowed back under the furs and linens again like a mole seeking darkness, and he was not at all sure she was yet awake. But that didn't concern him as much as the fact that he had absolutely no recollection of whether he'd consummated the wedding. In fact, he didn't even recall making his way up here to bed last night, which was troubling since he should. While his plan to abstain from alcohol last night had been forced off path by his father-in-law's claim that to not drink to a toast would be an insult on the whole clan, Alex had allowed them only to pour a small amount of whiskey in his mug before covering it with his hand. He had sipped that small amount slowly through the rest of the night, and it surely shouldn't have been enough to affect him as it had.

Unless his father-in-law had been topping up his mug when he was distracted, Alex thought suddenly, and was sure that must be the case. It seemed the only explanation for the state he'd been in last night.

"Ye *were* able to manage it, were ye no'?" Eachann Stewart asked with a sudden glower. "Ye were in rough shape last night and—" He paused abruptly and glanced to his sons when Brodie suddenly elbowed him. The younger man whispered something that made the older man's eyebrows rise, and then he turned back, his gaze honing in on Alex's groin. "Hmm, it appears ye managed all right after all."

Alex glanced down to himself, his own eyebrows rising as he saw the dried blood on his semi-erect staff. It did indeed appear he'd managed the deed, he thought with relief, and then found himself nudged to the side as the Stewart men pushed their way into the room, with Edda and the priest on their heels. It seemed they were impatient to get the deed over with. However, the sight of Merry sound asleep in the center of the bed brought them up short.

"How the devil did she sleep through the knocking?" Brodie asked with amazement as the small group came to a halt at the edge of the bed.

Eachann scowled at the sight, a tinge of concern on his face, but merely glanced to Alex and said, "Wore her out, did ye? Well, ye'll just have to move her out o' the way so we can retrieve the linen. We'll get out o' yer hair the moment we have it," he added.

Alex shook his head and moved around them to the side of the bed. If he hadn't managed the bedding last night, he'd send them all from the room and do it now. If he had . . . Well, frankly, he'd be grateful because he didn't think he could manage the task with his head as sore as it was.

"Merry?" he said softly, shaking her arm. When that gained no response, he shook her a little more insistently. "Merry, girl. Wake up. Your father and the others are here."

Much to his relief, she woke enough to grumble in her sleep and slap at his hand as if at a bee buzzing about her before snuggling back into the bed again and apparently drifting back to sleep.

Shrugging inwardly, Alex gave up on waking her and simply scooped her into his arms, taking the top linen at the same time. He carried her to the foot of the bed and out of the way, so distracted making sure the linen covered her decently that it took him a moment to notice the sudden silence in the room. Raising his head, he peered to the horrified faces of the group around the bed and then glanced toward the bed itself.

Alex immediately sucked in a breath of dismay, his eyes widening in horror as he took in the bloodstain that covered a good portion of the center of the linen.

"Dear God, what the devil did ye do to me daugh-

ter?" Eachann Stewart breathed with dismay and
the beginnings of anger. He then rushed forward to
grab Merry's face and turned it toward him. "Merry?
Merry, are ye alive girl?"

Merry blinked her eyes open, scowled, and
brushed irritably at her father's hands with a
grumpy, "Leave off."

Her father didn't seem to mind, but breathed out
a relieved "She's alive."

"Of course she's alive," Alex snapped, a bit affronted that they might think otherwise, but then
his gaze landed on the bed again and his irritation
left him, replaced by shame and worry. He must
have been incredibly rough with her to have made
her bleed like that. He might even have done serious damage. It was a sickening thought. Alex had
never in his life been rough with a woman, and the
thought that he might have been on his wedding
night, and to the warm, sweet-smelling woman in
his arms, was actually nauseating.

Suddenly furious, he glared at the silent people
staring so accusingly at him and growled, "Take the
linen and get out."

A moment of silence passed, and then Father
Gibbon began to strip the bottom linen from the
bed. Edda immediately hurried forward to help,
and then the group began to move out of the room
with the proof of his abusive treatment of his wife.
He couldn't help but notice that they were moving
extremely slowly, as if reluctant to leave Merry alone
with him, and that just made the shame in Alex
swell and grow. He was relieved when the door finally closed behind them, but not much. The image

of the blood-soaked linen was burned into his brain, and he peered down at Merry with regret and self-loathing.

She was a beautiful woman, sweet in sleep, with none of the frustration, anger, disapproval, and un-happiness that made up her expressions when she was awake. At that moment, it was his dearest wish that Merry always look as peaceful and tranquil as she did right then, that he somehow could soothe her wounded soul and make her happy. Unfortunately, he apparently hadn't made a good start on that last night. But he would make it up to her, Alex vowed silently. He would touch her only with the gentlest of intentions. He would never even speak a harsh word, and he would woo her, teach her to trust him, and make her forget their wedding night and the pain and misery he must have put her through.

Merry shifted sleepily in his arms, turning her head into his chest and exhaling against the naked skin there.

Despite his pounding head, Alex felt his body re-spond to the caress of breath against his skin and decided if he wished to keep those vows he'd just made to himself, he might do better to keep a little distance between them for a while. At least until she was healed and had forgiven him for their wedding night.

Moving back to the bed, he gently set her back in it, taking the time to cover her properly with both the linens and the furs on the bed. He then straight-ened and forced himself away from the bed to finish donning his clothes, his mind moving on to how his plans had changed yet again. The intention had been for him, Merry, and a dozen men to leave today along with her father and brothers and their men for the journey north into Scotland. They would have ridden with the Stewart party most of the way and then split the last day, with their own party continuing on to Donnachaidh while the Stewarts continued home.

That was out of the question now. He could hardly make Merry travel today. The amount of blood on the linen suggested he might have to give her several days to heal from his rough treatment, maybe even as much as a week before setting out for Scotland to check on his sister.

Guilt squeezed him at the realization that his sister, Evelinde, might be suffering mightily and would continue to suffer a week longer than necessary because of his own behavior, but he was already so soaked in shame and guilt it made little difference. Finished dressing, Alex scrubbed his hands wearily over his face and then cast one last glance toward the woman in his bed before making his way to the door. He would make it all up to her.

Four

The bed was empty when Merry woke up. She sat up and glanced sleepily around the room in search of her husband, but he was gone. Tossing aside the linens covering her, she started to slip her feet off the bed when a sudden sharp tug of pain from her right thigh reminded her of the night's events. It made her glance down, and Merry noted with surprise that the bottom linen of the bed was gone. She then turned her attention to her leg and saw that her thoughtless movement had started the larger cut on her inner thigh oozing blood again. Judging by the smeared bloodstain on her leg, it wasn't the first time.

Grimacing, she eased more carefully from the bed and stood to move to the basin of cold water on a small table by the window. Merry quickly washed, cleaning up the blood on her inner thighs last, and then pressed the bit of damp cloth against the wound until the bleeding stopped again. Her gaze slid back to the bed as she held the cloth there, and she found herself wondering how they'd managed to retrieve the bottom linen without waking her. She was still puzzling over it as she finished at the basin and moved to find a fresh gown to wear that day.

Merry had just pulled on a chemise and gown and was doing up the laces of the gown when her door eased open a crack and she saw Una's head poke in.

"Oh good! Ye're up," the maid said sounding relieved. She then pushed the door open farther and stepped in and to the side to make room for the servants who followed her.

Merry paused as two men carried in the bath she'd used the night before. They were followed by several servants carrying pails of water. Her eyes widened and she opened her mouth to refuse the bath, but in the next moment closed it again, the words unspoken. She was unwilling to send the servants away after they'd gone to all the trouble of hauling it above stairs for her. Supposing she'd just have to bathe again, Merry bit back her words and moved to one of the chairs by the fire to watch Una direct the servants. She was relieved when it was done and offered a quiet thank you as the servants then filed out, leaving only her maid behind.

Merry waited until Una had closed the door on

the last one before giving in to her curiosity and asking, "Who ordered the bath?"

"Yer husband was the first to order it," Una answered as she turned back from the door.

Merry's eyebrows rose slightly at the maid's grim voice and expression, but she merely asked, "The first?"

"Aye, he asked me in the hall outside the room when he came out. He said to let ye sleep and fetch ye a bath when ye woke. And then Lady Edda stopped me at the bottom of the stairs and suggested ye may want one when ye woke. She was followed by yer father, who approached me when I sat down to break me fast and made the same suggestion, and then finally Brodie came to me as I headed above stairs to check on ye some time ago and suggested it as well."

Merry's eyes were wide by the time the woman finished. It seemed everyone had thought she'd need to bathe this morning. She had no idea why. All she'd done was sleep since her last bath.

"I had no idea why everyone was so all-fired certain ye'd need a bath," Una said, echoing her thoughts. "Until I saw the linen hanging from the stair railing."

Merry gave a slight start at the hardness that had entered the maid's voice. She now noted the pity filling her face and bit her lip with worry as she wondered if she had not put enough blood on the cloth. "What is wrong with the linen?"

"What is wrong with it?" the maid gasped. "Why, 'tis covered in blood."

Merry waved that away with unconcern. "Well,

'tis expected. He was to break my maiden's veil last eve."

"Break it, aye, but to cause so much blood he must have done more than that. The maun must ha'e been an animal. I was surprised to open the door and find ye standing this morn. Does it hurt to walk?"

Actually, it did, she acknowledged to herself, but only because of the tender cuts on her thighs, not for the reason Una thought. Frowning, she asked, "Was there too much blood then?"

"Aye," she assured her firmly. " 'Tis normally just a bit of it."

Merry clucked irritably at this news as she began to strip her gown back off. "I wish ye'd told me so ere last night. That means I needn't have cut meself the second time at all."

"Cut yerself? Ye mean 'tis no' from the bedding?"

"My husband was so drunk he knocked himself out almost the minute everyone left the room," Merry said dryly, her voice muffled as she pulled the gown over her face. "He couldna bed anyone. But I kenned everyone would expect we consummate and be looking for the linen in the morning to prove it, so I cut meself and smeared the blood on the linen." She got the gown off and tossed it across the nearest chest with an irritated grimace. "I wasna sure how much blood there should be, but the first cut seemed to produce little, so I cut meself again. Only the second cut was deeper than I'd intended and bled quite freely."

Merry had tugged off her chemise as she spoke and now tossed it after the gown before turning to see Una's expression. The woman looked partly horrified at this news, partly admiring, and mostly like she was fighting to keep from laughing. Merry supposed it would be funny if she weren't still suffering a sore thigh from her efforts.

"What did yer husband say about it?" the maid asked finally, managing to stifle her amusement.

Merry shrugged. "Nothing. He was unconscious, as I said."

Una waved that away. "But what did he say this morn when he saw it?"

Merry didn't have any recollection at all of being woken and roused from her bed this morn, but she must have been for them to have taken the linen, she reasoned.

"I'm no' sure," she confessed unhappily. "I doona really recall waking this morning until just now."

Una pondered that briefly and then suggested, "Mayhap ye didna. Mayhap he just scooped ye up off the bed so they could take the linen and then set ye back to continue yer sleep."

Merry's eyebrows rose at the suggestion. She supposed that was most likely what had happened, else she'd have some memory of what had occurred, at least a sleepy, fuzzy one. However, it suggested a thoughtfulness and kindness on the part of her husband that she didn't generally equate with drunks. Their actions were usually selfish and thoughtless. At least they seemed to her to be. Although her own father and brothers had occasionally displayed a sweetness when sober that caught her by surprise.

Shrugging the matter away, she moved to the tub and leaned down to test the water. Finding it satisfactory, Merry then stepped carefully over the edge, grimacing as lifting her leg pulled on the wound again. Knowing the perfumed water was likely to sting the cut, Merry sucked in a breath and tried to steel herself against it, but still gasped in another breath as she settled to sit in the tub and the water covered her thighs. The pain was even worse than she'd feared, and she ground her teeth together and closed her eyes against the tears gathering there as she waited for it to pass.

Merry's eyes popped open again, however, when Una clucked with concern next to her.

"What did ye do to yerself, lass? There's blood in the water. Stand up."

Merry glanced down to see that there was indeed blood drifting through the water and it was coming from her right thigh. Grimacing, she stood up and let Una look at the wound.

"Dear God, what were ye trying to do? Cut off yer leg?"

"'Tis not that bad," Merry responded a bit irritably, for truly it did hurt and standing up had hurt, but sitting back down for the water to cover it again was going to hurt even more. Besides, she hadn't meant to cut so deeply, but the deed was done now, and she felt foolish enough knowing she hadn't needed to cut herself a second time at all.

Shaking her head, the maid straightened and gestured for her to continue with her bath.

Merry settled back in the tub, grinding her teeth against the return of pain as the water closed over her.

Una watched silently for a minute and then commented, "I wonder what he thought when he saw the blood this morn. Does he think he consummated the wedding? Or does he ken he didn't and has worked out that ye produced the blood for the linen?"

"I doona ken," Merry said as the pain finally began to ease.

"I think he thinks he consummated," Una decided. "He certainly looked guilt-riddled when he ordered me to let ye sleep and prepare a bath for when ye woke."

Merry felt a moment's guilt of her own at this possibility, but then shrugged. "Well, 'tis fine. Then mayhap he'll blame it on the drink and not drink so deeply ere he does try to bed me."

Una grunted at the suggestion and said, tight-lipped, "I wasna keen on the idea o' moving to England in the first place, but I damned near dragged ye out o' the keep and back to the horses when we saw the state of the man ye were to marry. 'Tis hard to believe that God and the fates could be so cruel as to take ye from yer whiskey-soaked father and hand ye ower to a whiskey-soaked husband."

"Aye," Merry said unhappily.

"The only thing we can hope fer is that fate has a plan and the man will do ye the favor o' gettin' hisself killed quick so ye can find some peace."

It was nothing more than Merry had thought last night, but hearing it from her maid made it sound terribly cold and heartless. She squirmed in her bath, ashamed of herself.

"We shall just have to make the best o' it," Merry murmured, and then added, "Lady Edda seems nice."

"Humph," Una muttered, drawing her curious glance. The maid had picked up her gown and was shaking it out to set down more carefully so that it would not wrinkle.

"Has Lady Edda been unkind to you?" she asked with a small frown.

"Oh, nay," Una assured her, but then pursed her lips briefly, her eyes thoughtful before she said, " 'Tis jest there is something wrong there."

"With Lady Edda?" Merry asked slowly. In her experience, women were saints and men sinners. It seemed to her that such was the case here as well. Edda was sweet and kind and Alexander was a drunken fool. It seemed much as it had been at home with her own mother and the male members of the family.

"Nay, no' with Lady Edda exactly," Una said carefully, and then admitted, "I am no' sure. She seems fine and has been kind to ye, but the servants act a little queer about her."

Merry's eyebrows rose. "Queer how?"

Una hesitated and then said, "They go all quiet and watchful when she is about . . . and the old woman, Bet, seems to hate her though she'll no' say why."

Merry considered this and then asked, "Have the servants said anything to ye?"

"Oh, nay." She waved the very idea away. "I'm new here. They'll no' say aught until they're sure they can trust me. 'Tis jest a feeling I get. Something isna right."

Merry considered that briefly, but Una was prone to "feelings" that were often wrong. For instance, during her mother's last illness, the maid had assured her she had a "feeling" her mother would recover. Instead she'd died. And while Una had fussed about leaving Scotland and living in a foreign land full of Englishmen, she'd also had a "feeling" when they had set out that the future was much brighter here for Merry. That she would be happier with her husband than she'd ever been at Stewart. Considering what they'd found here, that "feeling" had obviously been wrong as well.

Shaking Una and her "feelings" out of her thoughts, Merry decided to judge Lady Edda on how she treated her. So far the woman had been kind and even sweet. Therefore, she would consider her a friend.

Merry was quick about the unneeded bath, and the water was still hot when she decided it was enough and stood up. She quickly dried herself off with the linen Una handed her, and then stood patiently as the maid fussed over the cuts she'd given herself. Merry then donned her clothes, fidgeted impatiently while Una tended to her hair, and then burst from her room like a horse charging from a burning stable and made her way below, walking a bit oddly in an effort not to rip open her wound again.

Late as it was, Merry had expected the great hall to be empty, but instead found her father, brothers, and Lady Edda still seated there, their heads close together as they conversed in quiet voices. Curious at the solemn expressions they wore and the stiff tension in their bodies, she headed to the table. The foursome were so wrapped up in their discussion that she had nearly reached them before anyone noticed her. The moment they did, however, their conversation came to an abrupt halt and they all sat up and turned to offer her bright smiles that were patently false.

"Good morn, Merry lass," her father greeted, standing to walk the few feet to greet her. Much to her amazement the old man actually gave her a quick, hard hug and then took her hands to lead her back to the table. Her brothers were on their feet as well, she saw, showing a courtesy she'd never before seen, and Brodie even moved out of the chair that belonged to the lady of the house for her to sit. She was made suspicious by all this fuss. Nevertheless, Merry allowed herself to be steered into her seat and then glanced around as they all started to talk at once, wishing her good morning and saying they hoped she'd slept well.

Merry murmured a general good morning in return and assured them yes, she had slept well. She then paused and sat back as a young maid rushed from the kitchens with some mead and a pasty for her and asked if she would care for anything else.

"Nay. Thank ye," Merry murmured, and watched the girl nod and curtsy and then hurry back to the kitchens before turning curiously in her seat to see what had kept the girl glancing wide-eyed behind and above her as she'd set down her offerings and asked if she would care for anything else. The only thing behind and above her was the linen hanging from the stair rail for all to see, and Merry grimaced as she noted the dried blood on the sheet. There really was a lot of it, even more than there had been when she'd gone to sleep. Obviously her wound had opened up again and added to the stain she'd made before lying down last night. But then she'd already figured that out when she saw the dried blood on her legs this morning.

Shaking her head, Merry turned back to the table, her eyebrows lifting when she saw the expressions on the faces of the others. They, too, had turned to peer at the linen, and while Edda was glowering with displeasure, her father and brothers looked absolutely furious.

"Alex is down on the practice field with the men," Edda announced suddenly, noting Merry's curious gaze. She then shifted in her seat and stood. "I suppose I should leave you to visit with your father and brothers. I shall be in the salon above stairs if you wish to speak to me ere you go."

Merry nodded and started to lift her mead to take a drink, but paused as the woman's words sank through her thoughts. *Ere you go?* Ere she went where? she wondered, and glanced around to call after the woman, but paused when her father touched her arm. Turning back to the table, she raised an eyebrow in question as she glanced to her father.

"He hurt ye, lass," Eachann Stewart growled.

Merry's eyes widened at the rage now in the man's face. She stared at him blankly for a moment, stunned by a show of emotion she rarely saw from the man, and then set down her mead and peered at her pasty, muttering with embarrassment, "I am fine."

"Ye're no fine. The linen bears the proof. The man is an animal. If ye're wantin' to have the marriage annulled and return home with us, I'll back ye up on it."

That made her glance up sharply. Her father looked grim and determined, and her brothers were nodding their agreement to his offer. Merry didn't know what to think. The men had been nothing but eager to see her go since learning of Lord d'Aumesbery's return from Tunis, so this offer was more than a little surprising. After a stunned moment, she managed to gather her thoughts, cleared her throat, and then pointed out, "The linen bears the proof that the wedding canna be annulled."

"We'll say ye cut yer leg, or that 'tis yer woman's time. D'Aumesbery was so fou with drink he probably doesna remember what he did last night."

Merry simply stared at her father for the longest time. An annulment at this stage would mean forfeiting her dower. Her mind was finding it difficult to accept that he would make this offer. Truly, he and her brothers had been sunk so deep in their cups these last years, she'd felt sure they cared for naught but themselves. It was startling to find that they did, after all, care for her. The realization even brought tears to her eyes. But she wasn't foolish enough to think this meant anything had changed. While she was tempted to accept the offer and escape her marriage, it would simply mean returning to Stewart and babysitting her father and brothers again until her father mustered himself to contract another marriage. If he ever did.

And did he, there was no guarantee she would

land in happier circumstances. At least at d'Aumesbery she knew what she had to deal with. Here she might have a drunken husband, but she was used to dealing with drunks, and here she also had Edda. Merry had missed the kindness, wisdom, and guidance of a woman since her mother's death. Here she had that in her mother-in-law. And Edda even reminded her somewhat of her dear, deceased mother. Not in looks. Maighread Stewart had been a beautiful woman even in death, whereas Edda . . . Well, she wasn't as pretty, Merry ended the thought lamely, unwilling to insult the woman even in her own mind.

Besides, her looks mattered little. The fact was Edda was English, and Merry's own mother had been born to a Scottish husband and English mother and raised in England. Every time Edda spoke, Merry heard the same rhythm and cadence to her words as had been in her mother's, and it reminded her of her youth when she'd felt safe and secure in her mother's care. She would not give up the unhappy lot she had here for what might be an even unhappier lot somewhere else.

"Nay, I am fine," she said finally, and then assured him, "He really was not so rough with me. I must just be a bleeder."

Eachann Stewart's eyes narrowed at her words and he then offered, "We will stay around here for a bit in case ye change yer mind."

Merry blinked at the offer, surprised again. Alex had mentioned the night before the wedding that he thought they should ride back to Scotland the day after the wedding with her father and brothers for the added safety the increased number of men would supply. But now her father seemed to be suggesting that— "I thought we were all traveling north today?"

Eachann Stewart looked affronted at the very suggestion. "Even d'Aumesbery isna base enough to force ye to travel today. Nay." He shook his head. "Yer husband announced this morn when he came below that he was giving ye a week to heal and that we should go ahead without ye."

Merry bit her lip, feeling bad that everyone was thinking so poorly of her husband over this business. Obviously, she had really miscalculated the amount of blood expected. Unfortunately, she didn't know what to do to change that opinion of the man, short of admitting what she'd done.

"But," her father continued, "we'll stay right here to be sure the bastard doesna kill ye next time."

That suggestion nearly made her wrinkle her nose. Did they stay, Merry knew it would mean nothing but a struggle for her as she fought to keep them from drinking, and embarrassing her or wrecking the place.

"Nay. There is no need for that," she said solemnly, and when her father opened his mouth as if to argue, added, "We shall be traveling north to Donnachaidh as soon as enough time has passed for me to heal. 'Tis close to Stewart and easy enough fer me to ride over there then do I change my mind."

Her father did not look pleased, but nodded after a moment and let his breath out. "Well then, I guess we may as well leave."

Merry blinked at the abrupt announcement as the men stood up. "Now?"

"Aye, well, we did plan to leave today," he pointed out. "Everything is ready. We were only waitin' to see which way the wind was blowin' with ye."

Merry recalled Una telling her while helping her dress that she'd heard Alex order the whiskey locked up and the Stewart men to be told it had been used up in the celebrations for the wedding. It seemed likely to her that this was the real reason her father was now eager to go. It made the fact that he'd made the offer to stay—and that her brothers had not protested—even more surprising.

Suddenly aware that while her father and brothers had got to their feet, they now stood waiting for something, Merry glanced at them uncertainly and then rose herself. The moment she did, her father wrapped her in a warm embrace. He hugged her tightly and whispered, "Send fer me if ye need me, lass," before releasing her and stepping aside.

Merry was still blinking in surprise at the unexpected embrace when Brodie took his place and caught her in a bear hug. His message was a little different. As he released her, he pointed at her chest and said, "If he gets too bothersome, a blade right here and twisted will end him fer ye."

She smiled crookedly at the advice and pointed out, " 'Twould put an end to both of us since I'd be hung fer murder."

"Aye," he acknowledged, and then suggested, "Jest push him down the stairs then so it looks an accident."

"Stop giving her advice, Brodie, ye're like to get her hung," Gawain muttered, displacing him to clasp her in a warm embrace of his own so he could whisper, "I ken we've been a pain, Merry. But we love ye fer all of that. I want a letter a month from ye so we ken ye're well. All right?"

Merry nodded silently, unable to speak through the lump suddenly lodged in her throat. They were like strangers to her, or perhaps it was more as if her true brothers and father had been briefly returned to her. The ones who had existed before the drink had got the better of them. It made her heart ache. This was what they could have been all these years had drink not muddled their minds and made them so selfish and hard to handle.

"Come," Laird Stewart growled, and Merry found herself jostled between Gawain and Brodie as they followed their father to the keep doors. A half sob, half laugh slipped from her lips when she was led outside to see their already saddled mounts, and the Stewart soldiers all milling about the empty wagon that had carried her belongings here. It didn't make her doubt the sincerity of their offer to stay, but it seemed obvious they'd expected her response. Merry walked them down to their mounts, hugged each man one last time, and then impatiently dashed away the tears blurring her eyes as she watched the party ride out.

She found it hard to believe that after so many years of yearning to free of these three men, she now was upset at their going. But she couldn't help but wonder who would look after them.

" 'Tis hard, I know."

Merry glanced around to find Edda beside her. She hadn't heard the woman approach, but was grateful to have the distraction of her presence.

Edda smiled at her gently and reached out to take her hand, squeezing it reassuringly as she urged her toward the stairs. "I left my family and friends when I came here, too. 'Twas very hard on me. I had no interest in marrying a man nearly old enough to be my father, and even less interest in living so far away from the excitement of court." She shook her head and then said, "Take my advice, Merry. Do not do what I did. Do not allow yourself to grow bitter and mean."

"Mean?" Merry asked with a small laugh. "I've found ye quite kind."

"Aye, well . . ." She paused, her lips twisting. "You have not been here long. No doubt you shall hear a tale or two from the servants and people here. I fear I was quite a horror for many years. Now everyone here hates me, and I cannot even blame them, for I brought it on myself with my previous behavior. Do not do that yourself. Accept your lot in life and make a place for yourself here."

Merry nodded silently, her mind on the claim that Edda had been a horror. She found that hard to believe, but then she'd been surprised by her father and brothers' behavior that day, too. Perhaps people were not all purely evil or purely good. Perhaps everyone had bad traits and better ones. Even herself.

"Merry?" Edda said softly.

She glanced at her in question, noting the discomfort on the woman's face, and suspected whatever was coming had something to do with the bedding. She was right.

"I realize that the bedding must have been hor-

rible for you, and I myself can hardly believe that
Alex would be so brutal, but—"

"'Tis no' what everyone thinks," Merry interrupted quickly, feeling guilty that her ignorance
of how much blood was needed had convinced everyone the man must have been cruel in his bedding. The man might be a drunk, but she had no
desire to paint him blacker than he already was.
Unfortunately, she suspected Edda would not believe the excuse that she was a bleeder as her father
and brothers had. She took a moment and then decided it would be best to stick as close to the truth
as possible in case her cut leg was ever discovered.
It wasn't likely, but not impossible. She might forget
about it and change in front of one of the maids or
something. They might note it and comment on it
to Edda, and that might bring about doubt that the
marriage was even consummated.

"Is it your woman's time?" Edda asked, obviously
trying to find another reason she might have bled
so much.

"Nay, I finished that two weeks ago," Merry admitted, and then almost smacked herself in the head
for not thinking of that lie herself. It was too late
now, however, so she said, "I have a wound high on
my leg. It must have opened last night without my
realizing it."

"Oh," Edda breathed, her eyes going wide. She
hesitated and then said carefully, "So he did not
hurt you last night? He was gentle with you?"

Merry knew she was really asking if the wedding
had indeed been consummated. This was where the

truth would no longer suffice, and she lied solemnly, "Aye."

"Good," Edda said, but was still looking uncertain, and Merry felt moved to add to her lie.

"He was very gentle with me during the bedding . . . and *very* quick," she added, recalling his exploding at her touch.

"Oh." Edda's eyes widened and then she patted her hand. "Perhaps that is for the best. Though I would not expect to be so lucky in the future. 'Twas probably just the excitement of the first time with you that had him finish fast."

Merry wrinkled her nose at the warning. While it had been a problem for her last night and prevented her actually accomplishing the consummation, she suspected had they actually been consummating at the time, she would have appreciated his speed. Merry truly saw no joy in the act and believed when it came to unpleasant tasks, the sooner done the better.

"Well." Edda patted her hand again. "I am relieved all went well. When I saw the linens . . ." She didn't finish the comment, but just shook her head, and then pulled the keep door open and ushered Merry inside, saying, "Come, Cook wishes to discuss the menu for the week ahead and see if it suits you."

Merry managed a smile of her own and allowed herself to be led across the great hall. She tried to walk as normally as possible, but the wound to her thigh made her walk oddly as she tried to avoid rubbing it. Noting the pitying glance Edda was giving her and knowing why the woman thought she was in pain, Merry flushed but said nothing. She was grateful, though, that she would have some time for the cut to heal before having to travel. The wait would also allow her to settle in here at d'Aumesbery, and she was grateful for that as well.

Five

Alex reached for his drink and somehow misjudged its position, nearly knocking it over rather than picking it up. After adjusting his aim and managing to close his fingers around it, he raised it to his lips, but paused when his eyes slipped to his wife. She, of course, had not missed his clumsiness, and a sigh slid from his lips as he saw the disapproving look she was casting his way. Brodie had been right, she *did* resemble a fish when she did that.

It had been three weeks since their wedding day, and still they had not left for Donnachaidh. Unfortunately, the planned trip had met with delay after delay. First there had been the week he'd decided he should allow his wife to heal from his drunken clumsiness on their wedding night. Alex had chafed at the delay, but made himself stick to it despite the fact that she seemed well enough after only a couple of days.

However, the day before they were to leave, illness had struck the castle, forcing another delay. It had been a cruel ailment, attacking a body so that the victims spent half their time tossing up whatever they'd eaten, and the other half running for the garderobe. The illness had struck in waves, taking out a couple dozen men, and then taking out another couple dozen when the first were just starting to feel better.

Alex grimaced at the memory, but then shook his head and acknowledged that it could have been worse. While it had kept him and the rest of the men busy trying to pick up the slack their absence left, at least it had not struck them all at once, leaving the castle completely unmanned. Still, he hadn't been able to head to Scotland without leaving d'Aumesbery shorthanded, something he hadn't been willing to do. But now, after two weeks, the illness appeared to have run its course. Unless you counted him. Alex had been suffering his own illness these three weeks since his wedding night, but his symptoms were different from those of his men. His stomach did not cause him trouble and he wasn't running for the garderobe. Instead, every evening he found himself feeling off-kilter and disoriented, sometimes even dizzy. It left Alex slurring some of his words, missing his mug or trencher when he reached for them, and staggering on occasion. In short, it left him appearing as drunk as he'd somehow gotten on his wedding night.

At one point, the fact that the symptoms occurred only at night had made him consider that someone might be drugging his ale at the sup. His wife had been the most likely suspect the moment that thought had taken hold. It had started only after her arrival, and—after his apparent brutality on their wedding night—she'd certainly have reason, he'd supposed. Alex had been so sure this might be the case that he'd entirely skipped drinking anything at all during two evening meals in a row. However, he'd still suffered the symptoms. That had reassured him and left him again to decide that he must be fighting off some sort of infection, perhaps even the one his men had been battling. If so, the reason he suffered symptoms only at night might be that after a full day of running about, filling in here and there, he was usually exhausted and at his weakest point.

Unfortunately, it was also when he saw the most of his new bride, and he very much feared she was completely mistaking his symptoms for a result of too much drink. Merry had watched him like a hawk every night since their wedding. She had not missed a single slip, stagger, or slurring of words, and he feared she was putting it all down to his being a drunk like her father and brothers. Alex did not blame her after their unfortunate first meeting, but that, too, was damned inconvenient. He'd intended to show her with his actions that he was nothing like her father and brothers; instead this damned illness was simply reinforcing her certainty that he was. He'd considered trying to explain that he hadn't been drinking and that he suspected his symptoms were the result of illness, but doubted she would believe it. Besides, he was having difficulty even attempting to converse with his wife. First there was his guilt and shame over his rough treatment on their wedding night, and then he very much doubted she would believe a word he said anyway. She had grown up with drunks and was probably used to their lies. Even if he pointed out that he didn't drink at the table, she would probably just assume that he was drinking down at the inn beforehand.

Aside from that, however, Alex found it impossible to speak to his wife for another very different reason. The fact was that as ashamed as he was of his behavior on their wedding night, and as certain as he was that she must loathe him, he couldn't be around the woman without growing as hard as a dead hen. Every night he sat at the table beside her, a need burning inside him and growing with each accidental brushing of arm or hand, each whisper of her voice as she spoke to Edda, and each inhalation of her scent that reached him. Knowing she probably feared and loathed the idea of his touch after the pain he must have caused her on their wedding night, Alex fought that desire. But while he won the battle in his mind and managed not to touch her when he joined her in their bed at night, he was definitely losing it in body. For the last three weeks he'd found himself sporting an erection that just would not die. The damned thing left him swollen and aching and nearly rabid with need. Not even in his youth had he experienced such rampant desire and it was getting progressively worse each night.

In the normal course of events, Alex would have thought this a grand thing. With marriages being business contracts signed and sealed when the individuals were but children, it was a rare thing for a man to desire his wife as he did. And he would have thought himself a lucky man indeed had he not mucked up everything so royally on their wedding night. Now, however, Alex found himself lusting after a wife who appeared to loathe him. And the worst part was he couldn't even resent or blame her. He hated himself for the shape he'd been in on their wedding night and what he must have done to her to produce so much blood. He found the matter preying on his mind most days like a venomous snake. Had she pleaded with him not to be so rough? Struggled to be free as his body had pinned her down? Had she wept?

Dear God, Alex had never in his life mistreated a woman. Not that he could recall, but now he worried if at another time while in his cups he'd hurt a woman. He'd rarely been in his cups, but even once was once too often if it meant he had hurt a smaller, defenseless woman. And how was he to make up for it?

Clearly, he had to. He could not stand a marriage that had become a cold war. Three weeks of it were wearing on his soul already, but he wasn't sure how to repair the damage he'd done.

Alex glanced to his wife as she suddenly excused herself to retire. He watched unhappily as she walked toward the stairs, his eyes sliding over the curve of her back, to the gown swaying around her hips. He wanted to get up and follow her. He wanted to trail her to their room, follow her inside, and catch her by the wrist to pull her back around as he pushed the door closed behind them. He wanted to kiss her eyes closed and then kiss her sweet mouth until the pursed look left, never to return, and then he wanted to strip away her clothes, kissing every inch of pale flesh revealed, and show her he wasn't the monster she thought he was.

Unfortunately, Alex suspected did he try it, Merry would stiffen up and bristle, and while he was sure she wouldn't refuse him, he doubted he could soothe her into relaxing, and if she didn't relax, no amount of coaxing would bring passion to life within her, and it would be a stiff, uncomfortable act for both of them. That wasn't what Alex wanted.

Turning back to his mug, he peered down into the liquid it held and fretted over what to do. Barring any more emergencies, they were to leave for Donnachaidh on the morrow, which meant days of travel ahead to reach his sister's new home. Alex didn't want to travel in the cold silence he'd lived with for three weeks, especially with his ever-present erection. Since the wedding, he'd been free of the damned thing only during the day while away from his bride, but they would be together for nearly a week straight during the journey, and he feared that would mean a very uncomfortable ride for him. Also, he didn't cherish the thought of arriving at Donnachaidh with such an obviously unhappy bride.

However, to avoid all that he had to somehow

repair things with his wife, and to do that he needed
to get her to let down her defenses around him. Getting her to drink excessively was completely out of
the question, of course, but the only time she wasn't
stiff and prickly around him was when she was
sleeping, and . . .

Alex paused in his thoughts as he considered
that. When she was sleeping, she was warm and soft
and had even cuddled up close to him in their bed
with a sleepy murmur. It had been torture for him to
lie there with her scent in his nostrils and her body
warm and sweet against him as he fought doing
what his erection urged him to do. But perhaps he
shouldn't fight it, Alex thought now. If he kissed and
caressed her while she slept and she woke excited,
perhaps he could show her that their wedding night
had been an aberration and that there was pleasure
and happiness to be found in the marriage bed.

"Are you not going to bed early, too, Alex?"
Edda's question drew his gaze her way as she continued, "You plan to leave early on the morrow, do
you not?"

"Aye," he growled, and stood abruptly. Had he
been thinking, he would have recalled the erection presently causing a rather large bulge in the
front of his braies and turned the opposite way to
leave the table. Unfortunately, he hadn't thought,
and standing up placed it right in Edda's face. Her
widening eyes and sudden flush, followed by the
way she turned her gaze quickly back to her food,
reminded him, however, and Alex grimaced as he
left the table. He followed his erection above stairs,
thoughts and images of what might follow rolling

through his head. He would be gentle, he would stir her passions, he would—

Dear God, let this work, Alex silently prayed as he reached the door to their room and eased it slowly open. A little breath of relief slipped from his lips when he saw that despite the fact that no more than ten or twenty minutes could have passed since she'd retired, his wife was abed and sound asleep. Perhaps it would work out after all.

That hope firm in his heart, Alex quickly snuffed out the lit torch by the door, leaving only the dying fire to light the room, and then—as silently as possible—stripped off his weapons and clothing and eased carefully into bed beside his wife.

Merry was slow to wake and wasn't sure what woke her. At first she thought she was having a warm fuzzy dream, but it was unlike any dream she'd ever before experienced. She was cocooned in warmth and semidarkness, just the flicker of the dying fire casting small dancing shadows across the wall before her when she eased her eyes open. They soon drooped sleepily closed again, however, and she released a little sound of pleasure and shifted slightly against the warmth at her back as something slid warm and caressing down over her hip and along her upper leg. The sleepy little sound of pleasure slid from her lips once again, but ended with a low moan as the caress moved back up and continued up her waist and then around to drift feather-light over the lower curves of her breasts before stopping to cup one and squeeze gently.

Some instinct in Merry was urging her to open

her eyes then and wake fully, but she fought it. This was too pleasurable and she didn't wish to wake up and have it come to an end, so she tilted her head back slightly as she felt lips gently brushing the side of her neck. The hand at her breast was kneading and sending an odd excitement tingling through her body. Merry found herself gasping in response, her behind shifting into the hips against her backside and unintentionally nudging a hardness resting there. It brought a moan from the questing lips now slipping up over her cheek and toward her mouth, and Merry could no longer pretend she was asleep. Her eyes blinked open and she turned her head to peer at who she knew must be her husband. Before she could speak, his lips covered hers and his tongue swept in to fill her mouth.

Merry was so startled by the invasion she went completely still, her mind filling with confusion as the combination of his caresses and kiss filled her with a sharp excitement that was almost overwhelming. She remained still and uncertain as his mouth explored hers, her hands balling into fists by her waist as he plucked at her nipples and sucked on her tongue, and then his hand drifted down over her stomach and a new, stronger wave of excitement swept over her, an almost anticipatory need that exploded into full-blown passion as his hand gently cupped the apex between her thighs. Merry gave a small jolt in response, her hips thrusting her against his hand, and then she felt one finger slip between the folds of her most private place, and the excitement spiked to a level that raised fear in her and had her grabbing at the hand to stop him.

Alex immediately stopped his caress, but he also broke their kiss to lift his head.

"I am your husband."

He whispered the words against her lips and she stilled again, uncertainty flowing through her. He was her husband and had every right to do whatever he chose, and really, this was . . .

"I will be gentle," Alex continued quietly, the brush of his lips and breath stirring little swirls of pleasure inside her despite the fears and anxieties rolling around inside her head. "I am sorry about our wedding night."

Merry opened her mouth to tell him the truth. She would not have him feel bad for something he had not done, and besides, if he continued as he was going he would surely find out the truth for himself. However, before she could speak the words, he added, "I only had one small whiskey that night. That was my intention, but your father must have topped up my drink when I was not paying attention and so I drank more than I intended. I am sorry for it."

Merry's intention to set the record straight about their wedding night died right there and she felt her mouth turn down with disbelief. "I would believe that were it not for the fact you passed out drunk the day I arrived and have been drunk every night of the last three weeks since."

Her voice was hard and cold, and Alex responded as if she had physically slapped him, rearing up enough that they could peer at each other. He was scowling, she saw in the dim light, and scowled right back. She would not pretend to believe his lies.

He might fool himself, but she would not allow him to think he fooled her.

They stared at each other silently for several moments and Merry saw several expressions flash across his face. Disappointment, resignation, unhappiness. For one moment she thought he might roll away from her and leave off what he had started, and she was surprised to find that part of her was actually disappointed at the prospect. Then his expression turned determined and he said, "I was indeed drunk the day you arrived. Very drunk. The blacksmith insisted on it before pulling my tooth, but it was a singular occurrence. I do not usually drink."

Merry started to shake her head in disbelief and opened her mouth to tell him what she thought of that line, but he covered her mouth with one hand and said solemnly, " 'Tis the truth. I am not sure what is happening, but I can assure you that I have not been drinking myself to drunkenness each night. In fact, the way you watch me, surely you have noticed that I have no more than one ale each night, and that twice these last weeks I have not had anything at all to drink, even mead during the meal, and yet am experiencing some slurring in my speech and disorientation."

Merry considered this silently. She had indeed noticed what, and how much, he was drinking, and had wondered over it briefly, but then had decided that he must have been drinking with the men before coming inside for the meal so that he was drunk before joining her at table. "Then what—?"

"I think I may be fighting off what the men have

been suffering. 'Tis the only explanation I can come up with for the symptoms when I have not been drinking," Alex said solemnly, and then admitted a tad wryly, "At one point I thought perhaps someone was drugging my drink, but I did not drink at all for two nights and it changed nothing, so . . ." He shrugged helplessly. "Exhaustion and fighting off an illness seem the only reasonable explanation."

When her eyes narrowed at the suggestion, he added, "Merry, I realize you do not believe me. And I am not trying to convince you, I am just telling you what I think. Hopefully, this disorientation and slurring will pass now that the illness is passing and I will return to normal. Just . . . give me a chance, Merry. Let me prove to you through my actions that I am neither a drunk nor the rough animal that I acted on our wedding night."

The words were not a plea, but a solemn request, and Merry stared at him silently, wishing there was more light in the room so that she might better see his expression. At table that night he had slurred and twice missed his mug when reaching for it. She had assumed that he was once again in his cups and yet he claimed he wasn't, and he had kissed her most thoroughly and there was no hint of alcohol on his breath. Besides, he had not been a rough animal on their wedding night as he had just said, so that part, she knew, was not true.

Merry peered at him for another moment, her thoughts in a whirl, but truly there was little to think about. He was her husband and as such had the right to her body when he chose. As for the rest of it, only time would tell if he was a drunk or not.

Letting her breath out slowly, she released her hold on his hand and forced some of the stiffness from her body, but that was the best she could do. The warm, fuzzy excitement he'd stirred had already died and she was now growing anxious at what lay ahead.

Alex seemed to realize this and didn't react to her silent acquiescence at first. When he slid his hand from between her legs, she thought he would roll over and leave her alone after all, but she was wrong. Instead, he shifted slightly to make room on the bed and then urged her onto her back.

Merry didn't resist, but allowed him to turn her over. However, her eyes were wary as she watched his head lower. When his mouth brushed over hers, she lay still, waiting, but he didn't deepen the kiss as he had the first time. Instead, his mouth trailed away across her cheek to her ear, and she blinked in surprise and clenched her fingers again as he began to nibble at her ear and neck, stirring a lazy excitement in her once more. So distracted was she by the reactions he was causing with the simple caress, it took Merry a moment to realize that his hand was moving again, running lightly along her hip and stomach. She had barely become aware of that soothing caress when his mouth returned to hers again. This time he brushed them lightly with his own once, twice, and then urged her lips open so that his tongue could explore.

Despite her worries about what sort of husband she had, Merry found herself melting under the combination. She was just about to kiss him back when his mouth drifted away and slid down along her throat to her collarbone. Merry turned her head to give him better access, and then bit her lip on a gasp when his hand found and began to caress her breast once more. It appeared her earlier excitement had not died as she'd thought, but the fire had merely been banked for their brief conversation. Now it flamed back to life wherever he touched and kissed her. Pleasure shivered across her collarbone and followed the trail of his lips as they moved over the mound of her breast. It then sparked white hot as his mouth closed over her nipple and he showed her that it was good for more than feeding babies.

Without realizing how it had happened, Merry found her fingers curled in his soft hair, holding his head close as he suckled at one breast. When his now displaced hand moved to the other breast and began to knead and squeeze there, she had to bite her lips hard to keep from moaning at the double assault. Nothing, however, could keep her body from arching and twisting beneath his ministrations.

By the time he finally raised his head and kissed her again, Merry's mind had given up her worries about her marriage and what sort of husband she had. This was all so new and overwhelming, she had trouble holding on to a thought, so simply let them go and kissed him back. She wasn't entirely sure she was doing it correctly, but emulated his actions to the best of her abilities and hoped that enthusiasm would make up for whatever she lacked in skill.

Alex's response was encouraging. He moaned into her mouth, and she felt his hand slide into her hair, holding her firmly and tilting her face as his kiss became harder and more demanding. Merry responded by opening her mouth further and clutching at his shoulders as her body began to quiver and cry for more. When she felt him shift and his leg slide between both of hers, she thought he would mount her then and instinctively opened her legs to make room for him, but that one leg was all he placed there. Merry was, at first, confused, but then he slid it up to rest against the very center of her and her hips bucked, pressing her against him as a fire burst to life there and began to grow with every movement of his leg.

He was still kissing her, and his hands had returned to her breasts to find and tweak and pluck her nipples. The three things together had Merry in a tizzy of excitement, her body arching and twisting under the assault as she was driven toward something she didn't understand. Need was pulsing through her, making her crave an end to this madness and—forgetting about their wedding night—she reached instinctively for the hardness pressing insistently against her hip and grasped it, somehow knowing it could end this sweet torture.

Alex stiffened at her touch and broke their kiss on an alarmed gasp. He also reached down to catch at her hand. It was too late, her fingers were squeezing around his shaft and it responded as it had on their wedding night, thrusting in her grasp and—like a cow's udder—producing milk.

Merry stiffened, her eyes shooting to her husband's face even as he jerked and threw his head back with a shout that ended on a curse. It was the curse part that told her she had done something wrong, and Merry released him and bit her lip as she watched him in his throes. She very much feared she'd hurt him and silently berated herself for ruining what had been—up until then—a very exciting experience. And then Alex collapsed against her, his head buried in her shoulder as he regained his breath.

Merry lay still, afraid to move and ruin things further. When he finally lifted his head, she eyed him warily, sure he was about to give her hell, but much to her surprise, the first words out of his mouth were an apology.

"I am sorry, Merry," he whispered with a wry shake of the head. "This has never happened to me before."

"'Tis I who should be sorry," Merry said quietly. "I didna mean to hurt ye."

His eyes widened slightly at her words. "Hurt me?" he asked with disbelief, and shook his head. "You did not hurt me. That was wonderful."

She must have looked as confused as this claim made her feel, because he shook his head, and then said, "I fear the excitement was too much for me. I have been sporting an erection ever since our wedding night and unable to do anything about it, and your touch . . ." He grimaced. "It was just too much. I should have warned you not to touch me, or—"

"Ye mean ye liked that?" she asked with amazement. "But ye looked to be in pain. I thought I'd—"

Alex silenced her with a kiss and then whispered, "Forgive me. I forget how innocent you are. I know your first time must have been painful and you probably think it was for me, too, but I will show you it does not have to be and that what I just experienced was anything but pain." He paused and offered her a wry smile and then added, "Unless you mean painfully embarrassing. I have not given such a bad showing since my youth. But now that it is out of the way, I can concentrate on you."

Merry wasn't at all sure what he meant or how he could possibly claim it hadn't been painful. The man had been cursing but moments ago and she knew there was supposed to be blood. How could there be blood without pain? she wondered, but then her thoughts were distracted as he began to kiss her again. Despite his shout and cursing of a moment ago, there was no lack of ardor to his kisses, and Merry felt her own passions shiver quickly back to life as he bombarded her senses. This time it was different. Where before Alex had seemed careful and almost tentative as if expecting her to pull away weeping for him to stop at any moment, this time he was a man on a mission, his concentration and determination apparently on the sole goal of driving her wild with desire.

Alex kissed her hard and eagerly even as he slid his hands to her shoulder and urged her up until she knelt on the bed before him, and then his hands were everywhere. They slid over her back, and then down her arms, and finally up to cup both her breasts at once. Merry immediately sat up a little straighter before him, a little gasp slipping from her lips as her breasts rose and pressed into his caress. In response, Alex merely kissed her more deeply, his fingers squeezing and kneading briefly before he broke their kiss to duck his head and catch one erect nipple in his mouth.

A gasp of surprise slipped from her lips, and Merry clutched at his head as his tongue rasped over the engorged nipple, lashing it in a way that made her toes curl where they rested beneath her bottom. Now free, the hand that had been at that breast immediately dropped to cup her bottom. He used that hold to urge her up so that she was upright on her knees, placing her breast at a more comfortable angle before him. Alex then pressed her lower body forward until her hips and pelvis pressed against his chest.

A little unbalanced, Merry grabbed at his head and shoulders and held on. Her breath was coming in little panting gasps as he laved and suckled her breasts, but it stopped briefly when his hand suddenly slid around and between her legs from behind to brush across the very center of her. When his fingers brushed over her a second time, her breath left her on a little puff of surprised excitement, and Merry found her nails digging into his flesh as he concentrated on driving her wild. Within moments her thighs were shaking and threatening to drop her, and her breathing was a frantic mix of gasps and pants and pleading mewls. This was a part of the bedding Edda had obviously forgotten to mention, and Merry was almost relieved she had. For surely she would have been much more upset with him on their wedding night had she realized what he was depriving her of when he'd knocked himself out.

Alex nipped gently at her nipple, not enough to hurt, but enough to draw her attention back to him and away from her thoughts. Merry lowered her head to peer at him, surprised to see his eyes open and watching her. Apparently, he'd seen her brief distraction and hadn't liked it. She opened her mouth to explain, but the moment she did, Alex released the nipple from his mouth and surged upward to claim her. He had to retrieve his hand from between her legs to do so, and Merry felt a moment's disappointment, but then his hand slid between them to work their magic from the front, sliding urgently over her slick, swollen flesh as he kissed her.

Merry groaned and gasped into his mouth, her hips instinctively thrusting forward. Her eyes popped open with surprise when she reached down to his hip for balance, misjudged, and her hand brushed against a hardness between them. It seemed her husband was excited again, she realized, and then gasped in surprise as he released the hold he had on her head to catch her hand and twist it behind her bottom. The action was to keep her from touching him again, she realized as Alex used their entwined hands to press her bottom farther forward so that her upper body was leaning backward under his and her hips were pushing forward, urging her into his touch. He had her totally in his control now, and Merry found it all a bit overwhelming and almost frightening as her body roiled with the desire he was building in her. A long line of tension seemed to run between her mouth under his and the spot where his hand worked so feverishly and it was growing tighter by the moment. She knew it would soon break and feared what she did not know would happen. At the same time, her body craved it like a starving man craved food. It left her struggling in mind and body, her hips thrusting into his touch while at the same time twisting in an effort to try to escape the caress.

Alex ignored her struggles and answered her thrusts with a more urgent caress that almost made her dizzy with excitement, and then he slid a finger inside her and Merry went still with shock at the alien invasion. In the next moment, she screamed out and jerked in his arms as the tension finally snapped and wave after wave of pleasure roared through her body, leaving her drowning under the foamy surface as he held her.

Merry was vaguely aware when Alex broke their kiss, pressed a gentle kiss to her nose, and then eased her to lie back on the furs on the bed, but her mind was rather taken up with the sensations still pulsing through her. She paid a little more attention, however, when he settled himself between her legs and she felt his hardness nudge where his hand had been moments ago.

She blinked her eyes open and peered at him a bit blankly, wondering what he intended next, and he smiled at her expression.

"See, that was not painful, was it?" he asked softly.

Merry shook her head lethargically from one side to the other, now understanding that the shout and curse had not been because she'd hurt him. On the other hand, it had been much easier for her to make him cry out than for him to make her scream. That was an observation she would have liked to think about, but Alex was speaking again.

"And this next will not hurt, either, now that the first time is out of the way," he assured her.

Merry's mind cleared abruptly as she realized what he meant to do next and that the first time wasn't out of the way at all. She opened her mouth to explain what had happened on their wedding night, but instead screamed in shock as he suddenly plunged into her, definitely tearing through the maiden's veil.

Alex stilled at once, shock on his own face. He stared at her a moment and then started to withdraw, but she grabbed at his hips to keep him in place for fear of the pain it might cause. The slight movement before she made him stop didn't cause pain, but the way he rubbed against her as he shifted surprised her by sparking her excitement again. Merry avoided the questions in his eyes by glancing down their bodies and then shifted her hips cautiously. Once again there was no pain but a trembling excitement building back to life within her as their angle made him rub against her again.

"Stop moving, Merry, or I'll not be responsible for—" His words ended on a gasp as she shifted beneath him again. Not only did her excitement pulse more sharply through her, but Merry was sure that he grew harder inside her. She raised her gaze to see that his eyes were now squeezed closed as if he was in pain, and his face looked tense.

Curious, Merry shifted her hips again, this time drawing a groan from his lips and forcing his eyes back open.

"Wife," he breathed in warning, but it was a warning she chose not to heed. Merry shifted beneath him again, raising her knees on either side of his hips so that she could tilt her hips more and make him surge into her. That was all it took. Alex's control snapped like a twig. A low growl slid from his lips and then he was raising himself up to kneel between her legs, taking her with him so that she found herself sitting facing him in his lap, her legs around his hips and his body filling her so completely she thought she might split from it.

"What—?" Merry began with confusion, unsure what she was to do in this position, or any position really, and then he clasped her by the bottom and raised her slightly and she breathed, "Ohhh" as his shaft slid partway out of her before he lowered her again and filled her once more.

Alex did this several more times, the angle rubbing him against the nub of her excitement, and then suddenly he laid her back on the bed. He immediately followed her down so that he could drive himself into her more easily. Merry had no idea what she was supposed to be doing, but dug her heels into the bed and arched herself into his thrusts, her hands moving down to clasp his behind and urge him on as he drove them both back to, and over, the brink once more.

ur wedding night."

Merry slowly opened her eyes to find herself peering at her husband's chest. She didn't fully recall how she had ended up there. While her mere touch had made him spill his seed earlier, once he'd gone hard again, he'd stayed hard a very long time and proven a vigorous lover. By the time Alex had screamed out his satisfaction, she'd found her own at least three more times herself and had been barely conscious when he'd rolled off her. She supposed he must have then pulled her to rest on his chest. Now she raised her eyes slowly to his face and

took in his grim expression. It appeared to be time
for explanations.

"On our wedding night," she began, and then
paused as his eyes sharpened on her. This was
probably going to annoy him, she knew. After all,
he—and everyone else—had seen the blood on the
sheets and jumped to the conclusion that he'd been
overly rough. She truly should have explained matters to him sooner, but—

"Merry," he growled.

Grimacing, she lowered her eyes to his chest and
began to toy with the hair there as she quickly explained, "When everyone left our room that night,
they didna close the door properly. Ye got up to
close it, stumbled on yer clothes on the way back, hit
yer head on the bed and knocked yerself out."

"I did?" he asked with surprise.

"Aye." Merry nodded solemnly and then rushed
on, "I kenned they'd come searching fer the bed
linens in the morn and ye were unable to . . . er . . ."
She shrugged and then continued, "So I cut meself
and smeared blood on the linens."

"All that blood was from a cut?" he asked, actually sounding more dismayed now.

Merry nodded warily, and then gasped with surprise as he suddenly whirled her onto her back on
the bed and shifted to kneel beside her, his gaze
scouring her naked body.

"Where is this cut?"

Merry grimaced but raised one knee, making
more of her injured leg visible. Her husband's eyes
immediately shot to her thigh and widened with
horror.

"Dear God, woman! What did you do? Stab yourself with a sword?"

Alex was now bending over to look more closely at the remnants of the cut, so missed the face she made at him. It had been three weeks. The wound was healed and now just a scar, a rather large and ugly scar, unfortunately, but a scar just the same. One that was more likely to remind her of this night than their wedding night, she suspected, as his fingers moved gently over the healed wound, sending a shiver up her back.

Trying to ignore that his face was down between her legs, Merry cleared her throat and explained, "I didna ken how much blood breaching a veil would cause and thought overdoing it was better than underdoing it."

Alex's head suddenly swiveled, his eyes stabbing her with accusation. "And you let me think I had caused all that blood on our wedding night?"

Merry bit her lip. "I would have explained, but ye always seemed drunk and—"

Her words died when he raised a hand for silence. A moment passed when she suspected he was too furious to speak, but after a moment he ran a weary hand through his hair and shifted to sit at the head of the bed, his back against the wall. Alex then caught her by the waist and lifted her to sit in his lap. Merry peered down at her hands and waited, unsure if he was angry or not. His voice did not sound angry, however, when he asked, "Did I hurt you very badly?"

Merry glanced at him with confusion, noted that his eyes were on the apex of her thighs, and flushed as she realized he meant when he'd broken her maiden's veil. Feeling her face heat with embarrassment, she shook her head. "It was barely more than a pinch."

"You cried out," he pointed out quietly.

Merry shrugged. "'Twas the shock. I kenned what ye were about to do, but it still felt very odd to have ye filling me, and then, too, I was expecting it to hurt like the very devil and was shocked that it didna."

"I see," he said quietly.

Merry let out a slow breath and peered at her hands, noting absently that she was wringing them like an anxious old woman. She wasn't terribly surprised. While she was glad he didn't seem angry, Merry was also terribly uncomfortable sitting there in his lap with the two of them naked. She supposed it was silly to feel that way after the intimate things they'd just done, but emotion was rarely logical, and to be fair, she didn't normally sit around naked in front of her maid, let alone in the equally naked lap of a man. Merry was trying to think of a way to remove herself and somehow scoot under the covers without it seeming as if she was too eager to do so when she became aware that Alex was running one hand up and down her back. It was a soothing gesture and really very nice.

"Merry."

"Aye?" She glanced at him reluctantly, a bit surprised to see that he was smiling, a soft glow in his eyes that she didn't understand.

"Thank you."

Merry glanced to him with confusion. "Fer what?"

"For seeing to the linens on our wedding night," he said, his words a soft growl. "And for tonight."

Merry glanced away with a shrug, aware that the blush staining her cheeks had darkened further. She had done little tonight but allow him to do as he wished, as a proper wife should. Well, unless you counted enjoying it. She'd done that, too.

"I know we started out poorly, but I hope this can be a new beginning for us. We can use the trip to Donnachaidh as a chance to get to know each other better. Will you give us that chance?"

Merry hesitated. Alex had said earlier that he hadn't been drinking and that he suspected his slurring of words and occasional stagger these last three weeks were the result of fighting off an illness like the men suffered. If so, the symptoms were not ones she'd heard of before. Still, it would be nice if that were the case. She had enjoyed what they'd just done so knew the marriage bed would not be a trial. And Alex had proven himself a hard worker these last three weeks, running about the keep trying to do the work of four men while his soldiers were ailing. That alone showed that he differed from her father and brothers in at least one respect. If he was telling the truth and his behavior these last weeks wasn't the result of drink . . . Well, she might just have herself a fine husband after all. It seemed only fair she give him the chance to be that.

Meeting his gaze, Merry nodded solemnly. "Aye. I'll give us a chance."

Alex smiled and then caught her face in both hands and pulled her forward for a kiss. Much to Merry's amazement, the moment he deepened that kiss she felt her earlier excitement stirring back to life again. Even more surprising to her was that she felt *his* excitement stirring to life as well as he grew hard beneath her bottom once more. Merry had barely begun to wonder if he could manage the bedding again when he caught her by the hips and lifted her, urging her to straddle his lap. He then eased her to sit so that his staff was caught between them, rubbing across her excited flesh.

"One more time," he whispered, breaking their kiss to trail his mouth across her cheek as his hands began to move over her body. "I have never wanted a woman with such an insatiable hunger as I want you, but only one more time and then we must rest for the journey tomorrow."

"Aye," Merry gasped as one of his hands found a breast and the other urged her hips forward so that she rubbed against his shaft, the action caressing them both. "One more time and then we must rest."

"Good morning."

Merry offered a smile in response to that greeting from Lady Edda as the older woman claimed the empty bit of bench next to her chair. "Good morn, my lady. I hope you slept well."

"Very well, thank you," Edda assured her and then paused, eyebrows rising as she peered at Merry's face. "You on the other hand, do not appear to have slept well at all. Are you well, dear?"

"Oh, aye, I am fine. I just did not sleep much last night. Most likely the excitement about the journey today," Merry muttered, and turned self-consciously back to the bread and cheese she'd been eating before the woman's arrival. It hadn't been excitement about the trip that had kept her up, it had been her greedy husband. While they had both collapsed and slept briefly after the promised "one more time" of bedding, Merry hadn't been asleep long when she'd awoken to soft caresses and passionate kisses. There had been at least three more "one more times" last night with bits of slumber between and she was absolutely exhausted this morn. Not that she was complaining. Merry had quite enjoyed every minute of it. In fact, her only complaint was that they had to leave their bed for this journey and could not simply stay abed and continue as they had been going.

"Well, so long as you are not coming down with what the soldiers had," Edda said, drawing her attention once more.

"Nay, truly, I am fine," Merry assured her, and then glanced to the door as it opened. A small smile immediately claimed her lips when she saw her husband enter and move toward them. While she knew Alex must be as exhausted as she after last night, he hid it well, looking just as vital and strong as if he'd slept a long restful sleep. He was also smiling, she saw, and felt her own smile widen as he reached her.

"Good morning, Edda," Alex murmured, but his gaze was on Merry and he immediately added, "The men are ready to go. Are you nearly finished?"

"Have ye broken yer fast already then?" Merry asked with surprise. Alex had already washed and dressed and arranged for a bath to be brought up for her before he'd awakened her that morning.

Still, she'd been quick about her bath, taking only the time necessary for a good washing rather than lounging for a soak, but there had been no one at the table when she'd first arrived below. She'd assumed Alex had gone to see about his men before breaking his fast.

"Aye, I grabbed some bread and cheese as soon as I came down, and ate it while I checked that all was in order," he answered.

"Oh." Merry popped the last bit of bread in her mouth and stood as she chewed and swallowed. "I'm ready, too."

Alex smiled and took her hand to lead her toward the door.

"I shall see you off then," Edda murmured, getting up to follow them.

Merry glanced to the woman and offered a smile of gratitude. Edda had been very kind to her these last three weeks, doing everything she could to help her feel comfortable at d'Aumesbery, and she would not want to leave without saying good-bye. When Alex led her outside and to her horse, then started to move as if to lift her onto it, Merry backed away and hurriedly gave the other woman a hug.

Edda seemed surprised by the affectionate gesture, but patted her back and wished her a good journey before stepping away to allow Alex to lift Merry onto her mount. In the next moment, Alex had mounted as well and they were off, Alex in the lead, Merry behind him, and a small army of soldiers at their back, surrounding the wagon that Alex had insisted they would need. Merry knew it held her small bag with a couple of gowns in it, but had no idea what all the other bundles under the tarp might be. The only thing she could think was that they were gifts for Alex's sister, Evelinde.

Once they were out of the bailey, Gerhard rode past her with a small nod and moved up to ride beside Alex. They moved at a fast and steady pace for the first three hours, and Merry spent that time running her eyes over her husband's back and wondering what the future held. At that moment in time she was cautiously hopeful about their future together. She wasn't completely convinced that her husband wasn't a drunkard, but was willing to give him the benefit of the doubt. She supposed only time would tell. In the meantime, Merry was caught up in the thought that she might already carry their child. They'd certainly performed the bedding enough times last night for it to be a distinct possibility.

The thought made her smile as Merry recalled Edda's hinting and questions in that regard the last week or so. The first time had been the evening Merry's stomach had been unsettled and she'd feared she might have caught the stomach ailment the soldiers were all suffering. Edda had been sure she hadn't and had suggested it might be something else. Not understanding what she meant, Merry had just let the comment go. It was only later, after another similar comment, that she'd realized the woman suspected, and was even hoping she was with child. That hadn't been possible, of course. Until last night, her marriage had not been consummated. But Edda didn't know that, and Merry hadn't been willing to tell her, so had simply ignored her comments and questions in favor of wondering what on earth would make the woman immediately assume she might be pregnant anyway.

That question had been answered several days ago when Edda had come right out and reminded her that on her wedding night she'd admitted that she'd had her woman's time two weeks ere the wedding. She had then pointed out it had been weeks since the wedding and yet she had not had her woman's time again. Edda was sure she was pregnant and was cautioning her to be careful and look to her health. She'd even suggested she might wish to bow out of this trip rather than risk the baby.

Merry had found the entire conversation terribly embarrassing and discomfiting. First of all, still a virgin at that point, she knew there was no way she was pregnant. As for her woman's time, the truth was it had always been somewhat undependable, sometimes not appearing for a month or two, and other times lasting twice as long as it should. Merry had worried over the fact when she was young until her mother had sat her down and assured her there was nothing wrong with her, that she herself had always been the same way. Her mother had said she'd found over the years that her moods affected her woman's time, so that in times of great stress she often missed one or even two. Finding the whole subject rather embarrassing, Merry hadn't explained any of this to Edda, but simply let her think what she wanted and found an excuse to escape the conversation altogether.

Now she wondered if Alex's seed had taken hold last night and if so, if this journey might not shake it loose. The thought was enough to make her peer down at her stomach and begin to fret.

"You look worried."

Merry glanced up to find that her husband had slowed to ride beside her and was eyeing her with concern.

"Is anything amiss? Are you feeling well?" Alex asked.

"Oh, aye," she assured him quickly, forcing herself to sit a little straighter in the saddle. She then explained away her mood by saying, "I'm just a wee bit tired."

"That would be my fault," he said wryly. "I do apologize. I knew we had to travel today and should have been more considerate of—"

"Did ye hear me complaining last night?" Merry interrupted abruptly to bring his apology to an end. She then reached out impulsively to squeeze the hand that rested on his pommel. "I am fine. I will just sleep well tonight."

"Aye," Alex said, but still looked guilty, and then he suddenly reached out and took her reins from her with one hand, while catching her about the waist and scooping her from her saddle with the other.

"What are ye doing?" Merry asked with surprise as he settled her sideways in his lap.

"You may ride with me," he answered, and then retrieved a length of rope from the bag hanging from his pommel. He tied one end of the rope to the end of her mare's reins and then fastened the other end of the rope to his pommel so that her mare could follow comfortably along behind his mount.

Merry peered over his shoulder at her mare. "I can ride. I'm a good rider."

"I know you are," he reassured her soothingly. "I have watched you this morning and you are indeed a fine rider, but this way you can sleep if you wish."

"Oh." Merry shifted a little before him, not at all used to—or comfortable with—being taken care of, and then muttered, "Well, ye must be tired, too, and it seems unfair that I get to rest and ye—"

"Tell me about your mother," Alex interrupted abruptly.

Merry blinked at the order and then turned to peer at him suspiciously. "Why?"

"Because you have great difficulty accepting any sort of assistance and I wish to understand why," he said simply.

"I doona ha'e trouble accepting—" Merry's denial was silenced when his mouth covered hers in a quick, hard kiss.

"Aye, you do," Alex assured her solemnly as he lifted his head once more, and then he repeated, "Tell me about your mother."

When Merry hesitated, torn between arguing the point further and simply answering his question, he added, "I know what your father and brothers are like and that they probably weren't very helpful over the years, but what of your mother? I've been told she ran Stewart until her death."

"Aye," Merry said at last. "Father liked to pretend he was laird, but in truth he was laird only in name. The servants and soldiers all came to me or me mother with their worries and questions."

"They came to you even while she lived?" he asked.

Merry was silent for a moment and then slowly nodded her head. "Mother was ill a long time. She did what she could, but she was often tired and weak at the end. Her mind was always clear, though, and she told me what to do, and I did it fer her."

"So, you have never really had anyone to depend on, have you?"

Merry bristled at once. "I could depend on me mother."

"But she was ill and you had to help her rather than the other way around," he pointed out gently.

Merry shook her head. "She was not always ill. She was healthy and well when I was a child. Besides, 'twas not her fault that she was ill. She did the best she could."

"Aye, but—"

"And there was Kade," Merry then interrupted quickly.

That made Alex pause. She could tell by his expression that he vaguely recognized the name but was having trouble placing who Kade might be, so explained, "He's the eldest of me three brothers and the best of the bunch."

"Oh, yes," Alex murmured, his expression beginning to clear as his memory began to supply missing pieces. "He was raised by your uncle as I recall."

"Aye, Mother sent him to Uncle Simon when he was but a boy. I suspect she feared the effect being raised by my father would have on him. Seeing how Brodie and Gawain turned out, I think she was right to send him away."

Alex nodded. "He is older than I?"

Merry considered the matter and nodded. "Aye, two years older, I think. Brodie followed two years later and then Gawain two years after that and then there was me."

"Brodie and I were both five when you were born and our fathers struck the marriage contract," Alex said with a nod and then asked, "Why did Kade not accompany you to d'Aumesbery as Brodie and Gawain did?"

"He joined the Crusades like you," she answered, and then admitted unhappily, "We havena heard from him since."

The silence that followed was full of unspoken words, but Merry did not encourage his speaking them. They hadn't heard from Kade in a couple of years. Messages were expected to be few and far between in such situations, but not completely non-existent. In her heart of hearts Merry feared he was dead, but until one of the other men who had ridden with him came to her and said so, Merry would believe he was alive. She had to. He really was her favorite brother. She and her mother had made the trek to Uncle Simon's to visit him at least once a year, and he had come home to stay for one week a year as well. Kade had always been kind and support-ive during those visits, and they had correspond-ed often between them.

While her father, Brodie, and Gawain had always seemed weak and stupid to her thanks to their trou-ble with drink, and her mother had been sweet and intelligent, but weak from her illness, Kade had been the shining star in her family; strong, intelligent, and sober. She'd looked up to him and admired him, and when her mother had died, Merry had wished with all her heart, and prayed until her knees were chapped from kneeling, that he would return from their uncle's and take over the struggle that both riding herd on her father and brothers and running Stewart was. She had even written, asking him to, but when Kade had arrived for a visit shortly after that and offered to help at Stewart, her father had refused to allow it, claiming he was the laird and would run his own castle. Never mind that he was too drunk half the time to manage it, she thought with disgust. However, Eachann was the laird and Kade had been forced to leave when he suggested it might be best he did. He'd sailed to Europe and written Merry frequently about his adventures, but she hadn't had a single letter since he'd gone on crusade.

"He may yet return."

Merry glanced to her husband at those soft words, only then realizing that tears now blurred her eyes. Embarrassed by this show of weakness, she started to raise a hand to wipe them impatiently away, but Alex brushed her hand away before she could and did it for her. He then caught her by the chin and tipped her head up so that he could kiss her.

For one moment, Merry remained still under the soft pressure of his mouth, but immediately blinked her eyes open when he raised his head. Before she could see his expression, he pressed her head to his chest and whispered, "Rest. You are tired."

Merry's head popped up the moment he released it, however. Tired as she was, she simply could not rest when he couldn't, especially since she knew Alex must be tired, too. She knew he was scowling at her for being difficult, but avoided meeting his gaze and said, "Tell me about your family."

Alex hesitated, and for a moment she thought he would repeat his order to sleep, but then he relaxed behind her and began to speak. Merry listened curiously as he told her about his mother, father, and sister, and recounted a childhood vastly different from her own. His childhood had been one filled with happiness and loving parents who were neither drunks nor ill and in need of care. It was only with his mother's death when he was in his teens that the tone of the recounting changed. Alex was careful in his wording, but even so it was obvious that life after his mother's death was much less idyllic than before. He never insulted Edda or accused the woman of anything, but Merry could tell that after the king had forced the marriage between her and his father, life had been fraught with tension and much less pleasant at d'Aumesbery. She wasn't terribly surprised. After all, Edda had told her that she'd been bitter and unhappy when she married and moved out to the "wilds" of Northern England, but it was apparent from Alex's change in tone that Edda's arrival hadn't made only her miserable.

Between the soothing rock of the horse and the natural rhythm of Alex's voice, Merry soon found herself curling sleepily into his chest. When he fell silent, she tried to open her eyes to ask another question that would keep him talking, but it seemed like far too much effort, and she finally gave in and allowed sleep to fully claim her.

Merry wasn't at first sure what startled her awake some time later. She then became aware of the chest she leaned on shaking slightly as if with laughter. Raising curious eyes, she peered at her husband, surprised to see that he was indeed silently laughing.

"What did I miss?" she asked, glancing about, but no one else rode near them and she didn't understand what had amused him until he shook his head and explained, "You were snoring."

"What?" Merry sat up a little straighter, embarrassment bringing color to her cheeks as she shook her head in denial and assured him, "Ye're mistaken. I'm a lady and ladies doona snore."

That just made him laugh again and Merry glared at him with irritation and insisted, "I doona snore."

"Aye, you do," Alex assured her and then added, "And not daintily. You woke yourself with your own snores."

Merry was scowling at the claim, when he bent and kissed her reassuringly. " 'Tis all right. I am told I have the affliction as well."

"Well, I do not," she assured him, unsoothed. "If I did snore, and I'm no' sayin' I did, then it must be the position I was sleeping in."

"Aye," he agreed at once, and then further mollified her by adding, "I have never noticed you snoring in our bed, so it may very well be down to having to sleep upright."

Merry relaxed a little at this concession, but was still embarrassed. Sitting a little straighter before him, she glanced at the path ahead. "Where are we?"

Alex glanced over the area surrounding them

and then answered, "About halfway to the Scottish border."

Merry nodded at this news, but Alex was looking behind them, back toward the men and wagon that followed. She followed his gaze to note that Gerhard had fallen back beside the wagon where he was talking and laughing with a couple of the men. Alex waited until the man glanced in their direction, and then gestured for him to come forward. Gerhard immediately broke off the conversation and urged his mount up to join them.

"My lord?"

"There is a clearing ahead by the river," Alex said quietly.

"Aye, I know which one you mean," Gerhard said at once. "We have used it in the past."

Alex nodded. "We will use it again this night and travel the rest of the way to the border tomorrow. Lead the men there and set up camp."

"Where will you be?" Gerhard asked with surprise.

"I am going to take Merry a little farther up the river so that she may take care of her ablutions without fear of being seen. We will rejoin you afterward."

"Very good," Gerhard murmured, and then turned his horse back to wait for the others to catch up as Alex urged his mount to a faster pace.

Merry peered around curiously as they rode. They followed the path for a short distance, and then Alex steered his mount to the side and the trees fell away around them, opening out into a clearing. She wondered if it was the one that he'd spoken of to Gerhard, but they were moving so swiftly now that she feared biting off her tongue did she try to ask the question, so held it back. The clearing was surrounded by a thin line of trees and foliage on all sides. Alex cut across it to a narrow path she didn't see until they were almost on it. Here the trees on their left were thin, allowing glimpses of the water beyond, but were a little thicker on the left side, almost a wall.

Alex turned his horse to the right and they traveled parallel to the river for several minutes until the narrow grass path ended at another clearing. This one, while smaller, also had a small, picturesque waterfall and a cliff that curved around the clearing, leaving only the path through which they'd entered between it and the river.

A small murmur of pleasure slipped from Merry as she peered around the area. It was quite lovely, a private little oasis, and appeared to her to be the perfect spot to tend their needs after a long day riding.

"I found this spot during my travels before going on crusade," Alex said as he slipped off the horse behind her. "I recalled it some distance back and thought you might like it."

"I do," she assured him with a smile as he lifted her down from the mount. The moment she was on her feet, Merry tried to move away to explore, but Alex held on to her. When she turned to glance at him in question, he smiled faintly and said, "Give your legs a minute to find themselves. You have been in the saddle all day."

"My legs are fine. I was not doing the riding, merely resting in your lap," she pointed out with a

laugh and pulled free of his hold, only to land on
her knees as her "fine" legs gave out under her. Grimacing, she glanced to Alex, fully expecting him
to laugh at her as her brothers would have done.
Surprisingly enough, however, his expression was
solemn and even slightly concerned as he reached
down to take her hand and help her back up.

"You need to learn to accept advice and aid from
others, wife," Alex said quietly as he set her back on
her feet. "Everyone needs assistance at one time or
another."

The words were softly spoken and nothing like
the sort of rebuke one would receive from a parent,
but it had as much effect as a yell. Merry was suddenly hot with an emotion that felt part shame, part
fear. It was the fear that bothered her most. She was
suddenly afraid he thought less of her, and that bothered her more than she would expect. This was the
man she'd thought was no better than her father and
brothers. Why should she care what he thought of
her? Merry didn't know, but she did care, and didn't
like that caring.

Biting her tongue on the sharp words that rose
up in her defense, Merry forced herself to suffer his
hold until he felt she could stand alone and then
quickly moved away once he released her.

"I shall tend the horses," Alex said as she moved
toward the water. "You go ahead and bathe if you
wish."

Any other time, Merry would have insisted that
she could tend her own mount, but still stung by the
mild rebuke and her own reactions to it, she didn't.
Instead she continued to the water's edge and began

to disrobe. Merry stripped off her gown and laid it across a boulder nearby, but then paused and cast a quick glance back to her husband. Finding he had his back to her and was busy with the horses, she then quickly stripped off her shift, too, and tossed it over her gown before rushing into the water.

Unfortunately, in her eagerness to be submerged before Alex turned around, Merry moved with more speed than care. She came to an abrupt halt, however, as she ran into a submerged boulder, banging her toes and shin under the water.

Merry hadn't realized she'd cried out until she heard Alex shout in response. She turned abruptly to see him rushing toward the water's edge. Realizing she was as naked as the day she'd been born, Merry immediately dropped to hide in the water.

"I'm fine, I'm fine," she gasped, the cold water taking her breath away.

"Did you hurt yourself?" Alex asked with concern, but came to a halt at the river's edge and didn't charge in as she suspected he'd been about to do.

"Nay," she lied. " 'Twas just surprisingly cold."

Alex eyed her briefly, not looking as if her lie had convinced him, but then he nodded and turned back toward the horses. "I am nearly done and then I shall join you."

Merry made a face at his back, finding the words more a threat than a promise at that moment, and then turned away to move more cautiously out into deeper water. She was not used to feeling in the wrong. Merry had spent years being the only one in the right at Stewart, or at least usually in the right, and didn't like that her husband found fault with her, even if it was something as small as her being unwilling to accept aid and advice.

Shaking her head at herself, Merry rubbed her arms under the water as her body began to adjust to the water. She took a moment simply to enjoy the cool feel of it caressing her skin, but then sucked in a breath of air and plunged forward in the water. While her body was now used to the cold liquid, her head was not, and Merry nearly opened her mouth on a gasp as it flowed over her. She managed to keep from doing so and swam down to scoop up some dirt from the river bottom. Once she had two hands full of the stuff, she continued forward in a somersault and then shot back to the surface, gasping with relief as her head broke through into the early evening air.

After a couple of breaths and a glance around to see that Alex was back at the horses, she raised her hands out of the water to peer at what she'd collected. Much to her relief it was gritty sand and not muddy dirt, which would have been useless to her. Merry quickly used the grit to wash herself, running it over her arms and chest so that the sand acted like an abrasive, washing away the day's dust from travel.

"I see you know about nature's soap." That approving comment from Alex made Merry whirl in the water to find him now naked, a bare few feet away in the water and moving closer.

"That is what my mother called it, too," she said, watching him warily. "She taught it to me on our first journey to visit Kade when I was young. She said it did the trick as well as the perfumed soap at home, but I think she preferred it."

Alex nodded, but continued forward until he could reach her. Catching her hand in his, he tugged her forward through the water toward him, murmuring, "Do not look at me with such bruised eyes. You make me feel an ogre for reprimanding you about accepting aid and advice."

Merry was slightly startled at his calling it a reprimand. It hadn't sounded like the sort of reprimand she was used to giving. But for all its soft couching, his words had certainly felt like one to her, she acknowledged, and wondered if perhaps she hadn't been approaching her father and brothers all wrong all these years. Perhaps a soft, firm voice and hard eyes would have been more effective on them as well.

Nay, Merry decided in the next moment. They would have listened to that no more than her snapping, barking, and yelling. Her father and brothers were simply incorrigible. She, however, was proving to be ridiculously sensitive. Something she would never have expected. Her father and brothers could call her a shrew without penetrating her hide, and yet this man showed his disappointment and disapproval with soft words and a look and she was hurt. It was all rather bewildering to her.

"Stop thinking so hard," Alex said, and Merry did at once, though not because he'd told her to. He had tugged her against his warm body in the water and she suddenly found it quite difficult to hold on to her poor thoughts.

Her ability to think was not improved when he began to kiss her. Alex was holding her up slightly in the water so that their heads were on a level. It meant he needn't bend to kiss her, but also that her feet were now groundless and floating free in the water. They immediately bumped against and tangled with his under water even as her breasts rubbed across his chest above, and Merry was actually startled by the sudden roar of desire that went through her.

"Should we no' go back and join the others?" she asked on a little breathless gasp when his mouth left hers and began to ease down her throat as he lifted her up farther out of the water. "They'll be preparin' the sup and makin' camp and may need help."

Alex's answer was to close his lips over her nipple and draw it into his mouth.

Merry shivered in the cool water and tilted her head back on a groan, giving up any further protest. If her husband wished to bed her again, it was her duty to submit, was it not? That thought had barely run through her mind when he was suddenly gathering her in his arms and carrying her toward shore.

"Are we going back?" she asked with surprise.

"Nay. I am hungry."

That answer merely confused Merry, but they had reached the shore, and her mind was taken up with further confusion when Alex moved to set her on a larger boulder next to the one she'd laid her gown on. While the water had felt cold on first entering, the evening air now felt chill on being out, and she shivered and quickly sat up to reach for her gown once he'd released her.

"I shall warm you," Alex said, taking the gown away. He tossed it back on the neighboring rock and then urged her to recline on the boulder as his warm body came down over her.

"Ye said ye were hungry," she reminded him in a whisper as he caught her hands and raised them over her head.

"Aye, and I am. For you," he explained in a low growl, and proceeded to try to devour her. At least that was how it felt to Merry. He started with a kiss, his mouth hard and demanding on hers as his hands released hers and slid to find her still wet breasts.

Merry gasped into his mouth and arched into his touch, and then moaned with disappointment as he broke the kiss to begin traveling down her body. That disappointment died a quick death when he paused to graze at her breasts again, drawing moans and mewls of need and pleasure from her that were quickly followed by renewed disappointment and then confusion as his lips continued farther downward. He trailed kisses down her stomach, making the muscles there jump and sing. Her eyes popped open, and she peered down at him with confusion, unsure why he would bother kissing her there, but that confusion was joined by something like alarm when his kisses continued farther and began to trail to her hip and then in toward her thigh.

"Husband, I—" Merry began uncertainly, for some reason feeling suddenly vulnerable. It was as far as she got, however. In the next moment, she was sucking in a startled gasp as his mouth dipped between her legs to trail up her thigh. Merry was too shocked to speak at that point, and then he reached and pressed a kiss to the very core of her, and she completely lost the ability of speech. Merry was sud-

denly torn between the urge to catch him by the hair
and tug his head away, and the equally strong urge
to catch him by the hair and urge him on. This was
like nothing she'd ever experienced, and certainly
nothing she'd ever imagined might happen between
a man and woman, but it was also . . .

"Dear God," she gasped, dropping back on the
rock and grabbing for something, anything to hold
on to as he began to lave and nibble at the very core
of her. He was eating her alive and she liked it.

Oh, this had to be a sin, she thought a bit hys-
terically, and then gave up thinking altogether as he
caught her by the hips and drew her closer to the
edge of the boulder so that he could bury his face
between her legs and do unspeakable things to her.
Truly, they were unspeakable. She had no idea what
he was doing, but it had just raised her temperature
almost unbearably high and left her mind a mass of
feverish mush in her head.

Merry found herself shaking her head madly
from side to side on the hard boulder, her nails
scraping over the stone she was trying to hold on to,
and legs shifting almost violently in his hold as she
tried to escape the caress and grind herself into it at
the same time.

It was more than a relief when the tension he
was stoking inside her suddenly snapped. Merry
screamed out as it poured over her, white lights exploding behind her eyes as her mind took a brief
hiatus and her body shuddered and pulsed with the
sensations coursing through her. When she came
back from her pleasure trip it was to find Alex standing between her legs and using his hold on her hips

to drag her across the boulder's surface until she reached the edge. Her eyes dropped to half mast as she spread her legs wider for him, and then he was thrusting himself into her and stirring her tender passions all over again.

Merry immediately sat up and wrapped herself around him. Still panting and gasping breathlessly from the first round, she clutched at him desperately as he drove her back into that land of pleasure again. This time, however, he joined her there himself.

chapter

Seven

We should rejoin the others." Alex spoke the words reluctantly as he watched Merry emerge from the river. She'd barely rested a moment after their lovemaking before scampering back into the water. He'd been more reluctant to move himself, and had simply sat on the boulder and watched her splash about in the chill water. Now his eyes swam over her body as she hurried back to shore, noting how the cold made her nipples erect and how the water shimmered like diamonds on her skin under the last rays of the dying sun.

It soon became obvious that, despite what they'd done last night and just now, his wife was still shy before him. Merry didn't actually raise her hands to cover herself, but did move quickly and then positioned herself so her back was to him as she swiftly used her shift to dry herself. Deprived of the vision of her generous breasts, Alex found his eyes dropping to her behind as she ran the cloth over her body in a cursory effort. His gaze slid over the rounded cheeks, remembering how they had felt in his hands, until she suddenly tossed the shift aside and tugged her gown on over her head.

Alex sighed with disappointment as the pale blue cloth dropped like a curtain, ending his view, but knew it was probably a good thing. Just those few moments of watching her naked had made interest slide through him again, stirring his shaft to half mast, and he knew that much more and he would have propelled himself off the boulder, strode over, and given her reason to clean up yet again.

Not that that was a bad thing, Alex thought, but it *was* growing dark and he *was* hungry for food, and they *should* really get back to the others before they sent out a search party. By now camp should be set up and a meal would be being prepared. Besides, he could always have her again later, in the comfort and privacy of their tent. Out here in the open, privacy was something of an uncertainty. Any of the men could have stumbled on them in their search for game to cook for the sup, or a private spot of their own to tend to personal matters.

A murmur from Merry drew Alex's gaze her way, and he frowned as he saw her moving off into the trees. He was about to call her back when he realized that she'd said something about tending to personal matters. Realizing she was looking for a private spot to relieve herself, he merely called out to her not to go far and then forced himself to get off the boulder and get moving himself. A quick dip in the river took care of the fledgling erection watching his wife had brought about, and then Alex, too, dried off and began to dress. He'd just donned his braies when he realized he, too, had some relieving to do.

Alex paused and glanced around. He was less concerned about privacy than embarrassing his new bride by accidentally stumbling onto her spot in the woods, so shrugged and moved to a small copse of bushes growing at the base of the small cliff that backed the clearing. He'd just finished tending to business and begun to tuck himself back in his braies when he heard a slight grinding sound from above. Pausing, Alex raised his head. He couldn't see anything but the face of the cliff from this angle, however, so started to step back, and then sucked in an alarmed breath and turned to run as a boulder suddenly rolled off the cliff and plummeted toward him.

He wasn't quick enough. While Alex managed to save himself from having the boulder slam down directly on his head, it still caught him on the edge of the shoulder. He grunted in pain as it struck and then grunted again as he fell under the weight and slammed his head on something hard.

Anxious at the idea of anyone stumbling upon her in such a private, undignified moment, Merry took her time about choosing her spot. She also went a little farther into the woods than she normally might have. But it wasn't a worry since she knew she merely had to follow the sound of the waterfalls to find her way back to her husband, so she wouldn't get lost. However, by the time Merry finished and headed back, she was sure Alex was probably dressed and waiting impatiently for her return. An apology was trembling on the tip of her tongue as she stepped back into the clearing, but it died unspoken as she heard a grinding sound and saw her husband peering up at the cliff he stood facing. She followed his gaze, eyes widening in alarm as she saw the boulder plunging down at him.

Merry thought she caught a glimpse of a figure disappearing into the trees on the cliff above, but paid it little attention, her concern with her husband as she saw the boulder crash down, hitting his shoulder in a punishing blow and knocking him to the ground.

Crying out, she rushed forward at once, flying across the clearing to kneel at his side and eye his still body where he'd sprawled. He lay on his stomach in only his braies, and the first wound she saw was the one to his shoulder and upper arm. The boulder had scraped away a layer of flesh and she knew it would be sore, stiff, and bruised by morning, but was more concerned by the blood just visible on the side of his forehead. She could see a good-sized rock sticking out from under his head and cursed as she realized his head had crashed into it as he fell, just worsening matters.

Merry turned Alex onto his back, the chore taking enough effort that she was a bit breathless by the time she finished. Truly, her husband was a large man, and limp as he was, turning him was difficult. But she managed the task and then leaned forward to peer at his head wound. It didn't look terribly bad. However, head wounds were tricky, and the fact that all her pushing and prodding to turn him hadn't woken him up was troubling.

Worry knitting her brow, Merry sat back and glanced around the clearing. She then got back to her feet and rushed over to grab her shift from where it lay across her mare's saddle. Alex must have put it there. She'd left it lying on the ground where she'd dropped it earlier, intending to pick it up when she returned. Now she carried the cloth to the water's edge and quickly wet it in the river before hurrying back to her husband.

Merry cleaned the blood away, her eyes narrowing on the wound left behind. It wasn't really very deep and looked much less nasty once the blood was gone, but that didn't make her worry lessen. Head wounds were a serious business and he was still showing no sign of waking. She held the cold damp cloth to his forehead and spoke his name, but he didn't even stir. After repeating both actions several times, she finally sat back and peered around the clearing again.

The sun was setting, the day darkening, and the clearing that had been so bright and sunny when they'd entered was growing chill and taking on shadows that were making her anxious. It would soon be full dark. While Merry was relatively sure that so long as there was light she could find her way back to the clearing where she thought Alex had intended to camp, she was less certain of being able to do so in the dark. It was so easy to get yourself turned around in the woods at night.

On top of that, she wasn't positive the camp would be where she thought. She hadn't asked at the time, but had just assumed. What if it wasn't there and she had to hunt up the camp? Would she find it in the dark? And even if she did, could she find her way back here to bring help to her husband?

Merry had barely had the thought when she recalled the grinding sound she'd heard as she'd entered the clearing and the quick flash she'd had of someone disappearing into the trees on the cliff above. Biting her lip, she lifted her head to peer up. The grinding suggested the boulder had been shifted deliberately, and she *had* caught a glimpse of someone hurrying away. Unfortunately, she hadn't seen the person clearly enough to even say if it had been a man or a woman. Whatever the case, it suggested this hadn't been an accident, which meant leaving Alex here alone while she went for help wasn't a good idea.

Merry fretted over the worries as she peered back at Alex. He looked so helpless lying there half clothed and unconscious. If she couldn't leave him here while she went for help, she would either have to stay here with him or find a way to take him with her.

Her gaze slid around the clearing again. It was probably her imagination, but it seemed to her to be even darker than it had been moments ago. She was also suddenly aware of a rustling in the woods. Her sensible self told her it was probably small animals moving about and foraging for a last bit of food before the day ended, but a less sensible part was imagining villains and wood sprites sneaking about, ready to pounce on her the moment the last light of day died.

A cool breeze brushed across her skin and hair, lifting several strands in what seemed to her to be an almost taunting manner, and Merry felt her lips compress. She had no desire to stay out here alone with her unconscious husband waiting either for him to wake, or for daylight to dawn. She had to somehow get him on his horse and go find the camp. But how was she to manage that?

Merry's gaze slid around the clearing again, looking for inspiration. There was no way she was going to be able to lift the man onto his mount using her own muscle. Just turning him over had proven to be an effort. Lifting him up and tossing him over his saddle . . . Well, she just couldn't do it.

A soft snicker drew her attention to the other side of the clearing where her mare, Beauty, and her husband's mount both waited patiently for their owners to reclaim them. Merry's eyes narrowed on the animals as she considered her options, and then she was suddenly on her feet and crossing the clearing once more.

Merry murmured soothing words and offered each horse a pat as she quickly untied their reins from the tree Alex had fastened them to. It was enough to soothe Beauty, but Alex's mount kept tossing its head and taking nervous sideways steps as she worked, and she wished she knew the animal's name. Unfortunately, if her husband had used it in her presence she hadn't been paying attention and caught it, so she had to waste a moment trying to soothe the beast before leading both horses back to her husband. Merry then tied the reins of Alex's mount to a nearby tree before leading her mare to stand on the far side of the stallion so that the larger horse stood between Alex and the mare.

The bit of rope Alex had attached to the end of her mare's reins earlier in the day was still fastened. Merry now passed the undone end of it over the stallion's back and then rushed around the animal to see that it was long enough to reach all the way to the ground where her husband lay. Relieved, she caught the end of the rope and then considered her husband.

Her thought was that if she tied the rope to Alex and then had her mare back away it should drag him up off the ground and across his saddle. That was if his stallion stood still and her mare cooperated and backed away when she ordered and then stopped when she ordered it as well. Otherwise, this could be something of a debacle.

Pushing away such negative thoughts, Merry began to tie the rope around his wrists, but then paused and undid that to wrap her shift around his wrists first as she realized that the rope might burn him and injure him further. Once satisfied that she'd done all she could to keep from further harming her husband, Merry straightened and moved around to her mare to begin urging her away from the stallion. She tried to watch what was happening to her husband as she worked the mare, but the stallion was in the way, and after only a couple of steps, she made the mare halt and then ran back around the stallion to look. Alex's arms were now raised, but that was about it.

Grimacing, she ran back to her mare and urged her forward half a dozen steps this time before running back to check. Merry was glad she had when she saw the peril her husband was in. While her trick seemed to be working and Alex was half off the ground with his wrists almost to the top of the saddle, his head was hanging down and forward just below his mount's belly. Another step or two and the back of his head would have caught on his horse's stomach, and if she'd continued to move the mare forward, forcing him upward . . . well, it was just a good thing she'd stopped to check.

Merry gave his stallion a pat for standing so perfectly still during the operation, and then moved to Alex's side to bring his head up and back a bit so that it wouldn't catch on the horse. However, the moment she released it, it fell forward again.

Cursing, she glanced around, her eyes falling on a branch that lay a few feet away. It was a good three feet long and about an inch thick and should do the trick. Letting Alex's head fall forward once more, she rushed over to grab the item. Returning to his side, Merry then lifted his head again, muttered an apology to her unconscious husband, and held his head in place by catching a handful of his hair while she placed the stick across his upper arms. She then eased her hold on his hair. A slow breath of relief slipped from her lips when his head moved forward, only to be stopped by the branch.

Satisfied that she'd taken care of the problem, Merry then ran around the stallion to urge Beauty forward another few steps and kept doing so, urging the mare forward a step or two and then rushing back to check on Alex before urging her forward again. The exercise took much longer than she'd expected and the sun was gone from the sky, its last dying rays casting a shadowy light by the time she had her husband lying across his mount's saddle.

Eager to get moving before that last bit of light was gone, Merry quickly untied the rope from her mare's reins and then bent to reach under her husband's stallion to fasten the other end to his ankles so that she needn't fear his falling off the beast and having to go through all this again on the way back. Once she had him trussed up to her satisfaction, she then caught his stallion's reins and mounted her mare.

While the sun was now gone, the moon was up and the clearing was still light enough to see in when she finally put her heels to her mare's side and urged her to move slowly out of it. However, the path along the river had thick woods on one side and a light scattering of trees along the water's edge on the other. It was enough to make it quite dark and a bit scary as she urged her mare forward at little more than a walk. Merry wanted to go faster but worried that doing so might jostle her husband enough that he might slide off the saddle. Tied as he was, he would merely hang under his horse's belly, but then there was a risk of his being unintentionally kicked by one of his horse's hooves as the animal walked, and she didn't wish that.

Still, Merry would have liked to go faster and found her gaze sliding nervously over the dark shapes surrounding them as they moved. She'd had the uncomfortable feeling that she was being watched as she'd worked to get Alex on his horse, and recalling the figure on the cliff, had kept glancing warily to the trees. But it had slowed her down, and she'd finally forced herself to ignore it and concentrate on what she was doing. Now, however, she eyed the darkness crouching all around her with more than a little anxiety.

She couldn't get the memory of the grinding sound out of her mind. If it weren't for that, she could have convinced herself the whole thing had been an accident, but the grinding suggested moving the boulder had been difficult, not a result of someone leaning against it and accidentally sending it plummeting off the cliff. Someone had deliberately pushed it down on Alex. She had no idea why anyone would want to do that, but it seemed to her to be the most logical deduction and raised a wagonload of anxieties and worries in her mind. Why would someone wish to kill Alex? And more importantly, might they still attack now despite her presence? Were she and Alex in danger?

Merry forced herself to take a few deep breaths to steady her nerves, telling herself that if they'd intended to strike with her there they would have done so back in the clearing while she was distracted with trying to get Alex onto his mount. She then concentrated on the dark landscape around her. Merry hadn't been paying much attention to where Alex had left the woods for the path along the river's edge, but it didn't seem to her that they'd ridden along the river for this long on the way to the clearing. She reminded herself that she was moving much more slowly now than they'd been riding on the way out, but was still starting to worry that she'd ridden right by the path without seeing it.

Merry was just starting to think she should stop and turn back when someone stepped out onto the path before her. She wouldn't even have seen him in the darkness had a stray ray of moonlight not caught on the sword he carried. Tense as she was, she couldn't hold back a short shriek of surprise as she yanked on her mare's reins to draw her to a halt.

"My lady?"

Merry let her breath out on a slow, embarrassed breath as she recognized the voice of her husband's squire.

"Godfrey," she breathed with relief.

"Aye, my lady." He put his sword away and moved up beside her mare's head. "Why are you alone? Where is—?" The second question ended on a gasp as Godfrey spotted his lord lying over the saddle on the second horse. He was at his lord's side at once, lifting his head to take in his unconscious face. His voice cracked with alarm as he asked, "What happened?"

"Someone pushed a boulder off the cliff in the clearing where we stopped to bathe," Merry said bluntly.

"What?" Godfrey asked, turning an alarmed face her way.

She nodded unhappily. "It struck Alex on the shoulder and knocked him down. He hit his head on a rock on the ground when he fell."

"He is not—?" Godfrey turned back to his lord, hesitating to even speak the fear that the man might be dead.

"Nay, of course not," Merry said at once, and then quickly dismounted. She joined the boy at her husband's side to be sure that was true. Alex had been alive when they'd left the clearing, but with head wounds one could not be certain. Thankfully, he was still breathing. His warm breath on her hand when she put it before his face told her that.

Merry let her hand drop and then glanced to Godfrey. " 'Tis glad I am ye came along. I was beginnin' to fear I'd missed the path back to the clearin'."

"Nay. 'Tis just ahead. You would have seen the fire through the trees in another moment."

Merry raised an eyebrow at this and asked curiously, "Where were ye headed?"

"To drain the dragon," he murmured, his distracted gaze still on his lord. Then, realizing what he'd said, he glanced at her quickly. "I mean—"

" 'Tis all right," Merry assured him with the first smile she'd managed since her husband had been knocked unconscious. "I ha'e brothers and they've said worse in me presence."

Godfrey did not look like her reassurance made him feel much better. Merry gave his shoulder a soothing pat and then turned back to gather her mare's reins in hand. She didn't ask why he'd had his sword out if he was just going to find a spot to relieve himself. She would have been grateful to have a sword for this ride through the dark woods. It would have eased her fears some, and she suspected that was the reason for it with him. Not wishing to

embarrass him further by making him admit it, she
wished him good eve and began to urge the horses
forward again, but then glanced to him with surprise when he remained beside her.

"I shall see you safely back," Godfrey said, his
shoulders up and back and his head held high in a
fashion she supposed he thought was manly.

"There's no need to trouble yerself. If 'tis close by
I will find it. Ye go on about yer business," she urged
quietly, but wasn't surprised when he ignored her
suggestion and continued at her side.

They'd walked no more than half a dozen steps
when Merry spotted the path as well as the glow of
firelight through the trees. Another couple of steps
and the smell of roasting meat reached her and then
they were stepping out of the trees and into the
clearing.

Merry's eyes widened as she glanced around. A
lot had been accomplished while she and Alex were
by the waterfall. The horses were all tended, several
rabbits had been caught and now roasted over the
fire, and a tent now stood on the far side of the open
area. Her eyes widened further with surprise at the
luxury of a tent and then moved over the men who
had all suddenly stopped moving and were now
peering back as wide-eyed as she was. And then everyone started moving and talking at once.

Merry took a step back at the confusion of questions suddenly shot at her. It was a relief when Gerhard suddenly came from the side, his voice louder
and carrying more authority than the others as he
asked, "What happened?"

"I believe someone pushed a boulder down on

Alex after we finished bathing," Merry admitted as he lifted Alex's head to peer at his face. She then explained what had taken place before adding, "I didn't actually see the person push the boulder down, but . . ." She shrugged unhappily.

Expression grim, Gerhard nodded and released Alex's head, allowing it to hang down again as he bent to untie the cloth from his hands and feet. Several men stepped forward to help ease Alex off his horse's back and then they glanced to Gerhard in question.

"The tent," Merry said before he could respond.

The men immediately moved that way with their lord, and Merry followed.

The soft glow of candlelight filled the tent when they entered, and Una was just straightening from making a bed of furs on the floor. When she turned to find the men carrying an unconscious Alex inside, her eyes widened in surprise and then shot to Merry full of questions.

"I need my medicinals," Merry said quietly as she waited for the men to set Alex down and get out of her way. Fortunately, they didn't dally, but filed out of the tent the moment they'd laid her husband down. She immediately knelt at his side, made anxious by how still and pale he was.

"Here."

Merry glanced around to see Una holding out her bag of medicinals. Taking it with relief, she opened it to retrieve her various balms and salves.

"Should I be prayin' that he heals or that he doesna?" Una asked dryly.

The question surprised her, but Merry supposed

it shouldn't have. She hadn't exactly been overjoyed about her marriage these last three weeks, and on her wedding night the answer would have been a simple one: *Pray he dies and frees me of this marriage.* But things had changed. Merry found she quite liked this man, and—given the chance—thought she might just come to love him . . . and she had promised to give their relationship a chance.

Letting her breath out slowly, Merry nodded. "Pray he heals."

"I kenned it."

Merry noted the slow smile spreading the maid's lips. Eyes narrowing suspiciously, she asked, "Kenned what?"

"Ye're fallin' in love with him."

Merry stiffened at once. "I—"

"Oh, doona bother denyin' it. I've watched ye watchin' him these last weeks. He may drink a wee bit at night and slur his words, but he's naught like yer father and brothers. The man is a man. He doesna shrug his responsibilities and leave them to ye to carry. He's fair with his people, and cares about them, and that shows in all he does." She nodded solemnly, and patted her shoulder. "No one's perfect, and he's a good man despite his drinking. He'll treat ye right."

The words had barely left her lips when the tent flap opened and Gerhard ducked inside.

"How is he?" the soldier asked.

"Still unconscious," Merry answered grimly as she returned to sorting through her medicinals, searching for something that might be of use. She had salve that would soothe the soreness of his shoulder and encourage it to heal, but was more concerned with the head wound. Unfortunately, there was little she could do for that but keep a cold compress on it to try to keep the swelling down. The rest was up to Alex.

Alex was beginning to think that he might be cursed. He'd been plagued by headaches for the last three weeks. Most mornings he woke up with a dull throb at the back of his head. Of course, none of them had been as bad as the headache that had woken him the afternoon of his tooth pulling when he'd downed a pitcher of whiskey . . . until now. The headache that greeted him when he woke up and forced his eyes open in the tent was easily as bad as that one, but this time it was centered on the left front side of his head, and it was bad enough to force a low groan of pain from him as he squinted his eyes closed, trying to force the pain back.

"Ye're awake."

That brilliant bit of deduction sounded like it came from his wife's sweet lips and made him blink his eyes open again to find her bending over him. He scowled when he got a look at her, not because of the relieved expression on her face, but because of the dark circles under her eyes.

Alex was about to ask why she looked so weary when a rustle drew his gaze past her to see that they were in his travel tent. He didn't normally bother with it when he traveled on his own, but had decided to bring it to make the trip more bearable for his wife. That thought spurred his memory, making him recall the journey that day, taking Merry to the waterfall, and all that had followed. Including the boulder crashing down toward him.

"How diya feel?" Merry repeated. He was a tad surprised to hear the amount of concern in her voice. While they had got along relatively well since consummating the wedding last night, the three weeks before that had been somewhat difficult, and he wouldn't have been surprised had she treated him more cavalierly instead of sounding like she cared.

"My head hurts," he said honestly and then asked, "What time is it?"

"Near dawn, I think," Merry answered, her gaze moving to the open tent flap and the grey light of predawn visible outside. She then suddenly turned away to pick up something. When she turned back he saw that it was a mug of liquid. She slipped an arm beneath his head and used it to help lever him up and then held the mug to his lips, promising, " 'Twill help with yer poundin' head."

Alex hesitated, but then opened his mouth to allow some of the brew to slip inside. A grimace immediately tried to claim his lips, and he had a very strong urge to push the drink away, but he resisted and drank as much as he could before his stomach threatened to rebel. He then raised a hand to let her know it was enough, relieved when she immediately removed the mug and eased him back to lie down.

Alex did grimace now, his lips working and tongue rubbing itself against his teeth and palate in an effort to scrub away the awful taste coating it.

" 'Tis vile, I ken, but 'twill help," Merry said sympathetically.

Alex merely nodded and closed his eyes, waiting

for the pounding in his head to ease. If Merry's medicinal was anything like Bet's, Alex knew it should begin to work after a quarter hour or so. And it certainly tasted as vile as Bet's so should work, he thought with disgust, and wondered why things that were said to be good for you always tasted so horrible.

The moments passed slowly for Alex. He had several questions he'd have liked to ask, but his mind was taken up with the pain consuming him and he kept his mouth shut. A long time seemed to pass before he became aware that Merry was running her fingers soothingly over the uninjured side of his brow. When he noticed that, Alex knew the brew was starting to work. He blinked his eyes cautiously open then, relieved when the pain didn't ratchet back up, and then released a small breath and closed them for another few minutes. When he began to be aware of a need to relieve himself, however, he decided it was time to get up.

"What are ye doin'?" Merry asked with dismay when he started to sit up. "Lie back down, ye've had an awful blow to the head and been unconscious all night. Ye need to lie still and let yer body recover."

"As you just said, I have been unconscious all night. 'Tis plenty of recovery time. Now I need to get up and about," he said firmly.

"Ye've no business being up and about," she snapped, placing her hands on his shoulders and pushing in an effort to force him back into a supine position. Much to his amazement, the action worked, and Alex found himself collapsing back onto the linens and furs he lay on. The fact that he was so weak, however, merely made him more determined to get up, and he immediately started trying to rise again. His wife merely kept her hands on his chest, holding him in place. Disgusted by his own weakness, he admitted, "I need to relieve myself."

"Oh." She bit her lip and glanced around, and then brightened and peered down at the mug in her hand. "Mayhap ye could—"

"Do not even suggest it," Alex said grimly, positive she was going to say he should relieve himself into the mug rather than get up. He might be weak, but it would be a cold day in hell before he would willingly do something like that.

Merry set the mug aside, then scowled at him and bit out impatiently, "Verra well, I'll ha'e to help ye then."

She sounded incredibly testy. Considering that he was the one whose head was still pounding, Alex thought that wasn't well done of her, but then he once again noted the circles under her eyes and the pallor to her face and thought perhaps she had every right to testiness after all. He was suddenly sure she hadn't slept at all, but had sat up all night watching over him like a mother hen watching her chicks.

Alex wasn't sure how to feel about that. One part of him was grateful and glad she cared enough to bother, and the other was annoyed and thought she should have slept and taken care of herself. He started to shake his head at his contrary thoughts, but caught himself at the last moment and saved himself the pain.

"Come, let me help ye," Merry murmured.

Alex considered refusing her offer of help, but

the moment he was sitting upright the tent showed a terrible tendency to spin, and so he gave in gracefully and accepted her assistance. Once upright, he'd hoped he could manage on his own, but that also proved not to be the case and he had to let her help him out of the tent.

"Where to?" she asked in a whisper as they staggered outside. Both of them had been forced to hunch over to get through the low opening the tent flap offered, and the action nearly saw them crashing to the ground. Certainly, Alex would have, had Merry not quickly bent herself forward and turned so that he fell across her back when he started to stumble.

Shaking his head at the state he was in, Alex used her back to push himself upright again, and then suffered her to slip under his arm to support him once more.

"Behind the tent is far enough," Alex muttered, eager to get this done and get back inside the tent where he at least did not need aid to lie down. Truthfully, falling down was probably the thing he was best at, at the moment, Alex acknowledged unhappily. Certainly, his mind didn't seem to be up to much in the way of thinking. Here he was, staggering around, unable to even walk upright, yet one glance down toward his wife found his eyes landing on her generous cleavage, and he was suddenly aware that little Alex, too, was awake, with his head half raised and pushing against the front of his braies.

Dear God, what the devil was the matter with him? Alex wondered with self-disgust. Wanting his wife was one thing, but this was just ridiculous. Abnormal, even, he was sure. His head hurt less than it had, but it was still pounding something awful. He was also weak as a babe and should have absolutely no interest in anything of the like. In fact, his mind didn't . . . but his body did.

"How is this?"

Alex tore his thoughts from his body's ridiculous wants and glanced around to see that while he'd been busy thinking, his wife had managed to steer him around the tent to a small copse of bushes behind it.

"This will do. I can— What the devil are you doing?" he gasped with dismay as she immediately began to work at the tie of his braies. Alex tried to push her hands away, but weak as he was, the effort wasn't very successful.

"I'm merely tryin' to help ye," she said dryly. "Trust me, me laird, I'm too weary to ha'e anything else in mind and ken ye're in no shape to— Oh." Merry paused as she managed to get his braies untied and his now almost full-blown erection sprang out into evidence. "Well, that is— Mayhap ye're feeling better than I gave ye credit fer," she muttered.

"I can manage the rest on my own," Alex growled, embarrassed and frustrated all in the same moment. Truly, his head was pounding, his shoulder throbbing, and despite the hours he'd been unconscious he thought he could sleep standing up at that moment, and yet, little Alex was waving in the night air like a flagpole eager to raise a banner. "Just go back to the tent. I shall return once I have finished."

Merry hesitated, but then slipped out from under his arm, waited just long enough to be sure he wasn't going to fall on his face, and moved away with a slight rustle.

Relieved that he no longer had a witness to this humiliation, Alex quickly relieved himself. It was only then he realized his wife had not obeyed and returned to the tent as he'd ordered. He'd tucked himself away and was struggling to retie his braies when Merry was suddenly there doing it for him.

"I can manage on my own, thank you, wife," he snapped.

Merry ignored him long enough to finish tying the laces and then straightened and eyed him solemnly before saying, "Ye need to accept aid and advice from others, husband. Everyone needs assistance at one time or another."

Alex stared at her, a slow smile curving his lips, and then he gave a slight bow. "Touché."

He thought he caught a glimpse of a quick smile claiming her lips, but it was dark out, and Merry ducked her head quickly as she repositioned herself under his arm and then they were moving back toward the tent. By the time they got back inside Alex was more than grateful for her assistance. He never would have made it on his own. His legs were shaking like a plucked harp string.

The moment they reached the fur, he collapsed on it with relief. Alex was so exhausted he didn't even protest when Merry settled herself beside him and raised him up to press the mug of her vile liquid to his lips, but merely gulped it down until it was gone. When she then laid him back on the furs, he closed his eyes and went right to sleep.

chapter

Eight

Merry woke to the rhythmic rock of the horse, found herself in her husband's arms, and at first thought it was still the first day of their journey. At least until she glanced up, spotted the bruise and cut on his forehead, and recalled all that had happened. Merry immediately sat up and turned an accusing glare on her husband.

"What are ye doing up?"

"Riding," Alex answered reasonably enough, but she didn't miss the twitch of his lips and knew he was amused. That just made her angrier.

"Ye've no business being up and about after the trial ye went through yesterday."

This time he didn't bother hiding his amusement, but smiled at her in a way that seemed almost affectionate and said, "You are adorable when you act the shrew, Merry Stewart."

"Merry d'Aumesbery now," she reminded him, putting a little more snap in her voice. She then warned, "And I *am* a shrew, and as such, like to make ye miserable do ye no' explain—"

"I feel fine," Alex interrupted patiently. "Good as new in fact. It must have been that vile mixture you made me drink, 'tis surely a miracle cure. I slept another hour or two, woke up pain-free, and decided I was fine for traveling today. So here we are, halfway through the day and another half day closer to Donnachaidh."

Merry was sure he was lying. While she didn't doubt the tonic she'd given him might have helped him feel a bit better, it would hardly make him feel good as new. She had no doubt his head was probably still pounding at least a bit, and his shoulder was probably tender. He, however, was apparently unwilling to admit it. She didn't know what to think of that. Merry was used to men who whined and carried on at the least little ache or pain . . . and then used it as an excuse to drink to excess.

"You were exhausted from watching over me last night," Alex went on. "So I let you sleep as we broke camp and then brought you onto my mount again so that you could continue to catch up on the sleep you'd missed."

Merry grimaced. Only complete exhaustion would have allowed her to sleep through it all, but then she supposed she *had* been pretty exhausted.

Her husband had kept her awake most of the night before the journey with the bedding . . . or beddings. The few hours of light sleep she'd managed to snatch in his lap during the afternoon the day before had hardly made up for it, and then she'd stayed awake to watch over him through last night. Aye, Merry supposed, she shouldn't be surprised that she'd slept through the men breaking camp and part of the ride today.

Raising her head, she suddenly asked, "Did Gerhard and the men find out who pushed the boulder down on you?"

Alex was silent so long, she thought he might not answer, but then he said, "Nay. He had the men search the area. It was probably just some bandits who saw me alone and thought I would be easy pickings. Your arrival must have scared them off."

Merry eyed him doubtfully at the suggestion, finding it hard to believe that her presence would scare off anyone. It was possible, though, that they'd thought him alone, and her arrival had made them realize he wasn't, and fear that others were with them and might follow.

"'Tis well past the nooning hour," Alex announced, distracting her from such thoughts. "Are you hungry?"

Merry glanced to him, started to open her mouth to answer, but paused as her stomach emitted a loud rumble at the thought of food. She flushed with embarrassment, but he grinned and retrieved a small bag from his pommel.

"There is food in there for you," Alex said quietly as he gave it to her.

Merry managed not to rip and tear at the cloth bag, but just barely. She hadn't eaten a thing last night as she'd watched over Alex and was terribly hungry. She paused in surprise, however, when she got the bag open and began to remove item after item. There was a bit of bread, cheese, an apple, and even what she at first thought was leftover roasted rabbit from the night before.

" 'Tis quail," Alex told her quietly as she unwrapped the cloth around the meat and saw that it was indeed a small, full bird. "I was up before everyone else and caught and cleaned it and then put it over the fire to roast while the men broke camp this morning, thinking you might like it when you woke."

Merry swallowed the lump that had suddenly lodged itself in her throat at his taking such effort for her and then, not knowing what else to do, raised the bird toward him in offer.

Alex shook his head. " 'Tis for you. Eat."

Merry hesitated, but then lowered the offering and began to do just that. She couldn't possibly eat everything he'd packed for her, however, and when that became obvious, Alex did accept one of the bird's legs. Once they had both finished and the remains had been once more packed away, Alex began to ask her questions about her childhood again. She answered them willingly enough, but asked questions of her own in return, and the afternoon passed surprisingly pleasantly, with their conversation then moving on to other topics. Even as they talked, Merry couldn't help but note to herself that it was a much different journey than the one she'd undertaken to reach England from Stewart. That had been silent, uncomfortable, and grim, with her father and brothers avoiding talking to her, let alone showing any concern for her well-being or comfort. Once again she was forced to acknowledge that Alex was different from the males in her family. Perhaps she had married into a happier situation after all.

Alex's hand suddenly went up and Merry glanced around to see Gerhard urging his horse up beside them. The man had been riding behind them since she'd awakened, his eyes on her husband every time she'd glanced his way. But then Alex had talked a little about his time on crusade that afternoon and told her how the man had saved his life a time or two in Tunis and looked out for him. He obviously looked up to the older man, and it appeared, despite their being back in England, Gerhard, too, still felt the need to look out for him.

"Keep an eye out for a likely spot to camp," Alex said once Gerhard reached them. "We are nearing the border and I would rather spend this last night in England and cross the border tomorrow."

Gerhard nodded. "I shall ride ahead and see what I can find."

The soldier waited just long enough for Alex to nod his approval and then headed off up the lane.

"Gerhard was worried about ye last night," Merry murmured as the other man disappeared around a bend in the path. "He must have come to the tent to check on ye at least twenty times. He even offered to sit with ye so I could rest."

"There was no need for either of you to miss your

sleep just to watch me snore the night away," he said gruffly.

"Head wounds are tricky," Merry said firmly. "Someone had to watch over ye."

"Then you should have let Gerhard take half the night, so you both at least had some sleep."

Merry snorted at the suggestion. "Oh, aye. As if I could sleep while worried about ye. Besides, I'd have been lying right there beside ye, and I'd ha'e never managed to sleep with him sitting there watching anyway."

"Aye, and he might have heard you snore, too," Alex said solemnly.

Merry turned a glare on her husband, but it became a reluctant smile when she saw the teasing glint in his eyes. In the next moment, she stifled the smile and said primly, "I hate to be the one to tell ye, me laird, but if ye're trying to be amusin', ye're failing miserably." When he arched an eyebrow at that, she added, "The English are no kenned fer their sense o' humor."

"Is that so?" he asked dryly.

"Aye. Everyone kens the English are all grumpy sods who walk around bemoanin' everything and lookin' like they just buried their brother."

"What?" he asked with disbelief.

Merry shrugged. "Deny it if ye will, but 'tis the truth. The English haven't a clue how to have a good time or enjoy life."

"Ha!" he barked with a laugh. "That sounds more like the Scots to me. They are the ones who are sour-faced, dour, and forever bemoaning. We English are *renowned* for our sense of humor."

"In yer own minds, mayhap, but then the world kens ye're all mad as well as dour," she said with a sniff, and raised her nose in the air in a superior attitude that was difficult to maintain when his jaw dropped at her sally.

"Why you—" he began, but stopped as Gerhard suddenly appeared on the lane before them.

"I found a spot not far ahead," the soldier said by way of greeting as they reached him. " 'Tis along the river and large enough for our party."

"Good." Alex nodded. "Lead on."

He waited until Gerhard had turned to lead the way to the spot he'd found before glancing down at Merry to say, "I shall punish you for insulting my countrymen later, wife."

The sparkle in his eyes and promise in his voice sent a little shiver down Merry's back. The man wasn't talking about spanking her bare bottom. Their mock argument had been all teasing, and while he promised punishment and it might include bare bottoms, she knew it would be a "punishment" that left her satisfied and smiling.

They soon reached the spot Gerhard had found, and Alex dismounted and helped Merry down. After giving the area a quick appraisal, he nodded his approval and gave some orders, then took Merry's hand to lead her farther along the river in search of privacy. It was late afternoon and early yet, but the sky was overcast and threatening rain, so they were quick about their ablutions. The men were just finishing erecting the tent when they returned. While Alex helped the men finish all that needed doing, Merry immediately headed to the tent to help

Una arrange things inside for the night. She'd just reached the tent flap when the first bit of rain began to spit down.

Merry glanced back to see the men moving busily about, ignoring it. She grimaced, but ducked into the tent with a shrug. There was little anyone could do about rain. It fell when it fell, and they, like the birds and forest creatures, would just have to put up with it. She did spare a moment to feel bad for the men, though. The Stewart party had been plagued by rain twice on the journey to England from Scotland, but they'd had their greased plaids and had all bundled up in them against the weather. The Englishmen didn't have that, however. Fortunately, rain never fell very hard or lasted long in England. It was probably why it fell so frequently. This would pass soon enough, and then the men would merely have to contend with the damp, an ever-present issue here.

"You look lovely by candlelight."

Merry glanced up with surprise at her husband's words. They were inside the tent, a meal laid out before them. Despite the rain, the men had managed to catch some game. The moment the rain had stopped they'd built a fire to roast it. However, when Merry had gone out to join them by the fire for the meal, Alex had pointed out that it looked as if it might rain yet again and suggested they should eat in the tent. She had agreed at once. Now they sat on a fur next to their bed of furs; roast meat, cheese, bread, and wine laid out between them.

"Thank ye," she murmured, noting the way shadow and light danced across his face. Candlelight was common at the castle, but normally there were also a fire and torches about, helping to chase back the night. Here there were just the two small candles she'd placed on the chest next to them to fight it off, and darkness was dancing with light, threatening to overwhelm it. It softened his features and added a glow to everything, and she would have liked to see him naked in this light, to watch the way the light would dance across his bare flesh, but knew that wasn't likely despite his promise earlier. After the wounds he'd taken last night, he would still be sore and wanting time to heal before indulging in anything as energetic as what her mind was thinking of.

"Why the frown?"

Merry glanced guiltily to her husband, but didn't tell him where her naughty mind had led her. Instead, she said, "I was just thinking of the incident in the clearing yesterday."

That brought a slight frown to Alex's face as well, and she added quickly, "I didna get the chance to ask ye if ye saw who pushed the boulder off the cliff."

"Oh." He shrugged and took a drink of his wine before muttering, "Nay. All I saw was the boulder plummeting toward me. I tried to get out of the way, but . . ." Alex grimaced at the remembered failure.

Merry stared at him silently, her teeth nibbling thoughtfully at her lips. She wished she'd got a better look at the person. She had no idea why, it probably had just been a bandit who had happened on them, but . . .

"Eat," Alex said suddenly.

Merry hesitated, but then let the matter go for

now. She popped a bit of bread in her mouth and chewed it, her gaze shifting to her husband and eyebrows rising as she noted that while he'd ordered her to eat, he himself was not eating.

"Are ye no' hungry?" she asked curiously once she'd chewed and swallowed her cheese.

"Aye, but my hunger can wait until after we eat," he said with a slow grin.

Merry's eyes widened, and she felt a flush of color claim her cheeks. So much for her thinking his arm and head must be paining him. Her gaze dropped, and she noted the bulge pressing insistently against the cloth between his crossed legs. His arm and shoulder might be paining him, but it didn't appear to affect his other parts. She swallowed the meat in her mouth and then quickly reached for her wine, downing some to help carry the meat down her suddenly dry throat as she contemplated the night ahead.

Her contemplations were interrupted when a loud throat clearing drew her gaze to the tent flap.

"Come," Alex barked.

He and Merry both then swiveled curiously to peer toward the tent flap as it lifted outward to reveal Gerhard. The soldier's gaze shifted briefly around the tent and then landed on Alex before he announced, "Allan says there is a problem with the mare."

"Beauty?" Merry asked with alarm, on her feet at once.

"Stay here and finish your meal," Alex said soothingly, getting up beside her. "I shall check on her for you."

Merry snorted at the very suggestion. Beauty was her baby. She'd been there in the stables when the mare had kicked her way out of her mother and into this world. It had been a difficult birth for both foal and mother and there had been some question as to whether either would survive. Having just lost her mother, Merry hadn't been willing to accept such news from the stable master and had gone down to the stables to help fight for both horses. When it had turned out the foal survived and was a female, Merry had claimed her for her own. She'd nursed her to strength, trained her, and hadn't gone anywhere without the animal since she'd aged enough to be a proper mount. If the mare was ailing, she would be there to nurse her through it again.

Alex merely shook his head at her determination as she moved toward the tent flap and then followed her out. They were halfway across the damp campsite when one of the men by the fire hailed Gerhard.

"Go ahead," Alex suggested. "Allan can tell us what is wrong."

"Allan went to . . . er . . . for a walk in the woods," Gerhard finished with a grimace, and Merry shook her head at the men's discomfit with simply admitting a fellow needed to relieve himself. She knew it wasn't considered polite talk in front of ladies, but her own father and brothers had never troubled themselves to watch their speech in front of her and it did seem silly getting so discomfited by a natural function. Forcing himself past the moment, Gerhard added, "You should be able to see the problem for yourself, however. She has a small cut just here."

He gestured toward his own shoulder. "'Tis not infected, but Allan wanted permission to put a salve on it to prevent the possibility of one settling in."

Alex nodded. "We shall find it."

Nodding, Gerhard turned away to move toward the fire, and Merry and Alex continued on to where the horses were gathered together at the end of the clearing.

As Gerhard had said, Beauty wasn't exactly ailing. She merely had a small cut on her withers on her right side. It was so small in fact that Merry and Alex had trouble finding it. Merry frowned when they did finally spot it. It was small, straight, and very thin. One could almost think it was from a blade rather than a branch as it must have been. She was actually amazed that Allan had seen it, but was grateful at the same time. Animals were as prone to infection as people, and the injury had to be tended to prevent it.

"Some salve ought to do the trick," Alex murmured as they peered at the injury.

"Aye," Merry agreed, running a soothing hand along her mare's side. "But I'd rather use me own. I'll fetch me medicinals and be right back."

"You shall return to the tent and find your salve and then wait for Godfrey to come fetch it from you," Alex countered firmly.

"But—"

"But nothing," Alex interrupted firmly. "'Tis starting to rain again and I'll not have you catching a chill. Allan can apply the salve as well as you. Just send it back with Godfrey."

Merry made an irritated face, but turned to head

back to the tent. She'd rather apply the salve herself, but it wasn't worth arguing over. The very fact that Allan, the fellow in charge of the horses for this journey, had spotted the tiny injury suggested he was capable and caring of the animals' well-being. He could smear it on as well as she could. That didn't stop her from resenting her husband's ordering her about, however. What did was the fact that it grew out of his concern for her well-being. He hadn't just been ordering her about for ordering's sake, but was worried about her catching a chill in the rain, and she thought that was incredibly sweet. Merry wasn't used to others caring for her well-being. She was generally the one taking care of everyone else. It made for a nice change.

The moment she reached the tent, Merry moved to the chest to retrieve her small cloth bag of medicinals. She had measured out what she felt would be needed and was waiting a tad impatiently when Godfrey announced his arrival by coughing himself silly outside the tent flap. Worried by the deep, wet sound of the cough, Merry moved to the flap and flipped it up, but rather than hand the boy the salve, she dragged him inside.

"My lord sent me"—he paused to cough long and deep before finishing breathlessly—"for your salve."

Merry bent to pick up a candle to get a better look at him, her mouth compressing when she saw the lack of color to his face and the almost blue tinge to his lips. "Ye've caught a chill and now have a chest complaint."

Godfrey grimaced at her accusing tone, but

shrugged wearily. "I am fine, my lady. A little sleep and I shall be as right as rain."

"Oh, aye," she muttered dryly, and moved to reclaim her bag of medicinals, muttering, "And me husband was worried about *me*."

"What was that?" Godfrey asked, and then burst into another round of coughing.

Merry didn't bother answering, but chose several items from her bag and then glanced around briefly before bending to grab up the nearest mug of wine from the furs. She quickly mixed in a selection of herbs and plants and then handed it to the boy.

"Drink," she ordered firmly. "'Twill taste absolutely vile, but will help strengthen ye to fight this off."

Godfrey started to shake his head, paused to bend forward as he was wracked by another round of coughing, and then straightened and accepted the drink. He paused after barely a swallow and opened his mouth, but whatever protest he'd been about to make died on his lips as soon as he saw Merry's grimly determined expression.

Giving in, he used the finger and thumb of his free hand to plug his nose and then stoically drank the liquid down.

Merry relaxed and nodded her satisfaction once he was done and took the mug back. "Now settle yourself in the corner there and try to sleep."

"Oh, nay," he cried at once, backing toward the tent. "My lord sent me for salve for your mare. I—"

"I'll take him the salve," Merry argued at once, turning to set the mug down and pick up the bit of salve she'd laid out on a piece of cloth. "But ye shouldna be out in the rain ailing as ye are, and ye certainly canna sleep out there in it."

"Well I cannot sleep in here," he squawked as she straightened.

"Aye, ye can," she said firmly, and then took pity on his panic and said, "I will explain things to me husband and he shall agree. Jest—"

Merry came to an abrupt halt as Godfrey, his face squinched up with panic, suddenly snatched the salve from her and fled the tent.

"Well, hell," she muttered, moving to the flap to see him racing through the rain to the horses at the end of the camp. She wasn't at all used to being disobeyed and simply watched with a scowl as he hurried to where Alex stood talking to Allan. The moment the boy had his lord's attention, he appeared to babble a string of words. She saw her husband's eyebrows go up, and then he reached out to press the back of his hand to Godfrey's head. The concern that suddenly claimed his features made her relax somewhat.

Merry let the tent flap fall into place and moved back to the furs then. She was sure Alex would agree with her and insist the boy sleep in the tent with them. And once he marched Godfrey back here, she would give the lad hell for flouting her instruction and running off like that. No one at Stewart would have dared disobey her so, and she wasn't going to have it at d'Aumesbery. The smooth running and very safety of the castle and its people depended on respect for their lord and lady and obedience when they gave an order. Merry knew she was still considered a stranger and would have to earn the respect, but she wasn't waiting for the obedience.

She was pacing the tent, working herself into a bit of a lather as she silently practiced what she would say to the boy. Merry disliked reprimanding anyone, but especially anyone she liked, and she rather liked Godfrey. He seemed a good lad to her, well, except for this disobeying her business. Merry was glowering over that when the tent flap rustled, announcing someone's arrival. Hand tightening on the empty mug she still held, Merry turned expectantly, but her husband entered alone. "Where is Godfrey?"

"I sent him to sleep."

Merry scowled at this news. "I told him he was to sleep in here with—"

"I know. He told me," Alex assured her with a faint smile. "But he did not seem comfortable with the prospect so I ordered him to go sleep in the back of the wagon with Una."

Merry's expression cleared at once. She'd quite forgotten Una telling her that the men had taken the tarp that covered the goods during the day and arranged it over the back of the wagon so that she had something of a tent of her own. Without their tent and the chests in it, there should be enough room in the back of the wagon for both Una and Godfrey without the pair being uncomfortable.

Realizing that Alex was awaiting her comment, she nodded and murmured, "That was a good idea."

"He also confessed that he disobeyed you and rushed out to me after you had ordered him to lie down and sleep. I did not reprimand him," he said, and when Merry stiffened, added, "Your order countermanded mine."

When Merry didn't hide her confusion, he reminded her, "I sent him to retrieve the salve from
you. To obey you, he had to disobey me. To obey me,
he had to disobey you. He was in a bit of a spot."

"Oh, aye," Merry agreed as she realized the truth
of his words. "I suppose the wagon is just as good as
the tent. At least he is out of the rain."

"Aye," he agreed, and caught her hand to draw
her closer. "And not in here preventing me from
doing this."

Merry's eyes widened and then drooped closed as
he lowered his head and kissed her. The kiss started
out sweet and questing, but soon turned passionate, and as she let the empty mug slip from her fingers and reached up to help her husband strip their
clothes away, Merry thought that his arm and head
must not bother him as much as she'd feared . . . and
that it was indeed a good thing the lad wasn't in the
tent with them.

chapter

Nine

"Where diya want this?"

Merry straightened from laying out the last of the furs and glanced to Una. The maid had been snappy ever since rising that morning. Even finally crossing the border back into their homeland of Scotland hadn't brought her mood around, and Merry was getting tired of her surly behavior. Her gaze shifted to the small cloth bag the woman held.

"Just set it on the chest there, please, Una," Merry answered, keeping her voice even and mellow. Her mouth tightened, however, and irritation got the better of her when the woman turned and tossed it carelessly on the chest. She snapped shortly, "Be careful with those, Una. You know they hold my medicinals."

Una scowled at the mild reprimand, but moved to check on the contents of the bag, and Merry eyed her with exasperation. "What is the matter with you today? You have been growling and snapping ever since you got up this morning."

"I didna get a wink o' sleep last night."

Merry's eyebrows rose slightly at this claim. "Was the back of the wagon so hard? If so, mayhap ye should take a couple of these furs for this eve then?"

"Nay, it wasna me back that was bothering me but Godfrey's front," Una snarled. She set the bag back on the chest with a little plunk.

"Was he snoring?" Merry asked, trying to get to the bottom of the matter. "Or was it his coughing?"

"Nay, it wasna his coughing though he did a fair bit o' that, too," she said dryly.

Merry clucked with exasperation and propped her hands on her hips. "Well, spit it out, woman. Ye've been in a foul temper all day and I would ken why."

"Because I spent the first part o' the night fightin' off Godfrey rather than sleepin' and then when I finally got free o' the lad, I crawled under the wagon to try to sleep there, but couldna because 'twas damp and cold. O' course I'm testy."

Merry's hands dropped from her hips, her eyes going wide with amazement. "Fightin' off Godfrey?"

"Aye." Una scowled and then explained in a low

growl, "The little bastard was as randy as a goat. And he understood the word 'nay' about as well as one, too. If he were not so fou with drink I'd ha'e no' got away."

"What?" Merry asked with shock. "But he was ill last night, 'tis why Alex had him sleep in the wagon."

"He wasna so ill he couldna muster the sword between his legs and try to make himself a man." She paused and bit her lip and then admitted, "He's well built in that area, by the way. The boy carries a claymore between his legs as compared to most men's short sword. Though I damned near snapped it off last night."

Merry bit her lip at this news, but then shook her head. "I just— Godfrey seems so sweet. I canna understand—"

"Oh, I know." Una shook her head. "I couldna credit it, either, 'tis no' like him at all. The boy's as shy as a bird around me and every other female. And after I got thinking about it today, I wondered if he wasna out of his head with fever . . . Though he didna seem that hot to me," she said, and then offered, "It could have been a mild fever combined with the drink."

"The drink?" Merry asked with surprise.

"Aye. I could smell wine on him."

Merry shook her head. "I am sure the only drink Alex brought was a couple of bottles of wine. They were to be a gift for his sister, but he opened one last night and—" She stilled and then said, "I gave Godfrey a tonic mixed in wine last night. I didna ha'e anything else at the time. But 'twas only half a mug.

Surely that little bit of wine wouldna affect him in such a way?"

Una shrugged. "Something affected him. He was slurring his words and clumsy as an ox, but hard and wantin' despite all that." She grimaced. "He definitely wasna himself, that is certain."

Merry was frowning over this when one of the men came to tell them that sup was ready if they wished to join the others. She murmured a word of thanks and followed Una out of the tent, her mind taken up with Godfrey. It was hard to imagine the lad behaving so badly, but she was sure Una wouldn't lie about something like that. Merry just didn't know what to think.

Alex stood to greet her with a kiss on the cheek as she reached the fire. Merry managed a distracted smile, but her gaze was searching for the boy who was on her mind. "Where is Godfrey?"

"I sent him to lie down in the wagon when we stopped. He seems worse today than he was yesterday and needs his sleep."

Merry noted the concern on her husband's face and knew the boy must be feeling poorly. She hesitated briefly and then said, "Mayhap I should check on him."

"After you eat," Alex said firmly. "I want you to take care of yourself so that you do not fall ill, too."

Merry nodded and settled to sit beside her husband. Had Una not just finished telling her what the boy had got up to last night, she might have insisted on going to check on him before she ate, but now . . . Well, frankly, she was a bit uncomfortable and embarrassed for the lad and unsure what she would say to him.

The meal seemed to pass quickly. Once done, she excused herself to go look in on the boy. She was desperately hoping that the lad would be sound asleep and there would be no need for her to take him to task for his reported behavior. She would have to talk to him eventually, but wasn't looking forward to the task and wouldn't mind putting off the chore. However, when she peered into the tarp to find that Godfrey wasn't asleep there, she was more concerned than relieved. Merry turned back to glance toward the men around the fire, and then she stilled and looked back to the wagon as a soft cough sounded behind her. Still the wagon was empty.

Merry was about to turn away again when there was another cough. This time she recognized that the sound came not from the wagon itself, but from under it. She knelt at once, her eyebrows flying up when she saw Godfrey all curled up under the cart, shivering in a thin blanket.

"Godfrey, what are ye doin' under there?" she asked with dismay. "Ye canna sleep on the damp ground, ye'll jest make yerself more ill."

A small grunt emitted from the depth of the blanket, and then Godfrey unbundled enough to peer out at her. Merry saw the shame on his face and felt sympathy slide through her before he'd even spoken. He looked as if he'd got caught doing something terribly naughty and was embarrassed by it.

"I am fine here, my lady," he assured her, and her concern deepened at the sound of his voice. The boy generally had a pleasant voice, but at the moment, it was a bare growl that spoke of a throat so sore he was like to lose the ability to speak altogether soon. "The wagon shall keep the rain off of me and—"

"That willna do, Godfrey," she said solemnly. "Ye must come out o' there and get in the wagon. Ye need to tend to yer cold ere it tends to you."

A moment of silence passed and then Godfrey whispered, "I cannot."

"Ye canna what?" she asked, and then, concern claiming her, crouched to crawl under the wagon with him. Feeling his forehead, she noted the heat pouring off his head and asked, "Are ye too weak to move? Shall I call for one o' the men to—"

"Nay, my lady," he said quickly. "I could not possibly sleep in the wagon tonight. Una would surely kill me in my sleep for my behavior last night."

Merry hesitated, but then, despite already having heard it from Una, asked, "And what did ye do last night?"

"I . . ." He paused, and even from that distance and in the dimness cast by the shadow of the wagon she saw him swallow unhappily before he gathered himself together enough to say, "I only vaguely recollect it, but I fear I may have tried to force her to . . ." The words died, and he bowed his head in shame and merely shook his head, unable even to speak the words aloud.

Merry bit her lip at the dejected and self-disgusted air about the boy and then quietly asked, "What were ye thinkin', lad?"

"I was not thinking at all," he admitted on an unhappy sigh. "Else I never would have . . . Truly, my lady. I do not know what came over me. I just—" He shook his head helplessly and then fell silent, misery plain on his face.

Merry tried to think of something to say to smooth the situation over, but truly, she was at a loss. And then Godfrey suddenly glanced up to say, "Would you tell Una how sorry I am? Truly, I would never have treated her so had I been in my right mind."

Merry hesitated, tempted to take the burden from him, but then said, "I think 'twould be better did you tell her yourself."

Panic immediately wreathed his face, and he shook his head a bit wildly. "She must hate the very sight of me now."

Merry felt her heart melt with sympathy and said, "Nay. She kens ye were ill and will most like accept yer apology."

"Aye, I will," Una said, and they both glanced to the side to see the maid crouched beside the wagon. It seemed obvious she'd been there awhile.

"I saw ye head ower here to talk to the boy and thought I'd best make sure ye were all right," her maid explained. "If the lad was out of his head again and foolish enough to attack ye, the laird would surely break his scrawny neck."

"Una, I am so sorry—" Godfrey began earnestly, but the maid waved him to silence.

"I heard everythin'. And I'll forgive ye this time. Ye may even sleep in the wagon tonight, but ye'd best nay try anything or ye're like to lose that claymore ye keep hidden in yer braies."

Godfrey flushed with embarrassment, and Merry bit her lip to keep from laughing. It was hard to imagine he'd attacked Una as he had when he could not even discuss the act or handle references to his body parts without acting like the embarrassed virgin he probably was. The whole thing was just beyond understanding really. She'd have bet her life that Godfrey was the last male in her husband's ranks who would have attacked a woman. This just didn't make sense. Obviously, Una was of the same mind, else she'd have not been so forgiving.

"Come along," Merry said. "Let us get ye off this damp earth and in the wagon."

"Aye, my lady," he whispered, and unrolled to crawl out from under the wagon, dragging his tattered blanket with him.

Merry bit her lip at the sad state of the article as he straightened next to the wagon and then glanced to Una. Before she could speak, the woman assured her, "There are furs and a couple of blankets in the wagon. He will be fine."

Merry nodded, but then asked, "Are ye sure? Ye could sleep in the tent with Alex and me if ye—"

"Oh, aye, he'd like that," Una interrupted dryly even as Godfrey groaned his mortification. She spared him a glance and then shook her head. "Nay, he seems fine. His eyes are clear and he isna slurring like he was last night."

Merry raised her eyebrows, but before she could comment or ask about the clear-eyed business, she noted Alex moving toward her and narrowed her eyes at the slight stagger to his step.

Una followed her gaze and commented dryly, "Yer husband, on the other hand, doesna look clear-eyed at all. Ye'd best get him to his bed ere he falls over and sleeps where he stands."

Merry's gaze instinctively lifted to Alex's face then and she stilled as she saw that there *was* something odd about his eyes. It looked more to her as if the blacks of his eyes had grown to take up most of the space, so that the blue was just a thin line around it.

"Husband," she began with concern, but that was as far as she got. The rest of her words were lost in a gasp as he reached her and suddenly scooped her up into his arms. Merry grabbed at his shoulders, afraid she'd be dropped or that they'd fall before she was safely back on the ground. Her husband wasn't exactly steady on his feet at the moment.

Her gaze shifted over his eyes as he walked, and she again found her concern growing as she took in the way the black had overtaken the clear bright blue of his eyes. For the first three weeks of their marriage, Merry had pretty much avoided looking straight at her husband. Instead, she'd mostly watched him out of the corner of her eye, looking for signs of drunkenness; his missing something he reached for, or stumbling in his step. Now she wished she'd looked at his face more, specifically his eyes, so that she would know if this strange dilation of the black centers had ever occurred during the day when he always appeared sober, or if it only coincided with each time he'd appeared drunk to her. It was an important point. Alcohol did not cause this reaction, and she didn't know of an illness that did, either, but Merry did know that some herbs and tonics could cause it.

Alex bent slightly to carry her into the tent, and suddenly overbalanced and careened forward, stumbling several steps.

Merry groaned and squeezed her eyes closed, sure she was in for it, for she was the one who would hit the ground first with his weight crushing her afterward. However, Alex managed to regain his footing after several steps, and she released a small breath of relief and opened her eyes once more as he carried her to the bed of furs.

Much to her relief, he set her on her feet then. Merry immediately turned to face him. She was eager to find out just how he was feeling and try to sort out what had caused the dark of his eyes to grow and might have brought about the symptoms she until now had thought were signs of drunkenness. But she'd barely opened her mouth to ask her first question when his lips covered hers. She tried to turn her head away, but he would not be denied and his mouth stayed fastened to hers like a leech, his tongue slipping out to anchor it.

Merry raised her hands to his chest to try to end the kiss and ask her questions, but it was like trying to move a mountain. There was absolutely no give under the pressure she exerted, and then she became aware that while he was unmoving, his hands were not. They first cupped her bottom through the skirt of her dress, raising her up to press against the demanding hardness between his legs as he kissed her. Holding her in place with one hand, he then moved the other to first one breast and then the other, squeezing and kneading eagerly through the cloth of her gown. In the next moment, Alex had eased her back to the ground and was tugging at her dress, impatient to remove the obstruction.

Merry found it all rather overwhelming. Almost frightening. His tongue filled her mouth so completely, she feared she might choke on it, and his behavior was more of an all-out attack than the sensual assault she was used to from him.

Apparently frustrated by the trouble her gown was giving him, Alex finally tore his mouth from hers to get a look at the matter, and Merry sucked in some much needed air. She then caught at his hands and gasped, "Husband, please."

Her plea fell on deaf ears. Alex didn't even acknowledge it, and her fear turned to anger as a ripping sound filled the air and her gown dropped away, leaving her in only her chemise. Merry didn't even think about what she was doing, she just suddenly balled up her fist and plowed it into her husband's face.

That got his attention, and he turned a shocked face to meet her gaze. Merry immediately noted that besides being dilated, his eyes were slightly glazed now.

"Alex?" she asked with concern, some of her anger dropping away. "What's wrong? What is happening?"

He gave his head a shake like someone trying to awake from a dream and then pulled her into his arms. "I need you Merry. Now."

"All right," she said soothingly, trying to ease the tight hold he had on her. Merry could hardly get air into her lungs he was squeezing her so close. She'd never seen him like this, she'd never seen anyone like this, but it seemed obvious to her that he was not himself. " 'Tis all right."

She was trying to soothe him, but Alex took that for permission though she didn't realize it until he growled, "Oh, thank God," by her ear and suddenly carried her down to the ground.

Merry stiffened in surprise and raised her hands to try to push him away again, but he was already gone, raising himself to kneel before her and begin tearing at his own clothes.

"Husband, ye need to stop and think," she said anxiously, sitting up on the furs. "Something is wrong. Ye're actin' like a madman."

"Aye," he growled, tearing his tunic off over his head and tossing it aside. " 'Tis what you do to me. You are making me crazy."

"Nay," she said quickly as he began to work at the ties of his braies. "I think ye may have been given something. Ye're no' right in the head at the moment. Ye—"

Her words ended on a gasp as he got his braies untied, let them drop to his knees, and then suddenly pushed her back on the furs. In the next heartbeat, he'd fallen on her like a starving man on a feast. His mouth was on hers, silencing her again, and his hands were everywhere even as he tried to slide his leg between hers and force them apart. But knowing she wasn't ready for him and afraid he would hurt her, Merry fought him. She hooked her ankles around each other to keep her thighs tightly closed and twisted half onto her side beneath him so that, short of forcing her, he could not do what she wished.

Apparently, he wasn't so far gone he was willing to force her. After a brief struggle, Alex lifted his head, freeing her mouth again to say, "Please, Merry."

"I'm no' ready. Ye'll hurt me," she cried, desperate to get the words out before he renewed his attack.

Alex froze at once and raised himself up slightly to peer at her. Merry knew there was fear in her eyes and suspected that more than anything reached through whatever madness was claiming him. They were still for a moment, both panting slightly as they stared at each other, and then she saw Alex's mouth tighten. At first, she feared he was about to renew his assault, and he did, but not as she'd expected. He took a deep breath, held it briefly, and then let it out as his mouth descended again. This time, however, he had more control over himself. His mouth on hers was firm and demanding, but not desperate and overwhelming as it had been. Despite herself, Merry felt herself slowly respond, a warm tingling running the length of her body and gradually warming her.

The moment she relaxed a bit beneath him with relief at this new approach, Alex drew his mouth away and began to slide it across her cheek and down her neck. When he reached the neckline of her shift, he didn't pause but simply kept going, his lips traveling across the cloth until it found and closed over one nipple, suckling on it through the material until the chemise was damp.

"Oh," Merry breathed with surprise as his tongue moved the damp material across her nipple, sending excitement shivering through her. Her hands moved to cup his shoulders rather than push at them as he did this, and her eyes drifted closed only to pop open again at the sound of rending material. It wasn't until he suddenly lifted his head out of the way that she realized he'd caught her chemise by the hem and was tearing it up the center.

Knowing it was too late to save the under tunic now, Merry bit her lip on the protest that tried to get out and lay still as he finished the task and pushed the two halves aside. She now lay bared to his view. His gaze slid over her pale skin and then to her face. Alex took in her wary expression and then renewed his assault, but it was nothing like that first one. The possibility that he would hurt her had got through whatever madness had claimed him, and while he still appeared focused on one goal, that goal had changed slightly. His determination now all appeared to be on rousing her passions.

Despite the frightening start, it took very little effort for him to do that. Merry soon found herself moaning and writhing beneath the magic of his fingers and mouth. It was only moments later when he thrust himself into her, but she welcomed him with a cry that had nothing to do with fear or pain and everything to do with pleasure. Unfortunately, he'd barely sheathed himself inside her warm body when Alex went stiff and spilled his seed.

When he then collapsed on top of her with a groan, Merry's breath left her on a disappointed exhalation. It did seem incredibly unfair that he finally took the time to get her all wound up and then left her feeling . . .

Well, actually, she was frustrated, Merry acknowledged unhappily and wiggled beneath him, wishing he'd get off her so that she could breathe. Alex murmured something she didn't quite catch, and thrust his hips reflexively. She stilled at once as she realized that he was still hard, or hard again. She wasn't sure which, but didn't think it was normal. The night they'd consummated the wedding he'd recovered himself and taken her back to the realms of pleasure a good five or six times, but there had been some time between each recovery.

Merry immediately forgot her frustration and started thinking about his dilated eyes and the possibility of his having ingested something that was affecting him this way.

"Husband?" she whispered, trying to turn her head to see his face, but it was buried in her neck and not visible to her at the moment. Still, she asked, "Husband, did ye drink or eat anything unusual this eve?"

Alex remained still for a moment and then levered himself up on his arms, only to pause as the movement made him shift deeper inside her. The action sent a shaft of pleasure shooting through her, and— judging by the expression on his face—through him, too. Merry held her breath and merely stared up at him as the shock waves of pleasure shivered through her. Just as they began to ease, Alex withdrew slightly and thrust back into her again.

Merry had been about to repeat her question, but instead, a groan slid from her lips and she grabbed at his upper arms, holding on as her body instinctively arched into the move.

"Husband," she gasped, trying to keep her body still when it wanted nothing more than to wrap itself around him and urge him on. "We need to—"

"Aye," he growled, and thrust again, this time with more vigor.

"Oh God," Merry gasped, and couldn't keep her knees from rising on either side of his hips so that she could angle herself to accept him more deeply. "We need to—to talk about— Oh God," she whimpered as he drove in once more, this time angling himself so that he rubbed against the nub of her excitement with the action.

"Later," he growled, withdrawing enough to plunge forth again.

"Later," Merry agreed on a groan, giving up the battle. It would be all right, she assured herself as he shifted to his knees, caught her hips, and began to thrust himself into her with deep, steady thrusts that soon left her unable to talk at all. If he was suffering under the effects of a drug or tonic, it didn't appear to be hurting him really. At least not that she could tell. She could ask her questions later, Merry decided, clasping his hips and arching herself into him as her ability to think gave way altogether.

Alex eased away from Merry, trying not to disturb her any more than necessary. She might not be asleep, but he wouldn't be surprised if she was and didn't wish to wake her if that was the case. He'd kept her up all night with his needs, taking her again and again, collapsing with satisfaction and exhaustion, only to find himself unable to keep from reaching

for her once more. It had been like a madness, one
he'd barely had control of.

In fact, at first, he hadn't had control at all, Alex
admitted to himself unhappily. He could still recall
her struggles, hear her cry of "I'm no' ready. Ye'll
hurt me," and see the fear that had been on her face
then. It was that fear that had helped snap him back
to some semblance of sanity. It had been the only
thing to help him leash in the all-consuming need
that had driven him.

Alex had never in his life experienced such an
overwhelming hunger. He'd been mindless with
it until that point, his entire focus only on sinking
himself deep in her body and driving into her until
the need ravaging him had been eased. The fear on
her face, however, had helped him gain enough control to take at least a few moments to stir her passions, too. Alex had held out as long as he could, but
feared she'd been only mildly excited by the time
he'd claimed her. He, however, had exploded the
moment her moist heat had closed around him. It
hadn't been satisfying for either of them, though,
and what was worse, the moment she'd moved beneath him his hunger had reared again, returning
almost fully blown.

It wasn't natural, Alex thought now, his mouth
going flat. And, even worse, that unnatural hunger
had reared inside him again and again through the
night, giving neither of them rest . . . Until now, he
thought wearily as he shifted off the furs and began
to feel around for his clothes. Now, finally, as night
came to a close, his body had decided it had had

enough and would not trouble him again with needs neither he nor his poor wife had the energy to meet.

That was truly a relief, Alex decided, giving up on finding his clothes in the dark and moving across the tent floor on his knees until he bumped into the chest where he knew a candle and flint waited. With a little effort and a few soft curses he managed to light the candle. Alex then turned, his eyes searching out his wife. Merry lay crumpled among the furs where he'd set her, skin pale but for the bruises under her closed eyes. She looked completely and utterly spent, and he mentally kicked himself for using her so hard through the night.

Not that he hadn't given her pleasure; Alex knew he had, but he'd also been relentless and demanding.

Blowing out a breath, he forced his eyes away from Merry and began to look for his braies. All he really wanted to do was curl up beside his wife and sleep for a week to make up for the energy expended this night, but his body, once again, cared little for what he wanted. It wanted to be emptied, and he knew he wouldn't rest until he'd relieved himself.

Spotting his braies, Alex moved to collect and don them. He considered donning his tunic as well, but then decided to save the energy and left it to head out of the tent. His eyes slid over the dark camp as he moved around the tent, noting that everyone was still sound asleep and all appeared well.

Eager to get back to the tent, and, he hoped, manage at least a little bit of sleep before the sun rose, he was quick about his business. Alex had just finished and was tucking himself back into his braies when the snap of a twig behind him made him stiffen and start to turn. That start was all he managed before pain suddenly burst in his head. It was such an all-encompassing explosion of agony that he wasn't even aware of falling to the ground as unconsciousness claimed him.

Ten

Merry was exhausted, and every single muscle in her body ached. That was her first assessment of things when she woke up. Not that she was sure she'd slept. She'd closed her eyes briefly, too tired to move after the last time Alex had bedded her, but she'd been aware of him stirring and listened to the rustle of his moving about while she lay completely supine. It was possible she'd fallen asleep briefly to those sounds, but not very deeply, and the sudden silence in the tent was enough to stir her back to wakefulness.

Now she forced her eyes open and ignored their gritty, irritated state. For one moment Merry was actually relieved to find her husband gone. While he'd been insatiable on the night they'd consummated the wedding, at least then she'd managed to snatch bits of sleep between each bout, recovering a little before he'd woken her with passionate kisses and caresses. This night he'd offered her no quarter. Alex had spilled himself into her repeatedly. Each time he had, she'd thought she might now rest, only to have his hands and mouth begin to wander and stoke her fire once more.

Her husband had been so relentless Merry had actually begun to wonder if one might die from such a persistent pursuit of pleasure. And at one point, her heart pounding furiously and feeling faint, she'd worried that he was about to do just that and drive her to the point that her heart might give out. Fortunately, she'd survived, but knew she would pay today with exhaustion and sore muscles. She ached in places she'd never really thought there were muscles.

Slowly becoming aware of a need to relieve herself, Merry forced herself to sit up. It seemed she would not get any rest at all this night, for she had no doubt that was the reason for her husband's absence, too. There was little else he could be doing at this hour. However, if things continued as they had been going, she feared he would reach for her the moment he returned.

A low, self-mocking laugh slipped from her lips as she realized her thoughts suggested she hadn't enjoyed the night's endeavors. If she tried to claim that, it would be a bald-faced lie. She *had* enjoyed it. Immensely. But it had taught her that there truly could be too much of a good thing, and she was in desperate need of sleep and recovery time.

Merry forced herself to her feet, grimacing as some of her aches and pains intensified. She simply stood there, looking around. A candle flickered where it sat on the chest, and she vaguely recalled the sound of Alex cursing and muttering as he worked to light it moments ago. She was grateful for it as she peered at the ruined remains of her gown and chemise where they lay next to her husband's tunic.

The clothes she'd worn that day were as good as rags now, she thought with a grimace, and then glanced to the chest once more. Merry briefly considered going to the trouble of moving the candle and her medicinal bag to dig through the chest's contents for a fresh, intact gown, but it seemed like much too much effort at that point, so she bent to snatch up Alex's tunic instead and quickly tugged that on. It fell to her knees, not quite respectable, but covering all the important bits, so she decided it would do and made her way to the tent flap.

One glance outside brought an immediate scowl to her lips. The sky was already lightening with the approaching dawn. Whether her husband reached for her or not when he returned, she wasn't likely to get any sleep at all this night. Merry glanced around the camp itself at the thought of her husband. It was still rather dark. All she could make out were the shapes of sleeping men. There was no sign of anyone walking around as her husband would be. It simply reinforced her suspicion that he'd had a need to relieve himself, too.

Very aware of the skimpy nature of her present

dress, she slipped quickly from the cover of the tent. Her nose wrinkled at the feel of dew-damp grass beneath her bare feet as she hurried around the side, but she rushed on, eager to reach the privacy offered at the back of the tent. She came to an abrupt halt, however, when she stepped behind the tent and found it empty. Alex wasn't here.

Merry glanced back the way she'd come, wondering where he'd got himself to, but then shrugged the matter away. She really did have a desperate need to relieve herself. She would worry about him once she'd accomplished that, Merry soothed her conscience as she found a likely spot and set about the task. Of course, once she was tending the matter and it became less urgent, her thoughts returned to her husband.

Perhaps he'd gone to hunt up something to cook over the fire, for them to take to eat at the nooning hour, she thought, and then shook her head at the possibility. Nay. She was presently wearing his tunic, which meant he was dressed only in his braies. He would hardly go hunting in naught but his braies, she thought as she finished the task that had brought her out.

Then perhaps he's gone down to the river to clean up, her mind offered. *Or perhaps—*

Merry's thoughts froze; indeed she, too, froze in the act of straightening as she became aware of a constant steady rustling coming from the woods to her left. The sound had been there when she'd first come back here, but she'd been so distracted with her body's needs she hadn't paid it much attention. Now that she was done and feeling better it sud-

denly came to the forefront of her mind, however,
and she peered in that direction, trying to sort out
what the sound could be.

It wasn't the usual crackle of undergrowth that
sounded the approach or fleeing of small wildlife,
but a steady, heavy rustle as if something weighty
was being dragged across the forest floor. Oddly
enough, the moment Merry had that thought, she
envisioned her unconscious husband being dragged
through the underbrush. And dragged away from
her since she was sure the sound had grown fainter
since her arrival and was continuing to do so now
with every passing heartbeat.

Merry tried to push that image away, but it was
stubborn and stuck with her until she finally could
not help but follow the sound to its source and reassure herself that it wasn't what her mind had suggested. She moved slowly at first, approaching the
woods behind and to the side of the tent with a bit
of caution. But when Merry reached the point where
the clearing ended and the underbrush began, she
found the waist-high weeds and grass pressed
almost flat as if something had indeed been dragged
over it. Her heart immediately leapt into her throat
and she began to move more swiftly.

Whatever it was she was following was moving
much more slowly than she, and Merry soon gained
ground, the sounds ahead of her growing louder. She
then found herself trying to move more carefully,
not wishing to make too much noise and announce
her approach. If what she was following truly was
her husband being dragged through the woods, she
doubted it would be good to run right into his at-

tackers without at least some sort of plan. In fact, the closer she got to her quarry, the more Merry began to think that she should have gone and roused the men for help. What was she going to do if her husband was being dragged off by someone?

"Ye'll think of something," she muttered to herself and knew she would. Merry had always been a bright girl. In fact, her mind was the one thing about herself she did have great faith in. Still, she set her mind to coming up with that something as she continued forward. She was so distracted with considering and discarding idea after idea that she did actually literally stumble upon the attackers, or at least upon her husband. She knew she was close, but it was only when she tripped on his feet and stumbled forward to crash down across his legs that Merry realized just how close.

"Husband?" she gasped with surprise.

A soft curse sounded over her head and then the man or men dragging him immediately released their hold on his hands and began to crash away through the woods. Merry pushed herself up off her husband to glance after them, but she was too slow and it was too dark in the woods. All she could make out were the dark shapes of trees and bushes surrounding them. Whoever had been dragging her husband away from camp had disappeared.

A groan from Alex drew her gaze back to her husband, and Merry shifted next to him again, finding his head by feel in the dark.

"Husband?" she whispered, running her fingers gently over his face and hair until a groan of pain and the feel of something warm and sticky made her stop.

"Blood," Merry muttered unhappily, wishing she had a candle or torch and could better see the wound.

"Merry?" Alex growled, his voice sounding alarmingly weak to her.

"Aye. Can ye stand?" she asked. Getting him back to the safety of camp was her main concern. Her arrival had obviously startled and scared off his attackers, but they could always come back, and might very well do so did they realize she was by herself. Besides, Merry could not take care of his head wound in the dark. She wanted to get him back to the safety of the tent as well as the candlelight it offered so that she could tend his injury.

"Stand?" Alex echoed, and concern rose up in her at the vague sound to his voice.

"Aye," Merry said grimly, and hooked her arm under his to help him sit up. "Come. We ha'e to get back to the tent, husband."

"Aye, the tent," he muttered, and with her help managed to get to his feet, but Merry was taking most of his weight and it was hard work. She could tell he wouldn't be able to stay on his feet long and just hoped it would be long enough.

There were several times Alex stumbled and Merry was positive they would fall and she wouldn't be able to get him back up, but they did make it in the end.

The candle was still burning brightly when they staggered into the tent. Merry was a bit breathless and her arm and leg muscles were trembling from the night's activities as they staggered to the bed of furs.

"Here," she said breathlessly, pausing beside the pallet. "Lie down and—"

Her words died on a murmur of concern as Alex just suddenly collapsed. It seemed obvious that determination alone had got him back here and he didn't have a lick of energy left. Merry wasn't surprised. She was done in herself and wouldn't have minded collapsing as well, but couldn't afford the luxury.

Fortunately, Alex had dropped across the furs so that he lay on them diagonally. That was good enough for her. While she'd prefer he be on them properly, she wasn't going to force him to further exertion to get on the furs the right way and didn't have the energy to try to move him around herself.

Leaving him where he was, Merry moved to the chest to collect her bag of medicinals as well as the candle and then returned to kneel beside him so that she could examine his head wound. While there was blood, she was relieved to note that the injury itself didn't look too deep or damaging. It was the second injury he'd taken to his head in a matter of days, however, so her relief wasn't complete.

Merry quickly tended the injury, cleaning it up and then placing a bit of clean cloth over it to act as a temporary bandage. She then sat back and simply peered at her husband. He appeared to be either sleeping or unconscious. Since he hadn't made a sound while she'd cleaned the head wound, she suspected he was unconscious, but did give his arm a little shake and whisper his name in the hopes of stirring him if he was only sleeping. She needed to know exactly what had happened and if he'd seen who had attacked him.

Unfortunately, her efforts were for naught, he was definitely unconscious.

She sat back on her haunches and merely stared at him, her mind now running through the different strands of information floating about inside her head. There were now three things to consider. Her husband had been attacked tonight and dragged away. Where his attacker was dragging him to and why was unknown, but she doubted it had been for a good purpose.

And then there was the previous incident. It might have been another attempt to knock him out and drag him off as had apparently happened tonight, but it could have killed him.

But then there was the matter of his dilated eyes and drunklike symptoms tonight. He'd been drugged, she was sure of that, and suspected it wasn't the first time. Recalling all those nights that she'd thought him drunk since their marriage, she now suspected he had instead been drugged. Merry took a moment to feel guilty for thinking so poorly of the man, but then pushed that aside. She could feel her remorse and apologize to her husband for it later. Right now she needed to get to the bottom of things. She needed to figure out what he'd been given and why. There were several things she knew of that might have caused the dilated eyes, and several other things that might have had the same effect as alcohol and made him appear drunk, but there were probably a lot more that she didn't know of. It would help if she understood what the drug he'd been given had been meant to do. Obviously, it hadn't been meant to kill him, for surely after more than three weeks he would be dead from it? Yet the only symptom he'd displayed was the drunkenness. Well, that and he *had* been terribly randy tonight, she acknowledged.

Merry suspected that was a side effect of whatever drug or tonic he'd been given as well. It just hadn't been natural. Last night had felt completely different from their passionate moments at the waterfall and the night before in their tent. Then he'd been passionate and excited, but slow and gentle. Last night he'd been almost mad with need and had taken her repeatedly . . . as he had on the night before this trip, when they'd consummated their marriage. But even that night he hadn't been as desperate and almost frightening as this night. He'd been like a man possessed tonight.

But it made no sense that someone would drug her husband to make him want to bed her. And how did that tie in to these attacks when he was knocked out?

A throat clearing behind her made Merry pause and glance toward the tent flap. The sun had obviously risen, for she could make out the shadow of someone standing outside the flap, and now that she wasn't lost in her thoughts, she could hear movement and voices coming from outside. Everyone was up and probably wondering when they would set off, she realized.

Standing, she moved to the tent flap and pushed it out and up to find Gerhard standing outside.

"Oh good, I did not wish to wake you, but— Oh." He paused abruptly, the look of relief that had crossed his face when she'd first appeared switching to discomfort and even embarrassment as he glanced over her dress.

It was only then that Merry recalled that she was still wearing naught but Alex's tunic. She felt herself flush and instinctively let the flap fall back into place, hiding her. Whirling from the flap, she then rushed to her chest, shouting, "I'll be just a moment. Don't go away."

"Er . . . Aye, my lady." Gerhard's voice came muffled through the flap and then was followed by "Actually, I just wished to speak to Lord d'Aumesbery. Is he already up and about? He is not in the clearing. Did he perhaps go—"

"He's here," Merry interrupted as she threw open the lid of the chest and quickly dug out the first gown that came to hand.

"Here?" Gerhard asked, and she could hear the uncertainty in his voice, and knew he was wondering why her husband had not gone to the flap rather than she. Then he cleared his throat and said more loudly, "My lord? The men are all up and wondering if we should break camp. What shall I tell them?"

Merry made a face, but merely dragged off her husband's tunic and swiftly pulled a chemise on over her head. The gown she'd grabbed followed quickly and she moved back toward the flap as she tugged it into place.

"My lord? Oh." Gerhard blinked and stepped back as Merry threw the flap up again. He opened his mouth to speak again, but whatever he said died on a startled gasp when she grabbed him by the arm and dragged him into the tent.

"My lady, what—?" The question died in his throat as she pulled him to the bed of furs and his eyes landed on Alex. "What in hell is going on?"

He was on his knees beside his lord at once, reaching to remove the cloth she'd covered Alex's head wound with.

"What happened?" Gerhard asked with dismay as he saw the bit of blood on the cloth. It was the only evidence there was. The new wound was barely visible through the thick strands of Alex's blond hair. "Is this from the other day? Did it open up again? What—?"

"Nay," Merry interrupted. "'Tis from last night. This morning really, I suppose. It happened only little more than an hour ago."

Gerhard turned hard eyes on her. "What did you do to him?"

"Me?" Her eyes widened with amazement, and she shook her head as she struggled with the anger that quickly followed. "I didna do this to him. Alex left the tent and I think someone hit him over the head and tried to drag him off. I stumbled upon them some distance away in the bushes and me appearance was enough to startle them off. He was semiconscious then and between the two o' us we managed to get him back here, but he blacked out soon as he hit the furs."

Much to her relief, he seemed to accept her word.

At least the accusation left his expression and he relaxed, and then muttered, "Damned Scottish bandits."

When Merry started to shake her head, he suddenly flushed, and said, "Sorry, my lady. 'Tis probably English bandits. We are still close to the border."

She clucked her tongue impatiently at the apology. She hadn't been offended at the accusation of Scottish bandits and there had been no need for him to apologize. "I doona think 'tis bandits at all. Not this time and not last time."

"Last time?" he asked with surprise, and then relaxed. "Oh, you mean the boulder by the waterfall. Alex said he thought 'twas probably an accident, or possibly a bandit thinking he'd found an easy target, but he saw no one near the boulder."

Merry clucked with impatience. "Well, I did see someone up there and I am sure 'twas no accident."

"Who did you see?" Gerhard asked at once.

She scowled at the question. "I am no' sure."

"Was it a Scot or Englishmen? The clothing should have told you that much," he pointed out.

"I doona ken," she admitted unhappily. "I just caught a glimpse of a figure moving away. But I did hear a grinding sound before I saw the boulder falling toward Alex. So did he. 'Tis what saved his life. It made him look up, see the boulder coming, and try to get out of the way, else it would ha'e hit him flat on the head."

Gerhard glanced to Alex at this news and admitted, "He did not mention that to me and so I thought—"

When he cut himself off sharply, she glowered and said, "So you thought I was just a panicky female. Well, this morning's events should prove otherwise." Merry was silent for a moment and then added, "It also makes me doubt 'twas just a bandit."

Gerhard raised an eyebrow in question and she gestured to Alex.

"The man is wearing naught but his braies. There's nothing to rob him of, and why would a bandit be draggin' him off through the woods?"

The soldier glanced back to Alex, his brow knitted with concern. "If what you said is true and the first time was not an accident, either, then—"

"There is more," Merry said before he could continue.

"More?" he asked with alarm.

"Aye." Merry peered down at her husband and then admitted, "I think someone's been dosing him with something."

"Dosing him?" Gerhard squawked. "What—?"

"Surely ye noticed that he was not well most nights back at d'Aumesbery. He was clumsy and slurring his words and so on?"

"Aye. He even complained of it to me. He thought mayhap someone was dosing him then," Gerhard admitted, and added reluctantly, "At the time I suspected you."

"Me?" Merry asked with surprise.

"You did not seem overly happy with your marriage," he said apologetically, and then quickly added, "But he drank nothing two nights in a row yet had the same symptoms, and we both decided he must simply be fighting off what the men had."

"Aye, he said as much to me the night before we left on this journey," Merry said slowly, and then added, "But he hasna shown the same symptoms again until last night." She paused, considering the matter, and then added, "Though the first night he was unconscious from the falling boulder. Last night he wasna hisself at all. He was slurring and stumbling again and was like a man possessed. The man gave me no rest. He—" She cut herself off and flushed, unwilling to explain how he'd been insatiable.

Gerhard looked curious, but merely asked, "And what of the night between? The night we had rain?"

"Oh, nay, he was fine then." She waved the question away and then added dryly, "'Twas Godfrey acting the drunken fool that night."

"Little Godfrey?" Gerhard asked with dismay.

"He was ailing and Alex had him sleep in the wagon, and apparently he kept Una up all night trying to . . ." Merry paused again as she thought on the matter. Godfrey had attacked Una, something completely out of character. The maid had also said she'd been sure he was drunk. Was that just because he'd reeked of wine when he'd tried to kiss her, or had he been clumsy and slurring like Alex? She had commented on his being clear-eyed last night while Alex was not.

"I need to talk to Una," she said abruptly, and turned away, only to pause and peer at Alex with concern.

"I will sit with him until you return," Gerhard assured her.

Merry nodded. "I'll no' be more than a moment." She continued on to the tent flap then, flipped it up, and started to step out, only to pause abruptly to keep from crashing into her maid. "Una. I was just coming to find ye."

"And I was a-comin' to see what was takin' so long. Are we ridin' today or no'?"

"I—" Merry bit her tongue on her answer that they most assuredly were not traveling that day when she realized Godfrey was only a step behind her.

"Allan sent me to fetch Gerhard," the boy said when he noted her attention on him. "He wishes to ask him something."

"I shall let him ken," Merry assured him, noting that he was looking bashful and avoiding even casting his eyes in Una's direction. He was obviously still embarrassed by his behavior the other night. There was nothing she could do about that, so Merry merely turned and peered into the tent to Gerhard. The man had heard, however, and was rising to approach.

"I shall return as soon as I can to finish our conversation. In the meantime, I shall set two men on the tent to guard Lord Alex," he said as he slipped past her.

Merry merely nodded and then caught both Una and Godfrey by an arm and tugged them into the tent with her.

"What—?" Godfrey began, his face flushing, but he paused, his expression stricken as his gaze fell on Alex. "Is Lord Alex sick?"

Merry pulled the flap down and turned to see the

lad hurrying to his lord's side, concern on his face. "Nay, he was attacked."

"Attacked?" Una echoed with dismay, moving closer to the bed of furs now herself. "By who?"

"That is what I am trying to figure out," Merry admitted, and then joined them by the bed. Her gaze slid over her husband's face, but he looked the same as he had since she'd got him here. Pale and still. She frowned at how vulnerable he appeared and then glanced to Una. "Ye said ye thought Godfrey was fou when he attacked ye in the wagon. Was it just because of the stink of wine?"

"What is fou?" Godfrey asked with confusion.

"Drunk," Merry answered, her gaze still on Una as she awaited her response.

"I was not drunk," Godfrey protested with affront. "At least I do not think I was. I had only had that half mug of wine you pressed on me, and that surely was not enough to—"

"Nay, 'twas not the stink of wine," Una answered, bringing the boy's protests to a halt. "Well, there was that, but it was mostly because he was slurring and clumsy and his eyes were all funny with the black almost takin' over the green o' his eyes." She shrugged. "I assumed he was drunk."

"I was not drunk," Godfrey snapped with irritation.

Merry ignored him for the moment and said, "Drink does not make the black of a person's eyes grow."

"It does yer husband's eyes when he's been drinking. His eyes looked like that every night since we arrived at d'Aumesbery," Una argued, and then admitted, "Though I ne'er noticed drink affecting yer father and brothers that way."

"Lord Alex is not a drunk," Godfrey said staunchly. "He was not drinking every night these last weeks."

"Oh, bollocks!" Una snapped. "He has been slurring and clumsy every night since we arrived at d'Aumesbery. He's as much a drunk as Laird Stewart and the boys."

"He is not," Godfrey insisted, chest puffing up like a rooster about to crow. "Lord d'Aumesbery is not a drunk and you cannot make me believe he has been drunk every night for all these weeks."

"Nay, he wasna," Merry agreed quietly.

"What?" Both Una and Godfrey asked with astonishment. Merry wasn't surprised by her maid's confusion, but the squire's surprise after defending his lord so staunchly made her smile wryly. It seemed, despite his firm defense, he hadn't been at all sure of his lord. She was happy to reassure him.

"Alcohol doesna make the eyes dilate like that," she said calmly.

"Then what does?" her maid asked.

"Some herbs and tonics will do it," Merry said, and then glanced to Godfrey and said, "I need ye to tell me exactly how ye were feeling when ye attacked Una and when it started."

"Oh . . . er . . ." The boy turned as red as a ripe apple and she knew he was embarrassed but she needed him to tell her.

"I'm no tryin' to embarrass ye, but 'tis important, Godfrey," she said solemnly.

He glanced down to the ground and then shook

his head. "I was just feeling poorly at first. Running hot and cold and coughing."

"Aye, 'tis why I gave ye the tonic," she reminded him.

He hesitated and then admitted almost reluctantly, " 'Twas not long after that that I started feeling a bit queer."

"All I gave ye was a tonic to help build yer strength," she assured him when suspicion quickly followed realization across his face. "But I suspect there was already something in the wine. We each had a little more than half a glass and Alex had only had a sip or so before the trouble with the mare came and you arrived at the tent with yer cold. I grabbed one of the mugs to mix yer tonic and only later realized it was my husband's."

"You think His Lordship's wine was drugged that night and I drank it?" Godfrey asked with dismay.

"Aye. Now, tell me what ye mean by ye felt queer? And how long after ye drank me tonic?"

Godfrey hesitated, obviously wanting to question her further on this drugged wine business, but then glanced to Una and away before clearing his throat and saying, "Well, I guess it started after I was in the wagon. Una was not there yet, and despite how poorly I felt I could not sleep. Ere that I feared I might drop off to sleep on my feet, but by the time I climbed in the wagon I was wide awake and wanting to move about. I knew you and my lord would be angry did I do so, so I just lay there, trying to sleep, but—"

"But?" she prompted.

"Well, I noticed that everything sort of seemed

blurred," he said, obviously struggling to explain. "I was staring out at the campfire and the men moving about and 'twas like I was looking through a veil at everything." He grimaced at the memory and then added, "And I was hot. Unbearably hot, I wanted to tear my clothes off to get relief, and then I . . ."

"Aye, go on," Merry prompted.

Godfrey groaned miserably and admitted, "My dragon woke up and wanted feeding . . . badly."

"Aye and 'tis a dragon too," Una said dryly. "Huge."

Rather than appear flattered at the comment, Godfrey looked like he wanted to sink through the floor of the tent. Merry gave the woman a silencing look, and patted the squire's arm encouragingly. "Go on."

The boy shrugged unhappily. "That is it. Once that started I could not seem to think of anything else but feeding the dragon. Una entered sometime after that and . . ." Godfrey shook his head. "All I could think of was gaining relief. Everything else, even Una's struggles, they did not seem as real as that. It was like they were being muffled by a veil." He turned to the maid with remorse. "I am sorry, Una. I do not know what was happening. I would never force myself on a woman like I tried to do with you. And yet I did."

"Aye, well . . ." She grimaced and shrugged. "If ye were drugged, 'twas hardly yer fault, and fortunately, ye're still a skinny lad and I'm bigger and stronger and managed to fend ye off. No harm done."

"How long did it last?" Merry asked.

Godfrey grimaced. "All night long. 'Twas near dawn ere the excitement eased enough that I could fall asleep and then 'twas from exhaustion."

"Aye," the maid said with remembered irritation. "I lay under the wagon listening to him rolling restlessly about until dawn. It made fer a miserable day o' noddin' in the wagon, I can tell ye."

Merry murmured sympathetically, but her mind was on her husband's behavior the night before. She couldn't ask him how he'd been feeling, but judging by his behavior he'd been suffering the same thing Godfrey had the other night after drinking his wine. And it, too, had appeared to wane near dawn. Although she couldn't say Alex might not have reached for her again on returning to the tent had he not been knocked out, she didn't think he would have. The last time he'd bedded her had been less urgent than ere that. Less driven.

She'd barely come to the conclusion that someone had indeed been dosing her husband with something since their wedding night when her mind began to niggle with difficulties to this theory.

"So, I gather ye're thinkin' yer husband wasna drunk all those nights, but dosed by someone?" Una asked, intruding on her thoughts.

"Aye," she admitted uncertainly.

"I hear a 'but,'" Una said curiously.

Merry shook her head unhappily. "Well, it would seem so. He had the slurring and clumsiness pretty much every night fer the last three weeks straight and yet claims he did not drink. And ye did say that ye noted his eyes dilated."

"But he didna bed ye those three weeks, either,"

the maid pointed out. Merry noted the way God-frey's eyebrows flew up at this news and grimaced, thinking that sometimes it was most inconvenient to have a maid living so closely and knowing so much.

"Aye, that is what I was just thinking. While he had the other symptoms, he didna attack me as Godfrey did you."

The maid glanced to the boy and shrugged, "Yer husband is a bigger man. Mayhap it has a lesser effect on him."

"Mayhap," Merry murmured. That could explain matters . . . except that last night he had acted much differently. And on the night they'd consummated the wedding, too, though that time while he'd reached for her again and again he'd not been nearly as aggressive as last night. He'd been more leisurely then and less driven and frightening than the man who had carried her into the tent and fallen on her with determination last night.

But who would want to dose her husband with something that would make him overactive in bed? Merry thought unhappily. In truth, it was some-thing a wife would do to a disinterested husband, and she had neither that problem nor the desire to dose him.

"What has this to do with His Lordship being attacked?" Godfrey asked suddenly, and Merry rubbed her forehead with her fingers as she recog-nized another flaw in her theory. If someone had dosed her husband with something that made him a ravenous lover, why would they then attack him and try to drag him off?

"I dinna ken," she admitted wearily. "I just thought surely the attacks and the dosing must be connected, but in truth, that makes little sense."

"None of it makes much sense," Una put in irritably. "Why would anyone wish to dose the man with something to make him an insatiable animal anyway? Are ye sure ye havena just mixed up yer herbs and accidentally made a tonic that—"

"The only time I have given me husband anything was the night he was felled by the boulder, and he was fine that night," Merry interrupted with a bit of snap to her voice.

"Aye," Godfrey said apologetically, and then added, "But you did mix me up that tonic and that is when I—"

"It must have been something already in the wine," Merry insisted. When Godfrey didn't look convinced, she threw up her hands with exasperation and moved to grab her medicinal bag. While Godfrey and Una watched, she opened it and sorted through the contents until she found the two herbs she'd used to mix up a tonic for him. Merry moved back to hold it out beneath his nose. "This is what I used on you."

"Ugh." Godfrey grimaced and backed away. "Aye. I recognize the stink and it tastes just as bad."

"Aye, well, this is what I gave ye, and both are only to help build yer blood to fight illness. Neither wid make ye attack Una," Merry said firmly.

Godfrey hesitated and then said, "Are you sure? I mean, mayhap you have simply mixed up two plants."

"I havena," she insisted impatiently, and then

added, "Besides, do ye no' think Alex wid ha'e noticed these in his ale did I put it in?"

"Oh, aye, definitely," Godfrey muttered with disgust.

"So now ye're sayin' he wasna drugged?" Una asked.

"I am sayin' he wasna drugged with this," Merry responded with exasperation.

"Aye, but would he not have tasted if his ale was off of a night?" Godfrey asked suddenly. "Surely he would have realized?"

"Not all tonics taste as bad as this. With some plants and herbs ye need so little he may no' ha'e noticed a difference," she said patiently, and wished she had a better grasp of herbs and could figure out what exactly had been used on him. Her mother had taught her what she would need to know, healing herbs. Her knowledge didn't go beyond that.

The rustle of the tent flap drew her gaze around to see that Gerhard had returned and was entering. Merry dumped her herbs back into the bag and closed it with a little jerk on the tie string.

"I have told the men we will be staying here until Alex recovers. I have also set two men to guard the tent and arranged for two more to relieve them during the night."

"That willna be necessary," Merry said quietly. "Ha'e the men start breaking camp. We'll leave as soon as 'tis done."

Gerhard wasn't the only one startled by this announcement. Both Una and Godfrey turned surprised glances her way as well.

"Twice now my husband has been knocked unconscious, and this night someone then tried to drag him off. I am not waiting for a third attempt where they might succeed in making off with him," Merry said before any of them could protest. "And I think 'tis better do we get him to Donnachaidh where the Devil can see to his well-being until we get this sorted out."

"But he cannot travel while unconscious. And I think 'twould be safer did we remain here and keep him guarded."

"What if one of his guards is the one behind this?" Merry asked, and the man stiffened as if she'd slapped him.

"None of Alex's men would attack him like this," he assured her staunchly. "He's well-loved by his people."

"And yet twice now he has been attacked," she pointed out.

"Then it must be a bandit or villain who is following our group," he said firmly. "None of our people would harm a hair on his head."

"It had to have been someone from d'Aumesbery," she said grimly. "Only someone from there could have been dosing him the three weeks before we left on this journey."

"Aye, well, that did not start until *you* arrived."

Una gasped in outrage at the words, but Merry reached out and caught her arm to warn her to silence. What the man said was true and she could not blame him for his suspicions. In fact, she could only think a healthy dose of suspicion on both their parts would be a good thing if it kept her husband alive while they sorted this out.

"Do ye trust Godfrey?" Merry asked suddenly.

Gerhard and Godfrey both looked startled at the question, but the man glanced to the boy and nodded slowly. "Aye. He's a good lad and looks up to Alex."

Merry nodded. "Then we will put Alex in the wagon with Godfrey to watch over him. I want no one near him without Godfrey present until this is settled. But we *will* travel on to Donnachaidh."

Gerhard was silent for a moment, and she knew he wanted to protest, but she was his lady now, in charge while Alex was incapacitated and could not give orders. He had to obey her. Finally, he nodded slowly. "So it shall be."

’T is Edda."

Merry tilted her head and peered at Evelinde Duncan. Alex's sister was tiny, blond, and lovely. She was also very upset at the moment and had been since the d'Aumesbery party had ridden into the Donnachaidh bailey with her unconscious brother in the wagon.

Merry had never had a sister before, but thought she might enjoy having Evelinde as one now that they were related by marriage. After only a half hour in her presence, she already liked her a great deal. The woman was warm, loving, intelligent, and welcoming. She also obviously loved her husband,

Cullen Duncan, better known as the Devil of Donnachaidh. And that Devil loved her in return. Neither of them was shy about showing their mutual affection.

However, Evelinde also obviously loved her brother, Alex, and appeared just as concerned as Merry by everything she'd learned since they'd seen Alex settled in a room above stairs with Godfrey.

"Aye," Evelinde said firmly. "Edda has to be the one behind all of this."

Merry noted both Una and Evelinde's own maid, Mildrede, nodding in agreement from where they sat a little along the table. Gerhard, and Cullen were there as well, and all of them were openly listening, but Merry didn't mind. It seemed to her that the more of them who were working on this problem, the better their chance of solving it. She considered the woman's words for a moment, but then merely said, "Edda warned me that ye hated her and with reason. She said she was terribly unhappy at d'Aumesbery and acted terrible to ye."

"Aye, she was," Evelinde said quietly. "Both to myself and the servants and people of d'Aumesbery."

Merry took in her expression and then changed the subject by saying, "Well, I wish I kenned what he's been being dosed with and why. I suspect that would shed some light on matters."

"Just a moment." Evelinde was suddenly on her feet and rushing for the kitchens.

Merry stared after her with surprise and then glanced to Cullen in question. The large man merely shrugged with indulgent amusement and picked up his ale. A bare moment after that, the kitchen door banged open and Evelinde rushed back, dragging an older woman behind her.

"This is Cullen's Aunt Biddy. Mine now, too," she added with an affectionate smile toward the woman as she urged her to sit at the table. Evelinde then sat down herself and turned to Merry to say, "Biddy is ever so smart. She may be able to sort out what Alex has been given."

"And then again, I may no'," Biddy inserted dryly. "But I'll do me best. First, tell me what makes ye think he's being dosed to begin with."

Merry nodded and quickly gave a brief summary of Alex's symptoms each night the last three weeks, and then told her how Godfrey had acted the night she'd mixed him a tonic in Alex's wine, as well as her husband's aggressive behavior the night after. When she finished, the older woman pursed her lips thoughtfully and stared off into space for a long time before shaking her head and saying, "I ken naught that'll cause all those symptoms. It must be a combination of two or three things. Something to increase his ardor, something to offset his self-control, and something else to boost his energy levels so he could . . . er . . . perform for such an extended period. And from what ye've said 'twas most like put in his ale at sup."

"Nay. At least not all the time," Merry said solemnly. "Alex suspected as much and apparently refrained from drinking anything at all for two nights in a row and yet suffered the same symptoms. Because of that he'd decided he was indeed fighting off an illness. 'Tis only when I used his wine to make Godfrey's tonic and he reacted so poorly that it became clear he was being dosed."

"That night it was in his wine?"

"It must ha'e been. 'Twas his wine I gave to Godfrey."

"But no' yours?"

"Nay," Merry said at once and then bit her lip.

"What is it?" Evelinde asked, leaning closer.

"Well, I had barely touched me wine ere Gerhard came to fetch us about me mare, and I didna get a chance to drink any when I got back." She shrugged helplessly.

"So the bottle may have been dosed," Evelinde said thoughtfully.

"That night, aye," she agreed. "But his drink could no ha'e been the culprit the two nights he refrained from drinking."

"Could it have been in his food? Or in a drink he consumed ere he sat to table?" Evelinde suggested and then asked, "Does he have an ale or mead on the practice field or at the inn ere the sup?"

"I doona ken," Merry admitted unhappily. In truth, she knew very little about her husband's habits and behavior . . . at least at home. They had spent a great deal of time together during the journey, but at d'Aumesbery, Merry had been busy getting used to her new home and people. While she knew Alex spent his days working hard, running his home and ruling his people, she had spent little time with him there and had no idea what he ate and drank away from the d'Aumesbery table.

Evelinde was frowning, but now nodded solemnly and suggested, "Mayhap 'twould be easier to figure out who is behind it than where or when."

Merry made a face at the suggestion. That did not seem the easier task to her. She had been at d'Aumesbery only three weeks and hardly knew the people. Well, other than her maid Una and Lady Edda, whom she'd spent a lot of time with. Keeping these concerns to herself, she asked, "And how are we to sort that out?"

Evelinde shrugged and asked, "Well, who benefited by his being dosed?"

"Well, I'm no' sure who would benefit from the accidents, but the only person who has been benefiting from the potion he's being dosed with is me," she said wryly, and then flushed as wicked grins covered every face at the table. Even Cullen Duncan was grinning, a twinkle in his eye. Merry ignored that and added, "But I didna dose him. And none o' this makes any sense. Why would anyone dose him like that and then try to kill him?"

"Well, he was injured not killed," Evelinde said slowly.

"Only by chance and his moving the first time," Merry pointed out grimly. "He very easily *could* have been killed. The boulder was huge and would have crushed his skull."

"But it did not," Evelinde pointed out quietly. "And his moving may have put him more in the way than he would have been had he stayed still. Mayhap they were hoping just to knock him out as they did later. Perhaps the intention has always been to kidnap him."

"Kidnap him?" Merry echoed dubiously.

"Aye." Evelinde appeared to be warming to the idea. "D'Aumesbery is wealthy. They may have planned to demand a rich purse in exchange for his safe return."

"Then why have they been dosing him?" Merry asked with bewilderment.

Evelinde bit her lip and then shook her head and suggested, "Are you sure the two are connected? Mayhap whoever dosed him was not behind the attacks."

Merry sighed unhappily at the suggestion. She had hoped with them all thinking on it, they might be able to sort out the matter, but it seemed to her they were no further ahead now than when they'd started talking.

"My lady!"

Merry stiffened and whirled on the bench at that strident shout. A panicked Godfrey stood at the top of the stairs, shouting his little heart out for her. The moment he saw he had her attention, he shrieked, "My lord is up. I told him you said he was to stay abed, but he will not listen."

She was on her feet, and rushing for the stairs at once.

Alex paused at the foot of the bed. His legs were shaking and threatening to give out, and he was so weak that his braies felt heavy as he lifted them off the chest at the end of the bed, but he rolled his eyes and muttered, "Tale carrier," as he heard Godfrey's shouts from the hall. The lad had tried to keep him abed himself, and—in truth—might have succeeded had he used more than words.

Alex grimaced with disgust at his weakness. He had no idea how long he'd been unconscious, but it must have been at least two days for them to have arrived at Donnachaidh, and that was where Godfrey had said they were. He'd apparently been unconscious the last part of the journey, carried in the back of a wagon with Godfrey next to him, his wife riding on one side of the wagon and Gerhard on the other. All three of them watching him like a hawk, Godfrey had said. The lad had also said Alex had started to stir shortly after noon on the first day and Merry had dosed him with something to make him sleep so that he wouldn't suffer during the journey. Gerhard had apparently protested, but as Lady d'Aumesbery, Merry was in charge when Alex was out of commission and she had prevailed, so he'd been dosed then, and several times afterward until they arrived.

He didn't know whether to thank or berate Merry for it. Alex didn't like the idea, but on the other hand, if his head was pounding as badly as this two days after the attack, he could only think he would have been suffering even worse these last two days had he been conscious. Still, he was awake now, and competent to make his own decisions, and he was getting up whether Godfrey got Merry up here to order him back to bed or not.

He was teetering on one leg and trying to get his other into the braies when Godfrey came rushing back into the room. Alex paused to send a glare the lad's way, and then gave up the task altogether to hold the braies in front of his groin as a herd of women followed a moment later. There were at least

five of them. Merry and his sister, Evelinde, were at
the head of the pack, but they were followed by both
their maids as well as another woman he didn't recognize. Alex stared at the small crowd askance and
thought they must have flown up the stairs to reach
the room so quickly.

It was the last thought he had a chance to think.
Alex was suddenly surrounded by women who
proceeded to peck and poke at him, plucking at his
braies, trying to get them away, tugging at his arm
to move him back toward the bed, and each of them
berating him at the same time in an incomprehensible babble that just made his head hurt worse.

Before he knew it, Alex found his hands empty
and his bare arse back in the bed as the five angry
women all fussed and tugged at the linens to cover
him up, still berating him for thinking himself
strong enough to be up and about.

It was deep male laughter from the door that
broke up the party. Alex glanced that way, hoping
for reinforcement, and froze as he took in the man
in the doorway. This could be none other than the
Devil of Donnachaidh. Alex had always thought
of himself as a good-sized man. He was usually
up to half a foot taller than those around him, but
this man was taller still, and he suspected a touch
wider as well. The top of Cullen Duncan's head
barely cleared the frame at the top of the door, and
he was wide enough to fill it from side to side with
little room left over. Despite his size, the man moved
with the grace of a panther, however, Alex noted as
Cullen Duncan eased into the room, his eyes taking
in the scene. Amusement still curved his lips, but

there was a serious look in his eyes that suggested it would be smart to obey as he surveyed the women and ordered, "Out."

Evelinde apparently was not intimidated by her husband. She scowled at the order and hurried to his side, saying, "But Cullen, we need to speak with Alex and find out what is going on."

Much to Alex's amazement, rather than becoming annoyed, the Devil's gaze softened as it settled on his wife and the man smiled and bent to press a kiss to her lips before straightening to say, "I will talk to him and get to the bottom of it."

"But—" Evelinde began, and fell silent when he raised a hand for silence.

"I let ye talk to yer new sister. Now let me talk to me new brother." When Evelinde hesitated and then cast a worried glance to Alex, he added, "And I'll make sure he stays abed."

His little sister relaxed and beamed at the great behemoth as if he'd just said the most clever thing in the world, Alex noted with amazement. She even then ushered the other women out of the room, including Merry, assuring her, "Cullen will sort it all out for us."

Alex watched the door close and then turned his gaze to his new brother-in-law. He peered at him silently, considering what he'd taken in in the last few moments, and then announced with some surprise, "She loves you."

"Aye." Cullen grinned widely, and then his expression became more solemn and he added soberly, "And I, her."

Alex merely nodded. The mutual love was obvious, and it seemed all his worry had been for naught. He smiled wryly and sat up to swing his feet off the bed, only to fall back with a grunt of surprise as Cullen quickly closed the distance between them and pushed him back flat.

"Keep yerself in that bed, else ye'll be wrestlin' with me," the Devil growled. He then smiled crookedly and added, "I did promise me wife, and I doona break me promises."

Alex considered the man and briefly toyed with the idea of making him keep him there, but then gave it up. Any other time he might do so just for the fun of it—and to see who would win—but there was no doubt who would win at the moment. He wasn't at his best and his head was a bit sore, so Alex nodded and then shifted around to sit up in the bed when the other man straightened.

"Good. As much as I enjoy a good battle, ye're in no condition to be much of a challenge." Cullen moved to grab one of the chairs by the fire. He placed it next to the bed and settled on it to peer at Alex.

Several moments of silence passed as the two men sized each other up, and then Cullen asked, "How was Tunis?"

"Hot and bloody," Alex said dryly and then smiled when the man laughed.

They shared a smile, and then Cullen said, "I gather ye've a bit o' trouble at d'Aumesbery. I can sympathize, we had a bit o' trouble when I first got yer sister here, too. I'm glad to say 'tis all tended now though," he assured him, and then asked, "So, diya want to hear what's been going on here, or tell me what's been goin' on with ye first?"

Alex was silent for a moment, thinking that it was a fair trade and he just might come to like this man, and then he suggested Cullen tell his troubles first. He listened silently as his new brother-in-law spoke of what had gone on when Evelinde had first arrived at Donnachaidh. The man didn't pull any punches or hold back anything, admitting to faults and his own blindness in some matters without mercy for himself. In fact, he was incredibly honest about all that had occurred, and Alex found his eyebrows flying up several times as the story progressed, and then lowering with concern. But then it was done, and it was his turn.

He could do no less than return the favor, and Alex was just as blunt and open about all that had occurred since Merry's arrival at d'Aumesbery. Cullen listened silently in return. When Alex got to the part about going outside to relieve himself and someone clubbing him over the head, that was where he fell silent. He didn't remember much after that; vague recollections of being dragged through the woods, Merry falling on him, her voice anxious, and then a pain-filled and nauseating trek back to the tent.

Cullen informed him of what Merry had told them, helping to fill in the holes, and then paused to rub his jaw thoughtfully before saying, " 'Tis no' yer wife dosin' ye."

"Nay, of course not," Alex said promptly, but was aware of a touch of relief sliding through him at the man's words.

Cullen merely smiled knowingly, and added, "Ye'd be forgiven fer thinking so since it only started after her arrival and since she's benefited from the dosing."

"Benefited?" Alex asked dryly.

"Well, some would think it a benefit to have a man chasin' after ye like a bull stud."

"Not if the bull was relentless and chased after you until you were both sore and aching," Alex said dryly.

"Mayhap no', but she's still no' the one behind it. She cares about ye."

"Does she?" Alex asked, and then felt his face flush as he heard the eagerness in his own voice. The idea that Merry might care for him was a pleasing one, and one he hadn't even dared hope for up until now. They had got off to such a bad start with her thinking him a drunk for so long . . .

"Aye, she does. I think she even loves ye, though she doesna ken it yet. Fer now, she's just at that mother bitch stage."

Alex stared at him blankly. "Mother bitch?"

"A bitch with a litter."

"Oh!" Alex relaxed. "You mean a dog."

"Aye. We call female dogs bitches," Cullen said, and then scowled as he added, "Ye're me dear wife's brother, I'd hardly be insultin' ye or yer wife with name callin'."

"Nay, of course not," Alex said with amusement because he suspected the man would insult anyone he pleased if he did not like him, though probably not in front of Evelinde if he thought it might upset her, but Evelinde wasn't here now to be upset. To change the subject, he asked, "So by mother bitch stage you mean she is protective of me?"

"Oh, aye, she is that," Cullen assured him, the smile returning to his face. "Stewart isna far from here and we've had occasion to meet ere this. Merry can be a right shrew when it comes to her father and brothers, but she's a good lass, and it's nothing less than they ask fer."

Alex nodded, he'd come to that conclusion rather quickly himself.

"But she wasna overprotective of them, mostly exasperated from what I could tell. But with you, she's showin' the same caring as she did with her ma. Maighread was a good woman and Merry loved her dearly. She was like a mama wolf around that woman, not lettin' anyone or anything bother her could she help it and tendin' her like a mother with a bairn rather than the other way around." He nodded and then said, "She's the same with you. Rode in here next to yer wagon, shoulders straight, a mean look in her eye, and her *sgian-dubh* at her waist where 'twas handy. Demanded to see me at once and didn't even bother with a greeting ere she asked me to see to it that ye were placed in a safe room with guards at the door and Godfrey at yer side until she could sort out who was tryin' to kill ye."

Alex's mouth softened as he imagined the scene.

"She had Evelinde all aflutter," Cullen added with a laugh and shake of the head and then said more seriously, "I didna like that too much. Evelinde's had enough to upset her recently, but what can ye do? Merry was lookin' out fer ye. She's a good woman."

"Aye, she is," Alex said with a smile. He certainly hoped Cullen was right and Merry did care for him. The more he got to know her, the more he was sure he could come to love his wife, and it would be painful not to have that love returned.

"So, ye need to figure out who wid want ye busy beddin' yer bride all night long," Cullen said suddenly. He thought for a minute and then asked, "Is there anything ye normally do o' a night that bedding yer bride has kept ye from?"

"Sleep," Alex said dryly.

"Then mayhap that's what 'tis. Keep ye tired and reduce yer concentration and ability to think so ye're an easy target. Although . . ." he added thoughtfully.

"What?" Alex asked.

"Well, Merry said whatever it is ye're given makes ye slur and stumble about like a drunk, too, and at first she even thought ye were like her brothers and father."

"Aye," Alex said with a grimace, and then blinked as he realized where the man's thoughts were headed. "And so mayhap whatever I have been ingesting is not meant to make me bed her so much as appear like her father and brothers and cause strife between us."

Cullen nodded. "She'd hardly welcome ye to her bed did she think ye little more than a drunk."

"And under the influence of this drug I might very well have forced her had I not felt so bad about what I'd thought happened on the wedding night."

Cullen raised an eyebrow. "She said the need didna appear to be there the first three weeks though the slurring and clumsiness were."

"Oh, aye, 'twas there," Alex assured him dryly, and then added thoughtfully, "Though 'twas not as bad as last night, or the last night we were together," he corrected himself as he realized at least two days must have passed since the night the need had ridden him so relentlessly. "I could control it the first three weeks. But this last time . . ." He paused briefly, but then decided the man had been honest with him and he owed him the same back and admitted, "Had she refused me, I fear I would have ignored her refusal. I was barely able to slow down when I realized I was scaring her and she was not ready to accept me."

Cullen nodded solemnly, and then pointed out, "Medicinals and drugs are often a woman's weapon."

Alex eyed him narrowly. "I thought you did not think Merry behind this?"

"Nay. I doona," he assured him. "But I wouldna put it past Edda. That woman is a viper."

Alex wouldn't have put it past his stepmother, either, but pointed out, "She is back at d'Aumesbery, so could not have dosed me on the journey."

"But mayhap she has enlisted one of yer men," he pointed out. "If so, he may ha'e got the dose wrong and given ye too much. It may be why ye reacted so strongly this last time."

"Mayhap," Alex allowed, though he didn't like the idea that one of his men might be behind this. "Why would Edda bother? Causing trouble between Merry and me merely makes for a battle zone for a home. 'Tis not as if we can dissolve the marriage. And if the attacks are connected to the dosing, then what are they about? I'd swear that boulder incident was an attempt to kill me. Had I not moved it would have landed on my head. But the second time they knocked me out and tried to drag me away. I had just regained consciousness and was preparing to struggle when Merry found and fell on me."

"Did ye see who had ye?" Cullen asked, leaning eagerly forward.

Alex grimaced. "Nay. I was conscious but just barely and hadn't yet gathered the strength to lift my head."

Cullen nodded. "Mayhap they really didna mean to kill ye the first time, or mayhap they were dragging ye away to try to make yer death look like an accident the second time."

"Aye," Alex said thoughtfully. Either was a possibility. "An accident might have been believed . . . Still, why? Merry would be widowed, but still hold the title, and the king would see her married as quickly as possible to place a man there to hold the castle. Edda would hardly benefit from that."

"What would happen if both o' ye died?" Cullen asked curiously. "Wid Edda gain d'Aumesbery?"

Alex stiffened at the very suggestion, and then relaxed and shook his head. "Nay. Evelinde would inherit and d'Aumesbery would be your problem."

Cullen grimaced at the idea. "I ha'e me hands full with Donnachaidh. Ye can keep d'Aumesbery."

"Thank you," Alex said dryly, but found a reluctant smile claiming his lips when the man laughed.

"Well, 'tis quite a puzzle," Cullen said unhappily and then added, "And it appears I'm goin' to disappoint me wife by no' bein' able to help ye solve it."

"Well, you tried," Alex said quietly. "And I appreciate it."

"Hmm." Cullen nodded. "And the women ha'e tried, too. Merry has been fretting o'er it with me wife below. The trouble is that the two things, the attacks and the dosin', doona appear to work toward the same end." He shook his head. "I'll continue to give it thought, but in the meantime, I advise ye to be careful, keep a guard with ye, and no' to drink anything unless ye're sure it hasna been tampered with."

"Aye," Alex agreed.

"Good, then ye'll keep yerself alive and me wife happy as well as yer own."

"Then we shall all be happy," Alex said dryly.

chapter

Twelve

Alex was absolutely miserable.

He closed his eyes and clutched his head against the pain that was being exacerbated by the arguing in the room. He finally covered his ears to block it out, but it helped little. His room had been full of people ever since Cullen and he had finished their talk. The Devil of Donnachaidh had left the room to speak to his wife, and the next thing Alex knew, Merry was there with Gerhard and Godfrey hard on her heels, and Evelinde; her maid, Mildrede; and Merry's maid, Una; as well as a woman introduced to him as Cullen's Aunt Biddy, not far behind.

It had been fine at first. The women had done most of the talking, and he'd actually enjoyed the light chatter and easy banter between his wife and sister. Gerhard and Godfrey had merely listened as Evelinde apprised Alex of all that had happened in the three years while he'd been away on crusade and of her life here at Donnachaidh. She was so obviously happy here that it warmed his heart. He'd also noted and enjoyed the easy affection she seemed to share with Aunt Biddy, though he wasn't surprised by it. The charm of the older woman and the twinkle in her eye as she'd told tales about life at Donnachaidh when Cullen was a boy made him quite like her.

Out of it all, however, the thing Alex had enjoyed the most was when Merry had opened up and told little anecdotes about her own childhood. It had helped him get to know her better, too, and the more he learned about his wife, the more he liked her.

When it was time to sup he tried to get up, but Alex found himself immediately pushed back into bed as Merry insisted she would bring him his meal there. She'd added that she would eat with him, and Evelinde suggested they would all eat above stairs. The next thing Alex knew, Cullen had joined them and maids were trooping in with trenchers piled high with food for one and all. The conversation continued to flow while they ate and then afterward . . . until a few moments ago when Merry caught him yawning and suggested it might be time for everyone to leave and let him rest.

Gerhard proposed that he remain and sleep on a pallet by the door to be sure Alex remained safe. The soldier's eyes had been fixed firmly on Merry and her maid when he'd said that. In the next moment, all hell had broken loose, with everyone talking at once and accusations and suspicions flying every which way.

Since covering his ears didn't help any, Alex wearily let his hands drop back to his lap and scowled at the people filling his room, as Gerhard said sarcastically, "Well, begging your pardon, my lady, but 'tis notable that the dosing and attacks did not start until after you and your maid arrived at d'Aumesbery."

"That *is* rather upsetting," Evelinde put in, biting her lip.

Merry turned a hurt expression to the woman. "Ye believe I would harm Alex, too?"

"Nay, of course not," his sister said quickly, and then added reluctantly, "But mayhap your maid, thinking you were married to a drunk and miserable—"

Merry brought her words to a halt with an irritated wave of the hand. "Oh, Una would never do that. Especially once she realized I was beginning to care for him."

"You care for me?" Alex asked, perking up on the bed.

Merry flushed, but scowled at him and murmured, "Hush."

"Still," Gerhard insisted, waving a finger at Merry. "The attacks did not start until after you arrived and *you* are the only one who would benefit from his death."

"Diya point that finger at me again, Gerhard, I'll surely snap it off," Merry said coldly. "Has it escaped yer notice that *I* am the one who dragged me husband's very heavy and unconscious body back from the waterfall? And what o' the other night when I scared off the one dragging him away and helped him stumble back to camp? I would hardly knock him out just to have to lug his huge, heavy body back."

"Mayhap you would, to steer the suspicion elsewhere when he is finally killed the next time," Gerhard snapped back, and then added, "And who would believe that a lady as little as you would scare off an attacker anyway? Why did he not just knock you out, too?"

"I have no idea," she said stiffly. "But I ken I didna harm Alex and never would. You on the other hand seem to be busy pointing the finger at me. Mayhap that is yer attempt to keep suspicion off yerself."

"Me?" Gerhard barked with disbelief. "Why the devil would I harm Alex? And I certainly would have no reason to dose him . . . unlike you."

"Oh, aye, but mayhap the dosin' was merely to point the guilty finger in me direction. As fer why ye'd harm him?" Her eyes narrowed. "I keep recallin' the day me family and I arrived at d'Aumesbery and ye had trouble introducing yerself. Ye hesitated and then just settled on referring to yerself as 'his man' and *that* a tad bitterly."

Alex glanced to Gerhard with surprise. "You are my first, Gerhard. Why would you even hesitate to say so?"

The soldier looked uncomfortable and then grimaced and admitted, "I was not sure I still was your first."

"What?" Alex asked with amazement.

"Well," he said a bit bitterly, "as your first, I should have been the one left behind to tend to d'Aumesbery while you were away on this journey, so when you trained someone else to run the keep while away and brought me along on this trip, I thought mayhap you felt I am too old for the position of first and were looking to replace me."

Alex clucked his tongue with irritation. "Why did you not just ask me? I left another in charge and brought you because d'Aumesbery is relatively safe and threat-free at the moment, but I was riding into an unknown situation here. If Evelinde was miserable and being abused I could not simply leave her here and not do anything about it, so brought my best and most trustworthy men, including *you*, my *first*, with me in case we had to battle to get her away."

"Oh, Alex, that is so sweet," Evelinde said, smiling on him widely.

Cullen looked less impressed and said dryly, "Ye'd need more men than ye brought with ye fer that, brother."

Alex grimaced. "I most like would have tried sneaking her away somehow rather than take on you and your men could it not wait until I could bring back my full army."

"Hmm." Cullen nodded and then glanced to the others. "'Tis obvious no one is above suspicion here."

Though his words and tone were hard, Alex noted that the man cast an apologetic glance Merry's way as he said it and recalled his stating his opinion that she was a fine woman. He didn't think Cullen truly thought her behind these attacks on him and was glad for it.

"And," Cullen went on, distracting him from his thoughts. "Since Alex needs his sleep and I *like* mine, and I ken I won't be gettin' any if Evelinde is up half the night fretting ower her brother, no one is sleeping in here with him. Merry, we'll fix ye a fine room down the hall," he said gently and then turned a less gentle glance to Gerhard and Godfrey. "And ye two may get yer arses below with the rest of yer men. I already have two of me own best men on the door guarding it and they'll remain there all night. Now, everyone out."

Alex saw Merry hesitate, but then she nodded and moved toward the door, only to pause there and wait until everyone else but Cullen and Evelinde had left before nodding a somewhat stiff good night to them and leaving herself.

"I fear I have hurt her feelings," Evelinde murmured as she watched her go.

"She will get over it," Cullen said gruffly and slipped his arm around his wife's shoulders to lead her to the door. "She kens is only out o' worry fer yer brother."

"Aye." Evelinde leaned into her husband as they walked. "Still I feel bad. I like her and truly do not think that she is behind it, but this all started after the wedding. I get the feeling that means something, but cannot sort out what. None of it makes any sense really. Why make Alex randy and then try to kill him? If they *are* trying to kill him," she added, worrying the problem fretfully.

Cullen rubbed his hand over his wife's back as he urged her through the door before him. "Let it go, wife. Ye'll no sort it out tonight. 'Twill just keep ye awake fretting, and I have better things fer ye to be doing in our bed than fretting."

"Oh, Cullen, I do love you." Evelinde chuckled as the door closed behind them.

Alex stared at the closed door as blissful silence fell around him and then shook his head with mild disgust. It seemed that taking a blow to the head made people think you'd lost your wits, because no one seemed to care what he thought or felt. They'd snapped and snarled at one another as if he was not even there, his wife even going so far as to hush him when he'd tried to speak. And Cullen hadn't even asked how he felt the sleeping arrangements should go. The man was laird here and his word was law, but not over Alex or his people. As Lord D'Aumesbery, he was the one in charge of them, but apparently the Devil of Donnachaidh didn't think so, and Alex suspected that was all down to his being stuck in this bed all day, appearing an invalid.

Well, Alex thought, he would correct that impression on the morrow. He was getting out of this bed first thing in the morning and taking charge of matters. And he would also sort out what was happening and who was behind it, he decided firmly and then blew out the candle still burning on the bedside and settled under the linens and furs.

However, it was a long time before Alex was able to find sleep. The room was incredibly quiet and the bed seemed extremely empty without Merry there. After tossing and turning for a while, he slipped from the bed and—relieved to find he wasn't quite as weak as the first time he'd tried to rise—made his way to the chair by the fire to think over the problem some more. It was near dawn before Alex gave it up and slipped back into the big empty bed. As he drifted off to sleep he decided he just didn't like not having Merry there and wasn't going to sleep alone again . . . even if he had to leave Donnachaidh to do it.

"I truly am sorry, Merry," Evelinde said for the third time in the last half hour since Merry had joined her at the trestle table to break her fast. "I really do like you and I do not believe you are behind any of these attacks on Alex, but—"

"'Tis all right," Merry interrupted quietly. "I do understand. Ye love yer brother and so ye're doing what's in his best interests."

"Aye, but I feel bad you went to bed last night thinking I suspect you. I just—"

"Well, I was a little hurt," Merry admitted quietly. "But I still understood even then. Ye've no need to keep apologizing like this." She patted her hand soothingly and then added, "Besides, 'twas Cullen who ordered the sleeping arrangements last night, and his suspicions were fair. He kept Gerhard from staying with Alex, too, and I am grateful for that."

"Aye."

Merry quirked one eyebrow at her troubled expression. "What is it?"

"'Tis just . . . Well, Gerhard was at d'Aumesbery

my whole life and I thought I knew him well, but . . ."

"But?" Merry prompted.

"His time on the Crusades seems to have changed him somewhat. He is harder than I recall and yet softer in some ways as well." Evelinde scowled as she tried to explain and then burst out, saying, "Do you know when I came to the table this morning, he was telling Cullen he did not think there was any way Edda could be behind all of this. That she was not as bad as everyone thought, had nothing to gain from it, and was basically an unhappy woman who was sadly misunderstood."

Merry's eyebrows rose slightly at this news and she glanced around the great hall in search of the man.

"He was up talking to Alex with Cullen earlier and then went out to the bailey for some reason," Evelinde muttered unhappily, sending a glare in the general direction of the stairs. "I cannot believe the man would take her side like this. He saw how Edda was all those years after she married my father. Granted, he left with Cullen on crusade ere my father died and Edda did keep herself somewhat reined in while he still lived, but she was still unpleasant and cold to everyone. And yet he appears to be falling for her line about being unhappy and behaving badly and now regretting it. I mean, I understand you believing it. You never met her ere a month ago, but how Gerhard could—" Apparently realizing she was ranting, Evelinde reined herself in and smiled wryly. "I am sorry. I shall give you indigestion with such talk while you are trying to break your fast."

Merry smiled faintly but asked, "Is it not possible she has changed?"

Evelinde considered the suggestion and then nodded reluctantly. "I suppose 'tis possible. Howbeit it was only weeks ago that she arranged the marriage between Cullen and myself."

"Aye, and that obviously worked out well," Merry pointed out.

"But that was not her intent when she petitioned the king to arrange the marriage," Evelinde said solemnly. "All we knew of Cullen was that silly reputation he has as the Devil of Donnachaidh."

Merry had to repress a smile. That silly reputation was well-earned. Cullen had gained it in battle and he truly was a Devil under such circumstances, wielding his sword with deadly speed and accuracy. He was an opponent to be feared and respected. However, it appeared he was a much different person with those he cared about.

"Nay," Evelinde assured her solemnly, "Edda's intent when she arranged to marry me off to Cullen was not to see me happy. I merely got lucky that way. Howbeit, if you wish to see Edda's true face, then when you return to d'Aumesbery, you should tell her how blissfully happy I am. I doubt she will be able to maintain a sweet disposition then."

" 'Twill make her furious," Evelinde's maid, Mildrede, said solemnly, drawing Merry's gaze to where she sat. The woman looked grim and knowing, and Merry glanced down unhappily, finding it difficult to imagine that the sweet dear woman who had been so kind to her and made her feel welcome at d'Aumesbery could be the same one these women knew.

"I can see what we are saying is not sitting right with what you know of Edda," Evelinde said sadly, and then added, "But mayhap you could err on the side of caution for now? For Alex's sake?"

"Aye," Merry agreed. She would be happy to err far on the side of caution to keep her husband alive. Her feelings for the man were growing by leaps and bounds since the night before they'd set out on this trip. She was now certain he wasn't a drinker, but had been suffering the effects of some drug, and having got to know him as she had, Merry was starting to think she could be as happy with Alex as Evelinde was with Cullen, and that was saying something. The day she'd arrived at d'Aumesbery she was sure she'd been landed in hell, but now her future was showing the possibility of being closer to heaven.

If her husband could care for her in return, Merry thought suddenly, knowing the future might not be so bright if he didn't. It would be hard indeed loving someone who did not love her back, but he did seem to like her, and always showed her courtesy and consideration, and she hoped over time that could turn to love.

Merry's main concern at the moment was this business of the dosing and the attacks. While she feared losing him before they could enjoy the happiness Evelinde and Cullen had found, she also feared the possibility that Alex might believe Gerhard's accusations and suspect she was behind it all. Love did not come without trust, and she wanted that love and trust.

"What do you suggest?" she asked quietly, determined to do anything she could to earn Alex's trust and love.

"Mayhap you could just be cautious and when you return to d'Aumesbery, suggest Alex send Edda away."

Merry nodded unhappily at the suggestion, willing to do so to earn her husband's trust, but displeased with the possibility of hurting the woman who had been so kind to her.

"Not forever," Evelinde said quickly, apparently spotting Merry's reluctance. "After all, she may very well have turned a new leaf."

Merry couldn't help but laugh at the doubt Evelinde couldn't hide.

Grimacing, the blond rushed on, saying, "Perhaps you could just suggest she go to her sister's for a visit."

"She has a sister?" Merry asked with surprise.

"Aye. Lady Helen. She married Lord Alfred Duquet some twenty years ago, long ere Edda and my father were ordered to marry," Evelinde told her, and then added, "I do not think the two get on well, though. At least Lady Duquet never visited d'Aumesbery and Edda never went to visit her. Actually," she added dryly, "Edda has never visited anyone at all in all the time I have known her. I suspect she has no friends. I have always put it down to her unpleasant demeanor."

Merry murmured something of an acknowledgment, but she was wondering to herself why Edda had never mentioned having a sister. They had spent a lot of time talking the three weeks before this journey had parted them, and Alex's stepmother had told her much about her childhood and life at court, but had never once mentioned having siblings. Strange, she thought, but then shrugged the matter away. From what Evelinde had just said, it seemed obvious the two were not close; perhaps that was why.

"Sending her to visit her sister would not give her offense did you frame the suggestion right," Evelinde went on. "And it need not necessarily be permanent. Once you and Alex have sorted out this mess and caught her ally—I mean, the one responsible, and determined whether he worked alone or with someone else." She shrugged. "If 'tis not she he was working with, you could have her back."

"Aye," Merry agreed, but she was still wondering why Edda had never mentioned having a sister. It seemed an odd bit of information to leave out. The woman had always given the impression that she was alone in the world but for Alex and herself. Strange, Merry thought, and then glanced around in question when Godfrey suddenly appeared at her side, a fretful look on his face.

"What is it, Godfrey?" she asked, concerned by his expression.

"My lord Alex is up," he announced in an exasperated tone. "I told him you would not be pleased, but he insisted I help him dress. I did, but then came directly to you to tell—"

His words died, and the boy turned away with alarm as a crash and commotion sounded behind Merry.

She followed suit and swiveled abruptly on the bench in time to see her husband tumbling down the stairs, Merry was on her feet at once and rushing toward him.

Alex landed at the bottom of the stairs with a curse, followed by a groan as his body announced the various new aches and pains he could add to the one in his head. He then thanked his lucky stars that he had been clever enough to hold on to the banister as he descended. He'd done so just in case his legs weren't as steady beneath him as he'd hoped, but that hold on the sturdy wooden rail had probably saved him breaking his neck. When his foot had slipped on something on the stairs, his grip on the rail had kept him from pitching headfirst to the bottom. Instead, he'd slid down the steps on his behind and back, gaining more bruises, but keeping his neck intact.

"Husband!"

"Alex!"

He cursed under his breath again as he recognized the worry and upset in his wife's and sister's voices as they rushed across the great hall toward him. Godfrey and the maids were following. Of course, they had witnessed his clumsy moment. No doubt this would simply reaffirm their view of him as an invalid, and that was the last thing he wanted at this moment. Alex had determined to dress and rise this morning with the express purpose of appearing capable and in charge so that no one would kick up a fuss when he once again exerted his position as Lord of d'Aumesbery. He was determined he was not going to sleep alone again tonight, but knew he had to appear strong and able to be sure his decisions were not overridden. This was not a good start.

"Husband?"

"I am fine," Alex said firmly, forcing himself to sit up as Merry dropped to her knees on one side of him and Evelinde on the other. "Truly. I merely slipped on something on the stairs. It could have happened to anyone."

"Mayhap your legs are not yet quite strong enough to carry you," Evelinde suggested quietly. "We should return you to your bed for another day or two and—"

"Nay," he said sharply, and then forced himself to smile to ease the effect of the snap in his voice. Getting to his feet, he spoke more calmly as he added, "Nay. That is the last thing I need. I need to be up and about. I am not an invalid, Evie."

She smiled faintly at the old nickname, but also tried to put herself under his right arm, even as Merry moved to wedge her shoulder under his left. Alex sighed inwardly, but merely stepped back from them both.

"My legs are perfectly fine. I am just clumsy," he assured them both solemnly. Though that wasn't absolutely true. After the tumble he'd taken his legs were a little shaky, but he'd die before admitting that and being forced back to his bed. "Allow me to escort you back to the table, ladies."

Alex crooked out his elbows so that both his wife and his sister could slip their arms through his, and after a brief hesitation, each did. He let out a relieved breath then and walked them back to the table where they'd been seated when he'd made his grand entrance.

"How are ye feelin'?" Merry asked anxiously as they paused at the table and each began to reclaim her seat.

"Fine," Alex assured her as he settled to sit on the end of the bench between his wife and the chair where his sister sat. "I have a bit of a headache, but otherwise I feel fine."

"I shall mix ye up a tonic to ease it and—" Merry had started to rise, but paused and glanced to him in question when Alex caught her arm.

"I do not want a tonic," he said firmly, noting the worry and hurt this brought to her face.

He didn't understand it until she settled to sit again and said a bit stiffly, "Then perhaps Evelinde or her Aunt Biddy would be kind enough to mix one up fer ye."

Alex realized then that she thought he was refusing because he didn't trust her and might suspect she was behind the dosing. He didn't wish to address the issue there in front of everyone so merely said, "I do not wish a tonic at all. The headache will pass in its own good time, and I wish to maintain a clear head for our journey."

"Journey?" Merry and Evelinde asked together.

Alex could feel them peering at him wide-eyed from either side of him, but didn't glance to either woman. Instead, he smiled at the maid who had arrived with some mead, bread, and cheese to break his fast and merely said, "Aye. Gerhard is gathering the men together right now so that we can return to d'Aumesbery."

He did glance to Merry then to see how she was taking the news. His wife looked briefly startled, but then her eyebrows drew together as she apparently tried to work out what this meant. It was Evelinde who protested, "But you have only just got here."

"Aye," he said solemnly, turning an apologetic gaze to his sister. "And I wish that we could stay longer to visit. But I have found you happy and well, which was my main concern, and it has become obvious on this journey that there are some matters I myself need to address to reach that same happy state. It does seem best do I handle them now before whoever is behind these attacks succeed at their efforts. And since it all started at d'Aumesbery, I think I need to return there to sort it out."

Evelinde looked like she wanted to protest further, but held her tongue, and Alex was grateful for it. He knew she was disappointed, but suspected staying would simply draw out the matter presently plaguing them, and until it was resolved, Alex would have Gerhard accusing Merry and her maid, and Merry accusing Gerhard and the rest of his men. Alex knew he wouldn't be able to concentrate on his relationship with his wife until he had this out of the way.

The thought made him glance to Merry to see her looking thoughtful and unhappy. Before he could ask what she was thinking, Evelinde asked, "When do you plan to leave?"

Alex took a breath, knowing this was going to

upset her even more than the fact that he was leaving and then admitted, "As soon as Gerhard returns and tells me the men are ready."

Merry gave a start at his side, drawing his attention to her surprised expression.

Alex raised an eyebrow and asked quietly, "Is there anything you wished to do ere we leave?"

"Nay," Merry murmured and peered down again.

Alex opened his mouth to ask her if she was all right, but then paused and glanced across the room as the doors to the bailey opened. Cullen was the first to enter, but he was followed closely by Gerhard. The soldier walked a deferential step behind the Laird of Donnachaidh as they crossed to the table, but while Cullen merely nodded in greeting and then passed by to reach and kiss Evelinde good morning, Gerhard paused beside him before he, too, nodded.

"All is ready?" Alex asked.

"Aye. The wagon is packed, the horses are saddled, and the men are waiting."

"Go ahead and mount up then. We will join you directly," Alex said. He waited for the man to turn and make his way back out of the great hall, and then stood and reached down to help Merry to her feet before glancing to his sister.

Evelinde was already standing when he turned toward her and Cullen. His sister hesitated briefly and then threw herself into his arms and hugged him soundly, saying, "You must come again once everything is settled. In the meantime, write often so I know you are well."

"Of course," Alex murmured, pressing her close before releasing her. Cullen immediately pulled his wife to his chest, encompassing her with one brawny arm even as he reached out his other to offer Alex his hand.

"Safe travels and good luck with the matter. I will be curious to find out how it all works together in the end."

"As will I," Alex said wryly, and the two men smiled.

He started to retrieve his hand then, but Cullen tightened his grasp on it and held him in place as he said seriously, "Ye're welcome to come back fer a proper visit when ye're ready. Evelinde and I'd both enjoy that."

Alex felt his eyebrows rise slightly at the solemn words and knew he had just received a large compliment from his new brother-in-law. In man-speak, he'd just been told Cullen liked him. Since the feeling was mutual, he could do no less than offer, "And the same goes for you. You are welcome at d'Aumesbery at any time. I would enjoy the chance to get to know you better."

Cullen smiled and released his hand to look down at Evelinde. "The Scots blood in yer family shows through. Two such fine specimens couldna be produced by pureblood English parents."

"Oh, Cullen." Evelinde laughed and hugged him briefly even as she shook her head at her brother. "Ignore him. He is sure the English are weak and foolish."

"Aye, I am. And that's how I ken the two o' ye are no' pure English," Cullen teased.

Evelinde clucked her tongue with mock irritation, and Alex found himself smiling over the pair and then stepping aside to make room when Evelinde gave him a gentle push to get past him. Eyebrows rising slightly, he watched her hug his wife, pleased when Merry hugged her in return. He also noted that Evelinde whispered something to Merry and that she nodded solemnly in response, and then the two women linked arms and headed for the door, heads together as they walked.

"They like each other," Cullen commented as they started to follow the women.

"Aye," Alex agreed with a smile as he watched the pair, one petite and blond, the other a little taller and with long, gleaming chestnut hair. He had always thought Evelinde had been graced with lovely hair, but now thought that his Merry had the loveliest hair he had ever seen. Long and flowing, it shone with good health and seemed to capture bits of the sun with red and blond highlights as they stepped out under the midday sun.

"Ye're no' feeling a tad drunk and likely to start slurrin', are ye?" Cullen asked suddenly.

Startled by the question, Alex glanced to him with surprise. "Nay. Why?"

"Well, the randy way ye were just lookin' at Merry made me think mayhap ye'd been dosed again," the man teased.

Alex chuckled at the suggestion, but shook his head. "Trust me, I need no dosing to look at her like that."

Cullen smiled slightly and nodded, but then said more seriously, "Mayhap ye'd best reassure Merry o' that at some point in the near future. Women can be a strange breed and get the oddest ideas in their heads. 'Twould no' surprise me that she's now thinkin' the only reason ye'd bed her was if ye'd been dosed."

"That had not occurred to me. Thank you, Cullen," Alex murmured, now peering at his wife thoughtfully. He had been so concerned that she might think he had suspicions regarding her being involved in his attacks, he hadn't even considered what she might have made of this dosing business and whether he would be interested in her that way without it. It was definitely something he would have to see to, however. He wouldn't have Merry doubting his attraction for her and thinking he'd bedded her only because of some tonic.

The issue made him doubly glad he'd decided to leave Donnachaidh today. He could hardly prove he was attracted to his wife were they forced to sleep apart to ease everyone's worries and suspicions.

Merry was thinking of home. She supposed that shouldn't surprise her since she was on Scottish soil, but what did surprise her was the fact that she was feeling a little blue, and even longing for her childhood home at the moment. After so many years spent wishing and praying to get away from Stewart, it did seem ironic that she was now homesick for the place. But the fact was, at Stewart the only people trying to kill anyone were her father and brothers, and they were only trying to kill themselves. There was no great, incomprehensible plot afoot there, and no one in her childhood home, from her father and brothers down to the lowliest servant, would ever have even imagined that she might be capable of dosing anyone with something or attempting to kill him . . . except perhaps for her father and brothers, she acknowledged, but then only under great provocation.

It wasn't just that, however. While it was troublesome to think that her husband might now suspect her of being behind this ridiculous plot, as Gerhard did, what bothered her most was something Evelinde had said while they'd hugged and said good-bye before leaving. Evelinde had whispered in her ear, reminding her of her request to send Edda away to visit her sister once they'd returned to d'Aumesbery, and then had added, "And never fear, I am sure whatever Alex has been dosed with is not the only reason he . . . er . . . likes you in that way. I am sure he finds you attractive."

Alex's sister had pulled back to smile at her encouragingly then, but Merry had merely stared back blankly and then allowed herself to be led from the keep. She'd hardly heard a word Evelinde had said as she'd chatted on about the things they would do when next they visited as they'd walked out to the horses. Merry's mind had still been stuck on her reassurance. Until that moment, it had never occurred to her that her husband's desire for her might be tonic-induced. Certainly, the night she'd noted that his eyes were dilated, she'd realized that his aggressive behavior was due to being dosed. But surely the other times hadn't been . . . Had they? she wondered now with worry, recalling that according to Una his eyes had been dilated for the entire three weeks ere the journey, and yet he hadn't touched or even looked at her as he had on this journey. But they suspected the dosage had been increased since then and that this was why he'd acted as he had. Was it only whatever he'd been given that had brought him to her bed? she worried.

"You look very thoughtful."

Merry glanced up with a start to find that her husband had slowed to ride beside her again. They had started out the journey side by side on their mounts, but she had been so distracted by her thoughts she hadn't been able to respond to his comments and repeated efforts to strike up a conversation. After a bit, Merry had allowed her mare to fall back some, leaving Gerhard to take her place and talk with her husband. Now, however, Alex had dropped back to ride beside her again, and she forced herself to stop fretting about things she could not control and managed to offer him a smile.

"Does this area look familiar?" Alex asked suddenly, and Merry glanced around, her eyes slipping with little interest over the woods they were traveling through. It looked much like the rest of the woods they'd been passing through for the last hour, she thought, and then noted the hills ahead and stilled in her saddle, her head tilting slightly as she stared at them.

"Stewart." She breathed the word, amazed to see the place she'd just been pining for.

"Aye." Alex smiled gently. "I thought you might wish to stop and greet your family and old friends since we were passing so close by. But we can avoid it if 'twould bring up unhappy memories for you."

Merry smiled at the man, thinking she truly had

a thoughtful husband, and then glanced toward the
hills ahead as she considered her answer. Finally,
she nodded her head. "If you do not mind taking the
time, I would be pleased to check in on my father
and brothers on the way by."

"Then we shall," he said with a smile, and Merry
smiled back, but then glimpsed Gerhard riding on
his other side and noted the scowl on the man's face.
It seemed he was not pleased with the stop, and judging by the suspicion on his expression, did not think
she should be, either. She supposed she should not
be surprised. No doubt he was imagining she had
some grand plan to finish off her husband in the familiar surroundings, but there was little she could
do about his thoughts, so she merely ignored him
and looked toward the hills ahead and home.

The men on the wall were, of course, the first
to see their approach, and she noted the way they
each stiffened and grew still at their posts as they
watched them draw near. Their party was nearly
to the wall before the men were able to recognize
her riding at the front at her husband's side, and the
difference in them was immediate. They all relaxed,
breaking out in smiles of welcome; most even waved
and called out.

Merry felt a happy laugh slip from her lips as
she waved back, and then they were passing under
the gate into the bailey and their party was almost
brought to a grinding halt as the people of Stewart
rushed forward to greet her.

"Ye're back!"

"Are ye staying, lass?"

"Ye're lookin' fine and healthy, lass."

"Is this yer man, lovey? He's a fine-lookin' maun."

The calls came from every side, and Merry laughed as she urged her mare to continue slowly forward even as she tried to answer that aye, she was back. Aye, this was her husband, and no, she was not staying, just visiting. The warmth and welcome from the people of Stewart was a balm to her soul compared to the tension and suspicion of the last few days, and it was only then that Merry realized how upset she had been to be under that suspicion. She had understood it, but that apparently hadn't prevented it from hurting her.

The moment they drew their mounts to a halt at the steps to the keep and Merry dismounted, she found herself surrounded and caught up in one embrace after another by the women who had trailed them across the bailey. Things like " 'Tis good to see ye lookin' so bonnie, lass" and "We're missin' ye here at Stewart, my lady" were repeated to her over and over, and Merry would have liked to load every single one of them into her wagon and take them home to d'Aumesbery with her. At least then she would not feel so alone for, despite Una's accompanying her, it had been a lonely three weeks directly after her arrival in England. She had felt quite lost and alone and had clung to the kindness Edda had shown her. Now, however, she was questioning that kindness and the woman who had shown it and felt she had no ally at all.

Just as Merry acknowledged that thought to herself, Alex suddenly appeared at her side, making his way gently but firmly through the women to get to her and slip an arm around her shoulder. For one moment, she fancied he looked a little worried, as if he thought she might disappear into the crowd of women and not return, but then he managed a smile and suggested, "Mayhap we should go in now. One of the men said your father and brothers are inside."

Merry nodded agreement and Alex began to maneuver them toward and up the steps while she apologized and made her excuses for leaving, and then they were inside. The keep doors closed behind them, blocking out the chatter and noise, as well as the sun. Merry and Alex both paused to give their eyes a moment to adjust, and suddenly she was reminded of her arrival at d'Aumesbery, for while she was briefly blind, she was not deaf and heard the men in the room before she saw them. The overloud laughter and slurring words that hit her ear made her heart drop at once, erasing all the pleasure of a moment ago, and Merry mentally raised her shoulders and stiffened her resolve as Alex took her arm and led her slowly, almost reluctantly forward.

As her eyes focused and her gaze landed on the three men seated around the trestle tables with several empty, overturned pitchers lying around them, Merry began to wish she had thanked Alex kindly, but rejected the idea of stopping. In her brief moment of melancholy on the hill, she had remembered only the people who lived and worked here and the good of her childhood home. She'd quite forgotten the three men who had been burrs in her behind since her mother's death.

She and Alex were halfway across the floor when Merry suddenly found her feet would no longer move her forward. Alex paused at once, a questioning gaze on his face, and she said unhappily, "Mayhap 'twould be better did we just continue on our journey."

"I'd say so," Gerhard muttered behind her, drawing her attention to the fact that they had not entered alone.

Merry stiffened and felt her face flush with shame for her family, but did not miss the scowl Alex turned on the man. His expression was neutral when it returned to her and he said, "If you wish it, Merry. We will do what you like."

"Aye," she said solemnly. "I wish—"

"Merry! As I live and breathe! Here we were just talkin' about ye and ye appear as if by magic!"

Merry's shoulders drooped at that loud shout from her father, knowing it was too late now and they would have to carry this debacle forward. Taking a deep breath, she turned and forced herself to approach the table as the three Stewart men staggered to their feet to greet them.

"Damn me, Merry!" Brodie greeted. He was the first to reach them and immediately caught her up in a bear hug. "Ye're lookin' fine, lass. We've been fretting ower that husband o' yers and how he's treatin' ye. Is he givin' ye any trouble? We can kill the bastard and bury him and his men in Cook's herb garden and no one would be the wiser."

Merry forced a smile, treating the words like a joke though she suspected they weren't. She managed to ease from his embrace as she assured him, "There's no need fer that, me husband is verra kind to me."

"Well, that's all right then," her father decided as he displaced Brodie to embrace her himself. "We'll let the lad live then, shall we?"

"Aye," Merry said firmly, and wondered what madness had made her wish for this visit. Surely this was only going to add to the suspicion the English already had of her. Certainly, Gerhard had an expression on his face that suggested this was nothing less than he'd expected. As for Alex, his face was still in that neutral state and she could not tell what he was thinking.

And then her father was displaced by Gawain, who gave her a quick, hard hug and then tugged her toward the table saying, "Ye've got to come celebrate with us Merry. We've the most wonderful news."

"Oh?" she asked wearily as she was urged to sit on the bench.

"Aye," Brodie assured her as he and Gawain both settled on either side of her at the trestle table. Merry was about to glance around to be sure Alex was still nearby when he stepped up behind her and settled his hands on her shoulders. He then used that touch to urge her to relax back against his legs and use him as a chair back. Merry tilted her face up to peer at him, relieved to find his expression kind, sympathetic, and reassuring all at once as he murmured, "Let us hear this wonderful news."

Merry had to swallow a lump in her throat, grateful that he hadn't snatched her back off the bench and run for the door. She would not have blamed him had he done so, and part of her almost wished that he had, but they were her family.

"Kade is a-comin' home."

This announcement from her father made Merry whirl to stare at where he stood on the other side of the trestle table. He had a full pitcher of whiskey in one hand, a mug in the other, and a grin on his face full of happy expectation as he awaited her response. She stared at him blankly for the longest time as she tried to accept that the brother she'd begun to fear was dead was not and then finally said, "He isna."

"Aye," Brodie crooned, throwing an arm around her and drawing her up against his side in an exuberant, if clumsy, hug that pulled her away from Alex. "He *is*, Merry. Kade is alive and will soon be home."

"But how?" she asked with bewilderment. "Where has he been? Why has he not—?"

"He was being held captive by one o' those damned infidel princes," her father said grimly. "Three years the poor bastard rotted in some foreign cage."

"Aye," Gawain said solemnly, but then cheered and added, "But he escaped. There's no keepin' a Stewart where they're no' wantin' to be. He escaped and is recuperating with friends. As soon as he's well enough to travel, he'll be on a ship home."

"Recuperating?" Merry asked with alarm, reaching up to cover one of Alex's hands with her own as she straightened, and his hands settled on her shoulders again. "Was he injured?"

"Nay, nay," her father assured her, and then admitted with some concern of his own, "At least there was no mention o' injury. From the letter we received it sounds as though he was weak and half starved is all. He'll be home soon enough."

Merry sank back against Alex's legs and chest as she absorbed this news. Kade lived. All would be well. At least here at Stewart. He would return and take her father and brothers in hand and run Stewart in her place. It would be one worry off her plate, for she truly had been fretting over how Stewart would continue on with three drunks running it, but once Kade was back . . . Well, this was the best news she'd had since her marriage.

Tilting her head back, Merry offered a beaming smile to her husband. "'Tis good news. All will be well."

"Aye," he agreed quietly, a small smile playing about his lips.

"Aye!" Eachann Stewart said gruffly. "'Tis the grandest news imaginable. And surely the two o' ye will stay to celebrate it?"

Alex glanced to the man, hesitated, and then peered down at Merry, lifting one eyebrow. "Do you wish to stay and celebrate? We could stop the night and continue on in the morning."

Merry smiled wryly at the offer, knowing he was no more comfortable with the idea than she. Grateful he had made it, she nevertheless shook her head. "I think I'd like to continue our journey. We've a long way to go and much to settle at d'Aumesbery."

Alex nodded and glanced to her father. "I fear Merry is right. We do have to return home. We only stopped to say hello on the way and let you know that we will return for a longer visit another time if we are welcome."

"Oh, aye, ye're welcome here, lad," Eachann Stewart assured him generously, and added brightly,

"Mayhap next time ye come, Kade'll be back and ye can meet the boy."

"I would enjoy that," Alex assured him solemnly, slipping a hand to Merry's arm to help her maneuver herself from the tiny space she was inhabiting on the bench between her brothers. The two younger men were far enough gone in their celebrations that it apparently didn't occur to them to give her the room necessary to extricate herself and, in the end, Alex simply lifted her up and off the bench and set her on her feet once she was clear of it. They turned to leave then, but Merry paused as Brodie suddenly caught her hand, bringing her to a halt.

Glancing back, she raised her eyebrows curiously when she saw his solemn expression.

" 'Tis oddly quiet here without ye, Merry," he confessed somberly.

"Aye," Gawain agreed, and then added, "I didna think we would, but we miss ye."

Merry felt her heart squeeze at the soft words and impulsively moved back to give both her brothers a hug.

"We will come back soon," she whispered as she squeezed them both, an arm around each of them, and then added gruffly, "Try no' to drink yerselves to death or break yer fool necks ere we do."

The two men grinned as if this was a fine joke, and Merry shook her head as she straightened, then turned and took the hand Alex offered, allowing him to lead her out of her childhood home. It took them several moments to make their way through the people crowded outside the keep doors. The size of the group had grown while they were inside, and none of them was shy about letting their disappointment be known that she wasn't staying any length of time. It made her feel a bit guilty, but did her heart good as well. At least she knew, did things go terribly wrong at d'Aumesbery, she had a home and people to return to who would welcome her with open arms.

" 'Tis good Kade is returning," Alex murmured once they were finally on their way again and traveling out of the bailey.

"Aye," Merry agreed, a smile stretching her lips. It truly was the best news she'd had in a long time.

"You will worry less about your father and brothers with him here to watch over them."

Merry glanced to him, surprised by the astute observation, but then merely nodded. "Aye. I will."

They rode in a companionable silence after that, Merry thinking about her brother and what it would mean at Stewart for him to return. She had no doubt he would take up the reins there. Her father had no interest in running the place. Merry only hoped Kade could somehow make the three men give up, or at least slow down, on their drinking. Perhaps with him there Brodie and Gawain could be reformed. At least they would have a strong male lead to follow rather than their father. It was a possibility . . . if her father allowed him to take over this time . . . and if Kade returned to Scotland unbroken by all he'd experienced, she added unhappily, and began to fret about what shape he was in.

Merry was so caught up in her thoughts and worries about her brother that she didn't notice when the sun began to set or wonder why they were traveling so late into the day. It was only when Alex called a halt and she released her worries to glance around that she saw it was now full night. They were in a clearing beside a loch, the moonlight reflecting off its surface and making it easy to see despite the hour.

Her gaze slid to Alex in question then, but he was already dismounting. Once on the ground, he paused for a moment while he waited for his legs to recover from sitting his horse for so long and then moved around to hold his hands up to her.

" 'Tis late," Merry murmured as he lifted her off her mare.

"Aye," Alex agreed, but didn't explain and merely said, "Take a minute to find your legs ere you try to move about, Merry. You will be stiff from the ride."

She nodded silently and clutched his arms as he held her up, and then released a breath and murmured, "Thank you" when her legs had recovered enough to hold her up without issue.

Alex then led her farther along the lake to tend to personal matters. He said she could bathe if she wished, but the water was cold so she made do with a quick wash. They then returned to camp and parted ways, he to tend to the men and she to see what she could do about the tent.

Una had been busy and the tent was already set up, the furs and their belongings laid out. Merry paused in the tent flap, aware that Gerhard stood not far away, his eyes burning a hole in her back, and then moved inside to collect the sack holding her dresses. She had no doubt that the soldier would raise a fuss with Alex about the possibility of her sleeping in the tent with him where she might kill him in his sleep. Merry had no wish to have to hear Alex asking her to sleep elsewhere or choosing to sleep elsewhere himself. At least if she simply did it now herself, she could avoid that, she thought unhappily, and turned to hurry back out of the tent with her belongings.

Una and Godfrey were both inside the wagon arranging things when she arrived. Merry suspected that the lad had also helped Una set up the tent and that was why it was all done so quickly. She knew the boy still felt bad about attacking the maid and had been doing such thoughtful little things in an effort at repentance. Seeing the single pallet of furs the two were now setting out, Merry cleared her throat and murmured, "Ye shall either need two o' those or to make that one bigger do ye no' mind sharing it with me, Una."

The maid and Godfrey both sat back on their haunches to peer at her with surprise. It was Una who asked, "Ye're no sleeping with yer husband?"

Merry grimaced. "What? And have Gerhard insistin' on sleeping in there with us? Nay. I shall sleep in here with you."

Godfrey and Una exchanged glances and then set silently to work rearranging the furs, and Merry was relieved that they were not questioning her further or commenting on these new arrangements. She set her sack of gowns just inside the wagon and then climbed inside and moved forward on her knees to help them.

The men had finished tending to everything else needed to ensure a relatively safe and comfortable camp when the trio climbed out of the back of the wagon. Several rabbits and a bird or two had been trapped or shot with a bow and arrow and set over the fire to cook. Merry's stomach gave a loud growl as they joined the men around the fire, and she was glad to see that the meal was nearly ready. She sat beside her husband when he gestured her over, but said little and ate quickly before excusing herself for the night and making her way to the wagon. Merry had burrowed herself under the top linens and furs on her side of the pallet when Una arrived. They both whispered a quiet "Good sleep" to each other, and then Merry was left to her thoughts and misery. In a desperate effort to stave off the misery trying to claim her, she was reminding herself that this was her choice and she had not been banished there when she heard the rustle of the bit of tarp hanging over the end of the wagon being moved.

"Una?" Alex's irritated voice came from the darkness. "Do you know where my wife is?"

Merry heard rustling as the maid shifted about beside her, but was already unburying herself from the furs and sitting up herself. "I am here."

"What the devil are you doing here?" Alex asked, sounding most annoyed.

Merry opened her mouth to respond, but then let it close, her eyes widening as he suddenly clambered into the back of the wagon with them.

"Husband," she began uncertainly, and then gasped in surprise as he scooped her up off the furs and turned to carry her back the way he'd come. It was an awkward business carrying her across the wagon on his knees, but he did so, and then leapt to the ground behind it with her held close to his chest.

Merry didn't say a word as he carried her around the outside of the camp to get to their tent. But then neither did he, and then they were inside the tent and he was setting her, none too gently, on the furs.

The man was obviously annoyed. If she'd doubted that, his sharp "You sleep with me, wife. 'Tis your place" would have cleared up the matter for her.

Merry lay where he'd left her and peered at him uncertainly, but he wasn't looking at her. He had apparently come to the tent and started to disrobe before realizing she wasn't buried in the furs. The man wore only his braies, and those were now quickly stripped away. He then paused to blow out the candle on the chest next to the pallet before climbing into the makeshift bed beside her.

She waited nervously for him to say or do something, but after a couple of moments of rustling as he shifted about to get comfortable, Alex merely threw his arm over her and drew her against his side and then gave a little grunt of satisfaction. The tent then fell into silence.

Merry considered simply going to sleep and not talking about what had just happened, but she could feel his irritation in the tension of the arm around her and said meekly, "After Donnachaidh, I thought ye felt safer without me in yer bed."

A long sigh ruffled the hair on the back of her head, and then Alex said, "Why do you think I wished to leave Donnachaidh so soon?"

"To tend to matters at home?" she suggested, repeating what he'd said to his sister and Cullen.

"There is that," he admitted, and then added, "But Merry, your sleeping in another room was not my choice."

"But ye didna protest it," she pointed out quietly.

"I had just woken up from a head wound, my head was throbbing, everyone was yelling, and no one was listening to me because they all thought me an invalid. You even shushed me," he pointed out dryly.

Merry bit her lip to keep from grinning at the affront in his voice.

"I knew there was no use in arguing, but did not like not having you in my bed. *And did not intend to spend another night like that.* So rather than deal with Gerhard's protests and Cullen's efforts to keep everyone happy, I decided 'twas time to leave so that I could now make my own rules about who slept where. And," he added firmly, "my rule is that you will always sleep with me. Understood?"

"Aye," Merry said meekly.

"Good."

She listened to him breathe, waiting for him to tell her that he did not suspect her, or . . . well . . . anything that would help erase some of the worries that were rolling around her head like great boulders, but he apparently had nothing more to say and no desire to bed her, because she soon realized his breathing had grown deep and steady and he was sleeping. It left her to wonder what exactly this all meant. He hadn't bedded her, but she *was* back in his bed. That last part had to be a good thing, did it not? Merry wondered, and then allowed her eyes to drift closed as she, too, fell asleep.

chapter

Fourteen

Alex woke to smoke, the loud crackle of flames, and someone coughing as they tugged and pulled on him. It was a rude awakening, and he had stumbled half to his feet and started coughing himself before he was fully awake and aware that he was being half pulled and half led from the tent that was now awash in flames.

At first, Alex thought the person pulling him was Merry, and he had the brief thought that this would be the third time his wife had had to save his hide, but then he became aware that the body that had shifted to brace his own as they stumbled out of the tent into the cool night air was much larger than his petite wife.

Another fit of coughing seized Alex the moment he sucked clean fresh air in on top of the smoke filling his lungs, and he found himself doubled over and helpless to resist all the hands now pushing and pulling at him as more bodies surrounded him. In this state, he and his savior were propelled a safe distance away from the fire, and then Alex found himself pushed to sit on a boulder to catch his breath.

"Thank God," Gerhard got out between hacking coughs of his own as he dropped to sit beside him. "I thought sure you were done for."

Alex gave one last cough to clear his throat and shook his head before glancing to the man. He took in his grim, soot-stained face and then glanced to the tent before peering around the clearing to see where they had dragged his wife to. She was much smaller than he, and he worried that the smoke might have harmed her more than him. He didn't spot her at once, however, and asked, "Where did they take my wife?"

"What?" Gerhard asked sharply. "She is in the wagon with Una. Godfrey said she planned to sleep there and I saw her go there myself last night after we ate."

Feeling the blood drain from his face, Alex turned toward him with dismay. "Nay! I found her there and carried her to the tent ere going to sleep. Surely one of you saw her there and brought her out, too?"

Gerhard was now looking alarmed as well, but shook his head. "I saw no one. You were alone."

Cursing, Alex leapt to his feet at once and rushed toward the tent.

"My lord!" Gerhard caught his arm and tried to stop him. "I saw no one. She cannot be there, and if she is, 'tis too late. I barely got you out. There is no way to save her."

Alex merely shrugged his hold away and charged forward. He would save his wife, or die trying. He would not leave her in that inferno to die a fiery death. Dear God, she was probably awake right now and bleating with fear, he thought with horror. Roasting to death was a terrible way to go.

The tent had appeared fully aflame when he'd wakened in it and was certainly no better now, but Alex ignored that, took a last gasp of smoke-free air, and then charged through the flaming tent flap. His eyes were nearly closed against the heat inside, but he knew his way to the fur pallet and rushed there so quickly he almost could not stop himself and nearly trampled his wife under the furs and linens.

"Wife!" he shouted, dropping to his knees beside the bump that was she, but she did not stir. Alex didn't take the time to see whether she lived or not, but scooped her up into his arms, furs and all, and turned to crash back toward the tent flap. His heart lifted with relief and a sudden mad desire to laugh as he reached the flap and rushed through to the sound of a loud, snuffling snore coming muffled from the furs he held. His wife was alive . . . and had slept through the whole damned thing.

* * *

Merry was not pleased to be awake. It had been a long day of riding, following several days of little sleep as she'd fretted over Alex, and she simply was not happy to be jarred awake by Alex's sudden desire to cart her about. In truth, she suspected she might have managed to sleep through that, had the big lummox's chest not been vibrating against her ear and his laughter not reached her through the muffling of the furs she'd curled herself in as usual.

She was going to ignore him and simply go back to sleep until it occurred to Merry to wonder where he thought he was carrying her to. The wagon came to mind, and she stiffened in his arms at the thought of being put back where she'd started out after he'd dragged her out of there to begin with. Had he changed his mind about wishing her to share his bed?

Upset at the possibility, Merry began to struggle to unravel the furs cocooning her and managed to push her arms and head out of the top like a child being birthed. Her head turned instinctively toward her husband and she noted the dark smudges on his face and how they stood out in relief against the sharp light coming from the torches surrounding them.

Nay, not torches, she realized as her eyes traveled past his face to the tent he was carrying her away from. Her eyes widened incredulously on the flaming abode and then turned sharply back to her husband as she cried, " 'Twas not me!"

Alex's laughter immediately died and was replaced with a soft expression of regret, but before he could speak they were suddenly surrounded by several men, Gerhard among them. The next several moments passed in a whirl of chaos as Gerhard herded them farther from the still burning tent before allowing Alex to pause. She expected him to set her down then, but Alex held her tightly and shook his head when Gerhard tried to take her from him.

"We need to check both of you over for burns or injuries," the soldier said reasonably.

"I have a few minor burns, but am otherwise all right," Alex said quietly and then glanced at Merry and added, "And I believe the furs protected my wife from injury."

When she nodded silently, he released a small breath of relief and then dropped to sit on the nearest boulder, still cradling her in his arms. Merry peered from him to the burning tent and then to Gerhard as Alex asked him, "What happened?"

The concern on Gerhard's face suddenly turned to fury as he spat, "What happened is someone obviously set the damned tent on fire . . . which wouldn't have happened had you listened to me and allowed me to set guards on the tent for the night."

Merry's eyes widened at the anger in the man's face and voice. 'Twas obvious he was upset and not afraid to show it. Alex, however, merely nodded. "Aye, you are right. It would not have happened. But how do you know it was set?"

Gerhard blew out an exasperated breath. "Well, I presume you were not foolish enough to leave a candle burning while you slept?"

"Nay," Alex agreed, even as Merry shook her head. She distinctly recalled Alex blowing out the candle before joining her in the pallet. It had definitely been dark inside the tent when she'd drifted off to sleep.

"Then someone obviously must have set it," the soldier snapped, and was so upset he began to pace in front of them. "It was a stupid effort to kill you, though it nearly worked. Fortunately, the fire upset the horses, and their nervous movement and whinnying woke Allan and he got up to soothe them, saw the tent was afire, and woke me."

"And you came in after me," Alex said solemnly. "Thank you, old friend."

Gerhard waved his words away with disgust. "Of course, I came in after you. 'Tis my job to keep you alive. But I would not have needed to, had you just listened to me and allowed me to put guards on you. Someone set that fire deliberately, trying to kill you. There is no way this could be an accident that we are misconstruing."

His eyes slid to Merry as he said that and she sat a little straighter in Alex's lap and said quickly, "I did not set it."

"Merry, love," Alex said softly, drawing her wary gaze to him. Lifting one sooty hand, he brushed the hair back from her face and said solemnly, "We know it was not you. Do we not, Gerhard?" he added in hard tones.

Merry glanced to the man, sighing inwardly when he hesitated. She was sure he was about to accuse her of starting the fire in another attempt to point the guilty finger elsewhere, but much to her surprise, he nodded solemnly.

"Aye. We know it is not you," he said dutifully, and then added, "You would hardly set the tent on fire and then go to sleep inside and remain there so long." He shook his head. "I do not know how you survived it. The heat and smoke were enough that I was sure you were dead when I realized you were still in there."

"My wife sleeps buried under the furs," Alex said dryly. "She burrows even her head under them. 'Tis probably the only thing that saved her."

"Ah." Gerhard nodded and then peered at Merry and said seriously, " 'Tis good you do. 'Tis probably the only thing that saved you this night. I thought you were in the wagon with Una, and the smoke was so thick in the air I never would have seen you there. We are just lucky that the furs were not set afire by a spark ere Alex realized you were still inside and got you out. Surely the angels were looking after you both tonight."

Merry nodded solemnly as her gaze slid back to the fiery tent as it collapsed. The angels had indeed been working hard tonight.

"My lady?"

Merry glanced back to Gerhard and she noted that his expression had gone even more solemn.

"Allow me to offer my apologies for my earlier accusations," he said with dignity. "My only excuse is that—"

"Lookin' out fer Alex has been yer job fer many years now," Merry interrupted, equally solemn despite the relief pouring through her. She had not enjoyed knowing she was under suspicion for hurting Alex and was glad to have that pall removed. She was so relieved she didn't need the apology, so said, "And everything did start after me arrival. I understand why ye suspected me. 'Tis all right."

"Thank you," he murmured, and then seemed to become aware of the men all standing around them, watching and listening to everything, and said, "Well? 'Tis morn now. Why are you not breaking camp?"

The men began to move away at once, and Gerhard turned to offer them both a slight bow before following suit.

Merry watched him go, feeling as if a great weight had been lifted from her shoulders. In truth, she thought it was nearly worth having almost been roasted alive to get that suspicion off her. She suspected she might feel differently had she not slept through the ordeal. However, the very fact that she had made her shake her head with bewilderment. Surely the heat or the smoke should have made its way through to her sleeping mind and roused her? Apparently not.

"Merry?"

She turned to Alex, surprised to see that he looked even more solemn than Gerhard had.

He caught her face in his hands and said, "I want you to know that I have never believed that you were involved in what has been happening." When Merry's eyes narrowed with doubt and she opened her mouth to say she was not sure that was true, he held up a hand and said, "If ever I did wonder, it was only a passing thought and quickly forced away by your own behavior."

"Mine?" she asked, wanting to believe him.

"Aye," he assured her, and then laughed slightly and said, "Merry, there is a reason you gained the name the Stewart Shrew."

Merry felt herself flush, but before she could get too embarrassed or upset, he added, "And you did not get it from sneaking around drugging people or knocking them out when their backs are turned. Anyone could tell that from watching you deal with your father and brothers."

"They could?" she asked dubiously.

"Do you recall the day I found you training the men in the bailey?"

"Aye," she said slowly, unsure where this was heading.

"Well, Merry, when you realized your father and brothers were drinking in the great hall, you straightened your shoulders and marched up there ready to do battle. You did not handle it in some underhanded sneaky manner."

Merry grimaced but said, "As much as I hate to disappoint ye and risk ye thinkin' I'm behind all this, I feel I should tell ye that I did actually slam me shield ower Brodie's head from behind when I got there."

"That was just to get his attention," Alex said, waving her words away.

"Ye saw it?" she asked with dismay.

"Aye. I followed and saw and heard everything, and you have nothing to be ashamed of. You hit him over the head, got his attention, gave him hell, and then knocked him out good and proper from in front."

Merry was busy cringing over the knowledge that he'd witnessed one of her shrewish moments, when he caught her face and turned her so that she was focused on him as he continued, "Merry, you handle everything in a forthright manner. You did not hide the whiskey from your father and brothers, but locked it away in the pantry and kept the key on your person, and *all knew you had it.*" He shook his head. "Nay. Did you want me dead, you would not choose strange potions and sneak attacks from behind to do it. You would choose a much more forthright manner."

"Thank ye, husband," Merry said quietly, touched that he thought so highly of her. She then frowned and added, "I think."

Alex chuckled at the disgruntlement now claiming her face and then hugged her close. "I am almost glad for this latest attack. It has allowed us to clear up the matter of your being under suspicion and—"

Merry tilted her head back to peer at him curiously when his words faltered. "And what?"

He grimaced, but then admitted, "It also gave me the chance to rescue you for a change."

"I . . ." She paused, her brow furrowed with confusion.

Alex smiled, but explained, "It was beginning to hurt my pride that my sweet little bride had saved my life twice when I am supposed to be the big strong, warrior husband."

"Oh!" Her eyes widened in realization and then she patted his shoulder soothingly. "Ye *are* a big strong, warrior husband, husband. I have never doubted that, and I kenned 'twas only a matter of time ere ye'd ha'e to be savin' me back."

Alex began to laugh so hard he fell back on the grass with her, and Merry gave a little squeal and clutched at his shoulders as they went. She then found her head pressed to his chest as he hugged her tightly and breathed, "Ah Merry, you are priceless."

Merry wasn't sure what he found so amusing. She'd been in earnest, but let the matter go and admitted, "I'm glad o' it, too, if it means Gerhard will stop suspecting me. But yer words have made me wonder."

"About what?" Alex asked, his hand moving soothingly over her back.

"Well, ye're right. It hadna occurred to me, but this whole ordeal is full of sneakin' about and such, and I think Gerhard too forthright to do that, too."

"Aye," Alex agreed quietly. "He is not the sneaky sort, either. Sometimes I think 'twould be better if he did learn a bit of sneakiness."

When she tilted her head to peer at him curiously, he explained, "The man has a sharp mind and is good with a sword, but diplomacy is not exactly his long suit, as you may have noticed. Were he just a touch less forthright, he could avoid insulting unnecessarily."

"Hmm," Merry murmured, but said, "Ye ken the people of d'Aumesbery better than I. Who do ye think is sneaky enough to do this?"

Alex was silent for a moment and then sat up, taking her with him. He took a moment to help when

Merry then quickly set to arranging the furs and linens around herself to be sure she was decently covered, and then admitted, "You are not going to like this."

Merry grimaced. "Ye're going to say Edda."

He nodded solemnly. "I know you like her and she has been good to you, but she has proven herself sneaky in the past. When my father lived and was home, she acted much as she does with you and me now. However, when he left on the occasional journey, her demeanor changed entirely. She was cold and even cruel to those left behind, including myself and Evelinde. And then he would ride through the gate and she was suddenly sweet and dutiful again. 'Twas like there were two of her, a good Edda and an evil Edda."

Merry considered this, upset at the possibility that Edda was not what she presented herself to be, and then admitted, "Evelinde made me promise to approach ye about sending Edda away to visit her sister for a while once we return."

"Sister?" Alex echoed with surprise, and then nodded. "Oh, aye. I had forgotten she had one."

"I didna even ken she had one until Evelinde told me," Merry admitted. "I found that surprisin' considerin' how often we've sat by the fire chattin' ower our mending on a night."

"'Tis odd she would not have mentioned it," Alex agreed, and then asked, "Would you mind did we send her away for a visit when we return?"

"Nay," Merry said quietly. "I shall miss her, but it need only be until we sort things out and can prove she's no' behind all of this nonsense."

"Aye," Alex agreed, hugging her.

"My lady!"

Merry pulled a little away from Alex to glance around as Una came stumbling up. The maid was a complete mess, her hair still sleep-rumpled and her gown laced up crookedly. It was obvious she'd been in a rush to dress.

"Godfrey woke me with the news of the fire. Thank God, ye're all right," the woman gasped dropping to her knees beside them. "Ye didna get burned at all, did ye? Godfrey didna think ye had, but—"

"I'm fine," Merry assured her quickly and then glanced to her husband with surprise when his chest began to rumble with fresh laughter.

"It does seem amazing to me that the women from your part of Scotland can sleep through such things. Surely the ruckus the men were making with their shouts and so on should have woken you, Una."

"Oh." The maid flushed, but waved that away. "I am a deep sleeper. Most o' the people at Stewart are. It comes from years o' Eachann and the boys stayin' up all night drinkin' and carousin' and makin' a hell o' a racket. We are used to sleepin' with noise."

"Ah, that explains a lot," Alex said with sudden understanding and eased Merry off his lap so that he could get to his feet. "I suppose we, too, should get moving. I have not done so ere this because I am not sure what we are going to do for clothing now that everything burned up in the fire, but the men are nearly finished breaking camp and I'd best look into the matter."

Merry opened her mouth to point out that her

gowns were safe and sound in the wagon where she'd taken them last night when she'd thought she'd be sleeping there, but swallowed the words and nearly her tongue along with them as she glanced up and found herself staring at her husband's naked chicken neck. Until then, she hadn't realized that he was naked as the day he was born. She should have, since that was how he'd climbed into bed last night, but . . . .

"Dear Lord, Godfrey's no' the only one with a claymore," Una muttered, bringing Merry abruptly to her feet to wrap the furs that had been covering her around her husband's waist.

"Merry, stop that and cover yourself," Alex snapped, trying to wrap the furs back around her even as she wrapped them around him. "You are not decent."

"I may no' be decent, but at least I'm in me chemise. Ye, on the other hand, are bare-arsed, husband," Merry snapped back in case he'd missed that fact.

"My men will not care about me being naked," he argued, pushing the furs back toward her.

"And I doona mind, either," Una assured her, ogling Alex.

Merry scowled at her. "Well, I do. 'Sides, they willna care about me in me chemise."

"They may not, but *I* do," Alex growled back, and then gave up trying to cover her and merely scooped her up in the furs and headed for the wagon, saying firmly, "You shall have to borrow a gown from Una for the rest of the journey."

Merry didn't tell him then that she had gowns.

She was too busy scowling over his shoulder at Una.
The maid had stood to follow, and her eyes were
fixed firmly on Alex's behind as she did. Judging
by the expression on her face, she was enjoying the
view, too. Merry thought it terribly rude and was
not enjoying her enjoyment.

chapter

Fifteen

It was a hard ride for the next couple of days.
With no tent to sleep in at night, they were forced
to sleep around the fire with the rest of the men,
and so Alex saw no reason to stop each day until
well into the night.

It troubled him that this latest attempt on his life
had nearly seen his wife killed, and that was another reason he rode them so hard to reach home.
He knew he was driving them all to exhaustion and
risked the wagon losing a wheel, but hoped that the
exhaustion would be enough to keep whoever kept
attacking him from doing so again and possibly succeeding this time, if not in killing him, then in kill-

ing his wife. He would not lose Merry now when things were starting to look up between them.

By the last day, the pace he'd set had everyone grumpy, and so when the sun set when they were only four or five hours from d'Aumesbery, rather than call a halt and sleep one more night in the open before finishing the journey the next morning, Alex kept them going.

It was a relief to every one of the exhausted group when the torches on the towers of d'Aumesbery were spotted through the thinning woods. Alex glanced down to Merry to point out that they were nearly there, but she was sound asleep in his lap. Unlike the journey out, she had ridden on her own for most of the way back. However, when he'd caught her starting to nod off in the saddle an hour ago, he'd pulled her before him on his mount and ordered her to sleep. He suspected it was a sign of how exhausted she was that she had not argued or even troubled herself about her mare, but had merely curled up and dropped off to sleep at once.

"She is dead to the world, poor thing," Gerhard said quietly from the side, and Alex glanced to where the man rode with Merry's horse trailing his own. The first had taken the mare's reins and attached them to his pommel to lead the beast when Alex had scooped Merry from her back.

"Aye," Alex agreed, and then added, "But dead to the world is better than just plain dead."

Gerhard nodded. "It has been hard the last few days, but 'tis better to reach d'Aumesbery quickly and avoid further possible problems on the trail."

"That was my thought," Alex agreed.

"I suspected as much," Gerhard admitted, and then added wryly, "But you may wish to explain that to your wife when she awakes. I think she and her maid thought you had lost your mind, riding us as you have."

Alex smiled wryly at the suggestion and nodded. They broke through the trees then and started up the sloping path to the castle gates.

The greeting here was much different from the one they'd received at Stewart. The men on the wall did not break out in smiles or wave and call out greetings as they let down the gate, and no one rushed across the bailey to crowd and meet them.

Alex told himself it was because it was the middle of the night, but knew even had they arrived during the day, they would not have been welcomed as they had been at Merry's childhood home. He had been away for years and only recently returned to a troubled keep, only to turn around and leave again, and Merry herself was altogether new here. But he hoped that someday their people would be as pleased to see them return from a journey as the people of Stewart had been to see Merry.

It was a goal for him to work toward, Alex decided. He would gain the trust and love of his people so that his return was always welcomed.

Alex drew his mount to a halt at the keep stairs and eased out of the saddle still clutching her close, and Merry did no more than stir and mutter unhappily before dropping off back to sleep. Shaking his head at his wife's ability to sleep through anything, he didn't bother to give any orders or instructions to Gerhard and the men, but left them to it. Secure

in the knowledge that they would do whatever was
necessary and tend to the wagon and horses before
seeking their own beds, he carried Merry inside
and moved quietly through the sleeping bodies in
the great hall to reach the stairs. He met no one as
he made his way up to their room. Once there, he
settled Merry on the bed and then simply collapsed
beside her, too exhausted even to think about un-
dressing either of them. They would just have to
sleep in their clothes this night, he thought as sleep
washed over him.

Merry woke to find herself alone in the room she
shared with Alex at d'Aumesbery. Her first reaction
was relief that she was not lying stiff and sore on
the cold hard ground but instead in her warm bed.
Her second reaction was to wonder when they had
arrived, where her husband was, and if he'd even
joined her in the bed. The last thought brought a
wave of depression over her, for while Merry had
slept at Alex's side every night since leaving Donnachaidh, that was all they had done. He had not
touched her in any way that could be construed as
sexual, or even kissed her since the night he'd been
so aggressive and they'd realized he was being
drugged.

It was all rather depressing to Merry, which
was ironic when she considered that on her wedding night she hadn't been at all impressed with
Edda's description of the bedding. At the time she
had thought it would be a grand thing did he not
bother her too often. Now she lay in that same bed
and fretted because he was not bothering her with

it. Life did seem to like to have its little jokes, she thought wearily, and started to sit up, only to drop back down and pull the linens a little closer as the bedchamber door opened.

She held her breath, but then expelled it when Alex entered. He wore clean clothes, and his hair was damp, as if he'd bathed recently. He was also leading a parade of servants who were carrying a tub and several pails of water, some steaming, some not. Merry lay still as her husband oversaw the operation. Alex did not even glance her way that she noticed, so she was somewhat surprised when the servants finished and he moved to close the door behind them as they left, saying, "Are you going to lie there until I come fetch you? Or will you get up to enjoy your bath?"

Merry hesitated, and then sat up, surprised to find that she still wore the clothes she'd donned the last day of the journey. She hadn't thought to look, but had just assumed she was naked, but now threw the linens aside and slid her slippered feet to the floor.

"I was too tired to undress either of us last night," Alex announced as he moved back to the tub and bent to test the temperature. Apparently satisfied, he began to pour perfumed oil into it.

"What time was it when we arrived?" Merry asked, moving around the end of the bed to join him.

"I am not sure," Alex admitted as he finished with his task and straightened. "Three in the morn, perhaps four."

"Oh." Merry's gaze fixed on the tub of steaming water. It did look inviting. She hadn't had a proper bath in days. By the time they had stopped at night, she'd been too tired to be bothered, and while she'd managed a quick wash here and there on one or two occasions in the morning, they'd been hurried and not very satisfactory. The idea of a proper soak and scrub now was an attractive one and made her smile gratefully at her husband.

"Thank you," she murmured, and then asked, "Did ye already have a bath yerself? I notice yer hair's wet."

Alex nodded as he set the oil aside and approached her. "I bathed in the kitchens to save the servants some work and keep from waking you."

Merry raised her eyebrows, thinking that must have given the kitchen staff a thrill, and then scowled as she recalled Una's ogling her naked husband after the fire, and imagined all the lovely little maids in the kitchen doing so.

"Behind a screen in the kitchens, so you can stop scowling," Alex added with amusement as he came to a halt before her. "Come, let us get you into your bath."

When he reached for her laces and began undoing them, she felt the blush of heat that rose up her cheeks and quickly brushed his hands away, muttering, "I can manage."

But Alex was not a bee to be brushed away. He ignored her fluttering hands and continued with his efforts, not only undoing the laces in a trice, but then removing her gown and setting to work on her chemise as well. Merry was a clumsy mess as she tried to help, her mind taken up with wondering where this might lead, and hoping . . .

However, the wondering and hope were all for naught. The moment he had her stripped naked, Alex picked her up like a child and set her in the tub. He then turned away and headed for the door, murmuring, "Take as long as you like. There is nothing of import we need do today."

Merry watched the door close behind her husband, disappointment claiming her. While she knew she needed a bath, she had hoped that he might aid her in the endeavor and then follow it up with some houghmagandy. But it seemed he had no interest in that with her now that he was no longer being drugged.

"'Tis enough to make me seek out what it was he was being dosed with and mix some up meself," she muttered to herself, but could not even manage a smile at her own joke. The situation was too dire and miserable in her mind for that. He had taught her the pleasure of the marital bed and now was not interested in enjoying it with her. 'Twas a sad state to her mind and made her feel ugly and lacking in whatever it was that attracted a man. It made her feel unworthy, she supposed, and that was a feeling she'd had often over the years.

While she knew her mother had loved her, Merry had done so much to aid and comfort the woman that she had always wondered if that love was for herself or for what she'd done. And then there were her father and brothers. While they were showing caring now, they had not always done so despite all she had done to keep things running smoothly at Stewart . . . and in her young mind, she'd always felt that if they'd loved her, they would have fought off the sick hold drink had on them and try to relieve some of her burden.

Now it appeared she was not satisfactory in her husband's eyes, either, without the tonic to make her so.

The salty taste of tears on her lips brought Merry to the realization that she was weeping, and she was suddenly furious with herself. Why should her husband want her when she was such a puling, pathetic creature that she wept for no reason?

Gritting her teeth, she raised her knees and slid her bottom forward so that she could dunk her head under the water and remove the evidence of her weakness. When she came back up a moment later, Merry immediately concentrated on washing herself, trying to distract herself from the ache in her chest. She had managed to do so and was composed and nearly finished with her bath when the bedchamber door opened and Alex reentered with a tray in hand. Merry glanced with disinterest at the food and drink on the tray and then again slid under the water, this time to rinse away the soap she'd just finished lathering in her hair.

When she reemerged, it was to find that Alex had deposited the tray on the fur before the fire and now stood beside the bath, holding open a clean, dry linen.

"Come, you can sit by the fire and eat while your hair dries," he said.

Merry hesitated at the thought of standing naked before him, but then reminded herself that he had seen every inch of her body ere this and forced herself to do so. Did he find her body so ugly and unattractive, hiding it was hardly going to make a difference. She stood grimly and was relieved when he merely wrapped the linen around her and lifted her out of the bath.

Alex set her on her feet on the floor and quickly dried her down with the linen in a perfunctory manner before wrapping it around her once again and urging her to the fireside.

Merry noted the two glasses and the pile of food and glanced around to ask if he planned to join her, but paused when she saw that he'd moved back to the door. She thought he was about to leave, but then he opened the door and several servants bustled in to use the pails to empty most of the water from the tub before carrying the tub and the pails away. The whole operation took no more than moments, and Merry had barely sat and was only just surveying what he'd brought for them to eat when Alex closed the door behind the last body and then crossed the room to join her.

"It looks lovely. Thank ye," Merry murmured, managing a smile as he joined her.

Alex nodded as he settled cross-legged opposite her on the fur, and then smiled wryly as he admitted, " 'Tis probably too much, but I was hungry when I was choosing what to bring."

Merry smiled faintly at the confession, but had no idea what to say so simply ate and pondered how she could be so uncomfortable with him after everything they had been through. She was more uncomfortable right that moment than she had been the day she'd met him, or even on their wedding night. But at that time she had not cared for the man so much. Her own opinion of him had been so poor, she hadn't worried what he thought of her. Now, however, loving him as she did—

Merry sucked in a breath as the thought started to flit through her mind, and nearly choked on the grape she'd just popped into her mouth. Loving him as she did?

Aye, Merry admitted. She'd fallen in love with the blasted man. He was caring and considerate, intelligent and amusing, and all the things she could have wanted in a husband. Well, but for the fact that he did not want her, she thought unhappily, and knew that this one thing was not just a wrinkle she could smooth away to enjoy happiness over the coming years. 'Twas a huge wolf in their bed that would rend her apart in time. 'Twould tear at her self-esteem and sense of worth, make her doubt that he cared for her at all, and leave her feeling alone and, once again, unworthy.

"Merry? What is it?" Alex asked suddenly, and the concern in his voice told her that her fears and unhappiness were showing.

"Nothing," she assured him, her voice husky with unshed tears. "I merely choked on a grape."

Merry then turned her face solemnly to the offering between them, but was aware that he was watching her, his eyes sharp and thoughtful.

She'd chosen an apple and was carefully paring the skin away with the knife that had been provided when he suddenly said, "Cullen said something to me as we were leaving Donnachaidh."

"Oh?" Merry asked, concentrating on the task at hand.

"He suggested I may want to reassure you that I was attracted to you and that it was not the dosing I was receiving that brought me to your bed."

The knife slipped, slicing into her thumb, and Merry gasped and popped it into her mouth as she stared wide-eyed at her husband.

"Let me see that," Alex said, sounding annoyed as he shifted around the food to her side. He pulled her thumb from her mouth and cursed at the wound she'd given herself and then applied pressure with his own thumb to stop the bleeding as he berated her. "You must be more careful, wife. Honestly, you are forever slicing yourself up and I will not lose you to some stupid infection or—"

Alex paused suddenly, his eyes meeting hers, and Merry stared back, surprised at the outburst over such a small thing. Suddenly, he closed his eyes and shook his head. "You do think that, don't you?"

Merry blinked in confusion, but after a moment realized that he had returned to the original topic and was asking if she did believe that his attraction to her had been only because of the tonic he'd been given. She was tempted to lie and deny it, but they were husband and wife, and had a whole life ahead to deal with each other. Lies did not seem a clever way to manage the situation. Swallowing the sudden knot of anxiety and shame in her throat, she murmured, "Well, ye've no' bedded me since the night we realized ye were bein' dosed and took precautions against it, and it has occurred to me that mayhap now that ye're no' being dosed ye've lost interest or—"

Her words died on a gasp of surprise as she found

herself suddenly pushed back on the furs. The gasp then died as well, as he followed her and covered her mouth with his own, swallowing the sound. Merry almost caught at his arms in surprise, but remembered the knife she held at the last moment and dropped it before reaching to grasp him. She had barely done so and begun to kiss him back when he broke the kiss as abruptly as it had started and suddenly leaned up so she could see his face.

"Look into my eyes, wife," Alex ordered grimly, and she did so with some confusion until he pointed out. "There is no dilation now. I am not drugged, but I want you, Merry." He ground the bulge between his legs against her to be sure she understood that he did indeed want her, and then added, "I have not bedded you for days because there has not been the opportunity. That first night in the tent my head was still pounding badly and I was exhausted from just riding."

"I knew we should ha'e waited another day ere travelin'," she muttered irritably at this news. "Evelinde and I both told ye 'twas too soon to be up."

"Aye," he admitted, and laughed at her irritation. "Mayhap it was, but I missed you in my bed and was happier leaving and at least being able to hold you, even if I was too exhausted to do aught else."

Merry went still. "Really?"

"Aye, really."

She took in his expression briefly and then said, "But then on the second night, why did we not—"

"Merry, the tent burned to the ground," he reminded her dryly. "We left the ruins there in the clearing and were forced to sleep around the fire with the men. Would you have me tumble my wife right there for all to see?"

"We could have slipped away to a private spot as we did on the way to Scotland," she pointed out.

"And risk having my head bashed in again?" he asked dryly. "Or worse yet, you getting in the way and getting hurt?" Alex shook his head and then admitted, "I was tempted, but in the end I was too afraid of losing you to my momentary greed."

"Well, we could ha'e slept in the wagon then," Merry suggested. "Una wouldna ha'e minded."

"Again, we would have been away from the men and more vulnerable to attack. I was not willing to risk you that way. 'Twas safer to stick close to and even sleep by the fire, surrounded by the men, and safety was my main concern. So I decided it was simply better to get us all home as quickly as possible." He smiled wryly and added, "I suppose you did notice that I set a punishing pace on the return journey? That was not wholly out of a concern for my, or even your, well-being. I was eager to get back here where we could be alone."

"Really?" she asked, her heart filling with hope.

"Oh, aye, Merry, really," he assured her grimly and then added, "Just think on it logically. While I imagine that dosing me did make me randier than usual, that was all it could do. It could not make me randy for you. I could have taken that randiness it caused elsewhere, had I wished. True?"

She scowled at the very suggestion, but nodded.

"But I did not. And I did not do so because my interest lay only with you," he told her solemnly and then assured her, "Merry, I find you beautiful and graceful and strong and intelligent. I am proud and happy to have you to wife, and were my father still alive I would be thanking him ten times a day for arranging this marriage. I want you, and none other than you. In fact . . ." He paused to take a breath and then admitted, "I love you, wife."

"Ye love me?" she asked, almost afraid she'd misheard him.

Alex's mouth tipped crookedly at her expression, and he said solemnly, "Aye, Merry. I love you. How could I help it? You are strong and determined and take on whatever needs doing when others will not. Yet, despite the hard outer shell you present to the world, your heart is still soft and you care for those around you. Aye, I love you, Merry d'Aumesbery."

Merry stared at Alex, a terrible sharp ache in her chest that she knew was love. She wanted to hold him so close that they would forever be one and never again part, but all she could do was swallow and blink away the tears that had risen to film her eyes, and then say equally solemnly, "And I love and want ye, too, husband. I find ye handsome and sweet and ever so considerate. I—"

He brought her list of his good attributes to an end with a kiss that took her breath away. Merry did not fight him. She could tell him how wonderful he was later. For now she wished to enjoy this newfound love in the most satisfying way she knew of. She wished to take him inside her body and feel him fill her up until they were one in body as well as heart.

* * *

Merry woke the next morning to sunshine and bird-song pouring through the unshuttered window . . . and Una standing over her, dry amusement on her face.

"I'm guessin' all is right with yer world," Una commented wryly as Merry blinked her eyes open and smiled at her.

"Aye," she admitted with a grin and sat up to glance around. "Where is me husband?"

"Up and off tendin' to castle business hours ago," Una informed her, moving away to open her chest and begin rooting through it for what Merry should wear that day. "I'd ha'e rousted ye from yer bed at the time, but he ordered me to let ye sleep as long as ye liked," she announced as she settled on a dark green gown and got to her feet once more. As she walked back toward her, Una added dryly, "He, too, was smiling like a fool. 'Tis obvious the two o' ye got up to houghmagandy while locked in here all day yesterday."

"Jealous?" Merry teased with a grin.

"Aye," she admitted sourly. "I need me a man with a claymore. Even that boy Godfrey is lookin' attractive to me just now."

Merry laughed at the suggestion as she tossed the linens aside and hopped from bed. "I think ye were right about yer feelin's ere we left Stewart, Una," she announced as she moved to the basin of water to wash up. "I believe I will be much happier here than I ever was at Stewart."

"Aye," Una agreed, and then added seriously, "And 'tis happy I am fer ye. Ye've a fine husband there and I foresee many happy years and braw children . . . do the two o' ye settle this nasty business o' druggin' and attackin' ere one o' ye is seriously hurt."

Merry's smile immediately began to fade at this reminder that there was a snake in paradise.

"I had forgotten about that," she admitted on a mutter, and wondered how she possibly could.

"Well, I wouldna feel too bad about it. It looked to me like yer husband had quite fergot it, too, this morn. 'Tis that rosy glow of love. It fogs yer mind and blankets anything unpleasant."

"Aye," Merry murmured, and thought that she must not forget again. In fact, she was suddenly determined to resolve the situation as quickly as possible and asked, "Where is Edda?"

"At the table in the great hall," Una responded heavily. "And I can tell ye the servants are acting even queerer around her than usual, especially old Bet. I suspect Edda was up to no good while we were gone."

Merry didn't comment, but pondered this news as she washed and dressed. The more she heard, the more her own suspicions turned reluctantly to the woman, and it did seem for the best did they send her away, at least until they sorted the matter out.

Una left her to her silence as she helped her dress, and then remained behind to make the bed and clean up the room. Merry was alone when she descended the stairs to the great hall. Edda was no longer at the table, but had moved to sit by the fire. She stood, however, when she saw Merry, and smiled widely as she crossed the room to meet her at the table.

"Welcome back!"

Merry smiled in return and felt a pinch of guilt for her suspicions when the woman bent to hug her where she sat. It was enough to make her hug her back a bit more enthusiastically than she was feeling. "Thank ye. I hope all was well here while we were away?"

"Oh, aye," Edda assured her as she settled on the bench to keep her company. "My, you were hardly gone long enough for anything to be unwell."

"We had some difficulties on the journey and Alex thought it best to return."

"So I heard." Edda shook her head. "Accidents, the tent in flames, and someone drugging Alex? 'Tis hard to believe."

"Aye," Merry murmured, offering a smile to Lia as the maid appeared with food and drink for her.

"I hope you found Evelinde well?" Edda asked as the maid left.

Recalling Evelinde's comment that she should watch Edda when she told her of her happiness, Merry turned to smile at her widely and watched her expression as she gushed, "Oh, aye. She is wonderfully happy. 'Tis obvious she and Cullen are very much in love. The man dotes on her and she on him. 'Twas enough to make me jealous."

"What a relief," Edda said, and the words seemed genuine, as did her concern as she admitted, "I fear I have been fretting over the girl. We were not close, but still, she was my husband's daughter and I did worry how she would get along with the Devil of Donnachaidh. By all accounts he is a cold, heartless bastard." She paused and shook her head. "But

I suppose such names mean little in Scotland, and these tales just spread and grow until they carry little truth. After all, they call you the Stewart Shrew and that title hardly fits, does it?" She laughed.

Merry smiled and then turned to her food, now thoroughly confused. The woman truly seemed happy and relieved that Evelinde was well. Either she was a much better actor than Evelinde had supposed, or the woman really had turned a new leaf. It made Merry feel guilty for the suspicions she'd allowed the others to bring about in her. She herself had been falsely accused and knew how hurtful it could be. Now she was anxious about her promise to see Edda sent away to visit her sister. She still intended to carry that plan through, but was troubled at the prospect and found herself unable to join in properly as Edda chattered away keeping her company. Fortunately, she had the excuse of eating and drinking to cover her silence, but she was grateful when she was done and could excuse herself to go check on how things had gone while she was away.

Merry's guilt and discomfort made her avoid Edda for the rest of the day, and it was not until supper that she spoke to the woman again. Her mother-in-law was as cheerful and happy to see her then as she'd been that morning, but—terribly aware of Alex beside her and knowing he suspected the woman as much as his sister did—Merry found herself extremely uncomfortable through that meal as well.

When the sup had ended and Edda suggested they relax by the fire to attend to mending, Merry forced a smile and promised to join her in a moment and then waited until she had moved away from the table before turning to Alex.

"You are finding dealing with Edda difficult," Alex said sympathetically the moment his step-mother was out of earshot.

Merry was surprised at his intuition, but nodded silently and managed a true if weak smile when he leaned forward to press a quick kiss to her lips. Once he'd straightened again, he peered at her solemnly and then suggested, "Mayhap it would be for the best did we send her away to her sister's as you suggested."

"Evelinde suggested it," Merry said quickly, feeling disloyal enough without taking the full burden of responsibility for sending the woman away. Still, she could not wholly shirk the responsibility. "But, aye, mayhap 'tis fer the best."

"Then I shall ask her sister's name and suggest a visit," he said simply.

"Evelinde told me the name," Merry murmured, but then paused. The sound of the great hall door opening had distracted him, and Alex was glancing toward it, a scowl claiming his lips as he saw who entered. Merry followed his gaze, her eyebrows rising slightly as she saw that it was Godfrey. The lad hadn't attended the sup and she'd thought he must be on a chore for Alex. Judging by her husband's irritated expression as he stood to meet the lad, if he had been on a chore for him, Godfrey hadn't been quick enough about the task.

"What the hell took you so long?" Alex asked irritably as the boy came to a stumbling halt before him. "I sent you to the village shortly after noon. You should have been back hours ago."

"I am sorry, my lord," Godfrey said quickly, and then, shamefaced, admitted, "I met a courier on the way, got turned around in the woods, and lost my way back. I have been wandering for hours. I— Here. He gave me this letter to bring to you."

Alex scowled, but took the letter and barked less angrily, "You missed the sup. Go to the kitchens and get yourself something to eat."

"Aye, my lord. Thank you, my lord." The boy hurried off, disappearing into the kitchens as quickly as his legs would carry him, probably more in a rush to escape his lord's angry glare than an eagerness to find food.

Merry's gaze slid back to her husband as he untied the ribbon around the scroll and then unrolled it. "What is it?"

" 'Tis just a letter from his father, checking on how he is faring," Alex said. "He frets about the boy unnecessarily. I think 'tis because he is so small for his age and looks so much younger than he is." He paused to glance at her and then added with a grin, "I hope our own sons inherit their size from me."

Merry smiled faintly, her mind immediately moving to ponder their possible children and what they might look like as she asked, "How old is Godfrey?"

"Sixteen. Near a man, really, and much older than most boys are when sent away to squire, but as I say, I suspect his size and young looks have made his parents overprotective," Alex murmured as he turned back to continue reading the missive.

Merry's eyes widened with surprise. "Godfrey is indeed small and young-looking for his age. I would ha'e guessed him to be no more than twelve or thirteen. He barely has any meat or muscle on him."

"Aye, well, he's stronger than he looks," Alex murmured, setting the letter on the table. He then gave her a quick kiss even as he got to his feet to move toward the kitchen. "Excuse me, wife, I forgot to ask him how he fared with the task I'd set him. We can continue this discussion about sending Edda away later in our room where prying ears will not hear."

Merry nodded her understanding and watched him head to the kitchens before moving to join Edda by the fire as she'd promised.

"Alex looked annoyed," Edda commented as Merry took the seat across from her and began to poke through the endless mending that needed doing. "Is Godfrey failing in his position of squire?"

"Nay. Well, I do not think so. Alex apparently sent the boy to the village after lunch and expected him back much sooner, but Godfrey got lost on the return journey."

"From the village?" Edda asked with a bark of disbelieving laughter. She shook her head. "That boy is forever getting himself lost. He needs a couple of lessons in navigating ere he's let loose again, else he'll find himself in the wrong place at the wrong time and beset by bandits."

"Aye," Merry said, and decided she would mention as much to her husband this evening when they retired to their room.

"I need a refill on my mead, Merry," Edda announced suddenly, setting her sewing aside. "How about you?"

"Nay. I am fine, but I can fetch it fer ye, if ye like," Merry offered, eager for an excuse to escape the mending. It was not one of her favorite tasks.

"Nay, nay, that is all right," Edda said, getting to her feet. "My fingers are sore and stiff from sewing and I could use the chance to stretch my legs. You go on and get started, I shall return directly."

Merry watched her go and then glanced down to the braies in her lap and grimaced. She really wasn't in the mood for sewing, but it had to be done. She set to work, her thoughts wandering as she sewed, and then glanced up eagerly when the kitchen door opened once more and she saw Edda returning.

"I have decided I am rather weary tonight, Merry," the older woman announced, pausing beside her chair. "I think I shall retire early and finish this to-morrow night."

"Oh, all right," Merry murmured, and then offered a smile. "Well, good sleep then, Edda."

"Thank you, dear. And you, too. See you in the morning."

Merry nodded and watched her head off, then glanced back to her sewing once more, but managed only one stitch before restlessness had her setting it aside and wandering to the trestle table. She thought she would wait there for her husband's return and then suggest they, too, retire early. She was not tired herself, but was bored, and they might as well retire to their rooms where they could discuss Edda in privacy and decide how they were to approach her on taking a visit with her sister.

Merry settled at the table and began to toy absently with the letter from Godfrey's father, rolling the scroll around on the tabletop as she waited. After another moment's passing, she then unrolled the scroll for something to do and glanced over the contents with a bored eye. It was exactly what Alex had said it was, a letter from Godfrey's father asking about his welfare and how he was working out as squire. It wasn't until her eye slid to the signature that Merry's ennui died an abrupt death.

"Lord Alfred Duquet," she breathed the name aloud, her mind suddenly in an uproar. Evelinde had said Duquet was the name of Edda's sister's husband. Godfrey was Edda's nephew? Surely Alex would have mentioned it, she thought, and then recalled his saying that he'd forgotten Edda even had a sister and could not recall her name. He didn't know, she realized. And neither Godfrey nor Edda had mentioned it. Why?

Not for any good purpose, she decided with grim certainty and headed for the kitchens. This was something she needed to talk to Alex about at once. If Godfrey was Edda's nephew, he might very well have been the one behind the attacks on their journey, she thought, and suddenly recalled that he was the first person she'd run into on bringing Alex back from the waterfall. He'd claimed—and she'd believed him when he said—that he was coming from camp to relieve himself, but now she wondered if he hadn't been checking to see if his attempt had succeeded and his lord was dead. He certainly hadn't continued on with his chore to relieve himself that she knew of.

Merry didn't like to believe the thoughts now crowding her head, for she liked Godfrey, but this news placed suspicion firmly on his head . . . and Edda's, she realized unhappily, suddenly sure the kind woman who had been so welcoming to her since her arrival was just a façade. Evelinde had been certain Edda could not have changed, but Merry had been sure she was wrong. Now, however, she tended to think her sister-in-law might be right. It still didn't all make sense, but with this new bit of information perhaps she and Alex could sort it out. Or at least question the pair of them and get to the bottom of matters, she hoped, pushing the kitchen door open and peering around the busy room for her husband.

Her mouth tightened with displeasure when she didn't spot either him or Godfrey, and then her gaze landed on Una chatting with the old servant, Bet, and she headed in her direction.

"Una? Have you seen Alex?"

"Aye. He took Godfrey up to the tower."

"Whatever for?" she asked with surprise.

"Well, he was in here asking Godfrey about something he'd sent him to the village for when Edda came in and teased the boy about his complete lack of direction. She said only a fool could get lost on the way back from the village, or someone completely ignorant of navigation. She then asked Alex had he not taught the boy to navigate by the moss on the trees during the day and the stars at night." Una grimaced and muttered, "The cow. She was making like 'twas all teasing, but she was criticizing him for all that."

Merry felt her mouth compress, knowing Edda's

words had probably felt as sharp to Alex as her own insult to his sense of responsibility when she'd suggested it was not well done of him to plan a trip to Donnachaidh without first tending to his men's fighting skills here.

"I thought he'd snap at her, but no such luck," Una said glumly.

Merry raised an eyebrow at the disappointment in her voice. Una's comments made it more and more obvious that not only was she not warming to Alex's stepmother, but instead she seemed to be growing a stronger antipathy to her, but Merry had no idea why that was. Even the maid could not explain it, claiming 'twas just a feeling she had about the woman.

"Anyway," Una went on, drawing her attention back to her explanation, "yer husband decided he'd teach the boy what he could tonight and ushered him off up to the tower to train him in how to navigate by the stars."

"I did not see them pass through the great hall."

"Nay, he used the back stairs." Una turned and gestured to a stairwell in the back corner of the room. "It meets up with the stairs from the second floor about halfway up."

"Is there a guard on that tower?" Merry asked sharply, a bad feeling flowing through her.

"Nay. Well, there was, but he came down to find a warm drink just as Edda entered, and when Alex decided to take Godfrey up there, he said he'd keep an eye out and suggested the guard give his legs a stretch. He's going to send for him when he's done."

"Then he and Godfrey are alone up there?" she asked with sudden alarm.

"Aye," Una answered, and then asked, "What is it? Ye've gone all pale."

"Godfrey is Edda's nephew," Merry muttered, and rushed for the stairs, suddenly sure her husband should not be alone with Godfrey.

erry was perhaps halfway up the wind-
ing tower staircase when Edda suddenly
stepped out of the shadows a step or two
above her. The woman's appearance brought an
abrupt halt to her headlong rush, and Merry eyed
her warily and pressed a hand to the stone wall to
steady herself.

"Edda," she greeted, managing to keep her voice
polite.

"Why, Merry dear, wherever are you headed in
such a hurry?" Edda asked lightly, gracing her with
one of her sweet smiles.

Merry considered her briefly, and then said, "I thought to go join Alex and Godfrey on the roof."

"What a lovely idea," Edda responded at once. "I could do with a bit of fresh air myself. Why do we not go up together?"

When she hesitated, wondering how to handle this, Edda suddenly slipped her hand out from behind her back, revealing a small but lethal-looking dagger with a jeweled handle. Her smile suddenly as sharp as the blade's edge, she suggested, "Why do you not lead the way?"

Merry's mouth tightened, but she had little choice but to do as Edda said and started forward. It wasn't until she was passing Edda that she saw the door she'd been standing in front of. The door to the second floor, Merry supposed, stiffening when she felt the tip of Edda's blade press into her back.

"I had a feeling you might be a problem when I saw your expression as you read the letter at the table. Godfrey told me it was from his father. You recognized the name, didn't you?"

Merry nodded. "Evelinde said your sister was married to a Lord Duquet. I thought it too much of a coincidence that Godfrey's father was also a Lord Duquet."

"Hmm. I thought so," Edda said, and Merry couldn't help but notice that the sweet, affectionate voice was gone, a cold and even smug one in its place.

"I thought ye'd gone to yer room," Merry muttered, continuing grimly up the stairs.

"I did, but only to fetch my knife. 'Twas as I was leaving my room and walking by the stairs that I happened to glance down and see you seated at the trestle table in the great hall, reading the letter from Godfrey's father."

"Ye mean yer brother-in-law, do ye no'?" she asked dryly.

"Aye, he is that, too," Edda admitted. "Though I've never had much use for either him or my sister. They are a pair of mealymouthed, whey-faced cows; perfect for each other, but hardly interesting otherwise."

"And Godfrey?" Merry asked grimly.

"Oh, he at least shows *some* promise," she said, and then clucked her tongue and added, "Unfortunately, he is young yet and prone to make mistakes."

Thank God, Merry thought unhappily. Those mistakes were probably the only reason Alex still lived, and if she was lucky, he might make another tonight and she and Alex might yet get out of this.

"Speaking of my nephew," Edda said suddenly, prodding her with the blade, "do move more quickly, Merry, I am eager to see that all is well in the tower. If Godfrey hasn't erred yet again, Alex should already be lying broken on the stones below the tower."

Merry prayed that wasn't true and paused to peer back at her as she asked, "Why are ye doin' all o' this?"

"Because I am not ready to give up my position as Lady d'Aumesbery," Edda said simply.

"Killing Alex would not achieve that for you," Merry pointed out. "Neither will killing both of us. D'Aumesbery will merely go to Evelinde and Cullen and their heirs."

"No, it will not," Edda assured her firmly, and

jabbed her angrily with the blade for the suggestion.

Merry winced as it made a shallow cut in her back,
but merely shook her head and continued walking.
To her mind, the woman's plan could never work.
D'Aumesbery certainly would go to Evelinde and
Cullen did Edda succeed in killing both Alex and
her this night. The woman was obviously mad, she
decided, and then reminded herself that being mad
merely made her more dangerous. She then gave up
trying to sort out Edda's reasoning in favor of trying
to anticipate what was coming and find a way to
save both herself and Alex.

Unfortunately, she had little time to think. They
had almost reached the tower by then, and all too
soon they were stepping out into the starlit night.
Merry immediately glanced around, searching out
her husband, but any hopes she might have pinned
on him died the moment she saw him lying unconscious before Godfrey. He had either fallen across
the top of the parapet when Godfrey had attacked
him unexpectedly, or he had fallen on the floor and
Godfrey had so far managed to get him half over
the bulwark. She could not tell if her husband was
dead or just unconscious, but knew he must be one
or the other for he was completely still and silent
as the boy pushed and prodded at his limp form,
trying to push him up and over the wall.

"Dammit, Godfrey! Can you do nothing right?"
Edda snapped, urging Merry across the tower
toward them. "Alex should be lying broken and
dead in the bailey below by now."

"Oh, aye," Godfrey grunted, not bothering to

look around as he worked. "And if you think 'tis that easy, why do you not get over here and try to push him off? I have no stomach for this bit of business anyway."

"That became more than obvious to me with your repeated failures to kill him on the way to and back from Scotland," Edda said dryly, catching Merry's arm and drawing her to a halt several feet from the pair. "Unfortunately, you shall have to manage it on your own as I am presently otherwise engaged."

"Ha ha," Godfrey snapped, sounding nothing like the sweet, shy lad she'd known since arriving at d'Aumesbery. It seemed Edda was not the only actor in the family. "Why do you not—"

Godfrey's words died as he finally glanced over and spotted Merry with Edda. He gave up pushing at Alex then and let him drop back to the ground in a heap as he turned to stare at her in horror.

"What is she doing here?" he asked with alarm, stepping in front of Alex as if to hide his body with his small frame.

"What do you think she is doing here?" Edda snapped with disgust. "She read the letter from your father and connected the names. Evelinde told her my sister was Lady Duquet," she added grimly. "Certainly Alex never recognized the name."

Godfrey bit his lip and then glanced to Merry, "My lady, I—"

"Oh, please," Edda interrupted with disgust. "Do not tell me you intend to grovel and plead for forgiveness. You are trying to kill her husband. She will hardly thank you for that when the little fool is so obviously in love with him."

Godfrey fell silent, his gaze returning reluctantly to Alex's prone form. Afraid he would now continue with his efforts to throw Alex off the wall, Merry asked quickly, "So you were the one behind the accidents and fire on the journey?"

"I thought you were in the wagon with Una when I set the fire," Godfrey said quickly.

"That is not what she asked," Edda said with amusement and then told Merry, "Aye, it was him. He is a good boy, more than eager to help out his auntie for my silence and a few coins."

That caught Merry's attention, and she glanced back to the woman to ask curiously, "Silence on what?"

"Our little Godfrey has something of a gambling problem. He got himself in some trouble earlier this year when he accompanied my sister and her husband to court and got himself in deep with usurers."

"Was he not in Tunis with Alex this last year?" Merry asked with surprise.

"Nay. Godfrey replaced Alex's last squire, who was finished with his training when he returned from Tunis," Edda explained.

Alex hadn't mentioned that, Merry thought with a small frown. But then why should he? She was sure there was much he had not mentioned and she hadn't thought to ask about.

"At any rate," Edda continued, "Alfred paid off Godfrey's debts and exhorted him to stop. Godfrey, of course, promised he would, but both Alfred and my sister were fretting that he would not be able to resist, and so I suggested he be sent here to be trained by Alex. I pointed out that here, far from court or even a large town for quite a distance, there would be little temptation for Godfrey to break his promise. And I, of course, would keep an eye on the boy." She grinned, and Merry felt pity for the sister who had been foolish enough to trust her son's well-being to this woman.

"And no one mentioned the connection between ye to Alex?" she asked quietly.

Edda pursed her lips as if in thought, and then clucked. "I do believe I may have forgotten to mention that. I may even have suggested to my sister that they might not wish to mention it, either . . . just so that Alex did not start asking questions, learn of Godfrey's gambling problems, and reject the request, of course."

"O' course," Merry said dryly.

"They thought it all a wonderful idea and petitioned Alex at once. He accepted, and Godfrey arrived here just the day before you." Edda smiled at the lad with satisfaction, to which he scowled in return, which made her laugh as she turned back to Merry. "Unfortunately, even in the village here there is gambling. Cockfights and other low-class games of chance that anyone who wishes may bet on." She shrugged. "He soon found himself unable to resist the temptation of gambling and in trouble again owing money he did not have. He came to me, of course."

"And ye were ever so helpful," Merry suggested dryly.

"Of course. He is my nephew. I promised to pay off his debts and not tell his father—who would surely disinherit him this time—all in exchange for one little favor."

"Little?" Merry scoffed. "Ye've blackmailed the boy to commit murder. And you!" She turned on Godfrey. "Diya really think being hung fer murder is better than taking a beating from the local moneylender?"

"Nay," he said grimly. "But 'tis better than being disinherited and left a pauper without title, home, or wealth . . . and then I will only be hung if I am caught."

"Ye're caught," she said coldly, and was satisfied by the fear that flashed in the boy's eyes if only for a moment before he glanced to his aunt.

"Aye. You are," Edda agreed. "What are we going to do about that?"

Godfrey hesitated, his eyes sliding back to Merry, and she thought she saw a brief struggle on his face, but then he said, "Kill her, too."

"Nay. Then I shall surely be left homeless and penniless," Edda said, and then added grimly, "And trust me, nephew, does that happen I will not keep my mouth shut about your gambling here."

"Well, we cannot let her live," Godfrey argued, his brief moment of regret apparently gone. "She will see us both hanged."

"And if she dies without producing an heir, the castle will go to Evelinde and her husband and they shall surely cast me out," Edda snapped. "'Tis why it was done this way if you will recall. She was to get with child, then Alex was to die, and she was to follow once the babe was born and I could remain as his or her guardian and Lady d'Aumesbery for a good twenty years more, or longer if I could manage it. I *will* remain Lady of d'Aumesbery."

Merry's eyes were wide as she suddenly understood what had seemed so incomprehensible before. "Ye *were* dosing Alex to make him randy, not appear drunk and cause trouble between us."

Edda waved that away with irritation. "The slurring and staggering were an unfortunate side effect. The tonic was a combination of things to make him bed you often and well and get you with child. I also dumped some emetic in the soldiers' ale in the barracks to ensure they became ill so that Alex had to delay the trip. *And* I was giving you a tonic as well to strengthen you to accept his seed." She smiled slightly and added, "However, your tonic had no side effects, unpleasant or otherwise."

Merry's eyes narrowed at these words, but she merely said, "That is why ye were askin' about me being with child ere we headed to Scotland."

Edda smiled. "On your wedding night you told me you'd last had your woman's time two weeks earlier. When three weeks passed after the wedding and—no doubt—repeated beddings without its return, I knew my tonic had worked and you were with child." She shrugged. "There was no reason to delay killing Alex. An accident on his journey to Scotland seemed the safest bet." She turned angry eyes to her nephew and added in harsh tones, "However, the boy messed that up like he does everything."

While Godfrey stiffened and puffed up with outrage at the angry words, Merry had no interest in them whatsoever and asked, "But why continue on with the tonic on the trip then if ye thought I was carryin'?"

"There was extra left over," Edda said with a shrug. "I had made up an awful lot, expecting to have to dose him for longer than I did, and it did seem beneficial that the side effects made him clumsy and slow thinking. I thought he would be easier for Godfrey to handle did he continue dosing him. Howbeit," she added, turning a glare on the lad, "he messed that up, too, dosing himself by accident."

"I told you, it was not an accident. I slipped into the tent and dosed Lord Alex's wine while they were out checking the cut I gave her mare—"

"The cut was yer doing?" Merry interrupted.

Godfrey nodded. "Just a small one, a nick. I had to point right at it before Allan even noticed it," he added with disgust. "But then you two came out to look as I knew you would and I slipped into the tent to put the tonic in his wine."

"Too much tonic," Edda said grimly and complained to Merry, "He doubled the dosage I told him to use and then was foolish enough to drink it himself."

"You told me two portions," Godfrey argued.

"I told you one."

"Two," the boy insisted, and then added, "And I knew what I was doing when she pressed the tonic on me, but what could I do? Admit there was tonic in the wine and refuse to take it?"

Edda opened her mouth to snap back, but paused and turned a confused and suspicious glance Merry's way as she suddenly began to laugh. "What are you finding so funny, Merewen Stewart?"

"Merry d'Aumesbery," she corrected, sobering only slightly, and then explained, "I am laughing because the two o' ye are ridiculous. Ye're a pair o' jesters, too clumsy and foolish to succeed at anything."

"Is that right?" Edda asked grimly. "And yet your husband is about to die."

"And ye'll still have naught," Merry said with a shrug despite the fact that her heart ached at the thought of Alex dying. It wasn't going to happen could she help it, but she was still searching for a way to save them both and it was not looking good.

"We shall have you, and the child you carry," Edda pointed out, and when Merry opened her mouth, quickly went on, "You are about to say that you will surely turn us in the first chance you get. Howbeit, you will not get the chance. The tonic I gave Alex is not the only one I know. My mother was a master of herbs and tonics, and all things healing as well as not so healing in nature. I shall simply keep you full of one of the many that will leave you silent and your mind scrambled until the babe is born, and then you shall die giving birth . . . even if I have to smother you with a folded fur to do it."

Merry nodded slowly at these words, but then said, "Actually, I wasna goin' to say I would tell. I was goin' to say I'm no' carryin' a child."

Edda blinked several times, her mind apparently having difficulty accepting this, and then disbelief filled her face and she shook her head, "Nay. Your woman's time—"

"—has always been undependable; sometimes late, sometimes no' coming at all," Merry said with a shrug. "It used to worry me, but me mither told me she was the same way and I should ha'e no problem conceiving. Howbeit, I havena yet," she added pointedly.

"But—"

"Alex didna even bed me until the night ere the journey to Scotland," she announced triumphantly.

"But the blood," Edda protested with alarm.

"I told ye I cut me leg."

"But you said—"

"I told ye what ye wanted to hear, Edda," she said dryly. "The truth is, though, that after ye'd all departed that night, Alex got out o' bed to close the door properly, stumbled over some clothes on the way back, and knocked himself out. He wasna conscious and couldna consummate." Merry smiled her satisfaction and then said, "So, ye can do what ye like, but there'll be no heir to keep ye here as Lady d'Aumesbery. Ye *will* be homeless and penniless, for Evelinde will inherit, and she kens ye too well to be fooled by yer sweet smiles and kind words. She'll put ye out ere Alex and I are even placed in the family crypt."

Fury crossed Edda's face, but 'twas like lightning, there and gone quickly. A look of determination followed that was somehow more frightening than the fury could ever be. "That little bitch will never put me out. There *will* be an heir," she announced grimly. "I shall just keep you dosed as planned and have Godfrey at you every night until you begin to grow with one. And then—"

"The hell you will!"

Merry glanced sharply toward her husband to see

that he had regained consciousness. In fact, judging by his expression and the speed with which he regained his feet now, she suspected he'd regained consciousness shortly after she'd arrived and had heard most of the explanations. He looked more than angry, he was enraged, and it was enough to make Godfrey back away, wide-eyed.

"Stop him, you fool, else we are both done for," Edda snapped, even as she grabbed Merry by the arm and jerked her against her. The knife was at her throat ere Merry had fully come to rest with her back against the woman's chest, and she winced at the pressure of the cold steel on her throat. Her eyes automatically sought out her husband. When she saw that Alex had paused, his sword only half drawn as he saw her peril, Merry knew she would have to do something. She would not have him give up his weapon to save her. That would only see them both dead.

Movement from Godfrey drew her eyes then and she saw that the lad was taking advantage of Alex's distraction and rushing him with his own sword drawn. Ignoring the knife at her throat, Merry shouted a warning and then grabbed for Edda's arm and slammed her slippered foot down on one of Edda's even as she forced the hand away. Merry's actions were instinctive, things she'd been helping to train the Stewart men in since she was sixteen. She didn't think, but simply followed the training, pushing against Edda's wrist, and whirling out from between her and the knife. Edda, of course, was pulling at the weapon, trying to stab at her with it and prevent her escape. The moment Merry was out from between the knife and Edda, she reversed the pressure, adding her own impetus to Edda's so that the woman actually stabbed herself.

Both of them froze as the knife slammed into the base of her throat, and Merry found herself staring into Edda's startled, angry eyes, and then the life slipped from them and Merry released her as she began to sink to the floor of the tower roof.

She turned immediately to her husband then to find him in battle with his squire. His attention had obviously been only half on the fight as he'd kept an eye on what was happening with her. She saw the relief on his face as he noted that she was no longer in danger, and then Alex turned his attention wholly to Godfrey.

"You cannot win, boy, you know that. Give it up and live."

"Live how?" Godfrey asked bitterly. "In one of the cells in d'Aumesbery's dungeon? I think not, my lord. You shall have to kill me."

"So be it," Alex said quietly, and Merry turned away, not wishing to watch him have to kill the lad. Her gaze dropped to the woman lying at her feet, and she felt her mouth tighten. This was all her fault. Edda had brought about her own death as well as her nephew's, and Merry had no idea how they would tell Lady and Lord Duquet what had come to pass.

In the next moment the clang of swords ended with a grunt of pain. It was followed by a silence that made her bite her lip and then glance around just to be sure the end she'd thought had come and that Godfrey had not somehow got in a lucky blow. She found Alex kneeling beside the lad, smoothing the hair from his face and listening to something the boy was whispering to him. Merry stayed where she was, not wishing to intrude, but knew the moment when the boy drew his last breath by the way her husband's shoulders slumped and he bowed his head.

She moved to him then and rested one hand on his shoulder. Alex didn't respond for a moment and then he lifted a hand to clasp hers, and they remained like that a moment. It was how Gerhard found them when he rushed onto the tower roof moments later. Merry glanced around at the clank of metal that announced his arrival and raised one surprised eyebrow as the man came to an abrupt halt, his gaze sliding from Edda's prone body to Godfrey's.

"Una told me what you found in the letter and I came to see that all was well," he answered the silent question, and then added, "I take it, it was Edda and Godfrey behind it after all."

Merry nodded silently and then glanced to her husband with surprise when he rose beside her and said, "The lad died saving us from his aunt."

Gerhard gave a slight start at these words, his eyes sliding from Alex to her, and Merry realized that her own expression would give away the lie, but had trouble controlling it just then.

Alex must have realized it, too, for he slid his sword back into his sheath and scooped her up into his arms, meeting her gaze briefly before telling Gerhard, "Edda had blackmailed him into helping her, but at the last moment he chose the side of right and died for his lord, and that is what we shall be telling his parents."

Gerhard nodded abruptly, accepting what was really an order. "So it shall be."

Nodding, Alex then moved past him, carrying Merry toward the door as he said, "Have both bodies prepared and carried to Duquet. They will no doubt wish to bury their son with honors and can decide for themselves what to do with Edda. She will no longer cast a shadow on d'Aumesbery, not even with her gravestone."

Merry caught a glimpse of Gerhard nodding, and then Alex stepped into the tower and began to descend the stairs. She slid her arms around his neck and peered at his silent, stern face as he negotiated the steps, waiting until he'd stepped out and started up the hall to their room before saying, "That was kind o' ye."

"Fear is an awful thing, and he feared more than anything losing the love and support of his parents."

"Still," Merry began, only to fall silent as he continued.

" 'Twas his last request as he lay dying: 'Pray, my lord, do not tell my parents what I have done,' " he quoted, and then added, "He was but a boy, Merry, led astray by his vile, corrupt aunt. He made his choice. 'Twas the wrong one, but I do not hold him responsible as much as Edda and will not have his parents carry his shame as well as their sorrow."

She nodded silently and leaned her head against his chest, thinking that she had a good man to husband.

Epilogue

"What has my wife looking so grim and unhappy?"

Merry tore herself from her thoughts and glanced up at Alex as he settled on the bed beside her. It had been eight months since the night on the tower, and she managed to avoid thinking much on it, but found herself pondering Edda and her machinations this day for some reason. She did not tell Alex that, however, but said dryly, "Oh, I do not ken, husband. Me legs are swollen, I am as big as a wagon, and yer bairn has a liking fer kicking me in the stomach that is most distressing. Why would I look grim and unhappy?"

Alex chuckled and bent to press a kiss to her round stomach through the linen covering it and then pressed a kiss to her lips as well, before asking, "Shall I give the boy a good lecture for kicking you?"

"Ye may lecture *her* diya wish, but I doubt she listens any better than ye," Merry said dryly, and then asked, "And why is it ye kissed the bairn first and me second?"

Alex hesitated and then smiled and offered, "Babe before beauty?"

Merry chuckled despite herself and shook her head, "Oh, ye're a charmer, you are, Alex d'Aumesbery. Let us hope yer son is, too."

Alex arched an eyebrow. "I thought ye were sure 'tis going to be a she?"

"I changed me mind," Merry said with amusement. "And diya give me a moment I shall change it again."

Alex chuckled and shifted up to sit beside her on the bed so that he could slip his arm around her. He then presented a scroll he'd kept hidden until then. "Guess what this is?"

"A note from Evelinde and Cullen sayin' they're comin' to visit?" she asked hopefully, and then pointed out, " 'Tis their turn."

"Aye, it is their turn," he agreed, and then added, "And they did indeed send a note saying they shall come, but that is not what this missive is."

Merry smiled happily at the news that the other couple was coming to visit, but asked, "So what news is it ye thought was more important than that?"

Alex opened his mouth to answer and then

paused and threw one leg over both of hers before admitting, "A note from your father announcing that Kade has finally arrived back at Stewart."

Merry sucked in a long draught of air, instinctively trying to push Alex's leg off so that she could leap off the bed and start preparing. "Get off me legs, Alex. I needs must pack. We must head to Stewart at once, and—"

"Merry," Alex interrupted, his expression stern as he turned her face to his. "I know you have waited forever for Kade to return, and I know you want to go see him, but you are due to deliver our babe any day now. You cannot travel."

"But Alex, 'tis Kade," she moaned miserably.

"I know, but he will still be there after you have had the babe. Or perhaps he will be here before that. There is no reason he could not visit us."

"Aye," Merry agreed at once, her expression brightening. "We could have him visit while Evelinde and Cullen are here. That would be nice."

"Aye, it would," Alex agreed, and they fell silent for a bit as Merry concentrated on what they would do and what she should have Cook make, and—

"Now," Alex interrupted her thoughts and drew her to rest against his chest as he asked, "why do you not tell me the truth about what you were thinking about when I entered?"

Merry hesitated, but then admitted, "I was thinking about Edda."

"I suspected as much," Alex said quietly. When she glanced at him with surprise, he shrugged. "You have done it very rarely since that night, but I think I have been aware each time you have thought of

her. You get this look of regret as if you felt sorry for
your part in her death."

"Aye." Merry sighed. As glad as she was that it
was Edda and not they, and as much as she would
do everything the exact same again if necessary, it
was hard to know she'd had a hand in ending a life.
It was a large responsibility to bear, and she found
herself occasionally fretting over there possibly
being another way she might have handled it that
might have prevented anyone dying. Merry shook
these grim thoughts aside and added, "But that was
not what I was thinking about this time."

"Nay?"

Merry smiled at his surprise. "Nay. Though ye're
usually right when guessin' what I am thinkin', husband, sometimes ye're actually wrong, and this is
one o' them."

Alex smiled and gave her a gentle squeeze. "Then
tell me."

"I was thinkin' on how I grew up sure that men
were usually evil sinners and women the saints."

Alex nodded solemnly. " 'Tis how it was in your
family."

"Aye," she agreed, and then said, "But nay."

When he pulled back to peer at her with confusion, she laughed and explained, "My father and
brothers may be drunkards and fools, but they are
no' truly evil like Edda was."

"Nay," he agreed solemnly.

Merry nodded and then added, "And I was realizing that me prejudice in thinking that men are
evil and women saints blinded me to Edda's true
nature."

"You could not know—"

"I was told repeatedly," she reminded him. "And yet even that last evening, after hearing what you thought and what Evelinde had to say, I still couldna believe Edda wasna a good woman until I read the letter and realized that Godfrey was her nephew. That prejudice nearly got us both killed."

"No, it did not," Alex said firmly. "Even had you suspected her, you could not have foreseen what would happen on that tower unless you had known who Godfrey's parents were and you did not know because I never told you."

Merry considered his words silently and felt herself relax a little inside. But she nodded slowly and said, "I see. Then 'tis really yer fault fer no' tellin' me things."

"Aye," Alex said. He then frowned as he realized what had been said, but caught the twinkle in her eyes and started to chuckle. "You are an evil woman, wife."

"And ye're a saint fer puttin' up with me," she said, smiling.

"Then we are a perfect match," he murmured, and kissed her again.

Turn the page for a sneak peek at

The Hellion and the Highlander
By Lynsay Sands

Available March 2010
From Avon Books

Kade's gaze slid over the woman lying on his bed. He and Will had been talking quietly when Bess had burst into the room and told them that Averill had punched Lord Cyril and all hell had broken out below. He and Will had headed down at once, only to encounter Averill on the stairs. One look at her pallid face and the way she was swaying as she clutched at the rail had distracted him from the shouting below. Leaving her father to deal with Lord Seawell by himself, he and Will had each caught one of Averill's arms and ushered her up the last few steps. Since his room at the top of the stairs was closest, they'd taken her there.

Averill now lay flat on her back on the bed Kade occupied this last week, a cold compress over her eyes as she told them what had happened. Much to his fascination she'd done so not only in slurred words but also in most unsweet ones. Kade found himself unable to take his eyes away from the creature in his bed. She was a changeling. Certainly not the sweet, passionless creature who had hovered over him since his waking. It seemed the girl had a temper after all and had a rather varied and vulgar list of curse words rattling around in her head, for she'd used several to describe the loathsome Cyril Seawell.

"Oh." Averill waved one hand weakly, then released a gusty sigh. "The old cow was ranting on about how ungrateful I was and how I should be kissing her son's feet and bathing them with my tongue in gratitude for even considering me to bride, and I was trying to keep down luncheon and dared not open my mouth to respond. However, I was so exceedingly sick to death of the old bitch's rambling and completely ridiculous rantings—" She paused to sneer with disgust, and muttered, "As if I would lick any part of that addle-pated oaf of a son of hers, let alone his feet."

Will's eyes widened in horror at her words, but Kade found himself grinning as she continued, "And then the old battleaxe snapped, "Well? Are you going to apologize for such heathen behavior?" and I opened my mouth to tell her to sod off. I got the words out, but before I could close my mouth, the rest of my lunch spewed out. I got the skirt of her gown that time." She sighed at the memory, the bottom of the damp cloth fluttering slightly, then her lips thinned out, and she added, "And I am not sorry. Can you imagine having that mean old harpy for a mother-in-law? Dear God, even without the whiskey to shake my reserve, I could never hold my temper with her."

"But Averill, you do not have a temper," Will protested with dismay, then frowned at the ridiculousness of the claim considering what he'd just heard. "I mean you have never shown a temper before. You have always been sweet and most temperate."

"Because Mother insisted I must be and helped me learn to control it," she said quietly. "The day after I tried to run away and kicked the captain of the guard, she started to teach me to control it."

"Run away?" Will looked shocked. It was obvious he knew nothing about any of it.

"How did she teach you, Averill?" Kade asked quietly. For teaching a five-year-old anything was quite difficult, but trying to make one go against her own nature was nearly impossible.

"Every time I lost my temper, she made me take a bath in cold water." Her voice was almost absent as she said it, with no sign of rancor at the punishment ... and punishment it would have been, Kade thought grimly. He couldn't imagine anyone forcing a child to sit in cold water. Aside from unpleasant, it was surely dangerous to risk her catching a chill like that.

Averill suddenly snatched the compress away and scowled up at her brother. "I suppose you hate me now."

"Nay, of course not," Will said at once, then grinned, and added, "Actually, I rather like you like this. Where did you learn to curse that way?"

"From you," she said dryly, dropping the compress back over her face. "And from the soldiers who man the wall. They are forever shouting curses back and forth, and I hear it all from my chamber when the shutters are open."

"Hmm, I shall have to take more care in future and perhaps speak to the men on the wall," Will muttered, but he seemed more amused than anything. He then turned to Kade and arched an eyebrow. "Is she still too sweet?"

Kade turned to peer at the girl. She had pulled the compress away again, and her beautiful green eyes were shifting from one man to the other with suspicion. The bonnet she'd worn to meet Lord Seawell had been discarded, and her tresses now lay splayed over the bed on either side of her head, fiery locks he'd like to gather in his hands and press to his face. Her cheeks were flushed with color from her temper, her sweet, soft lips twisted with irritation, and he'd never seen her look more beautiful.

"Nay," he growled. "I'll have her."

Will grinned and slapped his shoulder happily. "Welcome to the family."

At Avon Books, we know your passion for romance—once you finish one of our novels, you find yourself wanting more.

May we tempt you with . . .

- **Excerpts** from our upcoming releases.

- Entertaining **extras**, including authors' personal photo albums and book lists.

- Behind-the-scenes **scoop** on your favorite characters and series.

- **Sweepstakes** for the chance to win free books, romantic getaways, and other fun prizes.

- Writing **tips** from our authors and editors.

- **Blog** with our authors and find out why they love to write romance.

- **Exclusive content** that's not contained within the pages of our novels.

Join us at
www.avonbooks.com

A V O N

An Imprint of HarperCollins*Publishers*
www.avonromance.com

JOHN LESCROART

A NOVEL

BETRAYAL

A SIGNET BOOK

SIGNET
Published by New American Library, a division of
Penguin Group (USA) Inc., 375 Hudson Street,
New York, New York 10014, USA
Penguin Group (Canada), 90 Eglinton Avenue East, Suite 700, Toronto,
Ontario M4P 2Y3, Canada (a division of Pearson Penguin Canada Inc.)
Penguin Books Ltd., 80 Strand, London WC2R 0RL, England
Penguin Ireland, 25 St. Stephen's Green, Dublin 2,
Ireland (a division of Penguin Books Ltd.)
Penguin Group (Australia), 250 Camberwell Road, Camberwell, Victoria 3124,
Australia (a division of Pearson Australia Group Pty. Ltd.)
Penguin Books India Pvt. Ltd., 11 Community Centre, Panchsheel Park,
New Delhi - 110 017, India
Penguin Group (NZ), 67 Apollo Drive, Rosedale, North Shore 0632,
New Zealand (a division of Pearson New Zealand Ltd.)
Penguin Books (South Africa) (Pty.) Ltd., 24 Sturdee Avenue,
Rosebank, Johannesburg 2196, South Africa

Penguin Books Ltd., Registered Offices:
80 Strand, London WC2R 0RL, England

Published by Signet, an imprint of New American Library, a division of Penguin
Group (USA) Inc. Previously published in a Dutton edition.

First Signet Printing, January 2009
10 9 8 7 6 5 4 3 2 1

PRAISE FOR THE NOVELS
OF JOHN LESCROART

Betrayal

"*Betrayal* is provocative ... a tour de force of a legal thriller." —*The Providence Journal-Bulletin*

New York Times bestselling author John Lescroart returns with an ambitious, torn-from-today's-headlines thriller featuring his trademark blend of real people and unbearable suspense.

Lescroart's millions of fans have been waiting three years for the return of San Francisco defense attorney Dismas Hardy and his buddy Detective Abe Glitsky—and in that time Lescroart's popularity has continued to soar. Now Hardy and Glitsky reunite in a story filled with the big themes that are worthy of them: the intersection of love, betrayal, and a desperate search for the truth in a young man's life—and in a critical matter of national security.

"A first-rate addition to the author's ongoing series, this should please both longtime readers and new fans." —*Publishers Weekly*

"Grisham and Turow remain the two best-known writers in the genre. There is, however, a third novelist at work today who deserves to be considered alongside Turow and Grisham. His name is John Lescroart."

—*Chicago Sun-Times*

The Suspect
The American Authors Association
2007 Book of the Year

"An intriguing puzzle.... Developments in Stuart's case will keep the reader guessing until the very end."
—*Richmond Times-Dispatch*

continued ...

"*The Suspect* is one smooth ride, and a fine legal thriller to boot." —*The Philadelphia Inquirer*

The Hunt Club

"A fast-paced tale of high-society intrigue and street-savvy suspense." —*The Washington Post Book World*

"Stakeouts, fake-outs, make-outs, and shoot-outs ... [Lescroart is] a terrific yarn-spinner." —*Chicago Sun-Times*

The Motive

"Surpasses anything Grisham ever wrote and bears comparison with Turow." —*The Washington Post*

"Unfolds like a classic *Law & Order.*" —*Entertainment Weekly*

The Second Chair

"Lescroart gives his ever-growing readership another spellbinder to savor." —*Library Journal*

The First Law

"With his latest, Lescroart again lands in the top tier of crime fiction." —*Publishers Weekly*

The Oath
A *People* Page-turner

"A terrific crime story." —*People*

The Hearing

"A spine-tingling legal thriller." —Larry King, *USA Today*

Nothing but the Truth

"Riveting ... one of Lescroart's best tales yet."
—*Chicago Tribune*

The Mercy Rule

"Well written, well plotted, well-done." —Nelson DeMille

Guilt

"Begin *Guilt* over a weekend.... If you start during the workweek, you will be up very, very late, and your pleasure will be tainted with, well, guilt."
—*The Philadelphia Inquirer*

A Certain Justice

"A West Coast take on *The Bonfire of the Vanities* ... richly satisfying."
—*Kirkus Reviews*

"A gifted writer.... I read him with great pleasure."
—Richard North Patterson

The 13th Juror

"Fast-paced ... sustains interest to the very end."
—*The Wall Street Journal*

Hard Evidence

"Engrossing ... compulsively readable, a dense and involving saga of big-city crime and punishment."
—*San Francisco Chronicle*

Dead Irish

"Full of all the things I like. Lescroart's a pro."
—Jonathan Kellerman

To Lisa M. Sawyer,
Who shares my life and owns my heart

"A man's death is his own business."
                    —Aaron Moore, First Sergeant, U.S. Marine Corps

"Injustice is relatively easy to bear; it is justice that hurts."
                    —Henry Louis Mencken

PROLOGUE
[2006]

ON A WEDNESDAY EVENING in early December, Dismas Hardy, standing at the thin line of dark cherry in the light hardwood floor of his office, threw a dart. It was the last in a round of three, and as soon as he let the missile go, he knew it would land where he'd aimed it, in the "20" wedge, as had the previous two. Hardy was a better-than-average player—if you were in a tournament, you'd want him on your team—so getting three twenties in a row didn't make his day. Although missing one or even, God forbid, two shots in any given round would marginally lower the level of the reservoir of his contentment, which was dangerously low as it was.

So Hardy was playing a no-win game. If he hit his mark, it didn't make him happy; but if he missed, it really ticked him off.

After he threw, he didn't move forward to go pull his darts from the board as he had the last thirty rounds. Instead, he let out a breath, felt his shoulders settle, unconsciously gnawed at the inside of his cheek.

On the other side of his closed door, in the reception area, the night telephone commenced to chirrup. It was long past business hours. Phyllis, his ageless ogre of a receptionist/secretary, had looked in on him and said good night nearly three hours ago. There might still be associates or paralegals cranking away on their briefs or research in some of the other rooms and offices—after all, this was a law firm where the billable hour was the inescapable unit of currency—but for the most part, the workday was over.

And yet, with no pressing work, Hardy remained.

Over the last twenty years, Wednesday evenings in his home had acquired a near-sacred status as Date Night. Hardy and his wife, Frannie, would leave their two children, Rebecca and Vincent—first with babysitters, then alone—and would go out somewhere to dine and talk. Often they'd meet first at the Little Shamrock, about halfway between home on Thirty-fourth Avenue and his downtown office. Hardy was a part owner of the bar, with Frannie's brother, Moses McGuire, and they'd have a civilized drink and then repair to some venue of greater or lesser sophistication—San Francisco had them all—and reconnect. Or at least try.

Tonight's original plan was to meet at Jardinière, Traci Des Jardins's top-notch restaurant, which they'd belatedly discovered only in the past year when Jacob, the second son of Hardy's friend Abe Glitsky, returned from Italy to appear in several performances at the opera house across the street. But Frannie had called him and canceled at four-thirty, leaving a message with Phyllis that she had an emergency with one of her client families.

Hardy had been on the phone when Frannie's call had come in, but he'd been known to put people on hold to talk to his wife. She knew this. Clearly she hadn't wanted to discuss the cancellation with him. It was a done deal.

After another minute of immobility, Hardy rolled his shoulders and went around behind his desk. Picking up the telephone, he punched a few numbers, heard the ring, waited.

"Yellow."

"Is the color of my true love's hair," he said. "Except that Frannie's hair is red. What kind of greeting is 'yellow'?"

"It's hello with a little sparkle up front. Y-y-yellow. See?"

"I liked it better when you just said 'Glitsky.'"

"Of course you did. But you're a well-known troglodyte. Treya pointed out to me, and she was right as she is about everything, that growling out my name when I answer the phone at home was somewhat off-putting, not to say unfriendly."

As a lifelong policeman, Glitsky had cultivated a persona that was, if nothing else, self-protectively harsh. Large, broad-shouldered, black on his mother's side—his father, Nat, was Jewish—Glitsky's favored expression combined an unnerving intensity with a disinterested neutrality that, in conjunction with anomalous ice-blue eyes and the scar that ran through both of his lips, conveyed an impression of intimidating, barely suppressed rage. Supposedly he had wrung confessions out of suspects by doing nothing more than sitting at an interrogation table, arms crossed, and staring. Even if the rumor wasn't strictly true, Glitsky had done nothing to dispel it. It felt true. It sounded true. So it was true enough for a cop's purposes.

"You've never wanted to appear friendly before in your entire life," Hardy said.

"False. At home, I don't want to scare the kids."

"Actually, you do. That's the trick. It worked great with the first batch."

"The first batch, I like that. But times change. Nowadays you want the unfriendly Glitsky, you've got to call me at work."

"I'm not sure I can stand it."

"You'll get over it. So what can I do for you?"

The connection thrummed with empty air for a second. Then Hardy said, "I was wondering if you felt like going out for a drink."

Glitsky didn't drink and few knew it better than Hardy. So the innocuous-sounding question was laden with portent. "Sure," Glitsky said after a beat. "Where and when?"

"I'm still at work," Hardy said. "Give me ten. I'll pick you up."

PERVERSELY, TELLING HIMSELF it was because it was the first place he could think of that didn't have a television, Hardy drove them both to Jardinière, where he valeted his car and they got a table around the lee of the circular bar. It was an opera night and *The Barber of Seville* was probably still in its first act, so they had the place nearly all to themselves. On the drive down they'd more or less naturally fallen into a familiar topic—conditions within, and the apparently imminent rearrangement of, the police department. The discussion had carried them all the way here and wasn't over yet. Glitsky, who was the deputy chief of inspectors, had some pretty good issues of his own, mostly the fact that he neither wanted to retire nor continue in his current exalted position.

"Which leaves what?" Hardy pulled at his beer. "No, let me guess. Back to payroll."

Glitsky had been shot a few years before when he'd been head of homicide, and after nearly two years of medical leave from various complications related to his recovery, he got assigned to payroll, a sergeant's position, though he was a civil service lieutenant. If his mentor, Frank Batiste, hadn't been named chief of police, Glitsky would have probably still been there today. Or, more likely, he'd be out to pasture, living on his pension augmented by piecemeal security work. But Batiste had promoted him to deputy chief over several other highly ranked candidates.

In all, Glitsky pretended that this was a good thing. He had a large and impressive office, his own car and a driver, a raise in pay, an elevated profile in the city, access to the mayor and the chief. But the rather significant, in his opinion, downside to all of this was that the job was basically political, while Glitsky was not. The often inane meetings, press conferences, public pronouncements, spin control, and interactions with community groups and their leaders that comprised the bulk of Glitsky's hours made him crazy. It wasn't his idea of police work; it wasn't what he felt he was born to do.

Glitsky tipped up his club soda, sucked in a small ice cube, chomped it, looked across at Hardy. "Lanier"—the current head of homicide—"is retiring, you know."

"Nobody's that dumb," Hardy said.

"What's dumb? I'd retire myself if I could afford it."

But Hardy was shaking his head. "I'm not talking about Lanier," he said. "I'm talking about you."

"I'm not retiring."

"No, I know. What you're doing is thinking about asking Batiste to put you back in homicide. Isn't that right?"

"And here I thought I was being subtle."

"You and a train wreck." Hardy sipped some beer. "You talk to Treya about this?"

"Of course."

"What's she say?"

"You'll just do that eye-rolling thing you do, but she says whatever makes me happy makes her happy." At Hardy's reaction, he pointed. "There you go, see?"

"I can't help it," Hardy said. "It's eye-rolling material. Have you talked to Batiste?"

"Not yet. He did me a favor making me deputy chief. I don't want to seem ungrateful."

"Except that you are."

"Well, I've already put in three years there and it's not getting any better."

"And homicide would be?"

Glitsky moved his glass in a little circle of condensation. "It's who I am more. That's all. It's why I'm a cop."

FINALLY GETTING TO the reason they'd come out in the first place.

"It's just so different," Hardy said. "I mean, two years ago, I've got two kids and a wife waiting for me when I come home. We're playing Scrabble around the kitchen table, for Christ's sake. Watching videos together."

"If memory serves, you couldn't wait for that to end. It was so boring."

"Not that boring. And even last year, the Beck's off at BU but at least Vince was still around at home and we'd give a nod to a family dinner a few times a week. Now he's in San Diego and Frannie's a working fool and . . . it's just so different."

"Empty nest," Glitsky said.

"I thought I was going to love it."

"Well, there you go. Wrong again." He shrugged. "You'll get used to it."

"I don't want to get used to it. I want to love it the way it should be."

"How's that? Should?"

"You know, like go out on dates with my wife, and do fun nonkid things on weekends, stay over places, go back to being my carefree old self."

"Who? I don't believe I ever met him."

"You know what I mean. It just doesn't seem right."

"What? That Frannie's working?"

"No. No, she's wanted to go back to work forever after the kids moved out. I've been totally behind her. Going back to school and everything. I mean, we've been planning on it."

"But you just didn't think it would take so much time away from you?"

Hardy sipped beer, swallowed, blew out heavily. "She's a good woman," he said. "I'm not saying she's not."

"Few better. If you do something stupid with her around this, I'll hunt you down and kill you."

"I'm not going to do anything. I'm just trying to get my head around where we are now. It's like her job is her life all the sudden."

"You ever hang out with yourself during a murder trial? Miss a few dinners, did you?"

"That's not the—" Hardy's tone hardened. "I was bringing in all the money, Abe. I was supporting everybody. That's not the situation now."

"Oh, okay. You're absolutely right. It was different when you did it."

Hardy twirled his glass on the table and stared out across the dimly lit bar. Even going out with his best friend to talk about himself wasn't turning out to be such a party. Things were going to have to change, and as Glitsky said, he was going to have to get used to it. Hell, things had already changed under his nose and he'd barely seen those changes coming. "It's never easy, is it?" he said.

Glitsky chewed some more ice. "What was your first clue?"

AFTER YEARS OF AGGRAVATION and frustration, Hardy had finally broken down and rented some enclosed parking space in his neighborhood. The full double garage was still a long block and a half from his home and it cost him nearly four thousand dollars a year, but its door opened when you pushed a button on your car's visor, it was closer than most of the parking spots he would wind up finding on the streets anyway, it did double duty as a storage unit, and, perhaps best of all, it removed both the family cars from the immediate threat of theft or vandalism, both of which his family had been the victim of three times in the eighteen months before Hardy had plunked down his first rent check.

The walk home tonight wasn't bad, though. He'd stopped after the two beers with Glitsky; his caseload was light at the moment and so he was unencumbered by his usual forty-pound litigator's briefcase; the night was brisk and clear. His two-story "railroad" Victorian on Thirty-fourth Avenue up by Clement was the only stand-alone house on a blockful of apartment buildings. It sported a white picket fence and a neatly maintained, albeit tiny, lawn. A flower-bordered brick walkway hugged one side of the lawn; four steps led up to the small porch, a light on by the door. More flowers grew in window boxes.

Hardy let himself in and flipped on the hall light. The house was called a railroad Victorian because the ground floor was laid out like a railroad car. All of the rooms—living, sitting, dining—opened off the long hallway on Hardy's right as he walked through the house to the back rooms.

Turning on more lights in the kitchen and family room behind it—the house was dead still—he automatically checked in on his tropical fish, sprinkled some food on the water's surface, and stood in much the same attitude of passive repose he'd adopted after his last round of darts earlier that night. After a minute of that, he took a few more steps and found himself in the corner that held the doors to both Rebecca's and Vincent's rooms.

He opened the Beck's first. She'd slept in this room only a couple of weeks before when she'd been home for Thanksgiving, but there was, of course, no sign of her now. The bed was neatly made, the bookshelves organized. Vin had been home, too, and his room was pretty much the same as his sister's, although somehow louder in his absence—it was more a boy's room, with sports and music posters and lots more junk everywhere. Mostly, now, both of the rooms just seemed empty.

Checking the phone for messages (none), then his watch, Hardy called Frannie's cell and got her voice mail. She turned her phone off when she was with clients. He said, "Yo. It's quarter to nine and I'm just starting to cook something that I'm sure is going to be fantastic. If you get this and you're on your way home, let me know and I'll hold dinner. If not, you snooze, you lose. Love you."

Hardy's black cast-iron frying pan hung on a marlin fishhook over the stove, and he took down the ten-pound monster and placed it over one of the stove's burners, turned the gas on, grabbed a pinch of sea salt they kept on the counter next to the stove, and flung it across the bottom of the pan. Whatever he was going to make, salt wouldn't hurt it.

Opening the refrigerator, he rummaged and found mushrooms, an onion, a red pepper, some leftover fettuccine with a white sauce he remembered as having been pretty good. He threw away one heavily mildewed tomato, but that still left two that were probably salvageable if he cut them carefully. Unawares, by now he was humming the tune to "Baby, It's Cold Outside"—driving home, he'd been listening to Steve Tyrell's standards on his CD player. The freezer held a four-pack of chicken-and-basil sausages that he loved.

In five minutes, he'd chopped all the ingredients, put them in the pan, added some random herbs and spices and several shakes of Tabasco sauce and a half cup or so of the Zinfandel he'd opened. He'd just turned the heat down and covered it when the phone rang. Certain that it was Frannie, he picked up on the second ring. "Bob's Beanery."

A male voice replied. "I must have the wrong number."

"No, wait! I'm sorry. I thought it was my wife."

"Mr. Hardy?"

"Speaking."

"Mr. Hardy, this is Oscar Thomasino."

"Your Honor, how are you?"

"Fine, thanks. Am I bothering you at an inopportune time?"

"No, but whatever, it's no bother. What can I do for you?"

"Well, admittedly this is a little unusual, but you and I have known each other for a long time, and I wondered if I could presume slightly upon our professional relationship."

This was unusual, if not to say unprecedented, but Hardy nevertheless kept his tone neutral. "Certainly, Your Honor. Anything I can do, if it's within my power." A superior court judge asking an attorney for a favor was a rare enough opportunity, and Hardy wasn't going to let it pass him by.

"Well, I'm sure it is," Thomasino said. "Did you know Charles Bowen? Charlie."

"I don't think so."

"You'd remember him. Flashy dresser, bright red hair, big beard."

"Doesn't ring a bell. He a lawyer?"

"Yes, he was, anyway. He disappeared six months ago."

"Where'd he go?"

"If I knew that, he wouldn't be disappeared, would he? He'd be someplace."

"Everybody's someplace, Your Honor. It's one of the two main rules. Everybody loves somebody sometime, and you've got to be someplace."

During the short pause that ensued, Hardy came to realize that he'd overstepped. His tendency to crack wise was going to be the end of him yet. But Thomasino eventually recovered to some extent, even reverting to his own stab at not-quite-cozy informality. "Thanks, Diz," he said. "I'll try to keep those in mind. Meanwhile, Charlie Bowen."

"Okay."

"Yes, well . . . the point is that he was a sole practitio-
ner. No firm, no partners, but a reasonably robust caseload."

"Good for him."

"True, but his disappearance hasn't been good for
the court. Or for his wife and daughter, either, to tell
you the truth. His wife's hired her own lawyer to file a
presumption-of-death claim, which, between you and me,
has very little chance of getting recognized, in spite of the
fact that it would be convenient for the court."

"Why's that?"

"Because when sole practitioners die and go to heaven,
the bar inherits the caseload and has to dispose of it."

"What if they don't go to heaven?"

"Most lawyers argue themselves in, don't you think? I
know you would."

"Thanks, I think. Your Honor."

"Anyway, I know it's just housecleaning, but Bowen
had a ton of work outstanding, and that work needs to
get done. And while we're not going to issue any pre-
sumption of death until he's been gone a lot longer, last
month Marian Braun"—another of the city's superior
court judges—"ruled that his disappearance rendered him
legally incompetent, and just yesterday the state bar suspended his ticket at the court's request."

"So now they've got to farm out his cases. If he hadn't
returned my calls for six months and I was his client, I
would have fired him by now."

"I'm sure some of his clients may have done just that,
but not all by a long shot." Thomasino sighed. "Charlie
was a friend of mine. His wife's going to need whatever
he still has coming from his cases. I'd like to be sure that

the bar puts those cases in the hands of somebody who I know will do the right thing by her. Anyway, bottom line is that I ran into Wes Farrell today at lunch." This was one of Hardy's partners. "He said things at your place were a little slow. The good news is that you can probably count on some percentage of Mr. Bowen's clients hooking up with your firm. Not that any of 'em will make you rich."

Reading between the lines, Hardy knew what the judge was saying—that this was grunt administrative work. The court probably had appointed the majority of Charlie's clients, indigents up for petty crimes and misde-meanors. Nevertheless, the court would pay for every hour Hardy's associates spent on the criminal cases any-way, and if the civil cases made any money, the firm could expect reasonable compensation. And it was, again, an opportunity to do a small good deed for a judge, and that was never a bad idea.

"You could probably get them all assigned out or closed in the next couple of months."

"I'm sold, Your Honor. I'd be happy to help you out."

"Thanks, Diz. I appreciate it. I know it's not very sexy. I'll have it all delivered to your office within the week."

"How much stuff is it?"

Thomasino paused. "About sixty boxes." In other words, a lot. "But here's the silver lining. It's only half as much as it appears, since half the boxes are one client."

"Tell me it's Microsoft."

A soft chuckle. "No such luck. It's Evan Scholler."

"Why is that name familiar?"

"Because you've read all about it. The two guys who'd been over in Iraq together?"

"Ah, it comes flooding back," Hardy said. "They had the same girlfriend or something, too, didn't they?"

"I believe so. There's a bunch of juicy stuff, but you'll find that out soon enough, I guess. But in any event, Diz, I really appreciate you doing this."

"I live to serve the court, Your Honor."

"You're already up on points, Counselor. Don't lay it on too thick. Have a nice night."

Hardy hung up and stood for a moment, musing. The judge's line played back in his mind: "There's a bunch of juicy stuff" in the Scholler case. Hardy thought he could use some juicy stuff in his life about now. If his memory served, and it always did, Scholler's situation was even more compelling than the bare bones of the murder case, because of its genesis in chaos and violence.

In Iraq.

PART ONE
[2003]

[1]

A BURNT-ORANGE SUN KISSED the horizon to the west as twenty-six-year-old Second Lieutenant Evan Scholler led his three-pack of converted gun-truck support Humvees through the gates of the Allstrong Compound in the middle of an area surrounded by palm trees, canals, and green farmland. The landscape here was nothing like the sandy, flat, brown terrain that Evan had grown used to since he'd arrived in Kuwait. The enclosure was about the size of three football fields, protected, like every other "safe" area, by Bremer walls—twelve-foot-tall concrete barriers topped with concertina wiring. Ahead of him squatted three double-wide motor home trailers that Allstrong Security, an American contracting company, had provided for its local employees.

Pulling up to the central temporary building, over which flew an American flag, Evan stepped out of his car onto the gravel that extended as far as he could see in all directions. A fit-looking American military type stood in the open doorway and now came down the three steps, his hand extended. Evan snapped a salute and the man laughed.

"You don't need to salute me, Lieutenant," he said. "Jack Allstrong. Welcome to BIAP." Calling Baghdad

International Airport by its nickname. "You must be Scholler."

"Yes, sir. If you're expecting me, that's a nice change of pace."

"Gotten the runaround, have you?"

"A little bit. I've got eight men here with me and Colonel . . . I'm sorry, the commander here?"

"Calliston."

"That's it. He wasn't expecting us. Calliston said you had some beds we could use."

"Yeah, he called. But all we've got are cots really."

"We've got our own on board," Evan said. "We're okay with cots."

Allstrong's face showed something like sympathy. "You all been on the road awhile?"

"Three days driving up from Kuwait with a Halliburton convoy, four days wandering around between here and Baghdad, watching out for looters and getting passed off around the brass. Now here we are. If you don't mind, sir, none of my men have seen a bed or a regular meal or a shower since we landed. You mind if we get 'em settled in first?"

Allstrong squinted through the wind at Evan, then looked over to the small line of Humvees, with their M60 Vietnam-era machine guns mounted on their roofs, exhausted-looking and dirty men standing behind them. Coming back to Evan, he nodded and pointed to the trailer on his right. "Bring 'em on up and park over there. It's dorm style. Find an empty spot and claim it. Showers are all yours. Dinner's at eighteen hundred hours, forty minutes from now. Think your men can make it?"

Evan tamped down a smile. "Nobody better stand in their way, sir."

"Nobody's gonna." Allstrong cocked his head. "Well, get 'em started, then."

IT HAD COME TO DARKNESS outside through the windows, but even inside, the noise never seemed to end. Planes took off and landed at all times. Beyond that constant barrage of white noise, Evan was aware of the hum of generators and the barking of dogs.

He'd gotten his men fed and settled and now he sat in a canvas-backed director's chair in the spacious double-wide room at the end of a trailer that served as one of Allstrong's personal offices. His gaze went to the walls, one of which was filled with a large map. On the other, commendation and service plaques, along with half a dozen photographs with recognizable politicians, attested to what must have been Allstrong's illustrious military career—his host had been Delta Force, finally mustering out as a full-bird colonel in the Army. He'd received two Purple Hearts and the Distinguished Service Cross. No sign of marriage or family.

Evan, taking Allstrong's measure as he pulled a bottle of Glenfiddich from what appeared to be a full case of the stuff behind his desk, put his age as late thirties. He had an open face and smiled easily, although the mouth and eyes didn't seem in perfect sync with one another. The eyes tended to dart, as though Allstrong was assessing his surroundings at all times. Which, now that Evan thought of it, probably made sense after a lifetime in theaters of war. Allstrong wore what he'd been wearing when they'd met outside—combat boots, camo pants, a black turtle-neck. He free-poured a stiff shot into a clear plastic cup, handed it over to Evan, and splashed a couple of inches into a cup of his own. Pulling another director's chair over, he sat down. "Don't bullshit a bullshitter," he said.

"It's not bullshit," Evan said. "They weren't expecting us."

"Two hundred and ninety-seven men and they didn't know you were coming?"

"That's correct."

"So what did you do? What did they do?"

"They had us camp just about on the tarmac at a holding station in Kuwait. We had all our gear with us. They put us on the ground until they figured out what we were here for."

Allstrong shook his head, either in admiration or disbelief. "I love this glorious Army," he said. "Who's the commander down there? Still Bingham?"

"That was the name."

"So you're telling me they had you weekend warriors running your asses off stateside—hustling you out of your day jobs, rushing you through training—then packed you up in a 737, flew nonstop for twenty-two hours, Travis to Kuwait—and it's all hurry up! move it! we need you over here!—and you get here and nobody knows you're coming?"

"That's right."

"So what'd they do?"

"You know Camp Victory?" This was a sand-swept safe zone five miles north of Kuwait City where the Army had erected five enormous tents to hold overflow troops.

"Camp Victory!" Allstrong barked a laugh. "That kills me!" He drank off some scotch, coughed, shook his head. "And I thought I'd heard it all. How long before they found out who you were?"

"We camped there for a week."

"Christ. A week. So how'd you wind up here? What happened to the rest of your unit?"

Evan took a good hit of his own drink. For a few months after he'd graduated from college, he'd put away a lot of beer, but since joining the police force a few years ago, he'd been at most a light social drinker. Here and now, though, his first sip of real alcohol, though technically forbidden while he was on duty (always), seemed appropriate and even earned. "I don't know," he said. "Most of 'em are probably still back in Kuwait, working on the HETs they eventually found." These were the heavy-equipment transporters that hauled 2½- to 5-ton cargo trucks and other massive ordnance and equipment from the Iraqi or Kuwaiti air bases where they'd been delivered to where they were supposed to get used in the field. Evan's National Guard unit, the 2632d Transportation Company out of San Bruno, California, was actually a medium transportation unit that had been trained to move troops and equipment.

"So what happened to you guys? The nine of you."

The drink was kicking in quickly. Evan felt his body relaxing and leaned back into his chair, crossing one leg over the other. "Well, that was just dumb or bad luck, one of the two. Once Bingham found the fleet of HETs, it turned out most of 'em didn't work. Heat, sand, four months without maintenance—you name it. So about half the guys got assigned to repair-and-rebuild work, and Bingham farmed out the rest of us wherever he needed somebody. I was a cop back home, and prior service enlisted with the infantry, plus I was the only guy with any crew-served-weapons experience, so Bingham had a convoy going to Baghdad and me and my men got assigned gun-truck support."

"So your other guys, they're cops too?"

"No. I'm the only cop, and the only one trained on the M60, if you don't count the forty-five minutes of instruction we all got before they sent us out."

"Now you are shitting me."

Evan held up three fingers. "Scout's honor."

"Jesus," Allstrong said. "So where do you guys stand now?"

"What do you mean?"

"I mean, what's your mission? What are you doing tomorrow, for example?"

Evan sipped his scotch, shrugged his shoulders. "No clue. I check in with Colonel Calliston tomorrow morning at oh eight hundred and find out, I suppose. I don't see him sending us back to our unit, although that's what I'm going to request. The men aren't too hot on this convoy duty, maybe wind up getting shot at. That wasn't in the original plan."

A small knowing chuckle came from Allstrong's throat. "Well, Lieutenant, welcome to the war. Plans are what you work with before you get there. They give you the illusion you've got some control, and you don't."

"I'm getting a sense of that," Evan replied. "So the short answer is I don't know what's happening tomorrow, or next week, or anything. We seem to be the lost company."

Allstrong stood up with his drink and walked over to the map. Staring at it for a few seconds, he spoke back over his shoulder. "Maybe I can talk to Bill Calliston. Get you and your men assigned to us. How'd you like that?"

"Staying on here?"

"Yeah."

"Doing what?"

Allstrong turned. "Well, that's the bad news. We'd want you to support our own convoy trucks, but there's a lot fewer of them and we're not afraid to drive faster if we need to."

"Where to?"

"Mostly Baghdad and back, but we're hoping to open offices at other bases near Fallujah and Mosul too. Wherever we can get work and beat damn Custer Battles to the punch."

"Custer Battles?"

"New guys. Contractors like us and kicking ass at it. They got the other half of this airport gig and they're going for everything else we are. I'm thinking of having their people killed." Evan nearly choked on his drink as Allstrong came forward with a laugh. "That's a joke, Lieutenant, or mostly a joke. Anyway, as you might have noticed, we're staffing up here. In a couple of months, this place will be hopping. Calliston's going to want to assign us some protection in any event. I figured you guys are already here. It's a good fit. Besides, over time, it's only going to get safer here, I mean the road between Baghdad and BIAP."

"You mean, the one known as RPG Alley?"

Allstrong smiled. "You heard that one already, huh?"

"Rocket-propelled-grenade alley just doesn't sound all that safe."

"It's going to get better."

Evan wasn't about to argue with his host. "You guys don't do your own security?" he asked. "I thought guys like you were guarding Bremer." This was L. Paul "Jerry" Bremer, head of the Coalition Provisional Authority, or CPA, who had set up headquarters to administrate infrastructure and the economy and all nonmilitary aspects of the occupation in Hussein's Republican Palace in Baghdad a couple of weeks before.

Allstrong chortled again. "Yeah. True. Another absurd moment. Guys like us protect civilians and admin staff, but we're not supposed to carry heavy arms, so the military needs to guard our convoys."

"That's beautiful."

"Isn't it? Anyway, if you're interested, I could put in a call to Bill. At least get you guys attached here. Call it a short-term home."

"That might be a start to belonging somewhere," Evan said. "Sure. Call him."

[2]

"ROUTE IRISH" FROM THE AIRPORT to Baghdad proper was a thoroughly· modern freeway, three well-maintained lanes in each direction. From Evan's perspective, the main difference between it and an American freeway, aside from the apparently near-standard practice of driving the wrong way on any given lane, was that from many places cars could enter it anywhere from either side—the asphalt ended on a sand shoulder that usually proceeded without a demarcating fence or barrier of any kind out across an expanse of flat, marginal farmland. So once you got away from Baghdad, where on- and off-ramps and bridges were more common, traffic could and did enter the roadway willy-nilly and not necessarily at designated entrances and exits.

This became a major problem because of suicide car-bombers. In the four days since Colonel Calliston had attached Evan's unit to Allstrong, they hadn't gotten approached by any of these yet, but the threat was real and ubiquitous. On his way through Baghdad this morning, Evan had counted four burnt-out hulks of twisted metal, one of them still smoldering as he drove by after an hour's delay while the powers that be stopped all traffic and cleared the road.

Today his assignment was to pass through Baghdad and proceed up to Balad Air Base, nicknamed Anaconda, about forty miles north of the capital city, and pick up a man named Ron Nolan, a senior official with Allstrong who'd been scouting potential air bases to the north and west for the past week, assessing contracting opportunities. After collecting Nolan, they were to proceed back to downtown Baghdad and make a stop at the CPA headquarters for some unspecified business, then return to BIAP by nightfall.

The round-trip distance was give or take a hundred miles and they had about twelve hours of daylight, but Evan wasn't taking any chances. Movement Control had signed off on his convoy clearance and he had his full package—the three Humvees—out and rolling at oh dark thirty hours. Each of his Humvees had a driver and an assistant driver, who was also in charge of feeding ammunition to the gunner, whose body remained half-exposed through the hole in the car's roof. The heavily armed men alternated roles on successive trips. Evan could have claimed rank and never taken a turn as gunner—as a lieutenant his official role was to be convoy commander, or radio operator—but he made it a point to ride in each car and take a turn at the crew-serve weapon as the opportunity arose.

Today he rode as a passenger in the lead vehicle, in one of the two back seats. Because of the traffic delay, the package didn't pass Baghdad until eight o'clock and didn't make it the forty farther miles to the outer periphery of the enormous Anaconda base—soon to be named "Mortaritaville"—until eleven-fifteen. Even without car bombs, traffic on the road to the main logistics supply area close to Baghdad crept at a near standstill, not too surprising considering the sixteen thousand flights per month that Anaconda was handling.

When they got through the gate, Evan's driver and the second-in-command of their unit, Sergeant Marshawn Whitman, drove for a half mile or so through a city of tents and trailers before they came to an intersection with a sign indicating that the camp headquarters was a mile farther on their right. But Whitman didn't turn the car immediately. Instead, his window down, he stared out to his left at two of the corner tents, one sporting a logo for Burger King and the other for Pizza Hut. "Am I really seeing this, sir? Aren't we in a war here? Didn't we just make it into Baghdad, like, two months ago? Can I get out and grab a quick Whopper?"

WHEN EVAN SHOOK Ron Nolan's hand just outside the headquarters tent, he had an immediate impression of great strength held in check. He went about five ten and came across as solid muscle, shoulders down to hips. Square jaw under brush-cut light hair. Today he wore a sidearm at his belt and a regular Army camo vest with Kevlar inserts over his khaki shirt. "Leff-tenant," Nolan boomed, pronouncing the word in the British manner and smiling wide as he fell in next to Evan, "I sure do appreciate the punctuality. Time is money, after all, and never more than right here and right now. I trust the limo's got good air-conditioning."

Evan slowed, jerked his head sideways. "Uh, sir ..."

But with another booming laugh, Nolan slapped him on the back. "Joking with you, son. No worries. Ain't no part of a Humvee don't feel like home to me. You know we're planning to stop off in Baghdad?"

"Those are my orders, yes, sir."

Nolan stopped, reaching out a hand, laying it on Evan's arm. "At ease, Lieutenant," he said. "You a little nervous?"

"I'm fine, sir. But I'd be lying if I said Baghdad was my favorite place."

"Well, we won't be there for long if I can help it, and I think I can. Jack Allstrong's a master at keeping doors open." He paused for a second. "So. You regular Army?"

"No, sir. California National Guard."

"Yeah. I heard they were doing that. How big's your convoy?"

"Three Humvees, sir." They were approaching it now, parked just off the pavement. "Here they are."

Nolan stopped, hands on hips, and looked over the vehicles, bristling with weaponry. "Damn," he said to Evan, "that's a good-looking hunk of machinery." Nodding at Corporal Alan Reese, a former seventh-grade teacher now manning the machine gun on the closest Humvee, he called up to him. "How you doing, son?"

"Good, sir."

"Where you from back home?"

"San Carlos, California, sir."

"San Carlos!" Nolan's voice thundered. "I grew up right next door in Redwood City!" He slapped the bumper of the vehicle. "You believe this small world, Lieutenant? This guy and me, we're neighbors back home."

"We all are," Evan said, sharing the enthusiasm although he couldn't exactly say why. "Our unit's out of San Bruno. The nine of us, we're all Peninsula guys."

"Son of a bitch!" Nolan crowed. "I got hooked up with the right people here, that's for damn sure. How long have you guys been over here?"

"Going on three weeks," Evan said.

"Get shot at yet?"

"Not yet."

"Don't worry about it," Nolan said with a grin. "You will."

FOR AN OBSCURE and possibly impenetrable reason, they got routed through the mixed neighborhood of Mansour by Haifa Street rather than through the military-only secure road they normally took when coming in to CPA headquarters from BIAP. Ron Nolan's destination was Saddam Hussein's old Republican Palace in central Baghdad, and the line of traffic on Haifa waiting outside the checkpoint to get into the Green Zone—bumper-to-bumper with weapons off-safe, ready to react—stopped them cold. Nolan extricated himself from his seat and opened his door, stepping out into the street and stretching. Evan, loath to let his passenger out of his sight, overcame his own reluctance—Iraqi civilians were all over the street, any one of them possibly an armed insurgent—and got out as well.

It was late afternoon by now, sweltering hot with nary a freshening breeze. The air was heavy with the smells of roasting meat and fish, manure, oil, and garbage. Haifa Street was wide and lined with three- and four-story concrete buildings, most with at least some of their windows blown out. From the crowd on the sidewalks, including women and children, no one would conclude that they were in a war zone, though. Merchants had lined up where most of the traffic into the Green Zone had to pass, and the street had the air of a bazaar—makeshift stands sold everything from clothing to batteries, toilet paper to money to candy.

Nolan, taking it in, seemed to be enjoying it all. Finally, he caught Evan's eye and grinned over the hood of the car. "We can make it in half the time if we walk. You up for it?"

Evan, reluctant to leave his troops, would have much preferred the relative security of his Humvee, but he also had a responsibility to protect Ron Nolan and get him back to Allstrong, and if that meant braving the streets of Baghdad, this was something different he should do as well. The mutually exclusive options played across his features.

Nolan noticed the hesitation. "Come on, Lieutenant. No guts, no glory."

"Just thinking about my men, Mr. Nolan," Evan covered.

"Hey. If they get to the gate before we're done, have 'em pull over and we'll meet 'em there. But at this rate they won't even be there by the time we're through. And I'd like to make it back to BIAP before dark."

Their Humvee moved forward about six feet and stopped again.

"Either way," Nolan said, "I'm going. You with me?"

"Sure." Evan leaned inside the passenger window and told Marshawn what he was doing.

"I don't like being out of contact," his driver replied.

"I don't either, Marsh. This is all new to me too." He indicated their passenger with a toss of his chin. "But he's going. And things here look pretty calm."

"Yeah," Marshawn said, "the 'before' shot."

They both knew that he meant "before the bomb exploded in the crowded marketplace."

"Let's hope not," Evan said. "And the sooner we get done and leave Baghdad, the sooner we're back home."

"I'm not arguing, sir. If you got to go, you got to go. But what if you're not at the gate? What are we supposed to do? Where will you be?"

For an answer, Evan shrugged and held up his portable Motorola radio, which was good for about a mile. Nolan, who'd heard the exchange, leaned back to Marshawn. "Budget office, down in the basement of the headquarters building. You can't miss it. But a hundred bucks says we beat you back to the gate."

The traffic gave and Marshawn crept forward another five or six feet before stopping again. The line of cars stretched for at least a quarter mile in front of him. "That's a bad bet for me, sir," he said, "even if I had the hundred bucks."

"I think so, too, Sergeant. That's why we're walking." Nolan snapped his fingers, remembering something, and reopened his back door. Reaching in, he emerged a second later with his backpack, apparently empty. "Can't forget this," he said with another grin, and strapped it onto his back, over the Kevlar vest.

RON NOLAN WAITED for Evan to fall in next to him, then said, "And by the way, my name's Ron, okay? Mr. Nolan's my dad. You okay with Evan?"

"That's my name."

"Yeah, well, Evan, I didn't mean to put you on the spot back there with your men, and I apologize. But you can't afford to be tentative here. You've got to make decisions and run on 'em. That's the main thing about this place."

"I just made my decision. But I'm not sure that leaving my convoy was the right one. We've had it drilled into us that procedures are crucial to maintain order."

They were walking shoulder to shoulder at the curb. Nolan shook his head, disagreeing. "My experience says it's more important to trust your gut. And I'm not talking just about deciding in a split second who's a Muj and who's a Hajj"—these were the Mujahideen and the Hajji, the bad guys and the good guys, respectively—"which is life and death and I mean right now. But the business environment here . . . Christ, what a gold mine! But you've got to see the opportunity and jump, and I'm talking like yesterday, or it all goes away. Did you get a chance to talk to Jack Allstrong at all back at BIAP?"

"A little bit."

"He tell you how he got the airport gig? The one that got us on the boards?"

"No. He never mentioned it."

"Well, it's a perfect example of what I'm talking about. You know what our half of that contract's worth? If you guess sixteen million dollars, you're on it."

"To do what? I saw the trailers, but it wasn't clear what you guys were doing there."

"We're guarding the airport, that's what."

"What about us?"

"What do you mean, us?"

"I mean the military, the Army, the Marines. What about us? We're not guarding the airport?"

"No. You're fighting the insurgents—most of the regular units, anyway. Jerry Bremer, God love him, in his wisdom fired all the Iraqi police and disbanded the military, so nobody's left over here except us contractors to provide security for the people who are coming in droves to do oversight and infrastructure, which is, like, everybody else."

Evan had his hand on the weapon in the holster on his hip. Most of the local people in the street and on the sidewalk were simply stepping out of the way as the two Americans passed by, but many of the children were smiling and jogging along with them—Evan had already learned, along with the Iraqi kids, that U.S. servicemen were a common source of candy from their MRE kits. But Evan had no candy on him and he wanted to get inside the Green Zone as fast as he could, so he kept pressing through the crowd.

Meanwhile, Ron Nolan kept up the patter. "Jack really hadn't been doing too good after he cashiered out. He'd been trying to set up a security business in San Fran, looking into water supply issues and the whole domestic terrorist thing, but it wasn't going very well. So then Baghdad falls, and what did Jack do? Same thing as Mike Battles with Custer Battles. He hopped on a plane with his last couple hundred bucks and flew over here to suss the place out for business opportunities." Nolan spread his arms theatrically. "*Et voilà!* Couple of months later, sixteen million smackeroos."

"Just like that?"

"Almost. Jack still knew a few guys from when he'd been in, and they turned him on to the airport gig and talked the guy in charge into letting Jack bid on it."

"But how'd he get it?" In spite of himself, Evan found himself taken by the narrative, and by Nolan's enthusiasm. "I mean, I'm assuming he's bidding against the giants, right? Halliburton, Blackwater, KBR." KBR was Kellogg, Brown, and Root. Unbeknownst to Evan, KBR was itself a subsidiary of Halliburton, not truly a separate entity.

"Yep. And don't forget DynCorp and ArmorGroup International. The big boys. To say nothing of Custer Battles—actually, they gave us the toughest run for it. But Jack wrestled 'em down and pulled out half the gig." Even in the madness of Baghdad's afternoon market, Nolan beamed at the memory.

"So what did he offer?"

"Well, first, a low bid, but that was basically because he was clueless and didn't know what it was worth. But the main thing was time. He promised to have almost a hundred and fifty men on the ground out here within two weeks."

"Two weeks?"

"Two weeks."

They walked on for a few more steps, before Evan couldn't help himself. "How was he going to do that? What was he going to pay them with? In fact, who was he going to hire? Did you guys have a hundred and fifty employees in San Francisco you could fly out here?"

Nolan howled out a laugh. "Are you kidding? He had three employees in San Francisco. And he'd paid them off of his credit cards in June. It was the end of the road for him if this didn't work. But it did."

"How'd that happen?"

They'd come almost to the checkpoint while the traffic hadn't budged, and Nolan stopped and faced Evan. "That's the great part. Jack didn't have any more credit. Nobody would lend him any more money back home, so he flew back here and convinced the CPA that they needed to lend him two million dollars against his first payment on the contract."

"Two million dollars?"

"In cash," Nolan said. "In new hundred dollar bills. So Jack packed 'em all up in a suitcase and flew to Jerusalem, where he deposited it all in the bank, then called me and told me to get my ass over here. He was in business."

At the gate, in spite of the crowd pressing up to get admitted, Nolan flashed his creds and the two men breezed their way through the CPA checkpoint—even the grunt guards seemed to know who he was. He and Evan crossed an enormous, open, tank-studded courtyard—at least a couple of hundred yards on a side—that fronted a grandiose white palacelike structure that, up close, bore silent witness to the bombardment that had rained upon the city in the past months—windows still blown out, the walls pocked with craters from shells, bullets, and shrapnel.

Inside the main building, in the enormous open lobby, pandemonium reigned. In a Babel of tongues, military uniforms mingled with business suits and *dishdashas* as half a thousand men jostled and shoved for position in one of the lines. Each line wended its way to one of the makeshift folding tables that apparently controlled access to the inner sanctum of Bremer and his senior staff. The noise, the intensity, the hundred-plus temperature, and the general stench of humanity assaulted Evan's senses as soon as he passed through the front door.

To all appearances, Nolan was immune to all of it. He hadn't gone three steps into the lobby when he plucked Evan's sleeve and pointed to their right. So they hugged the back wall, skirting most of the madness and making progress toward a wide marble staircase that led down. The crowd on the stairs was far less dense here than in the room behind them.

"What's all that about?" Evan asked as soon as he could be heard.

Nolan stopped at the bottom step. "Those folks," he said, "are basically the ones who got here a day late and a dollar short. I'd say they're Jack's competitors, except most of 'em are angling for subcontracts with the big boys. Basically, the entire country's for sale and Bremer's trying to administer all the deals from this building, from those tables, each of which represents a different ministry, if you can believe that. Seventeen, twenty of 'em. I don't know. And with, as maybe you can see, mixed results. Everybody wants a piece. Thank Christ we're beyond that stage. Fucking bedlam, isn't it?"

But he didn't wait for an answer. Turning, Nolan continued along the wall, Evan tagging behind him, the crowd gradually thinning around them the farther they went along the hallway. After thirty yards or so, finally, they turned a corner. Another long corridor stretched out before them, startlingly untraveled. A man in a military uniform sat at a lone table a little more than midway along, and three other men, apparently civilians, stood in front of him. But otherwise the hallway was empty. The noise and craziness behind them still echoed, but suddenly Evan felt psychically removed from it in spite of the fact that there was still a terrible odor of human waste and—even with holes where the windows should have been—no ventilation.

Nolan never slowed down. If anything, checking his watch, he glanced up at the window openings high in the wall and speeded up. But as they approached the desk, he put out a hand to stop their progress and swore.

"What's up?" Evan asked.

Nolan swore again and came to a dead stop. "It would

be Charlie Tucker when we're in a hurry. Maybe your sergeant should've taken my hundred-dollar bet."

"Who is he?"

"He's a twerp. Senior Auditor for Aviation Issues. I think back home he was a librarian. Here, he's a bean counter, but mostly he's a pain in the ass for people like Jack and me who are actually trying to do some good and make things happen." But Evan was starting to understand that Nolan wasn't the type of guy to brood about stuff like Charlie Tucker or anything else. He pasted on a brave smile. "But hey," he said, "that's why they pay us the big bucks, right? We get it done."

In the short time it took them to walk to the desk, Major Tucker had processed one of the three men who'd been standing in front of his desk. As Nolan got closer, the man in the back of the line turned and took a step toward them and bowed slightly. "Mr. Nolan," he said in accented English, "how are you, sir?"

"Kuvan!" From the apparently genuine enthusiasm, Kuvan might have been Nolan's best friend from childhood. Kuvan seemed to be in his early thirties. The face was light-skinned, bisected by a prominent hooked nose, and featured the usual Iraqi mustache. Nolan came up to him, arms extended, grabbed him by both shoulders, and the two men seemed to rub noses with each other. They then exchanged what Evan had already come to recognize as the standard Muslim praises to the Prophet, after which Nolan continued. "Kuvan Krekar, this here is Second Lieutenant Evan Scholler, California Army National Guard. He's only been here a few weeks and I'm trying to make him feel at home." Then, to Evan: "Kuvan helped us with some of our Filipino personnel down at BIAP. He's a genius at finding people who want to work."

As Krekar put out a hand and offered Evan a firm and powerful grip, he smiled and said, "All people treasure the nobility of work. If everyone had a job, there would be no war."

"Then *I'd* be out of a job," Evan said, surprising himself.

Krekar took the comment in stride, his smile never wavering. "But not for long, I'd wager. Even my friend Mr. Nolan here, a professional soldier of some renown, has found meaningful work in the private sector. In any event, welcome to my country, Lieutenant. You're in good hands with Mr. Nolan."

"I'm getting that impression," Evan said.

Krekar brought his smile back to Nolan. "One hears rumors that Mr. Allstrong is going to be bidding on the currency project."

This was the contract to replace Iraq's old currency, thirteen thousand tons of paper that featured the face of Saddam Hussein on every bill, with one of a new design. Twenty-four hundred tons of new dinars would have to be distributed in under three months. This would involve hundreds of Iraqis in all parts of the country, all of whom would need to be housed and fed in new camps with new infrastructure and Internet services at Mosul, Basra, and many other sites—exactly the kind of work Allstrong was doing now at Baghdad Airport. It would also involve supplying a fleet of five-ton trucks to carry the people and the money.

"It's entirely possible," Nolan said. "Although I haven't talked to Jack in a couple of weeks. And you know, here, a couple of weeks the world can change."

"Well, when you do see him," Krekar said, "please mention my name to him. The paper and pressing plants as well as the design elements and the banking issues—I know some people with these skills and perhaps Jack and I could reach an arrangement, if Allah is willing."

"I'll be sure to let him know, Kuvan. If he's bidding at all, that is."

Behind them, Tucker cleared his throat. Krekar bowed a hasty good-bye to Nolan and Evan and then stepped up to the desk.

Backing up a couple of feet, bringing Evan with him, Nolan spoke sotto voce, "Talk about getting it done. If Kuvan's with us on this currency thing, we're going to lock it up. Taking nothing away from Jack's accomplishment, without Kuvan we don't have the airport, and that's no exaggeration."

"What'd he do?"

"Well, you know I told you it was all about getting a lot of feet on the ground here in a couple of weeks. Jack promised he could do it, and the CPA believed him—he's a persuasive guy. But still, push came to shove and Custer Battles was beating us getting guys to work for them at every turn. Jack had no idea where he was going to find guards and cooks and all the other bodies he was going to need. So, it turns out that one of Jack's old Delta buddies does security for KBR, and he turns him on to Kuvan, who's connected to this endless string of mules—Nepalese, Jordanians, Turks, Filipinos, you name it. You give these guys a buck an hour, they'll do anything for you—cook, clean, kill somebody ..."

"A buck an hour? Is that what they're making?"

"Give or take, for the cooks and staff. Guards maybe two hundred a month." Nolan lowered his voice even further, gestured toward the desk. "But don't let Tucker hear that. Jack bid it out at around twenty an hour per man, but as I say, Kuvan's a genius. His fee is two bucks an hour, which takes our cost up to three an hour, so we're hauling in seventeen. That's per hour, twenty-four-seven, times a hundred and sixty guys so far, with another two hundred in the pipeline. And the more we bring on, the more we make. Like I told you, you play it right, this place is a gold mine. How much they paying you, Evan, two grand a month?"

"Close. Plus hazard duty…"

Nolan cut him off with a laugh. "Hazard duty, what's that, a hundred fifty a month? That's what our cooks make."

"Yeah, you mentioned that." The news disturbed Evan—a hundred and fifty dollars extra per month and he faced death every day.

After a little pause, Nolan looked at him sideways. "You know what I'm making?"

"No idea."

"You want to know?"

A nod. "Sure."

"Twenty thousand a month. That's tax-free, by the way. Of course, I've got lots of experience and there's a premium on guys like me. But still, guys like you can finish up here, then turn around and come back a month later with any of us contractors, and you're looking at ten grand minimum a month. A six-month tour and you're back home, loaded. This thing lasts long enough, the smart-money bet by the way, and I go home a millionaire."

UP AT THE DESK, Major Charles Tucker looked like he could use some time in the sun. He'd sweated through his shirt. He sported rimless glasses, had a high forehead, and nearly invisible blond eyebrows—a caricature of the harried accountant. And he made no secret of his disdain for Nolan. "Let's see your paperwork. Who signed off on it this time?"

"Colonel Ramsdale, sir. Air-base security services co-ordinator."

"Another one of Mr. Allstrong's friends?"

"A comrade-in-arms. Yes, sir. They were in Desert Storm together."

"I'm happy for them." Tucker looked down at the sheets of paper Nolan had handed him. He flipped the first page, studied the second, went back to the first.

"Everything in order, sir?" Nolan asked with an ironic obsequiousness.

"This is a lot of money to take away in cash, Nolan." He gestured to Evan. "Who's this guy?"

"Convoy support, sir. Protection back to the base."

Tucker went back to the papers. "Okay, I can see the payroll, but what's this sixty-thousand-dollar add-on for"— he squinted down at the paper—"does this say dogs?"

"Yes, sir. Bomb-sniffing dogs, which we need to feed and build kennels for, along with their trainers and handlers."

"And Ramsdale approved this?"

"Apparently so, sir." Nolan leaned down and pretended to be looking for Ramsdale's signature. Evan stifled a smile. Nolan, punctiliously polite, somehow managed to put a bit of the needle into every exchange.

"I'm going to have somebody in audit verify this."

Nolan shrugged. "Of course, sir."

"Sixty thousand dollars for a bunch of dogs!"

"Bomb-sniffing dogs, sir." Nolan remained mild. "And the infrastructure associated with them."

But apparently there was nothing Tucker could do about it. Nolan had his form in order and it was signed by one of the Army's sanctioned paymasters. He scribbled something on the bottom of the form. Then he looked up. Behind Nolan, the line had grown again to four or five other customers. "Specie?" Tucker said.

"I beg your pardon," Nolan replied.

"Don't fuck with me, Nolan. Dollars or dinars?"

"I think dollars."

"Yes. I thought you would think that. You're paying your people in dollars?"

"That's all they'll take, sir. The old dinar's a little shaky right now."

Tucker made another note, tore off his duplicate copy, and put it in his top right-hand drawer. "This is going to audit," he repeated, then looked around Nolan and said, "Next!"

[3]

THAT NIGHT IN HIS TRAILER'S OFFICE, Jack All-strong sipped scotch with Ron Nolan while they tossed a plastic-wrapped bundle of five hundred hundred-dollar bills—fifty thousand dollars—back and forth, playing catch. Allstrong's office, nice at it was, remained a sore point with him. This was because the main office of his chief competitor, Custer Battles ("CB"), was in one of the newly refurbished terminals. When Mike Battles had first gotten here two months before, he found that he'd inherited several empty shells of airport terminal buildings, littered with glass, concrete, rebar, garbage, and human waste. He had cleaned the place up, carpeted the floors, wallpapered (all of his supplies bought and shipped from the United States), put showers in the bathrooms, and hooked the place up to a wireless Internet connection.

At about the same time, Jack Allstrong had had to start work on his trailer park to house his guards and cooks, although he still couldn't compete with such CB ameni-ties as a swimming pool and a rec room with a pool table. Allstrong knew that these types of cosmetics would be important to help convince his clients that he was serious and committed to the long-term success of the mission, but he was initially hampered by lack of infrastructure and simple good help.

But then that genius Kuvan Krekar had come up with the idea of dog kennels as another income source, and that was already working. Allstrong now had a decent number of the ministry people starting to believe that IED- and bomb-sniffing dogs would be an essential part of the rebuilding process in bases all over the country.

So all in all, Jack was in high spirits for a variety of reasons: Kuvan was in fact interested in going in with them on their currency-exchange bid, which gave it immediate credibility and might make them the frontrunners over CB; the CPA was still paying them in dollars (which meant Allstrong could buy his own dinars to pay his local workers at the deeply discounted black-market exchange rate); the bomb-sniffing-dog revenue wasn't going to be stopped, at least in the short term, by bureaucrats like Charlie Tucker.

The bottom line was that the two million dollars in cash that Nolan had retrieved today and carried here in his backpack covered approximately four hundred thousand dollars in the company's actual current expenses, including tips to Colonel Ramsdale and several other middlemen. Everyone was too busy and/or too afraid and the times were too chaotic for anyone to bother keeping close tabs on exactly what the money was used for, or exactly where it went. There was plenty of it, in cash, and the mandate was to get Iraq up and running again. Subtext: whatever it cost.

For example, in the first month of the contract, Allstrong's trailer park had run out of drinking water within a week, a true crisis. Jack had gone to Ramsdale and told him he desperately needed to buy more water immediately, but that he was out of money, what with payroll, housing costs, legitimate security equipment, weapons, and vehicles such as armored Mercedes-Benz sedans, and all other daily supplies for his now close to 150-man staff. Without a personal look at the situation and apparently without a qualm, Ramsdale signed off on an authorization for Allstrong to add six hundred thousand dollars to the original sixteen-million-dollar contract over its six-month life—peanuts considering the fact that the contract as written already was paying Allstrong a little bit more than eighty-eight thousand dollars a day, all of it in cash.

Allstrong had requested a total of a hundred thousand dollars from Ramsdale for the water, but the colonel had been so used to thinking in one-month units that he'd okayed six times the requested price, and Allstrong had seen no reason to correct him. And after all, the truth was that they were all working in an extremely hostile environment, where the danger of death was real and omnipresent. In Allstrong's view, that risk should not go without significant reward, even if much of it turned out to be under the table. It wasn't as though people like Ramsdale didn't know what was happening. In fact, Ramsdale was planning to retire from the active military before the year was out, and he'd already made a commitment to stay on in Iraq as one of Allstrong's senior security analysts at a salary of $240,000 per year.

Standing over by his wall map, Allstrong caught the latest toss of the packet of bills from Nolan and turned it over in his hands. "So." It wasn't a question. It wasn't an answer. The tone seemed to say, *I'm holding on to fifty thousand dollars in cash, when last year I was flat broke.* He smiled. "How sweet is this, huh, Ron?"

"Yes, sir." Nolan tipped up his scotch. "It's turning out to be a good year."

"Yes, it is." Allstrong crossed over to his desk, casually flipping the wrapped bills package over to Nolan. "And I think it could be even better, but I'm leery of burning out my best assets, which are men like you. No, no, no, don't give me any of that false modesty bullshit. I send you out to do a job and you get the job done. It's not every guy in the world can walk around with two million dollars and not be tempted to disappear with it."

This was more than just idle chatter. That exact temptation, though for far less money—a quarter of a million dollars—had proven too strong for at least one of Allstrong's other senior employees in the past two months. Beyond that, almost two dozen of his first crew of guard hires—from pre-Kuvan sources—had disappeared with guns and credentials almost as soon as they'd been issued them.

But Ron Nolan merely shrugged. "You pay me well, Jack. I like the work. It's nice to get a regular paycheck. Beyond which"—he broke his own smile—"I disappear with two million of your money, I'm pretty sure you'd hunt me down and kill me."

Allstrong pointed a finger at him. "You're not all wrong there. Nothing personal."

"No, of course not."

Allstrong put a haunch on the corner of his desk. "What I'm getting at is whether you're starting to feel stretched a little thin."

"No, I'm good."

"I ask because another opportunity has come up—I know, they're growing on trees nowadays, but if I don't pick 'em somebody else will. Anyway, I wanted to run it by you, see if you wanted to take point on it. I should tell you, I consider it pretty high risk, even for here."

"Taking a walk over here is high risk, Jack."

"Yes, it is. But this is in the Sunni Triangle."

Nolan tossed the package up and caught it. He shrugged. "What's the gig?"

"Pacific Safety—Rick Slocum's outfit; he's tight with Rumsfeld—just pulled in a contract through the Corps of Engineers to rewire the whole goddamn Triangle in three months. High-voltage wiring and all the towers to hold it. You ready for this? He's going to need seven hundred guards for his people."

Nolan whistled. "Seven hundred?"

"I know. A shitload. But I'm sure Kuvan can get 'em."

"I'm sure he can too. You gotta love them Kurds."

"Who doesn't? So . . . you want to hear the numbers?"

"Sure," Nolan said. "I haven't had a good hard-on in a couple of days." With the wrapped bills in one hand and his tumbler of scotch in the other, he got up and crossed over to Allstrong's desk.

His boss pulled over the adding machine and started punching and talking. "Let's assume two hundred a month for the guards, what we're paying now. Good? We've got seven hundred guys working for ninety days, that's four hundred twenty thousand. Plus food and ammo and other incidentals. Let's go wild and call that twenty bucks a man per day, so forty-two grand. Shooting high, call our whole expense five hundred grand. Slocum told me off the record that because of the high risk in the area, he expects the winning bid to come in at no less than twelve mil. Which is exactly what I'm going to bid it at and which, if you're doing your math"—he hit the calculator—"is a three-month profit of eleven million five hundred thousand dollars."

"I've definitely got wood," Nolan said.

"So you're in if we get it?"

"All the way, Jack. We'd be crazy not to."

"I agree. But I'm not sugarcoating it. I'm thinking we might lose a dozen guys. I'm talking dead, not deserted or disappeared."

"Okay."

"There'd be a significant bonus in it for you. Twenty a month sound good?"

"When do I start?"

"First, let's get the gig. But remember, I want you to be sure you're good with it. You'll have your bare ass hanging out there."

"And seven hundred guys guarding it, Jack. Can I bring my escorts? I like that guy Scholler. He runs a tight ship."

"I'll talk to Calliston, but I can't imagine there'd be any problem. He doesn't even know who those guys are."

"Poor bastards."

"Hey," Allstrong said, "they enlisted. What'd they expect?" He went around his desk and stood looking out the window at the airport outside. An enormous C-17 Globemaster III transport plane coasted by on the tarmac—several hundred more tons of supplies and equipment direct from the United States. Without turning around, he said, "So between now and then, what's your schedule look like?"

"When exactly?"

"Next couple of weeks."

"Pretty free. I got the message out up at Anaconda and

Tikrit. We've definitely got friends trying to hook us up in both places, but they've got to clear their own brass first. We might have to sub under KBR, but I got the sense they're generally open to us doing what we've done here. Whatever happens, it's going to take a little time. Why?"

Now Allstrong did turn. "I'd like to send you back to the States for a week or two. Clean up some problems in the home office. I'd go myself, but I don't feel like I can leave here just now if we want to pick up these jobs we're talking about. You'd be back in plenty of time for the Triangle thing if that comes about. And after today, payroll's covered until next time."

"What kind of problems?"

"Well." Allstrong tipped up the last of his scotch. "I hired a private eye and he's found Arnold Zwick. The idiot went back home to Frisco." Zwick was the company's senior executive who'd disappeared with a quarter million dollars of Allstrong's money about six weeks before. "I'd kind of like to get my money back. I was hoping you could talk some sense into him. After that, take a little well-deserved R and R wherever you want to go. Sound good?"

"When do you want me to leave?"

"I can get you on a plane to Travis tomorrow morning."

"Done."

Allstrong broke a smile. "You know, Ron, I hate it when you take so long to make your decisions."

"I know," Nolan said. "It's a flaw. I'm working on it."

At his desk, Allstrong picked up a manila envelope and handed it across to Nolan. "If what's in that doesn't answer all your questions, I'll brief you further in the morning. Now you'd better go do some packing."

"I'm gone."

Nolan executed a brisk salute and whirled around. His hand was on the doorknob when Allstrong spoke behind him.

"Aren't you forgetting something?"

Nolan straightened up and turned around as he pulled the packet of bills out from under his jacket. He was smiling. "Oh, you mean this old thing?" He tossed it back to his boss. "Just seeing if you're paying attention, Jack, keeping you on your toes."

"Pretty much always," Allstrong said.

"I can see that. Catch you in the morning."

Dear Tara –

So today I got to walk through some of the mean streets of scenic Baghdad with this crazy guy, Ron Nolan, who didn't seem to know or care that we were in hostile territory. He's one of the security guys for Allstrong, which, you may remember from my last letter, if you're reading them, is the contracting firm that we've somehow gotten semipermanently attached to. I find it ironic, to say the least, that I'm supposed to be out protecting him. This guy needs protection like a duck needs a raincoat.

It was too surreal. He's there to collect the company's payroll for this month. So I'm thinking we're going to go in someplace like a bank and get a check from Bremer's people that Allstrong can then go deposit in their bank. Wrong. They've got barbed wire and cement blocks set up in the hallway in front of this door. Nolan shows his

ID to the Marine sergeant on duty with his whole platoon. The place is a fortress.

Anyway, we pass the ID check—everybody knows Nolan—and they walk us into this tiny internal room—no windows out to the hall, even. Stucco is still all over the floors from when the building was bombed in April. No drywall either. After Saddam left town, the looters came in and took everything, and I mean everything. Rebar out of the walls. Internal wiring. You wouldn't believe it. There's not a desk in the whole ministry building—everybody uses folding tables like you get at Wal-Mart. I wouldn't be surprised if we bought 'em from Wal-Mart and had 'em shipped over.

Anyway, so we're in this small, dim, dirty room. Four lightbulbs. It's roughly a hundred and fifty degrees in there. And there's these two guys who take Nolan's papers, check 'em over, then disappear into what looks like a warehouse behind them. Ten minutes later, they're back with a shopping cart full of packages of hundred-dollar bills.

I'm standing there thinking, They're kidding me, right? But they count out these forty wrapped bags of fifty thousand dollars each and—you won't believe this—Nolan signs off on the amount and together, counting them a second time, we load 'em all up into his backpack!

Picture this. Nolan's got two million American dollars in cash in a backpack he's wearing, and we're walking out through this mob of not very friendly people in the lobby of the Republican Palace, and then we're back outside the Green Zone, strolling through the impoverished Baghdad streets that are crawling with citizens who make less than a hundred dollars a month and *who really don't like us. Was I a little nervous? Is this guy out of his mind, or what? And I got the sense he was loving it.*

Long story short, a couple of blocks along through this really really crowded marketplace and finally we hooked back up with my guys in the convoy and made it out of town and back to the base here, where Jack Allstrong has supposedly got a huge safe—flown in from America, of course—bolted into the cement foundation under his office.

Anyway, lots more to tell about some of the other insane elements of the economics of this place—all the cooks here at the base are Filipinos, and the actual guards out at the airport are from Nepal. We met a guy named Kuvan today who evidently supplies Allstrong with all these workers. Nolan tells me none of them make more than a hundred and fifty bucks a month, where he makes twenty thousand! He tells me that when I get done with my service here, I should volunteer to come back and work for Allstrong. Ex–American military guys make out like bandits here. You'd love it if I went that way, huh?

Okay, enough about this place. You hear about Iraq enough anyway, I'm sure. What I'd really like to know is if you're reading any of these, if I'm at least communicating with you a little. It's hard you not answering, Tara. If you've gotten this far on this letter, and you don't want me to write to you anymore, just tell me somehow and I promise I'll stop. If you've made up your mind and it's completely over. But some part of me holds on to the hope that you might be willing to give us another try when I come home.

I know, as you said a hundred times, IF I get home. Well, here's the deal. I'm coming home.

I'm just having a hard time accepting that our slightly different politics have really broken us up. It's true that I think sometimes it's okay to fight for something, either because you believe in the cause or because you've signed on to fight. You've given your word. It's as simple as that. Maybe you don't think that, and we can argue about it more someday, I hope.

If you could just write me back, one way or the other, Tara, I'd love to hear from you. I love you. Still.

"Hey! Evan."

He looked up to see Ron Nolan standing in the doorway that led back to the dormitory where his men slept. He had written his letter sitting in muted light at a table in the otherwise empty mess hall. Now he'd just finished addressing his envelope and put his pen down, nodding in acknowledgment. "Sir."

Nolan stepped into the room. "Hey, haven't we already been over this? You're Evan, I'm Ron. What are you, twenty-five?"

"Twenty-seven,"

"Well, I'm thirty-eight. Give me a break. You call me 'sir,' I feel old. I feel old, I get mean. I get mean, I kill people. Then you'd be to blame. It's a vicious circle and it would all be your fault."

The last words he'd written to Tara still with him, Evan had to force his face into a tolerant smile. "You'd just kill somebody at random?"

Nolan was up to the table by now, grinning. "It's been known to happen. It's not pretty. You want a beer?"

Evan had a nagging feeling that this recreational

drinking could become a slippery slope. It would make the second time he'd had alcohol since his arrival over here. But then really, he thought, what the fuck. With everything else that was going on over here, who really cared? Nevertheless, he took a half swing at reluctance. "We're not supposed to drink," he said.

"Oh, right, I forgot." Nolan cocked his head. "Are you fucking kidding me? Somebody here gonna bust you? You're in charge here, dude."

"I know. I'm thinking about my men."

"What's that, like a mantra with you? You see that in a movie or something? I don't see any of your guys around who are going to be scandalized. They won't even see. Don't be a dweeb. I'll get you a beer."

"One." Evan was talking to his back as he turned.

"Okay. For starters." Nolan walked back into the kitchen, opened an enormous double-doored refrigerator, and returned carrying two bottles of Budweiser. Twisting off the top of one, he slid it down the length of the table to where Evan stopped it and brought it to his lips. When he finished his first sip, Nolan was sitting across from him. "There's e-mail out here, you know." He pointed at the envelope. "Mom or girlfriend?"

"Ex-girlfriend. I e-mailed her all during training and she never answered. It's too goddamn easy to hit Delete. Or change your address. So now I write letters." He shrugged. "Stupid, but maybe some kind of physical connection."

"If she's your ex-girlfriend, why are you writing her?"

"I don't know. It's probably a waste of time. I'm an idiot." He took another pull at his beer. "I'd just like to know if she's even getting these damn letters."

"So that's not the first one?"

"It's like, the tenth."

"And she hasn't written back? Not even once?"

"It was a pretty bad fight. We disagreed about the war."

"People don't break up over that."

"We did." He looked across the table. "But then sometimes I think maybe something's happened to her. I can't believe she won't write me back. Maybe she's not getting them. If she's read 'em, I know she'd . . . maybe she died, or something happened and she can't . . ."

"Can't what?"

"I don't know."

Nolan spun his bottle slowly. "Dude," he said. "No offense, but you're sounding a little pathetic. Here you are laying your life on the line every day. You got bigger fish to fry."

"Yeah. I know." He slugged down a mouthful. "I know."

"You want to just give it up."

"If I heard from her, maybe it'd be easier."

"You *are* hearing from her. Think about it."

"Yeah, you're right. I know you're right." He tipped up his bottle and drained it.

Nolan got up and went back into the kitchen, returned with another round, twisted off Evan's cap, and passed it across to him as he sat down. "So where'd you go to school?"

"Santa Clara."

"College boy, huh?" At Evan's shrug, Nolan went on. "Hey, no crime in that. I went two years to Berkeley. Couldn't stand the place, though, so I went out and enlisted. Made the SEALs and life got good. You finish?"

"Yep."

"What'd you do after?"

"Became a cop."

Nolan cracked a grin and nodded. "I had a feeling you were a cop."

"Why's that?"

"You look like a cop."

"I know a lot of cops who don't look like me."

"You know what you're looking for, I bet they do." Nolan drank, his grin in place. "It's how you walk, how you carry yourself. You're a big guy. You keep yourself in good shape. I would have guessed a cop. Here's to good cops everywhere."

Nolan straightened up, raised a flat palm, and Evan reached up and slapped it hard enough that the clap rang in the empty room. Back down on his seat, Nolan raised his bottle and the two men clinked them together and drank them down in one long gulp.

When Nolan got back with the next round and they'd clinked again, he pointed down at the letter, still on the table between them. "You in touch with anybody else back home who can talk to her, find out what's happening?"

"Not really. This place isn't the best for communication, maybe you've noticed."

"You got family?"

"Yeah, but . . . what am I supposed to do? Ask my brother or my mother to go see if Tara's okay? That'd just be weird. She'd think I was stalking her or something."

"Well." Nolan tipped up his beer again. "Here's the deal. I'm flying back to San Fran tomorrow. You give me that letter, I'll go put the damn thing right in her hand, ask her if she's read the other ones. Find out the story. Be back here in two weeks."

"You're going home. What for?"

He waved away the question. "Just some logistics stupidity for Jack. Office problems. Show a presence and make sure the staff is on board with the big picture. We get either one of these new contracts, we're going to need a new building back at home." He shrugged. "Business stuff. But the point is I'll have plenty of time to drive down to Redwood City. Suss out what's going on with your babe."

"Ex-babe."

"Whatever." He reached out and turned the envelope around, looked down, and read, "Tara Wheatley. Cute name anyway."

"Cute girl," Evan said.

"I believe you."

"You really wouldn't mind going down and giving her the envelope?"

Nolan spread his hands expansively. "Hey! Dude. Please. Forget about it. It's done."

[4]

Ron Nolan sat on the top step of the shaded outdoor stairway that led to the second landing at the Edgewood Apartments in Redwood City, California. The shade came courtesy of a brace of giant magnolia trees that stood sentinel over the entrance to the apartment complex.

An hour ago, at about five o'clock, he'd climbed the steps and rung the doorbell at 2C, but no one had answered. He could have called first and made an appointment—Tara Wheatley was listed in the phone book—but he thought it would be better if he just showed up and delivered the letter in person. He didn't want to give her the option of saying she wouldn't see him, didn't care if she ever got another letter from Evan. That would have complicated the whole thing. It was better to simply show up and complete the mission.

He wasn't in any hurry. He'd give it an hour or two and if she didn't come home in that time, he'd come back either later tonight or tomorrow. Evan had told him that this time of the summer, she was probably spending most days in her classroom, preparing it for the start of the school year. Tara taught sixth grade at St. Charles, a Catholic school in the next town. Evan assumed that she wasn't dating anybody else, at least not yet, so he was reasonably sure she'd be around by dinnertime most nights, if everything was still okay with her—if she wasn't hurt or sick, or dead.

So Nolan waited, comfortable on the hard stone step. The weather was really ideal, an afternoon floral scent from the gardenia hedge overlying the auto exhaust from the busy street, the fresh-cut-grass smell from the lawn below him, a faint whiff of chlorine from the complex's pool, a corner of which was visible off to his left. If he closed his eyes, Nolan could almost fool himself that he was back for a moment in high school. People were laughing and splashing down at the pool, and the disembodied sounds combined with the softness of the air to lull him after a while, carrying him away from what had become his real world of dust and duty, danger and death.

Like the trained animal he was, he came back to immediate full consciousness as a new vibration from the steps registered with his psyche. He looked down and saw a woman in a simple two-piece blue bathing suit stopped now on the third step, turned away from him, exchanging some banter with other friends who'd obviously just left the pool too. From the shade of her wet hair, he imagined it would be blond when it dried. A thick fall of it hung down her back to a little below the halter strap. She'd hooked a finger through her beach towel and thrown it carelessly over one shoulder. Nolan's eyes swept over the length of her body and he saw nothing about it he didn't like. Her skin was the color of honey.

He shifted on his step to get a better look just as she turned and glanced up at him. Catching him in the act, she shot him a brief complicitous smile that was neither embarrassed nor inviting, then quickly went back to the good-bye to her friends. One of them left her with some parting remark that Nolan didn't quite hear, but her spike of carefree laughter carried up to him. He hadn't heard a sound like that in a while.

Then she was coming up the stairs toward him.

Nolan stood up. He was wearing black shoes, pressed khakis, and a tucked-in camo shirt. He was holding Evan's letter in his hand. Suddenly she stopped halfway up, all trace of humor suddenly washed from her face. As tears welled in her eyes, she brought her hand up to her mouth. "Oh, my God," she said. "It's not Evan, is it? Tell me it's not Evan."

Realizing what she must be thinking—that he was the Army's messenger sent to inform her of Evan's death in Iraq—Nolan held out a reassuring hand and said, "Evan's fine. Completely fine. I'm sorry if I startled you. You must be Tara."

Still knocked out of her equilibrium, she nodded. "Yes. But . . . this is about Evan?"

Down below, one of her male friends called up to her. "Tara? Everything okay?"

It gave her an instant to collect herself. Turning, she waved. "I'm fine. It's okay." Coming back to Nolan, her voice had firmed up. "Who are you, then? What are you doing here? You had me thinking Evan had been killed."

"I'm sorry. My name's Ron Nolan. I'm a friend of Evan's over there. I should have realized what I'd look like waiting here for you to show up. I'm sorry."

"Okay, you're sorry." She pointed at the envelope he held. "What's that, then?"

"It's a letter that Evan asked me to hand-deliver to you. He was worried about you."

"Why would he worry about me? He's the one in the war zone."

"Well, he hasn't received any letters back from you."

"That's right. That's because I haven't written any. We broke up. Maybe he didn't tell you that. What does he want me to say?"

"I don't know." Nolan held the envelope out to her. "I'm just the messenger here. My job is to give you this last letter and then to tell Evan that you're all right."

"I'm fine."

"Yes, I can see that. You want to take this?"

She didn't move.

He waited, the envelope in his outstretched hand, looking at her, taken by her remarkable face. Her hair was pulled back; it revealed a clear, wide forehead. She'd just come from swimming, so there was no makeup to cover the landscape of pale freckles under her widely spaced glacier-blue eyes that spilled over onto well-defined cheekbones. Even without lipstick, her mouth looked slightly bruised.

Nolan forced himself to look away. It took a serious effort.

Tara looked down at the envelope. "Does he think I haven't gotten his other letters?" she asked. Her shoulders settled as something seemed to give in her. "I don't want to start again with him. Doesn't he see that? It's never going to work."

"Because you disagree about the war?"

"It's not just that."

"No?"

"No. Why do you ask that?"

"Because he seems to think it is. Just about the war, I mean. Although I told him, and I'll tell you the same thing, people who love each other don't break up over that."

"Over agreeing about whether or not killing people is the way to solve the world's problems? Oh yes, they do, I think."

Neither of them moved.

"And I didn't say that I loved him," she said.

Cocking his head, he said, "When you thought I was here to tell you he was dead, it seemed like you cared about him more than a little bit."

"You can care about someone without either loving them or wanting them to die. Don't you think that's possible?"

"Sure." The woman was beautiful, but Nolan thought that a little attitude check wouldn't hurt her. "Anything's possible," he said. "For example, it's possible that you might even change your mind someday about the people who are risking their lives to guarantee your freedom."

He'd clearly hit a nerve. Her whole face went dark. "That's not fair," she said. "I have nothing but respect for the military."

His mouth smiled, but his eyes didn't follow. "Sure you do," he said. "You just wouldn't want to marry one."

"Besides," she went on, "this war isn't about guaranteeing anyone's freedom. It's just about oil."

Nolan shook his head. As though fighting for oil or anything you needed was wrong. He looked down at his hand and held it out. "Are you going to take this letter or not?"

Her mouth set in a hard line, she stared at the thing as though it were alive and could bite her. And perhaps in some sense it could. At last, she shook her head. "I don't think so. I haven't even opened any of the others. I'm not going to start reading them now."

He nodded again as though she'd verified something for him.

"What does that look mean?"

"Nothing. There was no look."

"Yes, there was. And it meant something."

"Okay. You said you weren't going to start reading Evan's letters now. I guess the look meant, 'Spoken like someone who's afraid that if she gets some facts about what she's already decided on, she might change her mind.'"

Perhaps suddenly aware that she was standing arguing with a man while she was wearing less than her everyday underwear, she pulled the towel up over her shoulders and held both ends of it closed over her breasts. Her voice went soft and low in anger. "I'm not afraid of getting facts, Mister . . . what is it again?"

"Nolan. Ron Nolan."

"All right, Mr. Nolan …"

"Ron, okay?" Again, he grinned, taunting her.

"Okay, Ron." He'd gotten her heated up, which was his intention. "For your information, as a matter of fact I do have all the facts I need about Evan and about this stupid war in Iraq. And I don't need his letters to make me feel sorry for him. He made the decision to go over there. He decided to leave me and do that. Now I've moved on and he can't just think he's going to explain his way out of it and if I'd just understand how hard it was for him, then somehow we'd get back together. I'm not going to do that."

"No. I can see that." Nolan held out the letter again. "Last chance." When she didn't move to take it, Nolan slipped it into the pocket of his shirt and said, "I'll tell Evan you're in fine health. Excuse me. Nice to have met you." Moving past her, he started down the steps.

When he got to the bottom, she spoke. "Mr. Nolan. Ron."

Turning, he looked up at her. "I'm not against the military," she said. "I'm against Evan being in this war. There's a difference."

Nolan raised his hand in a salute. "Yes, ma'am," he said. "If you say so."

AT SEVEN-THIRTY, he rang her doorbell again.

She answered the door in tennis shoes, a pair of running shorts, and a black Nike tank top. Her hair back in a ponytail. She still hadn't put on any makeup and it looked as though she'd been crying.

"I'm not going to read that letter," she said first thing. "I already told you."

"Yes, you did. I'm not here for that."

"Well . . . what?"

"Well, pretty clearly you're not with Evan anymore. I thought maybe you'd like to go get a drink somewhere."

She crossed her arms. "You're asking me on a date?"

"I'm asking if you'd like to go get a drink or something. Not that big a commitment."

"I thought I made it clear how I feel about getting involved with military people."

"You did, which would break my heart if I were a military person. Which, fortunately, I'm not."

"But you said you were with Evan over there?"

"I am. But I'm a civilian. I work for Allstrong Security. Evan's based with our headquarters group. I'm back home on assignment here for a couple of weeks and to-night I'm looking at dinner all by myself, which isn't my favorite."

"So, as a last resort …"

"Not exactly that, but we had a couple of issues we could have fun talking about if we left Evan out of it." He looked around behind her into her apartment. "It doesn't look like you've got much of a party going here any-way."

"No." She sighed.

Sensing that she was weakening, he asked, "Have you eaten?"

"No."

"You can pick the place," he said. "Anywhere you want, sky's the limit."

Sighing again, she broke a weak smile and nodded. "That's a nice offer. Eating by myself isn't my favorite, either, and I've been doing a lot of that." She met his eyes, then looked away, wrestling with the decision.

"I don't want to have another fight about this war or about Evan."

"I don't want to fight either. I just want to put myself on the outside of some good food and drink."

"That does sound good." She gave it another second or two, then stepped back a bit, holding the door open for him. "You want to come in and sit down a minute, I'll go put on some clothes."

SHE PICKED AN UNDERSTATED and very good Italian place on Laurel Street in San Carlos, maybe a mile from her apartment, a car ride short enough to preclude much in the way of conversation. Nolan, usually voluble in any situation, found himself somewhat tongue-tied from the minute she walked out of her hallway in low heels and the classic simple black spaghetti-strap dress. She wore a gold necklace that held a single black pearl, and matching earrings. She'd put her hair up, revealing a graceful neck, showcasing the face in relief.

Neither the bathing suit she'd been wearing when he'd met her nor the tank top, tennis shoes, and running shorts when she'd opened the door tonight had prepared him for the sophistication that she now exhibited. Before, of course, she'd been pretty enough to attract him—good-looking California-girl cheerleader—but now something in her style bespoke a worldliness and maturity that, frankly, intimidated him. Nolan's style, and his plan for that matter, had been to tease her about her political leanings and beliefs, wear her down, get her laughing and eventually tipsy, bed her, and report back to Evan that he was lucky she hadn't read his letters or written back—she wasn't worth the trouble.

Now, ten minutes of silence on the drive over pretty much shattered that plan. Try as he might, and as much as he might have wanted, he wasn't going to be able to take her that lightly. It wasn't just the bare fact of her substantial beauty, but a seriousness, a gravitas, that he couldn't remember ever having encountered before in the women he'd known.

Handing his keys to the valet in front of the restaurant, Nolan noticed that Tara remained seated, her hands clasped in her lap. A test? Would he be a chivalrous gentleman if he opened the door, or would that make him a chauvinist pig? He hadn't worried about a social nicety like that in ten years, and now suddenly he badly wanted to make the right decision, to look good in her eyes. But his only option was to be who he was, and his parents had raised him to have old-fashioned manners, so he came around and got her door for her. She rewarded him with a small smile in which, inordinately pleased, he read approval.

The tuxedoed maître d' knew who she was, at least by looks. He greeted her familiarly, kissed her hand, nodded at Nolan with respect and perhaps a soupçon of envy, and led them to a private banquette in the back. Lighting in the place was dim, with pinpoint lights onto the tables to facilitate reading the menu. Tara ordered an Italian-sounding white wine he'd never heard of and he asked for a Beefeater martini up.

The waiter left. Tara sipped her water. "I said I didn't want to fight, but we're allowed to talk if you want. If we don't, it might get to be a long night."

"I've been trying to avoid sensitive subjects."

"Okay, but you haven't said two words since my apartment."

"That's because everything I thought of seemed risky."

"Like what?"

Nolan hesitated, came out with it. "Like how lovely you look. See? I've offended you already."

"I'm not offended."

"I think you are. You frowned."

"I did?"

"Definitely."

"I didn't mean to frown. I'm not offended. It wasn't an offended frown. I'm even flattered. Thank you." She scratched at the napkin next to her plate. "I'm just not very comfortable with compliments, I suppose. Plus, I'm a little nervous. This might have been a mistake."

"What?"

"You and me. Going out for dinner. It just sounded so good to go out and. . ." Sighing, she killed a moment with another sip of water. "I don't want to give you the wrong impression."

"About what?"

"About if this is a date. Like a boy/girl date."

"Okay, I'll try not to get the wrong impression. What would be the right one?"

"That it's just dinner. Two people out at a restaurant together."

He smiled across at her. "As opposed to what? A romantic dinner?"

"I guess. I wasn't thinking this was going to be a romantic dinner. That's probably why I frowned."

"Back to that, huh? You frowned because I said you were lovely, which means I'm romantically interested."

"Something like that, I suppose."

The waiter arrived with their drinks, and Nolan waited until he'd moved out of earshot, then sipped at his martini and picked up where they'd left off. "Okay," he said, "I promise I'm trying not to be romantically interested. You're the girlfriend of a pal of mine, so that would be awkward, except you said that you're done with him."

"I think."

"Ah. A change in the story."

"No, not really. I just wasn't thinking that I was going to go out with anybody else so soon. I mean on a date."

"I've got an idea. How about we don't call this a date or anything else? Just let it be what it is. Do you have to decide that right away?"

"Maybe not. I just don't want to send you any mixed signals. I'm not really with Evan anymore, but I'm . . ."

"You still care about him."

She raised her shoulders. "I don't know. Not answering his letters is a decision. Not having feelings about him isn't something you just decide. I can't say I'm there yet. And now here we are, you and me. You asked me out and I said yes. I don't know why I did that."

"You were hungry?"

"We could have gone to McDonald's. I didn't have to get dressed up. This feels . . . different."

"Than McDonald's? I'd hope so." Nolan leaned in across the table, caught and held her gaze. "Look, Tara, it's not that complicated. I don't know you, and the only two things I know *about* you are, one, that we probably disagree about the military, which we're not allowed to talk about. And two, you're very pretty. That's just an observation, and risky because you might think I was coming on to you, which would put this more in the line of a date, I admit. So let's get that off the table right now." He straightened back up. "This is not a date. I'm way too old, and what are you, twenty-two?"

"Try twenty-six."

"Well, I'm thirty-eight, that's too much right there. I could be your father."

Around a small smile, she sipped wine. "Only if you were a very precocious eleven-year-old."

"I was," he said, and held out his stem glass. "Here's to precocious children."

She stopped, her glass halfway to his. "I don't know if I can drink to that. I teach eleven-year-olds. If they were any more precocious, we'd need bars on the windows."

Nolan kept his glass where it was. "All right," he said, "here's to peace, then. Is peace okay to drink to?"

She clinked his glass. "Peace is good," she said. "Peace would be very good."

NOLAN PULLED INTO A SPACE in the parking lot by her apartment. He killed the engine and his lights and reached for his door handle.

"You don't have to get out," she said.

"No, I do. A gentleman walks a woman to her door on a dark night."

"That's all right. I'll be fine."

He sat back in his seat, then turned to look at her. "You're trying to avoid that awkward here-we-are-at-the-door moment. Understood. You don't have to ask me in for a nightcap. I won't try to kiss you good night. Even if I am finding you marginally more attractive than before we'd had such a good time. That was a great meal."

"It was." But she spoke without much enthusiasm. Her hands clasped in her lap, she sat facing forward, stiff and unyielding.

"What is it?" he asked. "Are you all right?"

She exhaled. "Do you still have Evan's letter?"

"Yes, ma'am."

She didn't move. "I think I should read it. I should read the other ones."

"All right. It's in the glove box, right in front of you. Help yourself." He opened the car door and stepped out. The night smelled of gardenia, jasmine, magnolia—he'd forgotten how beautiful it could be here in California in the summertime. Walking around the car, he opened the passenger door.

Tara sat still another second, then opened the glove compartment, picked out the envelope, swung her legs, and got out. She said, "Really, Ron, I'm okay. That's my place, right up there, you can see it from here."

"Yes, you can, but it's against my religion to let you walk up there alone."

She sighed. "Okay."

"And no funny stuff," he said. "From you, I mean."

Amused in spite of herself, she looked up at him and shook her head. "I'll try to keep myself under control." Holding up the letter so he could see she had it, she turned and he fell in beside her—across the parking lot, up the outside stairs. Unlocking her door, she pushed it open and turned on the inside light. "Safe," she said. "Thank you."

"You're very welcome." He executed a small bow. "I had a great time," he said. "You sleep tight."

[5]

SATURDAY HE TOOK HER up to San Francisco. This one was a nondate, he told her, because it was in the daytime and a real date by definition had to be at night. He picked her up at ten-thirty in the morning and with the top down on his Corvette, they took Highway 280 up to the city, the beautiful green back way, Crystal Springs reservoir on their left, and then, farther on, the great expanse of the glittering Bay down to their right.

She didn't know the city as well as he did. She'd told him that at dinner, and he'd used it as his excuse to ask her out again: She couldn't live as close as she did to one of the world's great cities and not know very much about it. It was morally wrong.

So they hit the Palace of the Legion of Honor, then swung back through Golden Gate Park, stopping for tea at the Japanese Tea Garden after an hour inside the De Young Museum. The fine August weather was holding up, and parking at Ghirardelli Square, they walked back up Polk Street and ate baguettes and pâté and drank red wine at one of the outdoor tables of a French bistro. Taking a walk afterward, idly sightseeing, they essayed the descent of Lombard, the "crookedest street in the world"—although it wasn't in fact even the crookedest street in the city, Nolan told her. That distinction belonged to Vermont Street down in Potrero Hill. Nevertheless, Lombard was crooked and steep enough, and he told her that she might want to put her hand on his arm for balance, and she did.

In North Beach, at Caffe Trieste, Nolan brought their cappuccinos over and put them down on the tiny table in front of her. "Okay," he said, "risky-question time again."

This time, more comfortable with him by now, she smiled and said, "Uh-oh."

"Think you can handle it?"

"You never know, but I'll try."

"Evan's letters."

"What about them?"

"Have you read them?"

She looked down at her coffee, lifted the cup and took a sip, then put it down carefully. "Why don't you just tell me I'm pretty again and we'll run with that instead?"

"Okay. You're pretty again. After that ugly time you had back there for a while."

"Yeah, that was terrible." But the gag wasn't working. Her mouth went tight and she closed her eyes, sighing, then opened them and looked him full in the face. "Not yet. I tried starting to read them the other night, but I'm still too emotional about him. I haven't changed my mind about what he's doing, so there's really nothing he can say . . ."

Nolan took a long moment before he sipped his coffee, another one before he spoke. "You don't see anything noble or glorious or even good in the warrior, do you?"

She briefly met his eyes. "The *warrior*," she said in a derisive tone.

"The warrior, that's right."

She shook her head. "Evan's not a warrior, Ron. Evan's a simple soldier, a grunt who's taking orders from men he doesn't respect, fighting in a country that doesn't want us there, risking his life for a cause he doesn't believe in. I have a hard time with words like *noble* and *glorious* and *good* coming into that equation when I keep seeing waste and stupidity and ignorance."

"Okay," Nolan said. "We could maybe get in a good fight about this particular war. But that's not what I'm talking about. I'm talking about the philosophical concept of the warrior."

Her face was still set in stone. "I never think about the warrior, Ron. War is what's wrong with the world, and always has been."

Again, Nolan let a silence accumulate. "With all respect, Tara," he said quietly, "you owe it to yourself to think about this."

"To myself?"

"If you're dumping the guy you're in love with over it, then yes. To yourself."

"I've told you, I don't know if I'm in love with him anymore."

"Because he went to fight?"

She slowly turned her coffee cup around. "I told him we could go to Canada, or anywhere else."

"And what happens when Canada or wherever feels threatened and needs soldiers?"

"But that's the point, Ron. There was no threat. Iraq was no threat. It was preemptive, like Germany invading Poland. America doesn't do that—that's the point. There are no WMDs, you wait and see. The whole thing's a sham. It's about oil profits and that's all. Halliburton and those people. Can't you see that?"

"Defense contractors, you mean?"

"Yes. Defense contractors. Big business. Cheney and his buddies."

"Well, of course I see what you're saying, but I'm in a little bit of a bind here, because a defense contractor is who I work for. But from my perspective, we're the guys who are protecting the Army and the civilian admin guys over there. We're the ones feeding our troops, moving water and supplies, doing good work, saving lives, trying to rebuild the country."

"That we destroyed in the first place."

Nolan took a breath. "Look, Tara, war may be hell but that doesn't mean everybody involved in it is evil. I've seen evil, and believe me, it's a whole different animal than what you're thinking of. So let's not talk about this war. I grant you it's got some issues. Let's talk about the warrior."

"The warrior, the warrior. I don't want the warrior in my life, that's all. I don't want the warrior in the world."

"Ah, but there's the crux of it. Of course it would be wonderful if there didn't need to be warriors. Just like it would be great if there were no evil in the world. But here's the thing—there is evil. And without warriors, evil would triumph."

"How 'bout this, Ron: Without warriors, evil couldn't attack."

"So it's chicken and egg, is that it? Which came first? No"—he put his hand on hers, took it away as though it burned him—"listen. My point is this: There is always going to be evil and, yes, it will attract evil warriors. You buy that so far?"

She managed a small nod.

"Okay," he went on. "So evil and its minions are a given, right? Right. Come on, you admit that. You've just admitted it. And, P.S., it's true."

She hesitated, then said, "Okay. Yes. So?"

"So once evil's on the march, what's going to stop it except a greater force for good?"

She sat back and folded her arms. "The greater force doesn't always have to be physical. It can be spiritual. Look at Gandhi, or Martin Luther King. Fighting should be a last resort. I think a lot of so-called warriors are really warmongers picking fights to justify their own existence."

"Sometimes they are, yeah. And Gandhi and King, great men, both of them, no question. And both assassinated, I might point out. And neither used their nonviolence in an actual war. Okay, they fought evil, but it wasn't on the march. It wasn't to the warrior stage yet. But even so, for every King or Gandhi, you've got a Neville Chamberlain or somebody who doesn't want to fight. It's not till you get yourself a warrior—like, say, Churchill—that you really can stop active evil. You think Hitler would have stopped by himself? Ever? Or Saddam Hussein, for that matter?"

"We did stop him, Hussein," she said. "He wasn't a threat."

Nolan let his shoulders relax. His face took on a peaceful neutrality. His voice went soft. "Tara, please, you've got it backward. If he wasn't a threat, it was because we did already stop him once. Our warriors stopped him in Kuwait. That's the only thing he understood."

Tara was twirling her cup around in its saucer, biting on her lower lip. Eventually she raised her eyes. "I don't like to think about this, Ron. About evil's place in the world."

He kept his voice low, met her eyes, again put his hand over hers and this time left it there. "I don't blame you, Tara. Nobody likes to think about it. And some places, like here in the U.S., and on a gorgeous afternoon in this great city, it can seem so far away as to be nonexistent. Thank God. I mean, thank God there are islands where the beast is kept mostly at bay. It's in its cage. But the thing to remember is that somebody, sometime, had to put the beast in there, and has to keep it there. And that's why we need—we all need, the world needs—warriors. How did you feel about Evan being a cop?"

Her frown deepened, her head moving from side to side. "I don't think I was exactly thrilled, but that was different."

"How?"

She worried her lip for another moment. "Soldiers, their job is to kill. Cops, they mostly protect."

"And sometimes to protect, don't they have to kill?"

"But it's not the main job."

"Could that be because individual bad guys don't need an army to defeat them?" He took his hand away from hers and sat up straighter, lifted his cup to his mouth, put it back down. Looking at her, he saw that her eyes had gone glassy and tears hung in their corners. "I'm sorry. I don't mean to ruin your day and make you cry. We can stop talking about this."

One tear fell, leaving its streak on her face. "I don't know what I'm going to do. It's so hard."

"It is," he said. "I know."

"I'm trying to do the right thing."

"I can see that."

"I should at least read his letters."

"That might be nice."

"But I'm still…" She stopped, looked at him, shook her head again. "I don't have any answers. I don't know what I should do."

"You don't have to decide anything today. How's that?"

She gave him a grateful smile. "Better."

"Okay, then," he said. "I think that's about enough philosophy for one day. Why don't we blow this pop stand?"

ONE OF THE LANDMARKS of old San Francisco was Trader Vic's, the restaurant where the mai tai was purportedly invented and a favorite hangout for the famous columnist Herb Caen and his pals. The original Vic's had gone out of business decades ago, but a couple of years back, they'd opened a new one near City Hall. It had a great buzz and was the same kind of place—a Pacific-island-themed destination spot serving enormous "pu-pu" platters of vaguely Asian appetizers that could be washed down with mai tais or any other number of generous rum drinks, many of them served for two out of hollowed coconut shells.

Nolan and Tara had ordered one of these when they sat down and then had another with their dinner. Their relaxed sightseeing and later the intense conversations had drawn them closer somehow and blurred the distinction between date and nondate, and by the time the waiter cleared the dinner trays and left them the check, Nolan was beginning to let himself consider the possibility that this incredible woman might like something in him after all. Clearly, Tara had an ambiguous commitment, at best, to Evan Scholler, and she seemed to be enjoying his company—laughing, teasing, drinking. Not quite outright flirting, certainly not coming on to him overtly, but giving him a lot of her time and attention, her foot nowhere near the brakes. His personal code of honor regarding a fellow warrior wouldn't permit him to pursue her if she claimed any sort of allegiance to Evan, but she'd rather definitively avoided that, and if she responded to one of his overtures later, then that would be a clear answer in itself.

Nolan had known that they had valet parking at Trader Vic's, but as a general rule he wasn't too comfortable letting valet attendants get behind the wheel of his Corvette. So, keeping his eyes open, a few blocks before they'd reached the restaurant, he had spied a miraculous section of free curb and he'd pulled into it without much thought. It had still been warm, with a certain softness to the dusk light, and walking a few extra blocks with Tara had seemed both natural and appealing.

Now, outside, it had grown dark. In typical San Francisco summer fashion, the temperature had dropped twenty degrees in the past two hours and a chill, biting wind off the Pacific was scouring the dust off the streets and making the very air gritty. They were on Golden Gate Avenue, an east-west street that funneled the blow and intensified the unpleasantness.

Tara said, "How'd it get this nasty this fast?"

"The city got the patent on this weather back in the Forty-Niner days. It was supposed to keep out the riffraff. I don't think it's worked too well, but they've kept it up. Why don't you go back inside and I'll get the car and come back for you?"

"We don't have to do that. It's not that far. I can take it."

"You're not too cold?" Tara was wearing sandals and shorts and a T-shirt with the midriff showing—California summer gear. Now ridiculously inappropriate.

But she just laughed. "It's only a few blocks. It's invigorating, don't you think?"

Nolan, in civilian shoes, khaki-colored Dockers, and a Tommy Bahama silk shirt, nodded and said, "Invigorating. Good word. You sure?"

"Let's go."

At the first corner they hit, Polk Street, they stopped at the curb for the light. He noticed that her teeth were beginning to chatter. "It's closer going back to Trader Vic's than it is to the car. You're sure you don't want to do that?"

"You think I'm that much of a wimp?"

"I never said that. But you do seem cold."

"I'll be fine. Promise."

"Okay, then." He put his arm around her. "This is for warmth only," he told her. "Don't get any ideas."

Perhaps a little tipsy, she folded her arms across her chest and leaned slightly into him. "Warmth is good," she said, then added, "Come on, light, come on."

But just then, before the light changed, a break in the traffic opened up, and taking her hand, he squeezed it. "¡Vámonos!" And they darted out into the street. In the next block, and the one after that, the streetlights weren't working. Even though they were only a few blocks from City Hall, Nolan realized that they were entering the Tenderloin District, one of the city's worst neighborhoods, where services tended to need upkeep. They walked quickly, still holding hands, their footfalls echoing, and, at the next crosswalk—Larkin—had to stop again for traffic and the light. Behind them, a prostitute in a black minidress and fishnet top stepped out from the lee of a building. "Are you two looking to party?" From the voice, Nolan realized that the woman was a man. "I've got a place right here behind us."

"Thanks, but we're good." Nolan stepped between Tara and the prostitute. "Just going to our car."

"Isn't this the street, up to the left?" Tara whispered to him.

"One more."

They jumped the light again and moved into the next darkened block. Suddenly the glittering city they'd been enjoying all day had disappeared. The breeze carried on it the acrid smells of garbage and urine. In the passing cars' headlights, Nolan could see that nearly every doorway they passed held a person lying down, bundled up in cloth or newspaper. At a break in the traffic, they crossed over in midblock, all but running now with cold and adrenaline. They turned up Leavenworth toward Eddy, into the heart of the Tenderloin. But—the good news—they were now only a bit more than a half block from where they'd parked.

As it turned out, though, that distance wasn't going to be short enough.

THE THREE YOUNG AFRICAN-AMERICAN MEN appeared out of nowhere and blocked their way. Tara whispered, "Oh God," and moved in a step behind Nolan. All of the men wore heavy, hooded jackets and as they fanned to surround the couple, the one in front of them flashed the blade of a knife. "Where y'all hurryin' up to?" he asked.

Nolan, following the flow as the men moved into position, one to the side into the street, and the other behind them, let go of Tara's hand and put an arm protectively around her waist. "Our car's just up the street there," he said, pointing.

"The 'Vette, I'm guessing?"

"That's right."

"Nice ride?"

"Yes, it is. I'm hoping that it's still in good shape."

The leader spoke to his troops. "He hopin' it still in good shape. You hear that? Man worried about his wheels." Coming back to Nolan, he moved the knife to his other hand. "Thing is, we been watchin' it, make sure nobody mess wid it, you know what I'm saying?"

"I appreciate that," Nolan said. He turned now, placed the position of his other two assailants clearly in his mind, then moved sideways a bit with Tara so that he could see any movement from the man behind him in case he was getting ready to strike. Looking now directly at the three men, one at a time, he said, "But my girlfriend's cold and she really needs to get inside the car right away." He reached behind him, as though reaching for his wallet. "How much can I pay you gentlemen for watching over my car for me?"

"Ron..." Tara began.

"Just stay cool," he whispered, tightening his grip on her waist, holding her to him. Somehow he'd taken the keys from his pocket, and now he found one of her hands and pressed them into it. "When it starts," he whispered directly into her ear, "get to the car and get it running."

"When what starts? Ron, you can't..."

Nolan started to reply when, with no warning beyond a guttural obscenity, the leader suddenly lunged forward, leading with the knife. Nolan pushed Tara back out of the way, then ducked away from the attack, deflecting the knife, and kicked out behind him, hitting the trailing man in the knee. The man screamed and went down. Nolan whirled, kicked again, and caught the leader in the hip, knocking him into the third guy coming in from the street. It was only a temporary holding action, but it gave the couple an instant's reprieve and, for Tara, a clear run to the car. "Go!" he yelled to her.

She ran.

Nolan saw the shadow looming up in his periphery, and he ducked away and slashed backward as he turned. Seeing the glint of the knife, he came down with a chop on the wrist above it, and it clattered away on the sidewalk. He no longer knew whether he was fighting the leader or the second guy, but it didn't matter. Close enough to smell him now, he lifted a knee into the man's groin and when he doubled over, followed it with a rabbit punch to the man's neck. Knowing that he'd killed him, as much by the way he fell as anything, he saw that there was still another knife in the equation. The other man swung a wide broadside at him and Nolan stepped back, let it pass harmlessly in front of him, then stepped inside and delivered a flat-hand uppercut to the base of the man's nose, driving the cartilage back into the brain. The body straightened for an instant before crumpling back to the street.

Looking back at the first man whose knee he'd shattered, Nolan realized that while he was no longer a threat, he was a witness. And witnesses, Nolan firmly believed, were bad luck. A brief scan of his surroundings confirmed that there were no others—none of the homeless were huddling in doorways on this block. The man was still down, moving on the ground, pushing himself in a crab-like fashion back and away from the fight. It took Nolan only a few steps, a couple of seconds, to get back next to him.

"Dude," he said. He was breathing hard, but his voice was almost apologetic, devoid of any emotion. "This was a bad idea. You got to stop this shit. Your leg okay? Can you get up? You ought to get that looked at. Here, let me help you."

The young man hesitated for a minute, but then took Nolan's outstretched hand and allowed himself to begin to be lifted. But as soon as he had the leverage he needed, Nolan reached his other hand around the man's neck, found his chin, and gave it a vicious snap back and side-ways. Letting this last body fall back to the sidewalk, Nolan looked down at the carnage he'd wreaked. Satisfied, he broke back up the street at a jog, jumped over the fallen leader, and in a couple of dozen steps was where Tara had started the car and already maneuvered it out from the curb, ready to make a getaway. He knocked on the car's trunk as he was going around the back of it and then opened the passenger door and jumped in, breath-less. "Are you okay?" he asked her. "Can you drive?"

She was holding the wheel, shivering, and managed a nod.

"Hit it, then. Now!"

TARA DROVE IN SILENCE for about six blocks before she pulled over and stopped the car. "I don't think I can drive anymore," she said.

"I'll take it."

She looked over at him for the first time since he'd gotten in with her. "Are you hurt?"

"No."

"What happened to them?"

"I don't know. They got tangled up in each other and that must have slowed them down enough to give me a minute to come running."

After a minute, she said, "We could have been killed, couldn't we?"

"I don't know about that. I think maybe they were trying to feel us out, that's all. They didn't have guns. They probably would have just taken our money and other stuff if we would have let them."

She sat still and allowed the silence to gather there in the confined space. Then, letting out a staggered breath, she opened the car door and got out. Nolan took the cue and did the same on his side, waiting for her to get in the passenger seat before he closed the door behind her. Behind the wheel, he belted up and got back into traffic.

"God," she said after a while. "You're sure you're all right? I can't believe that just happened. It was so fast. Just suddenly they were there."

"Yeah. That's how it happens." He glanced across at her. "I shouldn't have parked there. I should have known better. I wasn't thinking. I'm so sorry."

"You don't need to be sorry. It wasn't your fault. In fact, if you hadn't been there..."

But he shook his head. "Then *you* wouldn't have been there. You would have parked at the valet station like any other thinking human being."

"Well, still ..." She hugged her arms to herself. "God, I just can't stop shaking."

"It's okay," he said. "It's just adrenaline." He took his

right hand off the wheel and held it out. "If it'll help," he said, "here's a hand you can hold."

It took her a moment to decide. She took in a breath and let it out, then reached over and put her hand in his, bringing both hands over the gearshift and into her lap, then covering them with her other hand. "Thank you," she said. "That helps."

THERE WAS NO ARGUMENT about whether he should walk with her to her door. She opened it, flicked on the inside light, and turned back toward him, her face reflecting her turmoil. Breaking a weak, somehow apologetic smile, she started to raise her hand then let it fall. "I was going to say, 'Thank you, I had a good time,' but"—she met his eyes—"I'm a little confused right now. Is that all right?"

"That's fine," Nolan said.

"I'm going to read Evan's letters."

"As well you should."

"I don't want you to think I'm being ungrateful."

"Why would I think that?"

"Well, for saving my life and everything. For being a warrior."

That brought the trace of a smile. "I wondered if that had occurred to you. But you don't owe me anything, Tara, and certainly nothing for that." He gently chucked her chin with his index finger. "Don't you worry about me. I'm fine. You've just had a trauma you're going to need to process. It's okay. You're home now. Have a good night." And with that, he came forward, quickly kissed her cheek, and backed away. "Close the door," he said. "That's an order."

* * *

UNABLE TO SLEEP, she finally got to the letters.

They were from Evan's heart and soul. The way she remembered him came through loud and clear in every one—mostly chatty and irreverent, but then always there with the real stuff at the end. He missed her. He loved her and wanted them to try again when he got home.

When.

But it wasn't when, she knew. It was *if.* There was no certainty that he'd come back alive or in one piece. She couldn't shake the idea that even as she was reading his words, he might already be dead. She wasn't about to commit to him again and then have him die over there. There would be no commitment, she knew, until they were back together in person, until these philosophical issues had been resolved one way or the other. To give him hope before that would just be counterproductive and stupid.

Tara was reading in her bed with blankets over her, wearing pajamas and her warmest bathrobe against her continued shivering, even though it was a balmy night in Redwood City. Finally, she put down the latest letter—it was the fifth or sixth one she'd read—and closed her eyes, trying to picture the Evan she had known in her mind, trying to dredge up a feeling from the time when she'd thought they were the perfect couple, that they'd marry and have a family and a wonderful life together. It wasn't coming easy.

Part of her, perhaps most of her, still believed that she loved him, that he would come home from this war and they'd start over and work out all the issues. But he'd been gone now for several months and she'd spent the time putting him behind her. When he came back—if he came back—they'd see where they were. She thought that if she and Evan were in fact the perfect couple, if they were meant to be together, then nothing could keep them apart. But in the meanwhile she had her life and her principles. She wasn't going to remain in a relationship where those principles were compromised from the beginning.

But tonight's object lesson with Ron Nolan had shaken some of those core beliefs. They had been set upon by bad people who wished them harm, and without Nolan to defend her, she might very well . . .

Suddenly the memory of the assault came over her again—the men surrounding them with knives glinting in their fists. The utter lack of warning when the unexpected first thrust came at them. If Ron hadn't been there . . . or, no, more than that . . . if he hadn't been who he was, it could have ended so badly. It could have been not just a robbery, but the end of her life, of everything.

A fresh wave of adrenaline straightened her up in the bed.

Throwing off her covers, she went to the window in the bedroom and pulled aside the drapes a couple of inches, just enough so that she could see out. The blue-lit water in the pool down below was still. No shadows moved on the lawn, in the surrounding hedges. All was peace and suburban serenity. Letting the drapes fall, she crossed her bedroom and, turning on lights as she walked, she went out into the living room. She opened the closet in that room, the other one by the front door, then she turned and went into the kitchen. The window over the sink looked down on the parking lot and she turned out the kitchen lights so that she could more clearly see outside.

In the puddle of one of the streetlights, Ron Nolan's Corvette faced away from her apartment, toward the entrance to the driveway that led into the parking lot. The top was down, and it was close enough that she could easily see Ron himself still in the front seat, his elbow resting on the windowsill. She looked at the clock—he'd left her at the door nearly forty-five minutes before.

"RON?"

He'd heard the footsteps coming up and had forced himself to remain still, facing forward, until she'd come abreast of him. Now he looked over at her, in her T-shirt, jeans, and sandals. "Hey." Low-key.

"What are you doing?"

"Just sitting here. Enjoying the night." She seemed to need more explanation and he gave it to her. "I was a little wound up earlier. I thought I'd decompress a little before braving the roads again. I thought you'd be asleep by now."

"No," she said. "I was wound up too." Pausing, she let out a small breath. "I read Evan's letters. I think he's still confused. I know I am."

"About what?"

"Us. Me and him. What I'm going to do."

"What do you want to do about Evan?"

"If I knew that, I wouldn't be confused, would I? I haven't been fair to him either. I should write and tell him what I've been feeling."

"And what is that?"

"That maybe we still have a chance if he's willing to try to get through all this stuff. But that has to be in the future, when he gets back, if he does get back. I can't commit again until then, till we see what we've got. Does that sound fair to you?"

"I'm not an unbiased source," he said. "It sounds to me like you just said you weren't committed to him."

"We broke up five months ago, Ron." She took in a breath. "What were you really doing out here?" she asked.

"I was enjoying the night, the smells, the absence of gunfire." He looked up at her. "I was also hoping you might not be able to sleep and you'd see me down here, and that you'd come down and that I'd see you again. Maybe walk you back to your door."

After a second, she said, "You could do that."

[6]

IN SAN FRANCISCO, Deputy Chief of Inspectors Abe
Glitsky entered the homicide detail at nine-thirty on the
following Monday morning. Darrel Bracco, one of Glitsky's early protégés, looked up from the report he was
writing and almost spilled his coffee when standing up to
attention, saluting, yelling, "Ten-hut!"

Glitsky felt the scar through his lips straining against
the rare urge to smile. In the end, as usual, the smile never
appeared. Some inspectors in the room looked up, of
course, though nobody else went military on him. But
Bracco was still on his feet, expectantly. He evidently had
some knowledge of why the head of homicide, Lieutenant Marcel Lanier, had summoned the deputy chief.
"Marcel told me to keep an eye out for you, sir. I was just
warning him that you're here."

Glitsky stopped. "On the off chance that he's misbe-
having in some way?"

"You never know," Bracco said. He fell in beside
Glitsky, then nodded at another inspector, a woman
named Debra Schiff, who looked up and was getting
to her feet while Bracco went on. "Schiff was in there
with him with the door closed for an hour already this

morning. To look at her, you'd never know she was a screamer."

Schiff, gathering some stuff from her desk, nodded at Abe and replied in a conversational tone, "Bite me, Darrel."

Glitsky kept walking, Bracco and Schiff behind him. At Lanier's open door, he knocked. The lieutenant was on the phone, feet up on his desk, and waved everybody in. His new office upstairs was at least twice as large as the cubicle he (and Glitsky before him) had inhabited one floor below. There was room for as many as half a dozen people in front of his desk, with four chairs folded up against the back wall with its "Active Homicides" blackboard. Glitsky unfolded one of the chairs and let the other two inspectors grab theirs.

"I understand," Lanier was saying into the phone. "Yes, sir. That's why I've asked Abe to come down and get briefed. No"—he rolled his eyes with the tedium of it all—"I realize we don't want to…" He moved the telephone away from his ear and Glitsky could hear a voice he recognized as Frank Batiste's, the chief of police. So whatever this was about, it had some profile already. "Yes, sir," Lanier repeated in the next pause, "that's the idea. I will. Yes, sir." Finally, he hung up, got his feet back down on the ground, and brought his upper body in close to the desk, elbows on it. "That was the chief."

"I got that impression," Glitsky said. "How's Frank doing this fine morning?"

"Frank's concerned about our citizenry, lest they panic."

"And why would they do that?"

"Well, that's what I asked you down to talk about, since the media's going to be all over this if it gets out, and I know how much you cherish all things that give you face time in front of cameras." Everyone appreciated the irony of Lanier's statement. Within the department, Glitsky was notorious for two things: He didn't tolerate or use profanity, and he hated interactions with any form of media. Unfortunately, this latter made up about eighty-five percent of his job.

Now, a tight look of resigned patience firmly in place, Abe sat back and crossed one leg over the other one, ankle on knee. "Okay. What do we got?"

Lanier glanced at his two inspectors, came back to Glitsky. "We've got the possibility of a serial killer."

"Ah," Glitsky said. "And we haven't had one of those for a while."

"Hence the panic," Lanier said, "which Frank would so like to avoid. Anyway, I thought I'd let Darrel and Debra get you up to speed and you can decide where we are exactly and how we handle things if it gets hot." He nodded at his female inspector, whose pretty face she tried to make invisible, with limited success, by wearing a tough expression most of the time. "Debra, you want to start?"

"Sure." Bent over slightly in her chair, she had her elbows on her knees, her hands clasped in front of her. Raising her chin, she shifted a little to face Glitsky. "It's not much of a story by itself, but last Wednesday, I got a late call down in the Mish, early a.m. There's a body in an alley down there around the corner from the Makeout Room. White male, decently dressed, his wallet's still in his back pocket. Turns out he's a thirty-six-year-old ex–Navy SEAL named Arnold Zwick. No criminal record, unmarried and unconnected, currently unemployed. But he'd evidently come back from Iraq recently where he'd done some work for Allstrong Security, which is based here in town."

"What kind of work?" Glitsky asked.

"Whatever they do over there with former military guys. I went back to Allstrong and they told me that their main contract right now is protecting Baghdad Airport. But they didn't know where Zwick had gone to. The manager of the office told me they thought that he might have been killed over there. One day he just disappeared. Except that we now know he came back here. And some witnesses I talked to—neighbors he'd made friends with—seemed to have had the impression that he had a lot of money. But it's not in a bank account that I've been able to find, and there wasn't any cash in his apartment, so robbery might still be a motive, either that or he had the stuff hidden pretty well."

Glitsky asked, "Do you think it's possible he stole money from Allstrong over there?"

Debra nodded, apparently pleased at the question. "That was my assumption, too, sir. Especially given the way he died."

"And how was that?"

"Somebody snapped his neck."

"Close work," Glitsky said. "Not that easy."

"It's even harder when you factor in Zwick's training and that there was no sign of struggle or a weapon from his attacker. And Zwick was heavily armed. He had a knife in a sheath on his leg and a forty-five carried loose in his coat pocket. Both still on him when I got to him."

"So his killer," Glitsky said, "was another commando. You were thinking probably with Allstrong, somehow, getting back their money."

Debra nodded. "That is kind of where I was going

until Marcel called me yesterday and told me about Darrel's latest."

Glitsky shifted his interest over to Bracco. "Talk to me," he said.

"Three street thugs, all with sheets. All of 'em young, strong, and armed, out for a good time on Saturday night in the Tenderloin. All of 'em killed by hand. Maybe they just decided to mug the wrong guy, the same guy who killed Zwick, but that's a stretch, don't you think?"

"The stretch is why he would have stayed around," Glitsky said, "if he's one of the Allstrong people."

"There aren't any Allstrong people, though," Debra said. "The whole staff is over in Iraq. They've got a woman manager over here in a tiny office by Candlestick and a couple of clerks. None of 'em had ever met Zwick personally. And I believe them."

"On the other hand," Lanier interjected, "maybe we got a bona fide wacko who's getting off on killing people with his hands. These Tenderloin meatballs, we got two broken necks and a septum jabbed up into the brain. But there's no connection we can come up with between Zwick and these dirtbags. None of the victims had anything stolen off them."

Glitsky scratched at his cheek. "How many broken-neck murders have you seen in the past twenty years, Marcel?"

The lieutenant nodded. "I know what you're saying, Abe. And every one of the very few was in the course of some kind of a fight. These guys, there was hardly a sign of a struggle. The problem is that we got reporters already onto the story—I got a call at home this morning, and so did Frank—and they're salivating over this serial killer possibility."

Glitsky chewed the inside of his cheek for a minute. "And Allstrong hires Navy SEALs and guys like that for their security work over in Iraq?"

"That's what I gather," Debra said. "They've got nice brochures, but really, as I said, no people."

"But let's not lose sight of the main question," Lanier said. "We don't want to spin this toward a serial killer loose in the city. Frank would have my balls. Excuse me, Debra."

But Glitsky was standing up. "I'm doing my very favorite Monday-morning press briefing in fifteen, Marcel. I'll put that fire out at least until we get another broken neck."

"What are you going to tell 'em?" Lanier asked.

"I'll say I can't comment on ongoing investigations, except to say that it would be irresponsible to print or run rumors of a serial killer when there is no evidence to support it. And none of these victims are high profile. We got three dead brothers in the hood and one dead unemployed white guy in the Mish. This stuff is unfortunate but it happens. And the story goes away."

"Even if this guy's the same guy," Bracco said, "who did all of them?"

"If it was," Glitsky said, "I've got to believe he's long gone by now and never coming back."

[7]

MAJOR CHARLES TUCKER, the Senior Auditor for Aviation Issues, didn't like to leave the Green Zone any more than anyone else did. But in the past ten days, since Ron Nolan had shown up downstairs at the Republican Palace with his $2 million requisition, he had signed off on another $3.3 million in cash to Allstrong Security—all of it approved by Airbase Security Services Coordinator Colonel Kevin Ramsdale.

Jack Allstrong himself had shown up at his desk four times, patiently explaining to Tucker that obviously, if he continued to question the need for money, he was unaware of the sheer vastness of the task that Allstrong Security had contracted to undertake. The airport itself, BIAP, was enormous—thirty-two thousand acres. Securing even half of all that land alone in a hostile country was a monumental job. Besides that, Allstrong needed immediate money to buy the cars and trucks that would deliver the new dinar cash all over the country on his latest contract. He also needed more money for the bomb-sniffing dogs, for his enormous payroll, for food for his constantly growing influx of employees.

In spite of the danger inherent in every trip outside of the Green Zone, Tucker decided he had to see for himself what was going on out at BIAP. Leaving the Republican Palace in the early afternoon, and in uniform, he was chauffeured through the city and out to the airport by a three-Mercedes convoy of KBR security people who carried only sidearms—the irony wasn't lost on him. Nevertheless, by the time they arrived at the first airport checkpoint, it was nearly four o'clock in the afternoon.

There was, as always, a long line of cars ahead of his convoy, all of them waiting to be searched and to have their papers inspected. At this rate, Tucker's convoy wasn't going to get inside for at least another hour. So to save himself the time, he decided to get out of his vehicle and enter the compound on foot. With any luck, he could complete his informal inspection and start back to Baghdad before his convoy even made it as far as the gate anyway. They could U-turn away and be gone with that much less of a hassle.

But no sooner had he gotten out of his car than he became aware of the sound of gunfire. Not distant gunfire, which was so common in Baghdad and often relatively harmless, but nearby gunfire that seemed to be coming from the neighborhood just to his left, adjacent to the eastern border of BIAP. In contrast to the airport's western edge, which bordered the Euphrates River and opened into a plain of flat and formless ditch-crossed farmland that gradually degraded into desert, this eastern no-man's-land was a densely populated area of the ubiquitous low-lying, dung-brown structures that seemed to make up so many of Baghdad's suburbs, and that Tucker knew to be home to hundreds of Saddam Hussein's former officers. Gunfire in this area wouldn't be good news. But still, if it was confined to the neighborhood, he knew that it needn't necessarily concern him here.

Squatting, moving along the safe side of the line of vehicles, Tucker had almost made it to the gate when he realized that the gunfire was in fact close by. Stopping, he saw a handful of men scurrying along just outside the compound, by the barricades that had sprung up along the perimeter's fence. All of the black-clad men had camo'd their faces—Tucker knew that they weren't regular Army. They all carried rifles and belts of ammunition, and they were firing out into the suburbs.

Still keeping low, he sprinted to the gate, where four men—also heavily armed, in matching dark fatigues— were manning the entrance, seemingly unconcerned with the firing going on behind them. Tucker walked up to the nearest of them. "Hey!" Holding up his hand. "Major Charles Tucker. What the hell's going on over there?"

The man, who was not American, looked over his shoulder, then back at Tucker. He shrugged and spoke in a stiltedly correct British accent. "We were taking some fire from over there. Jack Allstrong ordered our men to put them down."

"You're attacking them?"

"It appears so, yes."

"*You can't do that*. That's against policy."

Again, the man shrugged. "Mr. Allstrong called them out."

"Well, let's get Mr. Allstrong here so he can call them off. You can't conduct an offensive with nonmilitary personnel."

Another man, with the same accent as the first, broke away from his inspecting comrades and got in front of Tucker. "Is there a problem, sir?"

"You bet there's a problem." He pointed to the

shooters. "I'm assuming those men are working with All-strong. Who's in charge here?"

"I am."

"What's your name?"

"Khadka Gurung."

"Where are you from?"

"Nepal."

"Well, Mr. Gurung, I'm a major in the U.S. Army. Private military forces are not allowed to attack insurgent groups."

"But we were fired upon first. From over there." He pointed vaguely to the general neighborhood.

"You were fired upon?"

"Yes, sir."

Tucker pointed. "Was anyone in this line of cars hit?"

"I don't believe so. No, sir."

"But the cars were just sitting here, like they are now?"

"That's correct."

"And none of them were hit?"

"I don't believe so."

"And nobody's firing from over there now?"

"No. We must have driven them off."

"Either that, Mr. Gurung, or there wasn't much of a concerted attack, if they couldn't manage to hit stationary vehicles at less than a hundred yards. Maybe the attack was just celebratory gunfire, which we hear all the time in Baghdad. How about that?"

"That's not impossible."

At that moment, several of the group of commandos broke into a run across an open area toward the Iraqi buildings. "They're attacking, for Christ's sake! That's blatantly illegal. Where's Jack Allstrong now? He's got to call this off. I need to talk to him right away. Do you think you could manage to arrange that?"

Gurung, nonplussed by Tucker's apparent anger, said, "Of course. Please to wait here and I'll try to reach him." In no great hurry, he walked over to a small stucco building that looked as though it had recently been constructed just inside the gate. He picked up a telephone.

Tucker, meanwhile, whirled back to face the first man he'd talked to. "Who are you?" he snapped.

"I am Ramesh Bishta."

"Well, Mr. Bishta, while we're waiting for Mr. Allstrong, can you tell me what's holding things up so badly here? Why can't you get this line moving?"

"The drivers," he explained. "So many do not speak English. It is difficult."

"Of course they don't speak English. They're mostly Iraqis. They're delivering Iraqi goods, doing Iraqi business. Don't you have people here at the gate who speak Arabic?"

"No, sir. I'm sorry, but no."

"How about translators?"

"Again. No. Maybe someday."

Tucker brought his hands to his head and squeezed his temples. He'd personally overseen the transfer of nearly six million dollars to Allstrong Security in the past two weeks and apparently Jack Allstrong couldn't find one local worker to speak Arabic to the Iraqis who needed to get into his airport? To say nothing of the fact that against all regulations he was paying his private commandos to lead offensive military strikes against the civilian population. Tucker had come to believe that Allstrong was playing fast and loose with the chaos that was Iraq, but now he was starting to believe that he didn't understand the half of it.

Gurung returned and informed Tucker than Mr. All-strong was on the way. The next car at the gate finally got approval and moved on into the compound. The raiding party seemed to have stopped for the moment at the back line of the neighborhood buildings. Tucker took the opportunity to ask Gurung about the dogs.

"I'm sorry?" The unfailingly polite guard shrugged.

"The bomb-sniffing dogs. I would assume they would be here at the gate, checking the cars. The trunks."

"No. I haven't seen these dogs yet. Perhaps soon." Still smiling, the soul of cooperation, Gurung asked to be excused for a moment. He went over to Bishta, and after a short conversation, the two men went and had a few words with their other two colleagues. Almost immediately, they stepped away from the next car in the line and waved it through the gate. And then the next. And the next. The line was starting to move.

Tucker watched for a minute, then stepped in front of the next car up, holding up his hand to stop it. The driver laid on his horn, but Tucker kept his hand up where it was, holding him back. "Mr. Gurung!" he yelled out. "What's happening now? You've kept these people sitting here for hours and now you're just letting them in?"

This finally brought a disturbed frown to Gurung's face. "Mr. Bishta said you told him the line should be moving faster."

"Yes, but, well . . . you don't just wave 'em in now, for Christ's sake! You still gotta get their papers and check the cars. Maybe you get some Iraqis down here, at least a translator, somebody who can speak Arabic. You get your bomb-sniffing dogs . . ."

Gurung's expression changed in the middle of the tirade. His focus went to someplace out over Tucker's shoulder and then suddenly he was walking away across the parade ground to intercept Jack Allstrong, who was jogging up. The two men stopped maybe twenty yards from where Tucker stood. After a short exchange of words, Allstrong put a quick, reassuring hand on Gurung's shoulder and then went past him as he strode toward the gate.

At this moment, Tucker, still in the middle of the road, holding up the flow of traffic, got another blast from the horn of the car in front of him. By now truly enraged, he put his hand onto his sidearm and pointed the index finger of his other hand at the car's driver—the warning explicit and eloquent.

Behind him, he heard Allstrong's relaxed voice. "Maybe you want to step out of the way and let my men do their job, Major."

Tucker whirled on him. "How can they do their job and question these people when they don't speak the language?" he said. Without pause, he went on, pointing to the commando team, now hard up against the back of one of the buildings. "But before anything else, you've got to call those men off. They can't conduct an offensive sweep."

Allstrong glanced over to them. "We were being fired on, Major. It's defensive. We have to protect ourselves, and we have every right to."

"Your men here tell me that nothing's been hit. Which makes me doubt there was much of an attack."

Allstrong pulled himself up to his full height, his usually affable expression suddenly harsh. "Maybe you missed the mortar attacks last month, Major, that punched holes as big as Volkswagens into the runways out here and killed four of my workers and wounded twenty more. Or the rifle fire that shot my office up and, oh yeah, killed another two of my guys." It was Allstrong's turn to point to the low-lying buildings. "That neighborhood over there is a breeding ground for attacks on this airport, and it's my job to stop them."

Tucker stuck his chin out. "There's no attack going on now, Allstrong. You either call your men back or I swear to God I'll personally intervene with Calliston and even your buddy Ramsdale to cut your funding off. We don't need wildcat contractors playing cowboys out here. You play by the rules or you don't play at all."

By this time, Gurung had come up near them. Allstrong glanced again at his commandos, then nodded to his employee. "Radio them to come on back in," he said. "Fight's over for today." Then, back to Tucker, "But that isn't why you came out here."

"No, it's not. I came here to inspect what our money's being used for. You realize that your gate guards here don't speak Arabic? How are they supposed to get information from these drivers when they don't speak the language?"

Allstrong shook his head. "These men are British-trained Gurkha guards, Major, the pride of Nepal. They're completely capable of handling this mission. I've tried hiring locals a few times and you know what happens? They either steal my shit or they don't show up, or both. They're afraid if they take a job with me, their families will get killed, and they're not all wrong. My guys are thorough and they get the job done. If it's a little slower than American standards, well, excuse me all to hell, but we're in a war here."

"What about the dogs? The bomb-sniffing dogs?"

"What about them? We're still training them. I've got sixty trainers and a hundred dogs working full-time out behind the terminals. When they're ready, I'll put 'em all to work. Meanwhile, again, I go with my guys."

"I'm going to want to see your kennels. And your fleet of trucks and cars that we've coughed up the money for. In fact, you can just look on my visit here today as an unannounced, informal audit to see if we've got to come back with a full-on inspection. I've got preapproval both from Calliston and the Inspector General of the Army."

"Good for you." Allstrong backed away a step and crossed his arms over his chest. "But I'm afraid I can't allow you inside the compound."

"The hell you can't."

"You watch me, Major. You're forgetting that I don't work for the Army. My contract is with the Coalition Provisional Authority. Jerry Bremer, through Kevin Ramsdale. I don't hear a Calliston in there, do you? Or a Tucker. And my bosses are happy enough with the job I'm doing that I'm getting almost more work than I can keep up with. So, look. You want to check up on me, clear it with Ramsdale. I've got nothing to hide, but I'm not showing my books to anybody who doesn't have permission to see them. So thanks all to hell for your interest, Major, but I'm afraid this trip's going to turn out to be a waste of your time." He turned to his worker. "Mr. Gurung, Major Tucker is not to enter the compound today or any other day without my permission. Is that clear?"

Gurung nodded. "Yes, sir."

Tucker glared at Allstrong. "I'm going to go to Ramsdale, and even Bremer if I have to," he said. "If I were you, Allstrong, I'd get my books in order. I'm going to be back with all the authority I need. You just wait."

"I'll look forward to it. Meanwhile, you have a nice drive back to Baghdad, Major. And keep your head down." Allstrong broke his trademark smile. "You never know."

RON NOLAN HAD ARRIVED back in the compound earlier that same day, and now he and Evan Scholler sat on the steps to the chow trailer. A few minutes of natural sunlight remained in the hot August evening. Dust from the afternoon winds hung in the air, smearing it yellowish brown.

"Dude," Nolan said. "I'm telling you. She's moved on. You ought to do the same."

Evan didn't argue with Nolan this time about whether or not he'd have another Budweiser. He'd already had three—cans this time, not bottles. He popped the top and lifted the next cold one to his lips. He wiped foam from his lips. "Was there anybody else?"

"What? You mean with her? Did I see anybody? Haven't we been through this already? No." Nolan took a pull from his can. "But we're talking about a total time in her presence of about three minutes, all of it at the door to her apartment trying to get her to just take the damn letter. If there was some guy inside with her, I didn't see him."

"So maybe—"

But Nolan cut him off. "Maybe nothing, Evan, don't do this to yourself. You had to see her face—great face, by the way, so I know where you're coming from and you've got my sympathy—but if you'd seen her face you wouldn't have any doubts. She didn't want anything to do with you or that letter. You want to hear it again? She says, 'I'm not going to read it.' And I go, 'You don't have to read it, but I promised Evan I'd get you to take it from my hands. You can do that, can't you?' So she goes, 'I'm just going to throw it away.' And I go, 'That's your call, but I've got to give this to you.' So she takes it, says thanks, and looking straight into my eyes, she rips the envelope in half."

Evan sipped beer and blew out a breath. "Fuckin'-A."

"Right. I agree, it's a bitch. But, hey, the good news is you don't have to wonder anymore." Nolan hesitated, sipped his beer, shot a sideways glance across the steps. "I don't know if you want to hear this, my friend, but I've got to tell you or you'll never know. She put a move on me too." Holding out a restraining hand, Nolan hurried on. "Nothing I couldn't handle and I very reluctantly gave her a pass, but if you needed any more certainty..."

"No, that ought to cover it."

"I hear you. But you know, give me certainty anytime. I can deal with that any day over not knowing."

"Maybe you're right."

"Damn straight I am."

Evan looked over at him. "She really came on to you?"

Nolan nodded, solemn. "And I didn't get the impression it was the only time since you've been gone. The girl's a stone fox, Ev. You think she's sitting home alone nights watching TV? Come on, she's human, life's short, and she's got a life back there. This isn't rocket science. You guys broke up before you came here. It's over. Accept it."

Evan hung his head. He couldn't seem to muster the strength to lift it up.

* * *

SHIT, NOLAN WAS THINKING. *Maybe the guy's not going to get over her.* That possibility hadn't occurred to him. Nolan had told the small lie about Tara ripping up the envelope because he thought it made for a convincing story, brought the finality of Evan and Tara's breakup a bit closer to home. But now he saw that Evan might not accept it. He might keep trying to reach her again, might find out what had gone on in Redwood City, might even manage to snag Tara back away from him.

Nolan couldn't let that happen. He wanted Tara. He'd gotten her and he intended to keep her until he didn't want her anymore, which might be a very long time. However, Evan's reaction caught him off balance; now he'd simply have to adjust. Fine-tune the mission. Keep him away from her.

All was fair in warfare anyway. And the old saying was right: in love, the same thing. You needed to be willing and able to adjust to the unexpected.

Evan Scholler was stationed in a dangerous place, after all, where anything might happen to him. Nolan could tweak the odds just a bit, give Evan a little something else to deal with instead of Tara Wheatley.

He reached over and hit Evan's arm, hard but friendly. "You know what you need, dude? You need something to take your mind off all this, that's all."

"And that's always an easy call here at party central."

"Hey, there's things to do here. You just got to know where to look."

"Right."

"You doubt me?"

For an answer, Evan drank beer.

"The man doubts me." Nolan shook his head in disbelief. "Dude," he said. "Put your beer down. Come with me."

Evan took a beat, then tipped his can up, emptying the contents into his mouth. When he finished, he got to his feet. "Where we goin'?"

"Smoke-check party," Nolan said.

"What's that?"

"Smoke-check the Muj. You'll love it."

THE SPY FOR JACK ALLSTRONG in the airport's adjoining neighborhood was an educated ex–Republican Guard officer, a Sunni named Ahmad Jassim Mohammed. No one knew the exact game he was playing, and this was no doubt the way Ahmad preferred things, but the pretense was that he had accepted the new, post-Saddam status quo and wanted to work with America and its allies to help rebuild his country. He'd gotten connected to All-strong during the July mortar attacks on the airport, when under the guise of offering his services as an interpreter, he'd instead provided five thousand dollars' worth of information that had proved valuable in identifying several target houses in the airport's neighboring slum that had contained large caches of weapons, mortars, and other explosives.

Though no one, least of all Jack Allstrong, ruled out the possibility that Ahmad might in fact be a spy checking out airport conditions for the insurgents, and though the consensus among Nolan and the other executives at Allstrong was that Ahmad was using the American military presence to settle vendettas with his personal enemies among his former Republican Guard colleagues, the fact remained that his information tended to be correct. When the targets he'd provided were eliminated, the mortar attacks on the airport had abruptly come to an end. That was about as far as Allstrong or Calliston needed to take it. Allstrong had paid Ahmad for similar information several times now, and counted on the intelligence he supplied to keep a step ahead of the insurgency just outside his perimeter. And so far it was working.

No one had expected today's attack, but Ahmad had arrived at the compound in its aftermath. Now, in the sultry early night, he sat in the front seat of one of Allstrong's convoy vehicles. Ron Nolan was driving. Evan Scholler, in black fatigues, his Kevlar vest, and with four beers in his bloodstream, stood uncomfortably manning the machine-gun platform on the vehicle's roof. Behind him in the seats, two other black-clad Gurkha commandos checked their weapons.

The party rolled out of the main gate. Off to their right, they could sense, more than see, the slumlike contours of the mud-caked domiciles of the residents. A quarter mile or so outside of the compound, the Humvee veered suddenly right and began bouncing across the no-man's-land that separated the airport from the homes. Nolan killed the regular beams, leaving only the car's running lights on.

Evan squinted ahead into the night, unable to make out many details either to the sides or ahead of them. He wished he hadn't had those beers. He wasn't drunk, but he could feel the alcohol, and though Nolan had assured him that they faced little or no danger, just an awesome adrenaline rush, he'd also insisted that Evan wear his bulletproof vest, as all the others had done.

Evan thought he might in fact wind up needing all of

his faculties, and couldn't shake a keen awareness that his reflexes might not be there for him in a pinch. So his mouth was dry, his palms sweaty, his head light. He was alone up here, half-exposed. Behind him in the car, he heard nothing—and that didn't help his nerves either.

What the hell was he doing?

In another minute, they'd entered the town itself. As they'd approached, Evan thought for an instant that the car might just try to crash through one of the yards, but evidently Ahmad knew where he was directing them. Suddenly they were in a street so narrow it barely fit them. It was lit only by the lights from within the houses, but the place wasn't dead by any means. The locals were outside smoking, talking—their Humvee picked up some kids, running along beside the car, whistling, calling out for food or candy.

The foot traffic forced them to slow down. Nolan honked from time to time, never stopping, forcing his way ahead, making the populace move out of his way. Evan, sweating heavily now, kept his hands gripped tightly on the handles of his machine gun, even as he heard Nolan call up to him. "Stay cool, dude. Nothing happening here. We're not there yet."

They turned left, then right, then left again, now down unmarked and unremarkable streets, into more of what looked like a marketplace area, closed up for the night, with few if any pedestrians. Nolan accelerated through the space and entered another quarter of the suburb. People still milled about, but less of them, and with far fewer children. Nolan made another turn and pulled up to a stop at a large open space in front of what appeared to be a mosque. Here the foot traffic had all but disappeared. The only light or sound—television and music—came from a two-story dwelling at the next corner down on their left.

The passenger door opened and Ahmad got out of the car, closed the door gently, then leaned back in the window and said something to Nolan. Then he turned and ran, disappearing into another of the side streets. Nolan killed even the running lights next, and then immediately they were moving, only to stop again sixty yards along, after they'd passed the house Ahmad had pointed out to them.

This time the engine went quiet. The radio music from the house was louder down here, providing cover for whatever noise they made as Nolan and his two commandos opened their doors and got themselves and their weapons out into the street.

They all gathered now down under and just to the side of Evan's position. They'd blackened their faces and hung grenades on their vests since they'd gotten into the Humvee and these two details chilled Evan, who could barely make out anything but Nolan's teeth in the darkness. He seemed to be smiling. "I'm leaving the keys in the car," he said to Evan, "in case you need 'em. You remember how we got here, right?" A joke, even in this setting. Nolan went right on. "If you need to, hop in the driver's seat and get out any way you can. But this shouldn't be long. And, hey, remember, we're in black, but we're the good guys, for when we come out."

Then he illuminated the light on the helmet he wore, as did the other men. All of these were clearly well-rehearsed maneuvers. At a nod from Nolan, the men broke into a trot toward their target. In an instant, one stood on each side of the door of the house. Nolan took a position in front of the door and, without any warning or fanfare, opened fire with his submachine gun. This knocked the door open and Nolan kicked it and led his men in.

Immediately, bedlam ensued. Screams and yelling, shots and sporadic bursts of automatic weapons fire, then the three men assembling outside again—Evan thinking it was already over—when the night was split by a shattering explosion out of the lower window. And the men rushed in again, this time into pure darkness.

Evan's knuckles tightened on the handles of his machine gun. Behind him, he heard a sound and whirled. He couldn't make the gun turn a full one-eighty, and he suddenly realized that if anyone were to come up behind him, he had no defense. Drawing his sidearm, he ducked down for a second below the backseat and peered back behind him, but there was nothing in the street. In the house across the way, the yelling and the gunfire continued—again individual shots followed by bursts of automatic weapons. Another explosion ripped through the night, this one blowing out the upstairs windows, and then suddenly all went quiet.

A few seconds later, the three men in black fatigues appeared outside the front door again. Two of them bolted back toward the car, while the third reentered the building, then emerged on a dead run just as his two colleagues got to the car. Behind him, in the house, two nearly simultaneous explosions blew out any remaining glass in the downstairs windows and halfway knocked him to the ground, but he kept running until he, too, reached the car.

By this time, Nolan was back in the driver's seat, breathing hard, starting the thing up. Over his shoulder, he yelled up at Evan. "That was the place all right. That

Ahmad is okay. Must have been a dozen Muj in there, dude, maybe two hundred AKs. RPGs, you name it. But nothing that a few frag grenades couldn't cure. God, I love this work. How 'bout you? Was that fun or what? Hang on, we're rolling."

Behind him, fire and smoke were beginning to billow out of the building's windows. Evan couldn't take his eyes off the spectacle. He was vaguely aware of doors opening on the street around him, people pouring out into the night, more shouts, the screams of women. Behind them now, he heard the crack of what he imagined must be gunfire, but he saw nothing distinctly enough to consider it a target.

But then they had turned the corner and were headed back through the space in front of the mosque, then the marketplace. Evan swallowed against the dryness in his throat, his stomach knotted up inside him, his knuckles burning white on the handles of his machine gun.

[8]

A WHILE AFTER MIDNIGHT, Evan tried to carefully and quietly navigate the three steps up to the dorm trailer. Between the news from home about Tara and his involvement in the raid, he figured he had every excuse in the world to split most of a bottle of Allstrong's Glenfiddich with Nolan after they returned to BIAP, and now the ground was shifting pretty well under him. He was looking forward to lying down on his cot. Tomorrow he'd try to process most or all of what he'd been through tonight, the aftermath.

He and his reservists had worked it out with the Filipino cooks and clerical staff and now had a dorm section of their own, eight cots in a double-wide bedroom. When he pushed open the door, the greeting was like a surprise party without anybody yelling surprise.

Suddenly all the lights went on, and these nearly blinded him, especially in his inebriated state. Stumbling backward against the brightness, his hands up in front of his eyes, he might have tripped on the steps and fallen back out of the trailer if one of his guys, Alan Reese, hadn't been waiting there to grab him.

As the glare faded, Evan blinked himself into some recognition. Facing him, some sitting on their cots, some standing, was his squad. Marshawn Whitman, his sergeant and second-in-command, much to Evan's surprise, was standing at attention and even offered a legitimate salute before he began with a formality he'd never used before. "Lieutenant," he said, "we all need to have a talk."

Evan tried to focus so that he only saw one Marshawn, instead of two, looming there in front of him. He put a hand out against the doorjamb to hold himself steady. His tongue, too big for his mouth in any case, could only manage the word "Now?"

"Now would be best," Whitman said. "We need to get out of here."

"Where to?"

"Back to our unit."

"Our unit? How we gonna do that?"

"We don't know, Lieutenant. But being here just isn't right."

Evan, stalling for time, looked over first at Reese standing next to him, then around to Levy and Jefferson and Onofrio sitting forward on their cots, identical triplets—elbows on their thighs, hands clasped in front of them—and finally to Pisoni and Koshi and Fields, who were standing with their arms crossed, leaning against the wall. Whatever this was about, these guys were a unit, all of them in it together. And from the looks of them, all of them angry.

"Guys," Evan said, "it's not like we got a choice. They sent us here."

"Well, not really. They sent us up to Baghdad, then we wound up here."

"I'm not sure I see the difference, Marsh."

Corporal Gene Pisoni, a sandy-haired, sweet-tempered

mechanic for a Honda dealership in Burlingame, and the youngest member of the squad, cleared his throat. "We could get shot at doing what we're doing here, is the difference, sir. They shot up this base today. We've just been lucky out in the streets up until now."

Next to Evan, Reese piped in. "The casualty figures posted today list a hundred and sixteen dead this last week in Baghdad alone. Our luck can't hold much longer."

Corporal Ben Levy, a law student at Santa Clara, added to the refrain. "We've been here almost a month, sir. This was supposed to be a temporary assignment, wasn't it?"

Evan still felt the room swaying under him, but part of him was sobering up. "Well, first, our luck can hold, guys, if we just stay careful. But I'm not arguing with you. This isn't what we got sent over here for, I agree. I just don't know what we can do about it."

"Talk to Calliston." Nao Koshi was Japanese-American, a software engineer who'd been pulled out of what he'd thought was the world's best job at Google. "He assigned us here. He can assign us out."

"We shouldn't be doing this." A thick-necked Caltrans employee from Half Moon Bay, Anthony Onofrio was thirty-three years old. He had two young children and a pregnant wife at home. He was perennially the saddest guy in the group, but rarely spoke up to complain. Now, though, he continued. "This really is all fucked up, sir. They've got to have the trucks we're trained to fix at least down in Kuwait by now. We ought to be down there doing what we're trained to do, not standing up behind machine guns."

"I agree with you, Tony. You think I want to be here?

But I thought you guys were happy to have regular quarters, regular meals."

"The guys we came over with," Marshawn said, "they've probably got that by now, too, wherever they are. Maybe better than we got it here. We're all willing to risk it. Huh, guys?"

A general hum of affirmation went around the room.

"Bottom line, Ev," Whitman continued, "is what Tony said. Us going out in these packages every day is just bullshit. We don't want to die driving Jack Allstrong or Ron Nolan around to pick up money."

"Nobody does, Marsh. I don't either."

"Well, the way it's going now," Whitman said, "it's only a matter of time."

Evan shook his head in an effort to clear it, then wiped a palm down the front of his face. "You guys are right. I'm sorry. I'll talk to Calliston, see what I can do. At least get things moving, if I can."

"Sooner would be better," Pisoni said. "I got a bad feeling about this. Things over here are heating up too fast. It's only going to get worse."

"I'm on it, Gene," Evan said. "Promise. First chance I get. Tomorrow, if he's around."

"Oh, and sir," Whitman added. "It might be better, when you get to see Calliston, if you were sober. He'll take the request more seriously. No offense."

"No," Evan said. "Of course. None taken. You guys are right."

As it turned out, Colonel Calliston did not have a free seventeen seconds, much less fifteen minutes, that he felt obligated to devote to the problems of a reserve lieuten-

ant whose squad was gainfully employed doing meaningful work for one of the CPA's major contractors. Finally,
Evan took the guys' beef to Nolan, who listened with apparent sympathy to the men's position and promised to
bring the matter up with Allstrong, who in turn would
try to make a pitch to Calliston. But, like everything else
in Iraq, it was going to be a time-consuming, lengthy
process that might never show results anyway. Nolan suggested that, in the meanwhile, Evan's squad might want
to write to the commander of their reserve unit, or to
some of their colleagues in that unit, wherever they happened to be in the war theater.

In the few days while these discussions and negotiations were transpiring, things in Baghdad—bad enough
to begin with—became substantially worse, especially
for the convoys. One of the KBR convoys delivering several tons of dinars in cash from Baghdad to BIAP was
ambushed just outside of the city and barely limped into
the compound with one dead and four wounded. The
lead vehicle's passenger-side window was blown out, and
the doors and bumpers sported dozens of bullet holes.
The attack had been a coordinated effort between a sui-
cide-vehicle-borne explosive device—an SV-BED—and
insurgents firing from rooftops. The consensus was that
the damage could have been much worse, but the Marines in the convoy had shot up the suicide vehicle and
killed its driver before he had gotten close enough to do
more significant damage.

Earlier in the week, another convoy manned by
DynaCorp contract personnel had shot out the windshield of the Humvee carrying the Canadian ambassador
as a passenger, when his car hadn't responded to a
warning to stay back. Luckily, in that incident, because

the contractors had used rubber bullets, no one was badly hurt. But nerves were frayed everywhere, tempers short, traffic still insanely dense.

By now, most of the routes in and out of the city had been barricaded off and access to those thoroughfares was nominally under the control of the CPA and Iraqi police/ military units. All vehicles had to pass at least one and often several checkpoints to be admitted to these streets. Unfortunately, the inner city was a cobweb of smaller streets that fed into the larger main roads, and access to these was much more difficult to control. A convoy like Scholler's would be sitting in traffic downtown, essentially stationary, and a car with four Iraqis in it would suddenly appear out of one of these alleys and begin crowding the convoys in the slowly moving endless line of traffic.

Since many of these cars were in fact SV-BEDs, they, too, ignored escalation of the hand and audio signals in their efforts to get close enough to destroy the convoys they'd targeted. And of course, in these cases, the machine gunners standing through the roofs of the Humvees in the convoys had little option, if they wanted to save their own lives, but to open fire on the approaching vehicle.

Tragically, though, all too often the approaching car held innocent Arabic-speaking Iraqi civilians who simply didn't understand the English commands to back off, or the simple Arabic commands soldiers had been taught to give to help with the confusion. Or they failed to appreciate the urgency of the hand signals. In the first months after the occupation of Baghdad, these shooting "mistakes" had come to account for ninety-seven percent of the civilian deaths in the city—far more than the deaths caused by all the insurgents, IEDs, sniper fire, and suicide bombers combined. If a car got too close to a convoy, it was going to get shot up. That was the reality.

NOLAN, scheduled for the rear car this Tuesday with Evan, picked right up on the bad vibe that had been riding along with Scholler's squad for the past few days. Now, as he walked up to the convoy, he was somewhat surprised to see Evan outside his vehicle, having some words with one of his men, Greg Fields. Tony Onofrio, another of the guys, was standing by listening, obviously uncomfortable.

"Because I say so," Evan was saying, "that's why."

"That ain't cutting it, Lieutenant. I've been up there three days in a row. How about we put Tony on the gun today?" Fields was obviously talking about the machine gunner's spot, the main target popping out of the roof of their Humvee.

"Tony's a better driver than you are, Greg, and you're better on the gun, so that's not happening. Mount up."

But Fields didn't move.

Nolan had been aware that the unit's respect for Evan's leadership had declined over their recreational drinking coupled with Evan's inability to get them transferred, and now it looked as though Fields might flatly refuse his lieutenant's direct order. So he stepped into the fray. "Hey, hey, guys. No sweat. I'll take the gun. Greg, you hop in the backseat and chill awhile."

Nolan knew that the men might also be mad about his own role in Evan's drinking, plus driving him all over to hell and gone, but figured that neither as a group nor individually could they resent him if he took a turn in the roof. Although this was technically forbidden.

Caught in the middle, Evan felt that he had to assert his authority. "I can't let you do that, Ron."

"Sure you can." He gestured toward the machine gun. "I'm a master on that mother."

"I'm sure you are," Evan said, "but you're only allowed to use a sidearm."

Flashing the smile he used to disarm, Nolan stepped up and whispered into Evan's face. "Dude, the other night ring a bell? That's not your rule. That's the recommendation for contractors. Nothing to do with you. I'm betting Fields has no objection." He turned. "That right, son?"

The young man didn't hesitate for an instant. "Absolutely."

"Fields isn't the issue," Evan said, even as the guys from the other Humvees were moving down in their direction, wondering what the beef was about.

"I'm the issue to me, Lieutenant," Fields said. "It ain't right, me being up there every day. If Mr. Nolan wants a turn, I say tell him thanks and let's roll out of here."

Evan didn't want this to escalate in front of his other men. Nolan was throwing him a lifeline that could save his authority and preserve some respect in front of his squad. And maybe what he said was true. Maybe it was a rule for contractors, and none of the Army's business.

"All right," Evan said at last, lifting a finger at Fields. "This one time, Greg."

NOW EVAN and his very disgruntled guys were in a Baghdad neighborhood called Masbah, where Nolan was to meet up and conduct some business with a tribal chief who was a friend of Kuvan. They'd already passed the checkpoint into the wide main thoroughfare that was now choked with traffic. On either side, storefronts gave way to tall buildings. Pedestrians skirted sidewalk vendors who spilled over into the roadway on both sides.

But in contrast to many of their other trips through the city, today they'd encountered quite a bit of low-level hostility. Kids who, even a week before, had run along beside the convoy begging for candy, today hung back and in a few cases pelted the cars with rocks and invective as they drove by. Older "kids," indistinguishable in many ways from the armed and very dangerous enemy, tended to gather in small groups and watch the passage of the cars in surly silence. The large and ever-growing civilian death toll from quick-triggered convoy machine gunners—in Evan's view, often justifiable, if tragic—was infecting the general populace. And in a tribal society such as Iraq's, where the death of a family member must be avenged by the whole tribe, Evan felt that at any time the concentric circles of retribution might extend to them—all politics and military exigencies aside.

Riding along with Nolan on the big gun above him, Evan was more than nervous. He honestly didn't know his duty. He hadn't been briefed on this exact situation and had no ranking officer above him to tell him the rules. Should he have stood up to Nolan and forbade him to man the machine gun, alienating himself from his men even more? Could he just continue to let him ride up there and hope the problem would go away? But playing into all of his ruminations was the fact that since the unauthorized raid into the BIAP neighborhood, everything about Nolan had him on edge.

The more Evan reflected on it, the less defensible that attack seemed, the more like some variant of murder. Evan had been a cop long enough in civilian life that he was sensitive to the nuances of homicide, and the raid had certainly been at the very least in a dark gray area. If the house that Nolan and his Gurkhas had trashed had in fact been identified as a legitimate military target, shouldn't it have been a military unit that took care of it? Though it was possible that the house full of AK-47s and other ordnance could have been an insurgent stronghold, Evan couldn't shake the thought that the attack might have been more in the line of a personal reprisal—payback to one of Ahmad's (or Kuvan's) enemies, or even to a business competitor.

Now, stuck in traffic in the passenger seat on a sweltering morning in Masbah, and still hungover from the previous night's beers, Evan tried to get his thoughts in order. He had to figure out a way to get his troops out of this assignment; he had to stop drinking every night with Nolan; he had to accept that it was over with Tara; he had to get a plan for his life when he got out of here.

He closed his eyes against the constant dull awful throbbing. In the driver's seat, Tony Onofrio must have caught his moment of weakness, because he turned the music way up to a painful decibel level—Toby Keith's new hit "Courtesy of the Red, White, and Blue (The Angry American)." This was Tony's not-so-subtle punishment for the fact that Evan hadn't succeeded in getting them transferred yet. The other beautiful aspect of the earsplitting volume was that Evan couldn't acknowledge that it bothered him—to do so would be admitting to his hangover. Tony, of course, knew he had the hangover.

The message was clear enough—if Evan could jeopardize all of their safety putting more priority on drinking than on getting them out of here, then Tony could play his goddamned music as loud as he fucking wanted.

But suddenly, all the cogitations became moot. They were moving along at about ten miles per hour and they had just passed a side street when Nolan slapped three times rapidly onto the hood of their vehicle. "Heads up," he yelled down with real urgency, "bogey at ten o'clock. Ten o'clock."

Instantly jarred alert—this was a situation Evan had been trained for—Evan hit his radio and passed the word up to the rest of his squad. "Pisoni! Gene, any way to speed up?" Then he yelled at Nolan. "Hand signals first, Ron. Back 'em off. Back 'em off!"

From the radio, he heard, "Negative, sir. We're stuck up here."

Nolan shouted, "Comin' on."

"Don't fire! Repeat, do not fire."

He knew that he had to see how serious the threat was before he could formulate his response. If nothing else, he needed to make sure that this encounter went by the rules of engagement, the escalated warning process. But on the other hand if it was a suicide bomber who had targeted them, it would happen quickly and he couldn't be afraid to pull the trigger. He drew his own sidearm, the 9mm Baretta M9, and, turning half-around in his seat, stuck his head out the window. Behind them, just out of the alley and pulling out ahead of the backed-up traffic in the space behind them, was a beat-up white sedan with no license plates. The rear car in all of the convoys already sported relatively large signs, written in

English and Arabic, warning following vehicles to leave at least one hundred feet of space, and experienced drivers in Baghdad tended to err on the side of caution. And yet this car had entered the roadway at about seventy-five feet and was advancing.

Looking up, Evan saw that Nolan had drawn himself up to full height and was standing with both arms extended, palms out—the classic "stay-back" signal in any language. Trying to get a better glimpse of the car behind them, Evan stuck his body out even farther. With the sun beating down on the windshield, the view inside the vehicle was generally obscured, but Evan was fairly certain that he could make out two people in the front seats. The back window on his side was down as well, and he caught a glimpse of forearm for a moment, instantly retracted.

"There's three of 'em in there at least," he called up to Nolan. Then, into the radio again, "Gene, can you get to the side and go around? The sidewalk, even?"

"Clogged up, sir. Negative. In fact, slowing."

"Shit." Evan knew that they had a megawatt flashlight in the backseat for just this situation. He pulled himself back in and told Greg Fields, behind the driver's seat—who should have been up where Nolan was—to find it and shine it at the approaching driver's face. It was supposed to be for nighttime use, but it might do some good during the day as well.

Digging in his duty bag on the floor at his feet, Evan pulled out the airhorn klaxon they carried for just such a moment. Amazingly enough, it seemed that even this many months into the occupation, some people—even whole families—would simply take to the streets in their cars to go shopping or run an errand. They'd get to talking or arguing and never see the warning hand signals until it was too late.

Coming out the window again, airhorn in his hand, Evan looked quickly to the roof. Nolan had gotten down out of his extended position and now his palms were gripped around the handles of the machine gun. "Hold off, Nolan! Hold off! Wait for my order!"

The car had closed to under forty feet in ten seconds, and seemed to be accelerating. Like everywhere else in the civilized world, Iraq seemed to raise drivers who abhorred a vacuum between vehicles. Even in the bright sunshine, even with the glare off the windshield, Evan could see that Fields had trained his blinding light on the driver. From his own side, he held out the airhorn and let out a blast.

The radio squawked out. "Deadlock up here, sir. Slowing down."

Evan checked the position of the approaching car— was it, too, slowing down at last? Good, it had stopped in time, thank God. This crisis would pass. He reckoned that he had time for a quick look ahead of them. Turning, he was about to order Pisoni onto the sidewalk—the pedestrians would have to scatter and that was just too damn bad. Onofrio hit the brakes and they came to a complete stop.

All was still. Evan breathed a sigh of great relief.

And then, with a maniacal war whoop, right above him, Ron Nolan opened fire.

THE CAR DID NOT EXPLODE.

That alone was enough to cause Evan grave concern. That and the fact that in the seconds before Nolan had started shooting, the car had finally gotten the frantic message from the lights and airhorns and without a doubt had come to a complete halt. Only after the first hail of bullets had slammed into it had it started moving again— the dead driver's foot letting up its pressure on the brakes?—coming on, actually faster now, with Nolan continually pouring rounds into it, until it rammed into the back of Evan's car and shuddered to a stop.

"Don't leave the cars unattended!" Evan tried to keep his rising panic out of his voice. "Stay at the wheel! Man your guns! Who's riding shotgun in your car, Gene? Well, get Reese back here with us. Fields," he yelled at his assistant driver, "out with me!"

The street had first seemed to go eerily silent, but already now as he all but fell out of the car, Evan became aware of the upswell of volume that was growing around them. Back behind them, on the sidewalk, a man was screaming, keening, and there appeared to be a form down on the sidewalk next to him—one or more of Nolan's bullets had apparently hit a bystander as he or she was walking down the street. This was perhaps unavoidable once the shooting started, but it aggravated the situation terribly.

A man on the curb was yelling at him in English. "He was stopping! He was stopping!" Back at the shot-up sedan, Fields and Reese on the other side, Evan approached with great caution. Although the windshield was blown out and red streaks tinted the inside of the other windows, someone might still be armed and alive inside, or there might still be an unexploded bomb.

Evan came up to the passenger door, gingerly pulled it open, then spoke into the radio to Pisoni. "Gene. Get through to somebody somewhere and tell them about this. Give 'em our location and tell 'em we need support yesterday. Anything they can get to us."

Behind him, he became aware of more shouts, randomly laced with fury. He turned his attention to the body—a woman, judging by the bloodied shreds of the *niqab,* or veil, that now stuck to what had been her face. Now she sprawled partially out of the front seat, her upper body bleeding into the street. On the other side of the car, Fields had opened the back door and stepped back in disgust and horror. "Holy shit, Ev, there's kids back here."

A minute later, the first of the rocks hit his Humvee.

FOR PERHAPS TEN MINUTES, though it seemed more like an hour, Evan tried to direct events, even through the bombardment of projectiles that the entire convoy was beginning to endure. He gave his machine gunners, including and especially Nolan, strict orders not to fire into the crowd. He hoped that the reinforcements that Pisoni had called for would arrive in something like a timely manner, and he entertained the hope that this wouldn't escalate further, at least until the cavalry showed up.

But he couldn't keep the crowd from closing in around the white sedan, some members of it clearly recognizing the family that Nolan had just slaughtered. As Evan and his men retreated back to their own bunched-up vehicles, they heard from Pisoni that Iraqi police units, stationed nearby, were on their way.

Meanwhile, though, some of the crowd members had laid down blankets in the street and begun the process of removing the bodies from the car. First the woman, then her husband, who'd been behind the wheel, finally the three children—by the size of them, none older than six or seven. All of them were badly bloodied, but one was apparently still breathing, and someone grabbed that child and disappeared with it into the crowd.

Nolan, still up behind his gun, now had his eyes on the street in front of them, which had cleared as the forward traffic had begun to move. "Evan," he said, and when Scholler looked up, he pointed. "Check it out."

Evan turned. "What?"

"We're good to go, dude."

"What are you talking about? We're not going any- where. We've got a multiple fatality incident here, Ron. We stay till we're cleared."

"Bad idea, Lieutenant. We go while we can. These people will take care of their own, but we'd best be gone by the time word gets out around here."

"We *can't* be gone. We've got to report—"

"Report? To the local cops? And then what? No, man, what we've got to do is get out of here now, while we can, before it gets ugly and personal."

"Personal with us?"

"We killed 'em, Lieutenant."

"We didn't kill 'em, Nolan. You killed 'em."

"So split a straw. They're not gonna care. We're on the same side, is all that matters. This is a clan culture, so everybody in these poor fuckers' clan is honor-bound to kill us. It's going to get personal in about two minutes, I promise."

Evan looked off down the street at the still-receding line of traffic that had been blocking their way all morning. Behind them, the horns of a hundred other cars urged him to drive off, clear the road, get out of the way. He didn't know how he could in any kind of conscience leave the scene of an incident such as this one—all his police training went against it. There would have to be an investigation, photographs, testimony taken. They couldn't just see an opportunity to get away and run from all this, could they?

From across the car, Fields said, "I think Mr. Nolan's right, sir. We've got to get out of here. We get back to an FOB someplace." Fields was picking up the jargon. An FOB was a secure troop area, or forward operating base, with Bremer walls, crew-served weapons, and security checkpoints. "We make our report out of there."

Evan didn't respond and instead went to his radio. "Gene," he said, "what's it look like for getting out of here?"

"When?"

"Right now."

"Decent. There's an off-road to a barricade point another quarter mile up, and I can—"

At that moment, a low hum filled the torpid air around them. Nolan yelled out, "RPG. Down!" And sixty feet from where Evan stood, the first Humvee suddenly exploded in a ball of flame, knocking him, Fields, and Reese to the pavement. Nearly deafened, Evan still registered that Nolan had come up out of his crouch and turned his machine gun to the building from which he believed the rocket-propelled grenade had been fired.

Gene Pisoni and Marshawn Whitman had just taken a direct hit that they couldn't have survived. Across the hood of Evan's own Humvee, Reese stood back into his view, the left half of his face awash in blood. He was trying to say something, motioning to Evan, but either he wasn't saying any words or Evan couldn't hear them through the deafening roar in his head. Fields, too, finally got to his feet, apparently unharmed, and pointed to the

Humvee, then to the empty street yawning open before them, in an unambiguous gesture. It was past time for talking about it. They had to get out of there.

He was right. Now the second and third Humvees were open targets—possibly saved, Evan later realized, by their proximity to the white sedan or to the crowd that had initially gathered around it. But that wasn't any part of his consideration as he pointed Reese to the second Humvee and hopped into the third one just as a spray of bullets pinged off the street in front of them all, cutting across the hood of his vehicle. Nolan wheeled and fired into the buildings again.

Onofrio had his vehicle in gear and started forward. In the second Humvee just in front of them, Reese reached the open passenger door and half jumped, half fell inside, joining Levy, Koshi, and Davy Jefferson—a twenty-four-year-old In-N-Out manager from Sunnyvale—who was stationed on the machine gun. And perhaps because of fear, or maybe an understood complicity among the locals, Evan noticed the crowd had suddenly fallen back from around them, isolating them as targets even further. Up out of the roof of the Humvee in front of them, Davy Jefferson had opened fire at some rooflines as well.

Another spray of bullets kicked at the street between the two vehicles. Over Evan's head, Nolan fired another burst, which was followed closely by a terrifyingly close low humming vibration as another RPG somehow missed them and exploded into a storefront over on their left. Glass and stucco dust rained down over them.

Evan hit his driver's arm and pointed to the burned-out, still smoking remains of their #1 vehicle. He still could barely hear himself, although he was yelling. "Gene and Marsh! Gene and Marsh!" Telling Onofrio he wasn't going to leave his dead men behind to be mutilated by the mob, which was the way this scenario looked like it was starting to develop.

They pulled around next to their #2 Humvee and at Evan's signal, he and Fields jumped out into the street again. Evan motioned to Nolan and Jefferson, on the two still-working guns, to cover them as they ran to the destroyed, still smoking #1 Humvee. Whitman's charred and bloodied body had been blown clear out of his hole by the machine gun and now lay sprawled over the roof. Evan and Fields grabbed their fallen comrade by the arms and pulled him down, then began dragging him as fast as they could back to their vehicle.

For a few seconds, the firing ceased. Evan and Fields managed to load Whitman's body into the back of their car, then they turned and went to join Alan Reese, who had come out of the #2 Humvee and was trying to open the front doors to the first car and get Pisoni out. But the doors were still too hot to touch, as well as sealed shut. The windows, of course, had all been destroyed by the blast as well, so Fields leaned in on the driver's side and tried to get some purchase on Pisoni's lifeless body, but couldn't get it to budge.

"He's still got his seat belt on!" he called back.

The force of the grenade had all but knocked the back door on the driver's side off its hinges, and Evan was able to force it open further with a few kicks. They could get Pisoni out that way. Evan got Fields over next to him, put his shoulder to it, and had just started to push when more rounds of automatic weapons fire exploded from the roofs around them. Fields, at his elbow, made a sickening guttural sound, then spun around and collapsed to the ground in a sitting position.

On the other side of the car, Reese fired off a few use-less rounds with his sidearm just as heavy automatic weapons fire began coming from the roofs of buildings on Reese's side of the street as well. Somewhere behind them, Nolan was firing continuously now, back and forth, side to side, from the roof of his vehicle, but when Evan looked over, hoping he might be able to direct some covering fire from the other Humvee, he saw that Davy Jefferson had disappeared and that bullet holes had pocked across the #2 windshield as well. If Levy and Koshi hadn't been hit in their front seats, it was a miracle.

"Alan!" Evan yelled to Reese. "Get around here on this side!"

Reese looked at him over the Humvee's hood and nodded. Turning, still firing his sidearm at the rooftops on his side, he made it nearly to the back side of the car before several more automatic rounds straightened him up, threw him up against the car's body, and dropped him out of Evan's sight.

His own gun drawn, Evan sat next to Fields's crumpled body on the pavement in the partial cover of the Humvee. Up to his left, he could make out a couple of running figures at the edges of the roofline, but Nolan was doing a decent job of keeping them down, stippling the fronts of the buildings they occupied, holding their fire to a minimum. But Nolan was the only machine gunner left and at his firing rate, he would soon be out of ammunition.

Evan nudged at Fields. "C'mon, buddy, we've got to move." He pushed at Fields's shoulder again and the man's body slumped all the way to the side on the ground, the front of his shirt soaked in red. Another burst of machine-gun fire shattered the air directly behind him, and Evan turned and saw that it was his own #3 Humvee, Nolan on the roof, coming around in the street and running its own screen between the buildings to cover him.

But he had three men down here at the #1 Humvee, and three more in #2. He could only guess at Reese's condition. Perhaps he'd only been wounded. He'd have to get around the Humvee here to check that out. And then still there were Koshi, Jefferson, and Levy, over in #2. He'd have to order Nolan and Onofrio to help him load the dead and wounded into the backseat and cargo area of the one working Humvee. He couldn't leave his men out here in the street.

It wasn't possible that he'd lost so many of them in so short a time.

And then his own Humvee pulled up, the back door open, Onofrio behind the wheel, frantically gesturing that he should jump aboard, screaming at him although Evan could barely hear him. It was his only chance, their only chance.

But here was Fields right at his side, bleeding to death if not already dead. There was no option but to try to get him in the car first.

"There's no time!" Nolan yelled down from the roof at Onofrio. "Keep driving! Go! Go! Go!" He fired a short volley up into the rooflines. "Move!"

It seemed like Nolan was urging—ordering!—Onofrio to save themselves and abandon Evan with the rest of the men. But his driver slowed the vehicle as it came abreast of Evan, looked over in panic and desperation, reached out a hand across the seat.

Nolan yelled from the roof. "Leave 'em, leave 'em, there's no time! They're gone!"

The Humvee stopped now, and Onofrio leaned over further and pushed open the passenger door, his hand outstretched. Evan reached around, trying to get ahold of Fields to pull him along. Getting a purchase on his squad-mate's sleeve, Evan was halfway to his feet, his own free hand out to Onofrio's, when, deep in his bowels, he felt again the low hum of another incoming RPG.

It was the last thing he felt for eleven days.

PART TWO
[2003–2004]

[9]

FROM RON NOLAN'S PERSPECTIVE, there was just
no benefit to staying in Iraq and talking about it.

The inquiry into the incident looked like it was going
to be a tricky thing. Onofrio was the only witness left in
the immediate aftermath, and Nolan believed that his testimony wouldn't be harmful. Onofrio had been busy
driving and wouldn't have had a clue about whether the
following car was in fact stationary when Nolan had
opened fire on it. But the word from the street, the result
of Jack Allstrong's reaching out to the local Iraqi and
U.S. military cops, had already filtered back about what
had actually happened, and there was a reasonable chance
that Nolan would be arrested.

The good news was that the Abu Ghraib scandal had
just surfaced, and every American remotely connected to
law enforcement in Iraq had been assigned to that investigation. Even Major Charles Tucker, that pain-in-the-ass
bean-counter who'd been constantly in their shit about
money, found himself reassigned to that scandal.

But in spite of that, and though he knew that jurisdictional issues were problematic at best in Iraq, especially
when they involved contractors accused of criminal activity such as, in this case, murder, Nolan was unwilling to

risk his own arrest. You never knew what could happen then. The CPA might decide to use him as an example for other trigger-happy contractors, or give him to the Iraqi prosecutors, both nonstarters from Nolan's point of view.

In fact, Nolan didn't feel particularly bad about what he'd actually done—hey, you're in a war, shit happens. The dumbasses should've stopped sooner, or better yet, stayed off the street entirely. What the hell were they thinking? If he had it to do over again, he'd do the very same thing, rules of engagement or no. And although he did very much regret the loss of life among his own convoy, again this was just another turd in the gigantic shitpile that was this war. Who could have predicted such a massive local retaliation for such a small, localized event? And then again, how was he supposed to know that this particular Mohammed Raghead, the father who'd stupidly driven his whole family into the killing radius of Nolan's Humvee, was in fact Jahlil al-Palawi, a major tribal leader and the most influential Shiite in the Masbah neighborhood?

Anyway, clearly the intelligent thing to do was for Nolan to blow Dodge until this incident blended into the chaos of all the other ones that were happening somewhere in the country just about every day. In a few months, Nolan could always come back with Allstrong or with another security outfit and pick up where he'd left off. In the meanwhile, Jack Allstrong certainly didn't want an army of investigators coming into BIAP without his say-so. Who knows what they'd see that they didn't like, and report back to the CPA?

So within a week of the incident, Nolan was back in Redwood City. After negotiations with Jack Allstrong that consisted of a couple of glasses of Glenfiddich each, the company chose to construe his departure as caused by an act of God, which meant it would honor his contract for a six-month hitch at full pay. And with some of this apparently inexhaustible supply of money, Nolan put a down payment on a modern and elegant furnished town-house near the sylvan border between Redwood City and Woodside. Still employed by Allstrong, he was the company's chief Bay Area recruiter of ex-military personnel. He knew the kind of people Jack Allstrong needed over in Iraq and he generally knew where to find them.

TARA WHEATLEY WAS SURPRISED to see Nolan back so soon. She'd spent the weeks he was gone coming to grips with her nagging sense of guilt. Which was, she told herself, ridiculous. She was an adult who could make her own decisions, and she and Evan had been broken up for months. She hadn't betrayed anybody. She was moving on in her life. She'd finally gotten around to reading the last four of Evan's letters, but after the night when she had invited Nolan back to her apartment, she couldn't make herself get around to writing back to him.

What was she supposed to say?

Oh, and under local news I slept with your friend Ron who came to give me your letter. I didn't really mean to, but I was confused and lonely, really lonely, and scared to be alone, he'd just more or less saved my life that particular night and I never thought you and I would ever work out our problems anyway. It was just time to act on us being finally apart, okay? We weren't together anymore and weren't going to be together, so I could sleep with another man if I wanted and you had no say over it. Okay, okay, there could have been some element

*where I was punishing you for going off the way you did—if
you can leave me, then this is exactly what you're risking. And
now—you see, you dummy?—it's happened.*

No. She wasn't going to write that letter, not now, not
ever.

And Evan, of course, never wrote to her again either.

Ron Nolan was a strong, powerful, attractive older
guy and if her life wasn't going to work out with Evan,
and it clearly wasn't, then with his charm, experience,
confidence, and—admit it—money, Nolan would at the
very least be able to help her get over her first love.
She could use a simple, uncomplicated relationship until
the next real one came along.

As if there'd ever be another one as real as Evan.

NOLAN NEVER SAW the need to tell her about the ambush
at Masbah, what had happened to Evan, or the role that
Nolan himself had played in it all. As far as Tara knew,
Nolan had voluntarily made the decision to come home,
possibly even as a result of some of their discussions about
the morality of the war. Explaining it to her, he had kept
it all, as his old English teacher used to say, vague enough
to be true.

And in fact, all Nolan knew about Evan Scholler was
that he'd sustained a serious head wound from the last
grenade they had taken and, by the time Nolan had flown
out of Baghdad, still hadn't been expected to live. He
might in fact already have died, although Nolan suspected
that if that had happened, Tara would have heard about it
from somebody.

But whatever had happened to Evan, nearly three
months had passed. Tara had moved on. For Ron Nolan,

there just didn't seem to be any benefit to talking any more about it.

SHE WAS STANDING in front of the artichokes in the vegetable aisle of the grocery store, two days after the start of her school's Christmas vacation. The canned music coming in to keep everybody merry and bright had just changed from the ridiculous to the sublime—the Chipmunks' version of "Rockin' Around the Christmas Tree" segueing rather inharmoniously into Aaron Neville singing "O Holy Night." The latter had been her and Evan's favorite recording of any Christmas song, and suddenly, hearing the first notes, Tara's mind had gone blank. Looking down at the bins of produce arrayed in front of her, she suddenly had no idea why she was here, or what she wanted to buy.

Unconsciously, her hand came up to cover her mouth, and she sighed deeply through her fingers, her eyes welling beyond all reason. "God," she whispered to herself.

"Tara? Is that you?"

Letting out another breath, she started out of her reverie. "Eileen?"

Evan's mother was still quite attractive, and Tara had always thought it was not so much about her trim body or her pleasant, vaguely Nordic facial features, but because she exuded kindness. In Eileen Scholler's world, everybody was equal and everybody was good, even if the rest of humanity didn't think so, and she was going to like you and treat you fairly and gently no matter what. Now, her head cocked birdlike to one side, she frowned with concern. "Are you all right? You look like you're about to faint."

"That's what I feel like." Tara tried to put on a smile but knew it must look forced. "Wow. I don't know what just happened." Bracing herself against her shopping cart, she again forced an unfelt brightness. "Stress, I'm sure. The season. But how are you? You don't shop here normally, do you? But it's so good to see you."

"I was on my way home from work and remembered I needed some veggies. But I'm glad I stopped here now. It's so good to see you too." Her expression grew wistful. "We've missed you, you know."

Tara nodded, sober. "I've missed you too. I really have."

"Yes, well, I don't think you children realize what you put us poor parents through when you break up with each other. Here we were, considering you all but the daughter we never had, and the next thing you know, you're not in our lives anymore. It's the saddest thing."

"I know," Tara said. "I'm so sorry. I never meant that to be part of it."

"I know, dear, it's nobody's fault. It's just one of life's little heartbreaks. Or as Jim says, it's just another FOG." Lowering her voice, she came closer. "Fucking opportunity for growth. Pardon my French."

"It's pardoned. How is Evan, by the way?"

"Well, we still worry, of course, but he seems all right. There are still some issues, but we're going out to see him for Christmas, so we'll have a better idea how he's doing after that."

"You're going to see him for Christmas?"

"Yes. We're flying over next week."

"To Iraq?"

For an instant, Eileen Scholler went completely still. "No, dear." Her eyes narrowed—was Tara kidding her?—

although the kindness remained in them. "To Walter Reed."

"Walter..."

"You didn't hear? I was sure you must have heard. In fact, I was a little bit annoyed, to be honest, that you never called us. If I'd have known you didn't know, I would have—"

Tara waved her off. "That doesn't matter, Eileen. Heard what? Did something happen to Evan over there?"

"He was wounded," she said, "this past summer. Badly, in the head. He was nearly killed."

"Oh, my God." Suddenly her legs felt as though they weren't going to support her. She tightened her grip on the shopping cart, looked plaintively at Eileen. "What happened?"

"They got attacked someplace in Baghdad. Most of his squad was killed. They were all from the Peninsula. It was everywhere in the papers and on the news. Didn't you see anything about it?"

"I stopped reading all of those articles, Eileen, and watching the news on TV. It says Iraq and I tune out. I just can't stand it. I figured if anything happened to Evan, I'd hear about it. I couldn't face the news every day."

"Well, fortunately, he wasn't killed, and that's all they seem to report. It's like the wounded don't count. So you might never have seen his name anyway. But his squad . . . those poor boys."

"All of them died?"

"All but one, I believe. Two, counting Evan."

"Oh, God, Eileen, I am so sorry. How is he now?"

"Getting better every day. He's making more sense when he talks on the phone. The doctors won't say for sure, of course, but his lead neurologist predicts that Evan might be one of the very, very few to recover almost completely. Though it's probably going to be a while."

"He's what, doing therapy?"

"Every day. Physical and mental. But as I say, he's really coming along now. For a few weeks there, after he first arrived, we didn't even dare hope for that, so this is all really good news. Once they decided he was eligible for therapy, it's been better."

"Why wouldn't he have been eligible?"

Eileen pursed her lips. "There was some question about whether he'd had something to drink before he went out on his last convoy. Nobody said he was drunk, but . . . anyway, they had to clear that up first. If he was in fact under the influence, he might not have been eligible for benefits."

"Even though he was shot?"

Eileen took a calming breath. "He wasn't shot, Tara. It was a grenade."

That news stopped her briefly. "Okay, but even so, they weren't going to treat him?"

"If he'd been drunk, maybe not. Or not right away, anyway. And we've learned time is everything with his kind of injuries, believe me."

But Tara was still reeling from the revelation. "I can't believe they really might not have treated him. How could he not be eligible for benefits if he got wounded in a war zone?"

"It's one of the great mysteries, dear, but don't get me started on how they're treating some of those other poor wounded boys at Walter Reed. It's atrocious. But—you'll really love this—even after they ruled that he was eligible for benefits, the Army made it one of the conditions of Evan's treatment that he wouldn't complain about conditions at Walter Reed to the media or anybody else." She laid a hand on Tara's arm, forced a tepid smile. "So the thing to do now is be grateful that they're finally helping him, and we are."

"You are a way better person than I'd be, Eileen."

"I don't know about that. It's the only way I know how to be. Of course it's frustrating and terrible, but at least Evan's getting better now. I don't see how making a stink at this point would do anybody any good."

Closing her eyes, Tara blew out her frustration. She didn't believe Eileen was right—she thought that making a stink might in fact help things improve. But suddenly the country's culture seemed to have shifted to where everybody was afraid to make a stink about anything—it meant they weren't patriotic. It meant they supported the terrorists. And this whole mentality was, to her mind, just stupid.

But she wasn't going to get in yet another argument about this ongoing and disastrous war—not with Eileen, not with Ron Nolan, not with anybody else. At least it appeared that, bad though it might have been, the worst medical part of Evan's ordeal was over. "So he's been there how long now?" she asked.

"About three months. We hope he'll be coming home in a couple more, but we're afraid to move him too quickly. At least he's got quality care now, and we don't want to rush his recovery. When he comes back, we want him all the way back, you know?" Eileen's serene gaze settled on her might-have-been daughter-in-law. "And how about you, Tara? How have you been?"

"Mostly good, I think."

"Mostly good, you think? That's not the most enthusiastic response I've ever heard."

"No. I guess not. I'm just . . . kind of at a loss somehow. I don't really feel whole in some way. It's like I'm waiting for something, but I'm not sure what it is, or even if I'll recognize it when it comes along. Does that make any sense?"

"More than you think. Are you seeing anybody?"

"More or less. I'm a little conflicted about him too. In fact . . ." She stopped.

Eileen's head fell off angling to one side in her trademark gesture. "Yes?"

Tara sighed. This close to Eileen's physical presence, now, she almost imagined she could feel emanations of her son in the air around them. And it affected her still, this sense of some deep-rooted connection between them that she'd never approached with anyone else. Certainly not with Ron Nolan.

So why, then, was she still seeing Ron? Was it only because she'd given up on Evan after he'd clearly stopped caring about her? Or was there something simply easier about Ron? Love didn't have to be all-encompassing and overpowering, did it? True, deep, abiding love was a fairy tale, a myth. She'd found that out the hard way. Now she'd moved on into an adult, reality-based relationship that could never hurt her the way she'd been hurt with Evan. And that was smart. She was in a better place, all in all. She had to believe that.

Besides, Evan would never take her back now. Not after what she'd done. She knew that, and she didn't blame him.

"Tara?" Eileen stepped closer to her. "What?"

She tried to smile, mostly failing in the effort. "Nothing really. Just what I said, being conflicted about this guy."

"Well, if you'll take some advice from an old woman who loves you, don't do anything irrevocable unless you're sure."

"Oh, don't worry. I'm a long way from either of those—irrevocable, or sure. I keep thinking it's the Christmas season, those old high expectations that don't seem to pan out." She swallowed against a surge of emotion that suddenly had come upon her. "Maybe Evan and I shouldn't have had such good times with you and the family back in the day. I keep waiting for it to feel that way again at Christmastime."

"It still can, you know."

"Well, maybe. I can keep hoping, at least." Putting on a smile now, Tara reached for some vegetables. "Anyway, I don't mean to sound so negative. Next to what you're going through, my life's great."

"Ours is, too, dear," Eileen said. "Evan's alive and we pray he'll be fine someday. It's been a bit of a challenge, but the worst is definitely behind us. Having gotten through the worst of it, I don't know if we could be happier."

"Well, that's the best news I could hear. You deserve it."

"Everybody deserves happiness, dear."

"Good people deserve it more."

"I don't know about that." Eileen laid a hand on Tara's arm. "But either way, you do. You're a good person."

"Not as good as you think." Not even close, she thought. She could not shake the feeling that somehow she had cheated on Evan, even though they'd broken up, even though they weren't a couple any longer, even though she hadn't written him one letter since he'd gone overseas. "I shouldn't have been so pigheaded with Evan," she said. "I should have written him and..."

"Hey, hey, hey." Eileen moved up closer to her. "You two had a disagreement. You did what you thought was right and so did he. That's not either of you being a bad person. You're both good people." She rubbed Tara's arm reassuringly. "Maybe you could write him now, just a friendly little note. I'm sure he'd like to hear from you."

"No, I couldn't do that. Besides, it's too late for that now. He's better off without me."

"Don't you think he should be the judge of that? Maybe I'll just tell him I saw you and you said to tell him hello. I know he'd be glad to hear that. Would that be too much?"

"I don't know, Eileen. It might be."

"If he wrote you, do you think you could write back?"

Tara's head tracked a pathetic little arc. She bit at her lip. "I don't even know if I could promise that." She put her own hand over the other woman's. "We tried, Eileen, we really did. But now it's just"—she shrugged—"it's just behind us."

Eileen, ever serene, nodded. "And that's all right too. If you change your mind and want to see him when he gets back, you've got our numbers still, I'm sure. Or even if you'd like to drop by and see us before that, you're welcome anytime. You know that, I hope."

"I know that. Thank you." She leaned over and planted a kiss on Eileen's cheek. "You're great. I love you."

Eileen held herself against Tara for a moment, then pulled away. "I love you, too, girl, and you're also pretty great. Us pretty greats have to stick together. And try not to be so hard on ourselves."

"I'll try," she said. Tara's vision had suddenly misted over. "I'll really try."

"I know you will. It was wonderful seeing you, dear. Be happy." With a quick last little kiss on the cheek and a smile, Eileen pushed her shopping cart by behind Tara, turned the corner at the end of the aisle, and was gone.

NOLAN ARRIVED AT TARA'S PLACE within twenty minutes of getting her call. Now Tara sat in her big chair, drinking her second glass of wine. It was nearly dark inside, the only light in the living room coming from the kitchen. With his own drink of scotch in hand, Nolan sat with his elbows on his knees, way forward on the couch, intent. "You've got to be kidding me. It must have happened within a week or two after I left."

"You didn't know anything about it?"

"Nothing. Why would I know anything about it?"

"Don't get defensive, Ron. You were there, that's why."

"I'm sorry, but no. It must have been after I left. Evan was trying to get himself and his guys transferred out of the airport and back to their regular unit the last couple of weeks I was there. It sounds like that's what must have happened. If they were still with us, Jack Allstrong would have mentioned it to me, I'm sure." Pushing himself back into the cushions, he sat back and crossed his legs. "His mom says he's at Walter Reed now?"

"For the last few months."

"Jesus," he said, "that's unbelievable." But if Nolan's pose was relaxed, he felt far from it—his assumption had all along been that Evan was dead, or at least permanently rendered mentally incompetent. After the RPG hit at

Masbah, Onofrio had insisted that they pile Evan into the Humvee. Nolan had field-assessed the damage to Evan's head, and it didn't look like the kind of wound from which people recovered, so he'd let himself be persuaded.

Now Nolan drummed his fingers on the arm of the couch. "But his mother said they expect him to get better?"

"Completely, though maybe not soon."

"Well, that's good news, at least. And she told you all of the other troops were killed?"

"All but one, that's what Eileen said. And then Evan."

Nolan raked his palm down the side of his face. "God, those guys. They were good kids. I can't believe . . . I mean, they shouldn't have even been there. They should have been fixing big trucks." He looked across at her, so lovely and vulnerable in the dim December night. Her tears had begun again and now glistened on her cheeks. "How are you doing with this, T? You want to go see him?"

"No!" The word came out in a rush. Then, more reflectively, she said, "I don't know what good that would do. I just didn't really expect anything like this, that's all. Maybe I should have, you know, but it just . . . when it's someone you know, who you loved . . ." She let out a weary sigh. "I don't know what to do with it. I want him to be okay, but Eileen asked me if I wanted to get back in touch with him, and I couldn't say I did. Although sometimes I think . . ."

"What?"

"No, it just would sound bad. For us, I mean."

"I can take it."

"I know that, Ron. You can take anything. But maybe

sometimes a person doesn't need to say everything. You've just got to get through stuff."

He sipped his drink. "Sometimes you think you would want to go see him, or talk to him, if it wasn't for us. Is that it? Because if it is, I won't stand in your way. I really won't, T." He came forward. "But let me ask you this: Were you thinking a lot about him before you ran into his mother and found out he'd been hurt?"

"Not a lot, no. Sometimes."

"So maybe—just a thought here—maybe it's guilt. Maybe on some level you feel like you need his permission."

"To do what?"

"Move on. Have a life of your own."

She sat on the edge of her big chair, biting her lip, holding her forgotten wineglass in both hands between her knees. Eventually, slowly, she began to shake her head. "No," she said. "I don't think that's it."

"Okay," Nolan said. "I've been wrong before. Twice, I think." A quick smile, trying to break the tension. It didn't work. "What's your theory?"

"It's not a theory so much as it's a change in the facts I was living with. I thought he stopped writing to me because he'd stopped . . . loving me."

"Maybe he stopped writing to you because you didn't write back."

"Okay, maybe some of that too. But that wasn't really him, I don't think. He's a stubborn guy. I mean, he wrote me ten letters and I didn't answer any of them, so why would he stop at number ten? I think he would have kept on until I told him to stop. Except he got hurt and he couldn't."

"So he's still carrying a torch for you?"

"He might be."

"And that would make a difference?"

She blew out the breath she was holding. "I'd gotten comfortable thinking it was over, that's all. Mutually over. Thinking he was okay with it. It made it easier for me."

"With me, you mean?"

She nodded. "Which is really why I didn't write back to him. You know that."

"Yes, I do." He sat back, let out his own long breath, and took a drink. "Do you regret that? Us?"

Tara's head kept moving slowly from side to side. "I don't know, Ron. I just don't know. You're a good guy and we've had a lot of good times . . ."

"But?"

She raised her eyes and looked at him, her lovely face drawn with indecision and regret. "But I think I might need some time to sort this out a little." Her eyes widened. "God, I don't even know where those words came from. I'm not saying I want to stop seeing you. I don't know what I'm saying."

Nolan pushed the ice around in his glass with his index finger. Sitting back now, an ankle on its opposite knee, he let the silence hang for a few beats. "Here's the deal," he said at last. "You take all the time you need, do everything you think you need to do. The downside is I might not be around anymore if the deciding goes on too long. That's just reality. I don't want to lose you, but I don't want half of you either. Just so it's clear where I stand."

"It's always clear where you stand. That's one of the great things about you."

He leveled his gaze at her. "You're going to call him?"

"I don't know. I shouldn't, at least not right now. His mother made it sound like he still wasn't all the way back to normal. I don't want to hear him or see him and start to feel sorry for him. That wouldn't be good."

"No, it wouldn't. It's easy to confuse pity and love, but it's bad luck."

"But I've still got to figure out where to put him. For my own peace of mind. And to be fair to us."

"I get it," Nolan said. "Truly." He drained his drink and got to his feet. "But as I say, T, don't be too long. I want for you what makes you happy, but I'd be lying if I said I didn't hope that that was me."

"It might be, Ron, but I'm just all confused by this right now. Please don't hate me."

"I couldn't hate you, T. You get this settled, maybe we can start over."

"That'd be good."

"I hope it would." He offered her a cold smile. "Well, listen. You've got all my numbers. I'll wait for you to call." Nodding, he placed his empty glass carefully on the coffee table, crossed over to the front door, opened it, and stepped out into the night.

[10]

EVAN SCHOLLER WAS the enemy. Sometimes it was a split-second evaluation, and sometimes a long-considered one, but once you made the decision that an enemy had to be eliminated, it came down to tactics—how to do it. And in this case, there was no more time to be lost. Tara remained undecided about getting in touch with Evan, but that could change in the blink of an eye. For all of Tara's apparent reluctance, at some point she'd need to see or talk to him. And any contact between the two of them would be a disaster.

Nolan had lied to Evan about what Tara had done with his letter; he'd lied to her about the incident in Masbah and many other things. Those lies and all the other ones would come out and he'd lose her.

He couldn't let that happen.

So Evan was the enemy.

Nolan left Tara's, went home and packed a bag with a heavy jacket in it, and made it to the Oakland Airport by ten o'clock. In the mobbed waiting room at the JetBlue terminal, he found a likely looking college kid, chatted him up, and ended up giving him three thousand dollars in cash to cancel his own ticket so that Nolan could get his own last-minute ticket on the otherwise sold-out red-eye flight to Washington. He caught four hours of solid sleep on the five-hour flight.

The sky was deeply overcast, a light snow was falling, and the temperature hovered at twenty-six degrees at ten twenty-five when he arrived by cab from National Airport at the main entrance to the enormous complex that was the Walter Reed Army Medical Center. The place brought him up a little short. Though he had some general understanding of the numbers of injured service personnel being treated at the center, he had more or less assumed that the place was in essence just a big hospital—a building with a bunch of patients and doctors.

It was more like its own city. The main reception area throbbed with humanity. It reminded him in some ways of the main hall of Baghdad's Republican Palace. By the information board, he checked out a rendering of the facility and saw that there were nearly six thousand rooms—he figured probably fifteen to twenty thousand beds—spread out on twenty-eight acres of floor space.

Turning back to the mob, he scanned the cavernous lobby, hoping to get his bearings somehow. A large information booth commanded a good portion of the reception area's counter space, but Nolan was here to neutralize one of the hospital's patients. It wouldn't be a good idea to call any attention to himself. Returning to the rendering, he found a building labeled Neurology and decided to start there. Grabbing the map from its slot, he started out across the huge campus.

The snow had begun to dump more heavily by the time he reached his destination, and he stopped inside the door to shake out his jacket and stamp his feet. The lobby here wasn't nearly as crowded as the main reception lobby, but it still was far from deserted.

He was surprised to see four gurneys lined up against one of the walls, each of them featuring hanging drips and holding a draped body. The line for surgery? For a room? He didn't know and wasn't going to ask, but it struck him as out of place and terribly wrong. These guys had no doubt been wounded in the line of duty—the least the Army could do, he thought, was get them some rooms.

But he wasn't here to critique conditions at Walter Reed. The Army he knew was so fucked up in so many ways that he'd given up thinking about it. Besides that, he had been running on a mixture of adrenaline and low-level rage ever since he'd left Tara's apartment last night, and now, suddenly, the logistics of carrying out this particular mission demanded his complete attention.

As the tide of humanity continued to flow past him in both directions, Nolan experienced a rare moment of indecision: Why did he assume that Evan Scholler would be here anyway? The front door of the building identified it as the Neurology Surgery Center, but Evan's surgery had possibly been months before, and he was now probably somewhere among these fifteen thousand beds, recovering or in rehab.

How did Nolan propose to find Evan without asking directions, and without calling attention to himself? And then, once found, how did he propose to kill him, especially if—as seemed likely if overflow gurneys here in Neurology were any indication—he was in a room with other patients?

Of course, he could eliminate them all. Collateral damage was inevitably part of the equation in any military strike. But this wasn't Iraq, where he could simply disappear without a trace. Here, potential witnesses would have to inform him of Evan's location. Staff members or nurses might be mandated to accompany him if he visited any of the patients.

Beyond that, and perhaps most significant, Nolan had to consider that Lieutenant Evan Scholler wasn't some raghead nobody shop owner in Baghdad. If he were the victim of a murder here at Walter Reed, every aspect of Evan's life would come under the microscope, including the incident in Masbah, the scrutiny for which Nolan had thus far managed to evade. The authorities would find a reason to talk to Tara, and that would eventually, inevitably, lead back to him.

Bottom line: it was mission impossible.

Fuck that, Nolan thought. *The guy is going down.*

"EXCUSE ME." A young woman in a pressed khaki uniform smiled up at him. "You look a little lost. Can I help direct you somewhere?"

Nolan's face relaxed into a smile. "I'm afraid I'm having some trouble finding a friend of mine, one of your patients."

"You're not the first person that's happened to," she said. "I've got a directory over at the reception desk that is marginally up-to-date, if you'd like to come follow me."

He started walking next to her. "Only marginally up-to-date?"

Rueful, she nodded. "I know, but we're so slammed lately, sometimes it takes the computer a while to catch up."

"That darned computer," Nolan said.

"I know. But we're trying. The good news is if he's not where the computer says he is, at least there they'll probably know where he went."

"That would be good news."

"You're being sarcastic," she said, "and I don't really blame you. But believe me, good news around here is scarce enough. You take it where you can get it." They arrived at the reception desk. "Now, your friend," she said. "What's his name?"

"Smith," Nolan said. "First initial *J*. We called him 'J' but he might have been Jim or John. I know," he added, with a what-can-you-do look, "it's a guy thing."

EVAN SCHOLLER STARED OUT at the falling snow.

He had either been asleep or didn't remember when it happened, but somebody had tacked up some Christmas decorations on the wall. There was a tree and those animals that flew and pulled Santa's sled—he couldn't remember what they were called, but he was sure the name would come to him someday. Then there was Frosty the Snowman—he remembered Frosty and even the song about him, sung by that guy with the big nose. They'd also hung up by the door one of those round things made out of evergreen branches and ornaments.

It was making him crazy. He knew what objects were. He just often couldn't remember what they were called.

What he did recognize as a real memory was that he was in his third room since he'd arrived at Walter Reed. His first stop for about ten days had been the Intensive Care Unit, where he'd mostly been unconscious, and about which he had little recollection except that while he was there, he was unwilling to believe that he wasn't still in Baghdad. It didn't seem possible that he could have gone from squatting next to his Humvee in Masbah directly to the ICU here.

Of course, that wasn't what had happened. His speech and language therapist, Stephan Ray, had made his physical and mental journey a kind of recognition game that he'd memorized as part of his therapy. His first stop after Masbah had been to a combat support hospital in Balad, which was where they took out a piece of his skull. The operation, which gave his brain room to swell, was called a craniectomy—remembering that word had been one of Evan's first major successes in therapy. When he'd gotten it right, repeating it back to Stephan the day after he'd learned it, Stephan had punched his fist in the air and predicted that he was going to recover.

What the doctors did next, still in Balad, was pretty cool. They'd taken the piece of his skull that they'd cut out and put it into a kind of a pouch they cut into his abdomen. He could still feel it in there, a little bigger than the size of a silver dollar—they were going to put it back where it belonged in his head in the next month or so, when his brain had healed sufficiently.

From Balad, they'd evidently flown him to Landstuhl in Germany, where after a quick evaluation they decided to get him here to Walter Reed.

His second room here was in Ward 58, the Neuroscience Unit. His mom and dad told him that for his first days there, the doctors more or less left him alone while the Army decided if he was eligible for benefits. He didn't understand that—eventually they had worked it out—but nevertheless he had nothing but good memories of the ward because this is where he had met Stephan. Though Evan hadn't had a clear sense of where he was or what had happened to him, in fact his therapist was there to explain things and pull him through some of the tougher, disorienting times.

Basically, what they did in those first days was play games, do flash cards and puzzles and simple math exercises. Neither Stephan nor his doctors seemed to understand exactly why, but Evan's progress was surprisingly rapid, far better than that of most of the other soldiers who were in here for head wounds. After only about a week in the ward, they moved him again to the room he currently occupied, on the fourth floor above the Pediatric ICU.

THERE WERE NINETEEN J. SMITHS at Walter Reed, but only one with traumatic brain injury similar to Evan's. The nice nurse/receptionist at Neurological Surgery checked her monitor at the desk and told Nolan that his friend was listed as being in Ward 58, the post-op Neuroscience Unit, but that if he was still under observation there—it was only one step removed from the ICU—she didn't think he would be allowed to see visitors.

"That can't be right," Nolan said. "I know his mom and dad have already been in to see him." He gave her a warm smile. "Why do I sense computer issues again?"

"I'm sorry," she said. "I told you it might take a little patience."

He kept smiling, relaxed. "Patience is my middle name. Is there someplace they send brain injury patients when they're starting to get a little better, after this Ward Fifty-eight?"

She screwed her lips in frustration. "I don't really know. But wait." Picking up the telephone, she leaned down to read something from the computer monitor, then punched in some numbers. "Hi. This is Iris Simms at Neurosurgery reception. I've got a guest here to visit one of your patients, Jarrod Smith, and the computer's still got him in your unit, and the guest doesn't think he could still be there. In which case, where would he be?"

She covered the phone and conveyed the message to Nolan. "There's a lot of overflow, but they're saying maybe you could check the upper floors of the Pediatric ICU building, but wait..."

She raised a finger, went back to listening. "He is? Oh, I see. But I understand his parents were able to see him." She waited for the reply. "Okay, thank you. I'll let him know."

Hanging up, shaking her head in continued frustration, she came back to Nolan. "I'm afraid Jarrod is still in Ward Fifty-eight, but they say he's still pretty incoherent. And they don't allow nonfamily guests in that unit. I'm sorry."

"Nothing to be sorry about," Nolan said. "You gave it a good try. I'll call first before I come next time. Thanks for all your help."

"No problem," she said, "anytime."

EVAN MIGHT BE RECOVERING FASTER than most, but to him it was still agonizingly slow going. This morning, he'd tried to get once through all of his flash cards—he had six hundred of them now in a shoe box next to his bed—but by about number two hundred his head felt as though it was going to explode, so he'd closed his eyes just for a minute.

And opened them more than two hours later. All of his three roommates were gone, out with their rehab or other therapies. Outside, the snow was falling in heavy clumps, which he found depressing—so depressing, in fact, along with his failure to succeed earlier with his flash cards, that for a moment he succumbed to the blind hopelessness of his situation here. He was never going to recover, in spite of what they said. He'd never really be normal again. People would notice the dent in his head, even after they put his skull back together. He'd never again talk like a regular person. He'd never have another relationship like the one he had had with Tara. He wished the shrapnel had just cut a little deeper and had killed him, the way it had his troops.

So many of them gone now. So many gone. Regular guys. And he'd been leading them. To their deaths.

Sitting up in his bed, he closed his eyes against the unexpected sting of unwelcome tears. Bringing both hands to his face, he pressed hard against his eyelids, willing himself to stop. In an instant, before he was even aware of it, the self-flagellation and depression had turned, as it often did, to fury. He was goddamned if he was going to cry. But why had this happened to him? Why wouldn't they let him out of here? Why were we having this fucking stupid war anyway? Who cared if he ever learned his fucking flash cards? He turned his head, ready to slap the damn box of the things to the ground, when his eyes grazed the wall again, stopped for a second at the new decorations. Santa and . . .

Reindeer!

Those flying animals pulling the sled were reindeer. That was the word.

He started to laugh. At first it was just a small chuckle emanating from his throat, but it soon swelled to something completely out of his control, paroxysms that violently shook him until he could no longer catch his breath. His shoulders heaved and heaved some more as he tried to grab air into his lungs and now suddenly he was crying again, crying for real. Exhausted, his body shaking with the release of so much that he'd kept pent up, he collapsed back into his pillows, tears flowing unabated in a steady stream down his face.

STEPHAN WAS WIPING his face with a warm towel. "What happened here?"

"Nothing. What do you mean?"

"I mean, your face is wet. Are you all right?"

"I got frustrated. Then the reindeer."

"Right." Stephan, perhaps more attuned to absurdist dialogue than most people, nodded as if he understood the meaning of what Evan had just said. "But you're all right now?"

"Fine."

"You're sure?"

"Sure."

"Because I've got a staff meeting in ten minutes, but I'll bail on it if you need me here. Even just to talk."

"No. I'm good. Really, Stephan. Everything's okay."

NOLAN WAS THINKING that this was why you didn't waste too much thought on what could go wrong. You just kept moving forward, you kept your goal in your sights, you pushed the niggling doubts out of your mind.

Walter Reed wasn't wallowing in chaos by any means, but clearly it was an understaffed and overburdened institution. In theory, maybe somebody was supposed to inquire whom he had come to visit, somebody should have checked his ID—he had almost hoped for that, since he had a Canadian passport in his pocket that identified him as Trevor Lennon—but no one had. Beyond those oversights, the crowding had become so serious that in many areas, and specifically on the upper floors of the Pediatric ICU building that had been pressed into service for recovering brain trauma patients, there was no video surveillance.

He was invisible.

There was no need to be impatient. The building had six stories and he'd covered floors two and three already, walking the hallways with a purposeful stride, as though he knew exactly where he was going. He stepped into each room on both floors, checking for Evan. As he walked the halls between rooms, he nodded to patients lying on their gurneys, or shuffling with their walkers; gave a brisk hello to anyone who looked like a doctor or nurse or staffer. He even had a name, Jarrod Smith, if anyone asked him who he was coming to visit, but he didn't think that was going to prove necessary.

Turning in the third door down on the fourth floor, he saw Evan in the bed across the room, over by the window. The three other beds in the room were all unoccupied. He walked into the room and closed the door behind him, checking the terrain, thinking on his feet that the best way to do it would be out the window.

Depressed brain-injured guy, left alone by a high window. An obvious suicide.

"DUDE."

For some reason, Evan found himself tempted to laugh. Inappropriate laughter, Stephan called it, a normal symptom of his kind of brain injury—this time he was able to resist the impulse. "I know you," he said after a moment.

"Of course you know me. I'm Ron Nolan."

Evan nodded. "That's it. Ron. How you doin', Ron?"

"I'm good. The question is, how are you doing?"

"They tell me I'm a miracle in progress, but I don't much feel like it. What are you doing here?"

"I was in town and found out you were too. I thought I'd come by and say hi."

"What town?" Evan asked.

"Washington, D.C., or close enough. They don't tell you where you are?"

"No, they probably do." He smiled. "I don't remember everything the way I should yet."

"Well," Nolan said, "wait a second." He walked around the bed and over to the window. Looking left outside, then right, he suddenly threw up the bottom half of the double-hung window and stuck his head out. Bringing his body back in, he asked. "Can you get up out of bed?"

"Slow but steady."

"Well, check it out. Come on over here. Next time you forget where you are, look out here—you can read the Walter Reed logo out there on the—"

"What's a logo?" Evan had thrown off his covers and

was sitting on the edge of the bed. "I told you," he explained, "some words—"

Nolan reached out a hand, ostensibly to stop his talking. "Hey, a picture's worth a thousand of 'em. Come here." Taking him by the wrist, he pulled him gently off the bed to a standing position, then backed away from the window to let Evan look out.

Three steps and then . . .

Nolan put a hand on the center of Evan's back. A slight pressure, moving him forward.

Two steps.

"WHAT'S THAT WINDOW DOING open?" Stephan Ray yelled from the doorway. "You're going to freeze yourself and the rest of the room to death." Then, pointing at Nolan, "And who the hell is this?"

Nolan recovered without missing a beat. Pasted the smile back on as he turned. "Ron Nolan," he said. "I was with Evan over in Iraq."

"He was with me in Iraq," Evan repeated.

"Glad to hear it, but let's close that window, what do you say? And, Evan, you shouldn't be walking around too much without the walker, right?" He softened his tone, spoke to both of them. "Falling would not be a good thing right now."

"No. I hear you. My fault," Nolan said. "Sorry."

The door was still open to the hallway, and now another man came in with his therapist and the two started to get the patient arranged on his bed.

The moment had passed.

* * *

PLAN B WASN'T GOING to be nearly as satisfying, final, or effective. In fact, it might not do any kind of a job at all, but at least it would give Nolan time. And keep Evan and Tara apart. But he had to work his way into it—besides, it was about the only possibility left, with the other witnesses remaining doing their therapy on the other side of the room. And with Nolan identified for who he really was. "Your nurse seemed a little upset," he said when Stephan had left them.

"He's not a nurse. He's a ..." The word *therapist* suddenly wasn't there. Evan searched the corners of the ceiling for an instant and couldn't find it up there either. So he regrouped, came out with, "He's a ... helper. He's here to help me. And sometimes I get upset. TBI will do that to you."

"TBI?"

"Traumatic brain injury. That's what I've got. Or had. They tell me I'm getting better. I'm not sure I believe them." Evan picked up the sheet that covered him, he wiped some sweat off his brow. It was, if anything, still cold on his bed, but something about this man Nolan's presence stoked him up, made him sweat with nerves. "What are you really doing here, Ron?"

"I told you. I had some business in D.C. and thought I'd drop by and see how they're treating you."

"They're treating me fine." The snow out the window held his attention for a beat, then he came back to Nolan. "And you're not here from Baghdad?"

"No. I left about a week after you did."

"What for? Were you hurt?"

Nolan's cheek ticked. "No. Me and Onofrio, we picked you up, then made a run for it and got out clean. It was a lucky thing."

"You got me out?"

"Yeah."

"I don't remember any of that."

"No, I don't suppose you would. I didn't expect you to live. Nobody did."

"I should thank you."

Nolan shrugged. "Line of duty, dude. We couldn't have left you behind."

"What about the other guys? What happened to them?"

Nolan took a breath. "They were all killed, Evan."

"No, I know that. But what happened to them, their bodies? If we didn't get them out? Nobody will tell me anything about that."

"You don't want to know, dude. Really." He paused. "And that ought to tell you everything you need."

His jaw set, Evan looked over again at the snow, then came back to Nolan. "So why'd you leave? If you weren't hurt . . . ?"

"Politics. They were going to offer me up, maybe to the CPA, maybe to the locals. Either way, I lose. So I'm out of there, for a while, at least. Until it blows over or all the other shit that happens every day over there covers it up."

"What do you mean, exactly? What are they accusing you of?"

"Some lying witnesses over in Masbah said I fired too soon. That the car we hit had already stopped. Which is bullshit, since it kept coming and slammed into us way after I blew out the whole front windshield. But they were going to lay it all off on me. I didn't see any point in sticking around."

The nebulous memory in Evan's gut began to coalesce

around Nolan's words, the all-but-forgotten moments just preceding the attack coming back to him with a sickening urgency. It wasn't some lying witnesses in Iraq—it was people who had seen what had happened and were coming forth with the truth. And the truth was that this trigger-happy son of a bitch was responsible for everything that had happened in Masbah, for all of Evan's men's deaths, for all of his own suffering.

Nolan, oblivious to Evan's growing awareness, continued. "Anyhow, this way, I'm home for Christmas, doing business development over here for Jack Allstrong. You wouldn't believe how many soldiers like me want back in on the private side. The contractors' market is going through the roof over there and we get the pick of the litter."

Evan's blood pounded in his brain. Pinpricks of bright light danced in the periphery of his vision. The pain forced him to close his eyes, to bring his hands up to cover them.

"But you know," Nolan went on, his voice suddenly taking on a confiding familiarity, "what I'm really here for is to talk about Tara."

Evan opened his eyes. The throbbing inside his head squeezed itself down to a tiny pulsing silent ball of focus. Bringing his hands down slowly to avoid drawing attention to the internal violence of his reaction, he forced a curious expression to gather in his facial muscles. "Tara? What about her? Is she all right?"

"She's fine. She's terrific, in fact." Nolan cleared his throat. "The thing is, though, the main reason I wanted to see you in person, I thought I owed it to you …"

"What?"

"To tell you to your face that Tara and me, we're kind

of an item. We're going out together. I thought the right thing would be to let you know."

Evan felt his hands tighten into fists again under the sheets, but he couldn't find a response in words right away. Until at last he said, "All right. Now I know."

"I don't blame you for being pissed off," Nolan said.

Evan's nostrils flared and his breath seemed to be coming in ragged chunks. But he said, "I'm not pissed off. It's none of my business. We were broken up."

"Yeah, sure, but I met her doing an errand for you. That's got an odor on it. You being hurt makes it worse."

"So? You want some kind of forgiveness? You're barking up the wrong tree, *dude*."

"I don't think so. And I don't have a guilty conscience. I just wanted you to know how it happened, so you'd know it wasn't me. I didn't start it."

"I don't care how it happened."

"No. You'd want to know. It was when I came to tell her you'd been hit."

"You did that? What for?"

"I thought I owed it to both of you." Nolan raised his right hand. "I swear to God, I went over to her place as your comrade-in-arms. I told her the whole story, that you'd been talking about her the night before the attack, that you knew she'd ripped up your last letter and were still going to try to work things out with her."

Beyond the bare truth of Tara and Ron's involvement with each other, a far more important fact leapt out at Evan, and he wanted to make sure of it. "You're saying she knew I was hit from before I even got here to Walter Reed?"

Nolan nodded. "Within a week of it anyway. All she said was that this is what she assumed was going to happen when you went over in the first place. When you actually left, she was done. That's why she never wrote. It's why she never contacted you here. It was over, dude. When she knew I was coming out here this trip, I told her I was going to come see you and at least try to explain my side of it . . ."

"There's nothing to explain. Who wouldn't want her? You think I blame you for that? I barely knew you for a few weeks in Iraq. You didn't owe me squat, Ron. And, okay, you got her. Good luck. I mean it. Now get out of here, would you? Get out of here."

"I'm going," Nolan said. "But there's one last thing. I asked if there was anything she wanted me to say to you. You need to hear this. You know what she said?"

"I can't imagine."

"Here's the quote: 'I'm sad he got hurt, and I hope he's okay. But I've really got nothing to say to him. He made his bed, he can lie in it.'"

It took Tara three days to work up the nerve to call Evan. Still uncertain exactly about what she was going to say, even once she'd made up her mind to call, she actually wrote some ideas down so she'd hit all the notes—she didn't know he'd been injured, she missed him. Mostly—she wrote it five separate times—she was going to say she was sorry. She was going to tell him that when she'd found out what had happened to him, she was resolved to reach out and try to connect with him again. In spite of how badly she'd treated him by not answering his letters, she hoped he could forgive her. She had been wrong, and she was sorry, sorry, sorry. Now she had to know where she stood with him before she could go on with her life anymore. In spite of their philosophical differences, they'd had something rare and special. He knew that. She was sure they'd both changed since he'd left, and possibly it could never work between them, but maybe they could at least start talking again and see where that led.

Sitting in the big chair in her living room, she listened to the ring at the other end of the line, three thousand miles away. Her mouth was dry, her heart pumping wildly. She realized that she was holding her breath and let that go with an audible sigh, reminding herself to breathe again.

"Hello."

"Hello. Evan, is that you?"

"No. This is Stephan Ray. Do you want Evan Scholler? I'm his therapist."

"Yes, please, if he's there."

"Just a second. Can I tell him who's calling?"

"Tara Wheatley."

Stephan repeated her name away from the phone and then she heard Evan's voice, unnaturally harsh and unyielding. "Tara Wheatley? I don't want to talk to any Tara Wheatley. I've got nothing to say to her."

Stephan must have covered the mouthpiece with his hand, because his next words were muffled, but even through the muffling, there was no mistaking what Evan said next. It was loud enough they probably heard it at the Pentagon. "Didn't you hear me? I said I'm not talking to Tara Wheatley. Get it? I'm not talking to her! Tell her to get out of my life and stay out! I mean it." Next she heard what sounded like a heavy object being thrown against a wall, or knocked onto the floor. And swearing, Evan insane with rage.

Or just insane from what he'd been through.

Back in Redwood City, Tara stared at the mouthpiece that she held in her shaking right hand, then slowly, as though the violence she'd heard in it might escape and hurt her further, she lowered it into its cradle.

[11]

FIVE MONTHS LATER, at the main Redwood City police station, Evan Scholler sat waiting in a hard chair just outside the room to which he had been summoned, the small wire-glass-enclosed cage that was the office of his boss, Lieutenant James Lochland. Evan's shift had ended twenty minutes ago, at five o'clock. The summons had been taped to his locker downstairs. Now, as he sat, he could see Lochland at his desk, moving paperwork from a pile in the center of it to one of the trays at the far right corner. When the surface of the desk was clear, the lieutenant drew a deep breath, looked through his wired glass, met Evan's eyes and, in his no-nonsense style, crooked an index finger at him, indicating he should come on in.

Lochland was a young forty and considered a good guy by most of his troops, who, as patrolmen, were by and large, like Evan, young themselves. The scars from a severe case of teenage acne marred what would have been an otherwise handsome face, so that now he came across as approachable. He wore his brown hair a little long by cop standards, and cultivated a mustache that could use a trim. Now he told Evan to shut the door behind him, to take one of the two seats that faced his desk. He had his hands clasped loosely in front of him on the pale green blotter and waited while his visitor was seated.

"What's up, sir? You wanted to see me?"

"Yeah, that's why I sent the note. I thought maybe it'd be a good idea if we had a little informal chat and maybe nip a couple of habits, or tendencies, in the bud before they get you in trouble. But before we go into any detail on those things, I wanted to ask you how you think things are going in a general way. In your life, I mean."

"Pretty good, sir, I think. But, listen, if there've been complaints—"

Lochland held up a restraining hand. "If there have, we'll get to 'em, promise. But we're not there yet. Meanwhile, what I'm really asking about is your state of mind. How you feel about being back here, in the job."

"Pretty good. I feel okay about it. I'm glad to be back."

Lochland nodded, put on a tolerant look. "You sleeping?"

Evan let out a breath, started a smile that went nowhere. "Most nights. Whenever I can."

"You need help with it?"

"What's that?"

"Getting to sleep?"

"Sometimes I'll have a drink or two, yes, sir. When I can't get my mind turned off."

"What are you thinking about?"

Evan shrugged.

"Iraq?"

He let out a long sigh, lifted his shoulders again. "I can't seem to get it out from inside me. The guys I lost. My girlfriend. The whole thing."

"You talking to somebody?"

"A shrink, you mean?"

"Anybody."

"I talked to some woman at the Palo Alto VA until my discharge came through."

"And that was just before you started here, right?"

"April nineteenth. Not that I'll have a party on that date for the rest of my life or anything. So, yeah, a couple of weeks before I started here."

"And you're not talking to anybody since then? They didn't give you any referrals for when you were done with them?"

This brought a snort. "Uh, no. I'm reading between the lines here, but you're saying you think I've still got issues."

"I'm asking, that's all. I'm asking if maybe it's a little too soon. If you feel like you're under too much stress."

"You mean post-traumatic stress?"

Lochland shrugged. "Any kind of stress. Stress you don't need if you're trying to do a good job as a cop. What I'm saying is that there are programs we've got here, and people we could recommend if you think you need it."

"I don't want to go down that road."

"What road?"

"PTSD. You get that label, you're damaged goods. The Army says I'm good. Physically and mentally I'm the miracle child. Now, if one of our own shrinks says I've got PTSD, I'm done."

"That's not exactly accurate."

Evan shook his head. "It's close enough. Post. Traumatic. Stress. Disorder. *Disorder*, Lieutenant. That's a mental illness. I'm not copping to that, period. That's not what I'm dealing with. I'm fine, sir. Maybe I just need to let a little more time go by." Again, Evan let a long breath escape.

"There!" Lochland said. "That's what I'm talking about."

"What?"

"You don't feel that when you do it? You're sighing like a bellows, Evan. Every time you open your mouth, it's like you're lifting this burden and dropping it on the side before you can say anything."

After a second, Evan hung his head. He came close to whispering, "That's the way I feel." Raising his eyes, he looked across the top of the desk. "So how am I screwing up? On the job, I mean."

In spite of military guidelines supposedly guaranteeing that police officers who got deployed to active duty from the reserves or the National Guard would be returned to their civilian work without demotion or loss of time served, Evan's assignment since he'd come back to work as a Redwood City patrolman was roving grammar school officer for the Drug Abuse Resistance Education (DARE) program. In that role, he visited classrooms of fourth-, fifth-, and sixth-graders all over the city, spreading the doctrine of clean and sober living. Though it wasn't a technical demotion and paid what he was making when he'd been called up, it still was not a job normally held by someone with three full years on the force. But it was the only opening they'd had when he was discharged and ready to go back to work, and he had taken it.

Now Lochland reached out and took a small stack of papers from his top tray. Removing the paper clip from the top, he leafed through them quickly—there were perhaps a dozen pages—then put them all down on his desk.

"I don't think we have to go over these one by one, Ev. They're pretty much the same."

Evan sat stiffly, his back pushed up tight against the chair. He had little doubt as to what the complaints had been about. "I just can't stand to see these kids who've got everything—I mean *everything*, Lieutenant—iPods, two-hundred-dollar shoes, designer clothes—I can't stand to see how spoiled they are. How they don't take anything seriously. I mean, this whole DARE thing, it's a joke to them. And when I think of the kids I saw over there in Iraq, with *nothing*, no shoes, no food, begging for MRE handouts..." He shook his head, the rave worn down by its own momentum.

Lochland sat forward, elbows on the desk, hands templed in front of his mouth. "You're not there to yell at them, Evan. You can't let yourself lose your temper."

"They don't listen, Lieutenant! They don't listen to a word I say. They've got everything going for them in the whole world and they don't give a good goddamn!"

"Still..." Lochland pushed the papers around in front of him. "The point is, school's out soon enough anyway. Anywhere you get assigned next, I solemnly promise you'll have more aggravation than these kids could give you on their best day. Serious aggravation. You can't go out there on the streets half-cocked and ready to explode. That just can't be any part of the job." He pulled himself up in his chair, lowered his voice. "Look, Evan, we're all proud as hell of you, of what you've done, of the fact that you've come back at all. You're our poster boy too. But you've got to get yourself under control. You've got to let this stuff go."

"Yes, sir. I know I do. I'm sorry."

"Sorry's a good start, but I'm thinking maybe you

want to think about anger management, maybe take a class, maybe talk to somebody, some professional. I'm afraid that if I get any more complaints after this little talk, it won't be a request. And next time we'll have an HR person in here with us. Understand?"

"Yes, sir."

"You think you can do this?"

"Yes, sir."

"I think you can, too, Evan. But get some help. And some sleep."

"Yes, sir. Thank you, sir. I'll try."

HE WASN'T SUPPOSED to engage in any sports that had a physical risk or contact element for at least another year and, depending on his follow-up neurological examinations, maybe forever. This left out his favorites, softball and basketball—he'd been active at least a couple of nights every week on a city-league men's team in both sports before he'd been deployed. But the police department had a bowling league and while it wasn't much in the way of exercise, it was something to do to get out of the apartment at night and mix with some of his colleagues, even if they were generally from a somewhat different subset—heavier, slower, and older—from the softball and basketball guys.

The positive aspect of this population was that it included men who had attained seniority or rank—Evan's three teammates included two sergeant detectives and a lieutenant. All of whom were more than happy to have recruited a returning young war hero with an average of 191—they all thought the kid had a chance to seriously turn pro. He was a natural. Tonight his three-game score of 621 was fifty points better than any of them individually, and more than enough to ensure the Totems' victory over their opponents, the Waterdogs.

"So here's to the Totems," intoned robbery-division sergeant Stan Paganini, hoisting a gin and tonic in the Trinity Lanes bar after the games, "and their upcoming undefeated season."

Lieutenant Fred Spinoza raised his glass of bourbon on the rocks. "And to our own uncontested rookie of the year, *Doctor* Evan Scholler!" Spinoza often bestowed random honorifics, such as "Doctor," on his colleagues when he got enthusiastic or excited. "Six twenty-one! That's got to be close to the record set. I know I've never heard of a higher one. Three two-hundred games in a row! That just doesn't happen in this league. In any non-pro league."

"They ought to write you up, Ev. Get your name in the sports page." This was white-collar-division sergeant Taylor Blades, drinking a Brandy Alexander.

"Thanks anyway, guys." Evan had acquired a taste for scotch but couldn't afford any of the single malts, so he was drinking a Cutty Sark and soda on the rocks. "But I've been in the paper enough to last me for a while."

"Yeah, but not as a sports hero," Paganini said. "You get known as a sports hero, you become a babe magnet. It's a known fact."

"He's got a point," Spinoza acknowledged. "Your teammates could benefit too. We could pick off stragglers from the swarm around you. Think about that, what it could mean to us and our happiness."

"Yeah, but you guys are all married anyway," Evan said. "You'd just get in trouble. And besides which I think the whole babe-magnet question in an amateur bowling league, even if it's a really good article, is going to be more or less underwhelming."

"No!" Blades said. "There's got to be bowling groupies. In fact, I think I see a bunch of 'em coming in right now. Maybe the word got out about your set already." He snapped his fingers. "YouTube. Somebody was filming you on their cell phone, and they posted it right up, and all these chicks . . ."

But Spinoza was holding out a hand, stopping Blades midrant. "Ev?" he said. "Is everything all right?"

IN THE BATHROOM, Evan threw water in his face a few times, checking his reflection in the mirror to make sure nothing showed in his expression. When he went back to the guys, he told them that he'd just gotten whacked by a wave of dizziness—an occasionally recurring symptom from his head wound. He excused himself, apologizing for raining on the postgame parade, saying he thought he'd better go home early, like now, and lie down, if he was going to be any good for work the next day.

Instead, he went outside and moved his car to the back of the parking lot so they wouldn't see it when they left. A half hour later, after he'd seen them all leave, he got out of the car and walked back into the alley, where he took a stool at the bar and ordered another Cutty Sark, a double this time, on the rocks.

Tara's lane wasn't fifty feet from where he sat. She was with three girlfriends, all of them acting animated and happy. She wore a short white polka-dotted red skirt that showed off her shapely legs, and on top, a red spaghetti-strap silk blouse that he fancied he could see shimmering to the beat of her heart.

Drinking off his scotch in a couple of swallows, he ordered another double and watched the group of young men from the next alley strike up, if not a conversation, then from the body language a running, flirtatious banter. At least, Evan thought, she wasn't here with Ron Nolan. That would have been very hard to take, far harder than seeing her alone, which was difficult enough. Was she still seeing him, he wondered, or could she in fact be unattached again? And if she was unattached … ?

But what was he thinking? This was the woman who hadn't even cared about his near-death in Iraq. Whose self-righteousness made her write him off forever when he was simply trying to do his duty. Who never even wrote him one letter or returned one e-mail from the minute he left.

Looking at her now, so carefree, it suddenly seemed impossible to him that the person he'd known and loved for two years had changed so much. She had always had strong opinions, but one of her best traits, and what his mother had always loved about her the most, was her innate kindness. Tara had always been a good person. What had happened that had changed her so very much?

Well, he was going to find out.

Putting a twenty-dollar bill in the bar's gutter, he again emptied his glass like a man dying of thirst. When he stood up, the dizziness he'd invented for his teammates came and whopped him upside the head for real. He stood leaning against the bar for a few seconds, getting his bearings, surprised at how tipsy he'd become—he'd only had four or five beers during his games and then the five shots of scotch in the bar. Or were they all doubles? He took a step or two and had to grab the back of a nearby chair at one of the tables for support.

This wouldn't do.

He wasn't about to approach Tara as a stumbling and slurring drunk. He didn't want to make it easy for her to dismiss him out of hand as a common nuisance. He would pick another time, when he was sober. Looking down at her and her friends one last time, he concentrated on his walking and made it to the front door without mishap, then down the steps and out to his CR-V in the darkness at the back of the lot.

Settling into the front seat, he locked the car doors and fastened his seat belt, lowered the backrest nearly to horizontal, leaned all the way back, and closed his eyes.

EVAN HEARD THE REPORTS from heavy rifles, bullets pinging now off the asphalt all around him. He was screaming at Alan and Marshawn. "Get down! Get down! Take cover!"

The barrage continued, a steady staccato as the car was hit and hit again. He turned to look and the second car behind him now was a twisted wreck, the bodies of two more of his men bleeding out onto the street where they'd been thrown from the force of the blast. And then suddenly he was aware that it was dark and that the beam from Nolan's headlamp was on him, blinding him as he tried to get his Humvee moving from his position up on the roof of it. His hands up in front of his face, he yelled down to the driver. "Kill that light! Now!"

More bullets raked the car, but as the muffled sound filtered into his consciousness, it became more of a repeated thudding, a knocking. When he opened his eyes, the light was still in his face, but this time he recognized it for what it was—a flashlight outside the car. Still shaking from the fear and immediacy of the dream, he took another second or two before he knocked on his own driver's window, then held his hand up to block the light. He could see enough in the pool of the streetlight above them to make out a couple of uniforms.

Cops. His brethren.

He rolled down the window halfway. "Hey, guys, what's going on?" He shot a glance at his watch. It was three thirty-five.

The officer with the flashlight moved back a step or two. "Could you please show us your driver's license and registration, sir?"

"Well, sure. I, uh ..." He reached for the door handle and pulled it to open the door.

But the near officer outside slammed it back closed, spoke through the half-open window. "Please stay in your vehicle. License and registration, please. Where've you been, buddy?"

Evan stopped digging for his wallet for a moment and sat back, closed his eyes, tried to remember. "Trinity Lanes," he said at last. The view of a suburban street out his car's windshield had him disoriented. "I was bowling."

"And drinking."

"It would appear so."

"Which leads to the question of how you got *here*." But as he opened Evan's wallet, the officer would have had a hard time missing the badge. "Holy Christ," he said with disgust, and flashed it at his partner, handing him the ID. Then, back to the car, he said, "You know how you got here from the lanes? Somebody must have driven you, right?"

Evan just looked at him.

"Cause you wouldn't have tried to drive in the state you're in, would you?"

But then the second cop butted in. "You're Evan Scholler?"

This one he could answer. "Yeah."

Number two said to his partner. "The guy from Iraq." Then, to Evan, "Am I right, pal?"

"Right."

"You don't have your gun on you, do you?"

"Nope. In the glove box."

The first cop shook his head in frustration, then said, "You want to get out now, you can." He pulled open the door. "Smells like a distillery in there, pal."

"Not surprised," Evan replied.

"You might want to open the windows, let it air out for the next time you're driving," the first cop said. "So, for the record," he continued, "do you remember who drove you over here?"

By now, Evan knew where he'd gotten to and where he'd parked, although the piece of the puzzle concerning the actual drive over was a complete blank. "My girlfriend." He pointed to the apartment building across the way. "She lives right up there. We had a fight and she left me in the car to sleep it off."

"That's a good story," the first cop said. "You want to lock up here and go up there now, we'll stick around till you get in."

Evan leaned back against his car. He swayed slightly from side to side. "We're not living together. She won't let me in. I've got to get back to my place."

The second cop handed the wallet back to Evan. "How you gonna do that?"

Evan took a beat deciding whether he should laugh;

he decided against it. "Good question," he said. "*Excellent* question." He looked from one of them to the other. "I guess I'll walk. It's not that far. Thanks, guys. Sorry for the hassle."

He'd gone about five steps, none of them very steady, when one of them spoke from behind him. "Scholler. Maybe you want to lock up your car."

Stopping, he turned back to them.

The first cop said, "It'd be a bad idea to pretend to walk until we pulled out and then come back and try to drive."

"Yeah," Evan said. "That'd be dumb."

"Where's your place?" the second cop asked.

"Just up by the college," Evan said.

The second cop said to his partner, "Not that far. Only about four miles, all uphill."

The one with the flashlight said, "Get in the squad car with me and he'll follow us to your place in your wheels. You barf in my car, you clean it up."

"Got it," Evan said.

[12]

EVAN WAS AT HIS PARENTS' HOME for a Sunday dinner that had become a more or less regular event since he had come back out to California. Once Daylight Saving Time arrived every year, Jim Scholler barbecued almost every night, and on this warm evening in late May he'd grilled chicken, which they'd eaten with fresh spring asparagus, a loaf of sourdough bread, and Eileen's "famous" tomato-potato salad with cilantro and red onions. Now, still long before true dusk, they were sitting outside, in the Schollers' large backyard in the long shadows cast by their mini-orchard of plum, fig, lemon, orange, and apricot trees.

Over their last glasses of cheap white wine, and with Evan now reemployed with the police department, ensconced in his new apartment, and with the immediate physical danger from his head wound behind them, at long last Eileen had mustered the courage to ask Evan about his love life.

He dredged up a chuckle. "What love life?"

"You're not seeing anybody at all?"

"That's not been at the top of my priorities, Mom. I'm not really looking."

His father cleared his throat. "What about Tara?"

"What about her?" The answer came out more harshly than he'd intended. "Didn't I mention that she never answered one of my letters—not one, Dad!—and I wrote about a dozen of them? That said it all clear enough. Plus, last I heard, she had another boyfriend."

"When did you hear that?" Eileen asked.

"At Walter Reed. In fact, the guy came to see me."

"Who did?" Jim asked. "Tara's new boyfriend? Why'd he do that?"

"I don't know. Guilt, probably."

"Over dating Tara?" Jim asked.

"Over stealing my girlfriend after I sent him over with one of my last letters to hand deliver to her? And instead he snags her away while I'm half-dead in the hospital? Could a person feel guilt about that? Or maybe if you were the reason a whole squad got wiped out?"

"You mean your boys?" Eileen asked. "Are you saying that Tara's new boyfriend is the man in your convoy who shot too soon?"

"You got it, Mom. Ron Nolan. I believe I've mentioned him once or twice."

"Never nicely," Jim said.

Evan slugged some wine. "What's nice to say?"

"Evan." Eileen frowned and threw him a quizzical glance. "I don't think I'd heard before that he was seeing Tara."

"But wait a minute," Jim said. "I thought you and Tara broke up over the war. Wasn't this guy Nolan over there too?"

"Yeah," Evan said. "Funny, huh? So I guess maybe it wasn't the war with me and Tara after all. Maybe she just wanted out and that was a good excuse."

"No." Eileen's voice was firm. "That's not who Tara is. She would have just told you the truth."

He shook his head. "I don't think we know who the real Tara is, Mom. Not anymore, anyway."

But Jim came back with his original question. "So this guy Nolan came to Walter Reed to apologize, or what?"

"That was the spin he put on it. But you ask me, it was to rub it in."

"Why would he do that?" Eileen asked.

"Because that's who he is, Mom. He's a mercenary who shot up that Iraqi car because he wanted to, period. Because he could. And if you want my opinion, he came to Walter Reed, among other reasons, to show me he'd gotten clean away with it. And while he was at it, he stole my girlfriend. This is not a good guy, believe me."

"Then what does Tara see in him?"

"That's what I've been getting at, Mom. She's not who you think she is."

"I still don't see how you can say that."

Facing his mother's implacable calm, her hard-wired refusal to think ill of anybody, Evan suddenly felt his temper snap. He slapped a palm flat down on the table, his voice breaking. "Okay, how about this, Mom? When Nolan told her I'd been wounded, you know what she said? She said I made my bed, I could sleep in it. Her exact words." His eyes had become glassy, but the tears shimmering in them were of rage, not sorrow. "She just didn't care, Mom. That's who she is now."

For a few seconds, the only sound in the backyard was the susurrus of the breeze through the leaves of the fruit trees.

"I can't believe that," Eileen said finally. "That just can't be true."

Evan drew a deep breath and raised his head to look straight at his mother. Exhausted and angry, he nevertheless had his voice under control. "No offense, Mom, but how can you know that? That's what she said."

Eileen reached out across the picnic table and put a reassuring hand on her son's arm. "And when was this?" she asked.

"When was what?"

"When she heard that you'd been wounded and said you'd made your own bed and you could sleep in it."

"I don't know exactly. Sometime in early September, right after Nolan got back home, about the time I got to Walter Reed."

"No, that's not possible." She told him about meeting Tara just before Christmas in the supermarket. "I may be terminally predisposed to seeing the good in people," she said, "and I know that sometimes I'm wrong. But there is no possible way that she had heard about your being wounded before I told her. And that was in December."

"If that's true, why didn't she call me then? Just to see how I was doing? Wish me luck? Some—?" He stopped abruptly, suddenly remembering the reindeer on the wall across from his bed, and that her call to him at Walter Reed—when *he'd* refused to speak to her—had been just before Christmas.

Or, if his mother was right, within a few days of when Tara had heard for the first time that he'd been injured.

Eileen patted Evan's arm. "She didn't call you because maybe she was already going out with this Nolan man by then. Maybe she felt guilty about that, or maybe she just thought it would be too awkward. But my point is, she certainly didn't know back in September that you'd been hurt. And it really doesn't sound like her to say you'd made your own bed."

"But then why would—?"

Jim, who'd been listening carefully to the debate, suddenly couldn't keep the enthusiasm from his voice. He knew the answer before Evan finished asking the question. "Why would Nolan come all the way to Walter Reed to tell you a lie? Could it be so that you'd get to hate Tara so much that you wouldn't be tempted to call her when you got back?"

Evan's flat gaze went from his father, over to his mother, back to his father again. "You know, Dad," he said, "you've gotten pretty smart in your old age."

THE SUN WAS JUST SETTLING in behind the foothills as Evan ascended the outside steps at Tara's apartment building and rang her doorbell. When there was no answer, he walked down to the kitchen window and peered inside, where the lights were off and nothing moved. He should have called first and made sure she was home, but the determination to go directly from his parents' house and talk to her had come as an impulse, and acting on the impulse—he was mostly sober, well-rested, recently showered and shaved, there'd never be a better time—he'd told his parents good night, jumped in his car, and driven down.

Since she hadn't been with Nolan at the bowling alley, Evan had more than halfway convinced himself that her relationship with him was over. And if that were the case, he'd talk to her and see once and for all if there was any trace of a spark left to what they'd had, in spite of everything. At least they'd be dealing with the truth.

He'd parked not in the building's parking lot, but out in the street, in the same space his unconscious had apparently picked the other night. Now he went back to the car and got in. Taking out his cell phone, he began to scroll down to her numbers, both cell and home, but then stopped. If she was still going out with Nolan, or worse, if she was out with him at this moment, the timing would be disastrous.

He turned on the car's engine for a minute so he could roll down the driver's window, and saw that the clock on the dash read nine-fifteen. One of the inviolable rules of Tara's life while they'd been going out was that she wouldn't stay out too late, or party too hard, on a school night. And Sunday was a school night. Setting his seat back down a couple of notches, but to where he could still see above the ledge of the window, he turned the engine off and settled down to wait.

It didn't take long.

There was still a trace of natural light left in the day when a yellow Corvette, top down, turned into the lot. Tara was in the passenger seat and still with Nolan, all right. He got out and came around and opened her door and they walked, casually familiar, hand in hand, across the parking lot and up the stairs. She opened the door and they both went inside and Evan felt the blood pulsing in his temples. He put his hand gently over the area when he'd been wounded and imagined that it felt hotter than it had been.

In the apartment, the kitchen lights went on in the front window. A shadow passed into the frame, occupied it for a moment or two, then moved out. The room—and the entire apartment—darkened again.

Evan placed his shaking hands on the steering wheel

and tried to get some physical control back into his body. Swallowing was difficult. Sweat had broken on his brow and down his back.

What was he going to do?

"C'mon, c'mon, c'mon, c'mon, c'mon," he said to himself. But it was an empty imperative with no meaning. Seeing them together, knowing that they were in fact a couple, rendered unimportant the day's discovery that perhaps Tara hadn't cruelly ignored his injuries. What did that matter if she was sleeping with Nolan? If he was in her life, and Evan wasn't.

Suddenly, rocked with self-loathing and hatred, he allowed a steely calm to wash over him. Like most off-duty cops, he kept his weapon available for emergencies. His .40 semiautomatic was locked in his glove compartment, and now he took it out. Checking the chamber and the safety, he took a breath and then opened his car door, tucking the gun under his Hawaiian shirt into his belt.

He stepped out into the street.

EVAN SAT AT ONE of the computers at police headquarters. There wasn't much call for accessing the Department of Motor Vehicles database with his work in the DARE program, and this was the first time he'd actually had occasion to use the department's software. So far, it hadn't gone as quickly as he would have liked. In a perfect world, he could have already been in and out and nobody would have seen him, which would have been his preference.

But his world hadn't been perfect for a long time.

And sure enough, suddenly, at nine-thirty on a Sunday night, when the whole station should have been all but deserted, somebody called out his name from the doorway. Straightening his back, he hit the "ESC" button and jerked his head to the side so quickly he felt a crick in his neck as he looked over to see Lieutenant Spinoza from the Totems now coming toward him. Breaking a casual smile, he said, "Hey, Fred, what's going on?"

"People keep killing each other, that's what. So we poor public servants have to burn the midnight oil and then some." He gripped Evan's shoulder. "But, hey, how are you feeling?" he said. "I didn't like the way that dizziness came up on you all of a sudden the other night."

"No, I'm fine. I don't know what that was. My brain whacking out on me again."

"Well, whatever it was, you looked like you got hit by a train, and I mean that in the most flattering possible way." He pulled around the chair next to Evan and straddled it backward. "You're aware, I hope, that when you're not feeling good, you can call in sick. Everybody knows what you've been through. You don't have to push it. Nobody's going to bust your chops if you need a little time off. Plus, the major issue, just to keep life in perspective, we need you sharp for the game next Tuesday, rather than frittering away your energies trying to convince kids not to smoke dope."

"I'm all right, Fred. Really. I don't need to take time off."

"Obviously, if you're down here now. What's so important on a Sunday night?"

Evan gestured vaguely at the screen in front of him. "Honing up on my computer skills." He crossed his arms over his chest, all nonchalance. "But why are you here?"

"I'd say the usual, but it's not." Spinoza had clearly put in a long day already. "Does the name Ibrahim Khalil mean anything to you?"

"Should it? Is that an Iraq question?"

The response slowed Spinoza down. "No," he said, "but where you're coming from, I can see that's how it would hit you. But no. Mr. Khalil lives—lived—in this mansion in Menlo Park. He owns about half the 7-Elevens on the Peninsula. Owned. He and his wife don't own anything anymore, though. If it is him and his wife...."

"What do you mean? You don't know?"

Spinoza shook his head. "Well, we know it was their house. And we know there were two bodies in it. But it's going to be a while before we can put the pieces back together."

"The pieces of what?"

"Their bodies."

Evan digested that for a second, then asked, "Did somebody cut 'em up?"

"No. Somebody *blew* 'em up, like with a bomb or something. Which of course set the house on fire and burned half of it down around them. So we won't for sure know much of the details for a while. But the neighbors all heard an explosion and then saw the fire."

"Somebody trying to get rid of the evidence."

Spinoza broke a small weary smile of approval. "Not only does he bowl," he said, "he also thinks. I think I see a detective badge in your future, my son."

"Let's get me out of DARE first."

"That's a good idea. How much longer you on that?"

"Well, after school's out." Evan let out a tired breath. "I can handle it if I can just keep from strangling any of the kids."

"Yeah, don't do that. Parents get all upset." Suddenly Spinoza's gaze went to the computer and he clucked in a schoolmarm fashion a couple of times. "This, boys and girls, is a bozo no-no."

"What is?"

"'What is?' he asks. I'm sure. You think I'm an idiot?" He spoke in an exaggerated stage whisper. "We—and by 'we' I mean the department—we officially frown upon this method of meeting pretty young women." He lowered his voice further. "But really, privacy issues, don't go there. If you got busted, it wouldn't be pretty."

"I'm not trying to find a girl, Fred."

Spinoza nodded. "Of course you're not. Perish the thought. I just thought, on the off chance that you were, that I'd point out to you the department's policy. So whose address are you looking for, then?"

"Just this guy."

Spinoza raised his eyebrows. "Same rules go for cute guys," he said. "I know we're not supposed to ask about sexual orientation, but—"

"I'm not gay, Fred. Some of my DARE kids say this guy's selling dope."

"So why don't you just kick it over to vice?"

"'Cause they'd just put it on a back burner, and if I find out this guy is really selling drugs to my kids, I'm going to hunt him down and kill him."

"That's different, then. Why didn't you just say so?" Spinoza moved in closer to the keyboard. "So you got a plate number?"

FOR THE FIRST TIME since he'd left Walter Reed, Evan felt he needed to talk to his therapist, Stephan Ray. He didn't know if there was a technical term for what he was experiencing, but subjectively it felt somewhat similar to his inability to recall the names for things in the first months after his surgery. Except that now, and several other times in the past few days, he had found himself in the middle of some activity, or in the grip of some emotional reaction, and didn't seem to have a memory of how he'd come to be there. Or any control over his actions.

Earlier tonight by the Corvette with the gun, for example.

What did he think he was going to do with the gun? What did he *want* to do with the gun? He didn't know, didn't recall any moment of actual decision. First he was sitting in his car, waiting for Tara to come home so he could have a reasonable discussion with her. And the next thing he knew—the next thing he *remembered*—he was standing by the Corvette in the parking lot with his gun in his hand. *Wondering* why his gun was in his hand.

Surely he wasn't planning to shoot Nolan. Or Tara. Or, God forbid, both of them. Maybe he'd decided to shoot out one or more of Nolan's fancy-rimmed tires. In the dim light of early evening, that at least seemed like a semibaked idea. But his sentient mind realized that this would produce a loud noise and the very likely possibility that he'd at least be seen and possibly be recognized. It would also—perhaps—announce himself as interested in Nolan's activities in a way that he'd rather keep to himself, until he made some rational decisions about what he wanted to do with the rest of his life.

With Tara.

The stop at the police station had been a rational decision. He knew what he wanted there, though he wasn't sure *why* he wanted it, and he knew how to get it.

But now, having learned where Nolan lived and having driven up there, he found himself sitting in his car, parked curbside, again with his gun in his hand. If Nolan came home alone, it wouldn't be the same situation at all as it had been when Tara was with him. This was a quiet street, far less traveled than Tara's, lined with mature trees.

The address was a nice-looking, stand-alone town-home with attached garage amid a cluster of similar units. Separate, yet somewhat isolated. Perfect for . . .

For what? he asked himself.

And suddenly, again, the awareness of where he was, of what he was doing, flooded back. He was doing something here—figuratively staring at a drawing of a reindeer and wondering what the name of it was—but the exact nature of what he hoped to accomplish continued to elude him.

Looking down at the gun, he reached over and placed it back into the still-open glove compartment, then closed the door behind it, turned the key to lock it up. Then, the keys in his hand, he realized that he had to get out of here before he did something stupid. Something that he couldn't even explain to himself.

So he hit the ignition. The dashboard clock read ten forty-two.

Putting the car into gear, he pulled out from the curb and hadn't gone twenty feet when he jammed his foot on the brakes enough to make the tires squeal. His windows were down, he hadn't turned his headlights on, and running dark with a warm breeze over him sparked a jolt of familiarity.

In the months since he'd been injured, it had left the forefront of his memory, but now, suddenly, all the elements of this night rekindled a vision of the episode with Nolan when they'd raided the insurgents' lair in the neighborhood close to BIAP. The bright light and the terrific explosion blowing out the windows; the flames licking into the night as gunfire erupted behind him.

A mercenary mission to kill.

An explosion and then a fire.

A dog barked somewhere in the neighborhood.

Evan let out the breath he'd been holding, turned on his headlights, and eased his foot off the brake.

[13]

"WELL, MY SON, the latest theory, which might still be wrong," Spinoza said, "is that it was a thing called a fragmentation grenade. You ought to know about them. They're evidently using 'em in Iraq right now. Blow the shit out of everything so you need a snow shovel to pick up the pieces. Which pretty much fits what happened here, by the way." He sat back in his chair and picked up his sandwich. Putting his feet up on the desk, he took a bite. "So why do you want to know? You teaching execution techniques in DARE to the little fuckers?"

"No reason, really," Evan said. "I just thought it was interesting. I don't think I've ever heard of somebody being killed that way. At least not here in the States."

"Yeah, well." The lieutenant chewed thoughtfully. "It's not the norm, I'll give you that. Somebody wanted these people completely dead, in a big loud way. It wasn't some gangbanger taking potshots at a residence and hoping somebody gets hit."

"Could the guy, the victim, have done it himself?"

Spinoza shrugged. "Not impossible, I guess. There's no evidence pointing to anybody else. But also there's absolutely no sign so far of why Mr. Khalil would want to do that. The businesses were going great. He apparently loved the wife. No health problems. At least that's what we got from the rest of the family. And, believe me, there's a lot of the rest of the family. So I'm betting against murder/suicide, which leaves a pro. 'Cause I'll tell you one thing. Whoever did this did it right. At this moment, the only evidence we've got is—maybe—the bits of the frag grenade. And just between you and me, I'm kind of hoping we don't have that."

"Why not?"

"Because as we stand now, we've got a local murder of a businessman. At least we can get away with calling it that, since Ibrahim was a naturalized citizen."

"Where'd he come from?"

"I thought I told you that last night. Iraq. Half his family, evidently, still lives there. The other half has the 7-Eleven concession for the Bay Area wrapped up here."

"So what's the issue if you've got a frag grenade?"

"You can't own a frag grenade. It's a federal offense. Which means the ATF's involved. Which, in turn, sucks."

"So how do you find out if it was a frag grenade?"

Spinoza came down in his chair, brought his feet to the floor. "Fear not, my son. The ATF has already picked up samples from the scene. They'll have it analyzed by tonight and soon we'll all know for sure. If it is what it is, the FBI's in before morning. The preliminary call is yep, frags. So it's gonna be their case."

"Why's that so bad, Fred? Don't they have a lot more resources than we do?"

"Oh, no question," Spinoza said. "More resources, more money, more access to data, the whole nine yards. The thing is, though—they don't share. So we wind up spending a week finding stuff they already have. It's kind of a race to see who can get there fastest, but we've got one leg tied behind our backs."

"I don't think that's exactly the expression."

"No?" Spinoza popped his last bite of sandwich. "Well, that's what it feels like."

HE KNEW THE LOCKSMITH from Ace Hardware both from his high school class and from his men's softball team. Now, at a few minutes before two o'clock on an afternoon after Evan had told *his* lieutenant, James Lochland, that he was suffering from a migraine and needed to go lie down in his dark bedroom, Dave Saldar pulled up outside of Nolan's townhouse and parked in back of Evan's CR-V.

Evan, in his police uniform to reinforce his legitimacy, got out of his car and they high-fived each other on the sidewalk. After a couple of minutes of catching up—Saldar had heard some of Evan's story from guys on the team—they got around to what Evan had called Dave up here for.

"You didn't hide a spare under a rock or something?" Saldar asked.

"No. I didn't think I'd ever forget my keys. Who forgets their keys?"

"My wife does every time she leaves the house."

"Yeah, well, I don't. I never have before."

"I would love one thin dime for every time I'd heard those exact words. Why do you think the world invented locksmiths?"

"I never could figure that out."

"Well, now you know." Saldar inclined his head toward the townhomes. "Okay, which one's yours?"

They went down to Nolan's doorway, partially enclosed and blocked from the street by an L-shaped, glass-block privacy screen. Saldar got out his tools and went to work. Evan found that his legs were weak enough that he had to lean against the screen for support. With each passing second, the enormity of the implications of what he was doing worked on his system. He felt as light-headed as he'd been on Nolan's night raid outside of BIAP. A jackhammer pulse pounded where they'd cut open his skull. The migraine he'd invented for Lieutenant Lochland threatened to become a reality—pinpoints of light exploded at the outer edges of his vision. He kept looking to the street, nearly passing out when a yellow Miata convertible crested the incline and drove by.

Saldar, noticing something in his reaction, glanced up at him. "You all right?"

"Good," he said. In fact, he could feel the sweat breaking on his forehead. Summoning all the control he could muster, he brought his hand up and dragged it across his brow.

At last, Saldar turned the knob and pushed the door open. "There you go, a minute and fifteen seconds. This could be a new record."

"I'm sure it is, Dave. That's awesome."

Saldar was holding open the front door. "Hey, are you okay, Ev? You really don't look so good."

"I'm all right. The head's acting up a little, that's all." He reached back for his wallet, thinking, *I've got to get him out of here! What if Nolan shows up?* But keeping it casual, he said, "So what's the damage?"

"Let's call it thirty, since we're friends. You want, you can go grab your set of keys and I can make you a couple of quick copies right out of the truck, five bucks each."

"That's all right." Evan fished out two twenties. "I know I've got some dupes inside. I've just got to remember to put 'em out here somewhere for next time. But right now I think I'd better get in there and lie down a minute."

"Sure, okay. But let me run and get you your change."

"No, keep it."

"I can't take tips from teammates, Ev. It's one of my rules. I've got some cash back in the truck. Won't take me thirty seconds."

He put a firm hand on his friend's shoulder. "Dave, really, I'm hurting a little here. Thanks for your help, but I've got to get horizontal pretty quick or I'm going to get sick. Seriously. Take care of yourself. I'll see you around."

"You need a doctor?"

The effort for even half a smile was almost too much to bear. "You don't let me get inside pretty quick, you're gonna need a doctor. You hear me?"

"All right, all right. But stop by the field sometime. We're still playing Tuesdays and Thursdays."

"I will. Promise."

"I'll buy you some beers with your tip money."

"Deal," Evan said, stepping inside the door. "Later."

HE STOOD IN THE LIVING ROOM. Part of him had a hard time believing that he was truly here, illegally inside another man's home. It felt surreal. This wasn't who he was. It wasn't the kind of thing he'd ever done, or even thought about doing.

But now, once inside, he couldn't let those considerations slow him down. There was no telling when Nolan might return. Evan had no idea what hours he worked, or what he did on a day-to-day basis, or even if he had any regular schedule at all. If there was something incriminating to be found in this place, and Evan's gut told him there was, he had to find it and then get out fast. It wasn't a matter of finding evidence that could be used in court— he simply wanted the knowledge.

Or at least that's what he let himself believe. He would decide then how to use what he knew at his leisure.

The room he was in was Spartan, furnished with a leather couch and matching twin leather chairs in front of built-in, mostly empty, bookshelves on either side of the fireplace. A large mirror over the mantel gave an impression of space, but the room probably wasn't more than ten feet wide. Half of the back wall was a glass doorway that opened onto a small brick patio, shaded by large oak trees. A potted plant squatted in the corner. The first glance told him that there would be nothing of interest here, but he forced himself to slow down and make sure.

When he was done, he parted the blinds in the front window, saw nothing out in the street, and crossed the tiled entry area that led into the kitchen, which didn't have much more personality than the living room. It was, however, quite a bit more exposed, since the double-wide window over the sink looked out over the small lawn to the street beyond.

It didn't appear that Nolan did a lot of cooking for himself—the refrigerator had eggs, beer, a pack of American cheese, and milk, with tomatoes and lettuce in the vegetable bin, and some condiments, while the freezer held three boxes of frozen spinach, a carton of ice cream, and a few packages of chicken breasts and ground beef.

A door next to the refrigerator led out to the small single-car garage, where Nolan had hung his empty duffel bag and two empty backpacks on hooks on the far wall. An uncluttered workbench obviously hadn't seen much use, and neither had the drawers under it.

Back in the kitchen, Evan finally got his nerves under control as he scoped out the street again and then ducked under the window passing through. Just off the living room in the back of the house, he entered a decent-sized den with a desk and a computer. The wall featured a tacked-up map of Iraq with several color-coded pins stuck in various spots—Baghdad, Mosul, Kirkuk, Abu Ghraib, Anaconda. Evan tried the mouse first to see if the monitor screen came on, and when it didn't, he hit the button on the CPU. While it booted up, he went through the next door into the bedroom and stopped in his tracks.

Drawing a heavy breath, he crossed over to the bureau next to his enemy's perfectly made bed and picked up the photograph of Nolan and Tara in a heavy silver frame. They were hugging each other for the picture, obviously from the deck of a boat out on the Bay, both smiling out at him on a lovely day. He held the picture long enough that the urge to smash it against the wall came and went. Then, replacing it carefully in its original position, he went back to his searching in earnest. Dresser drawers, bathroom drawers, cupboards, and closets.

The headboard of the bed yielded up the first weapon, another M9 Beretta, the same weapon that Evan had carried in Iraq. He smelled the barrel and picked up no odor, then removed the clip and verified that it was full. But a pro like Nolan, if he had used the gun, would have cleaned it and reloaded immediately afterward.

The bedroom closet, neat like the rest of the house, contained another backpack on the top shelf. This one he emptied out on the bed piece by piece. It held another Beretta 9mm, ten clips of ammunition, and six hand grenades. Evan didn't know for sure if they were fragmentation grenades or the so-called flash/bangs, which were nowhere near as lethal. But either way, he was willing to bet that they were illegal in the hands of private citizens. Evan was sure that they would be of interest to the police, once he figured out a way to get some law enforcement person interested in Nolan as a suspect in the Khalil murders.

Replacing the backpack, he went back into the den and sat in front of the computer. Clicking on the icon labeled "Allstrong," he scanned through a few documents—mostly what appeared to be copies of or amendments to government contracts or work orders that the company had secured overseas. There were also a significant number of e-mail files, and several résumés of people who had served in the military, which attested to the kind of work Nolan was probably doing over here stateside. Evan entered a few more of the documents and searched for the name Khalil, but came up empty.

Lacking a password, though he tried several obvious ones, he couldn't get into Nolan's regular e-mail file. The icon named "My Pictures," by contrast, came right up. Immobilized by what he feared he might see there—more photos of Nolan and Tara in much more intimate settings than the deck of a boat—he finally clicked on the first folder and, finding not even one picture of Tara, sighed in relief.

These appeared to be shots Nolan might have taken when he was shopping for a house. Here was a tree-lined street just like the one he lived on, cars parked along the curb. Then different angles, in different lights, on another house, large and grandiose. In fact, on closer inspection, on the clearest picture from directly in front of the building, the place was actually a pink-hued monstrosity. What in the world, Evan wondered, could Nolan have seen in the place that would have prompted such a detailed study?

Suddenly recognition straightened him upright. In the paper that morning, Evan had seen a black-and-white picture of the remains of Mr. Khalil's house, which of course no longer looked very much like the residence in this picture. But in the article, hadn't he read something about the house being pink?

Hurriedly he started pulling open the drawers to the desk. There was a digital camera in the middle drawer and for a second he considered looking at what it contained. But he couldn't take the time. He checked his watch—two forty-five. He'd been in here too long already. In the lower right drawer, he found an open ten-pack of floppy disks. Four remained in the box, and with his hands shaking now, he took one out, inserted it into the A-disk slot, and copied the file from the "My Pictures" photo onto the disk.

Ejecting the disk, he put it in his breast pocket, then sat back, took a breath, and walked himself through turning the computer off the careful way, through the "Start" menu.

Keenly listening for the sound of the garage door opening, or of a car pulling up out in the street, he forced himself to wait until the terminal screen went black. Then he got out of the chair and replaced it where he hoped and thought it had been. He pushed all the desk drawers flush against their inserts. Checking one last time to make sure that he still had the disk in his pocket, he walked back up through the living room, locked the front door from the inside, looked out through the window, saw that it was safe, and let himself out.

[14]

THE LAST CHILD HAD GONE home two hours ago; the sounds from the hallway were small and distant. The occasional whirrings of the Xerox machine way down in the office barely registered on Tara's consciousness as she looked out at the view from her classroom window. She'd always considered it a particularly fine view, with the small grove of scrub oak hugging the hilltop just across the street. She could imagine that the hilltop was far from anything mundane or suburban—say, in Tuscany, where she'd never been. Sometimes in the late afternoon like this, with the springtime scents of lilac and jasmine coming up on the breeze mingling with the closer smells of pencil and chalk, this classroom was her favorite place in the world.

She felt that she could count on her fingers the times when she'd been the absolute happiest and most content, and many of them had been right here. Some of the longtimers here at St. Charles had gotten perhaps a little cynical over the years, but either Tara hadn't been here long enough yet, or she didn't have the genes for cynicism; she wasn't that kind of a person. She still loved her kids. Every year a new batch, and every year with fresh challenges—oh yes, thank you, challenges—but also with something new to learn, to connect with, to love. New clay. That was how she always thought of her classes when the year began. New clay.

Sitting back in her desk chair, she daydreamed, her face relaxed in contented repose, an almost infinitesimal upturn to her lips. It had been a day almost exactly like this one, soft and scented—had it been three years now? She remembered that the whole day she'd felt almost sick with herself since she'd been so easy on the first date with this new guy, Evan. Too easy. She'd been too attracted and let him know it and wasn't really inclined to fight herself. Not against that kind of heat.

But what if it turned out to be that old cliché and he didn't respect her and never called again? Hell, she was an intelligent woman with a fine career and knew that she would never build her world around some man, but the thought of never again seeing this man she'd met only one time just suddenly didn't seem bearable.

And she had gotten up from her desk, sick at herself, and went to smell the outdoor smells by the window, which always helped when she was worried or depressed, and she looked down and there Evan was, getting out of his car with a bouquet in his hand. The happiest single moment of her life.

Sighing, she opened her eyes, surprised at how quickly the contented daydream had retrieved enough emotion to nearly bring her to tears. Breathing deeply, she dabbed at her eyes and pushed back from her desk, thinking that, oh, well, it was time to go home. No need to dwell on the past. It was still a beautiful day, with the incredible floral perfume outside on the breeze.

She crossed over to the window to smell the day one last time. And then she looked down.

In the street, Evan was getting out of his car. No flowers. But it was him nevertheless, coming to see her at last.

Tears welled again, and her hand went to her mouth. Then, after a moment, she brought it down to rest over her heart.

"HI."

"Hi."

"I thought you might be here."

"You were right. It's a beautiful afternoon. My favorite time."

"I remember."

A silence. She'd been standing when he got to the classroom door, and now she boosted herself back onto her desk. "So how are you?" she finally asked. "You look good."

"I'm okay. I still get headaches, but basically I'm Mr. Lucky."

"That's what I've heard. I'm glad for you. Glad you're alive."

"Me too." He moved a step closer to her. "Are you all right? You look like you've been crying."

She shook her head, smiled with a false brightness. "Allergies. The downside of all these blooming flowers." She sucked in a quick breath and let it out, then tried another smile that died on the vine. "I tried to call you."

"I know. I was a shit. I could say I was still recovering and don't remember anything about it, but that'd be a lie. I'm sorry."

She shrugged. "I was a shit too. Too inflexible. Too stupid."

"Okay," he said, "we're a couple of shits."

"Stupid shits," she corrected him. And finally a small smile took.

"Better," he said. He looked away, over at the window to the oak-studded hillside. Coming back to her, his jaw somehow had a harder line. He drew a breath and blew it out sharply. "You still seeing Ron Nolan?"

Biting at her lower lip, she nodded, answered in a very small voice. "Sometimes."

"Love him?"

She shrugged, shook her head, shrugged again. "I don't know, Evan. We've had some good times, but I don't know. *Love*'s a big word."

"Yes, it is. What are we going to do about it?"

"What do you mean, 'we'?"

"You and me. We. The usual meaning. The fact that I love you."

"Oh, God, Evan." She shook her head from side to side. "Don't say that."

"Why not? It's true."

"Well …" She slipped herself off the desk and walked over to the windows again, stood still a moment, then turned back to him. "Please don't say that," she repeated. "I don't know what to do with that."

"You don't have to do anything. Although that's one of the reasons I came here. To tell you that. Just so that if you were wondering, you'd know."

Her gaze settled on his eyes. "Okay," she said softly. "Okay, now I know." Bringing her hand up to her forehead, she pushed until her fingers went white, then pulled her hand away. "Were there other reasons?"

"Other reasons for what?"

"For why you came here. You said one reason was to tell me you loved me. What was another one?"

Evan's brow clouded over—he couldn't remember. For an awful moment, he thought he might have forever lost the real reason he'd come to see Tara today. He hadn't come to tell her he loved her. He hadn't been sure of that until he was with her. But then they'd started talking and that had come out and now he was unable to retrieve the real purpose of his trip here. "I'm trying to remember," he said. "Can you give me a couple of seconds?"

This was the first time she was seeing an effect of his injury, and he was acutely aware that this moment might change everything forever between them. He might, in her eyes, now be damaged, challenged, handicapped—somehow not as sharp as he'd been, not quite exactly the same person. Not quite her equal.

He couldn't let that happen.

Closing his eyes, concentrating, he thought, *"Come on, brain, come on. Retrieve it."* Then he opened his eyes as the answer found its way to his tongue. "The other reason I came here," he said, "is I wanted to ask you a simple factual question."

At once, she was all the way with him again. Her expression now relaxed, she moved a few steps toward him, her arms crossed over her chest. "I can do simple factual," she said. A smile played around her mouth.

"Okay. Do you remember when you first heard about me getting hurt?"

Her quizzical look stayed on him for a long moment, as though she were surprised that he would have to ask that question at all. "Sure," she said. "I ran into your mom at the grocery store one night. I think it was a few days before Christmas. I know it was a few days before I called you."

"You mean called me at Walter Reed? When I didn't talk to you?"

"Right."

"You're sure of that? The time, I mean. Just before Christmas."

"Of course. That's when it was. When else would I have heard?"

"How about back when it happened? Say, September?"

"No way, Evan. How could I have known then?"

He shrugged. "Well, when did you start seeing Ron Nolan?"

"What does Ron have to do with that?"

"I would have thought he'd have mentioned it, that's all."

"He never knew about it, Evan. You guys all got transferred out of his base the week he got back."

Evan canted his head a bit to one side. Studying her expression, he read only sincerity, openness, perhaps a bit of confusion. But one thing was clear—she was telling him the truth as she knew it.

"We got transferred?"

"That's what Ron said."

"Where'd we get tranferred to, Tara? Did he tell you that?"

"No. I don't think he knew."

"Right. He didn't know. You know why? Because we weren't transferred. We ran our last mission out of Baghdad Airport, where we'd been with Ron all along. You can look it up."

The germ of confusion spread like a plague over her

features. Mouth tightened, brow furrowed, eyes darting, seeking a place to land. "But..." The word hung in the room between them. Her arms hung down, inanimate at her sides. "I don't get this."

"Ron was with us in the convoy, Tara. He was in my Humvee. He was next to me when I got hit."

"No. That can't be true."

"Why would I make it up, Tara?"

"I'm not saying you're making it up, Evan. Although I could see a reason why you might. But I don't think you'd do that."

"I wouldn't. I'm not making it up," he said. "It's what happened."

She held his gaze for a minute, and then, her voice barely audible, grabbed at the next straw. "Maybe . . . I mean, I'm just thinking, could it be with what happened to your head . . . maybe you don't remember it all exactly?"

He nodded—sober, patient, restrained. "That's a legitimate question. I have forgotten some stuff. I don't remember whole days and weeks from when I woke up. But Ron was with us in that convoy. I remember everything about that. If you still don't believe it, you can look it all up on the Web. Just Google Masbah." He spelled the name of the neighborhood in Baghdad. "It's all there. He's the reason it all went down. And that's the reason he had to get out of Iraq so fast. They were starting the investigation, and he knew it led straight to him."

The color had drained from her face. Her eyes flitted to the corners of the room as though she hoped to find some answer there. She brushed a strand of hair from her forehead. Placing her hand flat on one of the students' desktops for support, she lowered herself into the connected chair. "He told me he had no idea you'd been hurt," she said, "that he found out about it from me after I ran into your mom that night and she told me."

"Christmastime."

She nodded. "Definitely."

"And he told you he knew nothing about it before?"

"Nothing. I swear, Evan. No, he swore. He'd never heard a thing about it."

"He didn't have to hear about it, Tara," Evan said. "He was there. He fired the first shots."

SPINOZA POURED THEM both a cup of coffee and took Evan out into the backyard so they wouldn't interrupt the movie Leesa and their four young kids were watching in the family room. The day, with at least another half hour of light in it, continued warm and fragrant. The two men sat down at a picnic table under a vine-covered trellis. "So," Spinoza began, "did you get your dope dealer yet?"

"Not yet," he said. "He's out of town."

"Timing's everything," Spinoza said.

"I don't know," Evan replied. "Timing's important, but I'd give points for location too. A quarter inch either way and my story's different. That's been pretty good nightmare material."

"I'd imagine so." Then, going back to his original subject, Spinoza said, "You know he's out of town?"

Evan shrugged. "His car's gone. Nobody answers the door."

"Don't do anything stupid, Ev," the lieutenant said. "If you think there's really something to this guy, send him to the narcs." Spinoza blew on his coffee and took a sip. "And in other news, you know Mr. Khalil, who we talked about at lunchtime? As of a couple of hours ago, Mr. Khalil is officially a joint-jurisdiction case. You remember the frag grenade issue we talked about? Well, the feds have conclusively determined that that's what blew up the room and started the fire. So they're in the case, in spite of the fact that it also looks like Mr. Khalil and his wife were first shot in the head with a nine-millimeter bullet."

Evan's face must have betrayed something. Spinoza abruptly put his coffee cup down on the table. "What?"

"Nothing," Evan said.

EVAN LEFT SPINOZA'S HOME in great frustration. He'd planned—hoped—somehow to get the picture from Nolan's computer in front of Spinoza, but there was no way he could tell his lieutenant how he'd gotten it—that he'd broken into someone's home—and that rendered hopeless his entire ill-conceived plan. But cruising down to the Khalils' ruined house, Evan had satisfied himself that the house in the picture was in fact theirs, then decided that the thing to do would be simply to send the disk to the FBI. The Bureau would have Nolan in their database and know all about his history. The advantage to his new idea was that both the ATF and the FBI were known to play fast and loose with due process and probable cause. If they came to think that Nolan had killed the Khalils, especially if there was an Iraqi or terrorist connection, they would find a way to question him and perhaps even get inside his house, where they would discover the grenades, the other pictures, the guns. In any event, after they got the disk, Nolan would be on their radar. After that, it would only be a matter of time before they could take him down.

Now night had fallen. In his kitchen, Evan's head throbbed and again the pinpricks of bright light at the edges of his vision presaged the onset of a migraine. He'd already taken a couple of Vicodin, and as soon as he finished the last of his business, he had to get to bed if he was going to work tomorrow.

Wearing blue latex gloves, he pulled the self-adhesive manila envelope over closer to him. It had taken a while, left-handed, to write down both Nolan's address on a piece of notepaper and the FBI's address on the envelope. But now he was satisfied—the writing was legible yet unidentifiable as his own. He slid the slip of paper with Nolan's address into the envelope along with the disk, then pulled the paper strip from the adhesive and closed the top. He peeled off ten self-adhesive stamps from the roll he'd bought and stuck them on. Tomorrow he would stop off in another neighborhood and drop the envelope into a mailbox.

Now he set the thing on his table and gave it a quick once-over. Satisfied that it couldn't be traced back to him, he walked back through his apartment to his bedroom, turning off the lights as he went. Lying down on the bed, his clothes still on, he pulled a blanket up over his shoulders, turned on his side, and closed his eyes.

A LITTLE WHILE after it was truly dark, Tara called Evan's mother, Eileen, and got his address. She waited and thought and second-guessed herself and eventually left her place sometime after eleven o'clock and drove. Parking out in the dark street across from his apartment, she sat for another five minutes or so with her car windows down, her hands in a prayerful attitude in front of her mouth.

By the time she got to the door, she barely heard her own timid knocking over the beating of her heart. After a minute, she knocked again, harder. And waited.

A light came on inside and hearing his footsteps, she held her breath.

The door opened. He'd been sleeping in his clothes. His hair was tousled, his eyes still with that sleepy look she remembered so well. She looked up at him, realizing that she loved having to look up, had missed that; loving the size of him, so different from looking across at Ron Nolan. Everything was so different and so much better with Evan. How could she have forgotten that?

She couldn't get her face to go into a smile. She was too afraid, the blood now pulsing in her ears, her hands unsteady at her sides.

He just looked at her.

"Is it too late?" she asked. "Tonight, I mean."

"No."

"I needed to talk to you some more. Would that be all right?"

"Everything's all right, Tara. You can do whatever you want. You want to come in?" Stepping back away from the door, he gave her room to pass and then closed the door quietly behind her as she kept walking through his living room, stopping by the counter that delineated the kitchen and turning back to face him. Her shoulders rose and fell.

From over by the door, he said, "I can't guarantee talking too well. I've been having some trouble sleeping, so

I'm a little doped up. Plus I've had a couple of drinks. I'm drinking too much. I need to stop."

"Are you in such pain?"

He managed a small shrug. "Sometimes, but that's not it really." He took a second to continue. "I know that whatever they say, I'm not all the way back. Maybe I'll never be. To tell you the truth, it freaks me out sometimes. When I'm alone mostly. But I don't want to have anybody feel like they have to be with me all the time either."

"Your mom?"

"For one example, yeah. Anybody, really. But it's"—he shrugged again—"it's just what I'm doing now, Tara. Holding on. Getting better, I hope. Getting over what happened."

Evan still stood by the door, making no effort to close the space between them. She felt the distance tugging at her, causing a pain of its own, and took a step toward him, then another.

"But that's all just me," Evan said. "What did you want to talk about?"

"Ron. I never . . . I wanted to tell you that it was never like it was with us. It was just a completely different thing."

"Was? Past tense?"

She let out a heavy breath. "Yes. After what you told me today."

"Okay. And how was it with us that was so different?"

Tara put her hands together at her waist. She deserved that question. And he deserved the real answer. "Because we connected, Evan. So basically."

He nodded. "I know."

"I don't think that ever goes away."

"No. Me neither."

She looked across the living room into his eyes. "Why are you staying over there? It's almost like you're afraid of me."

"I am. As much as I need to be."

"How much is that?"

"That depends on how much being done with Ron means you're back with me."

She waited another few seconds and then closed the space between them. Looking up at him again, now the smell of him so close. "Does it hurt you to touch the scar?" she asked.

"It's just a scar." But he inclined his head so that she could see it. Almost a perfect circle, slightly indented.

Slowly, she reached out her hand and brought it up to his head. As soon as she touched it, she felt something give in her legs. As she traced the shape of the scar, tears sprang into her eyes and she made no effort to stop them. Evan brought his head down, leaning into her.

Bringing her other hand up into his hair, she cradled his head in both her hands.

Holding on to her, his arms behind her, he went to his knees in front of her, his face first pressed to one side against her thigh. But then, her hands on his head now directing him, she turned him to be up against her, his hands gripping her from behind, pulling her into him, while she pressed herself against him. She pulled him gently away for an instant, only long enough to let her step out of her clothes, and then brought him back to where he'd been.

Beyond any time, then, she was on the floor with her legs around his neck, until the surge of blood and heat she'd only known with him took her and then there was the taste of her on his mouth and his own cry as everything between them came back and came again and left them both flung out on the floor, wasted and sated, and connected in every part.

[15]

THE RELEVANT PORTION of the e-mail from Jack Allstrong that had put Nolan on the road had read: "When the CPA hands over the government to the Iraqis, Uncle Sam is going to be shipping over $2.4 billion—that's right, *billion*—in shrink-wrapped 100s. That's twenty-eight *tons* of greenbacks, Ron, almost all of it earmarked for infrastructure and rebuilding, which means us. My standing directive to you is to recruit as many qualified personnel as you can find. Starting now."

Now Nolan was just getting back home from a productive couple of days. Frequenting the bars around some of California's military bases—Pendleton, Ord, Travis—he'd recruited four men for Allstrong's ongoing and growing operations in Iraq. Though Allstrong's security work was dangerous and demanding, ex-officers who were bored or broke or both in civilian life often jumped at the chance to resurrect their careers, their self-esteem, and their bank accounts, and to once again utilize the special skills that had served them well in the military.

And nowhere were they needed more than in Anbar. As Jack Allstrong had predicted in August, the rebuilding of the electrical tower infrastructure in that province was turning out to be a gold mine for the company, albeit a costly one in terms of human life. Allstrong had by now put more than five hundred men to work on this latest contract, which initially bid out at forty million dollars, although it had grown to more than one hundred million in the past seven months. Allstrong Security, Jack liked to point out, was in 2003 the fastest-growing company in the world, outstripping Google, compliments of U.S. largesse and Jack's ability to surf the chaos of the reconstruction.

But in Anbar, the company also had already lost thirty-six of Kuvan Krekar's men, and Kuvan's supply chain of bodies was growing thin and dispirited. Beyond that, Kuvan had been facing severe competition from another broker named Mahmoud al-Khalil, who was not only supplying cheaper workers but was perhaps terrorizing and even killing Kuvan's people to discourage others from signing on. Why? So that Mahmoud and not Kuvan could pocket the extremely lucrative cash commissions. Well, with the recent untimely demise of his paterfamilias in Menlo Park, Mahmoud would hopefully soon conclude that competing directly with Allstrong's chosen subcontractor was not a sound business decision.

Hefting his duffel bag, Nolan let himself into his townhome through the garage door to the kitchen. He walked through the living room, stopped in his office and turned on his computer, then went into his bedroom, where he dropped the duffel bag on his bed, then returned to his desk and checked his e-mail and—first things first—made sure he'd been paid. He had.

With that taken care of, Nolan went back into his bedroom and started to unpack. Grabbing a pair of pants, he turned and opened the closet, and stopped short.

Something was not right.

Nolan didn't spend much time thinking about his military-ingrained penchant for order, but when he woke up in the mornings, he automatically made his bed with hospital corners so that the covers were tight enough to bounce a coin off them. The spare shoes were always shined and perfectly aligned on the floor of the closet. He hung his shirts and pants in order from light to dark, the hangers spaced with an automatic and practiced precision.

Now he stared at the row of hangers. He didn't specifically remember taking down the shirts and pants that he'd packed for his trip, but could not imagine that he would have taken down his clothes and left the hangers spaced unevenly as they were now. His eyes went to the backpack on the top shelf. He had lined it up exactly with the break in the hangers between his shirts and his pants, and now it was clearly centered over the shirts. Reaching up, he pulled it toward him, relieved by the familiar weight. He opened it and saw that nothing—not the grenades, the gun, or the ammo—was gone.

Which was weird.

Maybe he'd imagined that the hangers had been moved. It didn't seem possible that someone would have broken in here and not taken the grenades and the gun.

But it wouldn't be smart to take chances. Reaching into the backpack, he removed the Beretta and slammed one of the clips into place, then racked a bullet into the chamber. He dropped the backpack next to the duffel bag on his bed and went to check the bathroom, where an intruder might still be lurking. Finding no one there, he went back out into the living room to the front door, where the piece of Scotch tape that he'd laid over the connection between the door and its jamb was now stuck under the jamb.

Somebody had definitely been here.

Methodically now, he went back out to the garage, where he patted down the empty backpacks hanging against the wall. He was about to start opening the drawers when he straightened up, stopping himself.

He didn't see how it could be remotely possible, but it occurred to him that if one of the members of Khalil's extended family could have somehow traced the patriarch's execution back to him, their method of retribution might include a bomb—open a drawer and it goes off. By the same token, his experience with IEDs in Iraq told him that if there was a bomb, someone would have been hiding somewhere outside, seen him drive up, and sent an electrical pulse to detonate the device after he was inside. Alternatively, Nolan could trigger the bomb himself by switching on any one of a dozen electrical connections in the house. But any of those scenarios contemplated the possibility that someone had identified him as the Khalils' killer.

Which from Nolan's perspective was flatly not possible. He'd made no mistakes. Therefore, there was no bomb. He'd also already turned on his computer, and several lights. Walking back out to the garage, this time he opened all the drawers. Back in the kitchen, he did the same. Opened the refrigerator. He had no idea what, if anything, he was looking for, but someone had been in his house in his absence, and if it hadn't been to take something, what did that leave?

He just didn't know.

Back in his office, he sat at his desk, laid the gun on it, and stared for a minute again at his computer. Picking up his telephone, he got the pulsing dial tone that meant he had messages, and entered his password.

The first message was from an obviously very distraught, though composed, Tara, who had called him on Monday night. "Ron. Evan Scholler came by to visit me today at the school. We had a long talk with one another and he told me some things that shocked me—you probably have a good idea what they were.

"I don't know what to say to you, other than that I just want you to know how completely violated I feel. And how used. I don't know how you could have lied to me so much. I'm leaving this message on your machine on purpose because I don't want to talk to you, or even see you anymore. I can't believe you've done this. It just doesn't seem possible that anyone could be so cruel and so selfish. I'm so sorry for who you are, Ron, but not for what I'm saying. Good-bye. Don't call me. Don't come by. Just stay away. I mean it."

The phone still at his ear, he hadn't let up his grip yet on the receiver when the next message began. The call had come this morning, about six hours ago. "Mr. Nolan. My name is Jacob Freed. I'm a special agent with the Federal Bureau of Investigation, and I wondered if we might be able to take a few minutes of your time to talk to you about a routine matter involving national security that's come to our attention. I don't mean to be unnecessarily vague, but I'm sure you understand that these days some things are best left unsaid over the telephone. If you could call me for an appointment at your earliest convenience when you get in, or alternatively, I'll try to get back to you in the next day or two. My number is . . ."

When Nolan finally hung up, he sat unmoving with his right arm outstretched and his hand covering the Beretta. After a minute or two, he let go of the gun and moved his hand over to the mouse. As soon as he saw the "My Pictures" icon, he realized that he'd made an error by not erasing that file before he'd gone away. Opening it now, intending to close the barn door after the horse had escaped, he checked the access record and saw that someone had, indeed, looked at the file two days before—the same Monday that Tara had spoken to Evan Scholler.

Though it might be too late, he still thought it would be better to delete the file now, so that if the FBI came and looked . . .

Except he knew that there wasn't really any such thing anymore as truly deleting something. Experts could always retrieve whatever it was from the hard drive.

Still, his finger hovered over the mouse as he stared at one of the many pictures he'd taken of Mr. Khalil's house while he was working on access and egress. One click and all of that at least would be gone for now.

Sitting back, his eyes narrowing, he took his hand abruptly off the mouse. Suddenly, he decided that he did not want to delete the picture file after all. Although he would have to remove the memory chip from the digital camera in the desk drawer and get rid of it. Tapping his index fingernail against his front teeth, he sat as if in a trance for a full minute, and then another one.

The idea looked perfect from every angle.

He reached again for the telephone.

"AGENT FREED, please."

"This is he."

"Agent Freed. My name is Ron Nolan. You left me a

message about a national security matter and asked me to call for an appointment."

"Yes, sir, I did. Thanks for getting back to me."

"I think maybe I should be the one thanking you, sir. I've just returned from a business trip. While I've been gone, somebody let themselves into my house. I was going to call the regular police, but then I got your message. I don't know if you know it, but I do some sensitive work with Allstrong Security, a government contractor in Iraq, and I thought what you wanted to talk about might have something to do with that."

"Well, as I mentioned, perhaps it would be better to meet in person to talk about the issue that's come up with us, although if you're reporting a robbery or burglary, you should probably call the regular police. That's not really our jurisdiction."

"Agent Freed, this wasn't a robbery. Whoever it was didn't take anything. They left something. Plus, they messed with my computer. I don't know what it's all about, but it's almost like somebody's trying to plant something on me."

"Like what?"

"Well, I just found one thing, but there might be more. I'm afraid to look in case he's planted a bomb someplace."

"Who's he?"

"I don't know. I mean the person who broke in."

"Okay. So what's the one thing?"

"This is what's so weird. It's a backpack full of ammunition and, you're not going to believe this, it looks like about a half dozen hand grenades."

"Hand grenades?"

"Yes, sir. As you may know, I've been over to Iraq several times. I know the ordnance. And these look like fragmentation grenades to me."

FREED AND HIS PARTNER, a middle-aged fireplug named Marcia Riggio, sat with Nolan on the small, oak-shaded back patio. Inside the townhouse, a three-man team of forensics specialists, having already confiscated the backpack with its contents, were fingerprinting every clean surface and cataloging anything that might be of interest—Nolan's other gun from the bed's headboard, the digital camera in the desk drawer, downloading his hard drive.

Nolan didn't want to rush anything with these federal cops. He didn't want to appear to point them in any specific direction. But now, as Agent Riggio looked up from her notepad, Nolan decided that it was getting to be the time. "Let me ask you something," he said. "Is there any scenario you can think of that makes any sense of this to you?"

The two agents exchanged a glance. Riggio got the nod from Freed and took point. "Do you have any enemies?" she asked.

Nolan frowned. "Even if I did," he said, "what does this do to hurt me? Unless I pulled the pin on one of those grenades, which anybody who knows me knows I'm not going to do."

"Maybe it's not about hurting you," Riggio went on. "Maybe it's about framing you."

"For what?"

But Freed stepped in. "Before we get to that," he said, "let's go back to your enemies."

This time, Nolan broke a grin. "I don't see it, really. I

like people. I really do, and they tend to like me. My boss thinks it's a flaw in my character." He shrugged. "So I'd have to say no. No enemies."

"Okay," Riggio said. "How about rivals?"

"In business?"

"Business, pleasure, whatever."

He took his sweet time, savoring the anticipation. "The only even remotely..." He shook his head. "No, never mind."

Freed jumped on it. "What?"

"Nothing, really. Just a guy I knew in Iraq who used to date my girlfriend. But that was a long time ago."

"If he's in Iraq," Freed said, "he's out of this."

"Well, he's home now. Here."

"And he's not over her? Your girlfriend?" Riggio asked.

"I don't know. He had a hard time with it at first, but now I haven't seen the guy in months. But, look, this is a dead end. He's a good guy. In fact, he's a cop. He'd never—"

Freed interrupted. "He's a cop?"

"Yeah, here in Redwood City. His name's Evan Scholler. He got hurt over there and they let him out early."

"So he would have had access to these types of grenades over there?"

"Yeah, but he wouldn't have taken any home. He did a few months at Walter Reed before he came out here."

"Soldiers have been known to send illegal ordnance and contraband stateside as souvenirs on the slow boat," Riggio said. "It's a problem. It happens all the time."

"Well, I don't know what Evan would have . . . I mean, what's the point of putting hand grenades in my closet? I'm not going to blow myself up with them. It's not like they're going to get rid of me as his rival."

Riggio and Freed again shared a glance, and again exchanged the imperceptible nod. Riggio came forward, elbows on her knees. "Do you know a man named Ibrahim Khalil?"

"No," Nolan said. "Should I?"

"He was a local businessman with ties to Iraq. He and his wife were killed last weekend."

"Well, I'm sorry to hear that, but I've been out of town. I haven't heard about it."

"Would Evan Scholler have known you were gone?"

Nolan shrugged. "If he knew where I lived, he could have just checked to see if my car was in the garage. If it is, I'm home."

"Has he ever, to your knowledge, been up here?" Riggio asked.

"No. As I say, we're not exactly pals anymore." As though it had just occurred to him, Nolan added, "But he's a cop. He could find out where I live easy enough, couldn't he? That's what it looks like he's done."

Freed picked it up. "So Sunday morning early you were with this same girlfriend that this Evan Scholler likes?"

"Tara," Nolan said. "Tara Wheatley. And, yes, she's the one. So what's this all about?"

"Those pictures you couldn't identify on your computer?" Riggio said. "They were pictures of Mr. Khalil's house before somebody killed them and hit it with a fragmentation grenade, and before it burned down."

"A frag grenade..." Nolan didn't want to overplay his apparent naïveté. Both Freed and Riggio knew that he had seen combat, and they might even know more than that. This was about the moment in the interview that,

against his own deep-seated reluctance to believe ill of a
fellow soldier, he might finally come to accept the apparent truth. So he nodded somberly and met both of their
gazes in turn. "He's trying to set me up. Christ, he killed
them, didn't he?"

[16]

THE EARLY EVENING SUN BAKED the parking lot
and the landing outside Tara's apartment. She could feel
its warmth in her hand through the closed and locked
front door as she stood behind it. "I told you, I won't see
you. I don't want to talk to you."

"I need to talk to you, though, T. Please. I need to explain."

"There's nothing you can say to me. Nothing I'd believe. I can't believe you'd even come by here and try this.
You *lied* to me, Ron. You've been living a lie for all these
months."

"No. I've been living the truth. And the truth is that I
love you."

"You don't lie to someone you love."

"You're right. That was a mistake. I shouldn't have
done that. I am so sorry."

"Sorry's not enough. I don't want to talk about this. I
need you to go away now."

"I can't, T. I can't leave it like this. Could you please
open up? Just so I could see you." When she didn't answer, he went on, talking at the door. "Listen, I knew you
were confused about Evan, especially the timing about
how we started. I thought that if you heard he'd been

wounded . . . that you'd feel sorry for him, or like you owed him another chance . . . and that whatever happened, somehow I'd lose you."

"And now that's what's happened."

"I can't accept that, Tara. I didn't think he was going to live. I didn't think it would matter."

"That's not the question, Ron. You lied to me. Everything we did was false, don't you understand that? If you couldn't stand to have Evan in the picture on any level, even if he was dying, how were we—you and me—ever going to amount to anything anyway?"

"We did amount to something."

"No, we didn't. That's the worst part. We supposedly trusted each other. Now that can't ever happen again. Don't you see that?"

"Because of one mistake?"

"You really don't see it, do you?"

"I see somebody who was terrified he was going to lose the woman he loved, who wanted to make sure they had some time together without the distraction of a wounded ex-boyfriend, who might never be coming home alive anyway."

"That's all you thought Evan was to me, a distraction?" The chain lock rattled and the door opened the couple of inches that the chain allowed. "I'm not going to yell at you through the door anymore. I just need you to go. You're actually scaring me now, all right?"

"How can I be scaring you, T? I'm here begging you just to listen to me, to give me another chance." He shifted his weight. "Is it because of him?"

"Do I still love him, you mean? I don't know about that. I lost track of who he was, and now I don't know what I feel. But I know you're scaring me now. And why? Because you lied. And lied and lied."

"I lied once, T. Once to try to protect what we were starting to have, that's all."

"No, it isn't, Ron. What about Masbah?"

"What about it?"

"You firing on that innocent family. I Googled you and read all about it. You started that whole thing."

Ron hung his head, wiped his brow against the glaring heat. "I was trying to protect the convoy. I thought the car was on a suicide mission. You had to have been there, but I can't apologize for what I did."

"The report said they'd stopped way back."

"You can't believe everything you read. It was a damn close call and if I waited another two seconds, we all could have been dead."

"Most of you died anyway. How about that?"

"Not my fault. The point is that if I fired too soon, and I'm not saying I did, it was on the side of caution."

"Ron. You killed an entire innocent family! Doesn't that bother you at all?"

"It bothers me a lot, T. It makes me sick to think about it. But I can't say, given the circumstances, that I wouldn't do the same thing again. It was a split-second, life-or-death decision, and I decided I had to try to save my men."

"That's not what Evan says, Ron. And he was there too."

"I guess he doesn't mention the part about me pulling him out of the line of fire and getting him out of there alive."

"So now you're the hero?"

"I'm not saying that. I'm saying Evan's memory maybe

isn't the most reliable thing in the universe right now. I'm also saying that he's got a reason to make me look bad."

"He didn't make you lie."

"How many times do I have to apologize for that? However many it takes, I'll do it."

"And what about the other lies?"

"What other lies? There were no other lies."

"How about me ripping up that last letter that you delivered to me?"

"You didn't rip it up."

"Right. But you told Evan I did."

"No, I didn't. Did he tell you that?"

"Yes."

"Then he's lying."

"I don't believe that, Ron. And what about when you visited him at Walter Reed, when you told him I said he'd made his own bed and he could sleep in it?"

Nolan looked down and shook his head.

"What?" she asked him.

"That's not true, either, T. Why would I say that? I went to see him to see how he was doing, if he was going to be all right. That's all. He's the one who didn't want to hear anything about you."

"That's not what he told me."

"No, I guess not. And why, do you think, would that be?"

Through the crack in the opening, he saw her close her eyes, lean her head up against the wall next to the door. He was wearing her down, getting to her. "Do you want to hear something else?" he asked. "Something truly scary, especially if you think your friend Evan is so innocent and so nice. You want to hear what he left in my house after he broke into it last weekend?"

* * *

AFTER TARA WATCHED Nolan finally drive away, she went into her living room, sat down, and put her feet up on the coffee table. Templing her fingers over her lips, she closed her eyes and tried to get herself to breathe deeply. A whirlwind of conflicting possibilities and emotions was literally causing her body to shake.

Ron Nolan had maintained a sustained falsehood, but did that mean that every word out of his mouth was a lie? She hadn't expected him to show up here, or to own up to the lies upon which he'd based their relationship. Perhaps the truth was that he loved her and had made a mistake. A terrible mistake, yes, and one he sincerely regretted.

Just like killing the Iraqi family.

What was the truth in that story? Had he been justified shooting when he did? And, in fact, had he pulled Evan to safety and saved his life? They'd been outnumbered and surrounded. If there had been a bomb in the car, none of them would have survived. Might she have made the same decision to fire under the same circumstances?

It struck her forcefully that maybe it was she who was being unfair. Ron Nolan had always treated her well, better than well. He'd literally saved her life that time in San Francisco. And surely his appearance today to beg her forgiveness—even while admitting he'd done the unforgivable—spoke to a depth of character she'd never given him credit for.

People grew, people changed, people learned from their mistakes. And if what Ron had told her about Evan were true? He might himself be in danger.

No. She could not believe that. That was more of Ron's poison, trying to get inside her.

After seeing Evan in her classroom, and then the intimacy last night, she knew what she felt—not just the still-powerful physical bond, but a connection that went down to the bottom of her soul. It was irrational, chemical, fundamental, and she knew that she would never feel it with anyone else.

But now, according to Ron, Evan had lied to her too. A known liar accusing another of lying. It was like game theory, where "A" always told the truth, and "B" always lied, but you didn't know which was the truth-teller and which the liar. Who did you believe?

Could Evan have made up the story about Ron saying she'd ripped up his letter? Or the Walter Reed moment? Evan admitted that his memory had been faulty, especially early on. Could he have lied to her and not even known he was lying? Finally, could Evan have broken into Ron's house and tried to frame him for a murder? A murder that he himself had committed?

Tara could not believe any part of that. She knew who Evan was. Even after all this time and all of their problems, she knew his heart.

He was not a liar. He was not a murderer.

And this meant that Ron Nolan was lying to her again. And lying to the FBI. And possibly to the local police.

Liars deal in lies.

Suddenly she opened her eyes and sat up.

She needed to get to Evan. She needed to warn him.

[17]

THOUGH IT WASN'T really a hangout for cops, the Old Town Traven wasn't far from the police station downtown, and it served a decent-tasting though nutritionally suspect happy-hour spread of chicken wings, peanuts in the shell, tiny meatballs in gravy, and popcorn. Even though happy hour had officially ended more than two hours before, there was still plenty of food available. The Traven didn't exactly pack 'em in, and now Evan, who'd changed out of his uniform at the station, and his bowling partner Stan Paganini, also in street clothes, held down one end of the bar all by themselves.

Between his low-watt nervousness over the envelope he'd mailed to the FBI and his need to keep himself occupied so that he wouldn't do something stupid and try to get in touch with Tara until she'd dumped Nolan, if she actually was going to dump him after all, Evan felt that a drink or ten wouldn't be amiss. Pass the difficult night in a haze and see what tomorrow brings.

Now it was half past nine and he and Paganini were on to the name of the place. Due either to the marginal intelligence of its owners, a drunken mistake, a simple typo, or all of the above, the neon sign above the door read "Old Town Traven." The place's business cards also had *tavern* spelled incorrectly, so Evan decided it was probably that the proprietors just weren't too bright and certainly had not been the San Mateo County Spelling Bee champions, as he had been when he'd been in eighth grade.

"No, you weren't." Paganini stabbed the last meatball on his plate with a toothpick and washed it down with a good swig of his gin and tonic.

"Was too. I won on *hygiene,* which is almost unfair, it's such an easy word."

"Wait! Don't tell me." Paganini took in a little more of his drink. "H, Y," he began.

"Good so far."

"G." He paused, glanced at Evan.

"I before E." Evan tipped his vodka rocks all the way up. "Except after C."

"Don't tell me!"

"I just did. 'Or when sounded like *a* as in *neighbor* or *weigh.*'"

"Okay, trying the old head-fake double reverse. I get it. But I'm on to you, boy. So here goes, again. H, Y, G, E …"

"*Buzz!* You're out." Evan shook his head. "I just told you, *i* before *e,* Stan. I told you the whole damn poem. You think I was making that up?"

"I thought you were trying to trick me. And then *g* is close to *c* soundwise, so it was the exception."

"Nope. It's the rule." Evan spelled the word out.

"That doesn't sound right. I'm going to look it up at home."

"You want to bet?"

"No, I don't want to bet. But you're right, that's a pretty simple word to win the whole county spelling bee on."

"Well, harder than *tavern,* anyway. And they got that one wrong here. Twice. Three times? Who knows, maybe more. They might have it on the matchbooks."

"Yeah, well . . ." Paganini shifted his bulk and cried out. "Hey!"

"What?"

"Sat on something." Paganini slid himself off his stool and was digging in his pants pockets. Plopping down a large set of keys in the bar's gutter, he reached in again and produced a heavy item that he plunked onto the bar. "Knucks," he said.

At one of their bowling league nights, the cops had gotten into a discussion about various common enhancements to a man's natural defensive arsenal. Brass knuckles had featured large in Paganini's experience, and Evan said he'd never actually encountered them.

Now he picked up the hunk of fitted metal. "Heavy sucker."

"Get hit with it, you're clocked," Paganini said. "Although who fights with their fists anymore, huh? Nowadays, you know you're going to be in a fight, you pack heat, am I right?"

"Maybe you don't want to kill who you're fighting?"

Paganini chuckled. "Yeah, like that happens anymore. Go ahead, put 'em on. Keep 'em if you want. I collect the ones I get off perps. I got a half dozen like these at home."

As Evan was pocketing the brass knuckles, the bartender, a midthirties slacker with a wispy effort at a beard, suddenly appeared in front of them. Paganini looked down at his glass. "We empty again?"

"Seem to be," Evan said. "Let's double us up here, would you, Jeff?"

Jeff looked from one of them to the other. "You guys walking home from here? You pull a DUI, they can come back and get us."

"We're not going to get any DUI," Paganini said. He reached around into the back of his pants and pulled out his wallet, opened it to the badge. "Pour us a couple more, would you, please, and I won't report the obvious health violation keeping those meatballs out so long. Awesome meatballs, by the way. Remind me of my mom's." He cocked his head over toward Evan. "I believe the gentleman requested a couple of doubles."

Jeff took a beat, nodded, and then turned to get fresh glasses and ice.

Evan lowered his voice, leaned into Stan. "Am I slurring?"

"Nope. You're as eloquent as Cicero. How about me?"

"How about you what?"

"Am I slurring?"

"No."

"You keeping track of where we are?"

"The Traven," Paganini replied.

"Drinkwise, Stan. Drinkwise. I know where we physically are."

"Four, I think, maybe. Couple of doubles is six, and we've been here"—he checked his watch—"three hours. So I figure we're blowing point oh five, six, max, which means we're totally cool to drive and will be for the foreseeable future."

But Evan—all too familiar with the average cop's rationalization genius when drinking—was doing his own math. He was fairly certain they'd had more than four drinks already, maybe as many as six or seven, and if they had a couple of doubles on top of that, two doubles each, that would take him up to eleven generous pours. He was just about to say that maybe he'd better stick with singles to give them a better chance to metabolize off, when the bar's door opened. Glancing up at the mirror behind the bar, he put a hand on Paganini's arm and without a word stood up and turned around.

"YOUR MOM SAID this was where she might look for you." From their table in the back, where they couldn't be heard by anyone else, Tara looked around the seedy bar. "Nice place. You come here often?"

"Sometimes. Nights get long, and I go crazy at home. Some nights I bowl. Or read or something. Two days ago I was at Mom and Dad's. I've got a life."

"Of course you do. I didn't mean that."

"Yeah, you do." He sat back and folded his arms. "You disapprove of me being here." He looked at her, flat affect. "You come down here to bust my chops?"

"No," she said. "No. I don't mean to do that. I came down here to . . . well, just to talk to you again."

Jeff showed up with two drinks and put them down at their table. "And for the lady?"

"Maybe I'll just have one of his. And some cranberry juice."

When Jeff left, Tara pulled her chair up, reached out across the table, and touched Evan's hand. "I'm really not here to criticize you, Evan. It's just that the other night you said you'd been drinking too much and were trying to slow down a little."

"Yeah, well, I guess I'm not succeeding tonight. What's

that look? You don't think a couple of drinks is a good idea?"

"I didn't say that. If you need it, you need it." She pulled his hand from his glass and covered it with hers. "Look," she whispered, "I don't know even any small part of what you've been through. You're the one who said it would be better if you didn't need so much alcohol."

"That would be better. I agree." Defiantly, he picked up his glass and took a long drink. "But that doesn't seem to be what I'm doing right now, which is trying to keep things together."

"What things?"

"My job, for one. What happened with my guys in Iraq. Why I'm still alive. Anger. Guilt. You name it." He brought his eyes up, unfocused, heavy-lidded. "And all those are before we even get to you."

Jeff showed up with Tara's cranberry juice, placed it on the table in front of her, turned, and left. A silence settled. Evan again lifted his glass, then put it back down. "You want to tell me about you and Ron?"

"There isn't any me and Ron. Not anymore. How can you even ask that after . . . ?" She swallowed. "I called him after I saw you at school on Monday. It's over." Sighing, she went on. "But then this afternoon he came by."

"Didn't take the hint, huh? How did that go?"

"I never let him in. He told me he never said I'd ripped up your letter."

Evan took that in with a solemn nod. "The guy's a congenital liar."

"Evan, look at me." Her eyes bored into his. "You're swearing to me that he said that? You didn't make that up to make him look bad? I know it's awful of me to ask, but

I've got to ask you straight out. I've got to know for absolute certain."

Evan covered Tara's hand with both of his. "I swear to God," he said. "I swear on the memory of the lives of my men, I have never lied to you."

Tara let out a long, shuddering breath, as though something that had been squeezing her had suddenly let go. "He also denied what he told you I said in the hospital, about making your own bed and you could lie in it."

Evan shook his head, almost in admiration. "Old Ron was on a roll." Lifting his glass, he finished his drink, reached across, and took the second one from in front of Tara. "He said it, all right."

"He said something else today too."

"I can't wait to hear it. What? Did I kill somebody now?"

But Tara had straightened up. "God, Evan, why do you say that?"

"What?"

"That you'd killed somebody."

"I didn't. I was kidding. What?"

She started to talk and stopped herself, then started again. "Ron told me you broke into his house last weekend and left stuff that you'd somehow smuggled out of Iraq to make it look like Ron had killed this man and his wife, when in fact it was you who'd killed them."

Evan's shoulders sagged. He slumped in his chair. He lifted his drink and put himself on the outside of it in one gulp.

"Evan?"

"That fucker. That *motherfucker*."

She went on. "He said you'd brought over hand grenades and guns to his place that you'd smuggled out of

Iraq. And planted incriminating pictures on his computer."

Evan's body molded itself back into his hard chair. He spoke slowly, with great caution lest his thick tongue betray him. "This guy who got killed, Khalil. He was Iraqi. Think about it. Think about Ron's real job over here . . ."

"What do you mean? Ron's a recruiter mostly. He's . . ."

"No, listen. He's a mercenary mostly. Those were his weapons, his grenades, his pictures."

Tara sat back and crossed her arms. "You mean you *do* know about this? How could you know about this? Or about Ron?"

He just looked at her, opened his mouth, closed it again.

She came forward now. "Are you telling me he wasn't lying about you breaking into his house? Did you do that, Evan? Tell me you didn't do that."

"No, I . . ." Evan shook his head, hard, trying to clear away the fog of alcohol. "I mean, okay, I went in."

"You broke into Ron's house? And did what?"

"Nothing. I didn't do anything. No," he said, "that's not true. I got on his computer and got pictures of this guy's house before it burned down."

"Why did you do that?"

" 'Cause Ron's a murderer, Tara. He killed this guy and this was the evidence . . ."

"So what did you do with it?"

"Mailed it to somebody."

"The FBI, you mean?" She hit the table with her palm. "Did you send your diskette to the FBI, Evan? Because Ron had the FBI over at his house today, and he told them you'd planted all that stuff there. And now you tell me you were actually inside, so they'll find your hair or fingerprints or something, don't you see that? He's trying to have you framed for this." She ran both of her hands through her hair, over her scalp, down to her neck. "God, God, God, how can this be happening? They may be at your apartment right now, wanting to talk to you, do you realize that? And then what are you going to do? What are you going to tell them?"

He stared blankly at her for a long minute, then brought his hand up and chewed at the knuckle of his index finger. "Enough of this shit." His words starting to slur.

"Evan." She gripped at his hands. "He's already got the FBI in on it, don't you understand? It's already happening."

"Can't be. I've got to stop him."

"No. Don't you do anything. Get a lawyer or talk to one of your bosses. Maybe they can deliver a message, get something through to Ron. But you stay out of it personally. Ron's dangerous, Evan. And he's out to get you. You've got to be smart. Get sober and get a plan."

Evan slammed a heavy hand on the table. "What do you mean, get sober? Is that what everything's about, whether I'm sober or not? I'm sober right now, enough for fucking Ron Nolan."

"Evan," she pleaded, "you're not. Listen to yourself. You don't swear when you're sober. You don't slur when you're sober." She stood up, reached out, and touched his arm. "Look, why don't you come home now with me. I could drive us."

"And then what?" Evan's thick voice trembled with rage. "And then the FBI finds me there? Or at work tomorrow? What do I do then?"

"Come home with me. We can talk about it and work something out." She let her arm fall along his sleeve and took his hand. "Come on. Really."

"No!" He pulled his hand from hers, turned away. His shoulders rose and fell and then he turned back to her. "I am not fucking dealing with him anymore! This has got to end. It can't go on."

"You're right, but it can't end tonight, Evan."

"Yes, it damn well can."

Tara kept her voice low, conciliatory, restrained. "Evan, come on. There's no way you can do anything the way you are now, so don't be crazy. You're just really mad—"

"Way more than that, Tara. I'm going to kill the son of a bitch."

"Shh, shh, shh." She moved up and put her fingers to his lips. "Don't talk like that. That's just crazy drink talk. Let's just the two of us get out of here and—"

"Hey!" Taking her hand down, roughly, away from his mouth. "Listen to me!" Low and deadly earnest. "It's got to stop! It can't go on! It's not about fucking drinking. Are you hearing me? It's about honor. Who I am. What he's done to us! Don't you see that?"

"Yes, I do see that. You're right. You're completely right. But this isn't the time to fix all that." She moved in close and stood straight before him, arms at her sides. "Please, Evan. I'm going to ask you one more time. Please come home with me. Whatever it is, we'll work it out together. I promise."

But the glaze in his eyes was all that answered her. Standing, weaving slightly, he gripped the back of his chair. "Enough's enough," he said.

She looked him in the face one last time. "I'm begging you," she said. "Please."

If he heard her at all, he didn't show it. He stared blankly ahead at her, shaking his head, shaking his head. Then he started walking toward the door.

"Evan, please," she called after him. "Wait."

He stopped, and for a second she thought that she'd convinced him. He turned back to her. "Leave me alone," he said. "I know what I've got to do and I'm gonna do it."

And then he turned and again started walking unsteadily toward the door.

PART THREE
[2005]

[18]

TARA HAD NEVER FELT so grateful for her job.

It was getting to the end of the year, and her kids were handing in their big reports and concluding their projects on the ancient world in preparation for the school's open house on Friday night, when all the work would be displayed in the classrooms. In Tara's room, they had rearranged all the desks to make room for the papier mâché pyramids, the dioramas of the growing cycle along the Nile, the plumbing schemes for the residences of the pharaohs. Hieroglyphics, the early domestic cat, the library at Alexandria, Moses and the Exodus.

So all day and much of the nights of Thursday and Friday, Tara was busy organizing and tending to last-minute crises among her students and, often, their families. She had no time to contact Evan to find out what, if anything, had happened after he'd stormed out on her on Wednesday night. And, truth to tell, she wasn't too inclined to call him anyway. She thought she would let him take a few days to sober up and get over his embarrassment about how he'd acted. Then, after he'd called her and apologized, they'd see where they were. But in the meanwhile, she had her job and her kids. She thought that a couple of days' respite from the emotional turmoil and upheaval surrounding Ron and Evan might do every-body involved a world of good.

Saturday, she slept in until nearly ten o'clock, then went down to the pool and swam a hundred laps. Coming back upstairs to her apartment, she showered and threw on some shorts and a T-shirt, made a salad for lunch, and after that dozed off watching a tennis match on TV. When she woke up, she graded the last of the written reports for another hour or so. At a little after four, she was just finishing up the last one when her doorbell rang. Checking the peephole, she saw Eileen Scholler, her face blotched from crying.

LIMPING, SCABBED, AND BRUISED in his orange jail jumpsuit, Evan entered his side of the visiting room chained to twenty other men. Watching the line enter, Tara stood among a loose knot of mostly women in a kind of bullpen waiting area on their side of the Plexiglas screen that separated the visitors from the inmates. A row of facing pairs of talking stations bisected the room from one end to the other.

Tara had to fight to hold back her tears as they unfastened Evan from the chain of men to whom he'd been attached. He saw her and started to raise a welcoming hand, but his wrists were still attached to the chain around his waist. The guard directed him to one of the desks and Tara excused herself through the now-pressing crowd of visitors and sat herself at last facing him. There was a hole in the Plexiglas through which they were supposed to talk.

It was Wednesday, his fourth day in custody, and the first day that his injuries had healed enough to allow him to walk unaided and to see visitors. In the first moment, neither could find anything to say. They looked at each other, then away, and back again.

How could either of them be here? How could it have come to this?

Finally, Evan leaned forward, shrugged, manufactured some kind of brave face. "I guess I should have gone home with you after all."

Tara didn't trust herself to say anything.

"I am so sorry," he said.

Tara opened her mouth, but again no words came. Now, unexpectedly, tears began to overflow onto her cheeks. She didn't try to stop them.

"Oh, babe," he said. Then, "I don't think…" He shook his head and looked at her. His shoulders rose and fell. "I don't believe I killed him."

Tara was still reeling from the bare fact that Ron Nolan was dead. Putting Evan together with that on any level wasn't yet possible for her; the idea couldn't bear any scrutiny. Instead, she found herself fighting a sense of un-reality that permeated her waking hours as though she were living within a bad dream from which she couldn't will herself awake.

"I wouldn't have killed him," he said, then waited for her until he couldn't take it any longer. "Can you say something, please?"

"What am I supposed to say? What do you want me to say? I'm here. That says something, doesn't it?"

"I hope it does."

"I hope so too. But I'm not sure. Are you hurt?"

"I'll be all right."

"Will you? When will that be? What does that mean?"

He just looked at her.

* * *

TEN WEEKS PASSED before they saw each other again.

In that time, Evan was charged with the murder of Ron Nolan, but no charges were brought against him for the Khalil slayings—the district attorney, Doug Falbrock, decided that the evidence tying Evan to those murders wasn't strong enough to convict. As almost always in a murder case, bail was denied.

Tara had cleaned up her classroom and then hung around her apartment for the first couple of weeks of summer. On the Fourth of July, she went up to her parents' condominium to spend the holiday near Homewood on Lake Tahoe and decided on more or less the spur of the moment that she wasn't going to go back home. She couldn't bear reading about Evan every day in the newspapers down there. She needed to be away from the whole thing—the requests for interviews with reporters, her proximity to the jail, the expectations and/or accusations of people who didn't know her. She wound up staying alone at Homewood until late August—reading, running at altitude, dead sober, swimming in the cold lake.

Finally, it was time to come and get her classroom ready for the new year. She drove down on a Thursday morning, cleaned up the dust that had gathered in her apartment, stopped by the school, and started in again on the familiar yearly routine. And somewhere in the middle of it, she realized that she'd come to her decision. Finishing for the day at a little after three o'clock, she drove directly to the house Evan had grown up in, parked out front in the street, and knocked at the door.

Eileen greeted her as she always did—effusively,

sincerely—with a welcoming smile, a hug, a kiss on both cheeks. They went together into the airy, modern kitchen and made catch-up small talk until Eileen had poured them both iced teas and they were sitting across from each other at the table in the nook that looked out at the Eden that was the Schollers' backyard. At last, Eileen cocked her head in her trademark fashion. "So what brings you around today?"

"I wanted to ask you if you think Evan would want to see me again."

"I think he'd want that more than anything."

"I wasn't too good the one time, you know? Did he tell you about that?"

"He didn't give me too many details. He said it wasn't very easy between you two. But he didn't blame you. Nobody blames you—I mean we don't—you know that, don't you?"

Tara nodded. "I just didn't know where to put any of it. Everything happened so fast. Finding out about all the lies Ron told me, and then thinking Evan and I, we might get another chance. Then that last night in the bar . . . where I thought. . ." She stopped, swallowed, shrugged.

Eileen reached over and patted her hand. "It's all right. If it means anything, and I think it does, Evan has no memory of what happened over there. He doesn't believe he killed Ron. He says that's just not who he is. He never would have done that."

"I believe him."

"So do I."

"But somebody did."

"Maybe somebody connected to these Khalils. That's what Everett says he believes."

"Everett?"

"Everett Washburn. His lawyer." A rueful smile. "His *expensive* lawyer." She waved away the comment. "But that's all right. We've got enough savings, thank God. I can't think of anything better to spend it on."

Tara hesitated, then came out with it. "They want me to testify about that last night. Against him."

"Everett said they would. I think it'll be all right if you just tell the truth."

"The truth wasn't too pretty, Eileen."

"No, I understand. But you can't do anything about that."

Tara twirled the iced tea in its little ring of condensation. "I could marry him," she said.

Sitting back and straightening in her chair, Eileen drew in a big breath and let it out. "Well . . . and here I've been thinking these old bones would never be surprised by anything again. But I don't think you'll have to take it that far."

"Not just to keep from testifying, Eileen. I've had all summer to think about how I feel about all this stuff. And over the weeks, it's just gotten clearer and clearer. Whatever happens, I'm on Evan's side. If he still wants me. If he'll see me."

Again, Eileen patted Tara's hand. "Oh, I wouldn't worry about that at all, dear. Not in the least little bit. I'm going down there to visit him in the next fifteen minutes if you'd like to come along."

WHEN EVAN SAW TARA standing next to his mother on the other side of the room, he turned his face upward and closed his eyes. His body seemed to heave in relief. Tara came to the window—Eileen waiting in the back—and sat down across from him.

"Hi," she said.

"Hi."

"You look a lot better than last time."

"I feel a lot better too. How have you been?"

"Good. Gone. I'm sorry it's been so long."

He shrugged.

"I was trying to figure things out," she said.

"Any luck?"

"Pretty much. I finally got so I could see what ought to have been obvious all along."

"Which is what?"

"That if I'd have just gotten down off my high horse when this all started, when you deployed . . . I was just afraid I was going to lose you, that you'd be killed. I couldn't believe you'd be willing to sacrifice everything we had. I was so mad—"

He raised his palm. "Hey, hey, hey. We've been through that enough, haven't we?"

She nodded, almost letting a smile break. "Way enough. You're right."

Now he reached his hand out and put it against the Plexiglas separating them. "It's so incredibly good to see you. Do you know that?"

"You too." She leaned in toward him. "I came down here to tell you that I love you, you know, Evan Scholler. I've always loved you. All that other stuff, not answering your letters, everything with Ron—I was just young and stupid."

"No, the stupid award goes to me. Walking away from you that night at the Traven."

This time, a smile broke. "Okay, maybe we're tied on that one. But I'm not going to be stupid anymore."

He sat back, then came forward again, his voice raw. "You realize people might say that this is stupid, visiting me, getting involved again with me on any level. If you're going to be doing that."

"I am. And it's not stupid, it's right. This is what I need to be doing. This is who I am, who we are. I'm just sorry it took me so long to figure it out."

"You don't have to be sorry for anything," he said.

But she shook her head. "No, you're wrong. I'm sorry for everything that's got us to here. I'm just so, so sorry, Evan. I really am."

His eyes met hers. "I am, too, Tara," he said at last. "I am, too."

[19]

On Tuesday morning, the second week of September 2005, an assistant district attorney with the impossible name of Mary Patricia Whelan-Miille looked at her wristwatch in Department 21 of the San Mateo County Courthouse in Redwood City. It was nine forty-two A.M. This meant that court was starting a few minutes late, but the tardiness didn't bother her.

Mary Patricia's law-school friends had given her the nickname of Mills almost before she'd gotten her full name out for the first time, and now Mills, with excitement and some trepidation, took in the scene around her. She was exactly where she wanted to be at this moment—in a courtroom as a prosecutor about to begin the trial of her life, and one that had a chance to become a defining moment in her career.

Oh, there would undoubtedly be pitfalls ahead, as in fact there had already been. Her boss Doug Falbrock's decision to abandon the charges against Evan Scholler in the murders of Ibrahim and Shatha Khalil for lack of evidence, for example, had been a bitter pill for her to swallow in the early innings. Pulling Tollson, a multidecorated Vietnam combat veteran who'd lost a foot to an antipersonnel bomb in that war, as the trial judge perhaps wasn't the greatest bit of good fortune imaginable either. Probably fewer than two or three years from retirement, Tollson, as the prototypical éminence grise, had earned the sobriquet "His Griseness" from Mills's paralegal, Felice Brinkley, and it fit perfectly.

Outside of the courtroom, in the building's halls, Tollson limped along exuding a nearly boyish enthusiasm. He came across as preppy, favoring casual menswear instead of coat and tie. He wore blue contact lenses, his perfectly combed, silver-tipped, Grecian Formula hair nearly luxuriant in a man his age. But on the bench he wore the black robe and thick black eyeglasses that magnified a pair of rheumy, depthless black pupils. His hair remained permanently in disarray, as though he spent his time in chambers running his hands through it in constant despair at the human condition. Add the permanent scowl, which emphasized heavy brows, a prominent and aggressive nose, and the thin-lipped set of his mouth, and His Griseness was a formidable and vaguely menacing force that attorneys in court crossed at their own peril.

Nor was Mills entirely sanguine about the defense attorney who was now standing behind his desk fifteen feet to her left. Everett Washburn, somewhere north of seventy, white-haired, and in rimless glasses, wore a light tan suit that was at least one size too large. His shirt had had all of its wash-and-wear washed out of it. The tie was an orange-and-tan paisley design, three inches wide. His florid face was a creased dried apple, and his voice combined equal parts honey and whiskey. He had the teeth of a horse, yellowed with age, cigars, strong coffee, and wine.

Washburn, reportedly, had lost a murder trial once, but nobody remembered when. Mills herself had come down to court just to watch him perform several times and considered him tenacious, brilliant, ruthless, and unpredictable. A dangerous combination.

Plus, and this made it worse, he was a famous nice guy, a favorite of all the judges, bailiffs, clerks, and even prosecuting attorneys such as herself. He knew every birthday and anniversary in the building and reportedly spent in excess of fifty thousand dollars a year on political fundraisers, charity events, and lunches.

And that didn't include his bar tabs.

But all of that being said, Mills liked her chances. Greater forces were at work here, the first of which was the fact that some benign karma had delivered her to San Mateo County. Her first seven years as a prosecutor had been in San Francisco and in spite of always being prepared beyond reason and never seeing a suspect who hadn't committed the crime of which he or she had been accused, she had only managed four jury trials—the rest had been pled out by her superiors for far less than any sentence they would have received in a fair world—and her record in those trials had been three hung juries and an acquittal. San Francisco juries, she believed because it was true, just didn't convict.

But San Mateo County!

She loved San Mateo County as it in turn hated its criminals—its vandals, gang-bangers, burglars, petty thieves, and murderers all alike. San Mateo County wanted these people dealt with and trusted the system to deal with them. As did Mills, whose parents she'd loved in spite of the mouthful of moniker they'd laid on her at birth, and who'd been murdered in a carjacking when she was sixteen.

So there was San Mateo County, essentially on her

side. It was a miracle, given her record, that they'd hired her here. The interview had come on the particularly bad afternoon when the big fourth of her four losses had come in and she'd been in a quiet and reasonable fury in her interview with Falbrock—a real I-don't-give-a-fuck-what-happens mood. Karma again. She'd found herself launched into her take-no-prisoners tirade before she could stop herself, and much to her surprise and delight, after she gave her exceptions about people the state should put to death, Falbrock had smiled and said, "I don't know. I'm not so sure we shouldn't execute shoplifters. It's a gateway crime." And he'd hired her on the spot.

There was, next, her victim, Ron Nolan—a young, wealthy, clean-cut, handsome, and charismatic ex–Navy SEAL, recipient of three Purple Hearts, the Afghanistan and Iraq Campaign Medals, the Liberation of Kuwait Medal, the Global War on Terrorism Expeditionary Medal, the Meritorious Service Medal, and the Bronze Star. Mills, learning about the extraordinary life of Ron Nolan as she had investigated his death, had wondered more than once why she hadn't had the good fortune to have met him in her real life before he'd been murdered. She hadn't quite fallen in love with his memory, but she felt a fascination bordering on infatuation that she couldn't deny, and if she could avenge his senseless death in any way, she would consider it her privilege and duty.

Which brought her to her suspect.

She stole a glance over to where Evan Scholler stood. To her, he was the definition of scumbag, and it still galled her to see him in the courtroom now all cleaned up, with a dress shirt and tie and nice jacket. But she was convinced that by the time she was done, the jury would see beyond the façade that Washburn was so adept at creat-

ing, beyond the injured war veteran with the pretty and
supportive girlfriend and the loyal parents, to the alcoholic and Vicodin addict whose incompetent leadership
had led his squad of San Mateo County boys into their
fatal ambush in Iraq.

As she waited for the judge to enter the courtroom,
her heart was beating hard in anticipation. She was particularly keen to face some of the issues that were to be
adjudicated before jury selection was to begin, the most
important of which was going to be up first today. Mills
had prepared a 402 motion requesting a foundational
hearing to determine the admissibility of evidence related
to post-traumatic stress disorder.

From the outset, it had been clear that Everett Washburn intended to use PTSD as an integral part of his defense of Evan Scholler. After all, the young man had
endured exactly the kind of severe personal trauma during wartime that had produced volumes of literature on
the subject. He'd also exhibited, to a host of witnesses
over a substantial period of time, some, if not all, of the
classic symptoms of PTSD.

So for a while early on, Mills had let herself get
lulled into a grudging acceptance that PTSD, with its
expert-witness madness, media appeal, and the emotional
overtones it created, particularly in the context of the in-
creasingly unpopular war, was going to be part of the
trial.

And then one day it came to her that Washburn
couldn't have it both ways. Either he could argue that
Scholler had killed Ron Nolan but that PTSD was an ex-
tenuating circumstance or even a defense; or he could
maintain that Scholler hadn't killed Ron Nolan at all, in
which case he wouldn't, strictly speaking, need any other

defense. If Scholler didn't do it, then it wasn't PTSD or self-defense or anything at all that had made him do it. So, believing that she had logic on her side—not that it always mattered—Mills had written her 402 motion. She wanted a full-blown hearing on the issue and was prepared to argue heatedly for it.

"All rise. Hear ye! Hear ye! The Superior Court, State of California, in and for the County of San Mateo, is now in session, Judge Theodore Tollson presiding."

Now she stood up and brought her eyes forward. Tollson had ascended to the bench. The clerk said, "You may be seated." After fifteen months, interviews filling thirty-seven binders, twelve pretrial written motions, three boyfriends, and the hint that the proper outcome would garner a six-figure book-deal offer, they were about to get on the boards at last.

Tollson glared down from the bench to both attorneys' tables, back over the small bullpen partition, and across the packed gallery. He looked in no way amiable. He straightened his back and pushed his glasses up to the ridge of his nose. "Mr. Washburn," he began. "Ms. Miille. Are you ready to begin?"

Both intoned, "Yes, Your Honor."

"All right, then, before we get down to it, let's spend a few moments in my chambers." And with that, he was up again, off the bench, and through the side door. To Mills, there was an absurd quality to the judge's formal entrance minutes before, followed by his near-immediate retreat back to his private office, but it was far from the only absurd moment she'd spent in and around courtrooms.

By the time she'd gathered her papers, Everett Washburn had come over to her table and, like the cultured gentleman that he was, waited for her to come around.

She almost expected him to hold out his arm as a courtier might, for her to take it. But he merely bowed and let her precede him across the courtroom and to the back door, where the bailiff was waiting.

IN TOLLSON'S CHAMBERS, a faded green-and-gold pennant from the University of San Francisco took pride of place on the wall behind the large oak desk. A trophy case held more than a dozen ancient baseball and football trophies. A golf bag sat up against the bookshelf wall. A credenza sported a dozen or more framed photos of family members. Someone had arranged his diplomas, honors, and ceremonial pictures in a large rectangular pattern that covered the last empty wall.

The bailiff stayed until they were seated, then disappeared, leaving only the two lawyers and the judge. Tollson, in his robe and glasses behind his desk, nevertheless was his casual, out-of-the-courtroom self as he began. "So, I take it you two haven't reached a last-minute settlement, Mr. Washburn?"

The old lawyer sat back with his legs crossed—bemused, tolerant, good-natured. "That's correct, Your Honor."

"So what are we looking at for time?"

The question was asked of both of them, but Mills spoke up first. "The People's case, Your Honor, maybe four weeks, depending on cross. I've never worked with Mr. Washburn before, so I don't know how long he takes. I'll let him give you the estimate for the defense. I don't know about rebuttal." She paused, decided to hedge her estimate. "A lot will depend," she said, "on what you let in."

"We'll be getting to that here," Tollson said. "Jury selection?"

"Probably a couple of weeks, Your Honor. I would suggest a week of hardship, based on the length." She was suggesting that they first screen prospective jurors to see who could be with them, basically without pay, for what looked like a couple of months. The idea was that it was wise to eliminate the vast majority of prospective jurors whose employers would not pay for that length of jury service, or who could not otherwise handle the commitment. Only those who survived the initial screening would undergo the more complex and time-consuming questioning that would decide who would sit on the jury.

She went on, "So we've got twenty peremptory challenges each, and some hot-button issues such as the Iraq War and maybe some psych stuff, depending on your rulings. We use questionnaires, we should get our hardships done in three days or so, and the regular jury picked a couple days after that, give or take."

Tollson nodded. "Mr. Washburn? Sound about right to you?"

"Pretty close," he intoned. "I agree we should hardship first, and have the jury fill out questionnaires." He reached into his inside pocket and extracted a handful of paper, folded the long way. "And I just happen to have a proposed questionnaire for this case with me." Handing a copy to Mills and the judge, he added, "I'll need about a week for the defense, Your Honor."

Tollson, perusing the questionnaire, didn't look up, but said, "Motions?"

This time Washburn went first. "Limit the use of autopsy photos, Your Honor. They don't need a bunch of gory photos to prove this guy is dead."

"Your Honor," Mills said. "This *guy*, the victim, was in superb health. Somebody beat him to a bloody pulp. Not a robber or a burglar, but someone who hated him. The jury will need to see the savagery of the attack to appreciate that this was a personal killing."

Washburn shot back, "Too many autopsy photos might unduly prejudice the jury."

Tollson held up a hand. "Show me the photos you want to have admitted. I'll let you know which ones you can use before we start jury selection. Anything else?"

This was the moment. Mills produced copies of her 402 motion for Washburn and Tollson and said, "Mr. Washburn has discovered some stuff on PTSD, Your Honor, and has expert witnesses on his list. We would like a full-blown hearing on what you're going to admit before we get near a jury."

She wanted the judge to require Washburn to call his witnesses outside of the presence of the jury and have them testify under oath. Then the two sides could argue over whether such testimony was admissible, and the Court could rule on it. If the evidence was admitted, the same witnesses would have to give exactly the same testimony later in front of the jury.

If the Court refused to hold the hearing, testimony was heard for the first time with the jury present. In this case, if the Court then ruled that the testimony should not have been admitted, the only remedy was to instruct the jury to pretend they had never heard it. Popularly known as "unringing the bell," this was a notoriously ineffective way to deal with the problem.

Mills went into her pitch. "The defendant claims PTSD,

Your Honor, but the defense here is that he didn't do it. If he didn't do it, then his state of mind is irrelevant. All this is going to do is put his war record and injuries in front of the jury to excite sympathy."

Washburn, leaning back with his legs crossed, ran a finger around in his ear. "My client was blacked out during the period where it appears Mr. Nolan was killed, Your Honor. First, evidence of PTSD will support his claim that he can't remember anything about this period. Second, if he did kill someone and there is a doubt about his mental state because he might have been in a PTSD episode, then he is entitled to that doubt. The crime would certainly be less than premeditated murder, maybe voluntary or even involuntary manslaughter."

This brought the first sign of Tollson's courtroom testiness. "I believe I understand the issues, Counselor." He spent a few more seconds looking over Mills's pages, then squared them and put them down with Washburn's questionnaire. "I'm going to allow two weeks for motions. Until we know what the jury will hear, we can't tell them how long the case will be, so jury selection starts two weeks from today. Sound good?"

It sounded good to Mills. She'd gotten her hearing. A good omen.

Tollson continued. "My staff will have the jury commissioner start to put panels together. Six court days for jury selection, including three days of hardship. Six weeks of trial or so if you get into PTSD, probably four at the outside if you don't. Let's get outside on the record and get to work."

[20]

EVERETT WASHBURN STOOD in the center of the courtroom, addressing his first witness in the hearing on PTSD. Dr. Sandra Overton was a frizzy-haired, earnest psychiatrist in her midforties. She wore a dark blue business suit with low heels. She had already recited her credentials and experience as a psychiatrist—i.e., a medical doctor—specializing in veterans returning from active combat. "In your experience with these veterans, Doctor," Washburn asked her, "have you run across a condition known as post-traumatic stress disorder, or PTSD?"

She almost laughed at the question. "It's pretty much all I work with."

"Can you tell the Court exactly what it is, then?"

"Certainly." She looked across at the prosecution table, where Mills sat with her hands folded in front of her, then around and up to where the judge sat on the bench. "It's pretty much what the name says. It's a psychiatric disorder that occurs after an episode of traumatic stress."

"A psychiatric disorder? Do you mean it's a mental illness?"

She shook her head. "That's not really a descriptive term. Legally it would qualify as a disease, defect, or disorder. Medically it is more a range of continuing symptoms and reactions experienced by someone who's endured a traumatic event. The key word being *continuing*."

"In what way?"

"Well, almost everyone who experiences a traumatic event has a reaction to it. Shock, or depression, or insomnia. But with PTSD, the reaction first tends to be more serious and second, it persists for a lengthy period of time, sometimes forever. It becomes a disorder, not a reaction."

"And what is a traumatic event, Doctor?"

Again, Overton shook her head. "There's no one definition. What's traumatic for one person might be relatively innocuous to another. But certainly traumatic events would tend to include military combat, serious accidents, crimes such as rape, natural disasters, terrorist incidents, and the like."

"Military combat?"

"Yes. Very commonly. Although the disorder wasn't much studied until after the Vietnam War. Before then, when people talked about it at all, it was usually called Da Costa's syndrome. But since Vietnam, estimates of soldiers with combat experience suffering from PTSD have run as high as thirty percent."

"And what are some symptoms commonly associated with PTSD?"

"One of the main symptoms is a reliving of the original traumatic experience through either flashbacks, or in nightmares. Beyond that, there's insomnia, of course, and a sense of disconnect with life. Then depression, memory and cognition issues, abusive and self-destructive behavior. A huge range of personal and societal problems, actually."

"Doctor, you referred to abusive and self-destructive behavior. Could this include alcohol abuse?"

"Yes, of course."

"And memory issues? Do you mean blackouts?"

"Yes. Blackouts are not uncommon, especially if coupled with excessive drinking or drug use or both."

"I see." Washburn acted as though he were hearing all of this for the very first time in his life. Now he moved a step closer to his witness. "Doctor, is there a physical component to PTSD? Or is it simply what a layman might just call a mental problem?"

As Washburn intended, this question kept Overton from becoming lulled in her relatively straightforward recounting. This hearing hadn't been his idea, but since he was in it, he was dry-running her to play to the jury's sensibilities when and if she testified at trial. She sat up stiffly, her expression defiant. "Absolutely not! In the first place, a mental problem is a real problem. It's as real as a broken leg. Secondly, with PTSD there is measurable altered brain-wave activity, decreased volume of the hippocampus and abnormal activation of the amygdala, both of the latter having to do with memory. The thyroid's affected, as is production of epinephrine and cortisol. I could go on, but suffice it to say that there are many, many physical and neurological changes and reactions associated with PTSD."

"I see, Doctor. Thank you," Washburn said. "Now, have you had an opportunity to interview and examine my client, Evan Scholler, with regard to PTSD?"

"I have."

"What were your findings?"

"I found that Mr. Scholler clearly suffers from the

disorder. His memory, particularly, seems to be compromised, and this symptom has been aggravated by a traumatic brain injury he suffered in Iraq in August of two thousand three. He suffers from frequent migraine headaches. Beyond that, he has reported the experience of blackouts and episodes of rage, shame, guilt, and depression. Sleeping has been a consistent problem. Finally, he has spoken to me about a tendency to abuse alcohol and other painkilling drugs, such as Vicodin. All of these symptoms are not only consistent with PTSD, they are diagnostic of it."

"And what about the physical changes you've described—to the amygdala and hippocampus and so forth? Did you test Mr. Scholler for these?"

"Yes, I did."

"What were your findings?"

"I found decreased cortisol with increased epinephrine and norepinephrine levels. Together, these hormone levels impact the body's fear response and the startle reflex, both of which I found to be in the abnormal range with Mr. Scholler."

"And your conclusions as a medical professional? Does Mr. Scholler suffer from PTSD?"

Dr. Overton looked over at the defense table where Evan sat. "Yes. Unremitting and severe PTSD. Without a doubt, in my professional opinion."

"Without a doubt. Thank you, Doctor." Washburn inclined his head in a courteous bow. Facing Mills, he turned his palm up. "Your witness, Counsel."

"DR. OVERTON," the assistant district attorney began, "you've testified that blackouts are not uncommon among people with PTSD. Were you saying that PTSD causes blackouts?"

"Not exactly. I believe I said that blackouts were common, especially when drugs or alcohol were part of the picture."

"Oh, so PTSD does not in itself cause these blackouts, is that true?"

"Well, in a sense you can say that—"

"Doctor, I'm sorry. It's a yes or no question. Does PTSD cause blackouts?"

Overton frowned, glanced over at Washburn. "They are commonly associated with PTSD, yes."

"Again, Doctor, not my question. Does PTSD cause blackouts?"

Washburn cleared his throat and spoke from his table. "Objection. Badgering."

Tollson didn't take two seconds to make up his mind. "Overruled." He leaned over to speak to the witness. "Please answer the question, Doctor."

Mills jumped right in. "Would you like me to repeat it?"

Tollson transferred his scowl down to her. "Can the sarcasm, Counselor. Doctor, answer the question, does PTSD cause blackouts?"

"Yes, there are some reports of that."

"Some? How many of these reports are you personally familiar with?"

"I'm not sure. To the best of my recollection, a few."

"A few. All right. And do any of these few reports with which you're familiar speak to the duration of any of these rare PTSD blackouts?"

From behind her, Everett Washburn rumbled forth again. "Objection. Assumes facts not in evidence. The doctor's awareness of only a few reports on blackouts doesn't mean that the blackouts themselves are rare."

"Sustained."

But Mills came right back at Overton. "Doctor," she said, "do any of these few reports with which you're familiar speak to the duration of any of these PTSD blackouts?"

"Yes, they do."

Mills had her own expert witness on this topic, although she wasn't sure she was going to use him. In any event, she'd done her homework and knew her facts. "Doctor," she said, "isn't it true that these PTSD blackouts tend to be of very short duration?"

"Yes."

"Along the line of forgetting where you put your keys, for example?"

"I'm not sure I understand what you mean."

"You put your keys on your kitchen counter, for example, then are struck with a vivid post-traumatic flashback. When it's over, you can't remember where you placed your keys. That's the kind of PTSD blackout discussed in the literature, is it not? In other words, a memory lapse of relatively short duration?"

"I think so. Yes."

Mills walked back to her table, took a drink of water. Turning around to the witness, she asked, "Doctor, are you aware of any PTSD blackouts that extended for more than a day?"

"No. I've never heard of that."

"How about an hour?"

"No, I don't think so."

"Ten minutes?"

"Somewhere in that realm, I believe. The flashback, usually, tends to be intense but short-lived."

The gallery might not have understood exactly what Mills was getting at with this questioning, but the doctor's answer of ten minutes sent a buzz through the room. Galvanized by it, the prosecutor moved in closer to the witness. "Doctor, you've also testified about blackouts that are coupled with excessive alcohol and drug use, or both. Would you characterize these blackouts as caused by PTSD, or by the alcohol and/or drug use?"

"Well, they're related. The PTSD exacerbates the abusive behavior."

"But it is the drinking or the drug use that causes the actual blackouts, is it not?"

"I don't think we can say that."

"Well, Doctor, alcohol and drug use by themselves can cause blackouts, correct?"

"Yes."

"And this is a fairly common and well-documented phenomenon, is it not?"

"Yes."

"But blackouts associated with PTSD are both rare and of short duration, isn't that true?"

Washburn knew that this was a compound question, and hence objectionable, but saw nothing to gain by further interruption.

"Yes."

"So," Mills continued, "if you had a blackout for an extended period of time, Doctor, say a couple of days, there is scientific evidence that it could have been caused by alcohol, and no scientific support for the suggestion that it was caused by PTSD alone, correct?"

"Yes."

"Thank you, Doctor. Now, you've said that Mr. Scholler told you that he had abused both alcohol and Vicodin, isn't that so?"

Clearly frustrated now, Overton had come forward in the witness chair, her hands on the balustrade of the box. "That's right."

"Did he also tell you, Doctor, that he had abused alcohol in Iraq before one of these so-called traumatic experiences?"

"Your Honor!" Finally Washburn was moved to rise to his feet in outrage. "I object to Counsel's characterization. Most of us humans would consider sustaining a severe head wound during a rifle and grenade attack on foreign soil in defense of our country a traumatic event. There is nothing spurious or so-called about it."

This brought the gallery noise now to a full hum, and Tollson dropped his gavel for the first time. Without a word, he glared around the room until all the noise had ceased.

Mills broke the silence. "I'll withdraw the word *so-called*, Your Honor." But she wasn't backing down. "Perhaps the court reporter can reread my question without the offending word."

Tollson looked down over the bench at his reporter and nodded.

The woman pulled the tape up and read, "Did he also tell you, Doctor, that he had abused alcohol in Iraq before one of these"—a pause—"traumatic experiences?"

Overton, her mouth set, shot a glance at Washburn, then came back to her tormentor. "Yes, he did."

"In other words, Mr. Scholler's alcohol abuse preceded his PTSD, and by itself was capable of producing extended periods of memory blackout, isn't that so?"

"Apparently," Overton snipped out.

"That would be a 'yes,' then, is that correct?"

Through all but gritted teeth now. "Yes."

"And Mr. Scholler told you that the particular blackout after the death of the victim, Ron Nolan, lasted approximately four days, isn't that true?"

"Yes."

"Thank you, Doctor," Mills said. "No further questions."

LAWYER AND CLIENT sat knee to knee in a holding cell behind the courtroom during the lunch recess. Outside their two small wired windows, it was a bright and sunny day. Their view included a small city of media vans that had set up out in the parking lot. Washburn's mouth was full of liverwurst on rye, but it didn't shut him up. "It doesn't matter," he said. "What's important is she established the PTSD. Now we've just got to make sure we get Tollson to let it in. You gonna eat your pickle?"

"No. I'm not holding anything down. You go ahead."

Washburn stopped chewing. "You nervous?"

"Why would I be nervous? On trial for murder and all."

"You've got to keep your strength up." Washburn grabbed the pickle and took a bite of it. After he finally swallowed, he sipped from his bottled water and cleared his throat. "But we need to talk about what we do if he doesn't allow it."

"You mean Tollson?"

A nod. "And the PTSD. We get that, we're going to have the jury on our side. They're going to see what happened in Iraq, what you've been through . . . . it's decent odds they don't convict. On the other hand, this morning I was hoping Ted would rule to let the PTSD in without a hearing, but he didn't do that. Which means he's thinking about it, maybe he thinks it's bogus."

"Why would he think that? He lost a foot himself."

"Yeah. But remember, whatever else happened to him, he didn't get any PTSD from it. Which means, maybe, that to him it's just a bunch of mumbo-jumbo from weak-ass lesser beings. Or shyster lawyers like me."

"Is this supposed to cheer me up?"

Washburn shrugged, took another monstrous bite of his sandwich. "Just running down the possibilities. Look," he went on, "don't get down about this. Half the world's on our side."

"Which means half isn't."

"But we don't need half. We just need one out of twelve. So get over it. The fact is you're a wounded veteran who's the victim of an extremely—now—unpopular war. The more we get the war in as a villain, the more we got Nolan as a victim of the war himself. Without the war, nobody would have been killed. Your guys in Iraq, Nolan, nobody. Plus we got our big surprise when you testify, which will sway some hearts and minds, since it brings it all around and gives them an alternative theory to think about. But all that's counting on the PTSD, without which it's a different ball game." Taking another drink of water, Washburn swished it around. "So the question is, Tollson doesn't let it in, we might want to talk about a plea."

Evan closed his eyes for a second, then shook his head. "No way."

"Wait. Before you—"

"Everett, listen. Mills's last offer was forty to life. I can't do forty."

Washburn looked at his client. He'd been here with other clients more times than he cared to remember, but it never got easy. Tollson's ruling to hold a hearing on the PTSD evidence was unexpected and perhaps ultimately disastrous. Washburn had truly believed that his argument in chambers, casually though he had phrased it, would carry the day and that Tollson would allow the PTSD evidence at the trial.

But now, possibly, that wasn't to be the case.

Washburn wasn't giving up. It wasn't in his nature to do that. But he had to get it through to Evan that they might, after all, lose. "I'm sure I could get Doug Falbrock to drop the gun," he said. Any use of a gun in the commission of a murder in California added an automatic twenty-five years to the sentence. "Plea to a second. Get them down to, say, twelve to life."

Evan was sitting back, arms crossed. "Wasn't it you who said the immortal words 'Anything to life equals life'?"

"I was being glib," he said. "You'd be a model prisoner, out in the minimum."

"Still," Evan said, "twelve years."

Washburn unfolded his hands, took his last bite of sandwich. "I'm just saying"—he chewed a couple of times—"I'm just saying you might want to think about it."

[21]

WASHBURN'S PLAN TO GET the war into the trial at every opportunity was behind his decision to call Anthony Onofrio as his next witness. Onofrio had come home six months ago and had immediately contacted Washburn's office asking if and how he could help with Evan's defense. As an older veteran, a father of three who'd left his Caltrans job and home in Half Moon Bay to do his duty, as well as the lone military survivor besides Evan in the Baghdad firefight, he was in a unique position to recount the traumatic event that was at the heart of this hearing.

But no sooner had the clerk sworn in the thick-necked, friendly looking workman than Mills stood to object. "Your Honor, the last witness has already testified and established to the People's satisfaction that Mr. Scholler suffers from post-traumatic stress disorder. We are willing to concede that point, though we still contend that it's irrelevant. The People fail to see what probative value, if any, this witness can bring to these proceedings. He wasn't even here in the United States during the time of the murder and his testimony can have no bearing on the defendant's guilt or innocence."

Judge Tollson leaned back in his chair on the bench,

his eyes nearly closed. He inclined his head a quarter of an inch. "Mr. Washburn?"

"Your Honor, this witness is foundational. There can be no post-traumatic stress without an original trauma, and Mr. Onofrio was an eyewitness to the trauma that Mr. Scholler experienced and to the effects of which Dr. Overton just testified. We did not simply hire a rent-a-shrink to come in here and invent a condition following an event which never took place. Without the event, there can be no condition."

For a long moment, and against all reason, since he was basically correct, Washburn lived with the agonizing possibility that Tollson was going to dismiss his witness and call an end to his entire line of questioning.

He also had time to reflect that Mills's objection made little sense. In theory, by granting this hearing without the presence of a jury, Tollson had provided her with a bonus—she'd get to see all of his evidence before he could present it at trial. She should want to hear everybody he brought in so she'd, in effect, have two chances to take them apart—now and when the jury had been impaneled.

But then, he realized, she was probably running mostly on nerves and adrenaline herself. And the fact remained that if Tollson did side with her and preclude Onofrio from testifying, the same objection and rationale might get some traction regarding calling his following witnesses as well, and that would truly be problematic.

Tollson ended the suspense. "Ms. Whelan-Miille," he said, "this is a hearing. That means we get to hear what people have to say before we get to trial. Mr. Washburn is right. This witness's proposed testimony is foundational to the question of trauma. The objection is overruled. Mr. Washburn, you may proceed."

Trying to hide his sigh of relief from the Court, Washburn leaned his head forward, the merest hint of a bow. "Thank you, Your Honor." He turned to the witness. "Now, Mr. Onofrio, can you please tell the Court about your relation to Mr. Scholler?"

"Until he was wounded, he was my squad leader in Iraq in the summer of two thousand three."

Over the next few minutes, Washburn walked Onofrio through the makeup of the squad and its general duties as a military convoy unit, then came back to the main thrust. "Mr. Onofrio, you've said that Mr. Scholler was your squad leader until he was wounded. Would you please tell us how that came about?"

"Sure. We were escorting Ron Nolan to a meeting with—"

"Excuse me," Washburn said. "You were escorting the same Ron Nolan who is the victim in this case?"

"Yes."

"He was with you in Iraq, was he?"

"He came and he went, but basically, yes. He was working for Allstrong Security, which was handling the Baghdad Airport and doing other work over there. It was one of our regular jobs driving him where he needed to go."

"All right, so he was with your convoy on the day that Mr. Scholler was hit?"

"Yes, he was." Onofrio sat back in the witness chair and basically told it as he remembered it. The tension on the city's streets, Nolan firing on the purported suicide car, the discovery of what it had really been and who had been in it, the rock-throwing and then the sustained attack from the surrounding buildings and rooftops. "Just after it all started, though, the actual rifle firing and the first RPG, we had a chance where maybe we could have gotten out, but the lieutenant wouldn't give the order to pull out until we'd gotten the men who'd already been hit into one of our vehicles."

"He wasn't going to leave anyone behind?" This was important information, carefully rehearsed. Washburn wanted it to be clear in the jury's mind, when it came to it, that Evan was in grave danger, in the thick of it, and had acted nobly.

"No, sir. So he ran up to the lead car, which was still smoking, and tried to get out the guys who'd been hit."

"He did this while you were under heavy fire?"

"Yes, sir. But then the second car took a hit and a couple of the other guys went down, so it was obvious there wasn't going to be any chance for any of us to get out if we didn't move pretty quick. So Nolan kept firing through the roof and had me drive up to where Evan was pinned down. He still wanted to try to carry some of the guys out if he could get to them, but an RPG went off somewhere behind us and next time I looked over, he was down."

"What had happened?"

"He was hit by shrapnel, or something. In the head. There was blood everywhere. I thought he was dead. I thought we were all dead."

"All right, thank you, Mr. Onofrio. I'm glad you made it home alive." He half turned back to Mills. "Your witness."

*　*　*

Mills saw this as a no-win cross-examination and almost passed the witness, but decided she had nothing really to lose if she just took the judge's advice and heard what the man would say. No jury was listening now, and maybe she'd strike some promising vein that she could mine when she had him again during the trial. If Washburn was going to call up what she considered these largely irrelevant witnesses, she might as well take the opportunity to go fishing with them.

"Mr. Onofrio," she began. "First let me say that I, too, and all of us in the courtroom, are grateful that you made it home alive. Thank you for your service to our country."

Shrugging, embarrassed, Onofrio mumbled, "You're welcome."

"One of the things I was struck with in your testimony was the fact that you were not sent over to do convoy work. Did I get that right?"

Onofrio nodded. "That's right. We were supposed to be doing maintenance on heavy equipment transport vehicles, but when we got to Kuwait, they weren't there yet, so they farmed a bunch of us out as convoy units."

The questioning was getting far afield, but Washburn took his own advice and let it go. Better to hear the answer now than find out for the first time in front of a jury about some land mine in the witness's testimony.

"How did you feel about that?" Mills asked.

He smiled, either at her naïveté or at the question. "They didn't ask us. It wasn't like it was negotiable."

"No, I understand that. But the convoy work at the front, wasn't it more dangerous than the work you'd originally been scheduled to do?"

"Only by about a factor of ten. Maybe twenty."

"So? Much more dangerous, then?"

"Yes. Way more."

Mills paused, and kept casting. "Didn't you and the other men object to that?"

"Sure. But what were we going to do?"

"I don't know, Mr. Onofrio. What did you do?"

"Well, we complained about it to Lieutenant Scholler. We asked him to talk to the base commander and see if we could get transferred back to our regular unit."

"And did he do that?"

"He tried, but he couldn't get in to see him. Not in time, anyway." Then, trying to be helpful, Onofrio added, "He was going to see if Nolan could pull some strings with the brass, but again, that didn't happen in time."

"Mr. Scholler thought that Mr. Nolan might be able to pull some strings for him. Why was that? Were they friends?"

"I'd say so, yeah."

"Close friends?"

"Well, I don't know." He shrugged again, then unwittingly dropped his bomb. "Drinking buddies, anyway."

The words had barely registered as significant when Mills heard Washburn all but erupt behind her. "Objection! Irrelevant!"

But this was the purest bluff. No one in the courtroom thought the answer was even remotely irrelevant, and Tollson sealed that opinion in an instant. "Overruled."

Mills kept her mouth tight to avoid telegraphing her pleasure. "Thank you, Your Honor," she said. Then, back at the witness. "Mr. Onofrio, when you characterize the friendship between Mr. Nolan and Mr. Scholler as that of drinking buddies, do you mean that they literally drank together?"

Onofrio, picking up the panic in Washburn's tone, flashed a quick look over to the defense table. "Occasionally, I think, yes."

"Do you think they drank together, or did you see them drinking together?"

"Yes, they drank together."

"Mr. Onofrio, is there a rule in the military against drinking on duty, or in a war zone?"

"Yes."

"But Mr. Scholler broke this rule?

"I suppose so."

"You witnessed this yourself, personally?"

"Yes."

"How many times?"

"I don't know exactly. A few."

"More than five times?"

"Your Honor," Washburn said. "Badgering the witness."

"Overruled."

Mills nodded. "More than five times, Mr. Onofrio?"

"Maybe."

"More than ten?"

"I didn't count the times," Onofrio said. "I really couldn't say for sure."

"Once a day? Once a week? Once a month?"

"A few times a week."

"All right, then. Did Mr. Scholler drink to excess?"

"Objection," Washburn sang out. "Calls for a conclusion."

"Overruled," Tollson said. "A lay witness can give an opinion as to sobriety."

Mills slowed herself down. She was close to something very good here and didn't want to blow it. "Did

Mr. Scholler ever appear drunk to you when he was on duty?"

"Objection. Conclusion."

"Sustained."

Mills tried again. "Did you, personally, ever see Mr. Scholler intoxicated after he'd been drinking with Mr. Nolan?"

Onofrio threw another worried glance over to Washburn and Evan. "Yes, ma'am."

"And by intoxicated, do you mean that you heard him speak with slurred speech or saw him have trouble walking?"

"Yes, ma'am."

"Mr. Onofrio. When was the last time you remember noticing these things—defendant's slurred speech or the uncertain walk?"

Onofrio looked down at his lap. "His last night over there."

"The night before this incident at Masbah, is that what you're saying?"

He blew out and slowly nodded. "That's what I'm saying."

"Mr. Onofrio, on the day the shooting started, when Mr. Scholler was leading the convoy that got ambushed, did he appear to be intoxicated?"

"No, ma'am," Onofrio answered strongly.

Mills paused, then came out with it. "But he certainly was hungover, wasn't he?"

STEPHAN RAY, the speech and language therapist from Walter Reed, nodded enthusiastically at Washburn from the witness stand. "He is definitely one of the success stories. He worked very hard and was also very lucky. But his success doesn't take away from the seriousness of his injuries. There was a real question for at least a couple of months as to whether he'd live, and then a further question about how completely, if at all, he'd recover."

"What were the areas most affected?"

"Well, most obviously affected were speech and memory, although there were also some coordination issues early on that cleared up more or less on their own."

"So how did these memory problems manifest themselves?"

"Well, at first, just after the surgery, of course, he remained pretty much continually unconscious for three weeks—in fact, I believe they kept him in an induced coma until they were confident that he'd gotten sufficiently well to handle consciousness, although I'm not a hundred percent sure of that. I wasn't on his medical team. I'm not a doctor. But when I first encountered Evan, he had what I'd call severe memory and cognition issues. He didn't know where he was, he thought I worked for the CIA, he didn't know what had happened to him exactly. But mostly, he didn't have a vocabulary."

"No vocabulary at all?"

"At first, very little. But then over time, as the healing progressed, he recovered the use of most common words."

"Was this a natural event?"

"To some degree, yes. But a lot of it was a matter of training the brain again, or relearning what he'd once known. We used flash cards, just the way you would if you were learning a new language, and Evan made really remarkable progress, especially compared to many others of our patients who never recover their ability to talk or to reason."

Washburn nodded. "Even with all this progress, how long did Evan remain in therapy with you at Walter Reed?"

"Nearly six months."

"Six months. And during those six months, while he was progressing so well, did he also suffer from blackouts?"

"I'm not sure exactly what you mean by blackouts."

"Periods when he could not recall what he'd done or where he was. As you described when he'd first come out of surgery."

"Ah. Well, yes. They were not infrequent."

"Not infrequent. So they were common?"

"Yes, but that's always to be expected in a case of traumatic brain injury."

"And how long could a blackout period last?"

"Again, it would vary. I remember a time with Evan, this was after three or four months of therapy, when he woke up one morning convinced that he was in Baghdad. He didn't understand why there was snow outside when it was summer in Baghdad. I thought it was a serious enough setback to bring it to the attention of the doctors, but he woke up on the third morning and was fine."

"He didn't think he was in Baghdad anymore?"

"No. He knew he was in Walter Reed. He picked up just where he'd left off in terms of his recovery."

"But for those three days, he was different?"

"As far as he was concerned, he was in Baghdad."

"I see. Now let me ask you this, Mr. Ray. After Evan woke up, realizing that he was in Walter Reed and not in Baghdad, did you ask him about his memory of the time he'd imagined he was in Baghdad? In other words, did you ask him about his memory of his past three days?"

"Yes, I did. He remembered none of it."

"None of it?"

"None. In fact, he thought I was playing a joke on him. Those days were just gone, as though he'd never lived them."

"Thank you, Mr. Ray. Ms. Whelan-Miille, your witness."

"MR. RAY, did Ron Nolan visit Mr. Scholler at Walter Reed?"

"Yes, he did. I met him on that occasion."

"Did you play a part in their conversation?"

"Not really, no."

Mills went right on. "Would you describe Evan's demeanor after Mr. Nolan left?"

"He was very upset and angry to the point of tears. I remember distinctly that later he developed a migraine headache so severe that he had to be sedated for a time."

Mills stood still for a moment, wondering how far she could push this point. Surely, if she got Ray at trial, she could take Evan's anger and jealousy further, but today she didn't want to overplay her hand. She knew he'd be there for her if she needed him at the trial.

"Thank you, Mr. Ray," she said. "No further questions."

BECAUSE SHE WAS ON the People's witness list, Tara wasn't allowed in the courtroom. Now, at five-fifteen, in the jail's visiting room, she bit her lip and tried to keep up a brave smile every time she met Evan's eyes.

And then they were at the window that would be theirs for today, one chair on either side of it, the hole in the Plexiglas through which they had to talk. It was by now all so familiar, and still so awful. But Tara wasn't going to concentrate on the bad. She could take her cues from Eileen, upbeat and positive. "I saw you on TV in a coat and tie."

"I thought I told you. I get to look like a regular person in court."

"You look like a regular person now."

"If you took a poll, I bet most people would say I look like a regular jailbird, what with the jumpsuit and all. What'd they say about things on TV?"

"They said it was a mixed day. What do you think?"

He shrugged. "There's no jury yet, so really none of this counts, but it didn't feel too mixed to me. This prosecutor woman is pretty tough. She's pounding on the drinking theme."

"Why does she want that so much?"

"Everett says it's all positioning for the jury. They're not going to be disposed to like or believe a drunk. Whereas if I'm suffering from PTSD and blacking out, then I'm a wounded war veteran with a mental illness who's caught in a terrible situation he didn't really create, and the sympathy flows like honey. I know, it's a little cynical. But the point is, if we get the PTSD, then to some extent it explains the drinking. Not that I'm using that as an excuse for myself. The drinking, I mean." He lowered his gaze for a moment. "I still don't know what got into me that night, why I didn't just go home with you."

"Did it ever occur to you that maybe what Mr. Washburn's arguing is actually true and not cynical after all? That your physical brain wasn't healed yet so you weren't completely rational—your cognitive powers just weren't all there. And you put PTSD on top of all that, I don't see how a jury could ever get to first-degree murder."

"Well, let's hope." He fell silent, seemed as if he were about to say something, but held it back.

"What?" she asked.

He drew a breath and let it out. "At lunch today, Everett said that I might want to start thinking about if I wanted to take a plea bargain after this hearing phase if the judge doesn't let in the PTSD."

"A plea bargain? Why? He's been saying all along we were going to win."

"Apparently it's not such a sure thing without the PTSD."

"Well, why wouldn't the judge let it in?"

"I don't know. Everett didn't even think it would be an issue until Tollson ordered the hearing this morning. But now it is, and if we lose it..." He lifted his shoulders.

"What would you plead to?"

"Second-degree murder. Everett thinks he could talk them into dropping the gun charge."

"So how long would that be?"

He hesitated for a beat. "Twelve to life."

Tara's head dropped as though she'd been struck. After a minute she looked up again, her eyes brimming with tears. "If you do plead, isn't that admitting you did it?"

"Yeah."

"You can't do that."

"No, I don't think I can."

"You don't remember anything about those four days?"

"Tara, we've been over that a thousand times."

"Well, maybe the thousand and first ..."

He shook his head. "It's not going to happen. I remember going to Ron's after I left you. I remember hitting him and him hitting me back, both of us getting into it. Then nothing until I woke up in jail. I'm sorry. I'm just so sorry, but there's nothing there. It's like I disappeared into those damn bottles."

Tara bit down on her lip. "You can't plead that you did it, Evan. We can't let ourselves accept that we're going to get beaten here."

"That's what I was thinking too. But if we do—get beaten, I mean—then I'm going to be in prison for a lot longer than twelve years."

"I'd wait, Evan. I really would."

"I could never ask you to."

She was rubbing her hand back and forth over her forehead. "God, God, God."

"I don't think He's listening," Evan said.

OVER THE NEXT TWO and a half very tedious days of technical testimony, Everett Washburn called two psychologists who had administered batteries of tests to Evan over the previous several months. Personality tests, neuropsych tests, intelligence tests, perception tests, concentration tests, memory tests. Both agreed with Dr. Overton that Evan clearly suffered from symptoms that were consistent with PTSD. Washburn called several members of the Redwood City Police Department who had worked with Evan and who had specific recollections of times when he'd exhibited PTSD symptoms in their presence—particularly inappropriate laughter and speech aphasia—

an overlong pause in the stream of his conversation. Lieutenant Lochland described his irrational anger and some of the complaints he'd fielded about Evan related to the defendant's work in the DARE program.

Now it was Friday, the lunch recess was over, as was the PTSD hearing, and Judge Tollson had both attorneys back in his chambers. In contrast to his usual out-of-courtroom affability—perhaps worn down by the gravity of the issues, perhaps chastened by the enormity of the decision he had to make—today the judge sat all the way back in his chair, his arms crossed over the robe at his chest. Still and expressionless, he waited until both Washburn and Mills had taken their seats and the court reporter set up her machine.

Finally, he looked over, got a nod from her, and cleared his throat. "Mr. Washburn," he said, "for the record, have you called all your witnesses related to the PTSD evidence that you're seeking to place before the jury?"

"Yes, Your Honor."

"Ms. Miille, do the People have any evidence they wish to offer on this issue?"

"No, Your Honor."

"All right. And before I make my ruling on the People's four oh two motion, do you have any comments that you'd like to make?"

"Just what I said at the beginning, Your Honor. That my witnesses proved beyond a doubt that Mr. Scholler suffers from PTSD and this in turn supports his claim that he can't remember anything about this period."

Tollson turned to the prosecutor. "Ms. Whelan-Miille? Comment?"

"After hearing all the evidence, Your Honor, the People still believe the entire issue of PTSD is irrelevant and highly prejudicial to this case. The defendant's position here is that he didn't commit the murder. So he's not arguing a quarrel with the victim, or heat of passion, or even self-defense. The only possible result of allowing this PTSD evidence will be to create sympathy for the defendant with the jury."

Tollson sat still for another few seconds, then came forward and rested his arms on his desk, his hands clasped in front of him. "Mr. Washburn, I substantially agree with Ms. Whelan-Miille. I've given this matter long and hard thought in terms of weighing prejudice against probative value. And my ruling is that I'm not going to allow this PTSD evidence."

Washburn, staggered by the ruling, brought his hands up to both sides of his face, then rested them on the side of his chair while he got control of his emotions. "Your Honor," he said, "with all respect, this evidence needs to be admitted."

"For your purposes, perhaps, but not as a matter of law, Counselor. It's inadmissible because it has no relevance to the evidence related to Mr. Nolan's murder. Beyond that, it has the strong possibility of wasting a lot of time and confusing the jury. If I let in your expert testimony on psychological issues, the jury is necessarily going to have to hear about a lot of hearsay which would not otherwise be admissible, would not be subject to cross-examination, and would be likely to prejudice the prosecution by exciting sympathy for the defense and a dislike of the victim. When you balance that against the entirely speculative argument that the defendant *might* have been undergoing an episode of PTSD when he killed the victim, which by the way he entirely denies doing, the whole thing is just designed to turn this trial into a circus.

Until you tell me your client or somebody else is going to testify to a self-defense claim now at this eleventh hour, this evidence does not come in."

"Your Honor." Washburn uncrossed his legs and moved to the front of his chair. Normally unflappable, the old barrister had broken a sweat over a flush during the judge's monologue. He wiped at his neck with the handkerchief from his jacket pocket. Looking over at the court reporter, he sighed in pure frustration. "Of course, this guts the defense, Your Honor, and I hope the Court will keep an open mind toward reconsideration as the case comes in."

"Of course, Counsel." Tollson at his most brusque. "This Court's open-mindedness is legendary."

[22]

"LADIES AND GENTLEMEN of the jury." Today—a Wednesday, two weeks after the PTSD ruling—Mills wore a subdued blue suit over a white blouse, no jewelry, low black pumps. Jurors knew she had a government salary and she was expected to dress in a "lawyerlike, ladylike" fashion. Her presentation was supposed to be professional. Any sign of flamboyance might be taken for disrespect, or even arrogance. Representing the People of the State of California before this jury of seven men and five women, she wanted nothing to call any undue attention to herself. Neither aggressive nor hostile, she was to be the plainspoken voice of truth and reason, recounting the prosecution's case.

Starting in the middle of the courtroom, Mills walked a short course up to the foreman's position, along the front row of the jury panel, and then, after a quick stop at her desk to turn the page in her binder and check her notes, back to where she'd begun. She did this as a kind of timing device to slow herself down; she also believed in making eye contact with each and every member of the jury. The message was clear—she was leveling with them, person to person, looking them right in the eye and telling them the unblinking truth.

"Good morning. As you know from the questions you answered during your selection as members of this jury, we'll be here for the better part of a couple of weeks hearing the evidence that proves that this defendant"—here she turned and pointed to Evan—"murdered a man named Ron Nolan. The defendant hated Ron Nolan. There's no doubt about it. He thought Ron Nolan had stolen his girlfriend. He hated him for being a business success in Iraq, where Defendant had been injured while serving in the Army. He blamed Ron Nolan for the injuries he'd received, injuries that actually occurred because Defendant, after a long night of drinking, led his men into an ambush in Iraq. Evan Scholler hated Ron Nolan.

"He made no secret of it. He told his parents, he told his girlfriend. He hinted as much to some of the police officers with whom he worked. He stalked Ron Nolan by illegally using police information to keep track of his whereabouts. He broke into Ron Nolan's house and tried to frame him for the killing of two Iraqi citizens murdered in the United States.

"Finally, the evidence will show that Defendant carefully planned and premeditated this murder. Several days before his attack on Mr. Nolan, Defendant, *while on duty and in uniform as a policeman for the city of Redwood City,* contacted a locksmith and tricked him into letting him into Mr. Nolan's townhouse. The locksmith admitted Defendant into the home. In a subsequent search, the FBI found planted in that house evidence related to the murders of Ibrahim and Shatha Khalil. Unfortunately for Defendant, his plan failed when Ron Nolan found the evidence that was planted and called the FBI, who then discovered Defendant's fingerprints in Mr. Nolan's home.

"The defendant hated Ron Nolan, and when he couldn't frame him for murder, in a drunken rage he went to Ron Nolan's house and killed him. The actual cause of death was a single gunshot wound to the head. Not just to the head, mind you, but fired from a gun held just inches from the skull.

"But Defendant didn't just murder Ron Nolan. First, he administered a savage beating. He broke his jaw. He broke his wrist. He broke at least two of his ribs. He left bruises and cuts and injuries over a lot of Ron Nolan's body. The evidence will show that this defendant hated Ron Nolan, and he killed him.

"But if that is what happened, how do we know he did it? Well, for openers, he told his girlfriend he was going to. He left his fingerprint on the murder weapon found by the body. And within hours after Nolan's body was found, the police found Defendant cowering in his apartment, Ron Nolan's blood still on his hands and clothes, the injuries he'd received in the fight still unhealed, and the murdered man's blood still on the brass knuckles he used to inflict the beating I've described.

"This defendant hated Ron Nolan and he killed him. And he killed him in a way that the law defines as first-degree murder. At the close of the evidence in this case, I'll stand before you and that is the verdict for which I will ask."

Mills was doing it by the book, dispassionately laying out the elements of the People's case. Like all prosecutors, she would consistently refer to the deceased as "Mr. Nolan," and later, sometimes, even Ron, to humanize him to the jury—a living, breathing human being whose life had been prematurely taken from him. By the same token,

Evan Scholler would forever after remain "the defendant," or even, less familiarly, simply "Defendant"—a clinical term denoting the place in society to which he'd fallen. A nameless, faceless perverter of the social order who deserved only the most cursory acknowledgment as a human being and no sympathy.

In the center of the courtroom one more time, she paused, noting that Washburn had let her go on this long without objection. It was a calculated technique, she knew, to signal to the jury that, in spite of this apparently damning litany condemning the defendant, the defense remained confident—nay, unconcerned by these allegations.

Letting out a theatrical sigh, Mills again allowed herself a glance over to the defendant's table, but this look communicated sadness and resignation. No one would have enjoyed putting on the kind of recitation she'd just completed. The human condition was sometimes a terrible burden. Mills had done her disagreeable though imperative job, hoping to bring justice to the evil defendant and closure to the victim and to those who had loved him.

WASHBURN HAD THE OPTION of coming out swinging now with his defense opening statement, or waiting until the People had presented their case and delivering it then. After Mills had sat down, Tollson asked him what he wanted to do, and he said he'd be going right ahead with his statement now. He didn't like to let the jury sit too long with one story without being made aware that there was another one, or another version of the same one. He found that if the prosecution got to make an unrebutted opening statement and then followed it with up to a week or more of its own witnesses, all he could do was play defense. And this passive style didn't win too many cases.

But, furthering his earlier strategy of avoiding interruptions and objections, he no sooner indicated to the judge his decision to give his opening statement—enthusiasm to defend his innocent client!—than he got the gallery chortling by commenting, in his folksiest manner, "But after Ms. Whelan-Miille's eloquent opening statement, Your Honor, the bladder of a poor old country lawyer could sure use a short recess." Which of course, reflected his opinion that the prosecution's opening had not in any way threatened his client, or even called into question Evan's innocence. Washburn would get to all that in just a minute in his own opening statement and clear up any nagging little inconsistencies that might point to Evan's guilt.

But first he had to pee.

Though, actually, he didn't.

The judge gave them fifteen minutes, and Washburn and Evan took the opportunity to walk out the courtroom's back door to the small holding cell, where they sat across from each other on the cold cement blocks that served as benches. Washburn had shaved carefully but had missed a fairly obvious spot along his jawline for three days running now. Beyond that, never sartorially close to splendid, in a too-large wheat-colored suit with a ludicrous orange tie, he looked particularly disheveled today, as he would every day of the trial. His ten-year-old brown wingtips had frayed laces and holes in both soles, so he could cross either leg and get the regular-guy message out. Juries, he believed, didn't like fancy dressers as defense lawyers. They liked real people who talked straight and respected their intelligence. And it didn't hurt if you had a personality either.

But now his immediate concern was his client. Evan had cleaned up pretty good. In contrast to defense attorneys, juries tended to like handsome and decently dressed defendants. Not too handsome, especially in a jury with seven men, but respectable. Evan's body language already spoke with an accent of defeat and dejection—not unexpected, given Mills's effective castigation of him—but troublesome nonetheless.

They both sat with their elbows on their knees, heads nearly touching. "You don't look good," Washburn said. "That get to you?"

Evan raised his eyes. "I can't believe I did so many stupid things."

"You were injured," Washburn said with apparent sincerity. "You weren't back to yourself yet. You are now."

"You believe that?"

"I do."

A pause. "You believe *me*?"

"I wouldn't be here if I didn't."

"Is that true?"

Washburn took a long beat. "That is God's truth, my son. You may not know what you did, and you know what that's consistent with?"

"What's that?"

"Innocence. If you weren't there, you wouldn't know what happened, would you?"

Evan sighed. "Everett, I broke into his house."

"You did not break into his house. You let yourself into his house."

"Either way. That was just stupid."

"Granted. It's one of the things I find fascinating about this case, all the stupidity." He held up a hand. "No, I'm serious. You've admitted to a lot of stupid behavior, plus you were drinking way too much, which never helps, but you've never admitted planting that evidence at Nolan's, have you?"

"That's because I didn't."

"You know that. I know it. And that would have been another stupid move. So it's not the stupidity that's keeping you from copping to it. You see what I'm saying? Staying drunk for four days after your fight with Nolan was stupid. Not going to work all that time was stupid. But you didn't drive up to Nolan's in an alcoholic stupor, somehow get into his home without alerting him, get ahold of his gun, and kill him. You couldn't have done it. Your state of mind, pardon me, was too stupid. Whoever did this planned it, timed it, did it right. And call me a softhearted romantic, I don't see that being you."

Evan almost broke a smile. "You going to argue that?"

"If I can get the right spin on it, which might be a trick. But, listen, the main thing ..."

"I'm listening."

"I need you to buck up in there. You don't have to be indignant, or angry, or anything negative. But you've got to sit up straight and don't let the weight of all the shit she's piling on you get you down. You'll look guilty and pathetic."

"You want me to look happy?"

"No! God, no. You're unjustly accused. Nobody's happy with that. But you're a soldier. You're fighting the good fight. You've been through battle, betrayal, brain injury, bottle-epsy, and now this bullshit. You beat every other one of 'em, and now you're standing up to this one.

That's the message. Stick with it. Those jurors are going to try to be objective, okay, but they're twelve unpredictable human beings. Don't forget that. And if they're inclined to like you, that's not a bad thing. Every one of their votes is going to count equally. You get one of 'em on your side, it's over."

Evan sat up straight, his back against the wall. "You really think we can still win this thing?"

"We're not in it to lose, Evan. So when I go out and razzle-dazzle 'em in the next few minutes, it'd be good to have an enthusiastic fan in the peanut gallery. You think you can do that?"

"I'll give it a shot. If I knew what the peanut gallery was."

"You know. The peanut gallery. Howdy Doody, Buffalo Bob, Clarabelle the Clown. All those guys." But clearly, Evan was clueless about *The Howdy Doody Show*. Washburn hit him on the shoulder. "Anyway, so forget the peanut gallery. Just hang tough out there and remember that the jury's looking at you. We're doing good."

"If you say so, Everett. If you say so."

At that moment, the bailiff knocked and opened the courtroom door, telling them their time was up. Washburn let Evan precede him, then stopped short in the doorway. His heartbeat stuttered. And again. He'd had a heart attack about five years previously, and this did not feel like that. There was no pain. The arrhythmia caught his breath, that was all, and then the moment was over. But suddenly he found that the confidence he'd been exuding in his pep talk with Evan had vanished. The harsh reality, as his body took another opportunity to remind him, was that he was getting old. He persisted in living each day with the myth that he was still at the peak of his powers and would live forever. When in truth, he was even older than the Howdy Doody generation, maybe even older than Buffalo Bob himself, now long deceased. He'd lost the PTSD fight to a far younger opponent and now, no matter what he'd told Evan, he faced a far more difficult uphill battle against Mills. It struck him that he might not have the advantage this time, that age and treachery might not overcome youth and skill.

As he stepped into the courtroom behind his client, he realized that he'd allowed his shoulders to slump, that his right hand had lingered at his chest. He willed it down, squared himself away, caught the eye of the young and confident Mary Patricia Whelan-Miille at her table, and flashed her a mouthful of teeth that would have done a horse proud.

"MY FRIENDS, I'm going to speak to you for just a few minutes to tell you about the rest of the evidence in this case—things that the prosecution chose not to mention because they don't fit Ms. Miille's version of what happened, and things that at the close of this case will still be unexplained. This evidence will make you wonder whether Evan Scholler killed Ron Nolan, and will leave you with a reasonable doubt and will require you—require you if you fulfill your oaths as jurors—to find Evan Scholler not guilty."

Washburn stood with his hands in his pockets, relaxed and genial. He'd actually won a round or two with Tollson in chambers, though it really didn't feel like it. But the whole question of Iraq, he'd argued, had to be part of the trial. It was relevant on its face, and essential if the jurors were even going to begin to grasp any of the complexities surrounding both the defendant and the victim. And Tollson had agreed with him. To a point.

He intended to find out where that point exactly was.

"This case and the issues surrounding it began in Iraq," he intoned. "It's important to understand the significance that Iraq plays in the affair, because so much of the evidence presented by the People that appears to cast Mr. Scholler in a negative light in fact paints a very different picture when viewed in its true context, the context of what happened in Iraq.

"You will hear testimony that the deceased was a highly trained mercenary with a long history of both overt and covert operations in some of the most violent places in the world—Afghanistan, Kuwait, El Salvador, and Iraq. At the time of his death, he was working as a government contractor for Allstrong Security, which has offices both here in California and in Iraq. All of his adult life, the man was surrounded by death and violence. This was his livelihood and he was good at it.

"Evan Scholler, on the other hand, worked as a Redwood City police patrolman until he was called up for deployment to Iraq in the first months after the invasion. He served over there for about three months before he was involved in a firefight against Islamic insurgents in Baghdad in which he suffered a head wound and traumatic brain injury. In a coma that lasted eleven days, he was airlifted first to a field hospital in Iraq, then taken to Germany, and finally brought to Walter Reed Hospital. In March of two thousand four, he came back to work for the police department here in this city."

He paused to meet a few more eyes in the jury box. There it was, he thought with some satisfaction and relief. Short and sweet, and he'd gotten it in. He'd hoped that bringing in this information first thing and right up front might catch Mills in a first-inning lull, and sure enough he'd pulled it off.

Dang! He loved the drama of a trial.

Taking a breath, his heart palpitations forgotten, he moved on to the more pressing evidentiary issues. "Ms. Miille has described at some length the evidence that she says will compel you to convict Evan of first-degree murder. That evidence is neither as clear nor as uncontradicted as she might have led you to believe. She talked a lot about the day of the killing. Just for openers, we don't know the day of the killing. Mr. Nolan was last seen on Wednesday, June third. He was found dead on Saturday, June sixth.

"Now, the prosecutor says he was killed on Wednesday, the third. If so, that would be convenient for the prosecution because that is a date when my client spoke harsh words about Mr. Nolan. The evidence will show, and it is in fact undisputed, that Evan had too many drinks that night, at a bar a few blocks from here called the Old Town Traven. There he learned that the deceased had tried to implicate him in the murders of two Iraqi citizens. Tara Wheatley, Evan's girlfriend, will tell you that, drunk and in a rage, he told her that he was going to go to Mr. Nolan's house and kill him. And, in fact, Evan has never denied that he went to Mr. Nolan's house that night, and that the two men fought.

"So the prosecution says, and wishes you to conclude, that that's the night the deceased was killed. But as the saying goes, wishing don't make it so. There is no evidence that Mr. Nolan was killed on Wednesday, as opposed to Thursday, as opposed to Friday.

"And let's take the two motives that, according to the

prosecution, caused Evan Scholler to commit murder. First, jealousy. Ms. Wheatley will testify that on the evening of June third, she came to find Evan at the Old Town Traven. She invited him to come back to her apartment for the night. She told him that she had stopped seeing Mr. Nolan, and that she was in love with him."

As though taken by an apparition, Washburn stopped in his tracks, spread his palms to the jurors. "Now, it's been a few years since I've experienced some of the finer emotions such as young love, but if my memory serves, when a woman tells you she's dropped another boyfriend in your favor, that's when jealousy's much more likely to go away than to make you want to go and duke it out with your rival."

This last witticism produced a gratifying hum from the gallery. Several of the jurors broke smiles as well. Feeding off those vibes, Washburn went on. "Now, anger. The evidence will indeed show that Evan was angry— angry enough to drive to Mr. Nolan's house and engage him in a fistfight. He was angry, the evidence will show, because he believed he was being framed for a murder he didn't commit. That's a good reason to be angry," Washburn added. "It might make any of you angry."

"Your Honor! Objection."

Washburn turned and took the opportunity to glance out at the gallery, always a reasonable litmus for how he was doing. Nobody snoring yet, anyway. He produced his patented half bow, acknowledging the objection, and turned back to the jury box, without even waiting for the judge to rule. "I'll withdraw that last comment, Your Honor," he said.

And continued. "Why, you may ask, did my client

illegally let himself into his rival's house? He had come to believe that Mr. Nolan was in fact the killer of Ibrahim and Shatha Khalil. He will testify that he accompanied Mr. Nolan on a kill-and-destroy mission in Iraq that featured the same type of fragmentation grenades as were used in the Khalil murders. This might have been an error in judgment, but it was not a prelude to murder. Had he intended to kill Mr. Nolan, he could have simply waited in his home and done it instead of gathering evidence against him to send to the authorities.

"These are all points that the prosecution has presented to you as facts, and they simply are not.

"Did my client hate Ron Nolan? Yes, he did.

"Was Evan Scholler struggling to recover from the physical injury and mental anguish he sustained as a result of fighting for his country in Iraq? Yes, he was.

"As a result of the pain, both physical and mental, did he sometimes drink too much during the months of his recovery? Yes, he did.

"And as a result of the combination of these things, did he display bad judgment? Without a doubt.

"He did misuse his authority as a policeman to keep track of Ron Nolan's whereabouts. He did break into Ron Nolan's house in the belief that Ron Nolan had a hand in the deaths of the Khalils. He did give way to despair and alcohol and anger, and threaten Ron Nolan. He did go to Ron Nolan's house and fight with him on the night of June third. He did all of these things and has freely admitted doing all of these things.

"But these are not the things for which he is on trial.

"Ladies and gentlemen of the jury, at the close of all of the evidence, you will find that what Evan Scholler did not do was kill Ron Nolan. That is something the evidence does not show. And when, at the close of the evidence, you can see that this has not been proved against my client, you will be obliged by your conscience and by the laws of this state to find him not guilty."

[23]

AFTER THE OPENING STATEMENTS, they got right
down to it as Mills called her first witness.

The medical examiner, Dr. Lloyd Barnsdale, had been
in his position for fifteen years. Dry as dust, pale as the
corpses in his lab, the bespeckled and weak-chinned coroner wore what was left of his graying, dirty blond hair in
a combover. Today, though the warm Indian summer
days of September continued outside, he wore a cardigan
sweater over a plain white shirt and a snap-on bow tie.

Mills waited impatiently for the ME to be sworn in.
The confidence she'd felt in the morning when she'd
finished with her opening statement had pretty much
dissipated under the amiable onslaught of Washburn's
monologue. The truth was that she had her work cut out
for her. It would never do to become complacent. Washburn would eat her alive if she gave him any opportunity
at all.

"Dr. Barnsdale, you did the autopsy on Ron Nolan,
did you not?"

"I did."

"Would you please tell the Court your ruling as to the
cause of death?"

"Certainly. Death was caused by a gunshot wound fired at close range into the head."

Barnsdale had, of course, been a witness a hundred times before. This did not necessarily make him a good witness. He spoke with a wispiness that was very much of a piece with his looks. Mills, from halfway across the room, found herself straining to hear him.

She saw that the jurors had, to a person, come forward in their chairs. It did not help that outside the building, road construction continued unabated on Redwood City's never-ending downtown beautification project. The noise of the heavy equipment was nearly as loud as the building's air-conditioning.

Mills backed up a couple of steps, to just beyond the last juror in the box. If she could hear the witness, so could all the jurors. She raised her own voice, hoping to lead by example. "Doctor," she asked, "were there other marks or injuries to the body?"

"Yes. There were multiple signs of blunt-force and sharp-force trauma—contusions, bruises, and lacerations on the torso, the groin, and the face."

"Approximately how many separate injuries were inflicted on the victim?"

"I counted twenty-eight separate injuries."

"And did each of these appear to be a separate application of force?"

"There were a couple that might have been the result of a single blow. For example, the same blow with an instrument could have hit the victim on the forearm and the head. On the other hand, from the size and irregular features of some of the injury sites, it appeared that some bruises might have resulted from multiple blows landing in approximately the same place on the body. I would have to say the man was hit at least two dozen times."

Mills went back to her table and brought forward a large piece of cardboard on which she'd taped some 8½ × 11 color photographs from the autopsy and had it entered into evidence as People's Two, since the autopsy report was People's One.

When they had gotten to it, Judge Tollson had hand-picked the six autopsy photos that he was going to allow the jury to see. Mills considered his choice a partial victory for herself—whoever had done this to another human being barely deserved to be called one himself. Even without the head wound, the damage to Nolan's body was severe.

"Doctor," Mills began, "using the photographs to illustrate your testimony, can you characterize these injuries more particularly?"

"Well, yes," Barnsdale whispered. "As we can see in Photograph A, there were quite a few injuries that either raised bruises, or cut the skin, or both. Although the gunshot wound, particularly the exit wound in the back of the head, no doubt obliterated some of these, there still remained a profusion of them, particularly on the head."

Using the laser pointer, she walked him through the other five photographs.

"Do you know what caused these bruises and contusions?"

"Not specifically. It was my finding that there appeared to be more than one type of bruise, caused by different objects, some blunt and some less so."

"Doctor, were you given any implement or implements in an effort to determine whether they might have caused the injuries you observed?"

"Yes. I was given a fireplace poker and a pair of brass knuckles from the evidence locker of the Redwood City Police Department."

Two more exhibits marked and presented to the doctor.

"Yes," he said, "these are the items I compared."

"What was your conclusion, Doctor?"

"Several contusions, particularly on the jawline, appear to be the result of contact with the brass knuckles. These particular knuckles have a piece or fragment missing from one edge. You can clearly see the pattern injury in several locations that match this implement. Further, in a general sense, the damage inflicted at those injury sites is consistent with what one might expect from being struck with this sort of an object."

"And what damage is that?"

"They both cut and bruise. They leave a distinctive imprint."

"Were there a lot of these brass knuckle contusions?"

"Distinctly, there were three. Perhaps five. I could not rule them out as having been used to cause other injuries, but there was not enough detail to tell you definitively that this was the weapon used."

"What about the poker?"

"I could only find one injury across the forearm that definitively appeared consistent with the poker or something very like it. But all of the injuries to the top and side of the head were consistent with a blow from a hard, cylindrical object that could have been this poker. Further, I understand from the lab that the victim's blood and tissue was removed from the poker, which also supports the suggestion that this was the weapon used."

"As to the injuries you've discussed so far, were they consistent with having been inflicted with a man's fist?"

"No. I don't think so. The injuries I've attributed to the poker and brass knuckles were far too extensive typically to have resulted from a simple blow from the fist."

"But that leaves, Doctor, does it not, many other bruises on Mr. Nolan's body?"

"Yes, it does."

"Could they have been inflicted by a man's fists?"

"Well, yes they could, although they are very nonspecific and might have been inflicted by any blunt object, including a glancing blow by the poker or brass knuckles, or even by the impact of Mr. Nolan having hit the ground or a table or anything else as a result of one of the other blows."

"Doctor, could you describe the gunshot wound in any greater detail?"

"Yes, it was what is called a close contact wound, meaning the gun was fired right up against the skin of the forehead."

"Doctor, are you able to tell us the order in which the injuries were inflicted?"

"Not really. Logically, it would seem likely the gunshot wound would have to be last because it would have been immediately lethal. As to the blunt force trauma, it appeared that some had actually started to heal slightly, and therefore might have been inflicted before some of the others which showed less signs of healing. But the body heals more or less quickly at different times and at different places on the body. This isn't a very reliable way to sequence injuries. All I can say is that all of these injuries were *perimortem,* meaning that they were inflicted around the time of death."

"Thank you, Doctor. No further questions." Mills, apparently shaken by the photos and the testimony in spite of herself, had gone nearly as pale as the medical examiner. She turned back to the defense table. "Your witness."

WASHBURN HAD THE IMPRESSION that Mills had cut her questions short because she was getting sick. Beyond that, he'd barely heard the testimony of the witness from back where he sat, and he doubted that the jurors, intent on the photographs, had heard too much of it either. He normally didn't like to spend too much time with this more or less pro forma witness, the medical examiner, since typically all his testimony served to do was prove that a murder had been committed, and that wasn't at issue here. But this time, he thought he might pry a nugget loose from this normally unpromising vein.

And if he was going to go to that trouble, he wanted the jury to hear what the man had to say. So when he got to the middle of the room, he pitched his own volume down to the nearly inaudible. "Doctor," he said, "can you tell how old a bruise is?"

"I'm sorry," the witness replied, cupping his ear. "I didn't hear the question."

Washburn barely heard the response, but came back with his question just a few decibels louder than the first time.

Barnsdale leaned forward, his face scrunched in concentration. "Can I what?" he asked. "I'm sorry."

Behind Washburn, the gallery was getting restive. Tollson brought his gavel down one time firmly. "I want it quiet in this courtroom!" He brought his focus back inside the guardrail that separated the gallery from the bull-pen of the court. "And I need you two gentlemen both to speak up, is that clear?"

"Yes, Your Honor," Washburn straightened up and nearly shouted.

Shaking his head—this was rank theatrics, circus behavior—Tollson looked down at the witness. "Doctor?"

Barnsdale looked around and up at him. "Sir?" A whisper.

"Louder, please. The jury needs to hear you."

Back to Washburn. "Go ahead, Counselor."

"Thank you, Your Honor. Doctor." A smile meant they were friends. "You've talked about these bruises on the body of the victim, that we've seen now in these photographs. My question is can you tell the age of a bruise?"

"As I just said, only within very broad limits."

"Please humor me, Doctor. Explain in some detail how you can tell that one bruise is older than another."

Clearing his throat, Barnsdale complied. "Yes, certainly. Bruises begin healing as soon as they are made, so the degree of healing, diminishing of swelling, thickness and solidity of scabbing, color, and so on, can tell you roughly how long it is since the bruise was sustained. We all know that some people bruise more easily than others. And it's also true that the same person might bruise more easily on a different part of his body, at a different time in his life, or depending on his general health. But all things being equal, we can get some idea from the bruises themselves."

Tollson, from the bench, intoned, "Louder, please."

Washburn went on. "And these bruises to the victim, were they all the same age, so to speak?"

"No."

"No? What was the greatest difference you observed between them?"

"Impossible to say."

"Impossible, Doctor. You can't give us any information? Are you telling me one of these bruises could have been inflicted on Mr. Nolan when he was five years old, and another a few minutes before his death, and there would be no difference."

A small round of laughter from the gallery.

"Well, no, of course not."

"Then could some of these injuries been inflicted a month before Mr. Nolan's death?"

"No."

"A week before?"

Some hesitation. "I doubt that seriously."

"But it could have been a week before."

"I doubt it."

"Well, certainly, Doctor, some of the injuries could have been inflicted three or four days before Mr. Nolan's death. That's true, isn't it?"

Washburn knew he had the doctor, and knew what the answer had to be.

"Well, I'd have to say yes."

"And, Doctor, did you make any effort at the time specifically to note in your autopsy the age of the various bruises?"

"I didn't record a specific analysis of that for each bruise."

"Why not?"

"It seemed irrelevant at the time. It certainly was irrelevant to the cause of death."

"Because none of these blows killed him, isn't that

right, Doctor? Mr. Nolan died from the gunshot wound, whenever that was inflicted. True?"

"Yes."

"Thank you, Doctor. No further questions."

NEXT UP was Shondra Delahassau, a forensics sergeant with the police department. A dark ebony woman in her early thirties with her hair in cornrows, projecting competence and confidence, she couldn't have been more of a contrast to Dr. Barnsdale.

"We got the call on a Saturday afternoon after the groundskeeper, who was blowing leaves off the back patio, saw evidence of a fight and what looked to be splashes of blood in the living room."

"And what happened next?" Mills asked.

"Well, the first responders to arrive were a patrol team, who entered the townhouse to see if there were injured persons or suspects still on the premises. They found only a dead body and left without disturbing anything. Once the house was cleared, they waited out front for other officers. My unit, which is crime scene investigation, got there about the same time as Lieutenant Spinoza, who had obtained a search warrant, at around four-thirty."

"And what did you find inside?"

"First, of course, the blood, a lot of blood. In the rug and on the walls and so on."

"Did your unit take samples of this blood for analysis, Sergeant?"

"Yes. We took samples from every location for testing in the lab."

Mills spoke to the judge. "Your Honor, I believe the defense is prepared to stipulate that DNA testing matched blood samples from the premises to either the defendant or Ron Nolan."

This was bad news, and a buzz arose in the gallery, but Washburn had been only too happy to enter the stipulation after Mills had told him that the lab tech who had actually done the DNA testing was out on maternity leave. It wasn't to his advantage anyway to have a half day of scientific evidence putting Evan's blood and Nolan's blood all over Nolan's home.

"Thank you, Sergeant," Mills said. "Now, back to the townhouse itself, what else did you find?"

"Well, furniture had been knocked over in the living room and in the office. We found a fireplace poker that was stained with the victim's blood on the floor in the office. Then we discovered the victim's body on the floor in the bedroom. There was a nine-millimeter Beretta semiautomatic on the bed."

"What did you do next?"

"While Lieutenant Spinoza called the medical examiner's office, I supervised while members of my unit started taking photographs of the scene, collecting blood, hair, and fiber samples and fingerprints if any were available. My usual drill at a murder scene."

Mills duly marked and had her identify almost two dozen samples with the trace evidence from Nolan's place. When they'd finished, Mills pulled the gun out of a protective firearms box and gave it to the bailiff to clear, demonstrating on the record that it was unloaded and safe to handle. "Now, Sergeant, did you personally dust the gun for fingerprints?"

"I did."

"Did you find any usable latents?"

"Yes."

"And were you able to identify whose fingerprints were found on the gun?"

"We did. It held the fingerprints of Mr. Nolan, as well as those of the defendant, Mr. Scholler."

Again, a rush of comment swirled across the gallery. Mills let it go on for a satisfying moment before she turned to Washburn and gave him the witness.

WASHBURN HAD ALWAYS believed that there were basically only two ways to defend against a murder charge. The first was to present an affirmative defense case that, on its own merits, created either mitigation or reasonable doubt. This former approach had been Washburn's stock-in-trade over the years and he'd done exceedingly well with it. He would listen to all the prosecution's facts and theories, and then introduce his own defense case, which might include self-defense, diminished capacity, temporary insanity, or any other of the many psychiatric defenses (including PTSD). In San Francisco, over time, these became pretty much slam dunks. But even in San Mateo County, such a strong affirmative defense would often convince a jury to convict only of a lesser charge. Washburn believed this was because people basically wanted to believe in the goodness of their fellow man. Even if they had done something truly heinous, if there was a semiplausible reason that they'd been driven to it by events outside of their control, jurors tended to give them a break.

The second way to win was, in Washburn's experience, both far more difficult and far less effective; this was the reactive defense, which challenged every fact and assertion made by the prosecution. Naturally, good defense attorneys also did this automatically even when they had a strong affirmative case, but debunking a carefully built prosecution was never an easy task. In most cases, of course, this was because the defendant was guilty. But beyond that, it was a huge hurdle for most jurors to disbelieve government testimony and to doubt the sworn testimony of authority figures such as doctors, forensics experts, and the police.

When Tollson had taken PTSD away from him, Washburn knew he was stuck with a reactive defense, and this was what had filled him with such a sense of dread. Now here he was with his second witness on his first day—a woman whom he normally would have dismissed without a cross-examination because she had nothing of substance that would help his case—and he was rising to question her, grasping at straws just to keep up the charade that he was putting on an enthusiastic, even passionate, defense.

"Sergeant Delahassau," he began, "you've testified that you tested Mr. Nolan's townhome for fingerprints, blood, hairs, and fibers, isn't that so? Your usual drill, I believe you called it."

"Yes, that's right."

"And you discovered matches with Mr. Scholler's blood and fingerprints?"

"Yes."

"What about his hair?"

The gallery let out what seemed to Washburn to be a collective chuckle.

"Yes, we found samples of his hair too."

"Did you find any other hair, besides Mr. Nolan's and Mr. Scholler's?"

"Yes. We found traces of hair from at least three other individuals."

"Can you tell if that hair was from a male or female?"

"Under some circumstances, DNA can determine that. You need a follicle."

"And to your knowledge, did anyone run DNA tests on these hair samples?"

For the first time, Delahassau's face clouded. She threw a troubled look over to Mills, then came back to Washburn. "Uh, no, sir."

"Why not?"

Another hesitation. "Well. We had no other suspects with which to match samples."

"But these hair samples surely indicated that someone else had been in Mr. Nolan's townhouse, isn't that true?"

"Well, yes, but they could have been years old, or ..."

"But, bottom line, Sergeant, you do not know if the three hair samples found in the victim's home came from men or from women, do you?"

"No."

Unsure of what, if anything, he'd just proven, Washburn decided he'd take his small victory now and move on to his other minuscule point. "Sergeant," he asked, "did you recover the bullet that had killed Mr. Nolan?"

Letting out a sigh of relief that the other line of questioning had ended, Delahassau reverted to her confident self. "Yes. It was embedded in the floor directly under the exit wound in his head."

"So he was shot while he was already on the ground?"

"That appeared to be the case, yes."

"And did you run a ballistics test on the Beretta?"

"No. The bullet was deformed too much for that."

Washburn brought his hand up to his mouth in an

apparently genuine show of perplexity. "Sergeant," he asked with an exaggerated slowness, "are you telling me that you do not know for an absolute certainty that the bullet that killed Mr. Nolan came from the weapon that had my client's fingerprints on it?"

"No, sir, but . . ."

"Thank you, Sergeant. That's all."

He'd barely gotten the words out when Mills was on her feet. "Redirect, Your Honor?"

Tollson waved her forward. "Sergeant," she began before she'd even reached her place, "what was the caliber of the bullet that killed Mr. Nolan?"

"Nine millimeter."

"And what was the caliber of the recovered weapon?"

"Nine millimeter."

"And was the recovered weapon a revolver or a semi-automatic?"

"It was a semiautomatic."

"Now, Sergeant, when a nine-millimeter weapon is fired, what happens to the casing—the brass jacket behind the actual bullet that holds the gunpowder that propels the blast?"

"It gets ejected."

"You mean it pops out of the gun?"

"Yes."

"And did you find a casing for a nine-millimeter round in Mr. Nolan's bedroom?"

"Yes. It was among the sheets on the bed."

"Were you able to match that casing to the recovered Beretta?"

"Yes."

"So there was one nine-millimeter bullet and no others recovered from the scene, one nine-millimeter casing and no others recovered from the scene, and although the bullet itself was not capable of comparison, the only casing at the scene that could have contained that bullet was fired by the nine-millimeter Beretta with the defendant's fingerprints on it."

"Yes."

"Thank you."

[24]

WHEN THEY ALL GOT BACK to their tables after a short afternoon recess, Washburn noticed that Mills seemed to be losing her sense of humor as the day wore on. But whether Mills was enjoying it or not, she was putting on the kind of straightforward, linear case that juries tended to like. Her next witness was Evan's direct superior in the police department, Lieutenant Lochland, who, alarmed at Scholler's absence from work, had found him in his apartment, drunk and covered in blood, and eventually placed him under arrest.

"Lieutenant," she began, "Defendant was under your direct supervision while he worked with the police department. Isn't that so?"

But Washburn and Evan had talked about this coming testimony on the break, and the old lawyer was on his feet before she'd finished her question. "Objection! Relevance. Three fifty-two, Your Honor."

Tollson turned a questioning look down to Mills. "Counselor?"

"Foundational, Your Honor," she said.

"That's fairly broad. Can you be more specific?"

"Goes to Defendant's state of mind leading up to the act. Also foundational to the break-in at Mr. Nolan's."

The judge, in what Washburn was beginning to recognize as something of a pattern, pulled his glasses off to ponder for a minute.

Before he could put them back on and render his decision, Washburn said, "Your Honor, if you will, I'd like to request a sidebar." If Mills was getting tired or losing her chops due to low blood sugar, if this was her afternoon tendency—and her body language made it appear to be—Washburn wouldn't hesitate to use that against her.

A shorter pause this time, until Tollson nodded. "Very well. Counsel may approach." When the two attorneys had gotten in front of the bench, Tollson peered over it. "What's the problem, Everett?" he said.

"Your Honor, there's no possible relevance to Lieutenant Lochland's relationship to my client. The only thing this will get the People is negative character stuff. That Evan was angry, that he lied to his superiors when he broke into Nolan's place, that he disobeyed orders, maybe got drunk on duty. There's nothing possibly relevant there and even if it is, it's far more prejudicial than probative and opens up a whole number of cans of worms."

"Ms. Whelan-Miille?"

Clearly, Washburn's attack on this point had blindsided her. But she wasn't about to give up any ground without some kind of a fight. "The lieutenant's a hostile witness, Your Honor. You think he wants to be up here testifying against another cop, and one that worked for him? He's not going to say anything bad about Evan's character. At worst, he'll say he was mixed up and still recovering from the wounds in Iraq. And that will, if anything, incite sympathy from the jury. This is all part of Mr. Washburn's case anyway. How can he want to put it in through his own witnesses and keep it out with mine?"

"If it was all that sympathetic," Tollson said, "I doubt if Mr. Washburn would object to the testimony. And in that case, why do you want it?" the judge asked. When Mills couldn't come up with an answer in the next ten seconds, Tollson stepped back in. "Let's move on, shall we? How's that sound?"

Washburn inclined his head. "Thank you, Your Honor."

Back at the defense table, he pulled his yellow legal pad over in front of him and drew a happy face that he showed to his client under his hand. At the same time, Mills tried to pick up with her witness. "Lieutenant, it was you who arrested Defendant, was it not?"

"Yeah. That was me."

"Can you tell the jury the specifics?"

"Sure." He turned to face the panel and began in a conversational tone. "Lieutenant Spinoza—he's the head of the homicide detail—called me at home as a courtesy on that Saturday to tell me he was worried about Patrolman Scholler. He'd been called on the Ron Nolan homicide and remembered that Patrolman Scholler had looked up that name on the police computer in the past few days. Spinoza wondered if I'd heard from him and I told him I hadn't. Patrolman Scholler hadn't been in to work on Thursday or Friday, so when I got Spinoza's call, I was a little worried myself.

"I thought the best bet would be to go check out his apartment, so I drove up there—he lived in one of those units along Edgewood Road. All the blinds in the windows were pulled down, so there was no seeing in. I knocked and called out his name, and nobody answered, but I heard some movement inside, like something, some object, falling over.

"Now I'm starting to think something's wrong. I get out my cell phone and call his number and the phone inside starts ringing, and I start pounding on the door, calling for him."

Washburn could have objected to this narrative, but again knew it was coming in, and was just as happy to get through it as quickly as possible.

"And finally I hear, 'Yeah, one minute,' and a few seconds later Patrolman Scholler opens the door, just like that. Then I take a look at him and he's all beat up. So I ask him what happened? But he didn't seem to understand the question. So then I asked him if he knew about a guy named Ron Nolan, that he'd been killed." Lochland stopped, sat back, clasped his hands in his lap.

But Mills wouldn't have called him up if he didn't have something she needed. So she asked. "And did he have any reaction to that, Lieutenant?"

"Yes, ma'am. He swore."

"He swore. What exactly did he say, Lieutenant?"

Washburn knew the answer to this question, and came halfway out of his chair as he objected and, much to the displeasure of both Mills and Tollson, requested another sidebar.

When both attorneys were again in front of the judge, Mills started right in. "Your Honor, this is a frivolous objection if we've ever heard one. Mr. Washburn knows what Defendant's words were upon learning about Mr. Nolan's death, and the jury needs to hear them."

Washburn shot back at her. "There is no need to subject the jury to vulgarity, Your Honor. The defense will stipulate that Evan used language that some might find offensive, in spite of the fact that even that admission might taint him in the eyes of some of the jury members."

"Oh, please." Mills rolled her eyes. "The man's on trial for murder, Your Honor. He's broken into the victim's house. He's admitted to beating him with brass knuckles—"

"*Fighting* him with brass knuckles," Washburn replied calmly. "The evidence supports a fight between two professional warriors, not a beating."

"This is hair-splitting of the most obvious kind, Your Honor. And, in fact, on reflection, I wonder if Mr. Washburn didn't help prepare Lieutenant Lochland in his testimony so that he would set up this objection, rather than simply repeat Defendant's words, which he'd always used with me in my preparation."

"Your Honor." Washburn's face reflected his sadness that his opponent had stooped so low as to accuse him of coaching her witness, although of course he had done just that. If he could somehow keep Evan's unfortunate choice of words, uttered in an alcoholic stupor, out of the record, it would be a significant victory. "I strenuously object to Counsel's intimation that I may have acted unethically."

"I'm not saying that, Your Honor. I'm saying that the jury knows that Defendant did all these other pretty questionable things, plus he lied to his boss and his locksmith friend. The fact that he used a mild swear word isn't likely to stain his reputation at this point."

Tollson put his glasses back on and scowled down through them. "I agree, Counselor. The witness can answer the question."

"Your Honor," Washburn said, "allowing a witness to use vulgarity on the stand is a slippery slope that . . ."

"Counselor, I don't believe . . . we're not talking about the f-word, the c-word, or the n-word, are we?"

"No, Your Honor," Mills said.

"We can't know that yet, Your Honor, the witness hasn't answered yet."

But this last comment, finally, got under Tollson's skin. "Don't toy with me, Counselor. I've made my ruling. Stop wasting the Court's time."

"Of course, Your Honor. Apologies."

Tollson ignored him. "Ms. Whelan-Miille," he said, "you may proceed."

So after all that, Mills was back at her place ten feet in front of the witness. "Lieutenant, would you please tell the jury Defendant's exact words when you asked if he knew a Ron Nolan, and that he had been killed?"

"Yes, ma'am." Frustrated that he wasn't going to be able to keep it out, Lochland put the best face he could on it. He turned toward the panel and spoke directly to them. "He said, 'I kicked his ass.' And I said, 'Jesus, Evan, he's dead.' And he said, 'Goddamned right.'"

Mills dared a glance over to Washburn, and certainly knew that she risked incurring the judge's wrath as she nodded, directing the words as much to her opponent as to the jury. "'Goddamned right,'" she said. "Thank you, Lieutenant. No further questions. Your witness, Mr. Washburn."

Fresh as a teenage boy, Washburn all but hopped up and over to his place to begin his cross-examination. "Lieutenant Lochland, after Patrolman Scholler reacted to the news, what did he do next?" The decision to refer to Evan by his police rank with this witness was, of course, intentional.

"He kind of folded himself down to a sitting position, then lay back all the way."

"On the floor?"

"Yes."

"Was he resisting arrest?"

"No, sir. His eyes were closed. I rolled him over and put handcuffs on him and he still didn't wake up."

"So he was asleep, then?"

"Asleep, maybe, but also drunk. We tested him at the station and his blood alcohol was point two four."

"And what, Lieutenant, is the blood alcohol level at which a person is considered legally drunk in California?"

"Point oh eight."

"So Patrolman Scholler was at something like three times the legal limit for driving?"

"I don't know the math, but he certainly was very drunk."

"Incoherently drunk?"

Mills jumped all over the question. "Objection! Conclusion."

"Sustained."

Washburn took a short beat, came at it another way. "Did Evan respond immediately to your question about what had happened to him?"

"No."

"At his apartment, did he ever call you by name?"

"No."

"Was his speech slurred?"

"Yes."

"And did you have to repeat your questions before he answered?"

"Yes."

"Now, Lieutenant Lochland, he never said he killed Ron Nolan, did he?"

"No, he did not."

"The only thing he said was that he kicked Nolan's ass, correct?"

"Right."

"And to repeat that colorful phrase, Evan Scholler looked like he'd gotten his ass kicked as well, didn't he?"

"Yes. He was seriously beat up."

"Now he said something else," Washburn continued, "after he said he'd kicked Mr. Nolan's ass, didn't he?"

"He said, 'Goddamned right.'"

"Before he said that, you said that Ron Nolan was dead, correct? But you have no way of knowing whether he understood you when you said that, do you?"

"Well, no, not for sure."

"He was drunk, beat up, and more than a little incoherent, correct?"

"Yes."

"So to repeat my question, do you have any way of knowing whether he heard or understood you when you told him that Ron Nolan was dead?"

"He was pretty out of it. I can't honestly tell you that he understood anything that was going on."

"Did Patrolman Scholler say anything else while you were transporting him to the police station?"

"Nothing coherent. Just gibberish."

"Your Honor!" Now Mills was on her feet, truly enraged. "Sidebar, please."

Clearly, tempers all around were fairly raw by this time. Tollson gave the request a full thirty seconds before, muttering, he nodded and waved the two attorneys forward for their third sidebar of the afternoon.

When they got to the front, Tollson was waiting, pointing a finger at them as though he were a schoolteacher. "I'm getting more than a little tired of this bickering, Counselors. This is not the way we do a trial."

But Mills, fire in her eyes, came right back at him. "I'd prefer we didn't have these issues, either, but Mr. Washburn's conduct here is unconscionable! You just sustained my objection about the word *incoherent* and now the witness gets it in, barely disguised."

"In such a way that his answer was not conclusory as to my client's mental state, Your Honor. That was, I believe, the objection. Lieutenant Lochland is certainly qualified to call gibberish incoherent."

But Mills wasn't giving up. In a restrained voice, she said, "Your Honor. Obviously, if Defendant was incoherent, then his earlier words don't have nearly the same power."

Washburn had a great deal of experience in situations like this one. The temptation was to begin responding directly to your opponent, and this invariably infuriated judges. So he kept his eyes on Tollson, his voice modulated and relaxed. "That is, of course, more or less my intention in pursuing this line of questioning, Your Honor. The distinction between an incoherent epithet and an incriminating answer to a question, though perhaps too subtle for my opponent to grasp, is hugely significant."

"All right. That's enough of that, both of you. I'm going to allow the question and the answer to stand. Ms. Whelan-Miille, you, of course, may redirect." He pointed down at them once again. "I will not be entertaining any more sidebar requests today. This witness has been up here for nearly an hour, and two-thirds of that time we've been up here arguing about four or five words. It's got to stop. If you have objections, raise them in the usual way and I'll rule as best I can. But that's the end of this quibbling nonsense. Understood? Both of you?"

Washburn nodded genially. "Yes, Your Honor."

Mills stood flatfooted, apparently still too angry to talk.

Tollson brought his hard gaze to rest on her. "Counselor? Clear?"

At last she got the words out. "Yes, Your Honor."

LOCHLAND WAS STILL on the stand, having established that on the Saturday of his arrest, Evan had been a fount of incoherent and meaningless babble. Washburn could be forgiven for feeling that things were going his way. After he passed around to the jury the booking photo, Defense Exhibit A, in which a completely disheveled Evan stared blankly at the camera, further establishing his incoherence, Washburn, in his courtliest manner, half turned to Mills. "Redirect."

Mills looked up at the clock, which read four forty-five. She could probably get in a question or two about whether Scholler's "Goddamned right" had sounded coherent to the lieutenant, but in the end she decided that this would only serve to underscore Washburn's thrust—that nothing Evan said that day meant much of anything. Even "Goddamned right," which she had worked so hard to get in. It was what he'd said, and she had no doubt what it had meant—it was tantamount to an admission that he'd killed Nolan and Washburn knew it. But whether the jurors would come to see it that way was anyone's guess. She was going to have to trust that they would use their common sense.

All she wanted at the moment was to put this day behind her. She'd get another hack at Washburn tomorrow, and she had the cards—Evan Scholler was guilty and the jury was going to see it and that was all there was to it. Raising her eyes to the judge, she felt the urge to smile begin at the corners of her mouth. She looked over to the jury, to Washburn, back up to the judge. "No questions," she said.

Tollson brought down his gavel. "Court's adjourned until nine-thirty tomorrow morning."

[25]

FRED SPINOZA WAS a far cry from being a hostile prosecution witness.

In fact, he felt seriously abused that someone who worked for his department, played on his bowling team, got his help finding the address of the house he was planning to break into, where he would then commit murder, and had even come to his own home and played the war hero with his children . . .

Every time Spinoza thought about it, it roiled his guts. He believed that there was a special section in hell reserved for someone who could have done that to his kids.

Never mind what Evan Scholler did to Ron Nolan.

Resplendent in his dark blue uniform, Spinoza settled himself into the chair hard by the judge's platform. He'd put in a lot of time on the witness stand in his career, and rarely had he looked forward to the experience more than today. Now here came Mary Patricia Whelan-Miille up from her table in the packed courtroom, to a space about midway between him and the jury.

Mills and he had shared drinks on several occasions, once they'd gotten to know each other over this case. There had been a short time in the first weeks when he thought she might be coming on to him, but though he found her quite attractive, he loved Leesa and had made that clear enough to Mills that, if she was in fact trolling, she chose to back off.

But some chemistry, he knew, still sparked between them.

He knew that this would play well for a jury—it was just another one of those intangibles that sometimes came into play during a trial. A major People's witness and an assistant DA working in understated sync could bring a sense of rightness, of unassailable conviction, to a prosecution case.

Mills seemed rested and confident as she nodded to the jurors, then smiled at her witness as though she meant it. "Lieutenant Spinoza, what is your position with the police department?"

"I'm the head of the homicide detail."

After she went over the details of his service, she got down to it. "Defendant was a patrolman, was he not, Lieutenant?"

"Yes. He'd been a patrolman working a regular beat before he went overseas, and when he came back, he went back to his former position."

"How was it, then, that you came to know him?"

Spinoza shot half a grin at the jury, then shrugged. What was he going to do? It was the truth. "He was on my bowling team."

"Can you tell the Court, please, Lieutenant, about the first time you ran across a connection between Defendant and the victim in this case, Ron Nolan?"

"Yes. I was in the office on a weekend. The Khalil murders had just taken place, so I was working overtime. I happened to run across the defendant at one of the computers, and I asked him what he was doing. He told me he was trying to locate the address of a drug dealer."

"Did you ask him the name of that drug dealer?"

"Yes. He told me it was Ron Nolan."

"Is that against department policy?"

"Well, it's a gray area. Of course, police are not allowed to use computers for personal reasons. He could use the computer to follow up on a narcotics tip, although, strictly speaking, he should have referred the whole thing to vice."

"How about using the computer to locate a romantic rival?"

"That would not only be against policy, but completely illegal. If he were caught doing that, he could expect to be fired and probably prosecuted."

"So Defendant's use of the computer in this case was illegal?"

"As it turns out, yes."

"And yet you helped him?"

In his prep work with Mills, they had both acknowledged that this would be an uncomfortable moment that they needed to address head-on. "Of course, I didn't know the real reason he was using the computer at that time, but yes. He told me he was tracking a drug dealer and I believed him."

"So in what way did you assist him?"

Spinoza looked at the jury, spoke directly to them. "Well, I knew that he'd have to know how to work the system if he ever did need to find an address from a license plate. I suppose you could say I viewed it as more or less a casual thing, a training opportunity."

"Did Defendant tell you why he wanted to find Mr. Nolan's address?"

"Yes. But I thought his reason . . . I thought he was making a joke." This was an important clarification that Mills had wanted him to make sure he got in, since it served to underscore both Evan Scholler's arrogance and his premeditation.

"Nevertheless, what was the reason he gave you?"

"He said he wanted to hunt down Mr. Nolan and kill him."

A shimmer of reaction echoed through the courtroom, serious enough that Tollson dropped his gavel a couple of times.

Mills let the murmur die down and then resumed her questioning. "Did Defendant mention this killing of his rival any other times?"

"Yes."

"And where was that?"

Spinoza turned in the witness chair to face the jury again. "At my house. After work."

"Was this a usual occurrence, a patrolman coming to your home outside of work hours?"

"No. It was decidedly unusual."

"So what happened?"

"Well, we got ourselves some coffee and went outside and since it was something we'd joked about before, I asked him if he'd killed his dope dealer yet."

"And what was his answer to that?"

"He said he hadn't because Mr. Nolan was out of town."

"And yet you still considered this a joke?"

"Maybe not a funny joke, but it's the way we cops often talk to each other. It still never in a million years occurred to me that he was actually planning—"

Washburn was on his feet, not letting him finish. "Objection!"

Not missing a beat, Tollson nodded. "Sustained. Confine your answers to the questions, please, Lieutenant. Go ahead, Counsel."

Mills nodded, satisfied, and apparently ready to begin the next line of questioning they'd rehearsed, which was the aftermath of the murder itself, the FBI's involvement, and Scholler's arrest. But then, suddenly, she paused, threw a last glance at the jury, and must have seen something she liked, because her next words were, "Thank you, Lieutenant." And then to Washburn, "Your witness."

Spinoza knew Washburn well. As head of homicide in Redwood City, he'd sparred with the veteran attorney many times before, and he was particularly looking forward to it today. Confident that even a master like Washburn wouldn't be able to put a different spin on the events about which he'd just testified, Spinoza was settling himself in, getting psyched for a cross-examination he thought he'd actually enjoy, when Washburn lifted his head, shook it, and said to Tollson, "I have no questions for this witness."

"SPECIAL AGENT RIGGIO," Mills began with the next witness, "how did the FBI get involved in the Khalil case?"

Marcia Riggio had short, cropped dark hair. She wore a navy-blue suit that would not have looked out of place on a man. But the severe look was mitigated by a tan open-necked blouse of some soft and shimmery material, as well as by a plain gold chain necklace. She sat upright in the witness chair, her hands folded in her lap, and spoke with a formal and flat inflection. "Many witnesses at the scene reported hearing an explosion, which the arson inspectors concluded was consistent both with the damage to the bedroom and with the cause of the ensuing fire. Mr. Khalil and his wife were both naturalized citizens from Iraq, and so because of a possible terrorist angle, local officials deemed it prudent to contact Homeland Security, the Bureau of Alcohol, Tobacco and Firearms, and the Federal Bureau of Investigation. Subsequently, analysis of the shrapnel from the explosion revealed that the blast was caused by a device called a fragmentation grenade, probably of domestic manufacture, the possession of which is against federal law. Effectively, the FBI took jurisdiction of this case, although we of course shared our findings with local police."

"And what were your findings?"

"Very little in the first few days. Besides the fragmentation grenade, we discovered that both victims had been shot before the explosion, with nine-millimeter caliber bullets which, when we found them, were too badly formed for comparison to a firearm. We interviewed several family members, of course, in the wake of the attack, and were beginning to process that information when my partner, Jacob Freed, and I received an envelope in the mail that contained a computer diskette with a photograph file that focused our attention in a different direction. Among the pictures in that file were photographs of the Khalils' home taken from several angles, with a handwritten note that the pictures had been downloaded from a computer belonging to a Mr. Ron Nolan. Subsequently, Mr. Freed obtained Mr. Nolan's telephone number and left him a message that we would like to have a discussion with him on a matter that might involve national security.

There was no mention of the Khalils, or of the photograph."

"Did you in fact interview Mr. Nolan?"

"Yes."

"What did he tell you?"

Washburn was on his feet. "Objection. Hearsay."

Tollson looked at Mills. "Counsel?"

"You've already ruled on this, Your Honor," Mills said. "When Mr. Nolan's accusations to the FBI are repeated to Mr. Scholler, they give Mr. Scholler yet another motive to kill him."

Tollson looked over to Washburn. "She's right, Counsel. We did talk about this, and it's coming in. Objection overruled."

She went on in the same vein, meticulous as to every detail and nuance. Nolan's call to the FBI, his theory that his romantic rival, the defendant, might have broken into his house, his discovery of the frag grenades and 9mm Beretta weapon in his closet, the record of computer usage while he'd been away; then, following up on Nolan's theory, the FBI's discovery a day later of the defendant's fingerprints on the computer diskette. Finally, she came to an end.

"Trying to get the timeline correct, do you recall the day or date that you made the discovery about Defendant's fingerprints on the diskette?"

"Yes. Both. It was Thursday, June fourth."

Mills waited for more of a reply until she realized that Special Agent Riggio had answered her question and didn't need to deliver a speech about it. "And after you had that information, did you try to contact Defendant?"

"Yes, we did. We attempted to reach him through his

job as a police officer in Redwood City, but he had not come in to work that morning."

"Had he called in sick?"

"No."

"All right. Where did you try next?"

"We called him at his home, but there was no answer there. So we left a message on his answering machine."

"Did he ever answer that message?"

"No, he did not."

"Were you planning to place Defendant under arrest at that time?"

"No. At that time, we wanted to question him."

"Did you stake out his apartment?"

"No. We had no reason to suspect that he was avoiding us. We thought it likely that he would either call us or we would otherwise locate him in a day or so."

"Did you attempt to locate Mr. Nolan during this time?"

"No. He said he would call us if he got any more information. Beyond that, we had no reason to try and contact him during this period."

"So what did you do next?"

"We ran the fingerprints we'd picked up in Mr. Nolan's townhouse and determined that he had been correct. The defendant had been in his house. Further, the defendant's prints were on the Beretta that was in Mr. Nolan's backpack."

"Did you find his prints on the fragmentation grenades?"

"No. They have a rough surface and did not contain usable fingerprints."

"But the Beretta with Defendant's prints was in the backpack with the fragmentation grenades, was it not?"

"Yes."

"And could you tell if that gun had been fired recently?"

"We could only say that it had not been fired after its last cleaning. But we have no way to tell when it had last been cleaned."

Mills, in a rhythm, kept it going. "Was the gun loaded?"

"Yes. There was a full magazine and a round in the chamber."

Mills knew she had covered a lot of ground with Riggio, who was in many ways the ideal witness, an uninflected, just-the-facts-ma'am kind of presence. But she still had a ways to go. "Special Agent Riggio, how did you discover that Mr. Nolan had been killed?"

SPINOZA AND RIGGIO ate up the whole morning, and court didn't resume until nearly two o'clock in the afternoon.

Washburn, who'd remained silent throughout the lengthy direct, showed little of the enthusiasm he'd displayed the day before as he slowly rose from his chair and advanced to make his cross. "Special Agent Riggio," he began sonorously, "you've testified that in the immediate aftermath of the Khalils' shootings, you interviewed several family members. What did you talk to them about?"

"We had the usual preliminary interviews following this kind of event."

"And what are these interviews comprised of?"

"Developing knowledge of the relationships between the family members and the deceased, as well as business, personal, political, or any other issues that might throw light on the investigation of the crime."

"How many of these interviews did you have?"

Mills spoke from behind him. "Objection. Relevance."

"Sustained."

Washburn couldn't entirely camouflage a disappointed grimace. "The Khalils have widespread business interests, do they not?"

Again: "Objection. Irrelevant."

This time Washburn replied. "Not at all, Your Honor. The People, while never charging Mr. Scholler with the murder of the Khalils, are attempting to insinuate without proof that he was somehow involved in their deaths. I'm wondering if Special Agent Riggio had interviewed anyone among Mr. Khalil's vast business interests who had any connection to Mr. Scholler."

"All right. Overruled. You may answer that question."

To Riggio, it was all the same. Unruffled, she nodded. "Yes, the Khalils had widespread business interests."

"Just here in this country?"

"No. Overseas as well."

"In Iraq?"

"According to the children, yes."

"But you didn't check that information yourself?"

"We were beginning to verify all the information we'd gathered when Mr. Nolan was murdered."

"So," Washburn said, "the answer is no, you didn't check the information about the Khalils' business interests in Iraq, isn't that so?"

"Your Honor!" Mills tried again. "Relevance?"

Washburn said, "It'll be clear in a second, Your Honor."

"All right, but it had better be. Overruled."

"Special Agent Riggio, Mr. Nolan worked for an

American security contractor firm in Iraq, did he not? Allstrong Security."

Now Mills was on her feet. "Your Honor, please! We've discussed this before. This fishing expedition is going nowhere and the only purpose to eliciting this hearsay is to suggest a connection between Mr. Nolan and the Khalils, which is unsupported by any evidence."

Washburn knew he could probably get away with at least one outburst per trial. He figured this was as good a time as any, and whirled around on Mills. "There's a whole lot more evidence of Nolan's involvement with the Khalils' murders than of my client's. You just don't want the jury to hear anything that doesn't fit your theory."

Bam! Bam! Bam!

"Mr. Washburn!" Tollson exploded. "Both of you. Enough. Any more of this and somebody's going to get a contempt charge. You're to address your remarks to the bench and not to one another." Tollson stared them down, giving equal time to both. Then, glancing at the wall clock, he said, "I'm calling a ten-minute recess so everyone can cool off."

WHEN WASHBURN RESUMED, his was once again the voice of sweet reason. He produced a stack of documents received from the FBI and gave them to Riggio on the stand. "Special Agent Riggio. Using these business records, did you have an opportunity to investigate the fragmentation grenades that you discovered in Mr. Nolan's apartment?"

"Yes."

"And what did you discover?"

"These particular grenades were produced in late two

thousand two—if you want the stocking and serial numbers, I've got them, but—"

"That won't be necessary. Go ahead."

"And they were shipped to Iraq in the early weeks after the invasion."

"Do you know if they were delivered to Mr. Scholler's patrol?"

"No."

"No, you don't know, or no, they weren't?"

"They were delivered as part of a consignment to Allstrong Security in Iraq."

"Is there any evidence that Mr. Scholler at any time had possession of these grenades, or shipped them back, by whatever means, to the United States?"

"No."

"Special Agent Riggio, have you any witnesses that reported seeing these grenades in Mr. Scholler's possession at any time?"

"No."

Even though he'd gotten the right answer on the last several questions, Washburn knew it wasn't much. But it was probably all he was going to get. He smiled at the witness. "Thank you," he said. "No further questions."

[26]

By the following Tuesday afternoon, the weather had turned. A violent early-season storm toppled trees and flooded many of the low-lying streets around the courthouse, playing enough havoc with the morning's traffic patterns that court couldn't be called into session until nearly eleven o'clock, and then only to adjourn almost immediately for an early lunch.

In the previous two trial days, Washburn hadn't had much to say to the witnesses Mills called. The other FBI agent, Jacob Freed, provided pretty much the same testimony as his partner, Marcia Riggio. Washburn hammered a bit at the provenance of the frag grenades again, at the lack of real investigation into the lives and motives of possible other suspects in both the Khalil and Nolan murders after they'd identified Evan as their main person of interest. But he knew that he'd inflicted little if any damage to the prosecution's case—the fact, and Washburn hated to admit it, was that the FBI and Spinoza had coordinated very well, and had fashioned an evidentiary chain that was pretty damn compelling. In the end, Washburn just wanted to get Freed off the stand as quickly as possible, although he still took the better part of half a day.

Likewise, David Saldar, the locksmith, came to the stand and, by far the most nervous and uncomfortable witness to date, gave his testimony without any surprises. He was talking about an unarguable point in any event— Evan Scholler had done exactly what Saldar was saying he'd done. He'd lied to a friend, he'd used the police uniform to buttress his credibility, he'd let himself into a home that was not his. It wasn't exactly a high-water mark for the defense, but Washburn couldn't do anything about that either.

Mills's final witness, who'd taken up most of yesterday's—Monday's—time, had been Tara. In spite of clearly conveying to the jury that she was involved with Evan, she not only reaffirmed the fact that Nolan had told her he was concerned and worried about Evan's break-in, but she also provided the crucial testimony of the overt threat to Nolan's life that Evan had made at the Old Town Traven.

Coming from a woman who so obviously did not want to hurt the defendant, Tara's testimony seemed to resonate with the jury in an especially powerful way. And Washburn, try as he might, couldn't get a handle on what he could cross-examine her about—that she hadn't believed Nolan's assertion about Evan planting the weapons in his house? That Evan hadn't really meant what he'd said about killing his rival? Neither of those opinions would be admissible, since that's all they would have been—the opinions of a woman, the jury would feel, who would certainly lie if lying would help her lover's defense.

Now the prosecution had rested and Washburn would get his chance to present an affirmative defense. But in the absence of a client who could even deny that he'd committed the crime, in the absence of an alternative suspect, and with the plethora of motive and opportunity weighing in against Evan, he knew that this might be the legal challenge of his entire career. He didn't have much, and what he did have was dubious at best.

The first order of business was to try to get the jury, to the extent it was going to be possible at all, into Evan's camp. Reminding himself that he only needed one juror, he settled on a woman in the back row named Maggie Ellersby, who was about the same age, and pretty much had the same suburban-housewife look, as Evan's mother, Eileen. More than that, during jury selection she'd revealed that she had two sons of her own; that she was opposed to the war in Iraq, although she supported the troops there. She might have a liberal streak, which in turn might extend to perceiving Evan as some kind of a victim of something, and hence not completely culpable. Beyond that, she had been married to the same man for thirty years, and so might in her heart be rooting for Tara and Evan to put this problem behind them and have a life together. All of this, of course, was extremely nebulous, but it gave Washburn hope to have a "litmus juror" to whom he could target his defense.

"Your Honor," Washburn said as a fresh squall of rain tattooed the courtroom's windows, "the defense calls Anthony Onofrio."

"MR. ONOFRIO, you knew the defendant, Evan Scholler, in Iraq, did you not?"

Washburn wanted Onofrio for a variety of reasons, not the least of which because he exuded such an appealing "regular guy" quality. This was an inherently friendly man who worked with his crew on California's roads. He had some, but not too much, education. Good-looking in a casual way, he might be able to bring Mrs. Ellersby, for example, along in his regard for Evan Scholler.

"Yes, I did. He was my squad leader."

Over the next hour, Washburn led Onofrio over the same ground they'd covered during the PTSD hearing before jury selection. Mills objected to the same things she'd objected to at that time—that Onofrio wasn't even in the U.S. at the time of the murder and therefore his testimony couldn't possibly be relevant—but Washburn argued again that Onofrio's testimony was foundational to Evan's head injuries, which so far hadn't even made it into the record. Even without mention of PTSD, those head injuries were certainly relevant to his blackouts, and these, in turn, Washburn argued, and Tollson agreed, could be a core issue for the defense.

The gallery grew hushed as Onofrio began describing the firefight at Masbah, concluding with the observation, ". . . we could have gotten out, but two of our men had already been hit, and Evan wasn't going to leave without them."

"So what did he do?"

"He led a couple of the other guys up to the first Humvee and pulled out the driver of that vehicle, then carried him back to our car. Then they went back for the gunner."

"And was Lieutenant Scholler under fire at this time?"

"A lot of fire, sir. It was pretty hot, coming from all over."

"All right." Having established Evan's bravery as well as his concern for his men, Washburn let Onofrio get to the end of the Masbah story without further interruption.

Washburn was happy to see that Mrs. Ellersby needed to dab at her eyes with a Kleenex several times during the recitation. When Onofrio finished, Evan bleeding profusely from the head and surrounded by his dead comrades, several other jurors were having similar reactions.

Washburn stood still for several seconds, moved as the jurors had been by the story. Then he turned the witness over to the prosecution.

THE LAST TIME Mills had cross-examined Onofrio, during the 402 hearing on PTSD, she'd hit pay dirt with questions regarding Evan's alcohol use in the war zone. Accordingly, she wasted no time broaching the topic again as soon as she was in front of the witness.

"Mr. Onofrio, did you personally witness Defendant drinking alcohol in Iraq?"

But this time, Washburn was ready for her. "Objection. Irrelevant."

"Sustained."

Mills was halfway back to repeating her question when she stopped herself in almost a double-take fashion. "Your Honor," she said, "with respect, Mr. Washburn made a similar objection during our four-oh-two hearing in this matter, and at that time you overruled him."

Tollson removed his glasses, leaned over the bench. "Yes, I did, Counselor. At that time, the question of Defendant's alcohol use, or not, was germane to the issues involved in that hearing. Here, unless you can show me that Defendant's alcohol use, or not, in Iraq in some way refutes Mr. Onofrio's testimony, or relates directly to the crime with which Defendant is charged, I'm not going to allow it. It's irrelevant, as Mr. Washburn has noted."

Mills stood flatfooted, then walked back to her table, checked her binder, turned a page or two of it, and looked back up. "All right, then." Determined not to let the jury see she'd been caught off balance, Mills smiled through clenched teeth. "Well, then, thank you, Your Honor," she said. "I'll tie this up and we'll come back to it later."

DENIED HIS USE OF PTSD, Washburn's best hope was still some kind of a medical defense. If the jury didn't buy the fact that Evan had suffered a severe and extended black-out, then he was left with no defense whatsoever, except that he was lying. So, to that end, over the past weekend Washburn had spent several hours going over his next witness's testimony. He could only hope that it was going to be enough.

"Dr. Bromley," he began. "What kind of doctor are you?"

"I'm a neurologist at Stanford Medical Center and at the Palo Alto Veterans Center."

"A brain doctor, is that right?"

In his midfifties, though he looked ten years younger, Bromley dressed impeccably. With a strong jaw, a prominent nose, fathomless eyes, and a short, well-kept Afro, he exuded a steely confidence. Now he allowed a breath of a smile to grace his features as he nodded. "That's the lay term, yes."

"Doctor, did you know Mr. Scholler before his arrest?"

"Yes. He was a patient of mine at the Veterans Center after he was released from Walter Reed."

"According to your understanding, Doctor, what was his situation at Walter Reed?"

"He was admitted there in September of the previous year. When he arrived, he was still in an unconscious state from injuries sustained overseas. Doctors had already performed a craniectomy—removal of a section of skull to allow the brain to swell—and his condition was poor. They thought it highly likely he would die. Second prize was that he would survive, but be a vegetable."

Washburn noticed several of the jurors flinch at this brutally matter-of-fact account. He went on. "And when you first saw him here in California? When was that, by the way?"

"Mid-March, nine months after he was wounded. He had made, frankly, a nearly miraculous recovery."

"In what sense?"

"In almost every sense imaginable. They'd replaced the disk of his skull about three months before that, and already his speech patterns had returned to almost normal. His memory still suffered small short-term lapses, and specific words would evade him from time to time, but he seemed to be improving in these areas with each test we administered. His physical coordination was such that I had no problem recommending that he go back to his work as a policeman, so long as his assignment was neither too strenuous nor stressful. In short, his was the most remarkable recovery from traumatic brain injury that I've seen in my twenty years of medical practice."

Washburn nodded, delighted that he had fastened upon Bromley. He'd always been in the picture, of course, but the opportunities for Evan's defense that involved PTSD had always seemed somehow sexier and more compelling. Now, knowing what was going to come out, he started to entertain a small ray of hope that a straight-forward medical explanation could produce approximately the same results as a PTSD defense. If he could make his client any kind of a victim, he knew he still had a chance.

"Doctor, did you have an opportunity to examine Mr. Scholler after he was arrested?"

"Yes."

"How soon after?"

"A couple of days."

"And what was his condition at that time?"

"Well, mostly he was suffering from headaches. But he was also experiencing fairly severe disorientation as well as some speech aphasia. All of this is, of course, consistent with trauma to the brain."

"But you have testified that the symptoms of his traumatic brain injury had all but passed by a few months before that, isn't that so?"

"Yes."

"And yet these symptoms seem to have reappeared. Right?"

"Correct."

"And why is that?"

"Because of new trauma. At the time I saw him after his arrest, Mr. Scholler had sustained several new head injuries."

"And how did he get those?"

"He told me he had been in a fight with Mr. Nolan."

"A fight with Mr. Nolan." Washburn half turned to bring the jury along with him. He particularly noted Mrs. Ellersby, canted forward in her chair, rapt. "Doctor, could a mere fight produce these kinds of debilitating injuries?"

"Of course. Any knock to the head can cause severe injuries, or even death. And from examining Mr. Scholler's head, I found evidence—bruises and broken skin—of several such blows. He also had a new concussion."

"Were these injuries enough to make a person pass out?"

"Certainly."

"At the time they were inflicted?"

"It could be then."

"Could it also be later?"

"Yes."

"Thank you." Washburn risked another quick look at the jurors. Everyone was still with him. "Now, Doctor," he continued, "in a case like this one, where there had been previous traumatic brain injury within the past year, might the ramifications of a beating such as the one endured by Mr. Scholler be more serious than in someone without that history?"

"There's no 'might' about it."

"So the symptoms of this kind of beating would be more serious than they would be to someone who hadn't had the earlier trauma?"

"Well, not to say that a single beating couldn't be severe enough to cause significant damage, and even death. But certainly the history of recent trauma would exacerbate any symptoms from the beating."

"And why is that?"

"Because the brain is an extremely complicated and slow-healing organ." Bromley—bless him, Washburn thought—turned to address his remarks directly to the jury. "It's common, in fact it's the norm, for a TBI to cause neurological and physical problems forever. Other scenarios, particularly if they involve bleeding and clotting, can take two to four years to clear up entirely. And even then, there may be scarring and other complications."

"What about blackouts?"

"Yes, of course, blackouts too. Although typically, medical professionals don't refer to them as blackouts. It's not a very specific term."

"Is there a specific medical term, Doctor?"

"Well, there is syncope"—he pronounced it sin-co-pee—"which is more or less simple fainting. Then there are seizures, both epileptic and psychogenic, that is, non-epileptic. And finally there are alcoholic blackouts, where you have anterograde amnesia during or following a drinking binge. All of these would probably be called some sort of blackout by a layperson, and all of them might be affected by TBI."

"And what happens during any of these blackouts?"

"Either one or both of two things: temporary loss of either consciousness or memory."

"And how long can a blackout last?"

"Well, again, that depends. In some sense, laypeople might call a coma a blackout, and they've been known to last a decade or more. Most, like fainting or epileptic seizures, last no more than ten minutes."

And suddenly, with this answer from Dr. Bromley, Washburn felt a sickening hollowness in his stomach so acute that he thought for a moment that he might have a period of syncope himself. He had known of the weakness of this blackout information, of course, for the better part of the year, and had gone over it again with Bromley over the past weekend, intent on getting this medical evidence into the record.

Struggling to get to his next point, all at once he saw

this testimony now for what it was, and it was smoke. He could sense that it wasn't going to work. His idea had been to establish that Evan's loss of consciousness was a possible, and even common, result of his TBI, tying everything neatly back to Iraq, and the good-soldier sympathy vote from Mrs. Ellersby. After the beating Evan had taken on that night, Washburn had assumed that he'd be able to supply at least a colorable argument that Evan's coming testimony held water.

And now, with a great and terrible clarity, he could see it just wasn't going to fly. The fact that Evan might have blacked out at some point was no proof that he actually had spent any or all of that time in an unconscious state. In fact, given his blood alcohol level at the time of his arrest, it was indisputable that he'd had at least flashes of consciousness during that time when he'd drunk himself into oblivion. Washburn's thought that he could slip this past the jury or that it would get lost in a wave of sympathy was just wishful thinking. He had believed it might work because he needed it to work to have any hope of winning this case.

Washburn still had Bromley's testimony about much of what Evan had been through because of his traumatic brain injury. He might go on to suffer effects from that for the remainder of his life. A few of the jurors initially might still give Evan the benefit of the doubt because they took pity on his situation. But Bromley's testimony offered nothing at all in the way of proof that Evan had been incompetent or unable to commit the murder of Ron Nolan. And eventually, this simple fact was very likely to convict his client. He'd been deluding himself to think otherwise.

He walked to his table and took a sip of water. Turning, he came back to his place in the center of the courtroom. Still, he hesitated.

"Mr. Washburn," Tollson asked with some concern, "is everything all right? Would you like to take a recess?"

"No, Your Honor. Thank you." Then he executed his trademark bow, thanked Bromley, and turned him over to Mills.

The prosecutor got up and advanced to her place with an enthusiasm that told Washburn that she hadn't missed the issue. And indeed, her first question honed in on it. "Doctor, with regard to these blackouts you were discussing. You said they usually lasted a few minutes, is that right?"

"Normally, yes, although it can vary."

"So you said. So your testimony is that a blackout can last for a few days, is that right?"

"Well, again, the terminology of blackout isn't precise. If we're talking about fainting or a seizure, I'd say no. They don't last more than ten minutes usually. True unconsciousness, however, can of course extend indefinitely, though I would hesitate to call that a blackout."

"So is there any way that you can assure the jury that Defendant in fact suffered any kind of blackout at all on the night of the beating?"

"No, I can't say that."

Mills threw a plainly gloating look over to the jury, then came back to Bromley. "Thank you, Doctor. That's all."

"WAS IT just me," Evan asked, "or did that not go very well?"

They were in the holding area behind the courtroom again, for the recess. In a gesture that Washburn took to be one of sympathy, the bailiff had delivered paper cups filled with fresh, hot coffee for both him and his client. Normally, this wasn't allowed since a suspect with a cup of hot coffee was a suspect who could attack people with it, but today for some reason—the change in the weather? the pathetic Bromley testimony?—the bailiff had offered and both men had jumped at the chance.

Washburn, of course, downplayed the problem. Shrugging, he said, "Between Onofrio and Bromley we got in a whole lot of what you've been through. Somebody on that jury is going to care, you watch." He sipped at the brew. The bravado he'd put in his answer wasn't just to buff up his own self-image. Evan was going on the stand next, and Washburn needed him to project both relaxation and confidence while he was up there. He was going to get to tell his story at last and, more important, sell it to the jury.

But it wasn't much of a story, and both men seemed to understand that.

"Don't take this badly." Unruffled, collected, Washburn leaned back against the wall and crossed one leg over the other. "I still think we've got a decent shot, but I also think the Court would look favorably on an offer to plead."

Evan turned his head and fixed Washburn with a glare. "We've been through that."

"Yes, we have. And now you're going to tell the jury that you didn't kill Nolan."

"That's right."

"Any idea who did? Because I don't have one."

"It wasn't me."

"Because you don't remember doing it?"

"Everett. Listen. I can't believe I beat him with a poker, then shot him in the head, and have no memory of it. I would remember that."

Washburn sighed. "Well, as you say, we've been all through it. But we could say you went back to talk to him after the fight and he attacked you. You were weak from the earlier beating and you had no choice but to grab the poker..."

Evan was holding up his hand. "... and execute him with a point-blank shot to the head. I didn't do that. That is not who I am."

"Yes, and that may not be the point." He tipped up his coffee and swallowed. "There's absolutely nothing about those days that you remember?"

"You don't think I've tried? You don't think I want to remember any little thing?"

"Maybe you were drunk the whole time?" Washburn rubbed his palms on his pants legs. "I want you to think about this carefully, Evan. If that's what happened, at least that gives the jurors something more to think about."

"If I change my story now, then I'm a liar before, though, right?"

"No. If you just remembered, it's come back to you in the stress of the trial."

"Damn conveniently. They'll see through that in a heartbeat."

"Okay. Suppose it happened that you were home the whole time, suffering from the beating, drinking to kill the pain. You never left the apartment."

"And how does that help me? They'd still have to believe me."

"No." Washburn shook his head. "*They* don't have to

believe you. *One of them* has to believe you. It's a lot better to say 'I didn't do it' than 'I don't remember, but I probably didn't do it.' There's a real difference there."

Evan took a couple of breaths. "I thought it was about the evidence. Not what I say. What the evidence says."

"That's the problem," Washburn said. "The evidence, my friend, makes a very good case that you did it." Just at that moment, the bailiff appeared, and Washburn punched his client on the thigh. "Drink your coffee," he said. "We're up."

[27]

AFTER THE MONTHS OF BUILDUP, the endless coaching and strategy sessions, the arguments, disagreements, accords, and prognostications, Evan Scholler's time on the witness stand was really quite brief. Washburn saw no point in having his client go over again all of the reasons he might have had to loathe the victim. That had all been well-established by earlier witnesses. There were really only a couple of lines of inquiry that Washburn thought stood any chance of traction with the jury, if only because they provided an alternative theory to the case, and he got right to them.

"Evan," he said, "why did you break into Mr. Nolan's home?"

"First, let me say that that was wrong. There's no excuse, I shouldn't have done that. I should have advised the homicide detail of my suspicions about Mr. Nolan."

Mills got to her feet. "Your Honor, nonresponsive."

"Sustained." Tollson's glare went from Washburn over to Evan. He spoke to the defendant. "Mr. Scholler. Please only answer the questions that the attorneys put to you. You're not here to make speeches."

"Yes, Your Honor. Sorry."

"All right, Mr. Washburn, go ahead, and carefully, please."

Washburn posed the question again, and Evan responded. "Because I had found out about the Khalil murders from the paper, and then more about them from Lieutenant Spinoza. I had gone on a mission with Mr. Nolan when we were in Baghdad together, and he'd used frag grenades at that time. Then, knowing that Mr. Khalil was of Iraqi descent, and knowing what Mr. Nolan did for a living, it occurred to me that he might have had something to do with those murders."

"Why didn't you simply, as you say, go to homicide?"

"Because I might have been wrong, which would have made me look stupid both to the lieutenant and to Tara, and I couldn't have that."

"Why was that?"

"Well, one, I was a policeman myself. Two, I was hoping to reconnect with Tara."

"All right. So you broke into Mr. Nolan's home?"

"I did let myself in, yes."

"Trying to find evidence that Mr. Nolan had been involved in the Khalil murders?"

"That's right."

"Didn't you think that was a bit far-fetched?"

"Not at all. I'd seen Mr. Nolan kill other people."

Mills raised her voice. "Objection."

"Your Honor," Washburn responded. "Mr. Nolan was a security officer. Sometimes his job was to kill people. Mr. Scholler knew him in that setting in Iraq. There is nothing pejorative about it."

Tollson put his glasses back on. "Objection overruled."

"All right," Washburn continued. "Now, when you

went into Mr. Nolan's home, Evan, did you find anything which in your opinion might have been connected to the Khalil murders?"

"Yes."

Evan ran through his actions and motivations in a straightforward manner—the frag grenades, touching the gun both in the backpack and in the bed's headboard, the computer files. As Washburn had coached him, he kept bringing his narrative back to the jury, and particularly— without being too obvious—to Mrs. Ellersby, three over from the left in the second row.

"So you copied the photographic computer file?"

"Yes."

"Presumably, now, you had your proof, or at least some possible proof, of a connection between Mr. Nolan and the Khalil murders. What did you do next?"

"Well, I didn't want to take away any of the proof, so that it would still be there when the FBI searched the house—"

Mills pushed her chair back with a resonant squeal and said under her breath, "Give me a break."

Tollson banged his gavel with some force. "If I thought you'd done that on purpose, Ms. Miille, I'd hold you in contempt right now. There will be no histrionics in this courtroom! You will live to regret the next outburst of any sort and I'm admonishing the jury to disregard your unprofessional comment." Then, to Evan, "Go ahead, Mr. Scholler."

Evan let out a long breath, for the moment apparently, and perhaps actually, unable to remember where he'd been in his testimony.

Washburn took advantage of the moment. "I'm sorry,

Your Honor, my client seems to have blacked out for a second."

"Oh, Christ!" Mills whispered.

Bam! Bam!

"That's it, Ms. Miille, you're in contempt. We'll talk about what the sanction is going to be outside the presence of the jury." His mouth set in a hard line, Tollson pointed to both attorneys. "This ends here, I'm warning you. Mr. Washburn, does your client need a minute to compose himself?"

"Evan?" Washburn asked. "Are you all right?"

"Fine."

"All right," Tollson said, "let's have the reporter read back the last question, please."

The question got Evan back to where he was saying that he didn't want to take away any of the proof, so that the FBI would find it when they searched the house. "So I decided to make a copy of the photo file on the computer that held what I was sure was a picture of the Khalils' house. So I took one of the diskettes and made the copy and brought it home."

"Now, wait a minute. You were a policeman and you had what you considered strong evidence of a murder, and yet you didn't contact homicide?"

"Right, I didn't."

"And why was that?"

"Because I couldn't tell them what I'd found without admitting I got it in an illegal search. None of it would have been admissible in court."

"So what did you do?"

"I mailed the diskette to the FBI, who I heard were investigating the Khalil murders."

"And then what happened?"

"And then Mr. Nolan came home and must have realized that somebody had been in his house."

"In fact, he must have realized it was you, Evan. Isn't that so?"

"Well, the way it worked out. Yes, apparently. So he turned it all around to make it look like it was me who'd planted the evidence at his place and also, incidentally, killed the Khalils."

Washburn knew this was all inadmissible speculation but was betting that Mills, still reeling from the contempt citation and the reaming she had taken in front of the jury, would be keeping a low profile, at least for a while. He pressed on. "And did you, in fact, kill the Khalils?"

"No, I did not."

"Were you ever charged with killing the Khalils?"

"No."

"Did you at any time send fragmentation grenades or any other type of arms, ammunition, or ordnance from Iraq to the United States?"

"No, I did not."

"At any time, did anyone ever present you with any evidence that you had tried to send these items from Iraq to the United States?"

"No."

"Now, when you heard that Mr. Nolan had turned the tables on you and reported to the FBI, what was your reaction?"

"I was furious. I wanted to confront him and fight him."

"You did not want to kill him?"

"That never entered my mind. I was mad. I wanted to hit him."

"With brass knuckles?"

"I just happened to have them with me that night, and when I got there, I thought I might need them. Mr. Nolan had a great deal of training in hand-to-hand combat, more than me, and I wanted to level the playing field."

"So, by fighting him, did you want to stop him from telling his story to the FBI?"

"No. It was too late for that. He'd already done it." This was another critical point related to Evan's alleged motive. There would be no point in killing Nolan to stop him from turning over evidence to the authorities if that had already happened, which it had.

"So let me get this straight, Evan. On the evening of June third, two thousand four, Tara Wheatley told you that she had ended her relationship with Mr. Nolan and wanted to pursue one with you, is that correct?"

"Yes."

"And on that same night, you learned that Mr. Nolan had already supplied the FBI with evidence that supposedly connected you to the Khalil murders, right?"

"Right."

Washburn threw an open glance at the jury. Could his point be more plain? But it was, of course, necessary to nail it down in all its particulars so there could be no misunderstanding at all. "In other words, Evan," he said, "did you have any motive to kill Ron Nolan on account of your relationship with Ms. Wheatley?"

"No, I did not."

"And did you have any motive to kill Mr. Nolan to prevent him from talking to the FBI?"

"No. He'd already done that."

"So you had no motive to kill Mr. Nolan, is that right?"

"I had no reason to kill him."

Washburn cast one last sidelong glance at the jury box, fixed on Mrs. Ellersby for a second, and was pleased to note that she was nodding soberly, as if newly convinced of something. Evan's testimony had, he was sure, made a strong impression on her. And if on her, then maybe on one or more of the others.

MILLS ROSE SLOWLY from her table, her brow creased, her face set in an expression of deep concern. She came and stood in her spot and brought her right hand to the side of her face, then let it down. "Mr. Scholler, as you've testified, on June third, two thousand four, you went up to Mr. Nolan's townhome with the intention of fighting him, and then you did in fact engage in a fight with him, am I right so far?"

"Yes."

"What did you do after that fight ended?"

"I don't remember."

"You don't remember? Did you black out?"

"I don't remember."

"So it is not your testimony that you suffered a blackout, after all. Is it?"

"No. Whether I did or not, I don't remember."

"You suffered quite a beating yourself in this altercation, did you not?"

"Yes."

"And yet, with all the problems you've had, particularly with traumatic brain injury, you did not seek medical help?"

"Apparently not, but I don't remember."

Washburn raised a hand at his desk. "Your Honor, objection. Badgering. If he doesn't remember anything, it follows that he doesn't remember particulars."

This satisfied Tollson, and he nodded. "Sustained."

Mills pursed her lips and paused to phrase her question so it came at things from a slightly different angle. "Mr. Scholler," she said finally, "what is your first memory after you sustained your injuries on Wednesday night at the hands of Mr. Nolan?"

"I remember waking up in a hospital bed, I think it was Saturday night."

"So Wednesday night through Saturday night is a complete blank, is that right?"

"That's right."

"All right." Mills paused for another second or two, and then—just like that!—her posture changed. Her back straightened perceptibly, a wisp of a grim smile tugged at the corners of her mouth. Obviously, she had reached some decision, as though she'd done everything in her power to get to this point, and now the time had come to commit irrevocably to her strategy. "So now, Mr. Scholler, as you are sitting here in front of me and the members of this jury, maybe you killed Mr. Nolan and maybe you didn't. You just don't remember. Is that right?"

Evan sat with the question for a long moment.

"Mr. Scholler," she prompted him. "It's a yes or no question. Can you tell me that you did not kill Mr. Nolan?"

Evan's eyes went to Washburn, who returned his gaze impassively. Coming back to face his prosecutor, Evan leveled his gaze at Mills. "I don't remember," he said at last.

[28]

AT EIGHT-THIRTY THE NEXT MORNING, Mary Patricia Whelan-Miille sat on the corner of her desk in her small office. Behind her, outside the window, the freak storm was into its second day and showing no signs of clearing. In the parking lot just outside, the cold and heavy rain slanted nearly horizontal in gusting sheets. In front of Mills, her secretary, Felice Brinkley, sat with a notepad on a folding chair that she'd set up by the door.

Felice was a no-nonsense woman who wore minimal makeup and had let her hair go almost completely gray. Mills thought she'd done this as a defense against being hit on by guys—with her finely pored skin, sculpted cheeks, and a hooded, sensuous cast to her eyes, and even with the gray hair and lack of fuss, she was a strikingly attractive woman. The curvaceous figure didn't hurt either.

Thirty-six years old, she was the mother of two boys and a girl, all under twelve. Mills also believed that Felice was among the smartest people she'd ever met and constantly tried to persuade her to take the LSATs and become a lawyer herself, but Felice would have none of it—perhaps in itself, Mills had to admit, a testament to her intelligence. The way it was now, Felice was explaining for the fiftieth time, she could come in early, work her regular hours, skip lunch, and be home just about in time to be there for the kids when they got home from school. Her husband, John, worked a swing shift in maintenance for the city for the pay differential, so one of them was always there for the kids. "That's just our priority."

"But with the extra money, and there'd be a lot more of it, John wouldn't have to work at all if you got in with a high-ticket firm, which you would," Mills replied.

"Sure. But I'd have to work twenty-hour days. And how would that make him feel, not working? He wants to work. Or if I made more money than him? I don't necessarily think that's a recipe for a happy marriage."

"But it's okay for him to make more money than you?"

"He doesn't."

"But if he did, that would be okay?"

"Sure. But it would also be okay if I made more than him, if that's just the way our lives work out. But why should I go for a new job that I wouldn't like as much and would keep me away from my kids just for the money?"

"Because money is what makes you safe, Felice." She held up an admonitory finger. "Okay, and I know you don't want to think about this, but what if he leaves you?"

"Who, John?" She laughed. "John is never going to leave me."

"How can you be sure of that? He's a man, isn't he?"

Felice had heard all of this before, and found it mildly amusing. Her poor, sad, driven boss who worked impossible hours and was never in a stable relationship trying to tell Felice how to have a more secure and happy life—there was something inherently funny, if also somewhat pathetic, about the situation. "All men don't leave," Felice said. "Both the kids' grandfathers are still around, for example, and married to the grandmothers. It happens. In fact, in both of our families, John's and mine, it's kind of a tradition." She brushed her hair back from her forehead, opened the notepad on her lap, snapped her ballpoint a couple of times, checked her watch. "Now, how about you show me this closing argument?"

Suddenly wide-eyed, bushwhacked by the time, Mills boosted herself off her desk. "Oh, God, is it really eight-thirty already? We've got to…"

Felice raised her hand. "You've got to just calm down, MP, and tell the story. That's all you've got to do. Slow and easy."

"You're right." Mills blew a strand of her hair away from her mouth. "You're right."

"Yes, I am." Felice clicked her pen again. "Okay, hit it."

"LADIES AND GENTLEMEN of the jury." Mills held her legal pad with her notes as a prop, although she knew pretty much exactly what she was going to say. "At the beginning of this trial, I told you that the evidence would prove to you beyond a reasonable doubt that Defendant killed Ron Nolan with premeditation and malice aforethought. I'd like to take a last few minutes of your time now to talk about the law and explain how the evidence has done exactly that."

For the next forty-five minutes, she focused on the elements of murder to help the jury wade through the verbose and sometimes arcane instructions that the judge would give them at the end of the case. Then she got to the core of the argument.

"So now I've explained what murder is. We've talked a little about what the legal definition of premeditation is, and I hope my comments have helped you understand what precisely the law requires be proved before the defendant may be found guilty. Now I'd like to talk to you about the evidence, the specifics of the testimony in this case, the exhibits, the reasonable inferences to be drawn from that testimony and from those exhibits that show the defendant's conduct meets the definition of first-degree murder.

"And what is that evidence? First, Mr. Nolan and Defendant were rivals for the attention of the same woman, Tara Wheatley. The defense would have you believe that on the night of Defendant's attack on Mr. Nolan—one that he freely admits, by the way—Ms. Wheatley, after a six-month relationship with Mr. Nolan, decided to suddenly change her allegiance and affections in favor of Defendant, and that because of this shift, Defendant no longer had a motive to want to kill Mr. Nolan. I submit to you that this is simply untrue."

"Wait a minute," Felice said. "Not 'untrue.' Be more earthy. Why not, 'Does this make any sense to you?'"

Mills nodded. "Better." She made a note, then resumed her pacing and her argument. "The defense is telling you that a man who lost his girlfriend to another man, who believes that that man lied and cheated and betrayed him, who knows that the man has enjoyed an intimate relationship with the defendant's girlfriend while he was laid up in the hospital, is suddenly told by the girlfriend that she intends to come back to him, and now everything is okay. No bitterness. No animosity. No hate. That's what the defense is selling. I hope you're not buying.

"First of all, because your common sense tells you that's nonsense. Blood feuds don't end in a minute. Long-held hates don't vanish overnight, and the defendant must have known that Ms. Wheatley, who had already changed her mind once, could just as easily change it again tomorrow and prefer Nolan to him. But more to the point, all the evidence shows that as a simple fact, the defendant still did hate Ron Nolan.

"After he talked to Tara, he armed himself with a deadly weapon—and as you've heard from the evidence, those brass knuckles are a deadly weapon—and he went to Ron Nolan's place for the express purpose of beating him. Does that sound to you like someone who had given up hard feelings, someone who had forgiven his enemy, someone who did not still want revenge and to inflict pain? Of course not. That's just nonsense." She stopped by the window. "Is that enough on that?"

Felice nodded. "I think so. You don't want to beat it to death. Just move along."

Pacing again, Mills continued. "While I'm discussing motive, let me just say that motive alone is not…"

"No," Felice said. "The weight of motive evidence will be in the jury instructions. You don't have to go there."

With a nod, Mills started in again. "The defense would also have you believe that the second equally compelling motive—that Defendant wanted to stop Mr. Nolan from producing more evidence to connect him to the Khalil slayings—was moot because Mr. Nolan had already produced such evidence. This is a spurious argument." She stopped. "Is *spurious* okay?"

Felice considered for a second. "Maybe a little fancy."

"How about *specious*?"

"Maybe a lot fancy." The paralegal rolled her eyes. "How about going for the blue-collar vote and using *phony*."

"*Fake*."

"*False*."

Mills snapped her fingers. "That's it. *False*." She went back to her formal voice. "This is a false argument because first, Defendant may well have believed that Mr. Nolan had more evidence. But more to the point, none of what Mr. Nolan had told the FBI about the Khalil evidence could be used against Mr. Scholler if Mr. Nolan was dead. If there's one thing you've learned in this trial, it's that we need to produce live witnesses to give testimony. I suggest to you that the defendant had an even greater motive to kill Mr. Nolan once it was clear that Nolan had turned him in and was prepared to cooperate as a witness against him.

"If the defendant did kill the Khalils, adding one more murder to the list to protect him from being caught wouldn't have been a big deal."

"Whoa up," Felice said. "You better be ready. Washburn's gonna light up on that one."

"I know. But I'm allowed to argue, and I want the jury to hear it."

"The judge won't let it in."

"No, probably not. But I'll talk fast and get as much of it in as I can before they shut me down."

"So long as you know."

"I know. Okay, moving on." Mills consulted her notes briefly. "So let's get down to what actually happened, what the undisputed evidence proves happened. Arming himself with brass knuckles, and admitting to Tara Wheatley that he was going to quote put an end to this unquote, Defendant drove to Mr. Nolan's house and attacked him. A fight ensued, and both men were injured. Three days later, a gun bearing Defendant's fingerprints was found on the bed in Mr. Nolan's bedroom, near to where Mr. Nolan lay on the floor with a fatal gunshot wound to the head from the same caliber weapon.

"Exactly what happened on the night of that fight? The only person in this courtroom who could tell us that claims that he has no memory of that time. No memory at all. And this in spite of his own doctor's testimony that blackouts last no more than ten minutes. That leaves a lot of conscious time for which Defendant has no explanation, and no memory. The evidence you've heard, and from his own witness, does not support his testimony.

"So with a lack of absolute certainty, we are left with the task of asking ourselves what is the most reasonable explanation for the facts in evidence. Is it more reasonable to assume that Defendant finished his fight with Mr. Nolan and then, inebriated and with a concussion, drove himself to his apartment, where he continued to drink for the next two days, while some unidentified third party, for some inexplicable reason—"

"Maybe *unexplained*."

"—for some unexplained reason, entered Mr. Nolan's home, beat him with a fireplace poker, and then shot him?

"Or is it more reasonable to assume that, armed with his set of brass knuckles, Defendant got the better of Mr. Nolan in their fight and, when he had finished that exercise, simply shot him in the head with a handgun he found at the scene? Then, ladies and gentlemen, and only then, after he had murdered Mr. Nolan in cold blood, did he drive himself home and proceed to drink himself into an alcoholic stupor." Mills stopped, locked eyes with Felice, and shook her head. "I hate this guy," she said.

"It's not coming across," her paralegal answered. "It's very clean and objective. I buy it completely."

"Not too short?"

"Not for me."

Mills glanced up at the wall clock. "Almost showtime. Imagine if I actually pull off beating Washburn."

"Don't get ahead of yourself. Just take it a sentence at a time." Felice stood up and gave her boss a quick hug. "You feel ready?"

"As I'll ever be."

"Okay," Felice said. "Go get 'em."

[29]

BY LATE FRIDAY AFTERNOON, the tension was thick in the jury room. Ryan Cannoe, the foreman, had just counted the fifteenth ballot and the vote—from an original of eight to four to convict—now stood at eleven to one.

"Maggie," he said to Mrs. Ellersby, "we've got another forty-five minutes and then we're going to have to come back after a very long weekend. Now, I'm not trying to coerce any kind of a different vote from you, but if you're sure you won't budge, and you're never going to budge, maybe we should just send out the word that we're hung and leave it at that."

This brought a burst of invective from several of the other jurors. "After all the time we've put in on this!" "No way!" "That's bullshit!" "The guy's guilty as sin and we all know it."

"Maybe we don't all know it," Ellersby replied. The day—in fact, the whole jury experience—had been its own trial for her, especially since this morning when the last two defections from her camp had crossed over, leaving her as the lone vote to acquit.

"So that's your final decision, Maggie?" Cannoe asked again. "You really don't think he did it?"

"Not exactly that," she said. "I think he might have done it, as I've said all along. I just can't be sure in my heart that it's first-degree murder. If he went there to beat Nolan up and he died by mistake, that's second-degree."

Cannoe kept his patience. "Except he didn't die from the beating."

"No. I know that. Things got out of hand."

Juror #2, Sue Whitson, a woman of Ellersby's age who'd been an early voter for acquittal, now joined the argument. "Maggie, I'd be with you except that in the end, he put the gun up to the man's head and shot him. How do you explain that except to say that at some time, Mr. Scholler decided to kill him? And that's murder one."

"The point," Cannoe added, "is that you believe Scholler did it, don't you? Never mind all the legal distinctions. He pulled the trigger, right?"

Ellersby sighed and whispered, "I don't see how he didn't, but I don't know if they proved he did."

"It's not absolute proof, Maggie," Sue said. "It's proof beyond a reasonable doubt. And they've done that."

"You admit it yourself," Cannoe said. "You just said you don't see how he didn't do it."

"I know."

"Well, then. . ."

"Well, then, I just keep coming back to what Mr. Washburn said in his closing statement. That they could have come up with any number of other defenses that seemed to make more sense. Self-defense, for example, or heat of passion, or simply saying no, he didn't do it. But instead they went with the truth, which he admitted was maybe harder to believe . . ."

Sue reached out and put a hand on Maggie's arm. She

spoke with a surprising gentleness. "Maybe because it wasn't, in fact, true, Maggie. Maybe Washburn's just playing on our gullibility, figuring we'll want to believe that this young man, Evan, who'd had such a terrible time in Iraq, that somehow his injuries there are to blame for the fact that he can't say he didn't kill Nolan. If it wasn't for all the Iraq stuff, would you have any doubt about what really happened? Would his story have made any sense at all? That's what I finally came to see. It just doesn't. I wish it did, but it doesn't."

"He came to beat him up," Cannoe said, "and wound up staying to kill him. If that's not what you see, Maggie, and you don't think you can ever say otherwise, I'll call for the bailiff and tell him we're hung. You want me to do that?"

Ellersby looked around the table at all of her intelligent, well-meaning fellow citizens. None of them coldblooded, none out for vengeance. All of them had given nearly a month out of their lives to see that justice was done, that the system worked. And for her part, she knew that she had been irrationally swayed by the power of Washburn's simple argument in closing that he was too smart and too experienced to ever allow a ridiculous defense like Evan's "I don't remember" to be the centerpiece of his case, except that it was the truth.

That's why they had gone with that defense, because it was the truth.

And Maggie Ellersby's mind's eye could picture Evan passed out in his apartment, not from alcohol, but from his brain injury—not in a blackout but in a true state of unconsciousness, knocked out from the beating he'd taken.

But there was no evidence that that was what had happened. None at all. And what if Washburn, as another one of her colleagues on the jury had pointed out early on, was nothing more than a man who was paid to tell lies on behalf of his clients? That's what all lawyers were, right? She flashed on the O. J. Simpson case, the Dan White "Twinkie Defense" case in San Francisco. If she was the lone holdout, and her vote to acquit wasn't based on any evidence she could name, how would she be able to explain herself to her husband and her friends?

How could she live with herself?

"Maggie?" Sue softly squeezed her arm again.

"Do you want me to call the bailiff?" Cannoe asked.

Ellersby looked up to the ceiling, said a quick prayer for Evan Scholler's soul, and brought her eyes back down to the table. "No," she said. "I think we need to do one more ballot."

PART FOUR
[2007]

[30]

DISMAS HARDY'S WINDSHIELD WIPERS couldn't keep up with the downpour. They thwacked as fast as they could go, but this latest in a series of March squalls reduced his visibility to near zero. He could barely make out the first gate until he was at it. He loved his little two-seater Honda convertible with the top down in the summer and fall, but it wasn't made for this kind of weather. The plastic back window had long since gone opaque and even with the defrost fan blasting, the inside surfaces of the door windows were fogged over too. He pushed the button to lower his driver's window so he could present his identification to the guard and the rain misted in over his face.

Behind him, someone honked, then honked again. His rearview mirror was useless; he couldn't see his side mirrors, either, through the condensation on the windows. The rain pounded down on the cloth roof. He was inside a drum. Blinded, cocooned, he had to lower his window another few inches so he and the guard could see each other. Opening the window allowed more water in, enough to soak through the fabric of his suit in seconds.

Another blast from the impatient prick behind him. Hell, Hardy was already wet; he had half a mind to jump out and confront the guy, pull him out of his ride, deck him, dump him into the churning brown stream that ran over the road's gutters.

Instead, he squinted out to see the guard, flashed his driver's license, and spoke so he could be heard over the rain. "Dismas Hardy, to visit one of your inmates, Evan Scholler."

The guard, all but invisible through the downpour, spoke loudly, too, from his semienclosed space, "I'll have to see your ID better than that, please, sir. Sorry."

Seething, Hardy handed it out. Waited. He had time to decide that if the car behind him honked once more, he would go take the driver out, but then his wallet was back at the window and he heard a crisp "Thank you, sir. Ahead to your right after the next gate."

And he rolled up his window and let the clutch out simultaneously.

When he'd left the city a couple of hours ago, the sky had been light gray, but it hadn't even been drizzling. So he didn't have an umbrella or a raincoat with him.

After he found his spot in the parking lot, he turned off the motor and parked to wait out the worst of the squall. Regain some of his composure. Whoever had been behind him—some delivery guy maybe—didn't follow him to this lot. He thought it was probably just as well.

Composure was an issue. Even before the rain, Hardy's physical reaction to the scheduled visit to the prison had caught him off-guard. It had been a while since he'd had a client in prison, and he was out of practice. He kept having to reach for a breath, his palms were sweaty, an unaccustomed emptiness had hollowed out his lower rib cage. Closing his eyes, he leaned his head back and drew in a long breath through his mouth, which he then exhaled with a certain deliberation. He did it again. And again.

When at last the drumming of the rain stopped, he opened his eyes. Now, suddenly, it was just a light drizzle. Seizing the moment, he opened the car door and stepped out onto the asphalt.

HARDY HAD SEEN pictures of Evan Scholler in the newspapers, caught some glimpses of him on the TV news as the trial had gone on, so he thought he'd recognize him on sight. But when the guard first opened the door to the very small room to bring the inmate in, Hardy took a quick glance and decided that this couldn't be his man; the guard must have gotten it wrong and this shackled guy must be going to see another attorney in a different room.

For one thing, Evan was younger, just thirty-one now; this inmate looked at least forty. Further, in photos and on television, Evan was far better-looking, with a stronger chin, lighter hair, a better complexion, smaller in the gut and bigger across the shoulders. This guy here was big, casually buffed, physically intimidating, especially wearing a flat-affect expression that made his thin mouth look mean, even cruel. At first glance, this guy looked like a stone killer.

But the guard, checking the slip of paper in his hand, said, "Dismas Hardy?" A nod. "Here's your mope."

Evan took the slur without reaction. He stood at attention, but relaxed in the pose, seemingly uninterested in what, if anything, happened next. He looked Hardy up and down as he might a side of beef hanging in a cooler.

"You can take the shackles off," Hardy said.

For the obvious reason, guards in prison did not carry guns on their persons, so in any one-on-one encounter such as this delivery, shackles on prisoners tended to be the norm. Hardy knew several attorneys who visited their clients here and most of them were happy to let the shackles stay put. A shackled convict was a controllable convict, and with many of these inmates, you couldn't be too careful.

The guard hestitated for an instant, then shrugged. "Your call." With practiced precision, he unlocked the handcuffs from the chain that was threaded through the Levi's belt loops encircling Evan's waist. The cuffs still dangled from the waist chain at his sides.

Now, though, his hands free, Evan rubbed at his wrists.

The room was four feet wide by about seven feet long. A heavy, solid, industrial gray metal desk squatted against Hardy's right wall and stuck out two-thirds of the way across the space; in a pinch it could serve as a first-line barrier in the event of a surprise attack. Folding chairs sat on either side of it. Hardy had a door with a wire-glass window in it behind him and another door just like that facing him. The guard who'd let him in had cautioned him to stay on his side of the desk, "just to be safe." He'd also pointed out the small button low in the wall on Hardy's side that could be pressed in the event of any trouble.

Evan's guard said, "I'm right outside the whole time," and then that's where he was, closing the door behind him.

Hardy said, "You want to sit down?"

Evan thanked him and sat. He put his free hands on

the table, still looking through Hardy, until suddenly he focused. "You got a cigarette?"

"Sorry, I don't smoke."

"I didn't either," Evan said. "What a joke."

"What is?"

"Not smoking. Watching what you eat. Staying in shape. All that stuff outside. Then you wind up in here." Maybe he felt as though he'd given too much of himself away. As a cop or a soldier or at the prison or somewhere else, Evan had gotten good at the thousand-yard stare, and he reverted into it. After a minute inside himself, he came back to Hardy. "So who are you?" he asked.

"Dismas Hardy, your new attorney."

"Don't take this wrong," Evan said, "but it took you long enough."

"Yeah, well, it was a little complicated."

A beat. "What's that first name again?"

"Dismas. The good thief. On Calvary? Next to Jesus?"

Evan shook his head. "Don't know him. Dismas, I mean. I've heard of Jesus."

Hardy looked him in the face. If this was humor, it was damn subtle and wouldn't be a bad thing. But he couldn't tell. He could see, however, that his initial impression of the man's age was off—close up he came as advertised, thirty-one. Hard years.

"What happened to Charlie Bowen?" Evan asked.

"He went missing last summer. He's the equivalent of dead as far as the Court's concerned. My firm inherited his files, including yours. I got them about four months ago."

"You a slow reader?"

Hardy's glance came up at his new client again. The

guy wielded words efficiently, short punches inside. First a wave at humor, then a cutting jab. A lot going on behind unyielding eyes. Hardy figured he deserved the rebuke—four months while he decided whether or not to take on the appeal himself must have felt a lot different to him than those same four months inside the prison had to Evan.

But Hardy was here now, and that's what mattered. Evan's trial had ended nearly two years before. Charlie Bowen obviously hadn't gotten too far with the appeal in the fourteen or so months that he'd worked on it. Nobody else had done anything on it for six months after Bowen disappeared. The four more months that Hardy had taken while he made up his mind after he got the files were the least of Evan's real problems.

So Hardy ignored the question. It was irrelevant now. He pushed his chair back from the desk, crossed his legs, started in a conversational tone. "I used to be a cop," he said. "Before that, I was a Marine and did a tour in Vietnam. Sound familiar?"

"You enlist?"

"Marines," Hardy repeated.

"How old were you?"

"Twenty."

"Yeah, I was twenty when I joined the Guard, still in college."

"That was pre-nine-eleven?"

"Pre-everything," Evan said. "Different world. The Guard looked like easy money at the time. A good way to keep in shape. Who knew?"

"Did you go right into the Police Academy after school?"

"Pretty much. Couple of months off, maybe. You can

only drink so much beer and do nothing else before it gets old."

"I don't know. I spent ten years doing that. I had a kid who died."

Hardy wasn't fishing for sympathy. He wanted Evan to know a little bit about who he was, why he might be taking on this case personally. The young man's history struck a chord in him. With his life apparently over, Evan was still seven years younger than Hardy had been when he'd awakened from his own long alcohol-powered slumber after the death of his first son, Michael. Starting over from scratch at thirty-eight, Hardy had resurrected himself and his life in a way he would have been unable to predict—success, wife, kids, even happiness. So he knew it could be done. You didn't want to bet on it, but the slim possibility was there. Maybe this kid—like Hardy an ex-cop, ex-soldier—could get another chance. "So how long," he asked, "did you walk a beat before they recalled you?"

"Three years, give or take. This isn't in my file?"

"How's it relate to your case?"

Perhaps unconsciously, Evan scratched with his right index finger at the surface of the desk. "I don't see how it would."

"That's why it's not in your file," Hardy said. "Not in Bowen's, anyway."

"What about Everett Washburn's?"

"It might be there, I don't know. I haven't talked to him yet. I wanted to meet you first. See what you had to say."

"Like what?"

"Like your own testimony at your trial. Was that Washburn's decision, or yours?"

"I don't remember, exactly. I think we agreed on it together."

"I don't understand why, when you were on the stand, you didn't take the chance to tell the jury yourself that you didn't kill Nolan. If you didn't."

The scratching stopped. Evan stared across at Hardy. "Maybe I did do it."

"Okay. That'd be a good reason. Did you?"

"You really want to know?"

"It's why I'm here."

"Washburn never cared one way or the other. If I actually did it, I mean. Said it didn't matter."

"That's what makes the world go 'round. I do care if you killed him. Did you?"

"I don't know," he said.

THE SECOND OFFICE out of which Everett Washburn practiced law was the lower flat of a Victorian building on Union Street in San Francisco. It was really more of a personal refuge than a business office. Everybody in Redwood City knew Washburn; aside from his managing-partner role in his own firm, he was a fixture at the Broadway Tobacconists down there, and sometimes the constant familiarity, having to be "on" all the time, got to be a little much for the old man. In San Francisco, he kept a secretary who came in for about ten hours every week. Her main job was to keep the plants watered. There were a lot of plants.

The place he favored most in the flat was all the way in the back. Twelve feet in diameter, octagonal in shape, with windows on four of the walls and bookcases stuffed with leisure reading—no law books—on the other four, the room was intimate and comfortable. It held his roll-top desk and slat-back chair, two small upholstered couches, a love seat, a large, square coffee table of distressed wood, and a couple of wing chairs. All of the furniture sat on a cream-colored Persian rug that had set him back twelve grand five years before.

"This is a great room," Dismas Hardy told him as he followed him in and stopped to admire it. "I could live in this room."

"It has a certain feng shui, I must admit. I do love the place. Have a seat, anywhere you'd like." Washburn plumped himself down in the middle of one of the couches, fixing Hardy with an appraising stare. "I've heard your name come up several times over the past few years, Mr. Hardy, but seeing you, I think we've met before, haven't we?"

Hardy took one of the wing chairs. "Yes, sir. And it's Diz, please. About five years ago in Redwood City. You put me in touch with an ex-client of yours and she wound up saving one of my associates' lives."

"Literally?"

"Well, the information she gave me. It solved a murder case about ten minutes before the guy could do it again."

Washburn pulled a look of pleased surprise. "I must say I don't hear that kind of story too often. An actual solved murder? My side of things, that never happens."

"Well, it did once. I probably should have gotten back to you, told you about it."

"You're telling me now. It's good to hear when a case turns out well. Did I charge you for the referral to my ex-client?"

"No."

Washburn clapped his hands together. "So much the better. Although as we all know, no good deed goes unpunished."

"I know," Hardy said. "I avoid them at every opportunity."

"And yet you've done me the courtesy to come down here to see me."

"That's not a good deed. I needed to talk to you and it was either my office or here. It gave me the chance to get out into the air in the middle of the day."

"Well, regardless, I appreciate your flexibility." And then, suddenly, as though he'd flicked a switch, Washburn shifted into business mode. He came forward to the very edge of the couch with his elbows on his knees, his hands clasped loosely. "You said it was about Evan Scholler."

"It is. I'm doing the appeal."

"Ahh. So you're the guy who comes in after the battle to shoot the wounded."

"I hope not. I've reviewed the transcripts. So far, from what I see, I'm not inclined to go with incompetence of counsel."

"That's magnanimous of you. Though in all honesty that trial wasn't one of my finer moments, I'm afraid. But what are you going to do when your client won't plead? I know I could have gotten him a manslaughter, and he could be out by the time he's forty. Now..." He shook his head. "Anyway, when I heard it was about Scholler, I thought you were coming here as a courtesy to tell me in person that I'd fucked it up and that was the basis of your appeal."

"Nope."

"So what are you thinking? The PTSD?"

Hardy nodded. "The judge shouldn't have kept it out.

It had as much, if not more, relevance as the TBI evidence. And this was a murder trial, after all. I don't know what he was thinking."

"Maybe," Washburn said, "the trial judge just didn't want to deal with the reality of what this war is doing to our soldiers. And true, I'd rather have the Ninth Circuit on this"—a notoriously liberal federal district—"but even the First District Court of Appeal justices have to read the paper and see what the Veteran's Administration is dealing with."

"You know any of those guys?" Hardy asked. "The First District justices?"

"Some. The Presiding Justice, Frank Gast. Sixties Boalt grad, thoughtful guy. He's even taught evidence to new judges. So I would think you've got a good shot."

"And no doubt Scholler had a legitimate disability that the jury never got to hear about, right?"

"Oh, yeah. We had the experts. The diagnosis was solid."

"How could it not be relevant and inadmissible?"

"How indeed."

If the appellate court didn't see the error of the trial judge in excluding PTSD to explain Scholler's lack of memory, Hardy would eat his bar card. "Well." He held out his hands, palm up. "Need I go on?"

"Not to me," Washburn said. "I do think that PTSD's the best play, though that just might be my own self-interest talking. I've kicked myself a hundred times over some decisions I made in that case. If I were doing the appeal, I might go for incompetent counsel."

"What would you have done differently?"

"Well, fought harder with Evan to take a plea, is the main thing." Washburn focused on an empty space in the air between them. "Done more with the Khalil murders, maybe, although God knows what that would have been—I spent fifty grand on my private eye and he got nothing remotely usable. Then—this was my favorite—I got halfway through my own chief medical witness when I realized that his testimony, if anything, helped the prosecution. But the main thing, as I say, would have been a plea."

"But he wouldn't take one."

"Adamant. He didn't remember doing it and wasn't going to say he did. Period."

Hardy shook his head. "Dumb."

Washburn shrugged. "I don't know. Maybe he thinks he probably didn't do it."

"What do you think?"

The old man waved that off. "I never go there."

Going for levity, Hardy put on half a grin. "Even for fun?"

"Never, no how, no way, ever."

"I can't stand a man who won't express his opinions."

"No. Me neither." Washburn sat all the way back on the couch. "But the poor fucking guy. You met him yet?"

Hardy nodded. "I went down there last week." A beat. "I bet he'd take that plea now."

"Yeah, I bet he would." Washburn had already given Hardy about twenty minutes of his time, call it two hundred dollars' worth, although he wasn't charging him for this visit. Still, time was money and if there was no business to be done between these two men, Washburn would not make any until Hardy left. "So. How else can I help you?"

"I was hoping to pick your brain a little."

"How little?"

"Six to eight hours over the next month or so."

Washburn came forward again. "My professional courtesy rate is two hundred."

"Sounds reasonable," Hardy said. "I don't know how much time you have right now, and I don't want to impose…"

Washburn held up a hand and looked over at the grandfather clock that stood sentinel where the windows met the bookshelves. It was quarter to four. "I'm comfortable going till five," he said. "Feel free. Pick away."

A MONTH into his new old job, his second hitch as head of San Francisco's homicide detail, Lieutenant Abe Glitsky walked alone down the fifth-floor hallway and turned into the small room—itself bisected by a counter—that served as the unit's reception area. It was five-twenty, and both of the clerks stationed here had left, probably gone home for the day. Glitsky, after his initial disapproval, was getting used to the idea of hourly employees putting in their time and going home. While he'd been deputy chief of inspectors over these past few years, he'd always felt it odd that even the clerical jobs were so personal—you got in early and you stayed until your boss went home because if you didn't, someone else might get close to him and then you might not rise in the bureaucracy when he did. Or she, of course.

In another few steps, he was in his office—a small room stuffed with file cabinets, crammed with a large flat working desk, windows high enough in the wall along the right to allow in a bit of natural light but that afforded no view of Bryant Street down below. Coming around the desk, Glitsky glanced up at his bulletin board of active homicides—nine of them today, about average, crimes committed in the past month or so on which his inspectors were still working. Settling into his chair, he sat back and wondered anew if his request for what amounted to a voluntary demotion had been a mistake.

He'd been on the job for more than a month now, and besides some of the personnel issues that had been and continued to be a bit troubling, he found that, much to his surprise, he somewhat missed his large official office with its bookshelves and plaques and wall decorations, its brace of leather chairs for important visitors, its reception area that discouraged passersby from stopping in to say hello. The deputy chief's office was that of an Important Man, and while he had occupied it, Glitsky often had not felt, at base, like he belonged there. Now, as head of homicide, he still had what he believed to be an important job, but it was mostly an invisible one. Could it be, he'd been wondering, that he'd grown accustomed to being in the public eye, to having his opinion matter to others, to being consulted by the chief and even the mayor about important civic issues?

He kept telling himself that he was in a period of adjustment to the new surroundings, that was all. Change itself was never easy. But two or three times already, he'd entertained the thought that maybe he'd made yet another mistake in a recent history of poor career choices.

And there was no getting around it. These new digs were different and they made the whole job, once so familiar, feel different. First, this office was physically separated from the inspectors' room. When the detail had been on the fourth floor, the internal windows in the lieutenant's office looked out over the crowded room that held the desks of the troops. Here, even if his new office had internal windows, which it didn't, he wouldn't have been able to see the inspectors, since the computer room was in the way. Inspectors could and did come and go, they never had to pass his door, and Glitsky might never know they'd been around.

The good news was that, barring emergencies, Glitsky's own hours had stabilized. As deputy chief, he'd considered it his duty to set an example of rigor, discipline, and enthusiasm, and he'd made it a point to be at work at seven-thirty. At the other end of the day, department meetings, press conferences, and public appearances often kept him out until nine, sometimes later. His weekends rarely were his own either. Deputy chief wasn't a job; it was a life.

And Glitsky was at a juncture—the crux of it, really—his desire in life was to be with his wife, Treya, and their two young children, Rachel and Zachary. The last couple of years, since Zack had been born, had been something of a strain. Treya worked as the secretary for San Francisco's district attorney, Clarence Jackman. She was at her desk at nine and left at five. There had been weeks while Glitsky had been deputy chief that they'd basically only gotten to speak to each other in this building, the Hall of Justice.

Now, having made sure that his desk was cleared, Glitsky was getting ready to check out for the day. He went out his door, closing it behind him. Passing through the empty computer room, he entered the inspectors' area and saw that fully eight of the fourteen homicide inspectors were in the room. This was unusual, since most of the time, these people were out interviewing witnesses, assessing crime scenes, building cases, and working out rebooking details and/or charges with assistant DAs.

Darrel Bracco looked over and raised a hand in greeting—at least one person in the unit apparently okay with the new status quo. As the vibe of Glitsky's presence passed through the room, other inspectors looked up. Glitsky caught a few nods from veterans who went back to their conversations and coffee, was ignored by a couple of others.

This was the way it had been since he'd come down here, his people misunderstanding his reappointment to homicide, wondering if in reality he was some kind of spy sent down by the brass to shake up the detail, screw up their jobs.

Glitsky hoped that this was simply the effect of change on his people, and that it, too, would shortly pass. But until it did, he wasn't having a good time. Getting up to Bracco's desk, he summoned a neutral tone. "I'm out the door, Darrel. Anything happening I might want to know about before I go?"

Bracco thought a minute, then shook his head. "Nothing new, Lieutenant," he said. "Slow day on the prairie, I guess."

"I guess so." Glitsky did a quick scan of the room. He didn't want to seem to be checking on anyone. In fact, he wasn't, but that didn't mean people might not think he was. "See you tomorrow, Darrel."

"Yes, sir," Bracco said. "Have a good one." Glitsky had turned and gone two steps when Bracco spoke again. "Wait a sec, Abe. I just remembered. There was something you might want to put back on your board." This was the active homicide board in Glitsky's office. Usually, once a name left that board, it stayed off forever, either because a suspect in the case had gotten arrested, or because the trail had gone too cold to waste the inspectors' time anymore, or if the only eyewitness fell terminally ill with lead poisoning, or if, for any of a zillion reasons, the case wasn't being actively worked anymore.

"Back on the board?"

"Yeah. One of my old ones. Bowen. But it's been closed since before your time. We can get to it in the morning. Here, I'm writing myself a note so I won't forget."

"How 'bout if I just walk back in there and write it back up?"

Sheepish, Bracco nodded, getting to his feet. "That would probably work too. I didn't want to keep you if you were leaving."

"How long can it take?" Glitsky asked. "B-O-W-E-N, is that right? Five letters. Shouldn't take me more than a few minutes." He was already back at his door, turning the key in it. "So what's the case?"

"Hanna Bowen. Finally ruled a suicide by hanging."

Glitsky turned and faced his inspector. "What? She unhang herself?"

"It's more like I promised the daughter that I'd take another look at it. She can't seem to get her arms around it. That her mom killed herself, I mean."

"Okay. But the coroner ruled suicide? And you're going to help this daughter how?"

"I know it's a long shot, Abe, but the girl's still torn up. You know all the classes we take that tell us to be sensitive to the victim's pain, and all that. I figure what can it hurt, and it might help her."

"What, though, exactly?"

"Well, evidently the mother kept a diary. Or the daughter—her name is Jenna—Jenna thinks her mom might have kept a diary and she asked me if I could try to find it."

"And do what with it?"

"See if it gave us any reason to think her mom's death might have been a homicide."

Glitsky boosted himself back onto his desk. "This was your case originally?"

"Yeah."

"Anything point to homicide back then? When was this?"

"Maybe early February, and not really, no. Except that Jenna had such a hard time with accepting that her mother would do that."

"Well, God knows we've seen that before, Darrel. Not that I blame her. Your mother goes that way, you don't want to believe it. Maybe you honestly can't believe it, but that doesn't mean it didn't happen."

"I know. I told her I'd look, that's all. No promises."

"For this diary?"

"I don't know, Abe. That might not be all. I worked the case pretty hard when it was live. There were other elements at the time. Well, to be honest, mostly one other element, but it seemed worth checking out, although at the time I couldn't get anything on it."

"What was that?"

"The dad, Charlie. He disappeared last summer. That's supposedly why the wife killed herself."

"What do you mean, disappeared?"

"I mean poof, gone, vanished. No trace. Jenna thinks he wouldn't have just disappeared either. She thought he might have been killed."

"By who? Why?"

"No idea."

"Very strong, Darrel. So she thinks her father was killed, too, and that it's somehow connected to her mother's suicide?"

"Not suicide. She doesn't buy suicide. She thinks her mother was another homicide."

"Two homicides." Glitsky sat with it for another few seconds.

Bracco made a face. "The daughter lost both parents in the same year. If the diary turns up..." He shrugged. "Who knows. We might get something."

"So where are you gonna start?"

"I suppose I'll meet her and go through all the evidence again. Then maybe get to the father's files, which I never really looked into last time."

"What files?"

"His work files. He was a lawyer. Maybe it was something he was working on."

"What was?"

"The reason he was killed."

Glitsky scratched for a second at the corner of his mouth. Bracco had always been an enthusiastic cop, but he'd gotten promoted up to homicide originally because his father had been a driver to a former mayor, and sometimes his lack of experience showed. "You realize, I know, Darrel," Glitsky said, "that most middle-aged guys who disappear . . . I'm assuming this Charlie Bowen was middle-aged?"

"Fifty."

"There you go. Sometimes guys like him just walk away from it all on their own. They're not murdered."

"Right. I know that, Abe. Of course."

"And the wives of those men, who have been deserted by their husbands of, say, thirty years, might they find themselves depressed in the months following the desertion, even to the point of wanting to kill themselves?"

"Sure."

"Did we investigate Bowen as a homicide when he went missing?"

"No."

"And that was because . . . ?"

"He was considered a missing person."

"Not a homicide?"

"Not a homicide. No, sir."

"Okay, then. Just to make the point."

"I hear you." Bracco shrugged away his misgivings. "Anyway, I'll be logging some time to the case and I thought you'd want to know."

"Okay." Glitsky pushed himself off his desk and wrote the word BOWEN onto the board, with the name BRACCO in the investigating inspector's column. "But, Darrel?"

"Yes, sir."

"Maybe not too much time, huh?"

OVER THE PAST SEVERAL YEARS, Glitsky's grown boys—Isaac, Jacob, and Orel—and Treya's grown girl, Raney, had created a diaspora of their own to places as far-flung as Seattle, Milan, Washington, D.C., and—not so far-flung—Orel was living in San Jose. Now the new family unit with two toddlers ranged in the same old upper duplex on a cul-de-sac above Lake Street.

When Glitsky got home from work—driving his own car instead of being chauffeured by his driver in his city-issued vehicle—he and Treya and five-year-old Rachel had pushed Zack's baby carriage for a mile or so on the foot-and-bike path that ran behind their home at the edge of the Presidio's forest. In their backyard, in the still-warm evening, both kids swung on the new swingset Glitsky and Dismas Hardy and Hardy's son Vincent had built about three years before. Dinner was a store-bought roast chicken, the skin peeled off, with fresh steamed spinach and a side dish of noodles for the kids—since Glitsky's heart attack six years ago, Treya wouldn't let him eat anything with cholesterol in it.

By eight o'clock, both kids were asleep in their separate rooms down the hallway off the kitchen. Abe and Treya sipped tea sitting together in dim light on the leather love seat in the small living room. They had re-decorated the room for the birth of Rachel, and now what had been a worn and dark interior sported blond hardwood floors accented with colorful throw rugs, yellow Tuscan walls, Mission-style furniture, plantation shutters.

Taciturn nearly to the point of muteness, Glitsky was happy to let Treya carry the conversational ball as she told him about her day, the machinations of the DA's office, Clarence Jackman's dealings with the board of supervisors, the mayor, the chief of police. It was endlessly entertaining because they both knew all the players and because the city was in many ways such a truly loony and fascinating place to live.

Today's drama featured Treya's boss on a tightrope walk between Mayor Kathy West's edict that declared San Francisco a sanctuary city for illegal immigrants, and the U.S. attorney's response that he was going to cut off every federal law enforcement grant to the city if she did anything to hamper the Justice Department's crackdown on arresting and deporting these people.

"That I'd like to see," Glitsky said. "What's he going to do, arrest Kathy?"

"If she actually does anything other than talk the talk."

"You think she will?"

"I don't know. She's talking about it." Treya's laugh was a low contralto. "Talking about not just talking about it."

"Very bold."

"*Très*. But you never know. She might really do something."

"So what's Clarence going to do?"

Treya laughed again. Sometimes Glitsky thought that her talent for laughter was what had attracted him the most about her. After his first wife, Flo, had died, he had thought for a long while that he would never laugh again. "Clarence," Treya said, "has got eight lawyer positions funded by federal money, but the rest of his budget comes from the city. He is going to wait."

"He's a good waiter," Glitsky said.

"One of the best." She put a hand on his leg. "But here I've been, me, me, me. You seem—I don't mean to spook you—but slightly more upbeat than you've been."

Glitsky shrugged. "Just getting used to the new world order. I actually had a possibly productive talk with Darrel Bracco today."

"I like Darrel. And possibly productive? Wow. The man gushes."

Sipping his tea, Glitsky gave her a sideways look. "Maybe saved him some hours of slog, that's all."

"Okay, retract the gush." She squeezed his leg. "And

next you were probably going to tell me what Darrel talked to you about. If you were going to keep on talking, I mean. Not that you have to. No pressure."

This time his smile broke clear. "He was going to be spending half of forever looking into the case files of this lawyer who disappeared last summer because some poor heartbroken girl thinks maybe he didn't run away and desert her and her mother after all. Maybe he was killed instead."

"Is there any reason she thinks that?"

"Not that Darrel knows. But the thing that makes it so sad is that her mother killed herself over it a couple of months ago, and the girl just can't accept it."

Treya took a beat and sipped her tea. "And people say you're not really all that fun. How can that be?" She turned to him. "That heartening, upbeat story was what's made you feel better about the job?"

"Talking to Darrel," Glitsky said.

"Ah. The silver lining."

"I mean, first, you've got to believe Charlie Bowen was a homicide, which there's no sign of, so why are you even looking?"

"Charlie Bowen," Treya said. "Where do I know that name?"

"He's the father. The missing person."

"The lawyer? I knew him, Abe. He's the guy, Diz got all his files."

"Our own Diz?"

"Our own Diz." Treya gave his leg another squeeze. "Maybe Darrel ought to talk to him."

[31]

THE NEXT MORNING, Friday, May 4, Glitsky and Treya drove in to work together. Through the largesse of Clarence Jackman, Treya had a dedicated parking spot behind the jail that she considered perhaps the job's single greatest perk.

Yesterday's high pressure front had scoured the sky clean and banished the marine layer halfway out to the Farallones, so the sun packed an unseasonable warmth. Though there was no breeze at all, some fluke of nature had delivered a fragrant and powerful olfactory blast from the city's main flower market around the corner. Treya, getting out on the passenger side, looked over the car's hood at her husband and said, "This day is too beautiful. Do you smell that? If we were truly evolved spirits, no way would we go in to work today."

"No? What would we do instead?"

"Whatever we wanted. Dance, sing, take the ferry to Sausalito."

Glitsky met her in front of the car and took her hand as they started toward the Hall of Justice. "If we were truly evolved," he said, "we'd probably get fired. So, luckily, we're not."

"Well, maybe you're not." She ceased walking, effectively stopping them both, and sniffed the air aggressively. "But I'm at least taking one extra minute here to enjoy this."

"Smelling the roses, as it were."

"You should try it. Close your eyes a second, breathe it in."

Glitsky did as instructed, then opened his eyes. "Yep, roses," he said, "and then all that other stuff."

WHEN GLITSKY opened the door to homicide's reception area, he was looking at Dismas Hardy, who was dressed for work in his suit and tie and looking at his watch. "Two minutes late," Hardy said. "What kind of example is that to set for your team?"

"Treya held me up," he said. "We stopped in the parking lot to smell the flowers."

"How were they?"

"Really great. Flowerlike." Glitsky greeted the two clerks that sat at their desks and then swung open the door to the counter that divided the room, indicating that Hardy follow him in. Opening the door to his office, Glitsky asked, "Did we have an appointment?"

"No."

"I didn't think so."

"But you called me last night, if you remember, which I bet you do. I didn't get in till too late to call you back. Something about Charlie Bowen?" Hardy took one of the chairs from against the back wall and pulled it up to sit on it.

Glitsky got himself seated behind his desk. "His name got you down here first thing in the morning?"

"Not really. I've got a hearing downstairs at ten anyway." Hardy crossed a leg. "So you're going to tell me they found his body?"

"Why do you say that?"

"Let's see. You're homicide. You call me about a guy who went missing ten months ago. Call me crazy, but I figure maybe he's suddenly become a homicide."

"Nope. That's not it. Good guess, though."

"Thank you. You want me to make another one?"

"You could, or I could just tell you."

"Okay. Let's go with that."

Glitsky gave it to him in about ten sentences, at the end of which Hardy was frowning. "So your guy Bracco," he said, "wants to do what exactly?"

"Find this diary."

"Which may or may not exist?"

"Right."

"And then which may or may not have anything to do with Charlie's wife's death?"

Glitsky shrugged his shoulders. "This isn't my idea, Diz. Treya just thought you might save Bracco some running around."

"If I could, I'd be happy to. But we're talking like sixty large boxes of files, about a third of which we've already farmed out or returned to clients."

"Right. I know."

"Besides which," Hardy said, "the timing's wrong. If the wife died in February, I had the files in my office by mid-December. She couldn't have dropped the diary into any of them even if she wanted to. You want, though, I'll get one of my people to go through the boxes on everything we've got left, but I wouldn't get my hopes up."

"That's what I told Darrel."

"There you go," Hardy said, standing up. "Great minds. Oh, no, wait, that couldn't be it."

Glitsky was picking up his telephone. "Get the door on your way out, would you?"

HARDY HAD TAKEN up the habit of his now-deceased mentor David Freeman and, whenever the opportunity presented itself, walked the fourteen blocks between his office on Sutter Street and the Hall of Justice. Today, his morning hearing having ended sooner than expected, he was making pretty good time—not that it was a race or an opportunity for exercise or anything like that—when he got to Mission Street. There, a well-dressed, elderly woman caught his eye and moved just a bit over to get in his path. She looked into his face, beamed at him, and said, "Pardon me."

"Yes?"

"Are you all right?"

"I think so." She didn't look like it, but Hardy suddenly had no doubt that she was yet another in a city full of crazies.

"Then you ought to smile."

"Excuse me?"

"A day like this, a handsome man like you ought to be smiling."

"I wasn't?"

"Not really, no. More like frowning. More like the whole world's on your shoulders."

"Sorry," he stammered, trying to rearrange his expression. "Better?"

"Much," the woman said. "You watch. It'll help. Have a nice day."

After she disappeared into the crowd, Hardy stood for a long moment, unable to move. Catching his reflection in the store window next to him, he saw that the smile he'd dredged up had already faded completely away. Stepping all the way out of the foot traffic into the archway entrance to an ancient storefront, on an impulse he pulled his cell phone off his belt and punched in a number. "Hey," he said.

"Hey yourself. This is a surprise. Is everything all right?"

"Fine. Everything's fine. I just wondered what you were doing?"

"When?"

"Like, now."

His wife's laugh tinkled through the phone. "Like now I'm about to get in my car and go eat a salad someplace. Why?"

"Because I thought for a change of pace maybe you'd like to have some lunch with your husband."

Hardy waited out the short pause.

Then, "I would love to have some lunch with my husband. I think that's a great idea."

"You're not too busy?"

"I've got two hours and change. Where were you thinking?"

THEY DECIDED on Tommy's Joynt, Hardy by cab and Frannie by car, since it was about midway between Frannie's office on Arguello and Hardy's downtown. Fifteen minutes after the phone call, they sat down in one of the booths, Hardy with a bowl of buffalo stew and a beer and Frannie with a French dip and Diet Coke.

"You don't come to Tommy's Joynt and eat a salad," she said, biting into one of the place's homemade pickles. "I mean, it's legal and all, but it would be wrong."

"It's not that I don't agree with you," Hardy said. "But if you really wanted a salad, we could have—"

"Hey!" She put a hand over his. "We're here," she said. "This is the perfect spot right now. There couldn't be a better one."

Hardy looked around and nodded. "No." He sighed. "You said it. It's perfect."

Frannie cocked her head. "Dismas, are you all right?"

"You're the second person who's asked me that in the last half hour, so apparently not."

"The second one. Who else?"

He told her about the lady at the corner of Mission.

"You mean out of everybody walking down the street, she just stopped you and told you to smile?"

"Right. But first she asked me if I was okay. That I looked like I was carrying the weight of the world on my shoulders. Then after she left, I realized that that was pretty much the way I felt. I don't know why. I wasn't consciously down or anything. It's an absolutely glorious day . . ." He put down his fork, looked across at her. "Anyway, it hit me pretty good upside the head, almost like a message from on high."

"Saying what?"

"One thing, saying I ought to call you."

"I'm glad you did."

"Me too." He picked up his fork again, put it in the

stew, stirred a minute. "I never thought I'd say this, but I think I'm having some trouble with this empty nest thing."

She put her sandwich down and again covered his hand with hers. "Yeah."

"And then I've been pretty pissed off at you for not being home when I get there, so I arrange not to be home when you are. Maybe I don't even consciously know I'm doing that, but I think that's what's been going on. It's wearing me down."

"I know. It's wearing me down too." She brought a napkin up to her eye and dabbed at it. "I don't really miss them so much, you know. I mean, I don't want them living with us anymore, God knows. We did enough of that. I just don't seem to know what to do with myself, so I fill up all my time with work, and then when I come home and you're not there either..."

Hardy finally got some of the great stew into his mouth, followed it with some Anchor Steam. "I'm thinking maybe we ought to reinstigate Date Night. Make it sacred again."

"I think that's a great idea. Maybe even go wild and have two a week."

"I would if you would."

"Deal."

She put her hand out over the table and Hardy shook it.

AN HOUR LATER, Hardy ascended the steps into the wide, marbled, circular foyer that marked the reception area of the law firm of Freeman, Farrell, Hardy & Roake, of which he was the managing partner. He marched up to the waist-high mahogany bullpen that demarked the territory of Phyllis, the firm's receptionist, and, obeying the finger she held up, waited while she placed a call to one of the other offices.

When she finished her business, she turned to him with her usual expectant petulance. "I told an Inspector Bracco that you would be here at one o'clock," she said. "Which is when you told me that you would be here."

"I know, Phyllis. I'm sorry. Something came up."

"And your cell phone broke?"

"You know, now that you mention it"—Hardy held his jacket down over the holster for his phone—"I've been looking all over for the damn thing. Have you seen it? Maybe I left it in my office somewhere. Or the car. I bet I left it charging in the car."

She shook her head with an icy disdain. "He waited forty minutes."

"I'm sure he did. Did he leave a number? We can get back to him."

"Of course, but I wanted to be sure you were here."

"As well you should, Phyllis. As well you should."

"Would you like me to call him now? He may not be far away. It's only been twenty minutes, after all, since he left."

Hardy considered that for a second. He had thought about driving down the Peninsula and getting some unscheduled time to ambush Mary Patricia Whelan-Miille on his Scholler appeal, but if Bracco was still close to the office, he was all but certain that it would be a short meeting. "Sure," he said, "call him back if he can make it."

Phyllis started punching buttons. Hardy made it to the

door of his office when his cell phone rang on his belt, stopping him in his tracks as he lifted the phone and looked at the display screen. The call was from his office's main number. His shoulders fell and he turned around to face her.

Phyllis, her mouth set in disapproval, shook her head at him. "Maybe you left it charging in your car. Or maybe not."

Busted.

"I'll try to reach Inspector Bracco now," she said.

BRACCO COULD HAVE been the poster child for the good homicide cop. He went about five foot ten, a hundred and seventy pounds of muscle. He wore a tailored camel-hair sport coat over a pair of brown slacks, a light tan dress shirt with a plain brown tie. Under a close-cropped head of straw-colored hair, gray eyes animated his square, ruddy, clean-shaven face.

Now Bracco sipped a cup of freshly brewed coffee and sat comfortably in a leather chair by one of the windows that looked down on Sutter Street. This was in the more casual of the two seating areas that distinguished Hardy's office—the other, formal, more intimidating space with the Persian carpet, the Queen Anne chairs and lion's claw coffee table, complete with doily, claimed the area more or less in front of his large cherry desk.

Hardy went to the twin of Bracco's chair and sat down. He began on a conciliatory note. "I'm sorry you had to wait last time you were here. There was some confusion about my schedule."

Bracco turned up a palm, dismissing the apology.

"You're doing me the favor, seeing me at all. I appreciate it."

"Sure. But I told Abe it'd probably be pretty slim pickins."

"That's what he said. He also said you offered to have one of your people go through Bowen's files, but that you didn't expect to find Mrs. Bowen's diary in them."

"Only because she would have still been writing in it, I presume, when the files had already been removed here to our storage. Glitsky said you weren't even sure there actually was a diary."

"No. Well, Jenna—Bowen's daughter—she's pretty sure there was a diary. Although I went through the house again this morning with a comb and nothing turned up."

"Well." Hardy wasn't sure where he fit in this picture, but he didn't want to give Bracco the bum's rush after his wait earlier. Let the man at least finish his coffee. "I can't speak for the files we've already finished with, but if you want me to light a fire under this, we can probably get through the rest of them in a couple of days. I've just gotten back to the office, otherwise I would have had somebody on it already. Is there some kind of hurry I don't know about?"

Bracco shook his head. "Just Jenna, to be honest with you. For the first few weeks after her mom's death, she was pretty much out of commission with grief. Now she's trying to process it, close the book one way or the other. If there's a diary and some clue…" He shrugged. "Anyway, so no, there's no real hurry, but I feel like I owe her another look if it's that important to her. And it is."

Hardy sat back and crossed his legs. "So I take it you had the mom's case?"

"Right."

"And you were okay with the coroner's call?"

"Pretty much."

"Did you see anything or talk to anybody that made you think it wasn't a suicide?"

"Generally, no. I mean, her husband had vanished a few months before. She'd made plans to go to Italy this summer, but the general feeling was that that was to try to put the desertion behind her, not to party. Most of her friends, and I talked to a lot of them, described her as devastated and depressed."

"So what's her daughter's take?"

"I think pretty much the usual. Her mother just wouldn't have done that. That's not who she was. Then she points to the Europe trip. Hanna—the mom—was evidently pretty frugal. Tight as a drum, Jenna says. She would never have bought tickets to Italy and not used them. She would have killed herself afterward."

Hardy allowed a small grin. "I know some people like that. Although putting off your own suicide until after you get your money's worth might be stretching it. And that's it? That's the daughter's reason she thinks it wasn't suicide?"

"Originally, basically, yes." Bracco drank some coffee, stared out the window for a moment.

Hardy had the impression he was trying to decide if he should say any more and thought he could help him along. "That's a lot of disclaimer you're throwing around. Originally. Basically. Do you have some doubts yourself? Is that why you're digging here?"

Bracco's mouth pursed as he continued to wrestle with whatever it was. "It was their rope, she slung it over a beam in the garage, got up on a little step-up ladder, and dropped off."

"But . . . ?"

Noticing that his coffee was finished, Bracco came forward in his chair and put the cup and saucer on the low table in front of him. Now he looked straight across at Hardy. "None of this worried me too much at the time, you understand. I had three other actives. This one went to the coroner and went away in a couple of days. It wasn't until Jenna called me back a few days ago that I looked at it again."

"And?"

"And her neck was broken." He paused, then made his point more clearly. "Regular slipknot, no hangman's noose, fifteen-inch fall."

"You're thinking she should have strangled."

"Most people, those same conditions, that's what happens."

"But not always? Did you ask Strout?" This was the city's medical examiner, who'd ruled the death a suicide.

"He says he's seen a few where the fall and the weight breaks the neck."

"Well, there you go."

"Nobody who weighed as little as she did, though. A hundred and five pounds." Hardy made no response; by itself this was interesting, certainly, but not conclusive. "And then," Bracco went on, "there was the other thing Jenna didn't think about originally, but remembers now."

"What was that?"

"That her mother had decided that Charlie didn't just disappear. That he'd been killed."

"Someone in her position," Hardy said, "that could easily be wishful thinking. That he didn't leave her, he was taken from her instead. Big psychological difference."

"Yeah," Bracco said, "but the main thing is that Jenna says her mom was on a mission to find out who killed her dad and wouldn't have killed herself in the middle of it."

"Maybe she got to the end and found he'd really run out on her."

"I said the same thing to Jenna. She totally disagreed. If her mom would have found that out, even then if she decided to kill herself, she would have left a note for Jenna so at least her daughter would know the truth."

A short silence settled between the two men. "You're saying you think it's not impossible somebody killed Mrs. Bowen."

"It's not the kind of thing I'd try to sell to Glitsky. Not on what I've got now."

"You got a motive?"

"You probably won't love it."

"Try me."

"Somebody—the same person—killed the husband, too, and Hanna got too close to finding out."

Hardy shook his head, suppressed the start of a smile. "A bona fide conspiracy theory. You're right, that would be a tough sell to Glitsky."

"That's why I'd like to find that diary. It would be something real."

Hardy thought that even if it existed, it still would be considerably less than a smoking gun. Stealing a quick glance at his watch, he decided he'd given Bracco enough time and a good listen. Bracco didn't wear a wedding ring, and Hardy wouldn't be at all surprised to find out that the daughter, Jenna Bowen, was a pretty young thing. As for him, it was time to get back to work. He started to get up.

But Bracco suddenly came forward. "Anyway, the reason I wanted to see you in person. I'm just saying there might be something else in those files."

"Some reason Bowen might have been killed, you mean?"

"Right."

This time, Hardy let his grin blossom. "You know how many big moving boxes we're talking about here, Inspector? Something like forty-five or fifty to go. Last time I checked, when he disappeared Charlie Bowen was covering two hundred and thirty-two active files, of which we've off-loaded about eighty so far." He softened his tone. "Which is not to say we won't come upon something that looks fishy somewhere down the line, and if we do, I promise you'll hear from us. From me. But I think you're talking the original needle in a haystack."

Chagrined, Bracco sat back and nodded. "Yeah, I can see that. Well..." He pushed himself up to his feet.

Hardy, rising himself, said, "If you get anything specific attached to some probable cause, you could always subpoena the files and have a special master go through them."

"I could do that, but I don't have any idea what I'm looking for."

"Well, there's that." Hardy brightened. "Except the diary."

"Right. Except the diary."

"I'll get somebody working on that before you hit the street."

"I appreciate that," Bracco said, extending his hand. "Thanks again for your time."

Hardy nodded. "And we find anything on the other matter, you'll be the first to know. But as I told Glitsky, I wouldn't hold my breath on any of this."

Bracco broke a small smile. "I never do."

[32]

HARDY HAD A SPY in Redwood City.

His old law school buddy Sean Kelleher worked as an assistant district attorney in the same building as Mary Patricia Whelan-Miille and told Hardy that she wasn't calendared for any trials and should be in or about her office for the whole day. As soon as Bracco had walked out of his office, Hardy had made the day of Michael Cho, one of his paralegals, by assigning him to start looking through the boxes of Charlie Bowen's files for a woman's diary. Then he'd picked up the phone and called to make double sure about Mary Patricia, told Kelleher he owed him one, and hightailed it down to his garage.

Ten minutes later, top down on his S2000, Hootie blaring from his car's speakers, Hardy cleared Candlestick Point and twenty minutes after that was parking in the courthouse lot twenty-five miles south. If San Francisco had been warm and pleasant all day, Redwood City, in the mideighties, was positively balmy. As he brought the roof back up over the convertible, he found himself humming out loud. He felt like a different person from the stoop-shouldered slug who'd attracted the attention of the possibly-not-crazy elderly woman at the corner of Seventh and Mission that morning. The lunch with

Frannie, her receptiveness, maybe the start of the next phase of their lives together after the unexpected hollow emptiness of the recent one.

The little dance he was doing around Mary Patricia Whelan-Miille was not frivolous. He thought it so likely as to be certain that she would not consent to a regular scheduled appointment with him. After all, he was the man who was trying to undo all of the hard work she'd put in on what was to date still one of the most successful moments of her career. In fact, he considered it not impossible that even his planned ambush of her would be rebuffed. Certainly, there was no reason, other than professional courtesy, that she need feel compelled to see him. He wasn't kidding himself. He knew who he was. He was the enemy.

When he arrived in Redwood City, he called Kelleher, who came out and walked him past the receptionist into the offices in the back. He had a cup of coffee and shot the breeze a little and then asked Kelleher to point him toward the lair of Mary Patricia Whelan-Miille.

Her door was open and Hardy stood for a second in the hallway, trying to take her measure. Younger-looking than he'd expected, with a very appealing profile, she was sitting forward in her chair, her elbows on her desk, one hand playing with a loose tendril of blondish hair, apparently reading. Her feet, shoeless, were tucked back under her chair. It was a Friday-afternoon scene similar to one he'd seen a thousand times in the legal world—the alone, as opposed to lonely, time every good lawyer needed to keep up on facts, to study cases, to stay current on changes in the law, to recharge.

Part of him hated to bother her.

The rest of him stepped forward and knocked softly on her door. "Excuse me."

She turned to face him, her expression just short of querulous. Yes, it said, he was interrupting her. But she could be serene about it. The petulance gave way to a mild curiosity. "Can I help you?"

"I think so." He pointed to the name on her door. "If you're Mary Patricia Whelan-Miille."

"That's me."

"That's some name."

"Tell me about it. Sometimes I wonder what my parents were thinking. Mississippi and all of New York."

"Pardon?"

She straightened up in her chair, put her hands behind her lower back, and arched herself briefly. Getting out the kinks or showing off the merchandise. "Nine syllables," she said. "Mary Patricia Whelan-Miille. Mississippi and all of New York. Imagine having to ask people to say 'Mississippi and all of New York' every time they wanted to address you by name. You'd never talk to anybody." She broke a nice smile. "People call me Mills. Who are you?"

Hardy came forward and introduced himself.

"Dismas?" she asked.

"Dismas."

"I don't think I've ever met a Dismas."

"You're not alone. He was the good thief on Calvary, next to Jesus. Also, he's the patron saint of thieves and murderers."

"Good for him. I'm proud of him. I've always wanted to be patron saint of something, except I understand first you've got to be dead, and that's got limited appeal."

Mills swung in around to face him. "So, Dismas, how can I help you?"

"Well, speaking of appeal, I wanted to ask you for a few minutes of your time to talk about the Scholler case. I'm doing the appeal."

The mildly flirtatious personality dropped off her like the calving of a glacier, leaving only the cold, flat ice behind. "I have nothing to say about that. I won the case. I don't think there are any legitimate appealable issues."

"You don't think PTSD should have been let in?"

"If you've read the transcripts, you know I argued against just that and prevailed. That was the right call. And now, I'm sorry, but I'm in the middle of—"

"You spoke to Charlie Bowen. I'm only asking for the same courtesy."

"Charlie Bowen made an appointment with me and we set ground rules."

"I'll go with ground rules," Hardy said. "Same as Charlie's."

"Do you even know what they were?"

"It doesn't matter. I'll agree unseen."

"There's a desperate offer." She folded her arms over her chest. "Look, Mr. Hardy..."

"Dismas."

"Mr. Hardy, please. I don't want to be a hardass, but I'm not going to talk to you about Evan Scholler. He was guilty and I got him convicted and I hope he rots away in prison. That's all I've got to say, all right? Please."

Hardy counted five of his heartbeats. Of course, there always had been the make-an-appointment-and-set-ground-rules option, but he'd never before had a conference like that produce anything of real substance. If you wanted your soda to fizz and bubble, you had to shake it up.

But now he was looking at turning around and driving back home, facing a weekend with absolutely nothing to chew on and work with. The words and the idea came out of his mouth before he was aware that he'd thought of them. Anything to keep her talking with him. "How about if I don't talk about that case at all?"

She cocked her head, still wary. "Then what exactly would we be talking about?"

"Charlie Bowen."

"What about him?"

"Anything he might have said to you before he disappeared."

That stopped her. She combed her hand through her hair, made a face at him that could have meant anything, looked down at her desk, back at Hardy. "Why do you want to do that?"

"He disappeared while he was working on this appeal. Before I get too far with it, I don't want to have the same thing happen to me."

She shook her head, chortling. "Don't be ridiculous. He'd barely started even the preliminary work. I don't think he'd even finished the transcripts when I talked to him."

"So what did you talk about?"

"He wanted to review the evidence that hadn't been used at the trial. To see if I had any working papers not included in the defense discovery. Stuff like that. Just to make sure the record was complete while he was going ahead. Housecleaning."

"He didn't mention any personal conflicts?"

"No. If I recall, the meeting lasted under the hour. We didn't get too close."

"But he was going ahead with the appeal?"

"Of course. That's why we were talking at all."

"He didn't seem nervous or overly concerned with his safety?"

"Why would he be? The bad guy was already in jail." Shaking her head as if to clear away that thought, she went on. "I hate the appeals process, you know that. They ought to give our side an appeals process if we lose a case—try the scumbags again until we get 'em and put 'em away."

"YEAH, THAT'S MILLS," Washburn said. "She's a bit of a zealot, but she's also only the second person in thirty years to whip me in court, so she's got my respect." Hardy had thought it was late enough in the day that there would be a good chance he'd find Washburn at the Broadway Tobacconists, and he was right.

Now they sat in a cloud of cigar smoke in the back of the unpretentious little store. Except for Greta, the female proprietor, they had the place to themselves, a situation—Washburn assured him—that would change in the next hour, when his acolytes and his girlfriend would appear from their various offices to drink "from the vast fount of my knowledge."

Not entirely sure Washburn was poking fun at himself, Hardy said, "Well, whatever time you and I get together here, it's on the clock."

"Goes without saying." Washburn savored his smoke, drawing on it, exhaling another plume. He twirled the cigar around between his lips, then dipped the unlit end into a small glass of amber liquid that, from the bottle next to it, was Armagnac. "Sure you won't join me?"

"Thanks, but then I'd just want a little nip of your nectar, and I'm going to be driving."

"Probably wise. So how can I help you today?"

"Well, this is odd, but it came to me when I was trying to get to Mills. I didn't even see a draft of Charlie Bowen's appeal brief in the file, so I'm assuming he hadn't gotten to it. I'd also been assuming that he was going to go with the PTSD. But now I'm wondering if he'd mentioned anything about that to you."

"What?"

"What he was basing his appeal on. Especially if it wasn't PTSD."

Washburn sat back, drew on his cigar, held the smoke. "Actually," he said, "you raise a good point." Another pause while he dipped the cigar again in the Armagnac. "You know, he seemed to think that it might be more fruitful to attack the competency of the local constabulary as well as the FBI."

"How's that?"

"Well, the Khalil murders." Turning the cigar between his lips, Washburn sat back, pensive. "I mean, here you had two murders intimately connected with the Scholler case—there was no question of that—and a blatant assumption that Evan had committed them with the frag grenades and so on. But the DA never charged him with those murders. You see the issue?"

Hardy saw it plainly, and it struck him as unusually powerful. "So the police and the FBI never questioned anyone else?"

"And, on one hand," Washburn added, "why would they? They had a suspect they could convict, and may as well send him down for one murder as for three, without the risk of losing on the other two."

"You mean they never questioned anyone else about the Khalil murders?"

"I assume they must have, a few people anyway. But certainly not everyone they could have." He took in a huge lungful of the pungent air. "You're forgetting, though, and I wonder if Mr. Bowen did as well, that you can't base your appeal on evidence that isn't discussed in the record. The Court doesn't know anything that the court reporter hasn't taken down."

"I'm not forgetting that," Hardy said, "but then who killed the Khalils?"

"Well, if you believe Evan, Ron Nolan did."

"Did you believe Evan?"

Washburn seemed to be considering it for the first time in a long while. "You know, now that you mention it, yes, I think I do. Evan just didn't smuggle small arms and grenades out of Iraq as souvenirs. He was only over there a matter of weeks. In the brief time he had there, he couldn't have both found a source for these things and arranged to find a way to send them home. Especially when you consider he was airlifted out of there unconscious and with no warning. I'd be surprised if he got out with his own socks, much less all this hardware." He studied his cigar's lengthy ash. "No," he repeated, "it beggars belief. That just didn't happen."

"So where did that stuff in Nolan's closet come from?"

"It must have been from Nolan himself, wouldn't you think? He could move about a lot more freely, and he had both more time and a lot more contacts than Evan ever did."

Hardy sat back in his chair, his elbow on the armrest, his hand resting over his mouth, in deep thought. "Okay," he said in a faraway voice, "let's go with Nolan killing the Khalils for a minute. I don't want to jump too far ahead of ourselves here. Can we take that as fact?"

After a small hesitation, Washburn nodded. "I do."

"All right, then, here's the million-dollar question. Why did he do it?"

"I don't know."

"Was there any speculation you heard?"

Washburn shook his head, now troubled by this as well. "Somehow that just never became part of the discussion, did it?" Asking himself. He turned to face Hardy. "Even when everyone was taking it for granted that Evan had killed them, I don't remember anyone stopping to examine the why of it too closely." He drew on his smoke. "I think there was more or less an assumption that it was something that had happened in Iraq that we would never find out about. Maybe it was something personal or maybe he just hated Iraqis in general for what they had done to him. And at the same time he could frame Nolan for the murders and eliminate his rival for Tara. It was a great opportunity to kill two birds with one stone if you happened to be a psychopath, which some people thought Evan was."

"But nobody asked the hard questions?"

"Apparently not."

"Even though the FBI was all over this thing?" It wasn't really a question. "Does that strike you as the FBI we all know and love?"

Clearly, Washburn, too, had caught the bug. His eyes were alight with possibility. "If Nolan did in fact kill the Khalils," he said contemplatively, "then certainly anyone in the Khalil family—Iraq being the tribal culture that it is—would have had not just a motive but an obligation to kill him."

Hardy, low-watt electricity running through him, leaned forward, elbows on his knees. "What do you think are the odds that the FBI never talked to any of the Khalils?"

"Zero. And yet now that you mention it, all the interviews we got were from the Redwood City police. And it was a pretty perfunctory job."

"So you're telling me the FBI would have relied on the locals to talk to witnesses in a potential terrorism case? I don't think so."

Washburn nodded and nodded. "Son of a bitch," he said, unmistakable glee in his voice. "You're talking *Brady*."

Hardy, his mouth set, tried to keep his elation low-key. "You're damn right I am."

The reference was to what was commonly called a *Brady* violation. In *Brady v. Maryland,* the Supreme Court held that a defendant had a right to any evidence that was in the possession of the prosecution that might cast doubt on his guilt, whether or not it was eventually to be used at trial. The prosecution was absolutely required to turn over any background, testimony, evidence, interviews— anything—that could exculpate a defendant. If the prosecution withheld any of this discovery, *and the withheld material was reasonably likely to undermine confidence in a guilty verdict,* then these were grounds to reverse a conviction. Of course, evidence of such a violation was never found in the court's records. The whole point was that the prosecution had withheld the evidence and the defense didn't find out about it until sometime after the trial.

This opened up an entirely new strategic element.

Hardy and Washburn both keenly understood the situation. If in fact the FBI had interviewed witnesses in the Khalil killings and did not supply either the witnesses or the testimony, or both, to the prosecution, which the prosecution was then mandated to turn over to Evan's defense, it was highly possible that they were looking at a *Brady* violation. The added beauty of the situation was that Mills didn't even have to know about the withheld evidence. The FBI was legally construed to be part of the prosecutor's team and Mills was responsible for turning over that evidence whether or not the FBI told her about it.

Of course, proving not only that the FBI had held back evidence but also that the withheld evidence was likely to undermine confidence in the guilty verdict against Evan Scholler was another problem.

But Hardy would face that when he came to it.

For the moment, the *Brady* possibility, if he could get it off the ground by finding an FBI witness or two that hadn't made it into the Scholler record, meant that he could file a writ of habeas corpus with declarations and get it in front of the court of appeals in relatively short order. The court of appeals could then remand it back down to Redwood City, probably back to Tollson's courtroom, where—if they were hearing new evidence—anything might happen.

Washburn tapped Hardy's knee, snapping him from his reverie. "It's still going to be a long shot proving the evidence is exculpatory," he said. "Essentially you'll have to prove somebody else other than Evan might well have killed Nolan. Which, I must tell you from bitter experience, is a tough nut." He lowered his voice. "It might even be contrary to fact."

"Maybe not," Hardy said. "It might be enough for the court if I prove that somebody else had a reason to."

The old lawyer shook his head. "That, I'm afraid, is wishful thinking."

"Not at all. If there was another plausible suspect the jury didn't get to hear about ..."

Washburn frowned. "And the FBI, which withheld it last time, and which is immune to state process, is going to hand it over now? How are you going to make them do that?"

"I don't know," Hardy said. "It's a work in progress."

[33]

HARDY DROVE BACK up to the city on the 280 Freeway, got off on the ocean side of town at Nineteenth Avenue, and, at a couple of minutes after the official beginning of the cocktail hour, walked into the front door of the bar he partly owned, the Little Shamrock. Moses McGuire, his brother-in-law, out of rehab now this past year or more, was behind the bar at the far end by the beer taps. To Hardy, he looked impossibly fit, although maybe it was simply the fact that he'd lost thirty pounds and cleaned up his appearance along with his bloodstream.

Perennially shaggy and long-haired, often bearded, McGuire had cultivated more or less the look of a biker or a mountain man since his twenties—which is to say for nearly forty years. Faded, often tattered blue jeans and some crummy T-shirt seemed as much a part of his personality as his justly fabled temper, his casual disdain for convention, his fondness for altered states of consciousness.

Down at the end of the bar today, passing the time with a pretty young woman, he might have been a mid-forties banker on his day off. The still-full head of salt-and-pepper hair was short and neatly parted, the mustache trimmed in an otherwise closely shaved face. He'd tucked the tails of his blue dress shirt into a pair of khakis. He'd had his nose broken often enough in bar fights that Hardy thought he'd always look a bit battered, but today his eyes were clear, his skin nearly devoid of the capillary etching that had been a regular feature of his face in the heavy drinking days that had constituted the majority of his adult life.

As a sometime bartender and part-owner, Hardy could have gone around the bar and helped himself to whatever he wanted, but occasionally you got back there and found you couldn't easily get yourself out, and tonight was supposed to be the first of his new Date Nights with Frannie, and he didn't want to start it off on the wrong foot. So he pulled up a stool and gave McGuire a casual nod, which brought him right on down.

"What's the word, Counselor?"

"Hendrick's, over. One onion."

"That's four words, and I've got cucumber."

Hardy nodded. "Even better. And while you're pouring, I've got a question for you."

"Hazel." McGuire didn't miss a beat. "Although some people think they're more green. But I'd call them hazel. Kind of a bedroom hazel." McGuire grabbed a glass, threw in some ice, reached up behind him to the premium gin row, and brought down the round dark bottle of Hendrick's gin. After a quick free pour to an eighth of an inch below the rim, he cut a fresh slice of cucumber and dropped it on top. *"Santé,"* he said, placing it on the cocktail napkin he'd laid down on the bar. "Okay, what's your real question?"

"It's a long one."

McGuire scanned the length of the bar and around the

corners of the room, none of which were very far away. The Shamrock was a small, neighborhood place that had been in its same location at Lincoln and Ninth Avenue since 1893. The grandfather clock against the wall behind Hardy had stopped during the Great Earthquake of 1906 and nobody'd set it running again since. The pretty girl had gone back to her friends by the dartboards, and all of the other twenty patrons seemed comfortably settled at the bar or on the couches in back. "That's all right," McGuire said. "The crowd's pretty much under control."

On the drive up from Redwood City, after he'd wrestled with some of the problems raised by the *Brady* violation issues, Hardy had returned to the question that he still hadn't answered, and that, in his and Washburn's enthusiasm for *Brady,* they'd inadvertently let drop. So, after filling in his brother-in-law on some of the background—with a doctorate in philosophy from UC Berkeley, McGuire's ability to grasp facts and concepts had always been impressive even when he was in the bag; now that he was sober, it was formidable—Hardy came out with it again. "So, the question is, why did Nolan kill the Khalils?"

"Piece of cake," McGuire said. "It was his job."

Hardy drank off some of the rose-scented gin—he'd come to love this stuff. "Just like that, his job?"

"Sure. He's a SEAL, right? He's a trained assassin. You remember the SEALs in 'Nam. Shit. Killers. And now he's working for this security company in Iraq?"

"Allstrong."

"Right, Allstrong."

"But he was a recruiter over here, Mose, hiring people. No way was he doing wet work."

"Right. I'm sure. With his background? No way he wasn't, if it was needed."

"And why would it have been needed with the Khalils?"

"I don't know. Not enough information. But they were Iraqi, *n'est-ce pas*?"

"Yep."

"Well, then, you check it out, I bet you find they have family or something over there and they were somehow getting in the way of Allstrong's business."

"So they kill the father over here?"

McGuire nodded. "Sending a message."

"Pretty long distance, wouldn't you say?"

"The father was probably running the business from over here. Cut off the head, the body dies. This isn't brain surgery, Diz. All this didn't come out at the trial?"

"None of it did."

"Why not?"

"Well, the easy answer is that everybody on the prosecution team thought my guy had been the killer, and the motive was mostly personal, about him and Nolan."

"But you think it was Nolan?"

"I'm beginning to."

"And you're thinking, then, that this stuff about him ought to have been in the trial?"

"Precisely."

"Hmm. Let me think about it." He walked down the bar and saw to a couple of drink orders. Shooting himself a club soda from the gun, he came back down to Hardy. "Okay," he said, "I've got it all figured out."

"Hit me."

"Nolan killed these Khalil people, and then their family killed him in retaliation."

"How'd they know he did it?"

"They put it together that it was Allstrong because of what was going on in Iraq, whatever that was. Once they knew that, they found out Nolan was Allstrong's man over here. Even if he wasn't the actual killer, they were striking back and getting revenge."

"How'd they know where he lived?"

"Diz, please. It's cake to find people nowadays. You got a computer? They probably knew where he'd be living before he moved in. Come on, this doesn't sing for you?"

"No, it does, that's the problem."

"Why's it a problem?"

"Because if it happened the way you say, my client's innocent."

"And this is bad news because..."

"Because he's about three years into life in prison right now."

Moses tipped up his club soda. "Could be worse."

"True," Hardy said, "but it also could damn sure be better."

"BUT WHY didn't the prosecution look into that?" Frannie asked between bites of her calamari. "I mean, I can see them finally deciding it was probably your guy Evan, but you'd think they'd at least question some of the victims' family, too, wouldn't they? If only to find out some background on them."

"More than background, Frannie. These were two murders. Just thinking it was Evan shouldn't have been nearly enough. They would have wanted to prove it and maybe send him to death row."

They were at Pane E Vino, back on Union Street not far from Washburn's office, and here it had finally chilled down enough to make them decide to eat inside. They were up right in the window. Dusk hadn't yet progressed into dark. Frannie's shoulder-length red hair brought out the contrasting green in her eyes, which were the same color as the silken blouse she wore—a visual that, even after all of their time together, still captivated Hardy.

Dipping some of the fresh warm bread into the restaurant's little dish of olive oil, Hardy pinched some salt from the open bowl and sprinkled it over his upcoming bite. "But just because we have no record that anybody from the FBI talked to them doesn't mean that it didn't happen. Washburn and I have developed a theory about that."

"Which is?"

"That the FBI interviewed these people and didn't pass their information on to the police or the DA."

"Why wouldn't they do that?"

"Well, the simple answer is because they didn't have to. But another answer is maybe they just didn't want to. And finally, Washburn's personal favorite and maybe my own, is perhaps they were ordered not to."

"Why would that be?"

"Evidently, that is not a question for us mere mortals."

Frannie chewed thoughtfully, sipped at her Chardonnay. "So what are you going to do?"

"Well, first thing, I've already done it. Driving up, I called Wyatt"—this was Wyatt Hunt, Hardy's private investigator—"and asked him to try to find anybody in the extended Khalil family that the FBI actually talked to. And the beauty of it is that it doesn't even really matter too much what they said. If the FBI talked to them at all about the Khalil murders and didn't see fit to tell the DA, then we've got a real discovery issue." Hardy put his wine down. "Moses, you know, thinks Evan might even be innocent."

"And why does my brilliant brother think that?"

"Well, the great thing about Mose, as you know, is that he can build these complex theories without any reference to the facts. Or maybe with just one teensy little fact."

"And which one was that?"

"In this case, that Nolan killed the Khalils."

"You think that's a fact?"

Hardy considered, nodded. "Close enough. I don't think Evan did, that's for sure. So based on that, according to Mose, Evan didn't kill Nolan. The Khalils did."

Frannie's face grew dark. She placed her hands carefully apart on either side of her plate. "And these are the people you're hoping to go talk to? These same people who killed Nolan?"

"We don't know they killed Nolan. That's just Mose's theory." But even as he said it, Hardy knew where his wife was coming from, and why she suddenly was so concerned. He couldn't deny the sharp tickle of apprehension that washed over him as well.

And, he realized, it was not altogether ungrounded.

Frannie was already concerned, and she wasn't even aware yet that there was any question about what had happened to Charlie Bowen, whether he'd in fact actually disappeared or whether he'd been the victim of foul play.

Perhaps following the same path upon which Hardy was thinking to embark.

He sucked in a quick breath—he didn't want Frannie to worry about that—then picked up his wineglass and took a sip. "I know what you're saying," he told her, "but if these guys were a real problem on that level, I've got to believe the FBI, with all of its resources, would have gotten some inkling of it. Wouldn't you think?"

"I would think that, yes. But then what?"

"Then I'd think they would have arrested somebody. That's what they do, Frannie. They find bad guys and put them away."

"Except if this one time they, in fact, didn't."

"Why wouldn't they?"

"For the same reasons you just gave me why they didn't tell the DA about these interviews you're pretty sure they had." She ticked them off on her fingers. "They didn't have to, they didn't want to, or they were ordered not to."

Hardy acknowledged the point with a small nod. "Well," he said, "I've got to believe there's a quantum difference between not turning over interview notes and not arresting someone they knew was a killer."

"Dismas." She put her fork down and met his eyes. "I never actually thought I'd say this, but you don't watch enough television. On *The Sopranos,* the FBI turn mobsters all the time and leave them in place for years, hoping to scoop up the big fish. Meanwhile, all these other people are getting beat up and killed. This happens in real life too. Everybody knows this."

He nodded again. "True. It just seems a ways off on this case. At least at this point when everything's speculation."

"Do me a favor, would you?"

"Anything, my love."

"If it moves beyond speculation, take a little extra care. If these people killed Nolan, they could kill you."

Hardy knew that she might be right, but so was he—this was a long way from being established. "I'm not a threat to the Khalils," he said. "I don't want to prove anything about what they did or didn't do. I just want to know if the FBI talked to them and didn't tell the Redwood City cops about it. So I don't think we have to worry too much about anything happening to me."

"Oh, okay," she said with an edge, "then I'll be sure not to."

ANOTHER OF THE CHANGES in Frannie's life after her own children had moved out was that she had turned into a baby junkie, so after dinner, since they would be driving right by the Glitskys' flat on their way home anyway, she suggested that they should call their friends and see if they wanted company. Back a few years ago when Date Night had been truly sacred, especially during Rachel's first year, this postprandial visit had become a weekly ritual.

Now, while Frannie and Treya and even Rachel passed the infant Zachary back and forth with suitable enthusiasm in the living room, the two men sat on the steps overlooking their swingset project in Glitsky's small backyard and talked quietly, very quietly, about Charlie Bowen.

"You really think he's a homicide?" Glitsky was nowhere near as defensive as he might have been if either Bowen or his wife had disappeared on his watch, rather than on Marcel Lanier's. So Hardy's theories were interesting and maybe even fun to talk about, but they weren't—yet—Glitsky's problems.

"Not exactly," Hardy said. "It's just suddenly I'm

finding myself a little more curious about what happened to the guy."

"You're building the whole thing on a bunch of ifs. You see that, don't you?"

"Well, not all of them are ifs. Scholler didn't kill the Khalils, for example. That just didn't happen."

"That doesn't mean Nolan did."

"No. That's true." Hardy rubbed his palms together. "But let's say that a homicide professional such as yourself had a hunch somebody had been killed, even if there was no body and no evidence. How would you go about finding out if you were right?"

Glitsky didn't hesitate. "I'd trace his last days, his last hours if I could."

"So do you know anything about Bowen's? Last days? Last hours?"

In the light from the bulb over the back door, Glitsky turned to his friend. His face, partly in shadow, with its hatchet nose and the whitish scar coursing through both of his lips, might have been some kind of terrible tribal mask, fearsome and powerful. "I don't know anything about Bowen, period, Diz. As far as I'm concerned, he's a missing person."

Hardy sat, musing. He wasn't here to argue.

An animal scurried through the brush on the Presidio's grounds.

"Your man Bracco came by my office today too," Hardy said. "On this Bowen thing."

"Charlie?"

"No, the wife."

"Right," Glitsky said. "He wanted this alleged diary."

"He did. But he also had a few other concerns that had just come up." Hardy went into it in some detail, Bracco's discoveries that the very light Hanna Bowen had broken her neck in a relatively short fall without a hangman's noose, that she'd come to believe her husband had been murdered. Bracco also apparently did not think it inconceivable that Charlie Bowen had been murdered, and that it might have had something to do with one of the cases he'd been working on.

"I told him," Hardy concluded, "that Charlie had a couple of hundred cases and identifying any one of them as connected with murder was going to take a bit of doing."

"But now," Glitsky said, "you're starting to think it might be Scholler."

"I don't know if I'd go that far yet. I wouldn't try to take it to the bank, but there's starting to be a hell of a lot of questions, don't you think?"

After a minute, Glitsky nodded. "It's interesting," he said. "I'll go that far." Then, "You want me to do anything?"

Hardy shook his head. "I don't know what it would be, Abe. Bracco's already on it, even without the diary. Since you trained him, he's probably doing that last-hours-and-last-days thing with Mrs. Bowen. Maybe he'll come up with something."

"If Darrel finds something that leads back to Charlie, Diz, and he starts to look like a homicide, I'll jump all over it."

"That'd be good. I'd appreciate it." Hardy fell into a silence again.

"What are you thinking?" Glitsky asked after a minute.

"Nothing."

"Yeah, but it's a loud nothing."

Hardy took a breath. "I was just wondering if it was possible that the FBI knew who killed the Khalils and didn't say anything about it because it was part of a bigger case."

Glitsky looked over at him. "I missed a segue here. I thought we were talking about the Bowens."

"Now we're talking about the FBI. But it's still Scholler."

"Guy gets around."

Hardy shrugged. "It's a complicated case. But part of it is how much the FBI didn't tell the DA. Or even if they had another suspect they forgot to mention."

"Whatever it is," Glitsky said, "you'll never know."

"But you think it's possible they'd deliberately withhold that kind of evidence?"

"As my father would say, 'Anything's possible.' If it's the FBI, I'd go a little further. Nothing is impossible."

"They'd screw up a murder case on purpose?"

"Not every day, certainly. Not usually. But for the right reason..."

"Like what?"

"I don't know. Say maybe the guy's a valuable snitch. Or he's a mole in a terrorist group." Glitsky snapped his fingers. "There you go. He's giving the Feebs good information on a terrorist cell, I bet they wouldn't blink if he killed his girlfriend on the side. Say 'national security' to these guys and anything goes."

"You think?"

Glitsky chewed his cheek. "Would I bet on it in this case? Maybe not. Do I think it's ever happened? Definitely, and more than once."

And if it happened here with the Khalils, Hardy thought, perhaps Charlie Bowen hadn't figured it out in time as he was preparing his appeal. Maybe the Khalils had seen him—justifiably—as a threat, a loose cannon who wouldn't hesitate to accuse them of murder if it would help get his client off. And if they had, or if one of them had, in fact, murdered Ron Nolan . . .

"Okay, then here's another angle you might want to put in your pipe and smoke," Hardy said. "Moses is of the opinion—again, based on nothing, but still, he's not dumb—he thinks that Nolan killed the Khalils because it was his job. They were Iraqi, and he worked for this company that does a lot of business in Iraq. Allstrong Security, which is evidently—"

But Glitsky put a hand on his arm, stopping him. "Allstrong Security?"

"Yeah, headquartered here and in—"

"I know where they are, Diz. I know who they are." Unconsciously, he tightened his grip on Hardy's arm. "Nolan worked for Allstrong? How could I not have heard about that?"

"Maybe because it's a small detail about a trial in another county three years ago. Could that be it? And why would it have mattered, anyway?"

But Glitsky, a muscle working in his jaw, was inside himself, putting something together. He let go of Hardy's arm, staring ahead of himself into the darkness.

"Abe? Talk to me."

Slowly, he began to spin it out, as though to himself. "I'd bet my life it's close to the same time frame, something like three years ago, right? But I'll check that."

"What?"

Still, Glitsky hesitated. "We had a homicide here in the city of a guy who'd been over in Iraq working for Allstrong. His name, if memory serves, was Arnold Zwick.

Somebody snapped his neck in an alley down in the Mish. Left his wallet on him."

"All right. And this means..."

"No, wait. The same weekend, a day or two later I think, three more guys, all together, all muggers with sheets, turn up dead on the street in the Tenderloin. Two of 'em with their necks broken."

"Three broken necks?"

"That's what we said. Batiste thought it might be a serial killer starting out, but nothing else happened. No clues, no suspects. Eventually it all just went away."

"So what was the deal with Allstrong?"

"Nothing, really." Glitsky still trying to process his memory. "We never found anything, anyway. The investigation never went anywhere."

"But?"

"But witnesses told us Zwick seemed to be rolling in cash before he got killed. But we never found any of it, except a couple of hundred in his wallet. Debra Schiff thought he'd embezzled it from Allstrong in Iraq, then split. They were getting paid mostly in cash back then. Her theory was that Allstrong sent somebody back over here to find Zwick, make an example of him, get the money back. But as I say, we never got a lick of proof."

"And now you're thinking ..."

"I'm not thinking anything yet. Except maybe Moses might not be all wrong about Nolan."

Hardy sat, elbows on his knees, mulling over this new information. "Let me ask you this, Abe. You've got friends in the FBI, right?"

Glitsky hit a one-note chuckle. "Local cops like myself don't have what you call bosom buddies in the FBI, Diz. But I know a few guys, yeah."

"Maybe you could ask them a couple of discreet questions?"

"About this Khalil case?"

Hardy shrugged.

"And what," Glitsky asked, "makes you think they'd tell me anything at all about that? Especially if they've kept something about it hidden all this time?"

"Well," Hardy said, "I know the two agents who were involved in my case. Maybe you could just put in a good word and see if they'd talk to me."

"I could do that, sure. Which doesn't guarantee they will."

"No, I know that. But it might help."

Glitsky shrugged. "Couldn't hurt, unless it does. And we'll never know either way, anyway. But I'll put in the word."

At that moment, the back door opened behind them. Frannie was standing there holding Zachary, with Treya in the hallway behind her.

"What are you guys plotting out here?" Frannie asked.

"Violent overthrow of the government," Hardy replied. "It's time we took control and fixed everything."

"Good idea," Treya said. "Maybe Abe could start the revolution with that squeak in our refrigerator door. It's been driving me crazy for weeks."

WHEN THEY GOT HOME, while Frannie was in the bathroom getting ready for bed, Hardy moseyed on downstairs and picked up the telephone in the kitchen. After three rings, he got the answering machine for the Hunt Club, Wyatt's private investigation agency.

"Wyatt." His voice a whisper. "I just wanted to give you a heads-up about the Khalils. You might want to keep a low profile. And if you find out if and when somebody talked to the FBI, go easy from there. Get as much detail as you can, but if you meet any resistance at all, don't make anybody mad at you. Just report back to me. We don't want to raise any flags with them. If you're getting the impression that the risk factor's gone up around this thing, that would be accurate. So be careful. Just treat that as the word of the day—careful."

When he got back upstairs to the bedroom, Frannie was in her pajamas in the bed. She put her book down. "Where'd you go off to?"

"Just downstairs, locking up, that's all."

She gave him a quizzical look. "Is everything okay?"

"Fine," Hardy said. "Everything's fine."

[34]

THE QUESTIONS ATE AWAY at Hardy for the rest of the weekend, and at seven-thirty Monday morning he called Darrel Bracco on his cell phone from home. The inspector seemed glad to hear from him at such an early hour, and told Hardy that they still hadn't located Hanna Bowen's diary but that yesterday he'd talked to one of Hanna's best friends, a woman named Nora Bonner, and gotten what he called pretty strong corroboration for Jenna's opinion that her mother had not been suicidal. Bonner and Hanna had gone out to dinner two days before she died, and all she'd been able to talk about was what she kept calling her husband's murder.

"Hanna didn't by any chance mention who she thought had killed him?"

"She thought it was something he was working on, but didn't know what. Evidently, he didn't talk about his cases at home."

"So why did she think it was that?"

"The last couple of days, he told her he thought he was onto something big, that he might actually be doing some real good."

"But he didn't say what it was?"

"He didn't want to jinx it before he had some answers."

"So why didn't she, Hanna, tell that to the police earlier? If Charlie was looking into something big—"

"Because nobody was looking at Charlie's case, that's why. It wasn't a homicide, remember?"

"All right," Hardy said, "let me ask you this. If Hanna was trying to find what Charlie was doing, how was she investigating it?"

"That's what I'm trying to find out. If it were me, I'd probably have gone to Bowen's secretary. Or maybe he was using a private eye. But the problem is this is all ancient history now. Bowen's gone most of a year. Who's gonna know, or remember?"

"The secretary might."

"Right. And she was?"

"It'll be in his admin records. While we're looking in the files anyway. Then you just track her, or him, down. Hopefully still in town, probably with another firm. Or— here's a possible shortcut—maybe the daughter knew."

"That's worth checking. I'll ask her." Bracco paused. "Can I ask you one?"

"Sure."

"Last time we talked at your office, you didn't seem too enthusiastic about the odds of getting anything out of all this. Now you're calling me before I'm in at work. Did something happen I might want to know about?"

Hardy took a beat. "That's a fair question. The answer is yeah, although it's all still pretty nebulous. I'm working on the appeal for one of Bowen's cases that was hanging fire when he disappeared. Evan Scholler. Some of the witnesses I'm hoping to talk to might have developed a motive to kill Bowen."

"You're shitting me."

"It's a long way from established, but it's something I'm looking at. I talked to Glitsky about it over the weekend."

"What does he say?"

"What does Abe usually say?"

"Not much."

"That's what he said this time too. But I'm thinking if you can find some independent confirmation looking into Hanna's last days, maybe that she had tried to contact these same people—"

"What are their names?"

"It's a family. The Khalils." Hardy spelled it for him. "The father and mother were killed about four years ago in Redwood City, and everybody thought my guy Scholler had done it. Now, maybe not."

"So these Khalils killed their own parents?"

"No, but they might have killed the guy Scholler got sent up for. If you're keeping score, his name was Ron Nolan. Anyway, I've got my investigator looking into this too. So, yeah, I'd say it's heating up, but it might all fizzle and go away."

"I should talk to these people too. The Khalils."

"Well." Hardy temporized. "First we've got to find out exactly who we're talking about, and at this point, we don't have any idea. It's a big family. And you're already well along on Hanna's last hours. If you get something solid there, you're ahead of me and then you've really got something to talk to these people about. Meanwhile, I keep scratching. And call you if I get anything real."

"With respect, sir. If Charlie Bowen's a murder, it's police work."

"I couldn't agree more, Inspector. I'm just trying to

find grounds that'll fly for my appeal. But Hanna Bowen's murder, if it was that, is police work too. And it's way fresher."

Bracco paused a little longer this time. "We ought to stay in touch."

"That's my plan. If you notice, I made this phone call, for example. I've got no desire to work your case, Inspector. Really. I just want to get my client out of jail."

Bracco let out a little laugh. "God, that just sounds so wrong. My clients, all I want to do is put 'em *in* jail."

AT LUNCHTIME, Hardy was down the Peninsula again. Though he might have been able to get the information from his client, Everett Washburn also knew Tara Wheatley's address and phone number and even where she worked. He'd left a message, identifying himself as Evan's attorney, and she'd called right back on her break and agreed to meet him in front of her school at a quarter to noon.

As soon as he saw her, as she walked out of the building and got close to where he'd parked, Hardy understood a lot better what all the fuss had been about. He'd just read a book called *Silent Joe* by one of his favorite authors, T. Jefferson Parker, where one of the underlying concepts was the idea of the woman who possessed what one of the characters called "the Unknown Thing"—an attractive force so powerful that it altered the orbit of every man it encountered. It wasn't mere physical beauty or sexuality, though they both were part of it. It was something bigger, more inclusive, subtler, and far more dangerous.

Whatever the Unknown Thing was, Tara Wheatley had it in spades.

When she got to the passenger door, she stopped and beamed a smile down at Hardy that, at another time in his life, would have melted him. She wore sunglasses against the bright day. Her hair was down. The plain pale-orange cotton dress she wore revealed nothing—it came to below her knees—and yet stirred something that, to his old bones, felt primal.

"What is it about guys and convertibles?" she asked. "I'm assuming you're Mr. Hardy."

"That's me."

Hardy started to reach over the seat, but she opened the door on her own—bare tanned legs and sandals—and plopped herself in. Hardy had the rogue thought that it was lucky she was teaching fifth-graders—any further into adolescence and her boy students would probably riot.

"Where to?" Hardy put the car in gear, got moving. "Can I buy you lunch someplace?"

She shook her head. "I've only got one period off for lunch—forty-five minutes. Just away from here, anywhere. Wherever you find shade."

Out of the parking lot, he turned right and crested a hill, following the main road until it dipped into an area where the homes were surrounded with old oaks.

"You can turn anywhere in here," she said.

Hardy did as he was told, and parked at the curb on a shady street in an established neighborhood of large attractive homes set on small lots. As soon as he'd set the brake and turned the motor off, she turned toward him in her seat, her near leg tucked up under her. "Sorry to hustle you out of the lot back there," she said, "but people don't need to see me talking to another man outside the school. I'm already pretty much the fallen woman. I almost lost the job over it back during the trial."

"Over what? Having a boyfriend?"

"Having *two* boyfriends, Mr. Hardy. Not exactly at the same time, but close enough for some people."

"Who?"

"Suburban moms, Mr. Hardy. Never underestimate the power. Some of them really never liked me. I think I must have threatened them somehow, though I don't know how or why that would be." Hardy had a pretty good idea, but he said nothing. "Anyway, thank God the nuns supported me. I love the work. I love my kids. But you didn't drive down here to talk about me. What can I do for you? Is everything all right with Evan?"

This had been her first question to him on the phone this morning, too, as soon as she'd heard who he was. But this time the question prompted an unexpected one from him. "Have you not seen him recently?"

Clearly, the answer made her uncomfortable. "Two weeks."

"That's not so bad."

She shrugged. "It's not good. Not if he's the man you love, and he is. But he's already been in prison for two years, and in jail another year before the trial." She lowered her head, shook it slowly back and forth, let out a deep sigh. "It's a hard one, the whole thing."

"I can imagine."

"I mean," she went on, "if he stays in prison. I don't know what we're supposed to do. He won't marry me. I've offered that a hundred times. I think he's starting to lose hope. I don't know what he wants out of me anymore. Sometimes I'm not even sure what I want. I know

I wanted him—I *do* want him—but I wanted a life with him. You know? Not this." Suddenly her eyes flashed. "But I'm not giving up on us. I'm not. Don't think that. It's just . . . it's so hard. It's so endless."

"I believe you," Hardy said.

She raised her eyes and looked over at Hardy. "Do you think you're going to have any luck? Do you think he's ever going to get out?"

"To be completely honest with you, I don't know. I don't want to give you any false hopes, but I'm starting to think we might have a prayer."

"Is that what was so urgent?"

Hardy nodded. Maybe he'd exaggerated about needing to see her right away, but here they were now, and he couldn't feel bad about it. He felt that things had begun to move quickly, and he didn't want to lose his momentum. "There's a good chance that the FBI talked to the Khalils and didn't let the prosecution know. If that's true, we've got an appealable issue."

"Well, I'm glad. But I don't know anything about that."

"No. I didn't think you did." Hardy hesitated for a moment. "I wanted to ask you a few questions about Ron Nolan."

She rubbed her hand across her forehead, brushed a hair away. "I knew it was going to have to come to that again someday."

"Why did you know that?"

"I don't know. He was such a mistake. I still don't know why . . ." Letting the thought hang until there was no other way to complete it. "I feel like the whole thing is my fault."

"How is that?"

"If I hadn't gone and told Evan about Ron tipping off the FBI. Ron knew I'd do that once he told me. He just played me. And then Evan went up to his place . . ."

"So you think Evan did kill him?"

"Well, I mean . . . I don't think he was himself at the time. But I guess. . ."

"You guess so?"

She shrugged again, then nodded. "I don't know what else could have happened."

"A lot else could have happened, Tara. Nobody seems to know what happened. So unless Evan told you something that didn't make the trial—"

"No! He didn't do that. He didn't remember."

"I believe him. You might be happier if you believed that too. But what I'm wondering is if Ron ever talked to you about his work with Allstrong? You went together for how long?"

"September to May. How long is that? Eight months? What do you want to know about his work?"

"Whatever you can tell me."

"Well, he liked it, it paid very well, he was gone a lot."

"Back and forth to Iraq?"

"Sometimes."

"Even though he was under suspicion for causing the blow-up at Masbah?"

"I never knew about that until Evan told me just before Ron and I broke up. But that really didn't worry Ron. Nothing worried Ron. I'm pretty sure he went over to Iraq at least three, maybe four times. To get paid in cash if nothing else."

"In cash?"

"Yes." She adjusted herself in the seat. "He showed me

a wrapped-up brick of something like fifty thousand dollars in cash after one of his trips."

"What did he get that for?"

"I think it was just how he got his regular pay sometimes. That's what he told me."

"How did he get that back into the country?"

"What do you mean?"

"I mean, you can't enter the country with that kind of money in cash. You've got to claim it at customs."

She shook her head. "No. Ron didn't have any problem with that. He always flew by military transport out of Travis. He knew all the pilots and the commanders and everything. It was just part of how Allstrong did business."

"Tara," Hardy asked, "didn't it ever occur to you that Ron brought those frag grenades over from Iraq the same way, and that he'd killed the Khalils with them?"

"Of course. I knew Evan hadn't done that anyway. But there wasn't really any proof that Ron had either. But then, he was such a liar. He lied about everything to me. And to Evan."

"Did you ever hear him mention anything about the Khalils?"

"No. Not really. Not until they were dead, anyway." She looked at Hardy in a pout of frustration. "I wish I knew what you were trying to get me to say. If it would help Evan, I'd say it. But I didn't know much about Ron's work at all."

"I'm not trying to get you to say anything, Tara. I'm trying to get a handle on Ron Nolan, on what was going on around him. See if that leads me anywhere on this appeal."

"Well, for a handle, I can help you there. He said he was a warrior."

"A warrior. What did he mean by that?"

"Oh, we talked about that a lot. I really didn't like it, or agree with him, but when he talked he could make it sound like it made perfect sense."

"What did, exactly?"

"That the world needed warriors, and the job of the warrior was to kill. And that's who he was, how he defined himself."

"As a killer?"

"A killer." She nodded. "And I'm sure he was. One time . . . well, no, never mind."

"What?"

She paused, then shrugged. "Well, it was one of our first dates . . ."

[35]

GLITSKY WAS ON THE PHONE at his desk, talking to his closest connection in the FBI, Bureau Chief Bill Schuyler, with whom he'd had many previous, nearly amicable dealings. Now the tone didn't ring with cooperation and friendship.

"Bill," Glitsky said, "you're telling me both agents quit?"

"Yes, sir."

"At the same time?"

"I'm not at liberty to disclose that, Abe. They're no longer with the Bureau. That's all I know."

"Could I talk to their superior?"

"I am their superior, Abe. What else do you want to know?"

"I want to know where they are."

"I just told you. They quit."

"You just also told me that you were their superior. And two hours ago when we last talked, you didn't know they'd left the Bureau."

"I hadn't worked with them personally in a while, Abe. I guess they got away from me."

After a small pause, Glitsky tried again. "This is a murder case, Bill. Freed and Riggio testified a couple of years ago down in Redwood City and it would be helpful to know who they talked to."

"Wouldn't that all be in the record?"

"We were wondering if any of their reports dealing with that case happened not to get turned over to the DA."

"I'm sure they turned over everything they were supposed to. And you're investigating a homicide in Redwood City? Isn't that outside of your jurisdiction? And who is we?"

"The Redwood City case might be connected to a couple of San Francisco homicides, Bill. And we is me and the lawyer I've been working with on this stuff."

"Well, whoever it is, Freed and Riggio aren't going to be available."

"Because they've left the Bureau?"

"That's correct, Abe. Anything else?"

"When you say they left the Bureau, Bill, do you mean they joined another federal agency? Or are you telling me a couple of thirtysomething FBI agents opened a Dairy Queen in Texas and didn't tell you where?"

"Always a pleasure to talk to you, Abe. Have a nice day."

IN SPITE OF Schuyler's best wishes, Glitsky wasn't, in fact, having a nice day. He sat at his desk in the early afternoon. He had gotten up five minutes earlier and turned off his overhead lights, closing and locking the door behind him. Both of his hands were cupped on the blotter in front of him and from time to time, irregularly, he would drum the fingers of those hands. His mouth was tight and a muscle in his jaw worked at the side of his cheek.

He hadn't been kidding when he'd told Hardy that one didn't really have bosom buddies among the agents of the Federal Bureau of Investigation. But Hardy's request, to put the word out to Agents Jacob Freed and Marcia Riggio to talk to him if he called, had been so benign that Glitsky never expected any sort of bureaucratic runaround. He and Schuyler had worked portions of several cases together and, jurisdictional squabbles apart, had always before gotten along reasonably well as human beings.

When Hardy had told him on Friday night that the number of questions surrounding the Bowens, which might or might not be connected with the Scholler case, was sufficient to get his attention, Glitsky still had had no problem reserving his judgment. Questions came with the territory. They were what investigations were all about. Few people had the good taste to disappear or die in such a way as to leave all questionable issues in their lives resolved.

But now this unexplained and almost certainly spurious disappearance of the two FBI agents who'd been instrumental in the Scholler case forced Glitsky up against one of the other cardinal rules of investigation: There is no such thing as a coincidence.

It wasn't a coincidence that Ron Nolan worked for Allstrong, and so had Arnold Zwick.

Three broken necks in one weekend wasn't a coincidence.

Beyond those new and disturbing items, it was one thing to have Charlie Bowen, who was working on the appeal in the Scholler case, vanish without a trace. There was a reasonable and plausible explanation for the suicide of his wife six months later.

And certainly FBI agents had been known to leave their jobs.

But for all of these things to come together in an apparently random set of coincidences stretched Glitsky's credulity far beyond its normal capacity for elasticity.

A relationship existed here among these parts. He just didn't know what it was. But he was starting to get a good idea that it probably involved at least one homicide in his jurisdiction, possibly two. And maybe more. This made it his business.

But more than that, the FBI and Allstrong connections significantly enlarged the playing field. Whatever had originally happened in the Scholler case, and Glitsky was woefully ignorant of all but the most general of those details, it had appeared more or less parochial—essentially two guys duking it out over a woman. Now, suddenly, Hardy's theories involving the Khalils, and whatever business they were doing in Iraq, and perhaps even some kind of U.S. government involvement, did not seem so incredibly far-fetched. And though Abe's opinion of the FBI's methods included his belief that it would ignore the taking of a life by a snitch or a prospective witness if it suited its agenda, it did not extend to the possibility that its agents would actually sanction or commit murder.

So—the only conclusion he could draw—the FBI knew more about this case than they were willing to divulge. They possibly knew who had killed the Khalils. And who had killed Ron Nolan. And if it wasn't Evan Scholler, this meant that the FBI had let the wrong man be sent to prison for life.

If one of the Khalils instead had killed Nolan in retaliation, and then either or both of the Bowens because they'd picked up that trail, and the FBI knew about it . . .

He pulled over the phone on this desk, lifted the receiver, and punched in a number he knew by heart. "Hello, Phyllis," he said, "it's Abe Glitsky. I need to talk to Diz, please."

HARDY'S PRIVATE INVESTIGATOR, Wyatt Hunt, did his research primarily on his computer in the large converted warehouse by the Hall of Justice that he called home. He had no trouble finding the details of the Khalil murders on the Net. Over the weekend, he also spoke to Hardy to clarify exactly what his assignment was. It had evolved somewhat from Friday's first phone call, when Hardy merely wanted to know who, if anyone, among the Khalil family had had an interview with FBI special agents in regard to the Scholler case. Now, Hunt's personal priority had shifted to finding out, without putting himself in danger, what those interviews had been about.

By now, on Monday afternoon, he knew that the extended Khalil clan consisted of twenty-three separate families strung out between South San Francisco and San Jose, and then across the Bay over to Hayward and Fremont. The typical arrangement was that each family owned its own franchise of the 7-Eleven chain, although four of them owned more than one store. The family had been in the country since Ibrahim and Shatha had emigrated with their four children in 1989, before the first Gulf War.

The eldest surviving brother, Abdel Khalil, had been the spokesman for the family in the aftermath of the murders of his parents and seemed the likeliest source of information. Abdel owned three stores along the El Camino Real between the two northern Peninsula towns of Millbrae and San Bruno, but conducted his corporate business out of a low-slung stucco-and-glass building set down in a former landfill by San Francisco Airport.

Hunt got out of his Mini Cooper and walked in the flat glaring sunshine across a treeless parking lot and into the nondescript reception area of AMK, Inc. A swarthy, somewhat disheveled young man in shirtsleeves sat at the only substantial piece of furniture, a cluttered desk in the middle of the room. He was sorting some kind of paperwork. A cup of tea steamed at the side of his desk. The screen saver on his computer showed an artist's rendering of a 7-Eleven store in a typical urban strip mall. A radio, turned low, played what Hunt would have called Middle Eastern, perhaps Iraqi, music.

Hunt had made the appointment this morning, probably with this same young man, under slightly bogus conditions, saying that he was a writer who was doing an article on successful immigration stories. Now, after he introduced himself, the boy gave him a nervous smile and disappeared through a door behind him, leaving Hunt standing alone in front of the desk.

A minute later, Hunt was shaking hands with a good-looking man in his midthirties. With his mustache he bore a slight resemblance to Saddam Hussein, although he was dressed in American clothes—black slacks that looked to be the bottom portion of a man's suit and a light blue dress shirt with an open neck. "Mr. Hunt, I'm Abdel Khalil. Would you like something to drink? A cup of tea, perhaps, coffee, Coke."

"Coffee would be nice. Black, please."

"Fine. We can take it in my office." Khalil snapped his fingers twice quickly and the boy jumped, bowed, and disappeared.

Hunt followed Khalil to a more spacious room in the back corner of the building. From the chair he was directed to in front of the standard wooden desk, he had an unimpeded view of the Bay and of planes landing at the airport.

The room itself, like its counterpart outside, was functional in the extreme. An oversized map of the Bay Area was pinned to one of the walls above a low credenza. A computer had its own small table at a right angle to the desk, which Khalil went around and sat behind. He'd barely gotten settled when the receptionist knocked and entered with a cup of coffee and handed it to Hunt, then closed the door behind him on the way out.

"Now." Khalil clasped his hands on the desk. He spoke educated and uninflected English. "Mr. Hunt. How's the coffee? Good. Now, how can I help you? I understand you're writing an article of some kind?"

This was always the tough part. Hunt placed his saucer on the tiny table next to him. "Actually, sir, that's not the case, and I apologize. I'm a private investigator working with a lawyer who's doing the appeal on the Evan Scholler case and if you'd like to kick me out of here, I'd understand."

Surprised, but not completely unamused, Khalil waved that off. "You've barely gotten settled. Why would you think I wouldn't talk to you about Evan Scholler?"

"It could be a touchy subject."

"And why would that be?"

"I think the assumption was that he killed your parents."

"Yes." Khalil's face darkened. "That was a difficult time. But I hope we've put that behind us. Did you say Scholler was appealing his conviction?"

Hunt nodded.

"Well, I wish him luck."

"You do? That's a bit of a surprise."

"Why is that?"

"If he killed your parents."

"But he was never charged with killing my parents. And frankly, it didn't seem to make much sense at the time, unless you bought the idea that after what happened to him over there, he hated all Iraqis and just picked them as a random couple to sacrifice." Khalil shook his head. "I never really saw that."

"So who do you think killed them?"

"I think it must have been Ron Nolan."

"Why do you say that?"

"Well, the fragmentation grenades, for example. His work, I understand, brought him to and from Iraq frequently, where he would have access to that stuff and would have been able to bring it back here by military transport without having to bother with customs."

"But why?"

"Why what?"

"Why your parents? What was Nolan's motive?"

Khalil grimaced, the memory of it all beginning to play back. "I believe he picked up a contract to assassinate them in Iraq. Our family has business interests over there and I think—well, I had heard this, and when I told the FBI—"

"Wait a minute, please! Excuse me. You're saying you talked to the FBI, then?"

"Of course."

"And you told them that you believed Ron Nolan had killed your parents because of information that you got from Iraq?"

"Well, yes."

"And what did the FBI say?"

"They seemed to already know, and didn't disagree that that was probably what happened. They assured us they would look into it. But then, of course, after what happened to Mr. Nolan . . ."

"So they talked to you about the Scholler trial?"

This seemed to stump him for a minute. He half turned and looked out his window, his brow furrowed, then came back to Hunt. "I don't really recall that."

"So what did they talk to you about?" Hunt sat back, lost for a beat in his own perplexity. "But I'm sorry. I interrupted you. So you're saying the FBI didn't think Scholler killed your parents?"

"Right. That's probably a large part of the reason he never got charged with that. Everyone I've talked to in the FBI agreed that it was Nolan."

"But Nolan was never—"

"Nolan was dead, Mr. Hunt. What was anybody going to do about that? It was over, a done deal. Even if some of my brothers and cousins wanted to kill him, he was already dead."

"So you're saying Scholler did kill Nolan?"

Now Khalil showed genuine surprise. "Well, yes, of course. I don't believe anyone has any doubts about that. Do they?"

Well, as a matter of fact, yes, Hunt was going to say, *my boss does.* Which would have led to Khalil's next question, *Then who did kill Nolan?* And Hunt's answer—Hardy's answer—would have been: *Uh, you guys. The Khalils.* But suddenly, that was not how this was going.

Instead, Hunt scrambled. "Okay. Nobody doubts Scholler killed Nolan. And the FBI told you that Nolan probably killed your parents. Did they know why? Or who put this contract out?"

"The short answer is not at first. They couldn't find anything, although I heard from relatives that they interrogated a lot of people over there."

It was all Hunt could do to keep his mouth from dropping open in amazement. "In Iraq? The FBI interrogated people about your parents' death all the way over in Iraq?"

"Of course. That's where the trail led."

"But they didn't find out who did it?"

"Eventually, they believed they did, yes." Now Khalil allowed a small smile. "And we—my family—verified that they were right. Your FBI, they know what they are doing, you know. They're extremely competent and efficient."

Hunt sat back. "What did they find out?"

"Well, as I say, eventually it became more or less obvious. But first you have to know that my father, Ibrahim, was a brilliant businessman. He directed his youngest brother, Mahmoud, in some of his widespread business dealings in Iraq. Mahmoud was trying to supply contract workers on a reconstruction job over there, a very lucrative one, but the main supplier—Mahmoud's chief competitor, in fact—was a Kurd named Kuvan Krekar. The FBI became satisfied that Mr. Krekar took out the contract on my mother and father to disrupt our business over there, and to a large extent he was successful. In the short term." When Khalil's small smile returned, it had a chilling aspect. "I received word about two years ago that Mr. Krekar had died from an improvised explosive device. My country, as you know, is going through some very violent times. But the good news is that Mahmoud and his business have been thriving lately, and we believe we have turned the corner over there."

[36]

AT FIVE-THIRTY, Hardy and Hunt were sharing one of the window booths at Lou the Greek's, a bar and, in some people's opinion, restaurant located just across the street from the Hall of Justice. The squabble over whether it was in fact a true restaurant worthy of the name derived from the uneven quality of the food they served at the place. Many of the regular patrons came in only to drink at the tiny bar in the front, and didn't ever try to eat the constantly changing Special that Lou's wife, Chui, created every single day.

The Special was the only food item on the menu, and in deference to Chui's Chinese and Lou's Greek ethnicities, she most frequently tried to make different combinations of ingredients that included both of these two cultures' rather violently disparate culinary traditions. Thus, on any given day, the Lou's Special might be taramasalata (fish roe) wontons in an avgolemono broth, moussaka potstickers, or the oft-requested Yeanling Clay Bowl, the ingredients of which had once stumped a panel of six of the city's all-star chefs after DA Clarence Jackman had publicly referred to it as his "favorite lunch in the city."

Because Lou's was semi-subterranean—the entrance

off Bryant descended eight steps from the street level—
the booth where Hardy and Hunt sat had windows high
in the wall above them, which at the same time were at
the ground level of the alley that ran alongside the building on the outside. The view out the windows, which few
took advantage of, was of passing feet, garbage cans, the
occasional horizontal homeless person.

Today, neither Hardy nor Hunt was paying attention
to the ambience. Hardy, who had spent most of the afternoon working on the first draft of his argument on the
PTSD issue for Evan's appeal, sat with his shoulders
hunched over slightly as though he were brooding, his
hands cupped around a mug of coffee. Hunt sat sideways
in the booth, slowly revolving a pint glass of beer on the
table. Hunt had already made his report to Hardy at his
office, and this had prompted Hardy's call back to Glitsky,
and ultimately the decision that they should all meet
down here and see what they had.

"You don't think the fact that the Khalils talked to the
FBI is going to be enough for you?" Hunt asked. "Friday
that was all you wanted."

"I remember it well," Hardy said, "those halcyon by-
gone days. And absolutely I'm going to make the argument. The Khalils had a strong motive to kill Nolan. The
jury should have known about that and decided for themselves whether that caused them to have a reasonable
doubt about Evan's guilt. It's up to the jury, not the FBI,
to decide what's important and what's not. But for *Brady*
to work, the withheld discovery has to be reasonably
likely to cast doubt on the verdict. And the idea that some
unknown third parties had a motive to kill Nolan probably isn't going to convince the court to give Evan a new

trial. We're just going to need something stronger if we want to argue that the Khalils killed Nolan—"

"Which I just don't see, Diz. Really. Still possible, I know, but you had to have heard this guy. If he didn't absolutely believe Scholler killed Nolan, he's gotta get himself an agent."

"Well, if the alternative option was either himself or one of his relatives, it might sharpen his thespian skills a little bit, don't you think?"

Hunt shrugged. "Possibly. But still, it's against my gut."

"All right, then, let's go with that for a minute. Say whoever killed Nolan, it wasn't the Khalils and it wasn't Scholler. Who does that leave?"

"How 'bout the FBI? Maybe there was way more money involved and these two agents who have disappeared found it and left the country."

"Maybe," Hardy said without enthusiasm. "And a good story. But I kind of doubt it."

"Me too," Hunt said, pointing at the entrance. "And I hate that. But here comes Glitsky. Maybe he'll know something."

IT WASN'T ONLY GLITSKY. Bracco came in with him. Hardy introduced Hunt around—he hadn't met either of the cops before. Lou came from behind the bar and took their orders, Glitsky's green tea and Bracco's Diet Coke. In the next few minutes of show and tell, everybody got reasonably caught up. The story Hardy had heard from Tara about the mugging incident in San Francisco's Tenderloin, implicating Nolan in those three deaths, significantly upped the buzz quotient around the table.

Bracco went last, revealing to the civilians what he'd already told Glitsky—that he'd located Bowen's secretary, Deni Pichaud, and talked to her for an hour or more about what her boss had been working on during the last few days before he disappeared. Ms. Pichaud didn't have much to offer. Bowen, as everyone already knew, had a varied and substantial practice, and according to Pichaud he tended to flit from one case to another as clients called and demanded his attention. She had no special memory of anything about Evan Scholler or his appeal.

When Bracco finished, the four men sat looking at one another for a long moment. Hardy finally broke into the silence. "So where does that leave us?"

"Is shit creek already taken?" Hunt asked.

Glitsky, who eschewed profanity, gave the detective a quick bad eye but then blew on his tea, sipped, and said, "It's the FBI and Iraq. That's all that's left."

Hardy shook his head. "The FBI didn't kill Nolan, Abe."

"Maybe Scholler did." Bracco held up a hand. "I know he's your client and all, but—"

"Yeah, but that almost doesn't matter at this point," Glitsky said.

"I'm afraid it still does to me, guys," Hardy put in. "That's why me and Wyatt are here. So if everybody's good with it, maybe we can just leave the whole question of who killed Nolan open and see where that leads us."

"Good by me," Glitsky said. "I want who did the Bowens, and we know that wasn't Scholler."

"So you're going with the Bowens being murders?" Hunt asked.

Glitsky nodded. "Until I get proven otherwise." He pointed a finger across the table at his inspector. "Which means, while I'm thinking of it, Darrel, feel free to put in more time on both these investigations. Treat 'em both like they're righteous one eighty-sevens. Witnesses if you can find 'em, evidence ditto, phone and financial records, the whole ball of wax."

Bracco, determination written all over his face, nodded. "Got it."

"Meanwhile," Glitsky continued, "how are the FBI and Iraq connected to the Bowens?" In a rare display of humor, he channeled the line from *Ferris Bueller.* "Anyone? Anyone?"

"I've got a thought," Hardy said. "Let's go back to Nolan. The FBI talked to him in person and his employer works in Iraq, which puts FBI and Iraq in the same sentence anyway."

Hunt picked it up. "All right. And Abdel Khalil says Nolan picked up the contract on his parents in Iraq from a guy named Kumar or something."

Hardy, who rarely forgot anything, chimed in. "Kuvan."

"Okay, Kuvan. Kuvan paid Nolan forty or fifty grand to take out the Khalils. Then the Khalil family over in Iraq took out Kuvan."

The four men sat with their thoughts and drinks. Finally, Hardy cleared his throat. "My, what a tidy little package," he said.

Glitsky turned to him. "What are you saying?"

"I'm saying that this is all a nice cleanly closed circle, except for two little things—Charlie and Hanna Bowen. And I think we're all in agreement that, no matter what, the FBI didn't kill them. Right?"

Nods all around.

"Well, check me if I'm wrong on anything here, but

how about if the trail leads to Iraq, all right, but instead of Kuvan paying for the hit, the order came from All-strong?"

"The way it did with Zwick," Glitsky added.

"Do we know that for sure?" Bracco asked. "And even if we do, what does it get us?"

"Nothing with Zwick, as you say. The FBI never got involved in that investigation," Hardy answered. "But with the Khalils, it gets us the FBI covering for an American company with contracts over there, deflecting the blame—and the retaliation—on this Kuvan guy. Just another Iraqi businessman who got squeezed in the war. This totally satisfies the Khalils—they get their tribal revenge and they're happy. And over here, now nobody's looking at Nolan anymore, or at Allstrong. The story's completely over."

"And the FBI did this, again, why?" Glitsky asked.

"Because Allstrong is connected high up in the government, both over there and back here. High enough that they could call off the FBI."

"Uh-oh." Glitsky was shaking his head.

"I know, I know," Hardy said. "You hate this conspiracy stuff. Which doesn't mean, Abe, that it doesn't happen."

"I don't hate it," Bracco said.

Hunt chimed in. "Me neither. In fact, I kind of like it."

"Maybe I'm missing something," Glitsky said, coming back at Hardy. "So, Diz, you're saying that the FBI went over to investigate what? Nolan's murder?"

"No. The Khalil murders."

"I thought they'd concluded that was your client?"

"No," Hunt corrected Glitsky. "Redwood City, not the

feds, concluded that that was Evan. According to Abdel, the FBI thought it was Nolan pretty early on."

"So they went over to Iraq? Why?"

"To find the source of the frag grenades," Hardy said, "if nothing else. Interview Nolan's associates, maybe his boss, who has, it turns out, in fact actually ordered the hit."

"But again, Diz, why?"

"Well, and here I'm extrapolating a little bit, but see if it doesn't sing for you, because Allstrong had a profitable relationship with this guy Kuvan. And the Khalils were getting in Kuvan's way. This is all stuff, by the way, that Wyatt more or less verified this afternoon with Abdel. So Allstrong orders its guy, Nolan, to do the hit. Which is, P.S., what he basically did for a living anyway."

"So." Glitsky, trying to make the tumblers fall into place, slowly swirled his teacup in front of him. "How does this get us to Bowen?"

"Bowen gets Evan's appeal," Hardy said, "just like I did. He starts asking the same types of questions I've been asking, except instead of sending Wyatt here down to talk to Abdel Khalil, he starts with the assumption we're working with right now—that Nolan and not Evan killed the Khalils. So that changes his equation about who would need to cover that up if it comes out, and what's the answer?"

"Allstrong," Hunt said.

Hardy nodded. "Ten points."

"Who needs to cover what up?" Glitsky asked.

"Allstrong. They can play fast and loose all they want in Iraq and nobody asks too many questions as long as they're fulfilling their contracts. But if it comes out—and it would be a huge story over here—that they're killing naturalized American citizens on American soil to promote their business interests in Iraq, I've got to believe that as screwed up as things are over there, Allstrong would at least stop getting new contracts. They might even lose the ones they've already got, and that's if they don't get charged for murder first."

Bracco slurped at the end of his Diet Coke. "How much money are we talking about? For Allstrong, I mean, their contracts over there."

Hunt spoke up. "I got curious checking out some stuff on Nolan and Googled them over the weekend. Their first year in Iraq, when Nolan was on the payroll, they got about three hundred and fifty million dollars in government contracts."

"You've got to be kidding me," Bracco said. "Allstrong Security? I mean, who are they? Nobody's ever heard of them. They're not exactly Halliburton."

"No, but they're trying harder," said Hunt, "that's for sure."

"Maybe they'd actually kill to get work," Hardy deadpanned.

Glitsky sat back, his body language saying that he was still reserving judgment. "Okay, okay. So you're saying Bowen went to Allstrong first, not the Khalils, with these questions?"

"That's my guess," Hardy said.

"And Allstrong killed him?"

A nod. "Or had him killed, yes."

"That's pretty drastic, don't you think?"

"Maybe from our perspective, granted. But these guys are a bunch of mercenaries. They're hired guns. That's how they solve problems." Hardy came forward in his enthusiasm. "Look, Abe, Allstrong had already dealt with the whole Nolan thing and put it behind them. The world believed it was Evan Scholler who'd killed the Khalils for his own twisted reasons. Someone with the government who had major juice—a general, a congressman, I don't know, somebody who was in Allstrong's pocket and helping it get its contracts—had either ordered or convinced the FBI to offer up Kuvan privately to the remaining Khalils."

Glitsky was still shaking his head. "I know we're not all big FBI fans here, but I've got to say that I don't see them doing this. Ever. Sometimes they might get a little overzealous, but they're not going to frame an innocent Iraqi and stand back while someone else kills him."

Hardy nodded, conceding the point. "How about if they didn't know, Abe? How about if someone way up, like the general or senator or whoever I was talking about earlier, got to the director of the Bureau, say, and vouched for Allstrong, meanwhile selling him a bill of goods about Kuvan? So your agents solve the case and then they're ordered off it."

"And when somebody else wants to talk about it," Bracco said, "like you, this morning, sir, the agents don't work there anymore."

"And Allstrong stays off the hook," Hardy said.

"Until Bowen showed up," Hunt added.

"That's it," Hardy said. "And then here it was again, the threat to Allstrong, to its very existence, and a lot closer this time. So they had to make Bowen disappear before he could make any kind of public stink. Or even ask any more questions. He just had to go away." Hardy looked around the table. "Anybody see an egregious flaw here?"

Glitsky looked across at Bracco. "Don't worry about it,

Darrel, he always uses words like that." Then, back to Hardy. "Do you know that Bowen ever actually got in touch with Allstrong? I mean, any actual proof?"

"No, but we can find that out. Those phone records you were talking about." Hardy turned to Bracco. "And you might want to check Hanna's too."

Glitsky snapped out a curt defense of his inspector. "I'm sure Darrel's got some sense of the drill, Diz."

"Sorry," Hardy said to Bracco. "I tend to get excited. This may really be something."

"Let's get some evidence first," Glitsky said. He sipped at the last of his tea, put his cup down gently. When he spoke, his voice was heavy with discontent. "I really don't want to believe there's a conspiracy here. And a cover-up. From somebody high enough up to have influence with the FBI. I keep believing our guys don't do that kind of stuff."

"With all respect, are you kidding, sir?" Hunt said. "These are the same swell folks who brought us Abu Ghraib and all the other disasters over there. Giving up Kuvan for the greater good, and that means pumping more money into a hardworking, God-fearing company like Allstrong—that's a no-brainer. We're the good guys, remember, so whatever we do is right."

"Yeah," Glitsky said, "so let's hope we're wrong on this one."

Hardy, thinking about Evan Scholler doing life without parole in prison, didn't hope they were wrong. He didn't see another plausible alternative, and he'd long since lost faith in the essential goodness of man. Some were good, true, maybe most. But others, particularly those drawn to war zones and to chaos, would sometimes do anything—lie, cheat, and kill—for more money and more power, either or both. The basic rules of civilization did not apply.

That, Hardy was now all but convinced, was what had happened here. The moral rot that festered in Iraq and in the halls of power both here and abroad had poisoned the communal well over there. What distinguished Allstrong was that it had had the arrogance and irresponsibility to bring the rot and the chaos home.

And that, Hardy felt, could not be allowed to stand.

[37]

HARDY SAT IN HIS READING CHAIR, his feet up on the ottoman, in the dark living room in the front of his house. He wore the same black gym shorts that he'd put on before he'd gotten into bed six hours before. When he had started awake about an hour ago—he'd dreamed that he'd been pushed from an airplane out over the Pacific Ocean—tossing off the covers, he had lain still in the night until his heart slowed down, listening to his wife's breathing beside him, taking what comfort he could from the peaceful regularity of it.

Finally giving up on the idea of sleeping, he eased himself out of bed. Downstairs, he looked into the refrigerator out of habit, then closed it and went into the adjoining family room and watched his tropical fish swimming in their dim, gurgling home.

He'd spent most of the evening after dinner back next to his fish at his computer, finding out everything he could about Allstrong Security. Hunt's analysis of their financial success early in the war was accurate as far as it went, but he'd failed to mention that to date, the company's government contracts in Iraq totaled eight hundred and forty million dollars.

Allstrong was in charge of security at sixteen of the

country's airports, as well as guarding electrical grids in twenty-two administrative areas. They had been in charge of the currency changeover for the entire country as well as the rebuilding of the power lines in the extremely violent Anbar Province. The company's Web site boasted of 8,800 employees in Iraq, 465 of whom were former American military men, most of them officers.

The company had also become active in several other countries, with more than 500 ex-commando operatives in Indonesia, Afghanistan, Kuwait, Nigeria, and El Salvador, where it specialized in corporate as well as government logistics and security. Over 200 more employees worked at a sprawling new headquarters complex near Candlestick Point in San Francisco, where the concentration was mostly on programs to guarantee the integrity of municipal water supplies and, incongruously, on raising catfish as a sustainable and inexpensive food source for developing countries.

Jack Allstrong, the founder, president, and CEO, had evidently relocated back to the home office in March of 2005. He lived alone in a mansion in Hillsborough and presided over the business out of San Francisco, although the home page stressed that Allstrong was ready and able to embark to trouble spots anywhere in the world at a moment's notice in one of the corporation's fleet of private aircraft, which included two Gulfstream V jets.

When he went to bed, Hardy's brain had been spinning with the possibilities that Allstrong presented for his Scholler appeal. As soon as Bracco could forge the link tying Allstrong to Nolan's involvement in the assassination of the Khalils and to the deaths of the Bowens, Hardy would have an unassailable argument that the jury in the original trial never saw crucial evidence that reasonably could have affected the verdict. He'd get his appeal granted on the *Brady* violation, and then probably a new trial. And further, he doubted that a new jury, given the reversals in the case, would convict Evan again.

Now Hardy's subconscious had rejected all of these optimistic conclusions. As he sat slumped down in his living room chair he found himself scavenging for any kind of salvageable something that could tie Allstrong—either the person or the company—to any crime at all.

If Jack Allstrong had personally ordered Nolan to eliminate the Khalils, and paid him in cash, which is exactly what Hardy conjectured had happened, he could count on there being no record of it whatsoever. Especially after all these years.

Or—Hardy corrected himself—Charlie Bowen had come up with the only evidence there might have been, and perhaps had inadvertently passed it on to his wife. But by now, whatever that had been must be gone. And similarly, the murders of Charlie and Hanna had been carried out with professional efficiency.

Even if Bracco discovered that Charlie and/or Hanna Bowen had called or gone down to visit Allstrong on the last day of their lives, what would that prove? Would it lead to a discovery of Charlie's body, which had probably long since become fish food? Or would it place an Allstrong mercenary in Hanna's garage pulling her body down to make sure to break her neck as she dropped from her stepladder?

Hardy knew it wouldn't.

And so long as Allstrong didn't confess to anything—and if there was no proof he'd ever done anything wrong, why would he?—then in the face of all the accusations in the world, he'd remain untouchable. In fact, Hardy realized, with the size of the operation Allstrong was running, by now he'd undoubtedly have surrounded himself with protection—administrative assistants, senior staff, his own lawyers—to keep him insulated from riffraff such as Hardy himself or even Sergeant Bracco who might come calling on him with impertinent questions. Hardy might never even get to talk to him.

At the sound of the newspaper hitting the porch, he opened his eyes again. The darkness outside had lessened by a degree.

It was going to be a long day.

THREE AND A HALF HOURS into the work portion of that day, Hardy glared malevolently at the phone as it buzzed at his elbow. He was eight pages into his brief about the *Brady* violation. He made a good case that the FBI's information should have been disclosed to Washburn. This would have allowed him to cross-examine the now-disappeared, allegedly ex–FBI agents on the entire question of Nolan's involvement with the frag grenades. He'd turned off his cell phone and left strict instructions with Phyllis to hold all of his calls. He needed to concentrate.

But here was the phone, buzzing at him. Hence the glare.

He put his pen down and reached for the receiver. "This must be an emergency," he said in a mild tone. "Is the building on fire?"

"No, sir. But Lieutenant Glitsky said I should disturb you. Apparently somebody tried to kill Evan Scholler at the prison this morning. Lieutenant Glitsky is holding now. Shall I put him through?"

"That would be a good thing, Phyllis. Please." He heard the click of connection. "Is Evan all right?"

"He's alive, though he's cut pretty bad. He was lucky. The shiv hit a rib or he'd be room temperature by now."

"So he's going to live?"

"No promises, but good chance, evidently."

"So what happened, Abe? He get in a fight?"

"Well, finding out what really happened is always a little iffy there, but by first reports, it's starting to look like he was a target of some kind. The guy who went for him was a Salvadoran gangbanger out of L.A. named Rafael Calderon. Nobody had ever seen these two guys together before this morning."

"So you're saying somebody ordered this?"

"I'm not saying anything. I'm telling you what I've heard so far. And I've heard that your man Evan had been an ideal inmate. No word about any enemies, or what he might have done to make them."

"So the order came from outside?"

"Don't know. It could have been something personal we don't know about. I'd hesitate to conjecture. But maybe you've got something you want to tell me?"

Hardy, recalling his research the previous night, couldn't keep the thought from jumping to the front of his mind—Allstrong Security was developing a presence in El Salvador. Beyond his net surfing last night, he'd read several lengthy magazine articles and even pieces of a couple of books delineating the relationships between U.S. mercenaries and the Salvadoran gang networks in that country, and took it as gospel that the connections between them ran deep. He took a minute to get Glitsky up to speed, then asked, "Did they question Calderon?"

"Calderon wasn't as lucky as Scholler."

"Are you telling me he's dead?"

"That's right."

"Did Scholler kill him?"

"No. Scholler was on the ground, bleeding. When the guards heard the screaming and yelling from the assault and got there, they got Calderon surrounded and he went more or less insane. He still had his shiv on him and he charged them. They reacted with what, after the hearing, I'm sure will be called appropriate force in self-defense."

Hardy realized that he was gripping the phone so tightly that his knuckles were white. He knew that if Calderon had taken the job of assassinating Scholler in prison and either botched it or got caught afterward, both of which had happened in this case, he could expect to be killed by his handler or by another gang-connected inmate before he could be questioned and give anything away. And he knew that whoever had put out the contract would just as easily put out another one.

AFTER THE PHONE CALL, Hardy couldn't get his mind back on the draft of his brief. He decided to walk down to the Hall of Justice to clear his mind. The fine weather continued, and if Glitsky had already gone to lunch, Hardy could walk down a couple of blocks and catch a meal at any one of a number of the good new joints in SoMa, South of Market. But Abe was in, at his desk drinking a bottled water and eating a rice cake. Glitsky opened his desk drawer, pulled out a handful of peanuts in the shell, and slid them across his desk.

Hardy cracked a shell. "This is Allstrong again, Abe."

"Calderon? It might be at that."

"It is, absolutely."

Glitsky shook his head. "Don't get me wrong. I want it to be with all my heart, but I don't have enough, Diz. If makes you feel any better, I think it's possible, and I didn't think that a few days ago. I'm waiting for Darrel before I jump to any conclusions."

"I made that jump when I heard about the stabbing. There is no other conclusion."

"Not to be disagreeable, but don't kid yourself. You were all over this at least yesterday, maybe before."

Hardy chewed reflectively. "You want to hear how it works? Why it's Allstrong?"

"Sure, but the short version, please."

"Okay, six weeks ago Hanna gets killed. Allstrong's now had to kill two people involved in the Scholler appeal. He thinks it's probably all done as far as getting rid of evidence is concerned, but he knows that as long as Evan Scholler's in prison, there's going to be this appeal coming up again and its attendant risks, meaning people like Bowen or me coming around asking him provocative questions. Maybe there's even more evidence someplace that he was actively involved in a domestic homicide."

"Let's hope," Glitsky said.

Hardy nodded. "So Allstrong gets another idea."

"Kill Scholler."

"You're reading my mind." Another peanut. "Scholler dies, the appeal is over. Cuts it off at the source. But of course, the problem is that Scholler's in prison. Not untouchable, but more complicated, through El Salvador and backup through one of the L.A. gangs." Hardy held up his hands in a *voilà* gesture. "There's your six weeks between Hanna and now."

"Brilliant." Glitsky ate another peanut. "You've got it all figured out."

"I've got Bowen figured out too. They dumped him out in the ocean."

This brought Glitsky forward in his chair. "How do you know that?"

"I dreamed it," Hardy said, grinning. "But it's what happened, Abe. You're going to find his DNA in one of their airplanes, I promise."

"Just as soon as I get to look in one of them." Sitting back, Glitsky folded his hands on his lap. "I want to believe you, Diz, I really do. I'll jump on all of this with both feet as soon as I can go to a judge to give me a warrant. Or I get any other reason to send Bracco to talk to the guy. But until I do..." He shrugged. "I'm waiting on Bracco. He finds something or he doesn't. Usually, if something's there, he does."

"Yeah, but meanwhile, my client's still a target."

Glitsky glanced at the wall clock. "Diz. I think that's a reach. I really do. Or, at worst, by your own math, the next attack is six weeks away."

GLITSKY WAS HALF JOKING, but the next attack felt far closer than six weeks away to Hardy.

Back in his office, galvanized, he told Phyllis to hold his calls again and spent the next two hours working on his brief. One thing he could do, as a lawyer, was actually file his appeal and get things shaking. He, too, had been waiting for Bracco to come up with actual evidence that either of the Bowens had called Allstrong, but there was another, and much more direct, way to go about getting this information. He could pick up the phone and ask.

It wasn't Glitsky's way, and Hardy, in his enthusiasm to simply figure out what had happened, had gotten hung up with that process. But Glitsky was trying to solve two homicides in his jurisdiction and bring a killer to justice. Hardy, on the other hand, had only one job. He was working to free his client.

It was a crucial difference, and it now had gained added urgency with the prison assault on Evan this morning. Hardy had been hoping that once the police could somehow prove an Allstrong/Bowen connection, it would strengthen the argument in his appeal. But he really didn't need that to file—the FBI and the Khalils might eventually lead to Allstrong and Nolan, but the issue was whether those initial interrogations should have been part of the prosecution's discovery, and on this point there was little doubt.

Easy though it might be to make an actual phone call to Allstrong, there was another component to the equation that Hardy could ignore only at his peril. These guys had proven themselves seriously proactive about people who threatened their business interests. If Hardy's theories were correct, and he was by now all but certain that they were, they had killed both the Bowens and made an attempt on the life of Evan. And all of this without leaving behind a shred of evidence that would tie them to these crimes.

Hardy realized that as soon as he made that one simple phone call, the threat level in his own life was going to go up in a hurry. He would be putting himself exactly where Charlie Bowen had gone before he disappeared forever.

But he needed the information. He had to know for sure; he couldn't file his appeal until he knew.

Reward; risk.

Hardy had written the Allstrong office number down in his notes as a matter of course while he was doing his research last night. Returning from word processing where he'd dropped his draft marked URGENT, he closed his office door, went behind his desk, sat down, took out his notes, and pulled the phone over in front of him, punching the numbers with a steeled deliberation.

[38]

"JACK ALLSTRONG, please."

"I'll see if he's in. Can I tell him who's calling?"

"I don't know. How can you tell him who's calling if he's not in?"

"I beg your pardon?"

"You said you'd see if Mr. Allstrong was in. But if you were going to tell him who was calling, then you must know he is in. Isn't that right?"

Hardy hated to launch this logic assault on the poor receptionist, but with the attack on Evan, he believed he was running out of time. "Please tell Mr. Allstrong that my name is Dismas Hardy and that it's extremely important that I speak with him as soon as possible." He spelled his name out for her. "I'm an attorney working on the appeal in the Evan Scholler matter, with which I'm sure he's familiar. Please also tell him that I'm continuing the work begun last summer by a lawyer named Charlie Bowen. If he's busy, tell him I'll be happy to wait here on the line for as long as it takes."

As it turned out, it took less than a minute. A voice with an undefinably Southern accent and devoid of nervousness, anger, or fear came through the wire. "This is Jack Allstrong."

"Mr. Allstrong, my name is Dismas Hardy and—"

A big, booming laugh. "Yeah, I already know that. You made quite a first impression on our Marilou, I must say. And normally she is some kind of a tough nut to crack. She says you're working with Lieutenant Scholler?"

"Evan. Yes, sir."

"Evan, right. I always think of him as Lieutenant. That's what he was when he worked with us." He paused. "God, that whole quagmire with him and Ron Nolan just turned into a hell of a thing, didn't it? The messes people get themselves into. And two better young men you couldn't have imagined. But I don't suppose you ever had a chance to meet Ron?"

"No, I didn't."

"That's a shame. He was a fine man, a fine soldier, a loyal employee. What happened to him was just nothin' less than a goddamned tragedy, Mr. Hardy, I'll be honest with you. And I know it was because of the lieutenant's head wound to some extent, so I don't blame him the way I might otherwise. War, and this one's no exception, it can do horrible things to people. Anybody's been in one knows that for a fact. You a veteran, Mr. Hardy?"

"Yes, sir. Vietnam."

"Well, then, you know what I'm talking about. But at least this war, the soldiers themselves, the men on the ground, they're getting some respect. And about goddamn time, wouldn't you say?"

"Yes, I would," Hardy said. "But I'm calling because I'm about to file an appeal to see if I can get Mr. Scholler out of prison and—"

"Wait!" Allstrong's voice hardened up. "Now, wait just a second here. You say you're trying to get the lieutenant out of prison? I thought nobody doubted that he had killed Ron."

"Well, the jury thought it was beyond reasonable doubt, which is not—"

"Now, hold on. We don't need to be splitting hairs here, Mr. Hardy. I think I've made it clear that until he was injured and even after that, Lieutenant Scholler had my complete respect. He was a good soldier, a natural leader, good to his men. But I don't think I'm comfortable with the idea that the man who killed one of my first employees, and a damn good friend, is going to be out walking the streets again, a free man. And I certainly don't think I'm inclined to help with this appeal of yours."

"Sir, I don't believe Evan Scholler did kill Ron Nolan."

"Well, that's a good one. You might be in the minority with that opinion. I haven't talked to anybody else who thinks that."

"Not even Charlie Bowen?"

Allstrong didn't hesitate for an instant. "Not him either."

"So you talked to him?"

"Couple of times, at least. Last summer sometime, was it? I don't know. Whatever happened to him anyway? One day he's here asking me all kinds of questions, I'm thinking he's moving forward on this appeal like you are, and next thing you know he's gone."

"That's what happened," Hardy said. "He disappeared."

"Just like that?"

"Apparently." Hardy found his temper starting to flare, and decided it was time to push on Allstrong, see if he could get a bit of a rise. "Did you know Charlie Bowen's wife?"

"I don't believe so."

"She never called you there?"

"She might have called here, although I don't know why she would have. But if she did, she never talked to me. Why do you think I would know anything about her?"

Hardy laid out his conjecture as factual truth. "She was working on some of the files Charlie was working on when he disappeared. Then, I don't know if you've heard, but six weeks ago, she committed suicide."

For the first time, Allstrong hesitated, then made a little kissing noise. "Well, I'm sorry to hear that, of course. Over Charlie walking out on her?"

"That's the general assumption, I presume. Although there are other theories."

"About why she killed herself?"

"Not just why, but whether. There's some evidence that she might have been killed by someone who wanted to make it look like a suicide."

"Why would anyone do that? Want to kill her, I mean?"

"Maybe because she'd found out something to do with her husband's death. And in that case, maybe Charlie Bowen wasn't a simple disappearance either. Maybe he was murdered too."

"That's a lot of maybes."

"Yes, it is. And here's another one. Maybe Charlie's work on this appeal is what convinced somebody they needed to kill him."

"Who would that be?"

"Whoever actually did kill Ron Nolan."

"Ahh." Allstrong mustered up a kind of chortle. "And this is what brings us around to where you don't think it was Scholler who killed him."

"That's right. These are my theories about the Bowens, both of them. I think they were both murdered, and I think the person behind those murders also tried to have Evan Scholler killed this morning at Corcoran Prison. But that one didn't work." Hardy didn't know if Allstrong had already received this news from his sources within the prison, and he thought it wouldn't hurt to hear it now from him.

And while there was no sign that this information registered as anything but another unimportant detail about Hardy's case, by degrees the superficial warmth was leeching out of both men's tones. When Allstrong spoke next, his easy Southern geniality was entirely missing. "Well, all of this is interesting, I'm sure, but it really doesn't have shit-all to do with me. And I'm afraid, as I told you, I'm not going to be too disposed to help you get Ron Nolan's killer out of prison. So if there's anything else specific I can help you with, let's hear it. Otherwise, I got a business I'm trying to run here."

"I appreciate that," Hardy said. "I thought you'd be interested in finding Ron Nolan's killer in any event, though. Whether or not it was Evan Scholler, you'd want to know who really did it, I presume. And whatever you can tell me now might help me get to the truth. I'm basing my appeal on stuff I think the FBI discovered that they didn't reveal to Evan's prosecutors at the time of the trial. I assume you're familiar with fragmentation grenades?"

"Sure."

"Well, then, you may know that Nolan, who was in

your employ at the time, had several of these in his home."

"I understood that Scholler put them there to frame Ron."

"No, sir." Hardy easily came out with the next untruth. "Since the trial, that's been pretty much discredited. The FBI concluded there was no way Evan could have gotten these things back home, whereas Nolan could have just packed them in his duffel."

"And why would he do that?"

"Because he liked them to cover his tracks after he assassinated people."

Allstrong laughed out loud, although through the phone Hardy picked up as much nerves as humor in it this time. When he got his breath, he said, "That accusation is really beneath contempt, Mr. Hardy. Ron was my recruiter out here. He didn't assassinate people."

"Yes, he did. The FBI has made that clear enough to the Khalil family, who were among his victims. That's the evidence I'm trying to get in front of the court this time around. If Nolan was killing people on contract, then revenge becomes a motive for his own death, and that might give Evan an out."

Allstrong came out with the question Hardy had been leading him toward. "You say Nolan was killing people on contract? That's absurd."

"The FBI doesn't think so."

"So who was paying him?"

"Well, the FBI makes the case to the Khalils that it was one of your former clients in Iraq, a man named Kuvan Krekar."

"Kuvan is dead. He's been dead now a couple of years."

"I know that. He was killed by the Khalils over in Iraq, but I don't think Kuvan was paying Nolan anyway. For what it's worth, a couple of inspectors with San Francisco's homicide department think the same thing I do, and they won't be giving up on their investigation anytime soon. They think that whoever paid Nolan to kill the Khalils also had a hand in the deaths of Charlie and Hanna Bowen. You got any idea who that might be?"

"None at all."

"That's funny, because all of us have the idea that it's someone in your company, Jack. Allstrong Security."

After a long pause, Allstrong said, "If that ridiculous accusation ever sees the light of day, Mr. Hardy, I hope you're prepared to spend the rest of your life defending the lawsuit I'll bring against you."

"I'M GLAD I did it," Hardy said. "I had to shake something up. It was kind of fun."

Frannie sat next to him at the bar of the Little Shamrock. Her brother, Moses McGuire, was standing across from them both behind the bar. "It was kind of fun," Frannie said to Moses, mimicking Hardy's voice with heavy irony. "*I think it's kind of fun* to threaten a man who's already killed at least two people and tried for three in trying to keep this information from getting out. *I think it's kind of fun* that he can put me on his kill list next so me and my family can live in fear of being murdered every day from now on. I really think that's kind of fun." Frannie's color was high, her eyes shining with anger.

Hardy put a hand over his wife's. "That's not going to happen, Frannie. And you know why? Moses knows why, don't you, Mose?"

McGuire sipped his soda and lime. "Because you told Allstrong the cops were on it too. Killing you the way he'd done the Bowens wouldn't get him anything. But"— he held up a finger—"here's the tiny flaw my smart little sister has picked up on in your strategy, Diz. If this guy is juiced enough that he can pull strings inside the FBI, and apparently he is, what on God's good earth makes you think that he can't get around Abe Glitsky and Darrel Bracco?" He turned to Frannie. "Did I express that succinctly enough, you think?"

She bobbed her head once, still furious. "Perfectly," she said.

"Guys, come on," Hardy said. "He's not going to kill two cops, for Christ's sake. And who knows who else is in on the investigation. That's just not going to happen."

"He doesn't have to kill them," Frannie replied. "But what about if he has them ordered off from on high? Where does that leave you then?"

"Me, me, Monty, call on me." Moses wasn't smiling, either, though. He leaned over into his brother-in-law's face. "That leaves you hanging out there alone in the breeze, Diz."

"Okay, but if that unlikely event happens, which I doubt—"

"Then you'll have an accident, like Charlie Bowen did," Frannie said.

"No, Abe would never rest if—"

Frannie slammed her palm down on the bar. *"You'd already be dead, you idiot!"*

In the silence that descended, Hardy put his hand gently over Frannie's again. "Well," he said, "then I'd better get this whole thing done fast, shouldn't I?"

* * *

HARDY COULD BE GLIB all he wanted, but in fact Frannie and Moses weren't all wrong, or even mostly wrong. He knew that he'd possibly put himself in an elevated state of jeopardy and could live with that—he also thought he'd mitigated the problem dramatically by telling Allstrong that the police were already involved in this same investigation.

But the more he lived with it, the more he found himself worrying. He hadn't adequately considered that his phone call to Allstrong might also have put Frannie in danger. That had not been his intention, though it might very well be the result.

So Date Night, even at their old favorite restaurant Yet Wah, ended early. Frannie, still very upset over Hardy's call to Allstrong, went straight up to bed. Hardy went to his chair in the living room and punched up Darrel Bracco's number on his cell phone. The inspector picked up and Hardy told him his story—putting a press on Jack Allstrong in person—to a considerably more enthusiastic response than Frannie had given him. When he finished, Bracco said, "So we know both the Bowens were talking to Allstrong. I got that from the phone records too. But so what?"

"So what is what else this tells us."

"What's that?"

"This is close to him, personally. It's not just some corporate thing."

"How do you know that?"

"Mostly," Hardy said, "because he came to the phone to talk to me when there was no reason he needed to. He's got two hundred people under him down there. I guarantee he's got several levels of bureaucracy between him and the front desk. But I call him up out of thin air and mention Evan Scholler and the Bowens and he came right away. He wanted to know what I knew, to see how exposed he was. And I'm confident that I made it pretty clear."

"Why did you want to do that?" Bracco asked. "Warn him we're coming."

"My wife had the same question," Hardy said. "But maybe rattling his cage gets him to do something stupid."

"Something stupid to do with you, maybe."

"Maybe, but unlikely. I made it clear to Allstrong that now it's not just one lone attorney, and then several months later, his wife, also acting alone. The police are part of it now. If any of us disappears or has an accident, the heat only goes up on him. So he's got to figure another way out, make this investigation go away, and I'm trying to make it easy for him."

"He's not going to confess to ordering a domestic murder. Or anything to do with the Bowens."

"True. But I don't need that. I just need to get my client off. As far as he's concerned, that's going to be all I want."

"I want these murders," Bracco said.

"Of course you do," Hardy replied. "And you should. But you'll admit that building any kind of winnable case on the evidence we see so far after all this time is pretty long odds. Meanwhile, Allstrong knows this whole thing is driven by Evan Scholler. That's what was behind the attack this morning in prison. He already believes that if Scholler goes away, all his problems go away."

"I'm not going to go away," Bracco said.

"You won't have any choice if he's left you no evidence to work with. I got the feeling this guy's built his business by getting around local authorities everywhere he sets up shop. Now he's got political clout and the veneer of respectability. We're not going to take him head-on."

"So you've got a better idea?" Bracco asked.

"As a matter of fact," Hardy said, "I think I do."

As HE TIPTOED into his bedroom at a little after eleven o'clock, Frannie switched on the light next to the bed.

"Hey," Hardy said.

"Hey." She patted the bed next to her. "I'm sorry," she said. "I was worried. I'm still worried, but I don't want to fight about it."

He crossed over to her and sat down, put a hand on her shoulder. "I don't either."

After a minute, she let out a long breath. "So how'd it go?"

"I think I've got Darrel talked into it. He really wants this guy. As do I."

"What about Abe?"

"I didn't get around to talking to Abe. He might have reservations I'd rather not entertain at this point in time."

Frannie closed her eyes and sighed again. "It's really that important?"

"Charlie Bowen told his wife it was the most important thing he'd ever worked on. It was his biggest chance to do some real good in the world."

"In the world, huh?"

"The big old world, yeah." He kept rubbing her back. "I didn't pick this fight, Frannie. It just came and fell in my lap. And now it turns out that this guy's just the smiling face of evil in this world, and what makes it worse is he cloaks it all in patriotism and loyalty while he deals away lives so he can make another buck. It makes me puke."

"And it's all up to you? It's got to be you, Dismas Hardy?"

"I think I've got the cards," Hardy said. "I can beat him and take him down."

"And what about the people protecting him politically?"

"Well, with any luck, them too. But Allstrong's enough for my purposes. I'm just trying to do the right thing here, Frannie, mostly for my client."

"I'm not sure I believe you, babe. I think you want to save the world."

"But if I did that," Hardy said, "I'd need personal theme music."

[39]

HARDY DIDN'T SLEEP as well as he would have liked. He woke up for the first time at two-sixteen to the sound of squealing tires out on the street below his bedroom. Wide awake, he went downstairs to check that the house was locked up front and back, which it was.

Behind the kitchen, he turned on the light and went to his safe under his workbench, opened it, and brought out his own weapon, a Smith & Wesson M&P .40. He hesitated for a moment, then picked it up and slammed a full magazine into the grip, racked a round into the chamber, and took off the safety. Then, quietly and methodically, he went through the downstairs, checking the kids' rooms, the family room, back up through the dining and living rooms. Nobody there.

Back upstairs in his bedroom, the gun's safety on, he put it in the drawer next to his bed and lay down again.

The sound of a Dumpster slamming shut, or a garbage can being dropped—something loud and clanging—woke him up at four thirty-eight. He grabbed the gun again and made another tour of the house, with the same result.

Up for the day, he realized, he put on a pot of coffee and went out to get the newspaper, but stopped at the front door first and looked down the street in both directions. Only after satisfying himself that it was clear did he go outside and grab the paper.

This was not turning out to be the way he had planned it.

ABOUT FIVE MINUTES before Frannie's alarm was going to go off, he went upstairs again and laid a hand on her shoulder, gently waking her up.

"Is everything all right?" she asked him.

"So far everything's fine. But sometime in the middle of last night, my subconscious must have decided that you were right. I've been awake half the night worrying. I shouldn't have put us in this situation. I'm sorry."

She reached out and took his hand. "Apology accepted. So what do you want to do?"

"I don't think it would be the worst idea in the world to check into a hotel for a couple of days. Treat it like a vacation."

She sat up, letting go of his hand. "Did something else happen last night that I didn't hear about?"

"No. I've just had time to think about these guys some more. Until it's clear to Allstrong that Glitsky and Bracco are really in on this investigation with me, which I hope ought to be by today or tomorrow, it's like Moses said—we're hanging out there all alone in the breeze."

Frannie shuddered. "I think I liked it better when you were pretending there was nothing to worry about."

"Me too. But I don't think that's the smart move right now. I think we'd be wise to lie a little low."

Sitting with the idea for another moment, Frannie finally sighed. "A couple of days?"

"Probably no more than that."

"Probably." She shook her head. "Do you have any idea how much I wish you hadn't called him?"

"Pretty much, yeah. If it's any consolation, I didn't feel like I had much of a choice."

"Right," she said. "That makes me feel much better."

ALLSTRONG WOULD ALSO know that Hardy went in to his office every day, but Hardy had convinced himself that he could minimize his risk on that score by pulling directly into his parking place in the gated and locked parking garage underneath the building and taking the inside elevator up to his office. Once he was inside, he had a reasonable faith in his firm's security system.

As he pulled in about to park, though, he noticed a brown paper lunch bag lying against the wall just in front of his space. For a minute, the sight of the thing froze him. It was just the kind of harmless-looking item, he imagined, that might in actuality be an improvised explosive device. Turning on his lights, he illuminated the bag, which looked to be nothing more than what it was.

Setting the brake, Hardy opened his door and walked over to the bag, touching it gingerly with his foot, then leaning over to pick it up. It weighed almost nothing, and contained only a few napkins, an apple core, and a couple of Baggies.

Forcing a small nonlaugh at his paranoia, Hardy got back in to his car and parked, then crossed to the elevator and pushed the button to call it down.

* * *

IN HIS OFFICE, Hardy went over the final draft of his appeal, which explicitly laid out his argument on the *Brady* violation in such a way as to maximize Allstrong's connection to Nolan and to the Khalils. He attached a declaration from Wyatt Hunt detailing the conversation Hunt had had with Abdel Khalil. Included in the narrative was Tara Wheatley's information about the cash Nolan had brought back from Iraq, buttressing the idea that perhaps he'd been paid to carry out a contract on the Khalils. Of course, the FBI's interrogation of Abdel Khalil, which the agency had not seen fit to share with the prosecution team, was at the crux of his discussion.

In toto, Hardy believed that the appeal raised enough questions about important evidence that had not been admitted in the trial that he thought he'd at least get a hearing out of it. And possibly, if things worked out with Allstrong between now and then, a new trial for Evan.

Satisfied with his work, he sent one of his paralegals down to the court of appeals to file the brief, and then sent registered copies of it, as required, to Mary Patricia Whelan-Miille down in Redwood City, and also—although there was no mandate he do so—overnight to Allstrong Security marked "personal and confidential" for Jack Allstrong. He wanted Allstrong to know what he was doing, when he was doing it, and how it was likely to affect him if he didn't step in and do something to stop it.

Next, calling the prison, Hardy learned that Evan was still in the infirmary and that his condition had stabilized. There was some chance that he would be able to have visitors, perhaps as soon as the next day.

Hardy's cell phone went off—Bracco calling him. "It worked," he said. "I used the old 'Surely you'd want to cooperate in a murder investigation' and he opened up some time for me and I'm on the way down there right now."

"Have fun," Hardy said, "but be careful."

"Right." Bracco barked out a short, nervous laugh. "I'm all over it."

ALLSTRONG AND HIS ATTORNEY, who introduced himself as Ryan Loy, led Bracco back through a maze of hallways into a beautifully designed medium-sized oval conference room containing an apparently custom-made table with twelve matching chairs around it. An enormous spray of fresh flowers claimed the center of the table; at the counter under the tinted windows, someone had set up a full coffee service with pastries and fruit. When Bracco sat down at last with his coffee and Danish, he had a view of the entire South Bay as it shimmered in the sunshine.

Jack Allstrong had played the gracious host in his garrulous style as they moved back through the building, pointing with pride to the headquarters of the other divisions that now made up much of the company's work—computer security, water safety, privatization, logistics consulting, aquaculture. Loy, bookish and reserved in his suit and bow tie, nevertheless came across as another truly nice guy. Everyone they passed in the hallways was wellscrubbed, nicely dressed, young.

Loy closed the door to the conference room behind them and went around the table to Bracco's left while Allstrong sat two chairs over from him on the right. Bracco took out his pocket tape recorder and without comment placed it prominently on the table out in front of everyone.

"Excuse me, Inspector"—Loy had stopped in the middle of raising his cup—"but I understood this was to be an informal discussion and not a formal interrogation."

"Either way," Bracco said with a matter-of-fact tone, "I'm going to need a record of it. I understood that you wanted to cooperate. Mr. Allstrong doesn't have to answer any question he doesn't want to. You both understand that, right?"

Loy looked at Allstrong, who nodded.

Bracco picked up the tape recorder and spoke into it. "This is homicide Inspector Sergeant Darrel Bracco, Badge Number 3117, conjoined case numbers 06-335411 and 07-121598, talking with Jack Allstrong, forty-one, and his attorney, Ryan Loy, thirty-six. It's eleven forty-five on Wednesday morning, May ninth, and we are at the offices of Allstrong Security in San Francisco. Mr. Allstrong, did you know an attorney named Charles Bowen?"

"Yes."

"How well did you know him?"

"Not well at all. I met him two or three times here in these offices to talk about an appeal he was working on."

"Evan Scholler."

"Yes."

"How did you figure in that case, that Mr. Bowen wanted to talk to you?"

"One of my past employees, Ron Nolan, was the victim. Scholler was eventually convicted of killing him."

"Do you know the grounds that Mr. Bowen planned to base his appeal on?"

"No idea."

"But he talked to you two or three times?"

"Yes. Is that a problem?"

Bracco shrugged. "Was he talking to you about the same things each time you talked to him?"

"Yes."

"And what specifically was the subject of those conversations?"

"I think he may have been trying to connect Nolan in some way to another couple who had been murdered a few days before Nolan himself was killed. I have the memory that he was trying to implicate Nolan in those murders somehow, which was ridiculous, and I told him so."

"Do you remember specifically any questions that he asked?"

"No. I couldn't really give him answers to the questions. This was a long time ago, and it didn't seem very important."

"When was the last time you saw him?"

"I don't know. Sometime last summer."

"And when was the last time you spoke to him on the phone?"

"I don't remember."

"Do you know that Mr. Bowen disappeared last summer?"

"Yes, I believe I did hear something about that just recently. Certainly I stopped hearing from him."

"Were you aware that his records indicate that he called you on the morning that he disappeared?"

Loy decided he had heard enough. Holding up a palm, he said, "Just a minute, Jack. What's your point here, Inspector?"

"Mr. Allstrong was apparently contacted by Mr. Bowen on the day he disappeared. I was wondering if he remembers any of the substance of that last phone call."

Allstrong reached out his own hand. "That's all right, Ryan." Then, to Bracco, "I don't remember any last phone call at all. I didn't know until just now that this last phone call was on the day he was supposed to have disappeared. As far as I know, Mr. Bowen might have just called the office on a routine housekeeping matter. I wouldn't know that. In any event, I don't remember talking to him. And while we're on this, Inspector, why didn't anybody ask these questions last summer when they might have been a little fresher in my mind?"

"The Bowen case has been reopened as a possible homicide, and we're going into more detail than when it was a missing person."

Loy sat up straighter, as if prodded. "If Mr. Allstrong is a suspect in a homicide, Inspector, I'm going to advise him to stop talking to you right now."

"Mr. Allstrong can stop speaking to me anytime he wants. And I never said he was a suspect. But he does appear to be someone who might have had contact with Mr. Bowen on the day he disappeared." Bracco talked straight at Allstrong. "But this leads to my next question, about Mr. Bowen's wife. Did you ever meet her or speak to her on the phone?"

"No."

"Are you quite certain?"

"Yes."

"Well, it appears she made a number of phone calls to your number. Do you have any explanation for that?"

"Again," Loy said, "he already told you he doesn't remember speaking to her. Mr. Allstrong gets a hundred calls a day, Inspector. He doesn't have time to speak to most of those people."

"Mr. Loy. Your client indicated he wanted to cooperate

in this investigation. I have a number of questions I want to ask him." Bracco nodded. "He doesn't have to answer any questions, but what I need are his answers and not your suggestions as to what might or might not have happened. So again, Mr. Allstrong, do you have any explanation for phone calls that Mrs. Bowen made to your phone?"

"Well, of course, Mr. Loy is right. I get lots of phone calls."

"I can appreciate that. But the last call Hanna Bowen made in her life was to here. And it was the day before her death. I think you can understand why we are curious about two people who call Allstrong Security, one of whom disappears and the other dies immediately after the contact. It does appear an unlikely coincidence." It also wasn't true, but Loy and Allstrong didn't have to know that. Hardy's plan was simply to have Bracco show up and make it clear that the cops, too, were now part of the picture.

"Well, okay," Loy said. "You've asked your questions. Mr. Allstrong has told you what he knows. If you don't have anything further, I think it's time to end the interview."

But Bracco ignored Loy again. "Mr. Allstrong," he said, "if you didn't receive these calls, to whom in your company might Mrs. Bowen have spoken?"

Allstrong shrugged. "I could ask Marilou, our receptionist. She's the first line of defense. If Mrs. Bowen was hysterical or nonspecific about what she wanted or who she wanted to talk to, her calls would have stopped at the front desk. But as Ryan here says, we can always ask and make sure."

Bracco finally reached for his coffee and took a sip. It had gone tepid and he made a face.

"Is something wrong, Inspector?" Allstrong asked.

Bracco reached over and turned off his tape recorder. He decided he'd give the shit one last stir. "This doesn't seem to be going anywhere, gentlemen. I came here under the impression that you'd like to cooperate in these homicide investigations, but I'm not picking up much of a spirit of cooperation. In fact, frankly, you both seem pretty darn defensive for people who've got nothing to hide."

"That's ridiculous," Loy said. "We've answered every question you've asked. The plain fact is that Mr. Allstrong doesn't know anything about the Bowens other than what he's told you. He runs a huge corporation with branches all over the world. He doesn't have time to get involved in these small parochial matters. Look, Inspector, we're sorry Mr. Bowen disappeared, and about whatever happened to his wife. But to imply that there's any real connection between Allstrong Security and these events is just an absurd flight of fancy."

"Amen to that," Allstrong intoned.

"Well, then"—Bracco pushed his chair back—"thank you for your time."

AT THREE-FIFTEEN, Glitsky was standing in front of a video monitor in the tiny electronics room between the two similarly minuscule interrogation rooms that fed off a narrow hallway that, in turn, was separated from the homicide detail by a glass wall. "I give up," he said to Debra Schiff, "what is it?"

"That, sir, is the top of your head."

Glitsky looked again. He wore his graying hair short and close to his skull. Leaning over, he squinted into the seven-inch monitor. "Could be," he said. "I couldn't prove it isn't."

"You see any identifiable part of your face?"

"No." He turned to her. "This is all the camera got in there?"

"Yes, sir."

"Lord." Glitsky walked out of the electronics room, took one step to his left, and reentered the interrogation room he'd left a minute before.

The room was four feet by five feet, so it was really more like a closet. It had no windows. Suspects in homicide investigations were often brought in for questioning and placed in these rooms, where they could be left alone and theoretically observed as they fidgeted or talked to themselves or otherwise did things that might be both incriminating and admissible in court. The problem was that the camera that was supposed to record all of this activity was cleverly hidden within the ceiling and the room was so small that the only image captured on tape, ever, was the top of the head of the suspect. As Schiff had just demonstrated to Glitsky.

"It's hopeless," Schiff told him. "We can't do business like this. We need a new room."

"I thought this *was* the new room." Glitsky was right. The entire homicide department had transferred to the fifth floor from the fourth only a little over a year before. Newly designed and supposedly state of the art. "But you're right, it's a little small too. Who approved the plans for this thing?"

"Well, nobody, which is kind of the problem. There's a

couple of guys in robbery who moonlight doing construction here in the building."

"We didn't bid this out?"

Schiff laughed. "Are you kidding me? We have employees that do the maintenance in the building. We try to bid this out, the union's going to have a fit. We'd be taking their jobs."

"Well, then, why didn't we have the people in maintenance do it?"

"Because they said there's a three-year backlog on maintenance, and they'd need to charge us seventy-five thousand dollars from our budget. So we got the two guys from robbery to do it."

"Perfect," Glitsky said. "So where do you propose we put it, this new room?"

"I don't know, Abe. Anyplace else. Maybe out where the lockers are. Or take part of the computer room, which is way too big anyway. But this thing is just crazy."

"I agree with you." He tried a small joke. "I'll try to bring it up to somebody in facilities."

Schiff didn't laugh. "Sooner would be better, Abe."

"I hear you, Debra, I'll see what I can do. Really." But even as he was finishing up with this unwelcome bit of housekeeping, Glitsky saw that one of the clerks from reception was hustling his way. "Yo, Jerry," he said. "What up?"

"I've got Bureau Chief Bill Schuyler with the FBI holding for you, sir. He says it's important."

THE DOORBELL RANG in Hardy's hotel room. They'd gotten a small suite at the Rex, not far from Hardy's office, and Hardy had checked in at a little before five o'clock.

He crossed to the door and, taking no chances, looked through the peephole. Glitsky frowned at nothing in the dusky light. When Hardy opened the door, the lieutenant focused the dark look on him. "When Phyllis told me you were here, I thought maybe she was kidding me."

"Yeah, she's a great kidder, that Phyllis."

Glitsky threw a quick look around. "Obviously, you think this is necessary."

"Precautionary, that's all."

Glitsky nodded, his expression set and hard. "In any event, we've got to talk."

"And, lo, as if by magic, here we are talking right now."

Abe tightened his lips enough that his scar stood out in relief. "Would you like to know the result of your ill-advised encouragement to Darrel Bracco that he go down and have a chat with the Allstrong people?"

Hardy's face grew sober. "Is he all right?"

"Physically, he's fine." Glitsky pushed on the door and Hardy stepped back to let him in, then followed him into the sitting room. Grabbing the chair behind the desk, Glitsky spun it around and straddled it. "But he's slightly ticked off at you. As am I, I might add."

"And why is that?" Hardy sat down on the love seat.

"Because he was starting to get a feeling about this Bowen case, or cases. That he could crack them if he just had some time. And now that's not going to happen, ever."

"Why not?"

"Because I got a call this afternoon from Bill Schuyler. You remember Bill Schuyler? He's the FBI bureau chief who couldn't find the agents who'd testified in the Scholler trial."

Hardy's eyes lit up, although he tried to keep any sign of enthusiasm out of his face. "Tell me the FBI's taken over the cases."

"Lock, stock, and barrel."

"Citing national security issues?"

"Citing they're gonna do it and we can't stop them. I think the actual line was 'I don't got to show you no stinkin' badges.' But even Schuyler went so far as to say that he didn't really like it, but the order came from high up and there was nothing he could do about it. You know what a huge concession that was from him?"

"I can imagine."

"I bet you can. So you know how me and Darrel have spent the last three hours? Packing up all our files on both of the Bowens and delivering them over to the Federal Building. These are two now very probable homicides in my jurisdiction, Diz, and now I'm off them for no reason that I can understand."

"Which accounts for your less-than-stellar mood, not that you normally need anything specific. But that was faster than I would have thought." He held out a hand. "I'm not talking about the three hours. I'm talking about Allstrong getting someone to pull the FBI's strings. He's got to be seriously highly connected, which is what we figured, anyway."

"So you knew this was coming?"

Hardy nodded. "I hoped something like this would happen. This soon is a surprise, but that's not a bad thing either."

Glitsky's face remained hard. "Well, I'm glad you're so happy about it. Darrel and I are feeling just a little bit used and abused."

But Hardy shook his head. "I told Bracco last night,

and I'll tell you now, you weren't going to get Allstrong on either of the Bowens. Never. Those cases are old, Abe, what evidence there might have once been is gone. And since these guys are stone pros, I'm guessing there wasn't much in the line of evidence anyway to begin with. So this FBI takeover, it's actually very good news."

"Yeah, I'm trying to keep my celebration pretty low-key. But just for the record, what's good about it?"

Hardy sat up straight. "All of a sudden the whole situation, which from Allstrong's perspective was under control and stagnant, is fluid again. It's a live issue. He's going to have to react and keep reacting if he wants to keep it where he can control it, which means he's going to have to deal with me."

"Like he dealt with Bowen?"

Hardy shook his head. "Not if I can help it, Abe, not this time. He's tried that approach and now it's come back to bite him. He's going to see that."

"I hope you're right, but even so, if the FBI is protecting him from prosecution, what difference can anything you do matter to him? Best case, you're a nuisance. He's never going down for murder if the Feebs won't let anybody build a case."

"Ah, but that's just it, you see? I don't want him for murder. I want his help to try to get my client out of prison. Then I'll just go away."

Glitsky's brow came down and hooded his eyes. "I hope I'm not hearing that all this has been about all this time is getting your *damn* client off."

Hardy's head snapped at Glitsky's rare use of a swear word. If he'd come to that, he was far angrier than Hardy had perceived. "Abe," he said quietly, "listen to me. Like it or not, my client's the only leverage we've all got. The

Bowen murders pose no threat, they're ancient history. The attempt on Evan at Corcoran, same thing. That assailant's dead and it's never going to be anything more than a prison beef anyway. So what's the only other crime we know about that he's done here on U.S. soil? Putting out the hit on the Khalils, right? Which means Ron Nolan. And who's the only guy interested in connecting him to Nolan? Me. He's going to have to come to me."

"And then what?"

Hardy leaned forward in his chair. "Then I play him."

[40]

EVAN CAME TO THE VISITING ROOM in a wheelchair. He was going to recover completely, he told Hardy, although he joked that he never wanted to hear those particular words again. Still, it was a good sign that he could make a joke about anything. The attack, he told Hardy, had been completely unexpected and, except for his rib, professionally executed as he walked into what he thought was the empty bathroom. As far as he remembered, there were no witnesses.

Hardy brought him a copy of the brief to look over, and they discussed some of the finer legal points that he didn't understand at first, but in the end he seemed satisfied that this was an approach that possibly had legs. Hardy also brought him up-to-date on the developments in the Bowen cases, the FBI takeover, and they talked about who the mysterious higher-up might be.

"We may never know," Hardy said. "Somebody who believes that it's more important for guys like Allstrong to build companies that grow and prosper than worry about if they exactly adhere to the letter of the law. So they need to kill a few people? Look at all the jobs they're providing, the infrastructure. Totally worth the price, right? Damn straight."

"I love the national security angle. Like if Allstrong goes under, what happens exactly?"

"At the very least, it hurts the war effort, all the good work Allstrong's doing over there. That's always a good one they pull out." Hardy had his grin on. "But I'm also guessing that the big guy, whoever he is, loses a decent portion of his discretionary cash income."

Evan drew a pained breath. "I don't like to think that's really happening." He looked around at the prison walls. "But then again, I don't like to think that any of this is really happening either."

THE CALL CAME in at a little after one o'clock, just after Hardy arrived back at his office.

"Mr. Hardy. Jack Allstrong." He had his hearty good-guy voice back on. "This morning I received a copy of the appeal that you're filing in this Evan Scholler case. Mr. Loy says we can probably expect an application for a writ of habeas corpus to follow. He admires your work, Mr. Hardy, and advises me that there is a fair chance the court will at least order a hearing into your issue. I think we might have gotten off on the wrong foot in our last conversation, and I wondered if you might be free to come down to my headquarters office this afternoon."

Hardy didn't think it would hurt to play a little hard to get. "If you don't know anything about Mr. Nolan's connection to the Khalils, and last time you made it pretty clear that you didn't, I'm not sure we have much to talk about."

"Well, you seem fairly certain that Scholler didn't kill Ron Nolan, and if that's the case, there might be something we can do to help. I think it might be worthwhile to discuss it."

Hardy let him hang for a few more seconds. "I could give you a couple of hours this afternoon, but I really think this meeting should take place in my office."

HARDY SAT at his desk with his legal pad in front of him. He'd already written a few notes to remind him of things he needed to cover in his upcoming conversation. Feeling mostly embarrassed at himself for believing that he might actually have the need for it, he'd placed his gun in the top desk drawer on his left, in easy reach if in fact it came to that.

As Phyllis let Allstrong into the room, he pretended to be writing. Looking up—"Excuse me, a few more seconds"—he motioned to the straight-backed Queen Anne chair that he'd placed in front of his desk, indicating that Allstrong take it. While he did, placing his briefcase down next to the chair, Phyllis closed the door on her way out. Scrawling some more lines, Hardy finally put down his pen and pushed the pad to one side.

"It appears," Hardy said, "you've got a guardian angel someplace in Washington who's taken care of making the police investigation into the Bowens go away. But as long as Evan Scholler is alive and in prison, either me or someone like me is going to be digging into the connection between Allstrong, Ron Nolan, and the Khalils. Whoever tried to have Evan killed has missed his chance and, with him held in protective custody from now on, isn't likely to get another one. And as you've recently found out, appellate lawyers are interchangeable. And, trust me, Mr. Allstrong, anyone who reads my file and my notes, of which there are several copies, will start this inquiry right where I left off. Does that about sum up the situation?"

Allstrong, wearing alligator cowboy boots with his light green gabardine suit, sat back and crossed a leg, his facial features relaxed, nearly friendly. "It adequately elucidates your understanding, certainly," he said. "Although, as I said in our conversation the other day, any assumption you're making that I've committed any kind of crime at all is false. I'm sure that federal investigators will find no evidence implicating me or Allstrong Security in what's happened to either of the Bowens."

"I'm sure they won't," Hardy said.

"And likewise they'll find no evidence that I ordered Ron Nolan to kill anybody. That's not the way I do business." His pro forma pitch completed, he flashed a quick salesman's smile.

"Since you've arranged to have Stevie Wonder and Ray Charles assigned to the investigation," Hardy said, "I'd be surprised if they could find Allstrong in the phone book. But that's not the point. What I'm going to uncover is the evidence the FBI already gathered that connects Nolan and your company to whatever it was that happened in Iraq that got the Khalils murdered. And if, in getting to Nolan, your company gets mixed up in a very public scandal, that's just an added bonus."

Allstrong sat impassively. "What makes you think the FBI has evidence tying Allstrong to these killings?"

"The agents told the Khalil family. What the agents found, I can find."

"I understood that the agents further told them that the contract had come from Kuvan Krekar. Isn't that so?" Allstrong asked.

Hardy nodded. "That's my understanding too."

"Well, then?"

"Well, then, what?"

"Well, then, it's obvious where the contract originated, isn't it? With Kuvan, not with me, and not with Allstrong."

"That would be obvious except for one thing. Or rather, except for two people. The Bowens. The whole thing with Nolan and Kuvan and the Khalils was a closed circle until Charlie Bowen pried it open again. If the Bowens were still alive, I might have believed that killing the Khalils was Kuvan's idea and Kuvan's contract. But Kuvan was already dead when Charlie Bowen started sniffing around, and that kind of neatly eliminated the possibility that Kuvan was Bowen's killer. But somebody still needed Charlie dead because he was going to find out and expose who'd really put out the contract on the Khalils. And you know who that was, Jack. You know because that was you."

Allstrong let his shoulders sag for a moment. "Back to that," he said.

"I'm afraid so." Hardy met his adversary's eyes, unyielding.

Allstrong shrugged, nodded, leaned down, picked up his briefcase, brought it up to his lap, and snapped it open. "Regrettably," he said, "this has become a very inconvenient situation."

And for an irrational moment, Hardy thought he'd miscalculated and in another half second he would be dead. Before he could even react to reach for his own gun, which he'd so stupidly, stupidly placed in the closed top drawer, Allstrong's silenced bullet would explode with no warning at all through the expensive briefcase and blow Hardy into oblivion. That would put an end to Hardy's threat right here, right now.

Hardy's left hand went to his drawer, started to pull it out.

He wasn't going to have enough time.

It was over. His life was over.

But in the moment Allstrong would have taken his shot if he could, instead of firing a weapon he'd perhaps concealed in his briefcase, he simply continued talking. "I have to admire your tenacity and industry. In fact, I'd like to offer you a retainer to take on some of my legal work. Mr. Loy is a fine corporate attorney but lacks the killer instinct sometimes required in my business. Like all our senior employees, you will be paid in cash."

Allstrong turned the briefcase around, showing Hardy the neatly stacked packages of one-hundred-dollar bills. And no sign of a gun.

Hardy quietly exhaled and brought his shaking hands together, clasped now white-knuckled on his desktop.

And Allstrong continued. "This is two hundred thousand dollars, Mr. Hardy. I'd like to offer it to you against billings for the first year. If you prefer, I could arrange to have this deposited in an offshore account, a Swiss bank account, or any other place that you choose. You would in fact be retained by one of our Iraqi subsidiaries, who do not file tax returns in the United States. So whether you choose to report this to the IRS as income is completely up to you."

"I wonder how many of those are my tax dollars," Hardy said.

"Don't be naïve," Allstrong countered. "And don't trifle with me." The bribe offer having already, albeit tacitly, admitted his complicity in everything that Hardy had accused him of, he went on. "I'd strongly advise you to consider what I'm offering. As you yourself have noticed, other alternatives, though perhaps risky and more costly, are still available to me."

Hardy clucked and cracked a grin. "I really thought we'd moved beyond that, Jack."

Allstrong slowly and carefully closed up the briefcase, setting it down again beside him. Sitting back, he eyed Hardy for a long moment. "So, Mr. Hardy, do we have an understanding?"

"Oh, we understand each other, Jack. But, no, we don't have a deal. I thought I'd made it clear. I want Evan Scholler out of prison. I don't care how it happens, but that's my price."

"What if the FBI suddenly found evidence that did implicate Nolan in the Khalils' deaths? What if there were surveillance reports linking some members of the Khalil family to terrorist organizations? And wiretaps where they discussed killing Ron Nolan? Do you think that would do the job, Mr. Hardy?"

"I think it might. So what you have to do, Jack, is get me that evidence."

"And then what?"

"And then I lose interest in you."

But Allstrong still wasn't quite ready to give it up. "And what if the evidence just doesn't exist?"

Hardy inclined his head. "Ah, but we know it does. Remember? The FBI found it before they talked to the Khalil children. You saw it when you decided to sell out Kuvan."

A lengthy silence settled.

At last, Allstrong nodded once. "He should have never used the grenades," he said quietly, as though explaining a complicated process to a child. "That was his own decision and just tactically stupid. But he didn't care. He'd become a liability. He loved to blow things up. He thought it was fun. The fool thought he was invincible."

"YOU WANT my opinion," Hardy said, popping a peanut into his mouth in Glitsky's office, "he did Nolan too. Not personally. Allstrong himself was still over in Iraq back then. But one of his guys took out Nolan. Just another job."

"Why?" Glitsky asked.

"Allstrong said it himself. Nolan had become a liability. He used the frag grenades that could be traced back to Allstrong."

Bracco, sulking, stood against the wall, arms crossed over his chest. "You're not telling me he's giving you something that can be traced back to him? I'm talking about the frags."

"No. He won't do that. They might get back to the company, but old Jack will be able to say that Nolan stole them or something, that he was acting on his own when he killed the Khalils. It was a freelance gig."

"It doesn't matter anyway." Glitsky sat all the way back, exuding frustration. "He's got protection, remember? He might as well have immunity. I'm still having a hard time getting my arms around the fact that the Feebs are part of this. Schuyler wouldn't go along with any of this on his own."

"I wouldn't take it personally, Abe," Hardy said. "And it's not on his own. He's being told it's national security, too, and he believes his bosses. There's a greater good involved. So everybody winds up being good guys."

"Peachy," Glitsky replied.

"So what about the Bowens?" Bracco asked. "What about those murders? Collateral damage and we leave it at that? Does that seem right to either of you guys?"

Hardy turned to him. "You were never going to make the case anyway, Darrel. Never, ever, in a million years. Ask Abe if he agrees."

For an answer, Glitsky shrugged.

Hardy held up a hand. "I'm not saying I'm happy with that, but it's reality."

"It sucks," Bracco said. "What am I supposed to tell Jenna the next time she calls? That fat cats like Allstrong walk? Sorry, but that's reality. Your parents don't count." He slammed his hand hard against a metal locker. "This just pisses me off." And he walked out the door.

"It's not over yet," Hardy called after him.

In the ensuing silence, Glitsky growled. "It's not over. What's that supposed to mean?"

"I mean I'm going to be getting this evidence in the next few weeks. And the great thing about evidence is that it speaks for itself."

Glitsky glared at him. "Oh, yeah, your *client*. Good for him. Good for you too."

"Not just us," Hardy said.

"No?" Glitsky asked again. "Then who else?" Sitting up, he shook his head in disgust. "Get the door on your way out, would you? I've got real work I got to do."

[41]

HARDY WAS IN HIS OFFICE opening his mail, having just finished reviewing the documents that he had received over the past three weeks via registered mail from the local FBI office in San Francisco. The FBI had done its usual efficient and thorough job and, from fragments found at the Khalil home, had matched the grenades used in that attack to a cache of them at the Allstrong warehouse at BIAP. Beyond that, they had recovered a bullet from the Khalil scene and matched it to the gun that had been in Nolan's duffel bag with the grenades. Downloads from Nolan's hard drive revealed not just the photos of the Khalil house from various angles, but also photos of the eventual victims that looked as though they'd been scanned in. Nolan's bank records memorialized regular biweekly automatic deposits of ten thousand dollars and another deposit, four days before the Khalils were killed, of twenty-five thousand. There was a handwritten quarter page in Nolan's handwriting, noting the victims' names and address, some indecipherable scribbling and doodling, and the notation "$50,000" circled several times.

The evidence tying the Khalils to a plot to kill Nolan was equally impressive. The wiretaps arrived, accompanied by neat binders of translations from the Arabic. There were informant reports, with names blacked out due to national security, but which clearly identified some of the Khalils as involved in a plot to murder Nolan in retaliation for the Menlo Park killings.

Hardy had to admire Jack Allstrong's own thoroughness, as well as his caution. All of this evidence would be valuable to Hardy when the hearing came up for Scholler's appeal. And none of it directly implicated either Allstrong himself or his company.

Of course, during the same time period, Hardy had been reading in the local press about the agents involved in the FBI's handling of the Scholler case. The debate raged in the media about whether the agents had been merely grotesquely incompetent or criminally derelict in suppressing such critical evidence in the trial of a bona fide war hero. Agents were being transferred, suspended, and demoted.

Glitsky, following it daily with Hardy, could barely suppress his own glee. Hardy had tried to point out that it was unlikely that anyone truly culpable in the affair was ever really going to be punished, but Glitsky exulted in the random carnage the agency was inflicting on itself.

Now Hardy reached for an 8½ × 11 envelope. It had arrived addressed to him, personal and confidential, by regular mail with no return address, but postmarked in San Francisco. Reaching in, he pulled out two sheets of faxed copies of e-mail correspondence between *Rnolan@ sbcglobal.net* and *JAA@Allstrong.com*. Dated the day after the Khalil murders, it acknowledged that Nolan had accomplished his most recent assignment and requested payment of the remainder of his fee into a certain bank account. Allstrong should advise Mr. Krekar that "the situation has been resolved, as promised; Krekar should expect to move on the Anbar contracts without competition."

Although there was nothing remotely humorous about any of this, a ghost of a smile tickled the side of Hardy's mouth. Maybe he ought to tell Glitsky that Bill Schuyler wasn't the gullible, gutless G-man he needed to pretend to be if he wanted to keep his job. On the other hand, Hardy had no proof that Schuyler had had anything to do with this latest evidence. Any mention of his name would probably just get the man in more trouble. And, in fact, the evidence could have come from any other FBI agent between San Francisco and Baghdad who had a sense of what was happening and a disgust at the role that the Bureau had been forced to play in it.

Hardy realized that without a witness or some other way to authenticate the documents, what he had in his hand were just two pieces of paper, worthless in a court of law. He sat at his desk pulling the tight skin at his jawline as for the hundredth, the thousandth time he considered the ramifications of his intentions.

He had made no promises to Allstrong. To the contrary, he'd made it abundantly clear that whatever information he received would be his to do with as he pleased. Additionally, this wasn't information he'd gotten from Allstrong anyway. He owed Allstrong nothing. As Allstrong himself had said, it was an inconvenient situation.

He got up and, without a word to anyone, walked across his office and out to the copy room, where he copied the two pages. Coming back to his desk, he put the copy in his file and began searching through his notes for the address of Abdel Khalil.

*   *   *

HARDY AND FRANNIE were trimming the roses that bounded the fence in their backyard on a cool Sunday afternoon in the second week of June, talking about the arrival of their children, who'd both be returning home from their respective schools in the next couple of days. "I think they should both work," Hardy said. "I worked every summer of my life."

"Of course you did," Frannie said. "I can see you now, four-year-old Dismas out plowing the fields. To say nothing of walking ten miles to school every day, in deep snow."

"Leave out the snow part," he said. "This was San Francisco, remember."

"Yeah, but back when you were a baby, wasn't the climate different here?" Frannie enjoying the little joke at the expense of the eleven-year difference in their ages.

"You're a very funny person." He reached over and clipped a newly budded rose just at its base.

"Hey!" She turned on him.

"It's my old eyes," he said, backing away. "I was aiming for lower down on the stem."

"Yeah, well, keep it up and I'll aim for lower down too." She took a quick and playful swipe at him with her cutting tool.

Hardy backed up another step, then cocked his head, looking over her shoulder. "Well, look what the cat dragged in."

Glitsky was just emerging into the yard from the narrow walkway between their house and the neighbor's. He was in civilian clothes, hands in the pockets of his battered leather jacket. Getting up to them, he gave Frannie half a hug and accepted her kiss on the cheek, then turned to her husband. "You should leave your phone on."

"I know. It's bad of me," Hardy said. "But it's Sunday, I figured whatever it is can wait. But maybe not."

"Maybe not, after all. You know anything about this?"

"About what?"

"Jack Allstrong."

Hardy felt his stomach go hollow. He caught his breath, cleared his throat, tried to swallow. "No. What about him?"

"He got in his car this morning down in Hillsborough and turned it on and it blew up him and half his house. It's all over the news."

"I don't watch TV on Sunday either."

Glitsky just stood there.

Frannie touched Glitsky's arm. "Abe? What's wrong?"

"I don't know, Fran. I don't know if anything's wrong. I was thinking Diz might be able to tell me." He kept his eyes on Hardy.

Who drew another breath, then another, then blew out heavily and went down to one knee.

EPILOGUE
[2008]

On a warm late-summer day about fifteen months after Jack Allstrong's death, an excellent jazz quartet was doing arrangements of big band material in her backyard as Eileen Scholler came out of her house. She wended her way under the balloons and through the large crowd of well-wishers, touching an arm here, a back there, smiling and exchanging pleasantries and congratulations with her guests. At last she came to the table under one of the laden lemon trees where Dismas and Frannie Hardy sat drinking white wine with Everett Washburn.

"Ah, here you are, way in the back. Do you mind if an old lady pulls up a chair?"

"I don't see any old ladies," Washburn said, "but glowing mothers of war heroes are always welcome."

Hardy pulled out the chair and as she sat, her eyes started to tear up at Washburn's words. She smiled around the table. "War hero. I never thought I'd hear anybody say that about Evan again. And now..." She indicated the overflow crowd and turned to Hardy. "How am I ever going to repay you?" she asked.

"Believe me, Eileen," he said, "the result was plenty payment enough." After the court of appeals had ordered a new trial for Evan, the San Mateo County district attorney declined to prosecute further. The FBI, it seems, was reluctant to cooperate, citing national security and the need to keep its own internal investigation confidential. Over the impassioned objection of Mary Patricia Whelan-Miille, the DA had been only too happy to use that as a reason to dismiss the charges. "Seeing Evan walking around a free man. Look at him over there, laughin' and scratchin'."

They all looked to where Evan stood with his arm around Tara in a knot of people composed of his father, several other guys and women about his own age, Tony Onofrio, and even Stan Paganini.

"I still feel like it's a dream," Eileen said. "Like I'm going to wake up and he's going to be in prison again."

Frannie reached over and put a hand over hers. "That's not going to happen. What's going to happen is he and Tara are going to get married next month and I wouldn't be at all surprised if you become a grandmother in pretty short order after that."

Eileen squeezed Frannie's hand, looked briefly skyward, then came back to her. "Your mouth to God's ear," she said, "but I almost can't bring myself to hope after all this time."

"You'll get used to it," Hardy said.

"No." Eileen smiled across at him. "You don't understand. I never want to get used to it. I want to just be glad he's back in our lives every day and never forget how today feels and how lucky we are. We really never believed we'd see this, and now that it's here, it's just . . . well, it's just a miracle. We're living in a miracle and we can't forget that and I'm just so grateful."

Suddenly she stood up, walked around behind Washburn, leaned over and hugged Hardy for a long moment, then gave him a kiss on the cheek and straightened up. "Thank you," she said. "Now I think I'm going to go hug my son again."

"That's a great idea," Hardy said. "Hug him for me too."

When she'd gone off, Washburn sipped his wine. "I must confess to both of you that I feel a little awkward being here. She should have been able to have this party four years ago."

Hardy shook his head. "The government cheated, Everett. They cheated him out of a fair trial. I wouldn't beat myself up over it."

Frannie leaned over. "Yes, he would," she said. "But that doesn't change the fact that you shouldn't."

"Well, in any event," Washburn said, "justice delayed is justice denied and all of that, but today I've got to go with it's better late than never." He glanced back over in Evan's direction. "The boy's paid some pretty mean dues, I'll give him that. Whatever's up next, I've got to believe he's going to be able to handle it."

"Odds are good," Hardy said. "The odds are pretty damn good."

EVAN KNEW that he was dealing with an expert in hand-to-hand combat and couldn't afford to hesitate. As soon as Nolan started to open the door, he lowered his shoulder and rammed as hard as he could. The impact knocked Nolan backward, the back of his leg caught the edge of the coffee table, and he went over and down backward. Evan was on him, a knee into his chest, almost before he hit the floor, and he followed with two or three near-instantaneous metal-knuckled fists to the jaw.

But all the alcohol he had on board wasn't to his advantage. Nolan came up with a vicious karate chop to Evan's neck that pitched him off to the side and onto his back, by the fireplace, while at the same time it cut off his ability to breathe.

Nolan twisted and leapt across the distance separating them, maybe five feet. Evan swung wildly in a huge roundhouse that Nolan blocked with his arm, but scored with a knee to the groin that allowed him to go inside, then jab twice at Nolan's head with the knuckles, glancing blows that nevertheless moved Nolan back. But not for long. Nolan got to his knees and actually produced a vacant smile of determination. "You are so fucking dead," he said.

Scrambling to his own feet, still gasping for breath, Evan grabbed the poker by the fireplace and held it to the side for an instant and then stepped forward and slashed with it. Nolan jumped back out of the way and, as the poker got past him, twisted half around and delivered a kick to Evan's stomach that knocked more air out of him, though it left Nolan exposed to the backhand slash of the poker.

But between the loss of breath and his drunken state, Evan's reflexes weren't responding as they usually did. Nolan got his hands on the poker as it came at him and brought it over his own shoulder and he turned and leveraged himself into Evan's torso, pulling him over his back, slamming him down, judo-style, half against the coffee table and half onto the floor. Evan felt as though he'd broken his back, but if he simply lay there and let Nolan come at him, he knew that he would have no chance and that his enemy would kill him here and now. So in desperation he kicked out again, this time hitting Nolan hard in the knee, spinning him half around and down against the brick of the fireplace, clattering in the tools still left against the hearth.

When Evan tried to move to get up again, though, his body

wouldn't obey the frantic commands of his brain. Pushing against his own inertia, he rolled himself over and over again, hoping to use the coffee table as a shield as Nolan picked himself up, slowly now, as though sensing his advantage.

Still struggling for breath, the images of Nolan straightening up doubling and blurring before his eyes, Evan forced himself to a knee, hoping to get his hands on something he could use for a weapon. The only chance was the poker, on the floor midway between them. With an animal growl, lunging, he got his hands on it just as Nolan's one foot came down, pinning his hands to the floor, while the other foot cocked and exploded at Evan's left ear, knocking him headfirst against the wall, from where, now unconscious, he crumpled to the ground.

THERE WAS NO TIME. He woke up again and, with his swollen tongue, tasted blood in his mouth, felt its crusted residue on his dry and cracked lips. Through the room's door, although the room itself was dark, he could see Nolan fumbling in the closet, where Evan knew he kept the gun.

The pain in his head had now spread to his back, his neck, his legs. He could not move a muscle. The slightest effort— opening his eyes the smallest crack, a quarter-inch twist of his head, a twitch in his knee—and the world, for his sanity and protection, went black.

THE FOOTSTEPS came closer, almost shuffling with a slow deliberation.

Even in the darkness, Evan felt a shadow fall over him. Nolan had the gun in his hand.

Then the whispered words. "You stupid son of a bitch."

Evan did not move or respond in any way. Did not feel that he could.

Nolan stood over him. Whatever damage Nolan had done to him, and Evan realized that possibly it was severe enough to be life-threatening, the fight had not been without its own consequences for the commando. From the way Nolan was moving, he was clearly hurt, physically compromised. With one arm so badly injured, it took him a couple of tries to rack a round into the chamber.

Evan had no option but to attack again, and he twisted and kicked, hitting Nolan below his knees, knocking him down. Evan scrambled, grabbing for Nolan's gun hand with both of his. Getting ahold of it. With his one free hand, Nolan swung in tight again and again, hard jabs to the side of Evan's head.

But even to protect his head, Evan didn't dare release his grip on Nolan's gun hand. To let go of the gun was to die.

Grabbing the barrel with all of his strength, grunting with the exertion, he finally lifted enough to get the gun and the hand that held it off the ground. And then he twisted it, and twisted again.

And at last the gun was free and in his hand, the barrel now tight against Nolan's forehead.

It was over.

Nolan went limp, the fight suddenly all out of him. He held his arms out against the floor in an I-give-up gesture. For a full second that felt like a minute, neither man moved.

And then in a lightning strike, Nolan screamed and threw a last jab in the direction of Evan's head.

And the gun went off.

ACKNOWLEDGMENTS

In preparation for this book, I spoke to many veterans of the fighting in Iraq and read a lot of books about that country and the war that, as this book goes to press, is still claiming American and Iraqi lives every day. I'd particularly like to acknowledge and thank Mike Dufresne for his early insights into the role of the National Guard in Iraq; Don Currier for his general overview of the war and his terrific photographs; T. Christian Miller, author of *Blood Money: Wasted Billions, Lost Lives, and Corporate Greed in Iraq;* Aaron Moore, First Sergeant, U.S. Marine Corps; Craig Denton; and Rick Tippens.

Other books that contributed in one way or another to *Betrayal* include *Blood Stripes: The Grunt's View of the War in Iraq,* by David J. Danelo; *Ambush Alley: The Most Extraordinary Battle of the Iraq War,* by Tim Pritchard; and *Licensed to Kill: Hired Guns in the War on Terror,* by Robert Young Pelton. In spite of all of this research, it is of course possible that there may be inaccuracies and/or errors of one kind or another in this book, and any of these are the fault of the author.

As with all of my other Dismas Hardy books, I owe a huge debt of gratitude to my great pal Al Giannini, an assistant district attorney in San Mateo County. Al is brilliant, tireless, and endlessly enthusiastic, and he contributed mightily to every part of this book from its inception to its final draft. His knowledge both of the law and of human nature is second to no one's, and whatever verisimilitude this work contains, particularly in the legal realm, is because of Al's keen eye and sagacious judgment.

At Dutton, I am blessed with a wonderful sales, marketing, publicity, and editorial staff. My deepest thanks for their commitment, enthusiasm, taste, and intelligence goes out to my publisher, Brian Tart; my new and excellent editor, Ben Sevier; Lisa Johnson, Trena Keating, Beth Parker, Erika Imranyi, Kara Welsh, Claire Zion, Rick Pascocello, Susan Schwartz, and Rich Hasselberger for another superb book jacket design. Though he has moved on to another publishing house, I would also like to tip my hat one last time to Mitch Hoffman, who was my editor at Dutton for many years, and who was instrumental in getting this book off the ground.

My assistant, Anita Boone, continues to perform her yeoman's work on a daily basis, creating a sense of calm and efficiency in my writing environment that makes it all possible. She is a great person, and I'm blessed to have her with me. Peter S. Dietrich, M.D., M.P.H., contributes not only his medical expertise, but his knowledge of clear libations. Karen Hlavacek and Peggy Nauts are both world-class proofreaders. I'm also lucky to have several other friends to keep books and other things in perspective in my day-to-day life. These include the very talented writer Max Byrd, my perennial best man Don Matheson, Frank Seidl, and Bob Zaro. Also, I must acknowledge my two great children, Justine and Jack, both of whom continue to inspire and inform these novels in many ways.

Several characters in this book owe their names (although no physical or personality traits, which are all fictional) to individuals whose contributions to various charities have been especially generous. These people, and their charities, include Ryan Loy, the Borders Group Foundation; Marcia Riggio, the Santa Clara Valley Chapter of Brandeis University National Women's Committee (Science for Life Campaign); Felice Brinkley, the First Amendment Project; Mary Patricia Whelan-Miille, Yolo County Court Appointed Special Advocates (CASA); and Arlene and David Ray (for the respective character Stephan Ray), Stop Cancer.

My agent, Barney Karpfinger, embraced the idea for this book at the very earliest stage and guided me through many moments of its inception and structure. I consider him a great friend and true collaborator in my work and my career, which would be significantly diminished without him.

I very much love hearing from my readers, and invite all of you please to visit me with any comments, questions, or interests on my Web site, www.johnlescroart .com.

Read on for a preview of
John Lescroart's riveting new novel

A PLAGUE OF SECRETS

Coming soon in hardcover from Dutton.

FRIDAY, THE END of the workweek.

On the small deck outside his back door, a lawyer named Dismas Hardy sat with his feet up on the deck's railing and savored a rare moment as the sun spent the last hour of its day lowering itself toward the horizon behind his home.

The house cast its ever-lengthening shadow out over the neighborhood to the east—San Francisco's Richmond District—and it threw into relief the bright west-facing facades of the buildings in the city before him as it stretched away to downtown. The random window reflected glints of sunlight back at him, fireflies in the gathering dusk, shimmering in the Indian summer air.

He sipped his gin and ice, placed the glass down on the meshed metal of the picnic table they'd set up out here, and was suddenly and acutely aware that he could not be more content. His wife, Frannie, whom he still loved after twenty-three years, was inside the house behind him, humming as she did whatever she was doing. His two children were away and doing well at their respective schools—Rebecca at Boston University, and Vincent at UC San Diego. The law firm of Freeman, Farrell, Hardy & Roake, of which he was the managing partner, was humming along as though it were on autopilot.

Hardy looked for a moment into the blue above him, blinking against a wave of emotion. Then, being who he was, his mouth cracked into a small grin at himself and he lifted his glass for another sip.

Inside, the telephone rang twice and stopped, which meant that it was someone they knew and that Frannie had picked it up. Her voice, with notes of sympathy and understanding, floated out to him, but he didn't bother trying to make out any of the words. She had begun to have a somewhat thriving career of her own as a marriage and family therapist and often would wind up counseling her clients from home.

Hardy drifted, not off to anywhere, but into a kind of surrender of conscious thought. For a long moment, he was simply there in the same way that his drink or his chair existed, or the light, or the breeze off the ocean a little more than a mile west of where he sat. So that when the door opened behind him, he came back with a bit of a start.

Frannie put a hand on his shoulder and he brought his hand up to cover hers, half turning, seeing the look on her face. "What's up?" he asked, his feet coming down off the railing. "Are the kids all right?" Always the first concern.

She nodded a yes to the second question, then answered the first. "That was Treya." Treya was the wife of Hardy's best friend, Abe Glitsky, the head of San Francisco's homicide department. Anguish in her eyes, Frannie held and released a breath. "It's Zack," she said, referring to Glitsky's three-year-old son. "He's had an accident."

ACCOMPANIED BY HER five-year-old daughter, Rachel, Treya Glitsky opened the gate in the Hardys' white picket fence. Dismas Hardy, in his living room watching out through the plantation shutters of his front window, called back to his wife in the kitchen that they were here, then walked over and opened his front door.

Treya turned away and, closing the gate, reached down for a small duffel bag. By the way she picked it up, it might have weighed a hundred pounds. When she straightened up, her shoulders rose and fell; then she brought a hand to her forehead and stood completely still for another second or two. With her tiny hand, Rachel held on to the front pocket of her mother's jeans while she looked up at her face, her own lips pressed tight.

Hardy crossed his porch and descended three steps to the cement path that bisected his small lawn. The sun had gone down behind the buildings across the street although true dusk was still twenty minutes away. Treya turned and saw him now, and her legendary composure threatened to break. She was a tall woman—nearly Hardy's size—and strongly built. Her mouth, expressive and normally quick to smile, quivered, then set in a line.

Hardy came forward, took the duffel bag from her, and put an arm around her neck, drawing her in, holding her for a moment. Finally he stepped back and whispered, "How is he?"

She shrugged and shook her head. Then her voice was as quiet as his. "We don't know yet."

Frannie came up, touched his shoulder, and came around to hug Treya.

Hardy stepped to the side and went down to one knee to face Rachel at her level. "And how's my favorite little girl in the whole world?"

"Okay," she said. "But Zack got hit by a car."

"I know he did, hon."

"But he's not going to die."

Hardy looked up at the two women. Treya gave him a quick nod, and he came back to her daughter. "No, of course not. But I hear you're going to stay here for a couple of days while he gets better. Is that okay with you?"

"If Mom says."

"And she does. Is that duffel bag your stuff? Here, let me get it. If you put your arms around my neck, your old uncle Diz will carry you inside."

Then they were all moving up the path and into the house. "Abe went with the ambulance," Treya was saying. "We don't know how long we're going to have to be down there. I don't know how to thank you for watching Rachel."

"Don't be ridiculous," Frannie said. "We love Rachel." She reached out and touched the little girl's cheek where she rested it on Hardy's shoulder. "She's our favorite little girl."

HARDY AND FRANNIE walked Treya out after they got Rachel settled in with cookies and milk in front of the television. They stopped again on the path just inside the fence. "Was he conscious?" Hardy asked.

"No." Treya paused, then lowered her voice. "He didn't have his helmet on."

"What happened exactly?" Frannie asked.

"We may never know," she said. "Abe had just brought down his Big Wheel bike and Zack was on it, but Abe told him to just sit still and wait a minute while he turned around and got his helmet. Which he'd set down like two feet away on the stairs. But then as soon as his back was turned, Zack got aboard and either started pedaling or just rolling down the driveway just as another car was coming up the street. One of our neighbors. He was only going like five miles an hour but Zack just plowed into him and got knocked off the bike and into the street." She flashed a pained look from Hardy to Frannie. "He banged his head." She hesitated. "I've got to get down there now. You guys are great. Thank you."

"Go," Hardy said. "Call when you can."

* * *

"THE BEST BIT OF NEWS," Treya was saying to both of them as they listened on the two extension phones, "is that he's out of his twos. Evidently the younger you are, the worse the prognosis. Three is way better than two. And this is a level-one hospital, so they had a neurological resident in-house, which is also lucky since he could go right to work." Her voice, while not by any stretch remotely cheerful, was strong and confident-sounding. Conveying facts, keeping to the bearable news, she was keeping herself together the way she always did, by sucking it up.

"They've cooled him down to make him hypothermic," she went on, "which is what they always do, and taken some scans and they've got him on a continuous EEG and his vital signs are good, so that's all heartening."

"But he's still unconscious?" Hardy asked.

Frannie and Hardy heard Treya's quick intake of breath and flashed their reactions to each other. "Well, that's really not so much of an issue now, since they've induced a coma. He's going to be unconscious for a while. Maybe a week or more."

"He's in a coma?" Frannie, before she could stop herself.

"It's not as bad as it sounds," Treya said.

Silence collected in the line as this bit of horrifying, yet perhaps good, information began to sink in. Finally Hardy cleared his throat. "So how's Abe?"

Treya hesitated. "Quiet. Even for him."

"It's not his fault," Frannie said.

"I know that. It might not be so clear to him." Again, a stab at an optimistic tone. "He'll get to it."

"I know he will," Frannie said.

Hardy, not so certain of that, especially if Zachary didn't make it, turned to face away from his wife. The women's words continued to tumble through the phone at his ear, but he didn't hear any of them over his own imaginings—or was it only his pulse, sounding like the tick of a clock counting down the seconds?

* * *

BAY BEANS WEST enjoyed a privileged location, location, location at the intersection of Haight and Ashbury streets in San Francisco.

The large, wide-windowed coffee shop had opened in the summer of 1998 and from its first days became a fixture in the neighborhood. It opened every morning except Sunday at six o'clock, when it opened at eight, and stayed open until ten. Between the UCSF medical school a couple of blocks east, the University of San Francisco a few blocks north, the tourists visiting the epicenter of the birth of hippiedom, and the vibrant and wildly eclectic local neighborhood, the place rarely had a slow moment, much less an empty one.

The smell of its roasting beans infused the immediate vicinity with a beckoning aroma; the management provided copies of the city's newspapers—the *Chronicle,* the *Free Press*, and the *Bay Guardian*—for free on the honor system that they wouldn't be taken. The papers rarely disappeared before three o'clock. Even the homeless honored the custom, except for Crazy Melinda, who used to come in, scoop all the papers up, and try to leave with them. Until the patrons started setting aside a copy of each paper for her at the counter to pick up whenever she wanted them.

Comfortable, colorful couches were available as well as the usual chairs and tables; the ethic of the place allowed an unlimited time at your seat once you'd claimed it, whether or not you continued to drink coffee; for the past five years or so, customers could avail themselves of free wireless Internet service; and legal or not, pets were welcome. For many in the neighborhood, BBW was a refuge, a meeting place, a home away from home.

At a few minutes before seven o'clock on this Saturday morning, the usual line of about twenty customers needing their morning infusions of caffeine was already growing along Haight Street at the establishment's front door. A long-haired man named Wes Farrell, in jogging pants and a T-shirt that read "DAM—Mothers Against Dyslexia," stood holding in one hand the hand of his live-in girl-friend, Sam Duncan, and in the other the leash of Gertrude, his boxer. They, like many others in the city that morning, were discussing the homeless problem.

For decades, San Francisco has been a haven for the homeless, spending upward of one hundred fifty million dollars per year on shelters, subsidized rental units, medical and psychiatric care, soup kitchens, and so on. Now, suddenly, unexpectedly, and apparently due to a series of articles that had just appeared in the *Chronicle*, came a widespread outcry among the citizenry that the welcome mat should be removed. Wes finished reading today's article aloud to Sam and, folding up the paper, said, "And about time, too."

Sam extracted her hand from his. "You don't mean that."

"I don't? I thought I did."

"So what do you want to do with them? I mean, once you give them a ticket, which by the way they have no money to pay, so that won't work."

"What part of that statement—I hesitate to call it a sentence—do you want me to address?"

"Any part. Don't be wise."

"I'm not. But I'd hate to be the guy assigned to trying to diagram one of your sentences."

"You're just trying to get me off the point. Which is what you would do with these homeless people, who suddenly are no longer welcome."

"Actually, they're just as welcome. They're just not going to be welcome to use public streets and sidewalks as their campsites and bathrooms anymore."

"So where else would they go?"

"Are we talking bathrooms? They go to the bathroom in bathrooms, like the rest of us."

"The rest of us who have homes, Wes. I think that's more or less the point. They don't."

"You're right. But you notice we're loaded with shelters and public toilets."

"They don't like the shelters. They're dangerous and dirty."

"And the streets aren't? Besides, this may sound like a cruel cliché, my dear, but where do you think we get the expression 'beggars can't be choosers'?"

"I can't believe you just said that. That is so, so"—Sam dredged up about the worst epithet she could imagine—"so *right-wing*."

Wes looked down, went to a knee, and snapped his fingers, bringing Gertrude close in for a quick pet. "It's all right, girl, your mom and I aren't fighting. We're just talking." Standing up, he said, "She's getting upset."

"So am I. If you try to pet me to calm me down, I'll deck you."

"There's a tolerant approach. And meanwhile, I hate to say this, but it's not a right-wing, left-wing issue here. It's a health and quality-of-life issue. Feces and urine on public streets and playgrounds and parks pose a health risk and are just a little bit of a nuisance, I think we can admit. Are we in accord here?"

Sam, arms folded, leaned back against the windows of the coffee shop, unyielding.

"Sam," Wes continued, "when I take Gertie out for a walk, I bring a bag to clean up after her. That's for a dog. You really think it's too much to ask the same for humans?"

"It's not the same thing."

"Why not?"

"Because a lot of these people, they have mental problems, too. They don't even know they're doing it or where."

"And so we should just tolerate it? You send your kids out to play and there's a pile of shit on your front stoop?

Next thing you know, half a school's got hepatitis. You don't think that's a small problem?"

"That's not what's happening."

"Sam, that's exactly what's happening. They've got to check the sandbox near the merry-go-round in Golden Gate Park every morning for shit and needles. Some of these people think it's a litter box."

"Well, I haven't heard of any hepatitis epidemic. That's way an exaggeration."

"The point is the alfresco-bathroom kind of thing that's been happening downtown for years. I think you'll remember we had a guy who used our front stoop at the office every night for a month. We had to wash the steps down every morning."

"There," Sam said. "That was a solution."

"It's a ridiculous solution. It's insane. To say nothing about the fact that using the streets for bathrooms punishes innocent, good citizens and devalues property."

"Aha! I knew property would get in there."

"Property's not a bad thing, Sam."

"Which is what every Republican in the world believes."

"And some Democrats, too. Dare I say most? And for the umpteenth time, Sam, it's not a Republican thing. You can be opposed to Bush and still not want to have people shitting in your flowerpots. Those aren't mutually exclusive."

"I think they might actually be."

"Well, no offense, but you're wrong. Public defecation and homeless encampments on the streets and in the parks are gross and unhealthy and sickening. I don't understand how you can't see that."

Sam again shook her head. "I see those poor people suffering. That's what I see. We've got a fire department with miles of hoses. We could deploy them to wash down the streets. The city could get up some work program and hire people to clean up."

"What a great idea! Should we pay them to clean up after themselves or after one another? Except then again, where does the money to do that come from?"

"There it is again, money! It always comes down to money."

"Well, as a matter of fact, yes, sometimes it does."

"The point is, Wes, these people just don't have the same options as everybody else."

"And they never will, Sam. That's rough maybe, okay, but it's life. And life's just not fair sometimes. Which doesn't mean everybody else has to deal with their problems. They get rounded up and taken to the shelters whether or not they want to go, and I say it's about time."

Without either Sam or Wes noticing, several others in the line, both male and female, had closed in around them, listening in. Now a young hippie spoke up to Wes. "You're right, dude," he said. "It's out of control. It is about time."

A chorus of similar sentiments followed.

Sam took it all in, straightened up, and looked out into the faces surrounding her. "I just can't believe that I'm hearing this in San Francisco," she said. "I'm so ashamed of all of you."

And with that, she pushed her way through the crowd and started walking up Ashbury, away from her boyfriend and their dog.

SAM WAS THE DIRECTOR of San Francisco's Rape Crisis Counseling Center, which also happened to be on Haight Street. Her plan this morning had been to take her early-morning constitutional from their home up on Buena Vista with Wes and Gertie, share a cup of coffee and a croissant at BBW, then check in at the office to make sure there hadn't been an overnight crisis that demanded her attention.

But now, seething, just wanting to get away from all the reactionaries, she had started out in the wrong direction to get to the center. Fortunately, the line for the BBW stretched down Haight Street, and not up Ashbury, and she'd gone about half a block uphill when she stopped and turned around, realizing she could take the alley that ran behind the Haight Street storefronts, bypassing the crowd and emerging on the next block on the way to her office.

But first she stopped a minute, not just to get her breath, but to try to calm herself. After an extraordinarily rocky beginning to their relationship, she and Wes hadn't had a fight in six or seven years. She'd come to believe that he was her true soul mate and shared her opinions about nearly everything, especially politics. But now apparently not.

It shook her.

And okay, she knew that she was among those whom conservatives would include among California's "fruits and nuts." She certainly didn't too often doubt the rightness of her various stances. She was in her early forties, and had seen enough of the world to know that the dollar was the basic problem. The military-industrial complex. Big oil and corporate globalism. Republicans.

But here now Wes, who had registered Green and hated the right-wingers as much as she did, was arguing for something that she just knew in her heart was wrong. You couldn't just abandon these homeless people who had after all flocked to San Francisco precisely because of the benign political environment. That would be the worst bait-and-switch tactic she could imagine. She would have to talk to him, but after they'd both calmed down.

She crossed back to where she wouldn't be visible to Wes or anyone else in the line as she came down the hill. It was the kind of clear morning that people tended to expect when they visited San Francisco during the traditional summer months. Those people often left in bitter disappointment at the incessant fog, the general inclemency of the weather. But today the early sun sprayed the rooftops golden. The temperature was already in the low sixties. It was going to be a perfect day.

She got to the alley, squinting into the bright morning sun, when here was an example of exactly the thing she and Wes had been talking about: a pair of feet protruded from the back door area of BBW. Not wanting to awaken the poor sleeping homeless man, she gave him a wide berth and only a quick glance as she came abreast of where he slept.

But something about the attitude of the body stopped her. It didn't seem to be lying in a natural position, the head propped up against the screen door. She couldn't imagine such a posture would be conducive to sleep. Most of the weight seemed to be on his left shoulder, but under that, the torso turned in an awkward way so that both feet pointed up, as if he were lying on his back.

Moving closer, she noticed a line of liquid tracing itself down over the concrete and pooling in the gap between the cement of the porch and the asphalt of the alley. In the bright morning sunlight, from a distance it could have been water. But another couple of steps brought her close enough to remove any doubt on that score—the glistening wet stuff was red.

Leaning over, Sam shaded her eyes against the glare and she saw the man's face—a face she recognized, had expected to see this morning behind the counter where he always was at BBW.

Her hand, already trembling, went to her mouth.

Penguin Group (USA) Inc.
is proud to present

GREAT READS—GUARANTEED

We are so confident you will love
this book that we are offering a
100% money-back guarantee!

If you are not 100% satisfied with
this publication, Penguin Group (USA) Inc.
will refund your money!
Simply return the book before
March 6, 2009 for a full refund.

M193G0508